WILLA CATHER

WILLA CATHER

LATER NOVELS
A Lost Lady
The Professor's House
Death Comes for the Archbishop
Shadows on the Rock
Lucy Gayheart
Sapphira and the Slave Girl

THE LIBRARY OF AMERICA

Grateful acknowledgment is made to the National Endowment for the Humanities, the Ford Foundation, and the Andrew W. Mellon Foundation for their generous support of this series.

Contents

A LOST LADY

". . . . . Come, my coach!
Good night, ladies; good night, sweet ladies;
Good night, good night."

For
Jan Hambourg

I

THIRTY OR FORTY years ago, in one of those grey towns along the Burlington railroad, which are so much greyer to-day than they were then, there was a house well known from Omaha to Denver for its hospitality and for a certain charm of atmosphere. Well known, that is to say, to the railroad aristocracy of that time; men who had to do with the railroad itself, or with one of the "land companies" which were its by-products. In those days it was enough to say of a man that he was "connected with the Burlington." There were the directors, the general managers, vice-presidents, superintendents, whose names we all knew; and their younger brothers or nephews were auditors, freight agents, departmental assistants. Everyone "connected" with the Road, even the large cattle- and grain-shippers, had annual passes; they and their families rode about over the line a great deal. There were then two distinct social strata in the prairie States; the homesteaders and hand-workers who were there to make a living, and the bankers and gentlemen ranchers who came from the Atlantic seaboard to invest money and to "develop our great West," as they used to tell us.

When the Burlington men were travelling back and forth on business not very urgent, they found it agreeable to drop off the express and spend a night in a pleasant house where their importance was delicately recognized; and no house was pleasanter than that of Captain Daniel Forrester, at Sweet Water. Captain Forrester was himself a railroad man, a contractor, who had built hundreds of miles of road for the Burlington, — over the sage brush and cattle country, and on up into the Black Hills.

The Forrester place, as every one called it, was not at all remarkable; the people who lived there made it seem much larger and finer than it was. The house stood on a low round hill, nearly a mile east of town; a white house with a wing, and sharp-sloping roofs to shed the snow. It was encircled by porches, too narrow for modern notions of comfort, sup-

ported by the fussy, fragile pillars of that time, when every
honest stick of timber was tortured by the turning-lathe into
something hideous. Stripped of its vines and denuded of its
shrubbery, the house would probably have been ugly enough.
It stood close into a fine cottonwood grove that threw shel-
tering arms to left and right and grew all down the hillside
behind it. Thus placed on the hill, against its bristling grove,
it was the first thing one saw on coming into Sweet Water by
rail, and the last thing one saw on departing.

To approach Captain Forrester's property, you had first to
get over a wide, sandy creek which flowed along the eastern
edge of the town. Crossing this by the foot-bridge or the
ford, you entered the Captain's private lane, bordered by
Lombardy poplars, with wide meadows lying on either side.
Just at the foot of the hill on which the house sat, one crossed
a second creek by the stout wooden road-bridge. This stream
traced artless loops and curves through the broad meadows
that were half pasture land, half marsh. Any one but Captain
Forrester would have drained the bottom land and made it
into highly productive fields. But he had selected this place
long ago because it looked beautiful to him, and he happened
to like the way the creek wound through his pasture, with
mint and joint-grass and twinkling willows along its banks.
He was well off for those times, and he had no children. He
could afford to humour his fancies.

When the Captain drove friends from Omaha or Denver
over from the station in his democrat wagon, it gratified him
to hear these gentlemen admire his fine stock, grazing in the
meadows on either side of his lane. And when they reached
the top of the hill, it gratified him to see men who were older
than himself leap nimbly to the ground and run up the front
steps as Mrs. Forrester came out on the porch to greet them.
Even the hardest and coldest of his friends, a certain narrow-
faced Lincoln banker, became animated when he took her
hand, tried to meet the gay challenge in her eyes and to reply
cleverly to the droll word of greeting on her lips.

She was always there, just outside the front door, to welcome their visitors, having been warned of their approach by
the sound of hoofs and the rumble of wheels on the wooden
bridge. If she happened to be in the kitchen, helping her

Bohemian cook, she came out in her apron, waving a buttery iron spoon, or shook cherry-stained fingers at the new arrival. She never stopped to pin up a lock; she was attractive in dishabille, and she knew it. She had been known to rush to the door in her dressing-gown, brush in hand and her long black hair rippling over her shoulders, to welcome Cyrus Dalzell, president of the Colorado & Utah; and that great man had never felt more flattered. In his eyes, and in the eyes of the admiring middle-aged men who visited there, whatever Mrs. Forrester chose to do was "lady-like" because she did it. They could not imagine her in any dress or situation in which she would not be charming. Captain Forrester himself, a man of few words, told Judge Pommeroy that he had never seen her look more captivating than on the day when she was chased by the new bull in the pasture. She had forgotten about the bull and gone into the meadow to gather wild flowers. He heard her scream, and as he ran puffing down the hill, she was scudding along the edge of the marshes like a hare, beside herself with laughter, and stubbornly clinging to the crimson parasol that had made all the trouble.

Mrs. Forrester was twenty-five years younger than her husband, and she was his second wife. He married her in California and brought her to Sweet Water a bride. They called the place home even then, when they lived there but a few months out of each year. But later, after the Captain's terrible fall with his horse in the mountains, which broke him so that he could no longer build railroads, he and his wife retired to the house on the hill. He grew old there,—and even she, alas! grew older.

II

B UT WE WILL BEGIN this story with a summer morning long ago, when Mrs. Forrester was still a young woman, and Sweet Water was a town of which great things were expected. That morning she was standing in the deep bay-window of her parlour, arranging old-fashioned blush roses in a glass bowl. Glancing up, she saw a group of little boys coming along the driveway, barefoot, with fishing-poles and lunch-baskets. She knew most of them; there was Niel Herbert, Judge Pommeroy's nephew, a handsome boy of twelve whom she liked; and polite George Adams, son of a gentleman rancher from Lowell, Massachusetts. The others were just little boys from the town; the butcher's red-headed son, the leading grocer's fat brown twins, Ed Elliott (whose flirtatious old father kept a shoe store and was the Don Juan of the lower world of Sweet Water), and the two sons of the German tailor,—pale, freckled lads with ragged clothes and ragged rust-coloured hair, from whom she sometimes bought game or catfish when they appeared silent and spook-like at her kitchen door and thinly asked if she would "care for any fish this morning."

As the boys came up the hill she saw them hesitate and consult together. "You ask her, Niel."

"You'd better, George. She goes to your house all the time, and she barely knows me to speak to."

As they paused before the three steps which led up to the front porch, Mrs. Forrester came to the door and nodded graciously, one of the pink roses in her hand.

"Good-morning, boys. Off for a picnic?"

George Adams stepped forward and solemnly took off his big straw hat. "Good-morning, Mrs. Forrester. Please may we fish and wade down in the marsh and have our lunch in the grove?"

"Certainly. You have a lovely day. How long has school been out? Don't you miss it? I'm sure Niel does. Judge Pommeroy tells me he's very studious."

The boys laughed, and Niel looked unhappy.

"Run along, and be sure you don't leave the gate into the

6

pasture open. Mr. Forrester hates to have the cattle get in on his blue grass."

The boys went quietly round the house to the gate into the grove, then ran shouting down the grassy slopes under the tall trees. Mrs. Forrester watched them from the kitchen window until they disappeared behind the roll of the hill. She turned to her Bohemian cook.

"Mary, when you are baking this morning, put in a pan of cookies for those boys. I'll take them down when they are having their lunch."

The round hill on which the Forrester house stood sloped gently down to the bridge in front, and gently down through the grove behind. But east of the house, where the grove ended, it broke steeply from high grassy banks, like bluffs, to the marsh below. It was thither the boys were bound.

When lunch time came they had done none of the things they meant to do. They had behaved like wild creatures all morning; shouting from the breezy bluffs, dashing down into the silvery marsh through the dewy cobwebs that glistened on the tall weeds, swishing among the pale tan cattails, wading in the sandy creek bed, chasing a striped water snake from the old willow stump where he was sunning himself, cutting sling-shot crotches, throwing themselves on their stomachs to drink at the cool spring that flowed out from under a bank into a thatch of dark watercress. Only the two German boys, Rheinhold and Adolph Blum, withdrew to a still pool where the creek was dammed by a reclining tree trunk, and, in spite of all the noise and splashing about them, managed to catch a few suckers.

The wild roses were wide open and brilliant, the blue-eyed grass was in purple flower, and the silvery milkweed was just coming on. Birds and butterflies darted everywhere. All at once the breeze died, the air grew very hot, the marsh steamed, and the birds disappeared. The boys found they were tired; their shirts stuck to their bodies and their hair to their foreheads. They left the sweltering marsh-meadows for the grove, lay down on the clean grass under the grateful shade of the tall cottonwoods, and spread out their lunch. The Blum boys never brought anything but rye bread and hunks of dry cheese,—their companions wouldn't have

nant and uncomfortable, not knowing what to do. They were not especially sensitive; Thad was always on hand when there was anything doing at the slaughter house, and the Blum boys lived by killing things. They wouldn't have believed they could be so upset by a hurt woodpecker. There was something wild and desperate about the way the darkened creature beat its wings in the branches, whirling in the sunlight and never seeing it, always thrusting its head up and shaking it, as a bird does when it is drinking. Presently it managed to get its feet on the same limb where it had been struck, and seemed to recognize that perch. As if it had learned something by its bruises, it pecked and crept its way along the branch and disappeared into its own hole.

"There," Niel Herbert exclaimed between his teeth, "if I can get it now, I can kill it and put it out of its misery. Let me on your back, Rhein."

Rheinhold was the tallest, and he obediently bent his bony back. The trunk of a cottonwood tree is hard to climb; the bark is rough, and the branches begin a long way up. Niel tore his trousers and scratched his bare legs smartly before he got to the first fork. After recovering breath, he wound his way up toward the woodpecker's hole, which was inconveniently high. He was almost there, his companions below thought him quite safe, when he suddenly lost his balance, turned a somersault in the air, and bumped down on the grass at their feet. There he lay without moving.

"Run for water!"

"Run for Mrs. Forrester! Ask her for whiskey."

"No," said George Adams, "let's carry him up to the house. She will know what to do."

"That's sense," said Ivy Peters. As he was much bigger and stronger than any of the others, he lifted Niel's limp body and started up the hill. It had occurred to him that this would be a fine chance to get inside the Forresters' house and see what it was like, and this he had always wanted to do.

Mary, the cook, saw them coming from the kitchen window, and ran for her mistress. Captain Forrester was in Kansas City that day.

Mrs. Forrester came to the back door. "What's happened? It's Niel, too! Bring him in this way, please."

Ivy Peters followed her, keeping his eyes open, and the rest trooped after him,—all but the Blum boys, who knew that their place was outside the kitchen door. Mrs. Forrester led the way through the butler's pantry, the dining room, the back parlour, to her own bedroom. She threw down the white counterpane, and Ivy laid Niel upon the sheets. Mrs. Forrester was concerned, but not frightened.

"Mary, will you bring the brandy from the sideboard. George, telephone Dr. Dennison to come over at once. Now you other boys run out on the front porch and wait quietly. There are too many of you in here." She knelt by the bed, putting brandy between Niel's white lips with a teaspoon. The little boys withdrew, only Ivy Peters remained standing in the back parlour, just outside the bedroom door, his arms folded across his chest, taking in his surroundings with bold, unblinking eyes.

Mrs. Forrester glanced at him over her shoulder. "Will you wait on the porch, please? You are older than the others, and if anything is needed I can call on you."

Ivy cursed himself, but he had to go. There was something final about her imperious courtesy,—high-and-mighty, he called it. He had intended to sit down in the biggest leather chair and cross his legs and make himself at home; but he found himself on the front porch, put out by that delicately modulated voice as effectually as if he had been kicked out by the brawniest tough in town.

Niel opened his eyes and looked wonderingly about the big, half-darkened room, full of heavy, old-fashioned walnut furniture. He was lying on a white bed with ruffled pillow shams, and Mrs. Forrester was kneeling beside him, bathing his forehead with cologne. Bohemian Mary stood behind her, with a basin of water. "Ouch, my arm!" he muttered, and the perspiration broke out on his face.

"Yes, dear, I'm afraid it's broken. Don't move. Dr. Dennison will be here in a few minutes. It doesn't hurt very much, does it?"

"No'm," he said faintly. He was in pain, but he felt weak and contented. The room was cool and dusky and quiet. At his house everything was horrid when one was sick. . . . What soft fingers Mrs. Forrester had, and what a lovely lady she was. Inside the lace ruffle of her dress he saw her white throat rising and falling so quickly. Suddenly she got up to take off her glittering rings,—she had not thought of them before,—shed them off her fingers with a quick motion as if she were washing her hands, and dropped them into Mary's broad palm. The little boy was thinking that he would probably never be in so nice a place again. The windows went almost down to the baseboard, like doors, and the closed green shutters let in streaks of sunlight that quivered on the polished floor and the silver things on the dresser. The heavy curtains were looped back with thick cords, like ropes. The marble-topped washstand was as big as a sideboard. The massive walnut furniture was all inlaid with pale-coloured woods. Niel had a scroll-saw, and this inlay interested him.

"There, he looks better now, doesn't he, Mary?" Mrs. Forrester ran her fingers through his black hair and lightly kissed him on the forehead. Oh, how sweet, how sweet she smelled!

"Wheels on the bridge; it's Doctor Dennison. Go and show him in, Mary."

Dr. Dennison set Niel's arm and took him home in his buggy. Home was not a pleasant place to go to; a frail eggshell house, set off on the edge of the prairie where people of no consequence lived. Except for the fact that he was Judge Pommeroy's nephew, Niel would have been one of the boys to whom Mrs. Forrester merely nodded brightly as she passed. His father was a widower. A poor relation, a spinster from Kentucky, kept house for them, and Niel thought she was probably the worst housekeeper in the world. Their house was usually full of washing in various stages of incompletion,—tubs sitting about with linen soaking,—and the beds were "aired" until any hour in the afternoon when Cousin Sadie happened to think of making them up. She liked to sit down after breakfast and read murder trials, or peruse a well-worn copy of "St. Elmo." Sadie was a good-natured thing and was always running off to help a neighbour, but Niel hated to have anyone come to see them. His father was at home very little, spent all his time at his office. He kept the county abstract books and made farm loans. Having lost his own property, he invested other people's money for them. He was a gentle, agreeable man, young, good-looking, with nice manners, but Niel felt there was an air of failure and defeat about his family. He clung to his maternal uncle, Judge Pommeroy, white-whiskered and portly, who was Captain Forrester's lawyer and a friend of all the great men who visited the Forresters. Niel was proud, like his mother; she died when he was five years old. She had hated the West, and used haughtily to tell her neighbours that she would never think of living anywhere but in Fayette county, Kentucky; that they had only come to Sweet Water to make investments and to "turn the crown into the pound." By that phrase she was still remembered, poor lady.

III

OR THE NEXT few years Niel saw very little of Mrs. Forrester. She was an excitement that came and went with summer. She and her husband always spent the winter in Denver and Colorado Springs,—left Sweet Water soon after Thanksgiving and did not return until the first of May. He knew that Mrs. Forrester liked him, but she hadn't much time for growing boys. When she had friends staying with her, and gave a picnic supper for them, or a dance in the grove on a moonlight night, Niel was always invited. Coming and going along the road to the marsh with the Blum boys, he sometimes met the Captain driving visitors over in the democrat wagon, and he heard about these people from Black Tom, Judge Pommeroy's faithful negro servant, who went over to wait on the table for Mrs. Forrester when she had a dinner party.

Then came the accident which cut short the Captain's career as a roadbuilder. After that fall with his horse, he lay ill at the Antlers, in Colorado Springs, all winter. In the summer, when Mrs. Forrester brought him home to Sweet Water, he still walked with a cane. He had grown much heavier, seemed encumbered by his own bulk, and never suggested taking a contract for the railroad again. He was able to work in his garden, trimmed his snowball bushes and lilac hedges, devoted a great deal of time to growing roses. He and his wife still went away for the winter, but each year the period of their absence grew shorter.

All this while the town of Sweet Water was changing. Its future no longer looked bright. Successive crop failures had broken the spirit of the farmers. George Adams and his family had gone back to Massachusetts, disillusioned about the West. One by one the other gentlemen ranchers followed their example. The Forresters now had fewer visitors. The Burlington was "drawing in its horns," as people said, and the railroad officials were not stopping off at Sweet Water so often,— were more inclined to hurry past a town where they had sunk money that would never come back.

Niel Herbert's father was one of the first failures to be

crowded to the wall. He closed his little house, sent his cousin Sadie back to Kentucky, and went to Denver to accept an office position. He left Niel behind to read law in the office with his uncle. Not that Niel had any taste for the law, but he liked being with Judge Pommeroy, and he might as well stay there as anywhere, for the present. The few thousand dollars his mother had left him would not be his until he was twenty-one.

Niel fitted up a room for himself behind the suite which the Judge retained for his law offices, on the second floor of the most pretentious brick block in town. There he lived with monastic cleanliness and severity, glad to be rid of his cousin and her inconsequential housewifery, and resolved to remain a bachelor, like his uncle. He took care of the offices, which meant that he did the janitor work, and arranged them exactly to suit his taste, making the rooms so attractive that all the Judge's friends, and especially Captain Forrester, dropped in there to talk oftener than ever.

The Judge was proud of his nephew. Niel was now nineteen, a tall, straight, deliberate boy. His features were clear-cut, his grey eyes, so dark that they looked black under his long lashes, were rather moody and challenging. The world did not seem over-bright to young people just then. His reserve, which did not come from embarrassment or vanity, but from a critical habit of mind, made him seem older than he was, and a little cold.

One winter afternoon, only a few days before Christmas, Niel sat writing in the back office, at the long table where he usually worked or trifled, surrounded by the Judge's fine law library and solemn steel engravings of statesmen and jurists. His uncle was at his desk in the front office, engaged in a friendly consultation with one of his country clients. Niel, greatly bored with the notes he was copying, was trying to invent an excuse for getting out on the street, when he became aware of light footsteps coming rapidly down the outside corridor. The door of the front office opened, he heard his uncle rise quickly to his feet, and, at the same moment, heard a woman's laugh,—a soft, musical laugh which rose and descended like a suave scale. He turned in his screw chair so that he could look over his shoulder through the double doors into the front room. Mrs. Forrester stood there, shaking her muff at the Judge and the bewildered Swede farmer. Her quick eye lighted upon a bottle of Bourbon and two glasses on the desk among the papers.

"Is that the way you prepare your cases, Judge? What an example for Niel!" She peeped through the door and nodded to the boy as he rose.

He remained in the back room, however, watching her while she declined the chair the Judge pushed toward her and made a sign of refusal when he politely pointed to the Bourbon. She stood beside his desk in her long sealskin coat and cap, a crimson scarf showing above the collar, a little brown veil with spots tied over her eyes. The veil did not in the least obscure those beautiful eyes, dark and full of light, set under a low white forehead and arching eyebrows. The frosty air had brought no colour to her cheeks,—her skin had always the fragrant, crystalline whiteness of white lilacs. Mrs. Forrester looked at one, and one knew that she was bewitching. It was instantaneous, and it pierced the thickest hide. The Swede farmer was now grinning from ear to ear, and he, too, had shuffled to his feet. There could be no negative encounter, however slight, with Mrs. Forrester. If she merely bowed to you, merely looked at you, it constituted a personal relation. Something about her took hold of one in a flash; one became acutely conscious of her, of her fragility and grace, of her mouth which could say so much without words; of her eyes, lively, laughing, intimate, nearly always a little mocking.

"Will you and Niel dine with us tomorrow evening, Judge? And will you lend me Tom? We've just had a wire. The Ogdens are stopping over with us. They've been East to bring the girl home from school,—she's had mumps or something. They want to get home for Christmas, but they will stop off for two days. Probably Frank Ellinger will come on from Denver."

"No prospect can afford me such pleasure as that of dining with Mrs. Forrester," said the Judge ponderously.

"Thank you!" she bowed playfully and turned toward the double doors. "Niel, could you leave your work long enough to drive me home? Mr. Forrester has been detained at the bank."

Niel put on his wolfskin coat. Mrs. Forrester took him by his shaggy sleeve and went with him quickly down the long corridor and the narrow stairs to the street.

At the hitch-bar stood her cutter, looking like a painted toy among the country sleds and wagons. Niel tucked the buffalo robes about Mrs. Forrester, untied the ponies, and sprang in beside her. Without direction the team started down the frozen main street, where few people were abroad, crossed the creek on the ice, and trotted up the poplar-bordered lane toward the house on the hill. The late afternoon sun burned on the snow-crusted pastures. The poplars looked very tall and straight, pinched up and severe in their winter poverty. Mrs. Forrester chatted to Niel with her face turned toward him, holding her muff up to break the wind.

"I'm counting on you to help me entertain Constance Ogden. Can you take her off my hands day after tomorrow, come over in the afternoon? Your duties as a lawyer aren't very arduous yet?" She smiled teasingly. "What can I do with a miss of nineteen? one who goes to college? I've no learned conversation for her!"

"Surely I haven't!" Niel exclaimed.

"Oh, but you're a boy! Perhaps you can interest her in lighter things. She's considered pretty."

"Do you think she is?"

"I haven't seen her lately. She was striking,—china blue eyes and heaps of yellow hair, not exactly yellow,—what they call an ashen blond, I believe."

Niel had noticed that in describing the charms of other women Mrs. Forrester always made fun of them a little.

They drew up in front of the house. Ben Keezer came round from the kitchen to take the team.

"You are to go back for Mr. Forrester at six, Ben. Niel, come in for a moment and get warm." She drew him through the little storm entry, which protected the front door in winter, into the hall. "Hang up your coat and come along." He followed her through the parlour into the sitting-room, where a little coal grate was burning under the black mantelpiece, and sat down in the big leather chair in which Captain

Forrester dozed after his mid-day meal. It was a rather dark room, with walnut bookcases that had carved tops and glass doors. The floor was covered by a red carpet, and the walls were hung with large, old-fashioned engravings; "The House of the Poet on the Last Day of Pompeii," "Shakespeare Reading before Queen Elizabeth."

Mrs. Forrester left him and presently returned carrying a tray with a decanter and sherry glasses. She put it down on her husband's smoking-table, poured out a glass for Niel and one for herself, and perched on the arm of one of the stuffed chairs, where she sat sipping her sherry and stretching her tiny, silver-buckled slippers out toward the glowing coals.

"It's so nice to have you staying on until after Christmas," Niel observed. "You've only been here one other Christmas since I can remember."

"I'm afraid we're staying on all winter this year. Mr. Forrester thinks we can't afford to go away. For some reason, we are extraordinarily poor just now."

"Like everybody else," the boy commented grimly.

"Yes, like everybody else. However, it does no good to be glum about it, does it?" She refilled the two glasses. "I always take a little sherry at this time in the afternoon. At Colorado Springs some of my friends take tea, like the English. But I should feel like an old woman, drinking tea! Besides, sherry is good for my throat." Niel remembered some legend about a weak chest and occasional terrifying hemorrhages. But that seemed doubtful, as one looked at her,—fragile, indeed, but with such light, effervescing vitality. "Perhaps I do seem old to you, Niel, quite old enough for tea and a cap!"

He smiled gravely. "You seem always the same to me, Mrs. Forrester."

"Yes? And how is that?"

"Lovely. Just lovely."

As she bent forward to put down her glass she patted his cheek. "Oh, you'll do very well for Constance!" Then, seriously, "I'm glad if I do, though. I want you to like me well enough to come to see us often this winter. You shall come with your uncle to make a fourth at whist. Mr. Forrester must have his whist in the evening. Do you think he is looking any worse, Niel? It frightens me to see him getting a little uncertain. But there, we must believe in good luck!" She took up the half-empty glass and held it against the light.

Niel liked to see the firelight sparkle on her earrings, long pendants of garnets and seed-pearls in the shape of fleurs-de-lys. She was the only woman he knew who wore earrings; they hung naturally against her thin, triangular cheeks. Captain Forrester, although he had given her handsomer ones, liked to see her wear these, because they had been his mother's. It gratified him to have his wife wear jewels; it meant something to him. She never left off her beautiful rings unless she was in the kitchen.

"A winter in the country may do him good," said Mrs. Forrester, after a silence during which she looked intently into the fire, as if she were trying to read the outcome of their difficulties there. "He loves this place so much. But you and Judge Pommeroy must keep an eye on him when he is in town, Niel. If he looks tired or uncertain, make some excuse and bring him home. He can't carry a drink or two as he used,"—she glanced over her shoulder to see that the door into the dining-room was shut. "Once last winter he had been drinking with some old friends at the Antlers,—nothing unusual, just as he always did, as a man must be able to do,— but it was too much for him. When he came out to join me in the carriage, coming down that long walk, you know, he fell. There was no ice, he didn't slip. It was simply because he was unsteady. He had trouble getting up. I still shiver to think of it. To me, it was as if one of the mountains had fallen down."

A little later Niel went plunging down the hill, looking exultantly into the streak of red sunset. Oh, the winter would not be so bad, this year! How strange that she should be here at all, a woman like her among common people! Not even in Denver had he ever seen another woman so elegant. He had sat in the dining-room of the Brown Palace hotel and watched them as they came down to dinner,—fashionable women from "the East," on their way to California. But he had never found one so attractive and distinguished as Mrs. Forrester. Compared with her, other women were heavy and dull; even the pretty ones seemed lifeless,—they had not that something in their glance that made one's blood tingle. And never elsewhere had he heard anything like her inviting, musical laugh, that was like the distant measures of dance music, heard through opening and shutting doors.

He could remember the very first time he ever saw Mrs. Forrester, when he was a little boy. He had been loitering in front of the Episcopal church one Sunday morning, when a low carriage drove up to the door. Ben Keezer was on the front seat, and on the back seat was a lady, alone, in a black silk dress all puffs and ruffles, and a black hat, carrying a parasol with a carved ivory handle. As the carriage stopped she lifted her dress to alight; out of a swirl of foamy white petticoats she thrust a black, shiny slipper. She stepped lightly to the ground and with a nod to the driver went into the church. The little boy followed her through the open door, saw her enter a pew and kneel. He was proud now that at the first moment he had recognized her as belonging to a different world from any he had ever known.

Niel paused for a moment at the end of the lane to look up at the last skeleton poplar in the long row; just above its pointed tip hung the hollow, silver winter moon.

IV

IN PLEASANT WEATHER Judge Pommeroy walked to the Forresters', but on the occasion of the dinner for the Ogdens
he engaged the liveryman to take him and his nephew over in
one of the town hacks,—vehicles seldom used except for funerals and weddings. They smelled strongly of the stable and
contained lap-robes as heavy as lead and as slippery as oiled
paper. Niel and his uncle were the only townspeople asked to
the Forresters' that evening; they rolled over the creek and up
the hill in state, and emerged covered with horsehair.

Captain Forrester met them at the door, his burly figure
buttoned up in a frock coat, a flat collar and black string tie
under the heavy folds of his neck. He was always clean-shaven
except for a drooping dun-coloured moustache. The company
stood behind him laughing while Niel caught up the whisk-
broom and began dusting roan hairs off his uncle's broadcloth. Mrs. Forrester gave Niel a brushing in turn and then
took him into the parlour and introduced him to Mrs. Ogden
and her daughter.

The daughter was a rather pretty girl, Niel thought, in a
pale pink evening dress which left bare her smooth arms
and short, dimpled neck. Her eyes were, as Mrs. Forrester
had said, a china blue, rather prominent and inexpressive. Her
fleece of ashy-gold hair was bound about her head with silver
bands. In spite of her fresh, rose-like complexion, her face was
not altogether agreeable. Two dissatisfied lines reached from
the corners of her short nose to the corners of her mouth.
When she was displeased, even a little, these lines tightened,
drew her nose back, and gave her a suspicious, injured expression. Niel sat down by her and did his best, but he found her
hard to talk to. She seemed nervous and distracted, kept
glancing over her shoulder, and crushing her handkerchief up
in her hands. Her mind, clearly, was elsewhere. After a few
moments he turned to the mother, who was more easily interested.

Mrs. Ogden was almost unpardonably homely. She had a
pear-shaped face, and across her high forehead lay a row of
flat, dry curls. Her bluish brown skin was almost the colour of

Mrs. Forrester last of the ladies but before the men, and to her, too, he said, "Mrs. Forrester, what part of the turkey shall I give you this evening?" He was a man who did not vary his formulae or his manners. He was no more mobile than his countenance. Niel and Judge Pommeroy had often remarked how much Captain Forrester looked like the pictures of Grover Cleveland. His clumsy dignity covered a deep nature, and a conscience that had never been juggled with. His repose was like that of a mountain. When he laid his fleshy, thick-fingered hand upon a frantic horse, an hysterical woman, an Irish workman out for blood, he brought them peace; something they could not resist. That had been the secret of his management of men. His sanity asked nothing, claimed nothing; it was so simple that it brought a hush over distracted creatures. In the old days, when he was building road in the Black Hills, trouble sometimes broke out in camp when he was absent, staying with Mrs. Forrester at Colorado Springs. He would put down the telegram that announced an insurrection and say to his wife, "Maidy, I must go to the men." And that was all he did,—he went to them.

While the Captain was intent upon his duties as host he talked very little, and Judge Pommeroy and Ellinger kept a lively cross-fire of amusing stories going. Niel, sitting opposite Ellinger, watched him closely. He still couldn't decide whether he liked him or not. In Denver Frank was known as a prince of good fellows; tactful, generous, resourceful, though apt to trim his sails to the wind; a man who good-humouredly bowed to the inevitable, or to the almost-inevitable. He had, when he was younger, been notoriously "wild," but that was not held against him, even by mothers with marriageable daughters, like Mrs. Ogden. Morals were different in those days. Niel had heard his uncle refer to Ellinger's youthful infatuation with a woman called Nell Emerald, a handsome and rather unusual woman who conducted a house properly licensed by the Denver police. Nell Emerald had told an old club man that though she had been out behind young Ellinger's new trotting horse, she "had no respect for a man who would go driving with a prostitute in broad daylight." This story and a dozen like it were often related of Ellinger, and the women laughed over them as heartily as the men. All the while that he was making a scandalous chronicle for himself, young Ellinger had been devotedly caring for an invalid mother, and he was described to strangers as a terribly fast young man and a model son. That combination pleased the taste of the time. Nobody thought the worse of him. Now that his mother was dead, he lived at the Brown Palace hotel, though he still kept her house at Colorado Springs.

When the roast was well under way, Black Tom, very formal in a white waistcoat and high collar, poured the champagne. Captain Forrester lifted his glass, the frail stem between his thick fingers, and glancing round the table at his guests and at Mrs. Forrester, said,

"Happy days!"

It was the toast he always drank at dinner, the invocation he was sure to utter when he took a glass of whiskey with an old friend. Whoever had heard him say it once, liked to hear him say it again. Nobody else could utter those two words as he did, with such gravity and high courtesy. It seemed a solemn moment, seemed to knock at the door of Fate; behind which all days, happy and otherwise, were hidden. Niel drank his wine with a pleasant shiver, thinking that nothing else made life seem so precarious, the future so cryptic and unfathomable, as that brief toast uttered by the massive man, "Happy days!"

Mrs. Ogden turned to the host with her most languishing smile: "Captain Forrester, I want you to tell Constance"—(She was an East Virginia woman, and what she really said was, "Cap'n Forrester, Ah wan' yew to tell, etc." Her vowels seemed to roll about in the same way her eyes did.)—"I want you to tell Constance about how you first found this lovely spot, 'way back in Indian times."

The Captain looked down the table between the candles at Mrs. Forrester, as if to consult her. She smiled and nodded, and her beautiful earrings swung beside her pale cheeks. She was wearing her diamonds tonight, and a black velvet gown. Her husband had archaic ideas about jewels; a man bought them for his wife in acknowledgment of things he could not gracefully utter. They must be costly; they must show that he was able to buy them, and that she was worthy to wear them.

With her approval the Captain began his narrative: a concise account of how he came West a young boy, after serving in the Civil War, and took a job as driver for a freighting company that carried supplies across the plains from Nebraska City to Cherry Creek, as Denver was then called. The freighters, after embarking in that sea of grass six hundred miles in width, lost all count of the days of the week and the month. One day was like another, and all were glorious; good hunting, plenty of antelope and buffalo, boundless sunny sky, boundless plains of waving grass, long fresh-water lagoons yellow with lagoon flowers, where the bison in their periodic migrations stopped to drink and bathe and wallow.

"An ideal life for a young man," the Captain pronounced. Once, when he was driven out of the trail by a wash-out, he rode south on his horse to explore, and found an Indian encampment near the Sweet Water, on this very hill where his house now stood. He was, he said, "greatly taken with the location," and made up his mind that he would one day have a house there. He cut down a young willow tree and drove the stake into the ground to mark the spot where he wished to build. He went away and did not come back for many years; he was helping to lay the first railroad across the plains.

"There were those that were dependent on me," he said. "I had sickness to contend with, and responsibilities. But in all those years I expect there was hardly a day passed that I did not remember the Sweet Water and this hill. When I came here a young man, I had planned it in my mind, pretty much as it is today; where I would dig my well, and where I would plant my grove and my orchard. I planned to build a house that my friends could come to, with a wife like Mrs. Forrester to make it attractive to them. I used to promise myself that some day I would manage it." This part of the story the Captain told not with embarrassment, but with reserve, choosing his words slowly, absently cracking English walnuts with his strong fingers and heaping a little hoard of kernels beside his plate. His friends understood that he was referring to his first marriage, to the poor invalid wife who had never been happy and who had kept his nose to the grindstone.

"When things looked most discouraging," he went on, "I came back here once and bought the place from the railroad company. They took my note. I found my willow stake,—it had rooted and grown into a tree,—and I planted three more to mark the corners of my house. Twelve years later Mrs. Forrester came here with me, shortly after our marriage, and we built our house." Captain Forrester puffed from time to time, but his clear account commanded attention. Something in the way he uttered his unornamented phrases gave them the impressiveness of inscriptions cut in stone.

Mrs. Forrester nodded at him from her end of the table. "And now, tell us your philosophy of life,—this is where it comes in," she laughed teasingly.

The Captain coughed and looked abashed. "I was intending to omit that tonight. Some of our guests have already heard it."

"No, no. It belongs at the end of the story, and if some of us have heard it, we can hear it again. Go on!"

"Well, then, my philosophy is that what you think of and plan for day by day, in spite of yourself, so to speak—you will get. You will get it more or less. That is, unless you are one of the people who get nothing in this world. There are such people. I have lived too much in mining works and construction camps not to know that." He paused as if, though this was too dark a chapter to be gone into, it must have its place, its moment of silent recognition. "If you are not one of those, Constance and Niel, you will accomplish what you dream of most."

"And why? That's the interesting part of it," his wife prompted him.

"Because," he roused himself from his abstraction and looked about at the company, "because a thing that is dreamed of in the way I mean, is already an accomplished fact. All our great West has been developed from such dreams; the homesteader's and the prospector's and the contractor's. We dreamed the railroads across the mountains, just as I dreamed my place on the Sweet Water. All these things will be everyday facts to the coming generation, but to us—" Captain Forrester ended with a sort of grunt. Something forbidding had come into his voice, the lonely, defiant note that is so often heard in the voices of old Indians.

Mrs. Ogden had listened to the story with such sympathy that Niel liked her better than ever, and even the preoccupied Constance seemed able to give it her attention. They rose from the dessert and went into the parlour to arrange the card tables. The Captain still played whist as well as ever. As he brought out a box of his best cigars, he paused before Mrs. Ogden and said, "Is smoke offensive to you, Mrs. Ogden?" When she protested that it was not, he crossed the room to where Constance was talking with Ellinger and asked with the same grave courtesy, "Is smoke offensive to you, Constance?" Had there been half a dozen women present, he would have asked that question of each, probably, and in the same words. It did not bother him to repeat a phrase. If an expression answered his purpose, he saw no reason for varying it.

Mrs. Forrester and Mr. Ogden were to play against Mrs. Ogden and the Captain. "Constance," said Mrs. Forrester as she sat down, "will you play with Niel? I'm told he's very good."

Miss Ogden's short nose flickered up, the lines on either side of it deepened, and she again looked injured. Niel was sure she detested him. He was not going to be done in by her.

"Miss Ogden," he said as he stood beside his chair, deliberately shuffling a pack of cards, "my uncle and I are used to playing together, and probably you are used to playing with Mr. Ellinger. Suppose we try that combination?"

She gave him a quick, suspicious glance from under her yellow eyelashes and flung herself into a chair without so much as answering him. Frank Ellinger came in from the dining-room, where he had been sampling the Captain's French brandy, and took the vacant seat opposite Miss Ogden. "So it's you and me, Connie? Good enough!" he exclaimed, cutting the pack Niel pushed toward him.

Just before midnight Black Tom opened the door and announced that the egg-nog was ready. The card players went into the dining-room, where the punch-bowl stood smoking on the table.

"Constance," said Captain Forrester, "do you sing? I like to hear one of the old songs with the egg-nog."

"Ah'm sorry, Cap'n Forrester. Ah really haven't any voice."

Niel noticed that whenever Constance spoke to the Captain she strained her throat, though he wasn't in the least deaf. He broke in over her refusal. "Uncle can start a song if you coax him, sir."

Judge Pommeroy, after smoothing his silver whiskers and coughing, began "Auld Lang Syne." The others joined in, but they hadn't got to the end of it when a hollow rumbling down on the bridge made them laugh, and everyone ran to the front windows to see the Judge's funeral coach come lurching up the hill, with only one of the side lanterns lit. Mrs. Forrester sent Tom out with a drink for the driver. While Niel and his uncle were putting on their overcoats in the hall, she came up to them and whispered coaxingly to the boy, "Remember, you are coming over tomorrow, at two? I am planning a drive, and I want you to amuse Constance for me."

Niel bit his lip and looked down into Mrs. Forrester's laughing, persuasive eyes. "I'll do it for you, but that's the only reason," he said threateningly.

"I understand, for me! I'll credit it to your account."

The Judge and his nephew rolled away on swaying springs. The Ogdens retired to their rooms upstairs. Mrs. Forrester went to help the Captain divest himself of his frock coat, and put it away for him. Ever since he was hurt he had to be propped high on pillows at night, and he slept in a narrow iron bed, in the alcove which had formerly been his wife's dressing-room. While he was undressing he breathed heavily and sighed, as if he were very tired. He fumbled with his studs, then blew on his fingers and tried again. His wife came to his aid and quickly unbuttoned everything. He did not thank her in words, but submitted gratefully.

When the iron bed creaked at receiving his heavy figure, she called from the big bedroom, "Good-night, Mr. Forrester," and drew the heavy curtains that shut off the alcove. She took off her rings and earrings and was beginning to unfasten her black velvet bodice when, at a tinkle of glass from without, she stopped short. Rehooking the shoulder of her gown, she went to the dining-room, now faintly lit by the coal fire in the back parlour. Frank Ellinger was standing at the sideboard, taking a nightcap. The Forrester French brandy was old, and heavy like a cordial.

"Be careful," she murmured as she approached him, "I have a distinct impression that there is some one on the enclosed stairway. There is a wide crack in the door. Ah, but kittens have claws, these days! Pour me just a little. Thank you. I'll have mine in by the fire."

He followed her into the next room, where she stood by the grate, looking at him in the light of the pale blue flames that ran over the fresh coal, put on to keep the fire.

"You've had a good many brandies, Frank," she said, studying his flushed, masterful face.

"Not too many. I'll need them . . . to-night," he replied meaningly.

She nervously brushed back a lock of hair that had come down a little. "It's not to-night. It's morning. Go to bed and sleep as late as you please. Take care, I heard silk stockings on the stairs. Good-night." She put her hand on the sleeve of his coat; the white fingers clung to the black cloth as bits of paper cling to magnetized iron. Her touch, soft as it was, went through the man, all the feet and inches of him. His broad shoulders lifted on a deep breath. He looked down at her.

Her eyes fell. "Good-night," she said faintly. As she turned quickly away, the train of her velvet dress caught the leg of his broadcloth trousers and dragged with a friction that crackled and threw sparks. Both started. They stood looking at each other for a moment before she actually slipped through the door. Ellinger remained by the hearth, his arms folded tight over his chest, his curly lips compressed, frowning into the fire.

V

N IEL WENT up the hill the next afternoon, just as the cutter with the two black ponies jingled round the driveway and stopped at the front door. Mrs. Forrester came out on the porch, dressed for a sleigh ride. Ellinger followed her, buttoned up in a long fur-lined coat, showily befrogged down the front, with a glossy astrachan collar. He looked even more powerful and bursting with vigour than last night. His highly-coloured, well-visored countenance shone with a good opinion of himself and of the world.

Mrs. Forrester called to Niel gaily. "We are going down to the Sweet Water to cut cedar boughs for Christmas. Will you keep Constance company? She seems a trifle disappointed at being left behind, but we can't take the big sleigh,—the pole is broken. Be nice to her, there's a good boy!" She pressed his hand, gave him a meaning, confidential smile, and stepped into the sleigh. Ellinger sprang in beside her, and they glided down the hill with a merry tinkle of sleighbells.

Niel found Miss Ogden in the back parlour, playing solitaire by the fire. She was clearly out of humour.

"Come in, Mr. Herbert. I think they might have taken us along, don't you? I want to see the river my own self. I hate bein' shut up in the house!"

"Let's go out, then. Wouldn't you like to see the town?"

Constance seemed not to hear him. She was wrinkling and unwrinkling her short nose, and the restless lines about her mouth were fluttering. "What's to hinder us from getting a sleigh at the livery barn and going down to the Sweet Water? I don't suppose the river's private property?" She gave a nervous, angry laugh and looked hopefully at Niel.

"We couldn't get anything at this hour. The livery teams are all out," he said with firmness.

Constance glanced at him suspiciously, then sat down at the card table and leaned over it, drawing her plump shoulders together. Her fluffy yellow hair was wound round her head like a scarf and held in place by narrow bands of black velvet.

* * *

The ponies had crossed the second creek and were trotting down the high road toward the river. Mrs. Forrester expressed her feelings in a laugh full of mischief. "Is she running after us? Where did she get the idea that she was to come? What a relief to get away!" She lifted her chin and sniffed the air. The day was grey, without sun, and the air was still and dry, a warm cold. "Poor Mr. Ogden," she went on, "how much livelier he is without his ladies! They almost extinguish him. Now aren't you glad you never married?"

"I'm certainly glad I never married a homely woman. What does a man do it for, anyway? She had no money,—and he's always had it, or been on the way to it."

"Well, they're off tomorrow. And Connie! You've reduced her to a state of imbecility, really! What an afternoon Niel must be having!" She laughed as if the idea of his predicament delighted her.

"Who's this kid, anyway?" Ellinger asked her to take the reins for a moment while he drew a cigar from his pocket. "He's a trifle stiff. Does he make himself useful?"

"Oh, he's a nice boy, stranded here like the rest of us. I'm going to train him to be very useful. He's devoted to Mr. Forrester. Handsome, don't you think?"

"So-so." They turned into a by-road that wound along the Sweet Water. Ellinger held the ponies in a little and turned down his high astrachan collar. "Let's have a look at you, Marian."

Mrs. Forrester was holding her muff before her face, to catch the flying particles of snow the ponies kicked up. From behind it she glanced at him sidewise. "Well?" she said teasingly.

He put his arm through hers and settled himself low in the sleigh. "You ought to look at me better than that. It's been a devil of a long while since I've seen you."

"Perhaps it's been too long," she murmured. The mocking spark in her eyes softened perceptibly under the long pressure of his arm. "Yes, it's been long," she admitted lightly.

"You didn't answer the letter I wrote you on the eleventh."

"Didn't I? Well, at any rate I answered your telegram." She drew her head away as his face came nearer. "You'll really have to watch the ponies, my dear, or they'll tumble us out in the snow."

"I don't care. I wish they would!" he said between his teeth. "Why didn't you answer my letter?"

"Oh, I don't remember! You don't write so many."

"It's no satisfaction. You won't let me write you love let-ters. You say it's risky."

"So it is, and foolish. But now you needn't be so careful. Not too careful!" she laughed softly. "When I'm off in the country for a whole winter, alone, and growing older, I like to . . ." she put her hand on his, "to be reminded of pleas-anter things."

Ellinger took off his glove with his teeth. His eyes, sweep-ing the winding road and the low, snow-covered bluffs, had something wolfish in them.

"Be careful, Frank. My rings! You hurt me!"

"Then why didn't you take them off? You used to. Are these your cedars, shall we stop here?"

"No, not here." She spoke very low. "The best ones are farther on, in a deep ravine that winds back into the hills."

Ellinger glanced at her averted head, and his heavy lips twitched in a smile at one corner. The quality of her voice had changed, and he knew the change. They went spinning along the curves of the winding road, saying not a word. Mrs. For-rester sat with her head bent forward, her face half hidden in her muff. At last she told him to stop. To the right of the road he saw a thicket. Behind it a dry water-course wound into the bluffs. The tops of the dark, still cedars, just visible from the road, indicated its windings.

"Sit still," he said, "while I take out the horses."

When the blue shadows of approaching dusk were begin-ning to fall over the snow, one of the Blum boys, slipping quietly along through the timber in search of rabbits, came upon the empty cutter standing in the brush, and near it the two ponies, stamping impatiently where they were tied. Adolph slid back into the thicket and lay down behind a fallen log to see what would happen. Not much ever hap-pened to him but weather.

Presently he heard low voices, coming nearer from the ravine. The big stranger who was visiting at the Forres-ters' emerged, carrying the buffalo robes on one arm; Mrs.

Forrester herself was clinging to the other. They walked slowly, wholly absorbed by what they were saying to each other. When they came up to the sleigh, the man spread the robes on the seat and put his hands under Mrs. Forrester's arms to lift her in. But he did not lift her; he stood for a long while holding her crushed up against his breast, her face hidden in his black overcoat.

"What about those damned cedar boughs?" he asked, after he had put her in and covered her up. "Shall I go back and cut some?"

"It doesn't matter," she murmured.

He reached under the seat for a hatchet and went back to the ravine. Mrs. Forrester sat with her eyes closed, her cheek pillowed on her muff, a faint, soft smile on her lips. The air was still and blue; the Blum boy could almost hear her breathe. When the strokes of the hatchet rang out from the ravine, he could see her eyelids flutter . . . soft shivers went through her body.

The man came back and threw the evergreens into the sleigh. When he got in beside her, she slipped her hand through his arm and settled softly against him. "Drive slowly," she murmured, as if she were talking in her sleep. "It doesn't matter if we are late for dinner. Nothing matters." The ponies trotted off.

The pale Blum boy rose from behind his log and followed the tracks up the ravine. When the orange moon rose over the bluffs, he was still sitting under the cedars, his gun on his knee. While Mrs. Forrester had been waiting there in the sleigh, with her eyes closed, feeling so safe, he could almost have touched her with his hand. He had never seen her before when her mocking eyes and lively manner were not between her and all the world. If it had been Thad Grimes who lay behind that log, now, or Ivy Peters?

But with Adolph Blum her secrets were safe. His mind was feudal; the rich and fortunate were also the privileged. These warm-blooded, quick-breathing people took chances,— followed impulses only dimly understandable to a boy who was wet and weather-chapped all the year; who waded in the mud fishing for cat, or lay in the marsh waiting for wild duck. Mrs. Forrester had never been too haughty to smile at him

when he came to the back door with his fish. She never hag-
gled about the price. She treated him like a human being. His
little chats with her, her nod and smile when she passed him
on the street, were among the pleasantest things he had to
remember. She bought game of him in the closed season, and
didn't give him away.

VI

IT WAS DURING that winter, the first one Mrs. Forrester had ever spent in the house on the hill, that Niel came to know her very well. For the Forresters that winter was a sort of isthmus between two estates; soon afterward came a change in their fortunes. And for Niel it was a natural turning-point, since in the autumn he was nineteen, and in the spring he was twenty,—a very great difference.

After the Christmas festivities were over, the whist parties settled into a regular routine. Three evenings a week Judge Pommeroy and his nephew sat down to cards with the Forresters. Sometimes they went over early and dined there. Sometimes they stayed for a late supper after the last rubber. Niel, who had been so content with a bachelor's life, and who had made up his mind that he would never live in a place that was under the control of women, found himself becoming attached to the comforts of a well-conducted house; to the pleasures of the table, to the soft chairs and soft lights and agreeable human voices at the Forresters'. On bitter, windy nights, sitting in his favourite blue chair before the grate, he used to wonder how he could manage to tear himself away, to plunge into the outer darkness, and run down the long frozen road and up the dead street of the town. Captain Forrester was experimenting with bulbs that winter, and had built a little glass conservatory on the south side of the house, off the back parlour. Through January and February the house was full of narcissus and Roman hyacinths, and their heavy, spring-like odour made a part of the enticing comfort of the fireside there.

Where Mrs. Forrester was, dulness was impossible, Niel believed. The charm of her conversation was not so much in what she said, though she was often witty, but in the quick recognition of her eyes, in the living quality of her voice itself. One could talk with her about the most trivial things, and go away with a high sense of elation. The secret of it, he supposed, was that she couldn't help being interested in people, even very commonplace people. If Mr. Ogden or Mr. Dalzell were not there to tell their best stories for her, then she could

be amused by Ivy Peters' ruffianly manners, or the soft compliments of old man Elliott when he sold her a pair of winter
shoes. She had a fascinating gift of mimicry. When she mentioned the fat iceman, or Thad Grimes at his meat block, or
the Blum boys with their dead rabbits, by a subtle suggestion
of their manner she made them seem more individual and
vivid than they were in their own person. She often carica-
tured people to their faces, and they were not offended, but
greatly flattered. Nothing pleased one more than to provoke
her laughter. Then you felt you were getting on with her. It
was her form of commenting, of agreeing with you and ap-
preciating you when you said something interesting,—and it
often told you a great deal that was both too direct and too
elusive for words.

Long, long afterward, when Niel did not know whether
Mrs. Forrester were living or dead, if her image flashed into
his mind, it came with a brightness of dark eyes, her pale
triangular cheeks with long earrings, and her many-coloured
laugh. When he was dull, dull and tired of everything, he
used to think that if he could hear that long-lost lady laugh
again, he could be gay.

The big storm of the winter came late that year; swept
down over Sweet Water the first day of March and beat upon
the town for three days and nights. Thirty inches of snow fell,
and the cutting wind blew it into whirling drifts. The Forresters were snowed in. Ben Keezer, their man of all work, did
not attempt to break a road or even to come over to the town
himself. On the third day Niel went to the post-office, got the
Captain's leather mail sack with its accumulation of letters,
and set off across the creek, plunging into drifts up to his
middle, sometimes up to his arm-pits. The fences along the
lane were covered, but he broke his trail by keeping between
the two lines of poplars. When at last he reached the front
porch, Captain Forrester came to the door and let him in.

"Glad to see you, my boy, very glad. It's been a little lonesome for us. You must have had hard work getting over. I
certainly appreciate it. Come to the sitting-room fire and dry
yourself. We will talk quietly. Mrs. Forrester has gone upstairs
to lie down; she's been complaining of a headache."

Niel stood before the fire in his rubber boots, drying his trousers. The Captain did not sit down but opened the glass door into his little conservatory.

"I've something pretty to show you, Niel. All my hyacinths are coming along at once, every colour of the rainbow. The Roman hyacinths, I say, are Mrs. Forrester's. They seem to suit her."

Niel went to the door and looked with keen pleasure at the fresh, watery blossoms. "I was afraid you might lose them this bitter weather, Captain."

"No, these things can stand a good deal of cold. They've been company for us." He stood looking out through the glass at the drifted shrubbery. Niel liked to see him look out over his place. A man's house is his castle, his look seemed to say. "Ben tells me the rabbits have come up to the barn to eat the hay, everything green is covered up. I had him throw a few cabbages out for them, so they won't suffer. Mrs. Forrester has been on the porch every day, feeding the snow birds," he went on, as if talking to himself.

The stair door opened, and Mrs. Forrester came down in her Japanese dressing-gown, looking very pale. The dark shadows under her eyes seemed to mean that she had been losing sleep.

"Oh, it's Niel! How nice of you. And you've brought the mail. Are there any letters for me?"

"Three. Two from Denver and one from California." Her husband gave them to her. "Did you sleep, Maidy?"

"No, but I rested. It's delightful up in the west room, the wind sings and whistles about the eaves. If you'll excuse me, I'll dress and glance at my letters. Stand closer to the fire, Niel. Are you very wet?" When she stopped beside him to feel his clothes, he smelled a sharp odour of spirits. Was she ill, he wondered, or merely so bored that she had been trying to dull herself?

When she came back she had dressed and rearranged her hair.

"Mrs. Forrester," said the Captain in a solicitous tone, "I believe I would like some tea and toast this afternoon, like your English friends, and it would be good for your head. We won't offer Niel anything else."

"Very well. Mary has gone to bed with a toothache, but I will make the tea. Niel can make the toast here by the fire while you read your paper."

She was cheerful now,—tied one of Mary's aprons about Niel's neck and set him down with the toasting fork. He noticed that the Captain, as he read his paper, kept his eye on the sideboard with a certain watchfulness, and when his wife brought the tray with tea, and no sherry, he seemed very much pleased. He drank three cups, and took a second piece of toast.

"You see, Mr. Forrester," she said lightly, "Niel has brought back my appetite. I ate no lunch to-day," turning to the boy, "I've been shut up too long. Is there anything in the papers?"

This meant was there any news concerning the people they knew. The Captain put on his silver-rimmed glasses again and read aloud about the doings of their friends in Denver and Omaha and Kansas City. Mrs. Forrester sat on a stool by the fire, eating toast and making humorous comments upon the subjects of those solemn paragraphs; the engagement of Miss Erma Salton-Smith, etc.

"At last, thank God! You remember her, Niel. She's been here. I think you danced with her."

"I don't think I do. What is she like?"

"She's exactly like her name. Don't you remember? Tall, very animated, glittering eyes, like the Ancient Mariner's?"

Niel laughed. "Don't you like bright eyes, Mrs. Forrester?"

"Not any others, I don't!" She joined in his laugh so gaily that the Captain looked out over his paper with an expression of satisfaction. He let the journal slowly crumple on his knees, and sat watching the two beside the grate. To him they seemed about the same age. It was a habit with him to think of Mrs. Forrester as very, very young.

She noticed that he was not reading. "Would you like me to light the lamp, Mr. Forrester?"

"No, thank you. The twilight is very pleasant."

It was twilight by now. They heard Mary come downstairs and begin stirring about the kitchen. The Captain, his slippers in the zone of firelight and his heavy shoulders in shadow, snored from time to time. As the room grew dusky, the windows were squares of clear, pale violet, and the shutters ceased to rattle. The wind was dying with the day. Everything was still, except when Bohemian Mary roughly clattered a pan. Mrs. Forrester whispered that she was out of sorts because her sweetheart, Joe Pucelik, hadn't been over to see her. Sunday night was his regular night, and Sunday was the first day of the blizzard. "When she's neglected, her tooth always begins to ache!"

"Well, now that I've got over, he'll have to come, or she will be in a temper."

"Oh, he'll come!" Mrs. Forrester shrugged. "I am blind and deaf, but I'm quite sure she makes it worth his while!" After a few moments she rose. "Come," she whispered, "Mr. Forrester is asleep. Let's run down the hill, there's no one to stop us. I'll slip on my rubber boots. No objections!" She put her fingers on his lips. "Not a word! I can't stand this house a moment longer."

They slipped quietly out of the front door into the cold air which tasted of new-fallen snow. A clear arc of blue and rose colour painted the west, over the buried town. When they reached the rounded breast of the hill, blown almost bare, Mrs. Forrester stood still and drew in deep breaths, looking down over the drifted meadows and the stiff, blue poplars.

"Oh, but it is bleak!" she murmured. "Suppose we should have to stay here all next winter, too, . . . and the next! What will become of me, Niel?" There was fear, unmistakable fright in her voice. "You see there is nothing for me to do. I get no exercise. I don't skate; we didn't in California, and my ankles are weak. I've always danced in the winter, there's plenty of dancing at Colorado Springs. You wouldn't believe how I miss it. I shall dance till I'm eighty. . . . I'll be the waltzing grandmother! It's good for me, I need it."

They plunged down into the drifts and did not stop again until they reached the wooden bridge.

"See, even the creek is frozen! I thought running water never froze. How long will it be like this?"

"Not long now. In a month you'll see the green begin in the marsh and run over the meadows. It's lovely over here in the spring. And you'll be able to get out tomorrow, Mrs. Forrester. The clouds are thinning. Look, there's the new moon!"

She turned. "Oh, I saw it over the wrong shoulder!"

"No you didn't. You saw it over mine."

She sighed and took his arm. "My dear boy, your shoulders aren't broad enough."

Instantly before his eyes rose the image of a pair of shoulders that were very broad, objectionably broad, clad in a frogged overcoat with an astrachan collar. The intrusion of this third person annoyed him as they went slowly back up the hill.

Curiously enough, it was as Captain Forrester's wife that she most interested Niel, and it was in her relation to her husband that he most admired her. Given her other charming attributes, her comprehension of a man like the railroad-builder, her loyalty to him, stamped her more than anything else. That, he felt, was quality; something that could never become worn or shabby; steel of Damascus. His admiration of Mrs. Forrester went back to that, just as, he felt, she herself went back to it. He rather liked the stories, even the spiteful ones, about the gay life she led in Colorado, and the young men she kept dangling about her every winter. He sometimes thought of the life she might have been living ever since he had known her,—and the one she had chosen to live. From that disparity, he believed, came the subtlest thrill of her fascination. She mocked outrageously at the proprieties she observed, and inherited the magic of contradictions.

VII

O N THE EVENINGS when there was no whist at the
Forresters', Niel usually sat in his room and read, — but
not law, as he was supposed to do. The winter before, when
the Forresters were away, and one dull day dragged after another, he had come upon a copious diversion, an almost inex-
haustible resource. The high, narrow bookcase in the back
office, between the double doors and the wall, was filled from
top to bottom with rows of solemn looking volumes bound
in dark cloth, which were kept apart from the law library; an
almost complete set of the Bohn classics, which Judge Pommeroy had bought long ago when he was a student at the
University of Virginia. He had brought them West with him,
not because he read them a great deal, but because, in his day,
a gentleman had such books in his library, just as he had
claret in his cellar. Among them was a set of Byron in three
volumes, and last winter, apropos of a quotation which Niel
didn't recognize, his uncle advised him to read Byron, — all
except "Don Juan." That, the Judge remarked, with a deep
smile, he "could save until later." Niel, of course, began with
"Don Juan." Then he read "Tom Jones" and "Wilhelm Meister" and raced on until he came to Montaigne and a complete
translation of Ovid. He hadn't finished yet with these last, —
always went back to them after other experiments. These authors seemed to him to know their business. Even in "Don
Juan" there was a little "fooling," but with these gentlemen
none.

There were philosophical works in the collection, but he
did no more than open and glance at them. He had no curiosity about what men had thought; but about what they had
felt and lived, he had a great deal. If anyone had told him that
these were classics and represented the wisdom of the ages, he
would doubtless have let them alone. But ever since he had
first found them for himself, he had been living a double life,
with all its guilty enjoyments. He read the *Heroides* over and
over, and felt that they were the most glowing love stories
ever told. He did not think of these books as something invented to beguile the idle hour, but as living creatures, caught

44

in the very behaviour of living,—surprised behind their misleading severity of form and phrase. He was eavesdropping upon the past, being let into the great world that had plunged and glittered and sumptuously sinned long before little Western towns were dreamed of. Those rapt evenings beside the lamp gave him a long perspective, influenced his conception of the people about him, made him know just what he wished his own relations with these people to be. For some reason, his reading made him wish to become an architect. If the Judge had left his Bohn library behind him in Kentucky, his nephew's life might have turned out differently.

Spring came at last, and the Forrester place had never been so lovely. The Captain spent long, happy days among his flowering shrubs, and his wife used to say to visitors, "Yes, you can see Mr. Forrester in a moment; I will send the English gardener to call him."

Early in June, when the Captain's roses were just coming on, his pleasant labors were interrupted. One morning an alarming telegram reached him. He cut it open with his garden shears, came into the house, and asked his wife to telephone for Judge Pommeroy. A savings bank, one in which he was largely interested, had failed in Denver. That evening the Captain and his lawyer went west on the express. The Judge, when he was giving Niel final instructions about the office business, told him he was afraid the Captain was bound to lose a good deal of money.

Mrs. Forrester seemed unaware of any danger; she went to the station to see her husband off, spoke of his errand merely as a "business trip." Niel, however, felt a foreboding gloom. He dreaded poverty for her. She was one of the people who ought always to have money; any retrenchment of their generous way of living would be a hardship for her,—would be unfitting. She would not be herself in straitened circumstances.

Niel took his meals at the town hotel; on the third day after Captain Forrester's departure, he was annoyed to find Frank Ellinger's name on the hotel register. Ellinger did not appear at supper, which meant, of course, that he was dining with Mrs. Forrester, and that the lady herself would get his dinner.

She had taken the occasion of the Captain's absence to let
Bohemian Mary go to visit her mother on the farm for a
week. Niel thought it very bad taste in Ellinger to come to
Sweet Water when Captain Forrester was away. He must
know that it would stir up the gossips.

Niel had meant to call on Mrs. Forrester that evening, but
now he went back to the office instead. He read late, and after
he went to bed, he slept lightly. He was awakened before
dawn by the puffing of the switch engine down at the round
house. He tried to muffle his ears in the sheet and go to sleep
again, but the sound of escaping steam for some reason excited him. He could not shut out the feeling that it was summer, and that the dawn would soon be flaming gloriously
over the Forresters' marsh. He had awakened with that intense, blissful realization of summer which sometimes comes
to children in their beds. He rose and dressed quickly. He
would get over to the hill before Frank Ellinger could intrude
his unwelcome presence, while he was still asleep in the best
bedroom of the Wimbleton hotel.

An impulse of affection and guardianship drew Niel up
the poplar-bordered road in the early light,—though he did
not go near the house itself, but at the second bridge cut
round through the meadow and on to the marsh. The sky
was burning with the soft pink and silver of a cloudless summer dawn. The heavy, bowed grasses splashed him to the
knees. All over the marsh, snow-on-the-mountain, globed
with dew, made cool sheets of silver, and the swamp milkweed spread its flat, raspberry-coloured clusters. There was
an almost religious purity about the fresh morning air, the
tender sky, the grass and flowers with the sheen of early dew
upon them. There was in all living things something limpid
and joyous—like the wet, morning call of the birds, flying
up through the unstained atmosphere. Out of the saffron
east a thin, yellow, wine-like sunshine began to gild the fragrant meadows and the glistening tops of the grove. Niel
wondered why he did not often come over like this, to see
the day before men and their activities had spoiled it, while
the morning was still unsullied, like a gift handed down
from the heroic ages.

Under the bluffs that overhung the marsh he came upon thickets of wild roses, with flaming buds, just beginning to open. Where they had opened, their petals were stained with that burning rose-colour which is always gone by noon,—a dye made of sunlight and morning and moisture, so intense that it cannot possibly last . . . must fade, like ecstasy. Niel took out his knife and began to cut the stiff stems, crowded with red thorns.

He would make a bouquet for a lovely lady; a bouquet gathered off the cheeks of morning . . . these roses, only half awake, in the defencelessness of utter beauty. He would leave them just outside one of the French windows of her bedroom. When she opened her shutters to let in the light, she would find them,—and they would perhaps give her a sudden distaste for coarse worldlings like Frank Ellinger.

After tying his flowers with a twist of meadow grass, he went up the hill through the grove and softly round the still house to the north side of Mrs. Forrester's own room, where the door-like green shutters were closed. As he bent to place the flowers on the sill, he heard from within a woman's soft laughter; impatient, indulgent, teasing, eager. Then another laugh, very different, a man's. And it was fat and lazy,—ended in something like a yawn.

Niel found himself at the foot of the hill on the wooden bridge, his face hot, his temples beating, his eyes blind with anger. In his hand he still carried the prickly bunch of wild roses. He threw them over the wire fence into a mud-hole the cattle had trampled under the bank of the creek. He did not know whether he had left the house by the driveway or had come down through the shrubbery. In that instant between stooping to the window-sill and rising, he had lost one of the most beautiful things in his life. Before the dew dried, the morning had been wrecked for him; and all subsequent mornings, he told himself bitterly. This day saw the end of that admiration and loyalty that had been like a bloom on his existence. He could never recapture it. It was gone, like the morning freshness of the flowers.

"Lilies that fester," he muttered, *"lilies that fester smell far worse than weeds."*

Grace, variety, the lovely voice, the sparkle of fun and fancy in those dark eyes; all this was nothing. It was not a moral scruple she had outraged, but an aesthetic ideal. Beautiful women, whose beauty meant more than it said . . . was their brilliancy always fed by something coarse and concealed? Was that their secret?

VIII

NIEL MET his uncle and Captain Forrester when they alighted from the morning train, and drove over to the house with them. The business on which they had gone to Denver was not referred to until they were sitting with Mrs. Forrester in the front parlour. The windows were open, and the perfume of the mock-orange and of June roses was blowing in from the garden. Captain Forrester introduced the subject, after slowly unfolding his handkerchief and wiping his forehead, and his fleshy neck, around his low collar.

"Maidy," he said, not looking at her, "I've come home a poor man. It took about everything there was to square up. You'll have this place, unencumbered, and my pension; that will be about all. The live-stock will bring in something."

Niel saw that Mrs. Forrester grew very pale, but she smiled and brought her husband his cigar stand. "Oh, well! I expect we can manage, can't we?"

"We can just manage. Not much more. I'm afraid Judge Pommeroy considers I acted foolishly."

"Not at all, Mrs. Forrester," the Judge exclaimed. "He acted just as I hope I would have done in his place. But I am an unmarried man. There were certain securities, government bonds, which Captain Forrester could have turned over to you, but it would have been at the expense of the depositors."

"I've known men to do that," said the Captain heavily, "but I never considered they paid their wives a compliment. If Mrs. Forrester is satisfied, I shall never regret my decision." For the first time his tired, swollen eyes sought his wife's.

"I never question your decisions in business, Mr. Forrester. I know nothing about such things."

The Captain put down the cigar he had taken but not lighted, rose with an effort, and walked over to the bay window, where he stood gazing out over his meadows. "The place looks very nice, Maidy," he said presently. "I see you've watered the roses. They need it, this weather. Now, if you'll excuse me, I'll lie down for a while. I did not sleep well on the train. Niel and the Judge will stay for lunch." He opened the door into Mrs. Forrester's room and closed it behind him.

Judge Pommeroy began to explain to Mrs. Forrester the situation they had faced in Denver. The bank, about which Mrs. Forrester knew nothing but its name, was one which paid good interest on small deposits. The depositors were wage-earners; railroad employés, mechanics, and day labourers, many of whom had at some time worked for Captain Forrester. His was the only well-known name among the bank officers, it was the name which promised security and fair treatment to his old workmen and their friends. The other directors were promising young business men with many irons in the fire. But, the Judge said with evident chagrin, they had refused to come up to the scratch and pay their losses like gentlemen. They claimed that the bank was insolvent, not through unwise investments or mismanagement, but because of a nation-wide financial panic, a shrinking in values that no one could have foreseen. They argued that the fair thing was to share the loss with the depositors; to pay them fifty cents on the dollar, giving long-time notes for twenty-five per cent, settling on a basis of seventy-five per cent.

Captain Forrester had stood firm that not one of the depositors should lose a dollar. The promising young business men had listened to him respectfully, but finally told him they would settle only on their own terms; any additional refunding must be his affair. He sent to the vault for his private steel box, opened it in their presence, and sorted the contents on the table. The government bonds he turned in at once. Judge Pommeroy was sent out to sell the mining stocks and other securities in the open market.

At this part of his narrative the Judge rose and began to pace the floor, twisting the seals on his watchchain. "That was what a man of honour was bound to do, Mrs. Forrester. With five of the directors backing down, he had either to lose his name or save it. The depositors had put their savings into that bank because Captain Forrester was president. To those men with no capital but their back and their two hands, his name meant safety. As he tried to explain to the directors, those deposits were above price; money saved to buy a home, or to take care of a man in sickness, or to send a boy to school. And those young men, bright fellows, well thought of in the community, sat there and looked down their noses and let your husband strip himself down to pledging his life insurance! There was a crowd in the street outside the bank all day, every day; Poles and Swedes and Mexicans, looking scared to death. A lot of them couldn't speak English,—seemed like the only English word they knew was 'Forrester.' As we went in and out we'd hear the Mexicans saying, 'Forrester, Forrester.' It was a torment for me, on your account, Ma'm, to see the Captain strip himself. But, 'pon my honour, I couldn't forbid him. As for those white-livered rascals that sat there,—" the Judge stopped before Mrs. Forrester and ruffled his bushy white hair with both hands, "By God, Madam, I think I've lived too long! In my day the difference between a business man and a scoundrel was bigger than the difference between a white man and a nigger. I wasn't the right one to go out there as the Captain's counsel. One of these smooth members of the bar, like Ivy Peters is getting ready to be, might have saved something for you out of the wreck. But I couldn't use my influence with your husband. To that crowd outside the bank doors his name meant a hundred cents on the dollar, and by God, they got it! I'm proud of him, Ma'm; proud of his acquaintance!"

It was the first time Niel had ever seen Mrs. Forrester flush. A quick pink swept over her face. Her eyes glistened with moisture. "You were quite right, Judge. I wouldn't for the world have had him do otherwise for me. He would never hold up his head again. You see, I know him." As she said this she looked at Niel, on the other side of the room, and her glance was like a delicate and very dignified rebuke to some discourtesy,—though he was not conscious of having shown her any.

When their hostess went out to see about lunch, Judge Pommeroy turned to his nephew. "Son, I'm glad you want to be an architect. I can't see any honourable career for a lawyer, in this new business world that's coming up. Leave the law to boys like Ivy Peters, and get into some clean profession. I wasn't the right man to go with Forrester." He shook his head sadly.

"Will they really be poor?"

"They'll be pinched. It's as he said; they've nothing left but this place."

Mrs. Forrester returned and went to waken her husband for lunch. When she opened the door into her room, they heard stertorous breathing, and she called to them to come quickly. The Captain was stretched upon his iron bed in the antechamber, and Mrs. Forrester was struggling to lift his head.

"Quick, Niel," she panted. "We must get pillows under him. Bring those from my bed."

Niel gently pushed her away. Sweat poured from his face as he got his strength under the Captain's shoulders. It was like lifting a wounded elephant. Judge Pommeroy hurried back to the sitting-room and telephoned Dr. Dennison that Captain Forrester had had a stroke.

A stroke could not finish a man like Daniel Forrester. He was kept in his bed for three weeks, and Niel helped Mrs. Forrester and Ben Keezer take care of him. Although he was at the house so much during that time, he never saw Mrs. Forrester alone, — scarcely saw her at all, indeed. With so much to attend to, she became abstracted, almost impersonal. There were many letters to answer, gifts of fruit and wine and flowers to be acknowledged. Solicitous inquiries came from friends scattered all the way from the Missouri to the mountains. When Mrs. Forrester was not in the Captain's room, or in the kitchen preparing special foods for him, she was at her desk.

One morning while she was seated there, a distinguished visitor arrived. Niel, waiting by the door for the letters he was to take to the post, saw a large, red-whiskered man in a rumpled pongee suit and a panama hat come climbing up the hill; Cyrus Dalzell, president of the Colorado & Utah, who had come over in his private car to enquire for the health of his old friend. Niel warned Mrs. Forrester, and she went to meet the visitor, just as he mounted the steps, wiping his face with a red silk bandanna.

He took both the lady's hands and exclaimed in a warm, deep voice, "Here she is, looking as fresh as a bride! May I claim an old privilege?" He bent his head and kissed her. "I won't be in your way, Marian," he said as they came into the house, "but I had to see for myself how he does, and how you do."

Mr. Dalzell shook hands with Niel, and as he talked he moved about the parlour clumsily and softly, like a brown bear. Mrs. Forrester stopped him to straighten his flowing yellow tie and pull down the back of his wrinkled coat. "It's easy to see that Kitty wasn't with you this morning when you dressed," she laughed.

"Thank you, thank you, my dear. I've got a green porter down there, and he doesn't seem to realize the extent of his duties. No, Kitty wanted to come, but we have two giddy nieces out from Portsmouth, visiting us, and she felt she couldn't. I just had my car hitched on to the tail of the Burlington flyer and came myself. Now tell me about Daniel. Was it a stroke?"

Mrs. Forrester sat down on the sofa beside him and told him about her husband's illness, while he interrupted with sympathetic questions and comments, taking her hand between his large, soft palms and patting it affectionately.

"And now I can go home and tell Kitty that he will soon be as good as ever,—and that you look like you were going to lead the ball tonight. You whisper to Daniel that I've got a couple cases of port down in my car that will build him up faster than anything the doctors give him. And I've brought along a dozen sherry, for a lady that knows a thing or two about wines. And next winter you are both coming out to stay with us at the Springs, for a change of air."

Mrs. Forrester shook her head gently. "Oh, that, I'm afraid, is a pretty dream. But we'll dream it, anyway!" Everything about her had brightened since Cyrus Dalzell came up the hill. Even the long garnet earrings beside her cheeks seemed to flash with a deeper colour, Niel thought. She was a different woman from the one who sat there writing, half an hour ago. Her fingers, as they played on the sleeve of the pongee coat, were light and fluttery as butterfly wings.

"No dream at all, my dear. Kitty has arranged everything. You know how quickly she thinks things out. I am to come for you in my car. We'll get my old porter Jim as a valet for

Daniel, and you can just play around and put fresh life into us all. We saw last winter that we couldn't do anything without our Lady Forrester. Nothing came off right without her. If we had a party, we sat down afterward and wondered what in hell we'd had it for. Oh, no, we can't manage without you!"

Tears flashed into her eyes. "That's very dear of you. It's sweet to be remembered when one is away." In her voice there was the heart-breaking sweetness one sometimes hears in lovely, gentle old songs.

IX

AFTER THREE WEEKS the Captain was up and around again. He dragged his left foot, and his left arm was uncertain. Though he recovered his speech, it was thick and clouded; some words he could not pronounce distinctly,—slid over them, dropped out a syllable. Therefore he avoided talking even more than was his habit. The doctor said that unless another brain lesion occurred, he might get on comfortably for some years yet.

In August Niel was to go to Boston to begin coaching for his entrance examinations at the Massachusetts Institute of Technology, where he meant to study architecture. He put off bidding the Forresters good-bye until the very day before he left. His last call was different from any he had ever made there before. Already they began to treat him like a young man. He sat rather stiffly in that parlour where he had been so much at home. The Captain was in his big chair in the bay window, in the full glow of the afternoon sun, saying little, but very friendly. Mrs. Forrester, on the sofa in the shadowy corner of the room, talked about Niel's plans and his journey.

"Is it true that Mary is going to marry Pucelik this fall?" he asked her. "Who will you get to help you?"

"No one, for the present. Ben will do all I can't do. Never mind us. We will pass a quiet winter, like an old country couple,—as we are!" she said lightly.

Niel knew that she faced the winter with terror, but he had never seen her more in command of herself,—or more the mistress of her own house than now, when she was preparing to become the servant of it. He had the feeling, which he never used to have, that her lightness cost her something.

"Don't forget us, but don't mope. Make lots of new friends. You'll never be twenty again. Take a chorus girl out to supper—a pretty one, mind! Don't bother about your allowance. If you got into a scrape, we could manage a little cheque to help you out, couldn't we, Mr. Forrester?"

The Captain puffed and looked amused. "I think we could,

Niel, I think so. Don't get up, my boy. You must stay to dinner."

Niel said he couldn't. He hadn't finished packing, and he was leaving on the morning train.

"Then we must have a little something before you go." Captain Forrester rose heavily, with the aid of his cane, and went into the dining-room. He brought back the decanter and filled three glasses with ceremony. Lifting his glass, he paused, as always, and blinked.

"Happy days!"

"Happy days!" echoed Mrs. Forrester, with her loveliest smile, "and every success to Niel!"

Both the Captain and his wife came to the door with him, and stood there on the porch together, where he had so often seen them stand to speed the parting guest. He went down the hill touched and happy. As he passed over the bridge his spirits suddenly fell. Would that chilling doubt always lie in wait for him, down there in the mud, where he had thrown his roses one morning?

He burned to ask her one question, to get the truth out of her and set his mind at rest: What did she do with all her exquisiteness when she was with a man like Ellinger? Where did she put it away? And having put it away, how could she recover herself, and give one—give even him—the sense of tempered steel, a blade that could fence with anyone and never break?

PART TWO

I

I<small>T WAS TWO YEARS</small> before Niel Herbert came home again, and when he came the first acquaintance he met was Ivy Peters. Ivy got on the train at one of the little stations east of Sweet Water, where he had been trying a case. As he strolled through the Pullman he noticed among the passengers a young man in a grey flannel suit, with a silk shirt of one shade of blue and a necktie of another. After regarding this urban figure from the rear for a few seconds, Ivy glanced down at his own clothes with gloating satisfaction. It was a hot day in June, but he wore the black felt hat and ready-made coat of winter weight he had always affected as a boy. He stepped forward, his hands thrust in his pockets.

"Hullo, Niel. Thought I couldn't be mistaken."

Niel looked up and saw the red, bee-stung face, with its two permanent dimples, smiling down at him in contemptuous jocularity.

"Hello, Ivy. I couldn't be mistaken in you, either."

"Coming home to go into business?"

Niel replied that he was coming only for the summer vacation.

"Oh, you're not through school yet? I suppose it takes longer to make an architect than it does to make a shyster. Just as well; there's not much building going on in Sweet Water these days. You'll find a good many changes."

"Won't you sit down?" Niel indicated the neighbouring chair. "You are practising law?"

"Yes, along with a few other things. Have to keep more than one iron in the fire to make a living with us. I farm a little on the side. I rent that meadow-land on the Forrester place. I've drained the old marsh and put it into wheat. My brother John does the work, and I boss the job. It's quite profitable. I pay them a good rent, and they need it. I doubt if they could get along without. Their influential friends don't seem to help them out much. Remember all those chesty old boys the Captain used to drive about in his democrat wagon,

57

and ship in barrels of Bourbon for? Good deal of bluff about
all those old-timers. The panic put them out of the game. The
Forresters have come down in the world like the rest. You
remember how the old man used to put it over us kids and
not let us carry a gun in there? I'm just mean enough to like
to shoot along that creek a little better than anywhere else,
now. There wasn't any harm in the old Captain, but he had
the delusion of grandeur. He's happier now that he's like the
rest of us and don't have to change his shirt every day." Ivy's
unblinking greenish eyes rested upon Niel's haberdashery.

Niel, however, did not notice this. He knew that Ivy
wanted him to show disappointment, and he was determined
not to do so. He enquired about the Captain's health, point-
edly keeping Mrs. Forrester's name out of the conversation.

"He's only about half there . . . seems contented
enough. . . . She takes good care of him, I'll say that for
her. . . . She seeks consolation, always did, you know . . .
too much French brandy . . . but she never neglects him. I
don't blame her. Real work comes hard on her."

Niel heard these remarks dully, through the buzz of an
idea. He felt that Ivy had drained the marsh quite as much to
spite him and Mrs. Forrester as to reclaim the land. Moreover, he seemed to know that until this moment Ivy himself
had not realized how much that consideration weighed with
him. He and Ivy had disliked each other from childhood,
blindly, instinctively, recognizing each other through antipa-
thy, as hostile insects do. By draining the marsh Ivy had obliterated a few acres of something he hated, though he could
not name it, and had asserted his power over the people who
had loved those unproductive meadows for their idleness and
silvery beauty.

After Ivy had gone on into the smoker, Niel sat looking out
at the windings of the Sweet Water and playing with his idea.
The Old West had been settled by dreamers, great-hearted adventurers who were unpractical to the point of magnificence;
a courteous brotherhood, strong in attack but weak in de-
fence, who could conquer but could not hold. Now all the
vast territory they had won was to be at the mercy of men like
Ivy Peters, who had never dared anything, never risked anything. They would drink up the mirage, dispel the morning

freshness, root out the great brooding spirit of freedom, the generous, easy life of the great land-holders. The space, the colour, the princely carelessness of the pioneer they would destroy and cut up into profitable bits, as the match factory splinters the primeval forest. All the way from the Missouri to the mountains this generation of shrewd young men, trained to petty economies by hard times, would do exactly what Ivy Peters had done when he drained the Forrester marsh.

II

THE NEXT AFTERNOON Niel found Captain Forrester in the bushy little plot he called his rose garden, seated in a stout hickory chair that could be left out in all weather, his two canes beside him. His attention was fixed upon a red block of Colorado sandstone, set on a granite boulder in the middle of the gravel space around which the roses grew. He showed Niel that this was a sun-dial, and explained it with great pride. Last summer, he said, he sat out here a great deal, with a square board mounted on a post, and marked the length of the shadows by his watch. His friend, Cyrus Dalzell, on one of his visits, took this board away, had the diagram exactly copied on sandstone, and sent it to him, with the column-like boulder that formed its base.

"I think it's likely Mr. Dalzell hunted around among the mountains a good many mornings before he found a natural formation like that," said the Captain. "A pillar, such as they had in Bible times. It's from the Garden of the Gods. Mr. Dalzell has his summer home up there."

The Captain sat with the soles of his boots together, his legs bowed out. Everything about him seemed to have grown heavier and weaker. His face was fatter and smoother; as if the features were running into each other, as when a wax face melts in the heat. An old Panama hat, burned yellow by the sun, shaded his eyes. His brown hands lay on his knees, the fingers well apart, nerveless. His moustache was the same straw colour; Niel remarked to him that it had grown no grayer. The Captain touched his cheek with his palm. "Mrs. Forrester shaved me for awhile. She did it very nicely, but I didn't like to have her do it. Now I use one of these safety razors. I can manage, if I take my time. The barber comes over once a week. Mrs. Forrester is expecting you, Niel. She's down in the grove. She goes down there to rest in the hammock."

Niel went round the house to the gate that gave into the grove. From the top of the hill he could see the hammock slung between two cottonwoods, in the low glade at the farther end, where he had fallen the time he broke his arm. The slender white figure was still, and as he hurried across the grass he saw that a white garden hat lay over her face. He approached quietly and was just wondering if she were asleep, when he heard a soft, delighted laugh, and with a quick movement she threw off the lace hat through which she had been watching him. He stepped forward and caught her suspended figure, hammock and all, in his arms. How light and alive she was! like a bird caught in a net. If only he could rescue her and carry her off like this, — off the earth of sad, inevitable periods, away from age, weariness, adverse fortune!

She showed no impatience to be released, but lay laughing up at him with that gleam of something elegantly wild, something fantastic and tantalizing, — seemingly so artless, really the most finished artifice! She put her hand under his chin as if he were still a boy.

"And how handsome he's grown! Isn't the old Judge proud of you! He called me up last night and began sputtering, 'It's only fair to warn you, Ma'm, that I've a very handsome boy over here.' As if I hadn't known you would be! And now you're a man, and have seen the world! Well, what have you found in it?"

"Nothing so nice as you, Mrs. Forrester."

"Nonsense! You have sweethearts?"

"Perhaps."

"Are they pretty?"

"Why they? Isn't one enough?"

"One is too many. I want you to have half a dozen, — and still save the best for us! One would take everything. If you had her, you would not have come home at all. I wonder if you know how we've looked for you?" She took his hand and turned a seal ring about on his little finger absently. "Every night for weeks, when the lights of the train came swinging in down below the meadows, I've said to myself, 'Niel is coming home; there's that to look forward to.'" She caught herself as she always did when she found that she was telling too much, and finished in a playful tone. "So, you see, you mean a great deal to all of us. Did you find Mr. Forrester?"

"Oh, yes! I had to stop and look at his sun-dial."

She raised herself on her elbow and lowered her voice. "Niel, can you understand it? He isn't childish, as some people say, but he will sit and watch that thing hour after hour. How can anybody like to see time visibly devoured? We are all used to seeing clocks go round, but why does he want to see that shadow creep on that stone? Has he changed much? No? I'm glad you feel so. Now tell me about the Adamses and what George is like."

Niel dropped on the turf and sat with his back against a tree trunk, answering her rapid questions and watching her while he talked. Of course, she was older. In the brilliant sun of the afternoon one saw that her skin was no longer like white lilacs,—it had the ivory tint of gardenias that have just begun to fade. The coil of blue-black hair seemed more than ever too heavy for her head. There were lines,—something strained about the corners of her mouth that used not to be there. But the astonishing thing was how these changes could vanish in a moment, be utterly wiped out in a flash of personality, and one forgot everything about her except herself.

"And tell me, Niel, do women really smoke after dinner now with the men, nice women? I shouldn't like it. It's all very well for actresses, but women can't be attractive if they do everything that men do."

"I think just now it's the fashion for women to make themselves comfortable, before anything else."

Mrs. Forrester glanced at him as if he had said something shocking. "Ah, that's just it! The two things don't go together. Athletics and going to college and smoking after dinner—Do you like it? Don't men like women to be different from themselves? They used to."

Niel laughed. Yes, that was certainly the idea of Mrs. Forrester's generation.

"Uncle Judge says you don't come to see him any more as you used to, Mrs. Forrester. He misses it."

"My dear boy, I haven't been over to the town for six weeks. I'm always too tired. We have no horse now, and when I do go I have to walk. That house! Nothing is ever done there unless I do it, and nothing ever moves unless I move it. That's why I come down here in the afternoon,—to get where I can't see the house. I can't keep it up as it should be kept, I'm not strong enough. Oh, yes, Ben helps me; he sweeps and beats the rugs and washes windows, but that doesn't get a house very far." Mrs. Forrester sat up suddenly and pinned on her white hat. "We went all the way to Chicago, Niel, to buy that walnut furniture, couldn't find anything at home big and heavy enough. If I'd known that one day I'd have to push it about, I would have been more easily satisfied!" She rose and shook out her rumpled skirts.

They started toward the house, going slowly up the long, grassy undulation between the trees.

"Don't you miss the marsh?" Niel asked suddenly.

She glanced away evasively. "Not much. I would never have time to go there, and we need the money it pays us. And you haven't time to play any more either, Niel. You must hurry and become a successful man. Your uncle is terribly involved. He has been so careless that he's not much better off than we are. Money is a very important thing. Realize that in the beginning; face it, and don't be ridiculous in the end, like so many of us." They stopped by the gate at the top of the hill and looked back at the green alleys and the sharp shadows, at the quivering fans of light that seemed to push the trees farther apart and made Elysian fields underneath them. Mrs. Forrester put her white hand, with all its rings, on Niel's arm.

"Do you really find a kind of pleasure in coming back to us? That's very unusual, I think. At your age I wanted to be with the young and gay. It's nice for us, though." She looked at him with her rarest smile, one he had seldom seen on her face, but always remembered,—a smile without archness, without gaiety, full of affection and wistfully sad. And the same thing was in her voice when she spoke those quiet words,—the sudden quietness of deep feeling. She turned quickly away. They went through the gate and around the house to where the Captain sat watching the sunset glory on his roses. His wife touched his shoulder.

"Will you go in, now, Mr. Forrester, or shall I bring your coat?"

"I'll go in. Isn't Niel going to stay for dinner?"

"Not this time. He'll come soon, and we'll have a real dinner for him. Will you wait for Mr. Forrester, Niel? I must hurry in and start the fire."

Niel tarried behind and accompanied the Captain's slow

III

NIEL HAD PLANNED to do a great deal of reading in the Forresters' grove that summer, but he did not go over so often as he had intended. The frequent appearance of Ivy Peters about the place irritated him. Ivy visited his new wheat fields on the bottom land very often; and he always took the old path, that led from what was once the marsh, up the steep bank and through the grove. He was likely to appear at any hour, his trousers stuffed into his top-boots, tramping along between the rows of trees with an air of proprietorship. He shut the gate behind the house with a slam and went whistling through the yard. Often he stopped at the kitchen door to call out some pleasantry to Mrs. Forrester. This annoyed Niel, for at that hour of the morning, when she was doing her housework, Mrs. Forrester was not dressed to receive her inferiors. It was one thing to greet the president of the Colorado & Utah *en déshabille*, but it was another to chatter with a coarse-grained fellow like Ivy Peters in her wrapper and slippers, her sleeves rolled up and her throat bare to his cool, impudent eyes.

Sometimes Ivy strode through the rose plot where Captain Forrester was sitting in the sun,—went by without looking at him, as if there were no one there. If he spoke to the Captain at all, he did so as if he were addressing someone incapable of understanding anything. "Hullo, Captain, ain't afraid this sun will spoil your complexion?" or "Well, Captain, you'll have to get the prayer-meetings to take up this rain question. The drought's damned bad for my wheat."

One morning, as Niel was coming up through the grove, he heard laughter by the gate, and there he saw Ivy, with his gun, talking to Mrs. Forrester. She was bareheaded, her skirts blowing in the wind, her arm through the handle of a big tin bucket that rested on the fence beside her. Ivy stood with his hat on his head, but there was in his attitude that unmistakable something which shows that a man is trying to make himself agreeable to a woman. He was telling her a funny story, probably an improper one, for it brought out her naughtiest laugh, with something nervous and excited in it, as if he were going too far. At the end of his story Ivy himself broke into his farm-hand guffaw. Mrs. Forrester shook her finger at him and, catching up her pail, ran back into the house. She bent a little with its weight, but Ivy made no offer to carry it for her. He let her trip away with it as if she were a kitchen maid, and that were her business.

Niel emerged from the grove, and stopped where the Captain sat in the garden. "Good-morning, Captain Forrester. Was that Ivy Peters who just went through here? That fellow hasn't the manners of a pig!" he blurted out.

The Captain pointed to Mrs. Forrester's empty chair. "Sit down, Niel, sit down." He drew his handkerchief from his pocket and began polishing his glasses. "No," he said quietly, "he ain't overly polite."

More than if he had complained bitterly, that guarded admission made one feel how much he had been hurt and offended by Ivy's rudeness. There was something very sad in his voice, and helpless. From his equals, respect had always come to him as his due; from fellows like Ivy he had been able to command it,—to order them off his place, or dismiss them from his employ.

Niel sat down and smoked a cigar with him. They had a long talk about the building of the Black Hills branch of the Burlington. In Boston last winter Niel had met an old mine-owner, who was living in Deadwood when the railroad first came in. When Niel asked him if he had known Daniel Forrester, the old gentleman said, "Forrester? Was he the one with the beautiful wife?"

"You must tell her," said the Captain, stroking the warm surface of his sun-dial. "Yes, indeed. You must tell Mrs. Forrester."

One night in the first week of July, a night of glorious moonlight, Niel found himself unable to read, or to stay indoors at all. He walked aimlessly down the wide, empty street, and crossed the first creek by the foot-bridge. The wide ripe fields, the whole country, seemed like a sleeping garden. One trod the dusty roads softly, not to disturb the deep slumber of the world.

In the Forrester lane the scent of sweet clover hung heavy.

It had always grown tall and green here ever since Niel could remember; the Captain would never let it be cut until the weeds were mowed in the fall. The black, plume-like shadows of the poplars fell across the lane and over Ivy Peters' wheat fields. As he walked on, Niel saw a white figure standing on the bridge over the second creek, motionless in the clear moonlight. He hurried forward. Mrs. Forrester was looking down at the water where it flowed bright over the pebbles. He came up beside her. "The Captain is asleep?"

"Oh, yes, long ago! He sleeps well, thank heaven! After I tuck him in, I have nothing more to worry about."

While they were standing there, talking in low voices, they heard a heavy door slam on the hill. Mrs. Forrester started and looked back over her shoulder. A man emerged from the shadow of the house and came striding down the drive-way. Ivy Peters stepped upon the bridge.

"Good evening," he said to Mrs. Forrester, neither calling her by name nor removing his hat. "I see you have company. I've just been up looking at the old barn, to see if the stalls are fit to put horses in there tomorrow. I'm going to start cutting wheat in the morning, and we'll have to put the horses in your stable at noon. We'd lose time taking them back to town."

"Why, certainly. The horses can go in our barn. I'm sure Mr. Forrester would have no objection." She spoke as if he had asked her permission.

"Oh!" Ivy shrugged. "The men will begin down here at six o'clock. I won't get over till about ten, and I have to meet a client at my office at three. Maybe you could give me some lunch, to save time."

His impudence made her smile. "Very well, then; I invite you to lunch. We lunch at one."

"Thanks. It will help me out." As if he had forgotten himself, he lifted his hat, and went down the lane swinging it in his hand.

Niel stood looking after him. "Why do you allow him to speak to you like that, Mrs. Forrester? If you'll let me, I'll give him a beating and teach him how to speak to you."

"No, no, Niel! Remember, we have to get along with Ivy

Peters, we simply have to!" There was a note of anxiety in her voice, and she caught his arm.

"You don't have to take anything from him, or to stand his bad manners. Anybody else would pay you as much for the land as he does."

"But he has a lease for five years, and he could make it very disagreeable for us, don't you see? Besides," she spoke hurriedly, "there's more than that. He's invested a little money for me in Wyoming, in land. He gets splendid land from the Indians some way, for next to nothing. Don't tell your uncle; I've no doubt it's crooked. But the Judge is like Mr. Forrester; his methods don't work nowadays. He will never get us out of debt, dear man! He can't get himself out. Ivy Peters is terribly smart, you know. He owns half the town already."

"Not quite," said Niel grimly. "He's got hold of a good deal of property. He'll take advantage of anybody's necessity. You know he's utterly unscrupulous, don't you? Why didn't you let Mr. Dalzell, or some of your other old friends, invest your money for you?"

"Oh, it was too little! Only a few hundred dollars I'd saved on the housekeeping. They would put it into something safe, at six per cent. I know you don't like Ivy,—and he knows it! He's always at his worst before you. He's not so bad as—as his face, for instance!" She laughed nervously. "He honestly wants to help us out of the hole we're in. Coming and going all the time, as he does, he sees everything, and I really think he hates to have me work so hard."

"Next time you have anything to invest, you let me take it to Mr. Dalzell and explain. I'll promise to do as well by you as Ivy Peters can."

Mrs. Forrester took his arm and drew him into the lane. "But, my dear boy, you know nothing about these business schemes. You're not clever that way,—it's one of the things I love you for. I don't admire people who cheat Indians. Indeed I don't!" She shook her head vehemently.

"Mrs. Forrester, rascality isn't the only thing that succeeds in business."

"It succeeds faster than anything else, though," she murmured absently. They walked as far as the end of the lane and turned back again. Mrs. Forrester's hand tightened on his arm. She began speaking abruptly. "You see, two years, three years, more of this, and I could still go back to California— and live again. But after that . . . Perhaps people think I've settled down to grow old gracefully, but I've not. I feel such a power to live in me, Niel." Her slender fingers gripped his wrist. "It's grown by being held back. Last winter I was with the Dalzells at Glenwood Springs for three weeks (I owe *that* to Ivy Peters; he looked after things here, and his sister kept house for Mr. Forrester), and I was surprised at myself. I could dance all night and not feel tired. I could ride horseback all day and be ready for a dinner party in the evening. I had no clothes, of course; old evening dresses with yards and yards of satin and velvet in them, that Mrs. Dalzell's sewing woman made over. But I looked well enough! Yes, I did. I always know how I'm looking, and I looked well enough. The men thought so. I looked happier than any woman there. They were nearly all younger, much. But they seemed dull, bored to death. After a glass or two of champagne they went to sleep and had nothing to say! I always look better after the first glass,— it gives me a little colour, it's the only thing that does. I accepted the Dalzells' invitation with a purpose; I wanted to see whether I had anything left worth saving. And I have, I tell you! You would hardly believe it, I could hardly believe it, but I still have!"

By this time they had reached the bridge, a bare white floor in the moonlight. Mrs. Forrester had been quickening her pace all the while. "So that's what I'm struggling for, to get out of this hole,"—she looked about as if she had fallen into a deep well,—"out of it! When I'm alone here for months together, I plan and plot. If it weren't for that—"

As Niel walked back to his room behind the law offices, he felt frightened for her. When women began to talk about still feeling young, didn't it mean that something had broken? Two or three years, she said. He shivered. Only yesterday old Dr. Dennison had proudly told him that Captain Forrester might live a dozen. "We are keeping his general health up remarkably, and he was originally a man of iron."

What hope was there for her? He could still feel her hand upon his arm, as she urged him faster and faster up the lane.

IV

THE WEATHER was dry and intensely hot for several weeks, and then, at the end of July, thunder-storms and torrential rains broke upon the Sweet Water valley. The river burst out of its banks, all the creeks were up, and the stubble of Ivy Peters' wheat fields lay under water. A wide lake and two rushing creeks now separated the Forresters from the town. Ben Keezer rode over to them every day to do the chores and to take them their mail. One evening Ben, with his slicker and leather mailbag, had just come out of the post-office and was preparing to mount his horse, when Niel Herbert stopped him to ask in a low voice whether he had got the Denver paper.

"Oh, yes. I always wait for the papers. She likes to have them to read of an evening. Guess it's pretty lonesome over there." He swung into his saddle and splashed off. Niel walked slowly around to the hotel for dinner. He had found something very disconcerting in the Denver paper: Frank Ellinger's picture on the society page, along with Constance Ogden's. They had been married yesterday at Colorado Springs, and were stopping at the Antlers.

After supper Niel put on his rubber coat and started for the Forresters'. When he reached the first creek, he found that the foot-bridge had been washed out from the far bank and lay obliquely in the stream, battered at by the yellow current which might at any moment carry it away. One could not cross the ford without a horse. He looked irresolutely across the submerged bottom lands. The house was dark, no lights in the parlour windows. The rain was beginning to fall again. Perhaps she had rather be alone tonight. He would go over tomorrow.

He went back to the law office and tried to make himself comfortable, though the place was in distracting disorder. The continued rain had set one of the chimneys leaking, had brought down streams of soot and black water and flooded the stove and the Judge's once handsome Brussels carpet. The tinner had been there all afternoon, trying to find what was the matter with the flue, cutting a new sheet-iron

After some exchanges with the Colorado office, he pointed her to the chair. "Sit down and I'll give it to you. He is on the wire."

He did not dare to leave her alone, though it was awkward enough to be a listener. He walked to the window and stood with his back to the desk where she was sitting.

"Is that you, Frank? This is Marian. I won't keep you a moment. You were asleep? So early? That's not like you. You've reformed already, haven't you? That's what marriage does, they say. No, I wasn't altogether surprised. You might have taken me into your confidence, though. Haven't I deserved it?"

A long, listening pause. Niel stared stupidly at the dark window. He had steeled his nerves for wild reproaches. The voice he heard behind him was her most charming; playful, affectionate, intimate, with a thrill of pleasant excitement that warmed its slight formality and burned through the commonplace words like the colour in an opal. He simply held his breath while she fluttered on:

"Where shall you go for your honeymoon? Oh, I'm very sorry! So soon . . . You must take good care of her. Give her my love. . . . I should think California, at this time of the year, might be right . . ."

It went on like this for some minutes. The voice, it seemed to Niel, was that of a woman, young, beautiful, happy,— warm and at her ease, sitting in her own drawing-room and talking on a stormy night to a dear friend far away.

"Oh, unusually well, for me. Stop and see for yourself. You will be going to Omaha on business next week, before California. Oh, yes, you will! Stop off between trains. You know how welcome you are, always."

A long pause. An exclamation from Mrs. Forrester made Niel turn sharply round. Now it was coming! Her voice was darkening with every word. "I think I understand you. You are not speaking from your own room? What, from the office booth? Oh, then I understand you very well indeed!" Niel looked about in alarm. It was time to stop her, but how? The voice went on.

"Play safe! When have you ever played anything else? You know, Frank, the truth is that you're a coward; a great,

hulking coward. Do you hear me? I want you to hear! . . .
You've got a safe thing at last, I should think; safe and pasty!
How much stock did you get with it? A big block, I hope!
Now let me tell you the truth: I don't want you to come here!
I never want to see you again while I live, and I forbid you to
come and look at me when I'm dead. I don't want your hateful eyes to look at my dead face. Do you hear me? Why don't
you answer me? Don't dare to hang up the receiver, you coward! Oh, you big . . . Frank, Frank, say something! Oh, he's
shut me off, I can't hear him!"

She flung the receiver down, dropped her head on the desk,
and broke into heavy, groaning sobs. Niel stood over her and
waited with composure. For once he had been quick enough;
he had saved her. The moment that quivering passion of
hatred and wrong leaped into her voice, he had taken the
big shears left by the tinner and cut the insulated wire behind
the desk. Her reproaches had got no farther than this room.

When the sobs ceased he touched her shoulder. He shook
her, but there was no response. She was asleep, sunk in a
heavy stupor. Her hands and face were so cold that he
thought there could not be a drop of warm blood left in her
body. He carried her into his room, cut off her drenched
clothing, wrapped her in his bathrobe and put her into his
own bed. She was absolutely unconscious. He blew out the
light, locked her in, and left the building, going as fast as he
could to Judge Pommeroy's cottage. He roused his uncle and
briefly explained the situation.

"Can you dress and go down to the office for the rest of
the night, Uncle Judge? Some one must be with her. And I'll
get over to the Captain at once; he certainly oughtn't to be
left alone. If she could get across the bridge, I guess I can.
By the way, she began talking wild, and I cut the telephone
wire behind your desk. So keep an eye on it. It might make
trouble on a stormy night like this. I'll get a livery hack and
take Mrs. Forrester home in the morning, before the town is
awake."

When daylight began to break Niel went into Captain Forrester's room and told him that his wife had been sent for in
the night to answer a long distance telephone call, and that
now he was going to bring her home.

The Captain lay propped up on three big pillows. Since his face had grown fat and relaxed, its ruggedness had changed to an almost Asiatic smoothness. He looked like a wise old Chinese mandarin as he lay listening to the young man's fantastic story with perfect composure, merely blinking and saying, "Thank you, Niel, thank you."

As Niel went through the sleeping town on his way to the livery barn, he saw the short, plump figure of Mrs. Beasley, like a boiled pudding sewed up in a blue kimono, waddling through the feathery asparagus bed behind the telephone office. She had already been next door to tell her neighbour Molly Tucker, the seamstress, the story of her exciting night.

V

SOON AFTERWARD, when Captain Forrester had another stroke, Mrs. Beasley and Molly Tucker and their friends were perfectly agreed that it was a judgment upon his wife. No judgment could have been crueller. Under the care of him, now that he was helpless, Mrs. Forrester quite went to pieces.

Even after their misfortunes had begun to come upon them, she had maintained her old reserve. She had asked nothing and accepted nothing. Her demeanour toward the townspeople was always the same; easy, cordial, and impersonal. Her own friends had moved away long ago,—all except Judge Pommeroy and Dr. Dennison. When any of the housewives from the town came to call, she met them in the parlour, chatted with them in the smiling, careless manner they could never break through, and they got no further. They still felt they must put on their best dress and carry a card-case when they went to the Forresters'.

But now that the Captain was helpless, everything changed. She could hold off the curious no longer. The townswomen brought soups and custards for the invalid. When they came to sit out the night with him, she turned the house over to them. She was worn out; so exhausted that she was dull to what went on about her. The Mrs. Beasleys and Molly Tuckers had their chance at last. They went in and out of Mrs. Forrester's kitchen as familiarly as they did out of one another's. They rummaged through the linen closet to find more sheets, pried about in the attic and cellar. They went over the house like ants, the house where they had never before got past the parlour; and they found they had been fooled all these years. There was nothing remarkable about the place at all! The kitchen was inconvenient, the sink was smelly. The carpets were worn, the curtains faded, the clumsy, old-fashioned furniture they wouldn't have had for a gift, and the upstairs bed-rooms were full of dust and cobwebs.

Judge Pommeroy remarked to his nephew that he had never seen these women look so wide-awake, so important and pleased with themselves, as now when he encountered them bustling about the Forrester place. The Captain's illness had the effect of a social revival, like a new club or a church society. The creatures grew bolder and bolder,—and Mrs. Forrester, apparently, had no power of resistance. She drudged in the kitchen, slept, half-dressed, in one of the chambers upstairs, kept herself going on black coffee and brandy. All the bars were down. She had ceased to care about anything.

As the women came and went through the lane, Niel sometimes overheard snatches of their conversation.

"Why didn't she sell some of that silver? All those platters and covered dishes stuck away with the tarnish of years on them!"

"I wouldn't mind having some of her linen. There's a chest full of double damask upstairs, every tablecloth long enough to make two. Did you ever see anything like the wine glasses! I'll bet there's not as many in both saloons put together. If she has a sale after he's gone, I'll buy a dozen champagne glasses; they're nice to serve sherbet in."

"There are nine dozen glasses," said Molly Tucker, "counting them for beer and whiskey. If there is a sale, I've a mind to bid in a couple of them green ones, with long stems, for mantel ornaments. But she'll never sell 'em all, unless she can get the saloons to take 'em."

Ed Elliott's mother laughed. "She'll never sell 'em, as long as she's got anything to put in 'em."

"The cellar will go dry, some day."

"I guess there's always plenty that will get it for such as her. I never go there now that I don't smell it on her. I went over late the other night, and she was on her knees, washing up the kitchen floor. Her eyes were glassy. She kept washing the place around the ice-box over and over, till it made me nervous. I said, 'Mrs. Forrester, I think you've washed that place several times already.'"

"Was she confused?"

"Not a particle! She laughed and said she was often absent-minded."

Mrs. Elliott's companions laughed, too, and agreed that absent-minded was a good expression.

Niel repeated this conversation to his uncle. "Uncle," he declared, "I don't see how I can go back to Boston and leave the Forresters. I'd like to chuck school for a year, and see them through. I want to go over there and clear those gossips out. Could you stay at the hotel for a few weeks, and let me have Black Tom? With him to help me, I'd send every one of those women trotting down the lane."

It was arranged quietly, and at once. Tom was put in the kitchen, and Niel himself took charge of the nursing. He met the women with firmness: they were very kind, but now nothing was needed. The Doctor had said the house must be absolutely quiet and that the invalid must see no one.

Once the house was tranquil, Mrs. Forrester went to bed and slept for the better part of a week. The Captain himself improved. On his good days he could be put into a wheel-chair and rolled out into his garden to enjoy the September sunlight and the last of his briar roses.

"Thank you, Niel, thank you, Tom," he often said when they lifted him into his chair. "I value this quiet very highly." If a day came when they thought he ought not to go out, he was sad and disappointed.

"Better get him out, no matter what," said Mrs. Forrester. "He likes to look at his place. That, and his cigar, are the only pleasures he has left."

When she was rested and in command of herself again, she took her place in the kitchen, and Black Tom went back to the Judge.

At night, when he was alone, when Mrs. Forrester had gone to bed and the Captain was resting quietly, Niel found a kind of solemn happiness in his vigils. It had been hard to give up that year; most of his classmates were younger than he. It had cost him something, but now that he had taken the step, he was glad. As he put in the night hours, sitting first in one chair and then in another, reading, smoking, getting a lunch to keep himself awake, he had the satisfaction of those who keep faith. He liked being alone with the old things that had seemed so beautiful to him in his childhood. These were still the most comfortable chairs in the world, and he would never like any pictures so well as "William Tell's Chapel" and "The House of the Tragic Poet." No card-table was so good for solitaire as this old one with a stone top, mosaic in the pattern of a chess-board, which one of the Captain's friends

grave. As Niel and his uncle were driving back from the cemetery with Mrs. Forrester, she spoke for the first time since they had left the house. "Judge Pommeroy," she said quietly, "I think I will have Mr. Forrester's sun-dial taken over and put above his grave. I can have an inscription cut on the base. It seems more appropriate for him than any stone we could buy. And I will plant some of his own rose-bushes beside it."

When they got back to the house it was four o'clock, and she insisted upon making tea for them. "I would like it myself, and it is better to be doing something. Wait for me in the parlour. And, Niel, move the things back as we always have them."

The grey day was darkening, and as the three sat having their tea in the bay-window, swift squalls of snow were falling over the wide meadows between the hill and the town, and the creaking of the big cottonwoods about the house seemed to say that winter had come.

VII

ONE MORNING in April Niel was alone in the law office. His uncle had been ill with rheumatic fever for a long while, and he had been attending to the routine of business.

The door opened, and a figure stood there, strange and yet familiar, — he had to think a moment before he realized that it was Orville Ogden, who used to come to Sweet Water so often, but who had not been seen there now for several years. He didn't look a day older; one eye was still direct and clear, the other clouded and oblique. He still wore a stiff imperial and twisted moustache, the grey colour of old beeswax, and his thin hair was brushed heroically up over the bald spot.

"This is Judge Pommeroy's nephew, isn't it? I can't think of your name, my boy, but I remember you. Is the Judge out?"

"Please be seated, Mr. Ogden. My uncle is ill. He hasn't been at the office for several months. He's had really a very bad time of it. Is there anything I can do for you?"

"Oh, I'm sorry to hear that! I'm sorry." He spoke as if he were. "I guess all we fellows are getting older, whether we like it or not. It made a great difference when Daniel Forrester went." Mr. Ogden took off his overcoat, put his hat and gloves neatly on the desk, and then seemed somewhat at a loss. "What is your uncle's trouble?" he asked suddenly.

Niel told him. "I was to have gone back to school this winter, but uncle begged me to stay and look after things for him. There was no one here he wanted to entrust his business to."

"I see, I see," said Mr. Ogden thoughtfully. "Then you do attend to his business for the present?" He paused and reflected. "Yes, there was something that I wanted to take up with him. I am stopping off for a few hours only, between trains. I might speak to you about it, and you could consult your uncle and write me in Chicago. It's a confidential matter, and concerns another person."

Niel assured him of his discretion, but Mr. Ogden seemed to find the subject difficult to approach. He looked very grave and slowly lit a cigar.

"It is simply," he said at last, "a rather delicate suggestion I wish to make to your uncle about one of his clients. I have several friends in the Government at Washington just at present, friends who would go out of their way to serve me. I have been thinking that we might manage it to get a special increase of pension for Mrs. Forrester. I am due in Chicago this week, and after my business there is finished, I would be quite willing to go on to Washington to see what can be done; provided, of course, that no one, least of all your uncle's client, knows of my activity in the matter."

Niel flushed. "I'm sorry, Mr. Ogden," he brought out, "but Mrs. Forrester is no longer a client of my uncle's. After the Captain's death, she saw fit to take her business away from him."

Mr. Ogden's normal eye became as blank as the other.

"What's that? He isn't her lawyer? Why, for twenty years—"

"I know that, sir. She didn't treat him with much consideration. She transferred her business very abruptly."

"To whom, may I ask?"

"To a lawyer here in town; Ivy Peters."

"Peters? I never heard of him."

"No, you wouldn't have. He wasn't one of the people who went to the Forrester house in the old days. He's one of the younger generation, a few years older than I. He rented part of the Forresters' land for several years before the Captain's death,—was their tenant. That was how Mrs. Forrester came to know him. She thinks him a good business man."

Mr. Ogden frowned. "And is he?"

"Some people think so."

"Is he trustworthy?"

"Far from it. He takes the cases nobody else will take. He may treat Mrs. Forrester honestly. But if he does, it will not be from principle."

"This is very distressing news. Go on with your work, my boy. I must think this over." Mr. Ogden rose and walked about the room, his hands behind him. Niel turned to an unfinished letter on his desk, in order to leave his visitor the more free.

Mr. Ogden's position, he understood, was a difficult one.

He had been devoted to Mrs. Forrester, and before Constance had made up her mind to marry Frank Ellinger, before the mother and daughter began to angle for him, Mr. Ogden had come to the Forresters' more frequently than any of their Denver friends. He hadn't been back, Niel believed, since that Christmas party when he and his family were there with Ellinger. Very soon afterward he must have seen what his women-folk were up to; and whether he approved or disapproved, he must have decided that there was nothing for him to do but to keep out. It hadn't been the Forresters' reversal of fortune that had kept him away. One could see that he was deeply troubled, that he had her heavily on his mind.

Niel had finished his letter and was beginning another, when Mr. Ogden stopped beside his desk, where he stood twisting his imperial tighter and tighter. "You say this young lawyer is unprincipled? Sometimes rascals have a soft spot, a sentiment, where women are concerned."

Niel stared. He immediately thought of Ivy's dimples.

"A soft spot? A sentiment? Mr. Ogden, why not go to his office? A glance would convince you."

"Oh, that's not necessary! I understand." He looked out of the window, from which he could just see the tree-tops of the Forrester grove, and murmured, "Poor lady! So misguided. She ought to have advice from some of Daniel's friends." He took out his watch and consulted it, turning something over in his mind. His train was due in an hour, he said. Nothing could be done at present. In a few moments he left the office.

Afterward, Niel felt sure that when Mr. Ogden stood there uncertainly, watch in hand, he was considering an interview with Mrs. Forrester. He had wanted to go to her, and had given it up. Was he afraid of his women-folk? Or was it another kind of cowardice, the fear of losing a pleasant memory, of finding her changed and marred, a dread of something that would throw a disenchanting light upon the past? Niel had heard his uncle say that Mr. Ogden admired pretty women, though he had married a homely one, and that in his deep, non-committal way he was very gallant. Perhaps, with a little encouragement, he would have gone to see Mrs. Forrester, and he might have helped her. The fact that he had done

that the silver dishes had reappeared on the dinner table, and the candlesticks and flowers. The young men who sat about in the twilight would not know the difference, he thought, if she had furnished her table that morning, from the stock in Wernz's queensware store. Their conception of a really fine dinner service was one "hand painted" by a sister or sweetheart. Each boy sat with his legs crossed, one tan shoe swinging in the air and displaying a tan silk sock. They were talking about clothes; Joe Simpson, who had just inherited his father's clothing business, was eager to tell them what the summer styles would be.

Ivy Peters came in, shaking his drinks. "You fellows are like a bunch of girls,—always talking about what you are going to wear and how you can spend your money. Simpson wouldn't get rich very fast if you all wore your clothes as long as I do. When did I get this suit, Joe?"

"Oh, about the year I graduated from High School, I guess!"

They all laughed at Ivy. No matter what he did or said, they laughed,—in recognition of his general success.

Mrs. Forrester came back, fanning herself with a little sandalwood fan, and when she appeared the boys rose,—in alarm, one might have thought, from the suddenness of it. That much, at any rate, she had succeeded in teaching them.

"Are your cocktails ready, Ivy? You will have to wait for me a moment, while I put some powder on my nose. If I'd known how hot it would be tonight, I'm afraid I wouldn't have had a roast for you. I'm browner than the ducks. You can pour them though. I won't be long."

She disappeared into her own room, and the boys sat down with the same surprising promptness. Ivy Peters carried the tray about, and they held their glasses before them, waiting for Mrs. Forrester. When she came, she took Niel's arm and led him into the dining-room. "Did you notice," she whispered to him, "how they hold their glasses? What is it they do to a little glass to make it look so vulgar? Nobody could ever teach them to pick one up and drink out of it, not if there were tea in it!"

Aloud she said, "Niel, will you light the candles for me? And then take the head of the table, please. You can carve ducks?"

"Not so well as—as my uncle does," he murmured, carefully putting back a candle-shade.

"Nor as Mr. Forrester did? I don't ask that. Nobody can carve now as men used to. But you can get them apart, I suppose? The place at your right is for Annie Peters. She is bringing in the dinner for me. Be seated, gentlemen!" with a little mocking bow and a swinging of earrings.

While Niel was carving the ducks, Annie slipped into the chair beside him, her naturally red face glowing from the heat of the stove. She was several years younger than her brother, whom she obeyed unquestioningly in everything. She had an extremely bad complexion and pale yellow hair with white lights in it, exactly the colour of molasses taffy that has been pulled until it glistens. During the dinner she did not once speak, except to say, "Thank you," or "No, thank you." Nobody but Mrs. Forrester talked much until the first helping of duck was consumed. The boys had not yet learned to do two things at once. They paused only to ask their hostess if she "would care for the jelly," or to answer her questions.

Niel studied Mrs. Forrester between the candles, as she nodded encouragingly to one and another, trying to "draw them out," laughing at Roy Jones' heavy jokes, or congratulating Joe Simpson upon his new dignity as a business man with a business of his own. The long earrings swung beside the thin cheeks that were none the better, he thought, for the rouge she had put on them when she went to her room just before dinner. It improved some women, but not her,—at least, not tonight, when her eyes were hollow with fatigue, and she looked pinched and worn as he had never seen her. He sighed as he thought how much work it meant to cook a dinner like this for eight people,—and a beefsteak with potatoes would have pleased them better! They didn't really like this kind of food at all. Why did she do it? How would she feel about it tonight, when she sank dead weary into bed, after these stupid boys had said good-night, and their yellow shoes had carried them down the hill?

She was not eating anything, she was using up all her vitality to electrify these heavy lads into speech. Niel felt that he must help her, or at least try to. He addressed them one after another with energy and determination; he tried baseball, politics, scandal, the corn crop. They answered him with monosyllables or exclamations. He soon realized that they didn't want his polite remarks; they wanted more duck, and to be let alone with it.

Dinner was soon over, at any rate. The hostess' attempts to prolong it were unavailing. The salad and frozen pudding were dispatched as promptly as the roast had been. The guests went into the parlour and lit cigars.

Mrs. Forrester had the old-fashioned notion that men should be alone after dinner. She did not join them for half an hour. Perhaps she had lain down upstairs, for she looked a little rested. The boys were talking now, discussing a camping trip Ed Elliot was going to take in the mountains. They were giving him advice about camp outfits, trout flies, mixtures to keep off mosquitoes.

"I'll tell you, boys," said Mrs. Forrester, when she had listened to them for a moment, "when I go back to California, I intend to have a summer cabin up in the Sierras, and I invite you, one and all, to visit me. You'll have to work for your keep, you understand; cut the firewood and bring the water and wash the pots and pans, and go out and catch fish for breakfast. Ivy can bring his gun and shoot game for us, and I'll bake bread in an iron pot, the old trappers' way, if I haven't forgotten how. Will you come?"

"You bet we will! You know those mountains by heart, I expect?" said Ed Elliot.

She smiled and shook her head. "It would take a life-time to do that, Ed, more than a life-time. The Sierras,—there's no end to them, and they're magnificent."

Niel turned to her. "Have you ever told the boys how it was you first met Captain Forrester in the mountains out there? If they haven't heard the story, I think they would like it."

"Really, would you? Well, once upon a time, when I was a very young girl, I was spending the summer at a camp in the mountains, with friends of my father's."

She began there, but that was not the beginning of the story; long ago Niel had heard from his uncle that the beginning was a scandal and a murder. When Marian Ormsby was nineteen, she was engaged to Ned Montgomery, a gaudy young millionaire of the Gold Coast. A few weeks before the date set for their marriage, Montgomery was shot and killed in the lobby of a San Francisco hotel by the husband of another woman. The subsequent trial involved a great deal of publicity, and Marian was hurried away from curious eyes and sent up into the mountains until the affair should blow over.

Tonight Mrs. Forrester began with "Once upon a time." Sitting at one end of the big sofa, her slippers on a foot-stool and her head in shadow, she stirred the air before her face with the sandalwood fan as she talked, the rings glittering on her white fingers. She told them how Captain Forrester, then a widower, had come up to the camp to visit her father's partner. She had noticed him very little,—she was off every day with the young men. One afternoon she had persuaded young Fred Harney, an intrepid mountain climber, to take her down the face of Eagle Cliff. They were almost down, and were creeping over a projecting ledge, when the rope broke, and they dropped to the bottom. Harney fell on the rocks and was killed instantly. The girl was caught in a pine tree, which arrested her fall. Both her legs were broken, and she lay in the canyon all night in the bitter cold, swept by the icy canyon draught. Nobody at the camp knew where to look for the two missing members of the party,—they had stolen off alone for their foolhardy adventure. Nobody worried, because Harney knew all the trails and could not get lost. In the morning, however, when they were still missing, search parties went out. It was Captain Forrester's party that found Marian, and got her out by the lower trail. The trail was so steep and narrow, the turns round the jutting ledges so sharp, that it was impossible to take her out on a litter. The men took turns carrying her, hugging the canyon walls with their shoulders as they crept along. With her broken legs hanging, she suffered terribly,—fainted again and again. But she noticed that she suffered less when Captain Forrester carried her, and that he took all the most dangerous places on the trail himself. "I could feel his heart pump and his muscles strain," she said, "when he balanced himself and me on the rocks. I knew that if we fell, we'd go together; he would never drop me."

They got back to camp, and everything possible was done for her, but by the time a surgeon could be got up from San Francisco, her fractures had begun to knit and had to be broken over again.

"It was Captain Forrester I wanted to hold my hand when the surgeon had to do things to me. You remember, Niel, he always boasted that I never screamed when they were carrying me up the trail. He stayed at the camp until I could begin to walk, holding to his arm. When he asked me to marry him, he didn't have to ask twice. Do you wonder?" She looked with a smile about the circle, and drew her finger-tips absently across her forehead as if to brush away something,—the past, or the present, who could tell?

The boys were genuinely moved. While she was answering their questions, Niel thought about the first time he ever heard her tell that story: Mr. Dalzell had stopped off with a party of friends from Chicago; Marshall Field and the president of the Union Pacific were among them, he remembered, and they were going through in Mr. Dalzell's private car to hunt in the Black Hills. She had, after all, not changed so much since then. Niel felt tonight that the right man could save her, even now. She was still her indomitable self, going through her old part,—but only the stage-hands were left to listen to her. All those who had shared in fine undertakings and bright occasions were gone.

IX

With the summer months Judge Pommeroy's health improved, and as soon as he was able to be back in his office, Niel began to plan to return to Boston. He would get there the first of August and would go to work with a tutor to make up for the months he had lost. It was a melancholy time for him. He was in a fever of impatience to be gone, and yet he felt that he was going away forever, and was making the final break with everything that had been dear to him in his boyhood. The people, the very country itself, were changing so fast that there would be nothing to come back to.

He had seen the end of an era, the sunset of the pioneer. He had come upon it when already its glory was nearly spent. So in the buffalo times a traveller used to come upon the embers of a hunter's fire on the prairie, after the hunter was up and gone; the coals would be trampled out, but the ground was warm, and the flattened grass where he had slept and where his pony had grazed, told the story.

This was the very end of the road-making West; the men who had put plains and mountains under the iron harness were old; some were poor, and even the successful ones were hunting for rest and a brief reprieve from death. It was already gone, that age; nothing could ever bring it back. The taste and smell and song of it, the visions those men had seen in the air and followed,—these he had caught in a kind of after-glow in their own faces,—and this would always be his.

It was what he most held against Mrs. Forrester; that she was not willing to immolate herself, like the widow of all these great men, and die with the pioneer period to which she belonged; that she preferred life on any terms. In the end, Niel went away without bidding her good-bye. He went away with weary contempt for her in his heart.

It happened like this,—had scarcely the dignity of an episode. It was nothing, and yet it was everything. Going over to see her one summer evening, he stopped a moment by the dining-room window to look at the honeysuckle. The dining-room door was open into the kitchen, and there Mrs. Forrester stood at a table, making pastry. Ivy Peters came in at the kitchen door, walked up behind her, and unconcernedly put both arms around her, his hands meeting over her breast. She did not move, did not look up, but went on rolling out pastry.

Niel went down the hill. "For the last time," he said, as he crossed the bridge in the evening light, "for the last time." And it was even so; he never went up the poplar-bordered road again. He had given her a year of his life, and she had thrown it away. He had helped the Captain to die peacefully, he believed; and now it was the Captain who seemed the reality. All those years he had thought it was Mrs. Forrester who made that house so different from any other. But ever since the Captain's death it was a house where old friends, like his uncle, were betrayed and cast off, where common fellows behaved after their kind and knew a common woman when they saw her.

If he had not had the nature of a spaniel, he told himself, he would never have gone back after the first time. It took two doses to cure him. Well, he had had them! Nothing she could ever do would in the least matter to him again.

He had news of her now and then, as long as his uncle lived. *"Mrs. Forrester's name is everywhere coupled with Ivy Peters',"* the Judge wrote. *"She does not look happy, and I fear her health is failing, but she has put herself in such a position that her husband's friends cannot help her."*

And again: *"Of Mrs. Forrester, no news is good news. She is sadly broken."*

After his uncle's death, Niel heard that Ivy Peters had at last bought the Forrester place, and had brought a wife from Wyoming to live there. Mrs. Forrester had gone West,—people supposed to California.

It was years before Niel could think of her without chagrin. But eventually, after she had drifted out of his ken, when he did not know if Daniel Forrester's widow were living or dead, Daniel Forrester's wife returned to him, a bright, impersonal memory.

He came to be very glad that he had known her, and that she had had a hand in breaking him in to life. He has known pretty women and clever ones since then,—but never one like her, as she was in her best days. Her eyes, when they laughed for a moment into one's own, seemed to promise a wild delight that he has not found in life. "I know where it is," they seemed to say, "I could show you!" He would like to call up the shade of the young Mrs. Forrester, as the witch of Endor called up Samuel's, and challenge it, demand the secret of that ardour; ask her whether she had really found some ever-blooming, ever-burning, ever-piercing joy, or whether it was all fine play-acting. Probably she had found no more than another; but she had always the power of suggesting things much lovelier than herself, as the perfume of a single flower may call up the whole sweetness of spring.

Niel was destined to hear once again of his long-lost lady. One evening as he was going into the dining-room of a Chicago hotel, a broad-shouldered man with an open, sun-browned face, approached him and introduced himself as one of the boys who had grown up in Sweet Water.

"I'm Ed Elliott, and I thought it must be you. Could we take a table together? I promised an old friend of yours to give you a message, if I ever ran across you. You remember Mrs. Forrester? Well, I saw her again, twelve years after she left Sweet Water,—down in Buenos Ayres." They sat down and ordered dinner.

"Yes, I was in South America on business. I'm a mining engineer, I spent some time in Buenos Ayres. One evening there was a banquet of some sort at one of the big hotels, and I happened to step out of the bar, just as a car drove up to the entrance where the guests were going in. I paid no attention until one of the ladies laughed. I recognized her by her laugh,—that hadn't changed a particle. She was all done up in furs, with a scarf over her head, but I saw her eyes, and then I was sure. I stepped up and spoke to her. She seemed glad to see me, made me go into the hotel, and talked to me until her husband came to drag her away to the dinner. Oh, yes, she was married again,—to a rich, cranky old English-man; Henry Collins was his name. He was born down there, she told me, but she met him in California. She told me they lived on a big stock ranch, and had come down in their car for this banquet. I made inquiries afterward and found the old fellow was quite a character; had been married twice before, once to a Brazilian woman. People said he was rich, but quarrelsome and rather stingy. She seemed to have everything, though. They travelled in a fine French car, and she had brought her maid along, and he had his valet. No, she hadn't changed as much as you'd think. She was a good deal made up, of course, like most of the women down there; plenty of powder, and a little red, too, I guess. Her hair was black, blacker than I remembered it; looked as if she dyed it. She invited me to visit them on their estate, and so did the old man, when he came to get her. She asked about everybody, and said, 'If you ever meet Niel Herbert, give him my love, and tell him I often think of him.' She said again, 'Tell him things have turned out well for me. Mr. Collins is the kindest of husbands.' I called at your office in New York on my way back from South America, but you were somewhere in Europe. It was remarkable, how she'd come up again. She seemed pretty well gone to pieces before she left Sweet Water."

"Do you suppose," said Niel, "that she could be living still? I'd almost make the trip to see her."

"No, she died about three years ago. I know that for certain. After she left Sweet Water, wherever she was, she always sent a cheque to the Grand Army Post every year to have flowers put on Captain Forrester's grave for Decoration Day. Three years ago the Post got a letter from the old Englishman, with a draft for the future care of Captain Forrester's grave, *in memory of my late wife, Marian Forrester Collins.*'"

"So we may feel sure that she was well cared for, to the very end," said Niel. "Thank God for that!"

"I knew you'd feel that way," said Ed Elliot, as a warm wave of feeling passed over his face. "I did!"

THE END.

THE PROFESSOR'S HOUSE

"A turquoise set in silver, wasn't it? . .
Yes, a turquoise set in dull silver."
—LOUIE MARSELLUS

lunched and had his tea in the garden. And it was there he and Tom Outland used to sit and talk half through the warm, soft nights.

On this September morning, however, St. Peter knew that he could not evade the unpleasant effects of change by tarrying among his autumn flowers. He must plunge in like a man, and get used to the feeling that under his work-room there was a dead, empty house. He broke off a geranium blossom, and with it still in his hand went resolutely up two flights of stairs to the third floor where, under the slope of the mansard roof, there was one room still furnished—that is, if it had ever been furnished.

The low ceiling sloped down on three sides, the slant being interrupted on the east by a single square window, swinging outward on hinges and held ajar by a hook in the sill. This was the sole opening for light and air. Walls and ceiling alike were covered with a yellow paper which had once been very ugly, but had faded into inoffensive neutrality. The matting on the floor was worn and scratchy. Against the wall stood an old walnut table, with one leaf up, holding piles of orderly papers. Before it was a cane-backed office chair that turned on a screw. This dark den had for many years been the Professor's study.

Downstairs, off the back parlour, he had a show study, with roomy shelves where his library was housed, and a proper desk at which he wrote letters. But it was a sham. This was the place where he worked. And not he alone. For three weeks in the fall, and again three in the spring, he shared his cuddy with Augusta, the sewing-woman, niece of his old landlord, a reliable, methodical spinster, a German Catholic and very devout.

Since Augusta finished her day's work at five o'clock, and the Professor, on week-days, worked here only at night, they did not elbow each other too much. Besides, neither was devoid of consideration. Every evening, before she left, Augusta swept up the scraps from the floor, rolled her patterns, closed the sewing-machine, and picked ravellings off the box-couch, so that there would be no threads to stick to the Professor's old smoking-jacket if he should happen to lie down for a moment in working-hours.

St. Peter, in his turn, when he put out his lamp after midnight, was careful to brush away ashes and tobacco crumbs—smoking was very distasteful to Augusta—and to open the hinged window back as far as it would go, on the second hook, so that the night wind might carry away the smell of his pipe as much as possible. The unfinished dresses which she left hanging on the forms, however, were often so saturated with smoke that he knew she found it a trial to work on them next morning.

These "forms" were the subject of much banter between them. The one which Augusta called "the bust" stood in the darkest corner of the room, upon a high wooden chest in which blankets and winter wraps were yearly stored. It was a headless, armless female torso, covered with strong black cotton, and so richly developed in the part for which it was named that the Professor once explained to Augusta how, in calling it so, she followed a natural law of language, termed, for convenience, metonymy. Augusta enjoyed the Professor when he was *risqué*, since she was sure of his ultimate delicacy. Though this figure looked so ample and billowy (as if you might lay your head upon its deep-breathing softness and rest safe forever), if you touched it you suffered a severe shock, no matter how many times you had touched it before. It presented the most unsympathetic surface imaginable. Its hardness was not that of wood, which responds to concussion with living vibration and is stimulating to the hand, nor that of felt, which drinks something from the fingers. It was a dead, opaque, lumpy solidity, like chunks of putty, or tightly packed sawdust—very disappointing to the tactile sense, yet somehow always fooling you again. For no matter how often you had bumped up against that torso, you could never believe that contact with it would be as bad as it was.

The second form was more self-revelatory; a full-length female figure in a smart wire skirt with a trim metal waist line. It had no legs, as one could see all too well, no viscera behind its glistening ribs, and its bosom resembled a strong wire bird-cage. But St. Peter contended that it had a nervous system. When Augusta left it clad for the night in a new party dress for Rosamond or Kathleen, it often took on a sprightly, tricky air, as if it were going out for the evening to make a great show of being harum-scarum, giddy, *folle*. It seemed just on the point of tripping downstairs, or on tiptoe, waiting for the waltz to begin. At times the wire lady was most convincing in her pose as a woman of light behaviour, but she never fooled St. Peter. He had his blind spots, but he had never been taken in by one of her kind!

Augusta had somehow got it into her head that these forms were unsuitable companions for one engaged in scholarly pursuits, and she periodically apologized for their presence when she came to install herself and fulfil her "time" at the house.

"Not at all, Augusta," the Professor had often said. "If they were good enough for *Monsieur Bergeret*, they are certainly good enough for me."

This morning, as St. Peter was sitting in his desk chair, looking musingly at the pile of papers before him, the door opened and there stood Augusta herself. How astonishing that he had not heard her heavy, deliberate tread on the now uncarpeted stair!

"Why, Professor St. Peter! I never thought of finding you here, or I'd have knocked. I guess we will have to do our moving together."

St. Peter had risen—Augusta loved his manners—but he offered her the sewing-machine chair and resumed his seat.

"Sit down, Augusta, and we'll talk it over. I'm not moving just yet—don't want to disturb all my papers. I'm staying on until I finish a piece of writing. I've seen your uncle about it. I'll work here, and board at the new house. But this is confidential. If it were noised about, people might begin to say that Mrs. St. Peter and I had—how do they put it, parted, separated?"

Augusta dropped her eyes in an indulgent smile. "I think people in your station would say separated."

"Exactly; a good scientific term, too. Well, we haven't, you know. But I'm going to write on here for a while."

"Very well, sir. And I won't always be getting in your way now. In the new house you have a beautiful study downstairs, and I have a light, airy room on the third floor."

"Where you won't smell smoke, eh?"

"Oh, Professor, I never really minded!" Augusta spoke with feeling. She rose and took up the black bust in her long arms.

The Professor also rose, very quickly. "What are you doing?"

She laughed. "Oh, I'm not going to carry them through the street, Professor! The grocery boy is downstairs with his cart, to wheel them over."

"Wheel them over?"

"Why, yes, to the new house, Professor. I've come a week before my regular time, to make curtains and hem linen for Mrs. St. Peter. I'll take everything over this morning except the sewing-machine—that's too heavy for the cart, so the boy will come back for it with the delivery wagon. Would you just open the door for me, please?"

"No, I won't! Not at all. You don't need her to make curtains. I can't have this room changed if I'm going to work here. He can take the sewing-machine—yes. But put her back on the chest where she belongs, please. She does very well there." St. Peter had got to the door, and stood with his back against it.

Augusta rested her burden on the edge of the chest.

"But next week I'll be working on Mrs. St. Peter's clothes, and I'll need the forms. As the boy's here, he'll just wheel them over," she said soothingly.

"I'm damned if he will! They shan't be wheeled. They stay right there in their own place. You shan't take away my ladies. I never heard of such a thing!"

Augusta was vexed with him now, and a little ashamed of him. "But, Professor, I can't work without my forms. They've been in your way all these years, and you've always complained of them, so don't be contrary, sir."

"I never complained, Augusta. Perhaps of certain disappointments they recalled, or of cruel biological necessities they imply—but of them individually, never! Go and buy some new ones for your airy atelier, as many as you wish—I'm said to be rich now, am I not?—Go buy, but you can't have my women. That's final."

Augusta looked down her nose as she did at church when the dark sins were mentioned. "Professor," she said severely, "I think this time you are carrying a joke too far. You never used to." From the tilt of her chin he saw that she felt the presence of some improper suggestion.

"No matter what you think, you can't have them." They considered, both were in earnest now. Augusta was first to break the defiant silence.

"I suppose I am to be allowed to take my patterns?"

"Your patterns? Oh, yes, the cut-out things you keep in the couch with my old note-books? Certainly, you can have them. Let me lift it for you." He raised the hinged top of the box-couch that stood against the wall, under the slope of the ceiling. At one end of the upholstered box were piles of note-books and bundles of manuscript tied up in square packages with mason's cord. At the other end were many little rolls of patterns, cut out of newspapers and tied with bits of ribbon, gingham, silk, georgette; notched charts which followed the changing stature and figures of the Misses St. Peter from early childhood to womanhood. In the middle of the box, patterns and manuscripts interpenetrated.

"I see we shall have some difficulty in separating our life work, Augusta. We've kept our papers together a long while now."

"Yes, Professor. When I first came to sew for Mrs. St. Peter, I never thought I should grow grey in her service."

He started. What other future could Augusta possibly have expected? This disclosure amazed him.

"Well, well, we mustn't think mournfully of it, Augusta. Life doesn't turn out for any of us as we plan." He stood and watched her large slow hands travel about among the little packets, as she put them into his waste-basket to carry them down to the cart. He had often wondered how she managed to sew with hands that folded and unfolded as rigidly as umbrellas—no light French touch about Augusta; when she sewed on a bow, it stayed there. She herself was tall, large-boned, flat and stiff, with a plain, solid face, and brown eyes not destitute of fun. As she knelt by the couch, sorting her patterns, he stood beside her, his hand on the lid, though it would have stayed up unsupported. Her last remark had troubled him.

"What a fine lot of hair you have, Augusta! You know I think it's rather nice, that grey wave on each side. Gives it character. You'll never need any of this false hair that's in all the shop windows."

"There's altogether too much of that, Professor. So many of my customers are using it now—ladies you wouldn't expect would. They say most of it was cut off the heads of dead Chinamen. Really, it's got to be such a frequent thing that the priest spoke against it only last Sunday."

"Did he, indeed? Why, what could he say? Seems such a personal matter."

"Well, he said it was getting to be a scandal in the Church, and a priest couldn't go to see a pious woman any more without finding switches and rats and transformations lying about her room, and it was disgusting."

"Goodness gracious, Augusta! What business has a priest going to see a woman in the room where she takes off these ornaments—or to see her without them?"

Augusta grew red, and tried to look angry, but her laugh narrowly missed being a giggle. "He goes to give them the Sacrament, of course, Professor! You've made up your mind to be contrary to-day, haven't you?"

"You relieve me greatly. Yes, I suppose in cases of sudden illness the hair would be lying about where it was lightly taken off. But as you first quoted the priest, Augusta, it was rather shocking. You'll never convert me back to the religion of my fathers now, if you're going to sew in the new house and I'm going to work on here. Who is ever to remind me when it's All Souls' day, or Ember day, or Maundy Thursday, or anything?"

Augusta said she must be leaving. St. Peter heard her well-known tread as she descended the stairs. How much she reminded him of, to be sure! She had been most at the house in the days when his daughters were little girls and needed so many clean frocks. It was in those very years that he was beginning his great work; when the desire to do it and the difficulties attending such a project strove together in his mind like Macbeth's two spent swimmers—years when he had the courage to say to himself: "I will do this dazzling, this beautiful, this utterly impossible thing!"

During the fifteen years he had been working on his *Spanish Adventurers in North America*, this room had been his centre of operations. There had been delightful excursions and digressions; the two Sabbatical years when he was in Spain studying records, two summers in the South-west on the trail of his adventurers, another in Old Mexico, dashes to France to see his foster-brothers. But the notes and the records and the ideas always came back to this room. It was here they were digested and sorted, and woven into their proper place in his history.

Fairly considered, the sewing-room was the most inconvenient study a man could possibly have, but it was the one place in the house where he could get isolation, insulation from the engaging drama of domestic life. No one was tramping over him, and only a vague sense, generally pleasant, of what went on below came up the narrow stairway. There were certainly no other advantages. The furnace heat did not reach the third floor. There was no way to warm the sewing-room, except by a rusty, round gas stove with no flue—a stove which consumed gas imperfectly and contaminated the air. To remedy this, the window must be left open—otherwise, with the ceiling so low, the air would speedily become unfit to breathe. If the stove were turned down, and the window left open a little way, a sudden gust of wind would blow the wretched thing out altogether, and a deeply absorbed man might be asphyxiated before he knew it. The Professor had found that the best method, in winter, was to turn the gas on full and keep the window wide on the hook, even if he had to put on a leather jacket over his working-coat. By that arrangement he had somehow managed to get air enough to work by.

He wondered now why he had never looked about for a better stove, a newer model; or why he had not at least painted this one, flaky with rust. But he had been able to get on only by neglecting negative comforts. He was by no means an ascetic. He knew that he was terribly selfish about personal pleasures, fought for them. If a thing gave him delight, he got it, if he sold his shirt for it. By doing without many so-called necessities he had managed to have his luxuries. He might, for instance, have had a convenient electric drop-light attached to the socket above his writing-table. Preferably he wrote by a faithful kerosene lamp which he filled and tended himself. But sometimes he found that the oil-can in the closet was empty; then, to get more, he would have had to go down through the house to the cellar, and on his way he would almost surely become interested in what the children were doing, or in what his wife was doing—or he would notice that the kitchen linoleum was breaking under the sink where the maid kicked it up, and he would stop to tack it down. On that perilous journey down through the human house he might lose his mood, his enthusiasm, even his temper. So when the lamp was empty—and that usually occurred when he was in the middle of a most important passage—he jammed an eyeshade on his forehead and worked by the glare of that tormenting pear-shaped bulb, sticking out of the wall on a short curved neck just about four feet above his table. It was hard on eyes even as good as his. But once at his desk, he didn't dare quit it. He had found that you can train the mind to be active at a fixed time, just as the stomach is trained to be hungry at certain hours of the day.

If someone in the family happened to be sick, he didn't go to his study at all. Two evenings of the week he spent with his wife and daughters, and one evening he and his wife went out to dinner, or to the theatre or a concert. That left him only four. He had Saturdays and Sundays, of course, and on those two days he worked like a miner under a landslide. Augusta was not allowed to come on Saturday, though she was paid for that day. All the while that he was working so fiercely by night, he was earning his living during the day; carrying full university work and feeding himself out to hundreds of students in lectures and consultations. But that was another life.

St. Peter had managed for years to live two lives, both of them very intense. He would willingly have cut down on his university work, would willingly have given his students chaff and sawdust—many instructors had nothing else to give them and got on very well—but his misfortune was that he loved youth—he was weak to it, it kindled him. If there was one eager eye, one doubting, critical mind, one lively curiosity in a whole lecture-room full of commonplace boys and girls, he was its servant. That ardour could command him. It hadn't worn out with years, this responsiveness, any more than the magnetic currents wear out; it had nothing to do with Time.

But he had burned his candle at both ends to some purpose—he had got what he wanted. By many petty economies of purse, he had managed to be extravagant with not a cent in the world but his professor's salary—he didn't, of course, touch his wife's small income from her father. By eliminations and combinations so many and subtle that it now made his head ache to think of them, he had done full justice to his university lectures, and at the same time carried on an engrossing piece of creative work. A man can do anything if he wishes to enough, St. Peter believed. Desire is creation, is the magical element in that process. If there were an instrument by which to measure desire, one could foretell achievement. He had been able to measure it, roughly, just once, in his student Tom Outland,—and he had foretold.

There was one fine thing about this room that had been the scene of so many defeats and triumphs. From the window he could see, far away, just on the horizon, a long, blue, hazy smear—Lake Michigan, the inland sea of his childhood. Whenever he was tired and dull, when the white pages before him remained blank or were full of scratched-out sentences, then left his desk, took the train to a little station twelve miles away, and spent a day on the lake with his sail-boat; jumping out to swim, floating on his back alongside, then climbing into his boat again.

When he remembered his childhood, he remembered blue water. There were certain human figures against it, of course; his practical, strong-willed Methodist mother, his gentle, weaned-away Catholic father, the old Kanuck grandfather, various brothers and sisters. But the great fact in life, the always possible escape from dullness, was the lake. The sun rose out of it, the day began there; it was like an open door that nobody could shut. The land and all its dreariness could never close in on you. You had only to look at the lake, and you knew you would soon be free. It was the first thing one saw in the morning, across the rugged cow pasture studded with shaggy pines, and it ran through the days like the weather, not a thing thought about, but a part of consciousness itself. When the ice chunks came in of a winter morning, crumbly and white, throwing off gold and rose-coloured reflections from a copper-coloured sun behind the grey clouds, he didn't

observe the detail or know what it was that made him happy;
but now, forty years later, he could recall all its aspects perfectly. They had made pictures in him when he was unwilling
and unconscious, when his eyes were merely open wide.

When he was eight years old, his parents sold the lakeside
farm and dragged him and his brothers and sisters out to the
wheat lands of central Kansas. St. Peter nearly died of it.
Never could he forget the few moments on the train when
that sudden, innocent blue across the sand dunes was dying
for ever from his sight. It was like sinking for the third time.
No later anguish, and he had had his share, went so deep or
seemed so final. Even in his long, happy student years with
the Thierault family in France, that stretch of blue water was
the one thing he was home-sick for. In the summer he used to
go with the Thierault boys to Brittany or to the Languedoc
coast; but his lake was itself, as the Channel and the Mediterranean were themselves. "No," he used to tell the boys, who
were always asking him about *le Michigan*, "it is altogether
different. It is a sea, and yet it is not salt. It is blue, but quite
another blue. Yes, there are clouds and mists and sea-gulls,
but—I don't know, *il est toujours plus naïf.*"

Afterward, when St. Peter was looking for a professorship,
because he was very much in love and must marry at once,
out of the several positions offered him he took the one at
Hamilton, not because it was the best, but because it seemed
to him that any place near the lake was a place where one
could live. The sight of it from his study window these many
years had been of more assistance than all the convenient
things he had done without would have been.

Just in that corner, under Augusta's archaic "forms," he had
always meant to put the filing-cabinets he had never spared
the time or money to buy. They would have held all his notes
and pamphlets, and the spasmodic rough drafts of passages
far ahead. But he had never got them, and now he really
didn't need them; it would be like locking the stable after the
horse is stolen. For the horse was gone—that was the thing
he was feeling most just now. In spite of all he'd neglected, he
had completed his *Spanish Adventurers* in eight volumes—
without filing-cabinets or money or a decent study or a decent
stove—and without encouragement, Heaven knew! For all

the interest the first three volumes awoke in the world, he might as well have dropped them into Lake Michigan. They had been timidly reviewed by other professors of history, in technical and educational journals. Nobody saw that he was trying to do something quite different—they merely thought he was trying to do the usual thing, and had not succeeded very well. They recommended to him the more even and genial style of John Fiske.

St. Peter hadn't, he could honestly say, cared a whoop—not in those golden days. When the whole plan of his narrative was coming clearer and clearer all the time, when he could feel his hand growing easier with his material, when all the foolish conventions about that kind of writing were falling away and his relation with his work was becoming every day more simple, natural, and happy,—he cared as little as the Spanish Adventurers themselves what Professor So-and-So thought about them. With the fourth volume he began to be aware that a few young men, scattered about the United States and England, were intensely interested in his experiment. With the fifth and sixth, they began to express their interest in lectures and in print. The two last volumes brought him a certain international reputation and what were called rewards—among them, the Oxford prize for history, with its five thousand pounds, which had built him the new house into which he did not want to move.

"Godfrey," his wife had gravely said one day, when she detected an ironical turn in some remark he made about the new house, "is there something you would rather have done with that money than to have built a house with it?"

"Nothing, my dear, nothing. If with that cheque I could have bought back the fun I had writing my history, you'd never have got your house. But one couldn't get that for twenty thousand dollars. The great pleasures don't come so cheap. There is nothing else, thank you."

II

THAT EVENING St. Peter was in the new house, dressing for dinner. His two daughters and their husbands were dining with them, also an English visitor. Mrs. St. Peter heard the shower going as she passed his door. She entered his room and waited until he came out in his bath-robe, rubbing his wet, ink-black hair with a towel.

"Surely you'll admit that you like having your own bath," she said, looking past him into the glittering white cubicle, flooded with electric light, which he had just quitted.

"Whoever said I didn't? But more than anything else, I like my closets. I like having room for all my clothes, without hanging one coat on top of another, and not having to get down on my marrow-bones and fumble in dark corners to find my shoes."

"Of course you do. And it's much more dignified, at your age, to have a room of your own."

"It's convenient, certainly, though I hope I'm not so old as to be personally repulsive?" He glanced into the mirror and straightened his shoulders as if he were trying on a coat.

Mrs. St. Peter laughed,—a pleasant, easy laugh with genuine amusement in it. "No, you are very handsome, my dear, especially in your bath-robe. You grow better-looking and more intolerant all the time."

"Intolerant?" He put down his shoe and looked up at her. The thing that stuck in his mind constantly was that she was growing more and more intolerant, about everything except her sons-in-law; that she would probably continue to do so, and that he must school himself to bear it.

"I suppose it's a natural process," she went on, "but you ought to try, try seriously, I mean, to curb it where it affects the happiness of your daughters. You are too severe with Scott and Louie. All young men have foolish vanities—you had plenty."

St. Peter sat with his elbows on his knees, leaning forward and playing absently with the tassels of his bath-robe. "Why, Lillian, I have exercised the virtue of patience with those two young men more than with all the thousands of young

ruffians who have gone through my class-rooms. My forbearance is overstrained, it's gone flat. That's what's the matter
with me."

"Oh, Godfrey, how can you be such a poor judge of your
own behaviour? But we won't argue about it now. You'll put
on your dinner coat? And do try to be sympathetic and agreeable to-night."

Half an hour later Mr. and Mrs. Scott McGregor and Mr.
and Mrs. Louie Marsellus arrived, and soon after them the
English scholar, Sir Edgar Spilling, so anxious to do the usual
thing in America that he wore a morning street suit. He was a
gaunt, rugged, large-boned man of fifty, with long legs and
arms, a pear-shaped face, and a drooping, pre-war moustache.
His specialty was Spanish history, and he had come all the
way to Hamilton, from his cousin's place in Saskatchewan, to
enquire about some of Doctor St. Peter's "sources."

Introductions over, it was the Professor's son-in-law, Louie
Marsellus, who took Sir Edgar in hand. He remembered having met in China a Walter Spilling, who was, it turned out, a
brother of Sir Edgar. Marsellus had also a brother there,
engaged in the silk trade. They exchanged opinions on conditions in the Orient, while young McGregor put on his
horn-rimmed spectacles and roamed restlessly up and down
the library. The two daughters sat near their mother, listening
to the talk about China.

Mrs. St. Peter was very fair, pink and gold,—a pale gold,
now that she was becoming a little grey. The tints of her face
and hair and lashes were so soft that one did not realize, on
first meeting her, how very definitely and decidedly her features were cut, under the smiling infusion of colour. When
she was annoyed or tired, the lines became severe. Rosamond,
the elder daughter, resembled her mother in feature, though
her face was heavier. Her colouring was altogether different;
dusky black hair, deep dark eyes, a soft white skin with rich
brunette red in her cheeks and lips. Nearly everyone considered Rosamond brilliantly beautiful. Her father, though he
was very proud of her, demurred from the general opinion.
He thought her too tall, with a rather awkward carriage. She
stooped a trifle, and was wide in the hips and shoulders. She
had, he sometimes remarked to her mother, exactly the wide

femur and flat shoulder-blade of his old slab-sided Kanuck grandfather. For a tree-hewer they were an asset. But St. Peter was very critical. Most people saw only Rosamond's smooth black head and white throat, and the red of her curved lips that was like the duskiness of dark, heavy-scented roses.

Kathleen, the younger daughter, looked even younger than she was—had the slender, undeveloped figure then very much in vogue. She was pale, with light hazel eyes, and her hair was hazel-coloured with distinctly green glints in it. To her father there was something very charming in the curious shadows her wide cheekbones cast over her cheeks, and in the spirited tilt of her head. Her figure in profile, he used to tell her, looked just like an interrogation point.

Mrs. St. Peter frankly liked having a son-in-law who could tot up acquaintances with Sir Edgar from the Soudan to Alaska. Scott, she saw, was going to be sulky because Sir Edgar and Marsellus were talking about things beyond his little circle of interests. She made no effort to draw him into the conversation, but let him prowl like a restless leopard among the books. The Professor was amiable, but quiet. When the second maid came to the door and signalled that dinner was ready—dinner was signalled, not announced— Mrs. St. Peter took Sir Edgar and guided him to his seat at her right, while the others found their usual places. After they had finished the soup, she had some difficulty in summoning the little maid to take away the plates, and explained to her guest that the electric bell, under the table, wasn't connected as yet—they had been in the new house less than a week, and the trials of building were not over.

"Oh? Then if I had happened along a fortnight ago I shouldn't have found you here? But it must be very interesting, building your own house and arranging it as you like," he responded.

Marsellus, silenced during the soup, came in with a warm smile and a slight shrug of the shoulders. "Building is the word with us, Sir Edgar, my—oh, isn't it! My wife and I are in the throes of it. We are building a country house, rather an ambitious affair, out on the wooded shores of Lake Michigan. Perhaps you would like to run out in my car and see it? What are your engagements for to-morrow? I can take you out in half an hour, and we can lunch at the Country Club. We have a magnificent site; primeval forest behind us and the lake in front, with our own beach—my father-in-law, you must know, is a formidable swimmer. We've been singularly fortunate in our architect,—a young Norwegian, trained in Paris. He's doing us a Norwegian manor house, very harmonious with its setting, just the right thing for rugged pine woods and high headlands."

Sir Edgar seemed most willing to make this excursion, and allowed Marsellus to fix an hour, greatly to the surprise of McGregor, whose look at his wife implied that he entertained serious doubts whether this baronet with walrus moustaches amounted to much after all.

The engagement made, Louie turned to Mrs. St. Peter. "And won't you come too, Dearest? You haven't been out since we got our wonderful wrought-iron door fittings from Chicago. We found just the right sort of hinge and latch, Sir Edgar, and had all the others copied from it. None of your Colonial glass knobs for us!"

Mrs. St. Peter sighed. Scott and Kathleen had just glass-knobbed their new bungalow throughout, yet she knew Louie didn't mean to hurt their feelings—it was his heedless enthusiasm that made him often say untactful things.

"We've been extremely fortunate in getting all the little things right," Louie was gladly confiding to Sir Edgar. "There's really not a flaw in the conception. I can say that, because I'm a mere onlooker; the whole thing's been done by the Norwegian and my wife and Mrs. St. Peter. And," he put his hand down affectionately upon Mrs. St. Peter's bare arm, "*and* we've named our place! I've already ordered the house stationery. No, Rosamond, I won't keep our little secret any longer. It will please your father, as well as your mother. We call our place 'Outland,' Sir Edgar."

He dropped the announcement and drew back. His mother-in-law rose to it—Spilling could scarcely be expected to understand.

"How splendid, Louie! A real inspiration."

"Yes, isn't it? I knew that would go to your hearts." The Professor had expressed his emotion only by lifting his heavy, sharply uptwisted eyebrows. "Let me explain, Sir Edgar,"

Marsellus went on eagerly. "We have named our place for Tom Outland, a brilliant young American scientist and inventor, who was killed in Flanders, fighting with the Foreign Legion, the second year of the war, when he was barely thirty years of age. Before he dashed off to the front, this youngster had discovered the principle of the Outland vacuum, worked out the construction of the bulkheaded vacuum that is revolutionizing aviation. He had not only invented it, but, curiously enough for such a hot-headed fellow, had taken pains to protect it. He had no time to communicate his discovery or to commercialize it—simply bolted to the front and left the most important discovery of his time to take care of itself."

Sir Edgar, fork arrested, looked a trifle dazed. "Am I to understand that you are referring to the inventor of the Outland vacuum?"

Louie was delighted. "Exactly that! Of course you would know all about it. My wife was young Outland's fiancée—is virtually his widow. Before he went to France he made a will in her favour; he had no living relatives, indeed. Toward the close of the war we began to sense the importance of what Outland had been doing in his laboratory—I am an electrical engineer by profession. We called in the assistance of experts and got the idea over from the laboratory to the trade. The monetary returns have been and are, of course, large."

While Louie paused long enough to have some intercourse with the roast before it was taken away, Sir Edgar remarked that he himself had been in the Air Service during the war, in the construction department, and that it was most extraordinary to come thus by chance upon the genesis of the Outland vacuum.

"You see," Louie told him, "Outland got nothing out of it but death and glory. Naturally, we feel terribly indebted. We feel it's our first duty in life to use that money as he would have wished—we've endowed scholarships in his own university here, and that sort of thing. But our house we want to have as a sort of memorial to him. We are going to transfer his laboratory there, if the university will permit,—all the apparatus he worked with. We have a room for his library and pictures. When his brother scientists come to Hamilton to look him up, to get information about him, as they are doing now already, at Outland they will find his books and instruments, all the sources of his inspiration."

"Even Rosamond," murmured McGregor, his eyes upon his cool green salad. He was struggling with a desire to shout to the Britisher that Marsellus had never so much as seen Tom Outland, while he, McGregor, had been his classmate and friend.

Sir Edgar was as much interested as he was mystified. He had come here to talk about manuscripts shut up in certain mouldering monasteries in Spain, but he had almost forgotten them in the turn the conversation had taken. He was genuinely interested in aviation and all its problems. He asked few questions, and his comments were almost entirely limited to the single exclamation, "Oh!" But this, from his lips, could mean a great many things; indifference, sharp interrogation, sympathetic interest, the nervousness of a modest man on hearing disclosures of a delicately personal nature. McGregor, before the others had finished dessert, drew a big cigar from his pocket and lit it at one of the table candles, as the horridest thing he could think of to do.

When they left the dining-room, St. Peter, who had scarcely spoken during dinner, took Sir Edgar's arm and said to his wife: "If you will excuse us, my dear, we have some technical matters to discuss." Leading his guest into the library, he shut the door.

Marsellus looked distinctly disappointed. He stood gazing wistfully after them, like a little boy told to go to bed. Louie's eyes were vividly blue, like hot sapphires, but the rest of his face had little colour—he was a rather mackerel-tinted man. Only his eyes, and his quick, impetuous movements, gave out the zest for life with which he was always bubbling. There was nothing Semitic about his countenance except his nose— that took the lead. It was not at all an unpleasing feature, but it grew out of his face with masterful strength, well-rooted, like a vigorous oak-tree growing out of a hill-side.

Mrs. St. Peter, always concerned for Louie, asked him to come and look at the new rug in her bedroom. This revived him; he took her arm, and they went upstairs together.

McGregor was left with the two sisters. "Outland, outlandish!" he muttered, while he fumbled about for an ash-tray.

Rosamond pretended not to hear him, but the dusky red on her cheeks crept a little farther toward her ears.

"Remember, we are leaving early, Scott," said Kathleen. "You have to finish your editorial to-night."

"Surely you don't make him work at night, too?" Rosamond asked. "Doesn't he have to rest his brain sometimes? Humour is always better if it's spontaneous."

"Oh, that's the trouble with me," Scott assured her. "Unless I keep my nose to the grindstone, I'm too damned spontaneous and tell the truth, and the public won't stand for it. It's not an editorial I have to finish, it's the daily prose poem I do for the syndicate, for which I get twenty-five beans. This is the motif:

'When your pocket is under-moneyed and your fancy is over-girled, you'll have to admit while you're cursing it, it's a mighty darned good old world.'

Bang, bang!"

He threw his cigar-end savagely into the fire-place. He knew that Rosamond detested his editorials and his jingles. She had fastidious taste in literature, like her mother— though he didn't think she had half the general intelligence of his wife. She also, now that she was Tom Outland's heir, detested to hear sums of money mentioned, especially small sums.

After the good-nights were said, and they were outside the front door, McGregor seized his wife's elbow and rushed her down the walk to the gate where his Ford was parked, breaking out in her ear as they ran: "Now what the hell is a virtual widow? Does he mean a virtuous widow, or the reverseous? Bang, bang!"

didn't get the son-in-law you wanted. And yet he was highly coloured, too."

The Professor made no reply to this. Lillian had been fiercely jealous of Tom Outland. As he left the house, he was reflecting that people who are intensely in love when they marry, and who go on being in love, always meet with something which suddenly or gradually makes a difference. Sometimes it is the children, or the grubbiness of being poor, sometimes a second infatuation. In their own case it had been, curiously enough, his pupil, Tom Outland.

St. Peter had met his wife in Paris, when he was but twenty-four, and studying for his doctorate. She too was studying there. French people thought her an English girl because of her gold hair and fair complexion. With her really radiant charm, she had a very interesting mind—but it was quite wrong to call it mind, the connotation was false. What she had was a richly endowed nature that responded strongly to life and art, and very vehement likes and dislikes which were often quite out of all proportion to the trivial object or person that aroused them. Before his marriage, and for years afterward, Lillian's prejudices, her divinations about people and art (always instinctive and unexplained, but nearly always right), were the most interesting things in St. Peter's life. When he accepted almost the first position offered him, in order to marry at once, and came to take the chair of European history at Hamilton, he was thrown upon his wife for mental companionship. Most of his colleagues were much older than he, but they were not his equals either in scholarship or in experience of the world. The only other man in the faculty who was carrying on important research work was Doctor Crane, the professor of physics. St. Peter saw a good deal of him, though outside his specialty he was uninteresting—a narrow-minded man, and painfully unattractive. Years ago Crane had begun to suffer from a malady which in time proved incurable, and which now sent him up for an operation periodically. St. Peter had had no friend in Hamilton of whom Lillian could possibly be jealous until Tom Outland came along, so well fitted by nature and early environment to help him with his work on the Spanish Adventurers.

When he had almost reached his old house and his study, the Professor remembered that he really must have an understanding with his landlord, or the place would be rented over his head. He turned and went down into another part of the city, by the car shops, where only workmen lived, and found his landlord's little toy house, set on a hill-side, over a basement faced up with red brick and covered with hop vines. Old Appelhoff was sitting on a bench before his door, making a broom. Raising broom corn was one of his economies. Beside him was his dachshund bitch, Minna.

St. Peter explained that he wanted to stay on in the empty house, and would pay the full rent each month. So irregular a project annoyed Appelhoff. "I like fine to oblige you, Professor, but dey is several parties looking at de house already, an' I don't like to lose a year's rent for maybe a few months."

"Oh, that's all right, Fred. I'll take it for the year, to simplify matters. I want to finish my new book before I move."

Fred still looked uneasy. "I better see de insurance man, eh? It says for purposes of domestic dwelling."

"He won't object. Let's have a look at your garden. What a fine crop of apples and sickle pears you have!"

"I don't like dem trees what don't bear not'ing," said the old man with sly humour, remembering the Professor's glistening, barren shrubs and the good ground wasted behind his stucco wall.

"How about your linden-trees?"

"Oh, dem flowers is awful good for de headache!"

"You don't look as if you were subject to it, Fred."

"Not me, but my woman always had."

"Pretty lonesome without her, Appelhoff?"

"I miss her, Professor, but I ain't just lonesome." The old man rubbed his bristly chin. "My Minna here is most like a person, and den I got so many t'ings to t'ink about."

"Have you? Pleasant things, I hope?"

"Well, all kinds. When I was young, in de old country, I had it hard to git my wife at all, an' I never had time to t'ink. When I come to dis country I had to work so turrible hard on dat farm to make crops an' pay debts, dat I was like a horse. Now I have it easy, an' I take time to t'ink about all dem t'ings."

on another line of work than his lectures, and was publishing books that weren't strictly text-books, had been used against him by Langtry's uncle.

As Langtry felt that the unpopularity of his course was due to his subject, a new chair was created for him. There couldn't be two heads in European history, so the board of regents made for him a chair of Renaissance history, or, as St. Peter said, a Renaissance chair of history. Of late years, for reasons that had not much to do with his lectures, Langtry had prospered better. To the new generations of country and village boys now pouring into the university in such large numbers, Langtry had become, in a curious way, an instructor in manners,—what is called an "influence." To the football-playing farmer boy who had a good allowance but didn't know how to dress or what to say, Langtry looked like a short cut. He had several times taken parties of undergraduates to London for the summer, and they had come back wonderfully brushed up. He introduced a very popular fraternity into the university, and its members looked after his interests, as did its affiliated sorority. His standing on the faculty was now quite as good as St. Peter's own, and the Professor wondered what Langtry still had to be sore about.

What was the use of keeping up the feud? They had both come there young men, fighting for their places and their lives; now they were not very young any more; they would neither of them, probably, ever hold a better position. Couldn't Langtry see it was a draw, that they had both been beaten?

IV

ON MONDAY AFTERNOON St. Peter mounted to his study and lay down on the box-couch, tired out with his day at the university. The first few weeks of the year were very fatiguing for him; there were so many exhausting things besides his lectures and all the new students; long faculty meetings in which almost no one was ever frank, and always the old fight to keep up the standard of scholarship, to prevent the younger professors, who had a sharp eye to their own interests, from farming the whole institution out to athletics, and to the agricultural and commercial schools favoured and fostered by the State Legislature.

The September heat, too, was hard on him. He wanted to be out at the lake every day—it was never so fine as in late September. He was lying with closed eyes, resting his mind on the picture of intense autumn-blue water, when he heard a tap at the door and his daughter Rosamond entered, very handsome in a silk suit of a vivid shade of lilac, admirably suited to her complexion and showing that in the colour of her cheeks there was actually a tone of warm lavender. In that low room she seemed very tall indeed, a little out of drawing, as, to her father's eye, she so often did. Usually, however, people were aware only of her rich complexion, her curving, unresisting mouth and mysterious eyes. Tom Outland had seen nothing else, and he was a young man who saw a great deal.

"Am I interrupting something important, Papa?"

"No, not at all, my dear. Sit down."

On his writing-table she caught a glimpse of pages in a handwriting not his—a script she knew very well.

"Not much choice of chairs, is there?" she smiled. "Papa, I don't like to have you working in a place like this. It's not fitting."

"Much easier than to break in a new room, Rosie. A work-room should be like an old shoe; no matter how shabby, it's better than a new one."

"That's really what I came to see you about." Rosamond traced the edge of a hole in the matting with the tip of her lilac sunshade. "Won't you let me build you a little study in the back yard of the new house? I have such good ideas for it, and you would have no bother about it at all."

"Oh, thank you, Rosamond. It's most awfully nice of you to think of it. But keep it just an idea—it's better so. Lots of things are. For the present I'll plod on here. It's absurd, but it suits me. Habit is such a big part of work."

"With Augusta's old things lying about, and those dusty old forms? Why didn't she at least get those out of your way?"

"Oh, they have a right here, by long tenure. It's their room, too. I don't want to come upon them lying in some dump-heap on the road to the lake. They remind me of the times when you were little girls, and your first party frocks used to hang on them at night, when I worked."

Rosamond smiled, unconvinced. "Papa, don't joke with me. I've come to talk about something serious, and it's very difficult. You know I'm a little afraid of you." She dropped her shadowy, bewitching eyes.

"Afraid of me? Never!"

"Oh, yes, I am when you're sarcastic. You mustn't be to-day, please. Louie and I have often talked this over. We feel strongly about it. He's often been on the point of blurting out with it, but I've curbed him. You don't always approve of Louie and me. Of course it was only Louie's energy and technical knowledge that ever made Tom's discovery succeed commercially, but we don't feel that we ought to have all the returns from it. We think you ought to let us settle an income on you, so that you could give up your university work and devote all your time to writing and research. That is what Tom would have wanted."

St. Peter rose quickly, with the light, supple spring he had when he was very nervous, crossed to the window, wide on its hook, and half closed it. "My dear daughter," he said decisively, when he had turned round to her, "I couldn't possibly take any of Outland's money."

"But why not? You were the best friend he had in the world, he owed more to you than to anyone else, and he hated having you hampered by teaching. He admired your mind, and nothing would have pleased him more than helping you to do the work you do better than anyone else. If he were alive, that would be one of the first things he would use this money for."

"But he is not alive, and there was no word about me in his will, and so there is nothing to build your pretty theory upon. It's wonderfully nice of you and Louie, and I'm very pleased, you know."

"But Tom was so impractical, Father. He never thought it would mean more than a liberal dress allowance for me, if he thought at all. I don't know—he never spoke to me about it."

St. Peter smiled quizzically. "I'm not so sure about his impracticalness. When he was working on that gas, he once remarked to me that there might be a fortune in it. To be sure, he didn't wait to find out whether there was a fortune, but that had to do with quite another side of him. Yes, I think I knew his idea would make money and he wanted you to have it, with him or without him."

The young woman's face grew troubled. "Even if I married?"

"He wanted you to have whatever would make you happy."

She sighed luxuriously. "Louie has done that. The only thing that troubles me is, I feel you ought to have some of this money, that he would wish it. He was so full of gratitude, felt that he owed you so much."

Her father again rose, with that guarded, nervous movement. "Once and for all, Rosamond, understand that he owed me no more than I owed him. Nothing hurts me so much as to have any member of my family talk as if we had done something fine for that young man, brought him out, produced him. In a lifetime of teaching, I've encountered just one remarkable mind; but for that, I'd consider my good years largely wasted. And there can be no question of money between me and Tom Outland. I can't explain just how I feel about it, but it would somehow damage my recollections of him, would make that episode in my life commonplace like everything else. And that would be a great loss to me. I'm purely selfish in refusing your offer; my friendship with Outland is the one thing I will not have translated into the vulgar tongue."

drama with God, glittering angels on one side and the shadows of evil coming and going on the other, life was a rich thing. The king and the beggar had the same chance at miracles and great temptations and revelations. And that's what makes men happy, believing in the mystery and importance of their own little individual lives. It makes us happy to surround our creature needs and bodily instincts with as much pomp and circumstance as possible. Art and religion (they are the same thing, in the end, of course) have given man the only happiness he has ever had.

"Moses learned the importance of that in the Egyptian court, and when he wanted to make a population of slaves into an independent people in the shortest possible time, he invented elaborate ceremonials to give them a feeling of dignity and purpose. Every act had some imaginative end. The cutting of the finger nails was a religious observance. The Christian theologians went over the books of the Law, like great artists, getting splendid effects by excision. They reset the stage with more space and mystery, throwing all the light upon a few sins of great dramatic value—only seven, you remember, and of those only three that are perpetually enthralling. With the theologians came the cathedral-builders; the sculptors and glass-workers and painters. They might, without sacrilege, have changed the prayer a little and said, *Thy will be done in art, as it is in heaven.* How can it be done anywhere else *as* it is in heaven? But I think the hour is up. You might tell me next week, Miller, what you think science has done for us, besides making us very comfortable."

As the young men filed out of the room, Mrs. St. Peter and McGregor went in.

"I came over to get you to go to the electrician's with me, Godfrey, but I won't make you. Scott wants you to run out to the lake, and it's such a fine day, you really should go."

"Car's outside. We'll just drop Lillian at the house, Doctor, and you can pick up your bathing-suit. We heard part of your lecture, by the way. How you get by the Methodists is still a mystery to me."

"I wish he would get into trouble, Scott," said Lillian as they left the building. "I wish he wouldn't talk to those fat-faced boys as if they were intelligent beings. You cheapen yourself, Godfrey. It makes me a little ashamed."

"I was rather rambling on to-day. I'm sorry you happened along. There's a fellow in that lot, Tod Miller, who isn't slow, and he excites me to controversy."

"All the same," murmured his wife, "it's hardly dignified to think aloud in such company. It's in rather bad taste."

"Thank you for the tip, Lillian. I won't do it again."

It took Scott only twenty minutes to get out to the lake. He drew up at the bit of beach St. Peter had bought for himself years before; a little triangle of sand running out into the water, with a bath-house and seven shaggy pine-trees on it. Scott had to fuss with the car, and the Professor was undressed and in the water before him.

When McGregor was ready to go in, his father-in-law was some distance out, swimming with an over-arm stroke, his head and shoulders well out of the water. He wore on his head a rubber visor of a kind he always brought home from France in great numbers. This one was vermilion, and was like a continuation of his flesh—his arms and back were burned a deep terra-cotta from a summer in the lake. His head and powerful reaching arms made a strong red pattern against the purple blue of the water. The visor was picturesque—his head looked sheathed and small and intensely alive, like the heads of the warriors on the Parthenon frieze in their tight, archaic helmets.

By five o'clock St. Peter and McGregor were dressed and lying on the sand, their overcoats wrapped about them, smoking. Suddenly Scott began to chuckle.

"Oh, Professor, you know your English friend, Sir Edgar Spilling? The day after I met him at your house, he came up to my office at the *Herald* to get some facts you'd been too modest to give him. When he was leaving he stood and looked at one of these motto cards I have over my desk, DON'T KNOCK, and said: 'May I ask why you don't have that notice on the outside of your door? I didn't observe any other way of getting in.' They never get wise, do they? He really went out to see Marsellus' place—seemed interested. Doctor, are you going to let them call that place after Tom?"

"My dear boy, how can I prevent it?"

"Well, you surely don't like the idea, do you?"

The Professor lit another cigarette and was a long while about it. When he had got it going, he turned on his elbow and looked at McGregor. "Scott, you must see that I can't make suggestions to Louie. He's perfectly consistent. He's a great deal more generous and public-spirited than I am, and my preferences would be enigmatical to him. I can't, either, very gracefully express myself to you about his affairs."

"I get you. Sorry he riles me so. I always say it shan't occur the next time, but it does." Scott took out his pipe and lay silent for a time, looking at the gold glow burning on the water and on the wings of the gulls as they flew by. His expression was wistful, rather mournful. He was a good-looking fellow, with sunburned blond hair, splendid teeth, attractive eyes that usually frowned a little unless he was laughing outright, a small, prettily cut mouth, restless at the corners. There was something moody and discontented about his face. The Professor had a great deal of sympathy for him; Scott was too good for his work. He had been delighted when his daily poem and his "uplift" editorials first proved successful, because that enabled him to marry. Now he could sell as many good-cheer articles as he had time to write, on any subject, and he loathed doing them. Scott had early picked himself out to do something very fine, and he felt that he was wasting his life and his talents. The new group of poets made him angry. When a new novel was discussed seriously by his friends, he was perfectly miserable. St. Peter knew that the poor boy had seasons of desperate unhappiness. His disappointed vanity ate away at his vitals like the Spartan boy's wolf, and only the deep lines in his young forehead and the twitching at the corners of his mouth showed that he suffered.

Not long ago, when the students were giving an historical pageant to commemorate the deeds of an early French explorer among the Great Lakes, they asked St. Peter to do a picture for them, and he had arranged one which amused him very much, though it had nothing to do with the subject. He posed his two sons-in-law in a tapestry-hung tent, for a conference between Richard Plantagenet and the Saladin, before the walls of Jerusalem. Marsellus, in a green dressing-gown

and turban, was seated at a table with a chart, his hands extended in reasonable, patient argument. The Plantagenet was
standing, his plumed helmet in his hand, his square yellow
head haughtily erect, his unthoughtful brows fiercely frowning, his lips curled and his fresh face full of arrogance. The
tableau had received no special notice, and Mrs. St. Peter had
said dryly that she was afraid nobody saw his little joke. But
the Professor liked his picture, and he thought it quite fair to
both the young men.

elder. St. Peter had thought that Scott McGregor was the sort of fellow Lillian always found tiresome. But no; within a few weeks after Kathleen's marriage, arch and confidential relations began to be evident between them. Even now, when Louie was so much in the foreground, and Scott was touchy and jealous, Lillian was very tactful and patient with him.

With Louie, Lillian seemed to be launching into a new career, and Godfrey began to think that he understood his own wife very little. He would have said that she would feel about Louie just as he did; would have cultivated him as a stranger in the town, because he was so unusual and exotic, but without in the least wishing to adopt anyone so foreign into the family circle. She had always been fastidious to an unreasonable degree about small niceties of deportment. She could never forgive poor Tom Outland for the angle at which he sometimes held a cigar in his mouth, or for the fact that he never learned to eat salad with ease. At the dinner-table, if Tom, forgetting himself in talk, sometimes dropped back into railroad lunch-counter ways and pushed his plate away from him when he had finished a course, Lillian's face would become positively cruel in its contempt. Irregularities of that sort put her all on edge. But Louie could hurry audibly through his soup, or kiss her resoundingly on the cheek at a faculty reception, and she seemed to like it.

Yes, with her sons-in-law she had begun the game of being a woman all over again. She dressed for them, planned for them, schemed in their interests. She had begun to entertain more than for years past—the new house made a plausible pretext—and to use her influence and charm in the little anxious social world of Hamilton. She was intensely interested in the success and happiness of these two young men, lived in their careers as she had once done in his. It was splendid, St. Peter told himself. She wasn't going to have to face a stretch of boredom between being a young woman and being a young grandmother. She was less intelligent and more sensible than he had thought her.

When Godfrey came downstairs ready for dinner, Louie was gone. He walked up to the chair where his wife was reading, and took her hand.

"My dear," he said quite delicately, "I wish you could keep

Louie from letting his name go up for the Arts and Letters. It's not safe yet. He's not been here long enough. They're a fussy little bunch, and he ought to wait until they know him better."

"You mean someone will blackball him? Do you really think so? But the Country Club——"

"Yes, Lillian; the Country Club is a big affair, and needs money. The Arts and Letters is a little group of fellows, and, as I said, fussy."

"Scott belongs," said Mrs. St. Peter rebelliously. "Did he tell you?"

"No, he didn't, and I shall not tell you who did. But if you're tactful, you can save Louie's feelings."

Mrs. St. Peter closed her book without glancing down at it. A new interest shone in her eyes and made them look quite through and beyond her husband. "I must see what I can do with Scott," she murmured.

St. Peter turned away to hide a smile. An old student of his, a friend who belonged to "the Outland period," had told him laughingly that he was sure Scott would blackball Marsellus if his name ever came to the vote. "You know Scott is a kid in some things," the friend had said. "He's a little sore at Marsellus, and says a secret ballot is the only way he can ever get him where it wouldn't hurt Mrs. St. Peter."

While the Professor was eating his soup, he studied his wife's face in the candlelight. It had changed so much since he found her laughing with Louie, and especially since he had dropped the hint about the Arts and Letters. It had become, he thought, too hard for the orchid velvet in her hair. Her upper lip had grown longer, and stiffened as it always did when she encountered opposition.

"Well," he reflected, "it will be interesting to see what she can do with Scott. That will make rather a test case."

VII

ARLY IN NOVEMBER there was a picturesque snow-storm, and that day Kathleen telephoned her father at the university, asking him to stop on his way home in the afternoon and help her to decide upon some new furs. As he approached McGregor's spick-and-span bungalow at four o'clock, he saw Louie's Pierce-Arrow standing in front, with Ned, the chauffeur and gardener, in the driver's seat. Just then Rosamond came out of the bungalow alone, and down the path to the sidewalk, without seeing her father. He noticed a singularly haughty expression on her face; her brows drawn together over her nose. The curl of her lips was handsome, but terrifying. He observed also something he had not seen before—a coat of soft, purple-grey fur, that quite disguised the wide, slightly stooping shoulders he regretted in his truly beautiful daughter. He called to her, very much interested. "Wait a minute, Rosie. I've not seen that before. It's extraordinarily becoming." He stroked his daughter's sleeve with evident pleasure. "You know, these things with a kind of lurking purple and lavender in them are splendid for you. They make your colour prettier than ever. It's only lately you've begun to wear them. Louie's taste, I suppose?"

"Of course. He selects all my things for me," said Rosamond proudly.

"Well, he does a good job. He knows what's right for you." St. Peter continued to look her up and down with satisfaction. "And Kathleen is getting new furs. You were advising her?"

"She didn't mention it to me," Rosamond replied in a guarded voice.

"No? And what do you call this, what beast?" he asked ingenuously, again stroking the fur with his bare hand.

"It's *taupe*."

"Oh, moleskin!" He drew back a little. "Couldn't be better for your complexion. And is it warm?"

"Very warm—and so light."

"I see, I see!" He took Rosamond's arm and escorted her to her car. "Give Louie my compliments on his choice." The motor glided away—he wished he could escape as quickly and noiselessly, for he was a coward. But he had a feeling that Kathleen was watching him from behind the sash curtains. He went up to the door and made a long and thorough use of the foot-scraper before he tapped on the glass. Kathleen let him in. She was very pale; even her lips, which were always pink, like the inside of a white shell, were without colour. Neither of them mentioned the just-departed guest.

"Have you been out in the park, Kitty? This is a pretty little storm. Perhaps you'll walk over to the old house with me presently." He talked soothingly while he took off his coat and rubbers. "And now for the furs!"

Kathleen went slowly into her bedroom. She was gone a great while—perhaps ten actual minutes. When she came back, the rims of her eyes were red. She carried four large pasteboard boxes, tied together with twine. St. Peter sprang up, took the parcel, and began untying the string. He opened the first and pulled out a brown stole. "What is it, mink?"

"No, it's Hudson Bay sable."

"Very pretty." He put the collar round her neck and drew back to look at it. But after a sharp struggle Kathleen broke down. She threw off the fur and buried her face in a fresh handkerchief.

"I'm so sorry, Daddy, but it's no use to-day. I don't want any furs, really. She spoils everything for me."

"Oh, my dear, my dear, you hurt me terribly!" St. Peter put his hands tenderly on her soft hazel-coloured hair. "Face it squarely, Kitty; you must not, you cannot, be envious. It's self-destruction."

"I can't help it, Father. I *am* envious. I don't think I would be if she let me alone, but she comes here with her magnificence and takes the life out of all our poor little things. Everybody knows she's rich, why does she have to keep rubbing it in?"

"But, Kitty dear, you wouldn't have her go home and change her coat before coming to see you?"

"Oh, it's not that, Father, it's everything! You know we were never jealous of each other at home. I was always proud of her good looks and good taste. It's not her clothes, it's a feeling she has inside her. When she comes toward me, I feel hate coming toward me, like a snake's hate!"

St. Peter wiped his moist forehead. He was suffering with her, as if she had been in physical anguish. "We can't, dear, we can't, in this world, let ourselves think of things—of comparisons—like that. We are all too susceptible to ugly suggestions. If Rosamond has a grievance, it's because you've been untactful about Louie."

"Even if I have, why should she be so revengeful? Does she think nobody else calls him a Jew? Does she think it's a secret? I don't mind being called a Gentile."

"It's all in the way it's done, you know, Kitty. And you've shown that you were a little bored with all their new things, now haven't you?"

"I've shown that I don't like the way she overdresses, I suppose. I would never have believed that Rosie could do anything in such bad taste. While she is here among her old friends, she ought to dress like the rest of us."

"But doesn't she? It seems to me her things look about like yours."

"Oh, Father, you're so simple! And Mother is very careful not to enlighten you. We go to the Guild to sew for the Mission fund, and Rosie comes in in a handmade French frock that cost more than all our dresses put together."

"But if hers are no prettier, what does it matter how much they cost?" He was watching Kathleen fearfully. Her pale skin had taken on a greenish tinge—there was no doubt about it. He had never happened to see that change occur in a face before, and he had never realized to what an ugly, painful transformation the common phrase "green with envy" referred.

"Oh, foolish, they are prettier, though you may not see it. It's not just the clothes"—she looked at him intently, and her eyes, in their reddened rims, expanded and cleared. "It's everything. When we were at home, Rosamond was a kind of ideal to me. What she thought about anything, decided it for me. But she's entirely changed. She's become Louie. Indeed, she's worse than Louie. He and all this money have ruined her. Oh, Daddy, why didn't you and Professor Crane get to work and stop all this before it began? You were to blame.

You knew that Tom had left something that was worth a lot, both of you. Why didn't you *do* something? You let it lie there in Crane's laboratory for this—this Marsellus to come along and exploit, until he almost thinks it's his own idea."

"Things might have turned out the same, anyway," her father protested. "Whatever the process earned was Rosamond's. I wasn't in the mood to struggle with manufacturers, I know nothing of such things. And Crane needs every ounce of his strength for his own experiments. He doesn't care about anything but the extent of space."

"He'd better have taken a few days off and saved his friend's reputation. Tom trusted him with everything. It's too foolish; that poor man being cut to pieces by surgeons all the time, and picking up the little that's left of himself and bothering about the limitations of space—much good they'll do him!"

St. Peter rose, took both of his daughter's hands, and stood laughing at her. "Come now! You have more brains than that, Kitty. It happens you do understand that whatever poor Crane can find out about space is more good to him than all the money the Marselluses will ever have. But are you implying that if Crane and I had developed Tom's discovery, we might have kept Rosie and her money in the family, for ourselves?"

Kathleen threw up her head. "Oh, I don't want her money!"

"Exactly; nor do I. And we mustn't behave as if we did want it. If you permit yourself to be envious of Rosie, you'll be very foolish, and very unhappy."

The Professor walked away across the snowy park with a tired step. He was heavy-hearted. For Kathleen he had a special kind of affection. Perhaps it was because he had had to take care of her for one whole summer when she was little. Just as Mrs. St. Peter was ready to start for Colorado with the children, the younger one developed whooping-cough and had to be left at home with her father. He had opportunity to observe all her ways. She was only six, but he found her a square-dealing, dependable little creature. They worked out a satisfactory plan of life together. She was to play in the garden all morning, and was not on any account to disturb him in his study. After lunch he would take her to the lake or the woods, or he would read to her at home. She took pride in keeping her part of the contract. One day when he came out of his study at noon, he found her sitting on the third floor stairs, just outside his door, with the arnica bottle in one hand and the fingers of the other puffed up like wee pink sausages. A bee had stung her in the garden, and she had waited half the morning for sympathy. She was very independent, and would tug at her leggings or overshoes a great while before she asked for help.

When they were little girls, Kathleen adored her older sister and liked to wait on her, was always more excited about Rosie's new dresses and winter coat than about her own. This attachment had lasted even after they were grown. St. Peter had never seen any change in it until Rosamond announced her engagement to Louie Marsellus. Then, all at once, Kathleen seemed to be done with her sister. Her father believed she couldn't forgive Rosie's forgetting Tom so quickly.

It was dark when the Professor got back to the old house and sat down at his writing-table. He would have an hour on his notes, he told himself, in spite of families and fortunes. And he had it. But when he looked up from his writing as the Angelus was ringing, two faces at once rose in the shadows outside the yellow circle of his lamp: the handsome face of his older daughter, surrounded by violet-dappled fur, with a cruel upper lip and scornful half-closed eyes, as she had approached her car that afternoon before she saw him; and Kathleen, her square little chin set so fiercely, her white cheeks actually becoming green under her swollen eyes. He couldn't believe it. He rose quickly and went to his one window, opened it wider, and stood looking at the dark clump of pine-trees that told where the Physics building stood. A sharp pain clutched his heart. Was it for this the light in Outland's laboratory used to burn so far into the night!

VIII

THE FOLLOWING WEEK St. Peter went to Chicago to give his lectures. He had engaged rooms for himself and Lillian at a quiet hotel near the university. The Marselluses went down by the same train, and they all alighted at the station together, in a raging snow-storm. The St. Peters were to have tea with Louie at the Blackstone, before going to their own quarters.

Tea was served in Louie's suite on the lake front, with a fine view of the falling snow from the windows. The Professor was in a genial mood; he was glad to be in a big city again, in a luxurious hotel, and especially pleased to be able to sit in comfort and watch the storm over the water.

"How snug you are here, Louie! This is really very nice," he said, turning back from the window when Rosamond called him.

Louie came and put both hands on St. Peter's shoulders, exclaiming delightedly: "And do you like these rooms, sir? Well, I'm glad, for they're yours! Rosie and I are farther down the corridor. Not a word! It's all arranged. You are our guests for this engagement. We won't have our great scholar staying off in some grimy place on the South side. We want him where we can keep an eye on him."

Louie was so warm with his plan that the Professor could only express satisfaction. "And our luggage?"

"It's on the way. I cancelled your reservations and did everything in order. Now have your tea, but not too much. You dine early; you have an engagement for to-night. You and Dearest are going to the opera—— Oh, not with us! We have other fish to fry. You are going off alone."

"Very well, Louie! And what are they giving to-night?"

"*Mignon*. It will remind you of your student days in Paris."

"It will. I always had *abonnement* at the Opéra Comique, and *Mignon* came round frequently. It's one of my favourites."

"I thought so!" Louie kissed both the ladies, to express his satisfaction. The Professor had forgotten his scruples about accepting lavish hospitalities. He was really very glad to have

dinner? Rosamond was presented with her emeralds, and, as St. Peter afterward observed to his wife, practically all the guests in the dining-room were participants in the happy event. Lillian was doubtless right when she told him that, all the same, his fellow professors went away from the Blackstone that night respecting Godfrey St. Peter more than they had ever done before, and if they had marriageable daughters, they were certainly envying him his luck.

"That," her husband replied, "is my chief objection to public magnificence; it seems to show everybody up in the worst possible light. I'm not finding fault with anyone but myself, understand. When I consented to occupy an apartment I couldn't afford, I let myself in for whatever might follow."

They got back to Hamilton in bitter weather. The lake winds were scourging the town, and Scott had laryngitis and was writing prose poems about the pleasures of tending your own furnace when the thermometer is twenty below.

"Godfrey," said Mrs. St. Peter when he set off for his classroom on the morning after their return, "surely you're not going to the old house this afternoon. It will be like a refrigerating-plant. There's no way of heating your study except by that miserable little stove."

"There never was, my dear. I got along a good many years."

"It was very different when the house below was heated. That stove isn't safe when you keep the window open. A gust of wind might blow it out at any moment, and if you were at work you'd never notice until you were half poisoned by gas. You'll get a fine headache one of these days."

"I've got headaches that way before, and survived them," he said stubbornly.

"How can you be so perverse? You know things are different now, and you ought to take more care of your health."

"Why so? It's not worth half so much as it was then."

His wife disregarded this. "And don't you think it's a foolish extravagance to go on paying the rent of an entire house, in order to spend a few hours a day in one very uncomfortable room of it?"

The Professor's dark skin reddened, and the ends of his

formidable eyebrows ascended toward his black hair. "It's almost my only extravagance," he muttered fiercely.

"How irritable and unreasonable he is becoming!" his wife reflected, as she heard him putting on his overshoes in the hall.

IX

For Christmas day the weather turned mild again. There would be a family dinner in the evening, but St. Peter was going to have the whole day to himself, in the old house. He asked his wife to put him up some sandwiches, so that he needn't come back for lunch. He kept a few bottles of sherry in his study, in the old chest under the forms. Fortunately he had brought back a great deal of it from his last trip to Spain. It wasn't foresight—Prohibition was then unthinkable—but a lucky accident. He had gone with his innkeeper to an auction, and bought in a dozen dozens of a sherry that went very cheap. He came home by the City of Mexico and got the wine through without duty.

As he was crossing the park with his sandwiches, he met Augusta coming back from Mass.

"Are you still going to the old house, Professor?" she asked reproachfully, her face smiling at him between her stiff black fur collar and her stiff black hat.

"Oh, yes, Augusta, but it's not the same. I miss you. There are never any new dresses on my ladies in the evening now. Won't you come in sometime and deck them out, as a surprise for me? I like to see them looking smart."

Augusta laughed. "You are a funny man, Doctor St. Peter. If anyone else said the things you do to your classes, I'd be scandalized. But I always tell people you don't mean half you say."

"And how do you know what I say to my classes, may I ask?"

"Why, of course, they go out and talk about it when you say slighting things about the Church," she said gravely.

"But, really, Augusta, I don't think I ever do."

"Well, they take it that way. They are not as smart as you, and you ought to be careful."

"It doesn't matter. What they think to-day, they'll forget to-morrow." He was walking beside Augusta, with a slack, indifferent stride, very unlike the step he had when he was full of something. "That reminds me: I've been wanting to ask you a question. That passage in the service about the Mystical Rose, Lily of Zion, Tower of Ivory—is that the Magnificat?"

Augusta stopped and looked at him. "Why, Professor! Did you receive *no* religious instruction at all?"

"How could I, Augusta? My mother was a Methodist, there was no Catholic church in our town in Kansas, and I guess my father forgot his religion."

"That happens, in mixed marriages." Augusta spoke meaningly.

"Ah, yes, I suppose so. But tell me, what is the Magnificat, then?"

"The Magnificat begins, *My soul doth magnify the Lord*; you must know that."

"But I thought the Magnificat was about the Virgin?"

"Oh, no, Professor! The Blessed Virgin composed the Magnificat."

St. Peter became intensely interested. "Oh, she did?"

Augusta spoke gently, as if she were prompting him and did not wish to rebuke his ignorance too sharply. "Why, yes, just as soon as the angel had announced to her that she would be the mother of our Lord, the Blessed Virgin composed the Magnificat. I always think of you as knowing everything, Doctor St. Peter!"

"And you're always finding out how little I know. Well, you don't give me away. You are very discreet."

Their ways parted, and both went on more cheerful than when they met. The Professor climbed to his study feeling quite as though Augusta had been there and brightened it up for him. (Surely she had said that the Blessed Virgin sat down and composed the Magnificat!) Augusta had been with them often in the holiday season, back in the years when holidays were holidays indeed. He had grown to like the reminders of herself that she left in his work-room—especially the toilettes upon the figures. Sometimes she made those terrible women entirely plausible!

In the early years, no matter how hard he was working, he had always felt the sense of holiday, of a special warmth and fragrance in the air, steal up to his study from the house below. When he was writing his best, he was conscious of pretty little girls in fresh dresses—of flowers and greens in the comfortable, shabby sitting-room—of his wife's good looks and good taste—even of a better dinner than usual under preparation downstairs. All the while he had been working so fiercely at his eight big volumes, he was not insensible to the domestic drama that went on beneath him. His mind had played delightedly with all those incidents. Just as, when Queen Mathilde was doing the long tapestry now shown at Bayeux,—working her chronicle of the deeds of knights and heroes,—alongside the big pattern of dramatic action she and her women carried the little playful pattern of birds and beasts that are a story in themselves; so, to him, the most important chapters of his history were interwoven with personal memories.

On this Christmas morning, with that sense of the past in his mind, the Professor went mechanically to work, and the morning disappeared. Before he knew it was passing, the bells from Augusta's church across the park rang out and told him it was gone. He pushed back his papers and arranged his writing-table for lunch.

He had been working hard, he judged, because he was so hungry. He peered with interest into the basket his wife had given him—a wicker bag, it was, really, that he had once bought full of strawberries at Gibraltar. Chicken sandwiches with lettuce leaves, red California grapes, and two shapely, long-necked russet pears. That would do very well; and Lillian had thoughtfully put in one of her best dinner napkins, knowing he hated ugly linen. From the chest he took out a round cheese, and a bottle of his wine, and began to polish a sherry glass.

While he was enjoying his lunch, he was thinking of certain holidays he had spent alone in Paris, when he was living at Versailles, with the Thieraults, as tutor to their boys. There was one All Souls' Day when he had gone into Paris by an early train and had a magnificent breakfast on the Rue de Vaugirard—not at Foyot's, he hadn't money enough in those days to put his nose inside the place. After breakfast he went out to walk in the soft rainfall. The sky was of such an intense silvery grey that all the grey stone buildings along the Rue St. Jacques and the Rue Sufflot came out in that silver shine stronger than in sunlight. The shop windows were shut; on the bleak ascent to the Pantheon there was not a spot of colour, nothing but wet, shiny, quicksilvery grey, accented by black crevices, and weather-worn bosses white as wood-ash. All at once, from somewhere behind the Pantheon itself, a man and woman, pushing a hand-cart, came into the empty street. The cart was full of pink dahlias, all exactly the same colour. The young man was fair and slight, with a pale face; the woman carried a baby. Both they and the wheels of their barrow were splashed with mud. They must have come from a good way in the country, and were a weary, anxious-looking pair. They stopped at a corner before the Pantheon and fearfully scanned the bleak, silvery, deserted streets. The man went into a bakery, and his wife began to spread out the flowers, which were done up in large bouquets with fresh green chestnut-leaves. Young St. Peter approached and asked the price.

"*Deux francs cinquante, Monsieur,*" she said with a kind of desperate courage.

He took a bunch and handed her a five-franc note. She had no change. Her husband, watching from the bakery, came running across with a loaf of bread under his arm.

"*Deux francs cinquante,*" she called to him as he came up. He put his hand into his pocket and fumbled.

"*Deux francs cinquante,*" she repeated with painful tension. The price agreed upon had probably been a franc or a franc fifty. The man counted out the change to the student and looked at his wife with admiration. St. Peter was so pleased with his flowers that it hadn't occurred to him to get more; but all his life he had regretted that he didn't buy two bunches, and push their fortunes a little further. He had never again found dahlias of such a beautiful colour, or so charmingly arranged with bright chestnut-leaves.

A moment later he was strolling down the hill, wondering to whom he could give his bouquet, when a pathetic procession filed past him through the rain. The girls of a charity school came walking two and two, in hideous dark uniforms and round felt hats without ribbon or bow, marshalled by four black-bonneted nuns. They were all looking down, all but one—the pretty one, naturally—and she was looking sidewise, directly at the student and his flowers. Their eyes met, she smiled, and just as he put out his hand with the bouquet, one of the sisters flapped up like a black crow and shut the girl's pretty face from him. She would have to pay for that smile, he was afraid. Godfrey spent his day in the Luxembourg Gardens and walked back to the Gare St. Lazare at evening with nothing but his return ticket in his pocket, very glad to get home to Versailles in time for the family dinner.

When he first went to live with the Thieraults, he had found Madame Thierault severe and exacting, stingy about his laundry and grudging about the cheese and fruit he ate for dinner. But in the end she was very kind to him; she never pampered him, but he could depend upon her. Her three sons had always been his dearest friends. Gaston, the one he loved best, was dead—killed in the Boxer uprising in China. But Pierre still lived at Versailles, and Charles had a business in Marseilles. When he was in France their homes were his. They were much closer to him than his own brothers. It was one summer when he was in France, with Lillian and the two little girls, that the idea of writing a work upon the early Spanish explorers first occurred to him, and he had turned at once to the Thieraults. After giving his wife enough money to finish the summer and get home, he took the little that was left and went down to Marseilles to talk over his project with Charles Thierault *fils*, whose mercantile house did a business with Spain in cork. Clearly St. Peter would have to be in Spain as much as possible for the next few years, and he would have to live there very cheaply. The Thieraults were always glad of a chance to help him. Not with money,—they were too French and too logical for that. But they would go to any amount of trouble and no inconsiderable expense to save him a few thousand francs.

That summer Charles kept him for three weeks in his oleander-buried house in the Prado, until his little brig, *L'Espoir*, sailed out of the new port with a cargo for Algeciras. The captain was from the Hautes-Pyrénées, and his spare crew were all Provençals, seamen trained in that hard school of the Gulf of Lyons. On the voyage everything seemed to feed the plan of the work that was forming in St. Peter's mind; the skipper, the old Catalan second mate, the sea itself.

One day stood out above the others. All day long they were skirting the south coast of Spain; from the rose of dawn to the gold of sunset the ranges of the Sierra Nevadas towered on their right, snow peak after snow peak, high beyond the flight of fancy, gleaming like crystal and topaz. St. Peter lay looking up at them from a little boat riding low in the purple water, and the design of his book unfolded in the air above him, just as definitely as the mountain ranges themselves. And the design was sound. He had accepted it as inevitable, had never meddled with it, and it had seen him through.

It was late on Christmas afternoon when the Professor got back to the new house, but he was in such a happy frame of mind that he feared nothing, not even a family dinner. He quite looked forward to it, on the contrary. His wife heard him humming his favorite air from *Matrimonio Segreto* while he was dressing.

That evening the two daughters of the house arrived almost at the same moment. When Rosamond threw off her cloak in the hall, her father noticed that she was wearing her new necklace. Kathleen stood looking at it, and was evidently trying to find courage to say something about it, when Louie helped her by breaking in.

"And, Kitty, you haven't seen our jewels! What do you think? Just look at it."

"I was looking. It's too lovely!"

"It's very old, you see, the gold. What a work I had finding it! She doesn't like anything showy, you know, and she doesn't care about intrinsic values. It must be beautiful, first of all."

"Well, it is that, surely."

Louie walked up and down, admiring his wife. "She carries off things like that, doesn't she? And yet, you know, I like her in simple things, too." He dropped into reflection, just as if he were alone and talking to himself. "I always remember a little bracelet she wore the night I first met her. A turquoise set in silver, wasn't it? Yes, a turquoise set in dull silver. Have you it yet, Rosie?"

"I think so." There was a shade of displeasure in Rosamond's voice, and she turned back into the hall to look for something. "Where are the violets you brought for Mamma?"

Mrs. St. Peter came in, followed by the maid and the cocktails. Scott began the usual Prohibition lament.

"Why don't you journalists tell the truth about it in print?" Louie asked him. "It's a case where you could do something."

"And lose my job? Not much! This country's split in two, socially, and I don't know if it's ever coming together. It's not so hard on me, I can drink hard liquor. But you and the Professor like wine and fancy stuff."

"Oh, it's nothing to us! We're going to France for the summer," Louie put his arm round his wife and rubbed his cheek against hers, saying caressingly, "and drink Burgundy, Burgundy, Burgundy!"

"Please take me with you, Louie," Mrs. St. Peter pleaded, to distract him from his wife. Nothing made the McGregors so uncomfortable and so wrathful as the tender moments which sometimes overtook the Marselluses in public.

"We are going to take you, and Papa too. That's our plan. I take him for safety. If I travelled on the Continent alone with two such handsome women, it wouldn't be tolerated. There would be a trumped-up quarrel, and a stiletto, and then somebody would be a widow," turning again to his wife.

"Come here, Louie." Mrs. St. Peter beckoned him. "I have a confession to make. I'm afraid there's no dinner for you to-night."

"No dinner for me?"

"No. There's nothing either you or Godfrey will like. It's Scott's dinner to-night. Your tastes are so different, I can't compromise. And this is his, from the cream soup to the frozen pudding."

"But who said I didn't like cream soup and frozen pudding?" Louie held out his hands to show their guiltlessness. "And are there *haricots verts* in cream sauce? I thought so! And I like those, too. The truth is, Dearest," he stood before her and tapped her chin with his finger, "the truth is that I like all Scott's dinners, it's he who doesn't like mine! He's the intolerant one."

"True for you, Louie," laughed the Professor.

"And it's that way about lots of things," said Louie a little plaintively.

"Kitty," said Scott as they were driving home that night, Kathleen in the driver's seat beside him, "that silver bracelet Louie spoke of was one of Tom's trinkets, wasn't it? Do you suppose she has some feeling for him still, under all this pomposity?"

"I don't know, and I don't care. But, oh, Scott, I do love you very much!" she cried vehemently.

He pinched off his driving-glove between his knees and snuggled his hand over hers, inside her muff. "Sure?" he muttered.

"Yes, I *do!*" she said fiercely, squeezing his knuckles together with all her might.

"Awful nice of you to have told me all about it at the start, Kitty. Most girls wouldn't have thought it necessary. I'm the only one who knows, ain't I?"

"The only one who ever has known."

"And I'm just the one another girl wouldn't have told. Why did you, Kit?"

"I don't know. I suppose even then I must have had a feeling that you were the real one." Her head dropped on his shoulder. "You know you *are* the real one, don't you?"

"I guess!"

X

THAT WINTER there was a meeting of an Association of Electrical Engineers in Hamilton. Louie Marsellus, who was a member, gave a luncheon for the visiting engineers at the Country Club, and then motored them to Outland. Scott McGregor was at the lunch, with the other newspaper men. On his return he stopped at the university and picked up his father-in-law.

"I'll run you over home. Which house, the old? How did you get out of Louie's party?"

"I had classes."

"It was some lunch! Louie's a good host. First-rate cigars, and plenty of them," Scott tapped his breast-pocket. "We had poor Tom served up again. It was all right, of course—the scientific men were interested, didn't know much about him. Louie called on me for personal recollections; he was very polite about it. I didn't express myself very well. I'm not much of a speaker, anyhow, and this time I seemed to be talking uphill. You know, Tom isn't very real to me any more. Sometimes I think he was just a—a glittering idea. Here we are, Doctor."

Scott's remark rather troubled the Professor. He went up the two flights of stairs and sat down in his shadowy crypt at the top of the house. With his right elbow on the table, his eyes on the floor, he began recalling as clearly and definitely as he could every incident of that bright, windy spring day when he first saw Tom Outland.

He was working in his garden one Saturday morning, when a young man in a heavy winter suit and a Stetson hat, carrying a grey canvas telescope, came in at the green door that led from the street.

"Are you Professor St. Peter?" he inquired.

Upon being assured, he set down his bag on the gravel, took out a blue cotton handkerchief, and wiped his face which was covered with beads of moisture. The first thing the Professor noticed about the visitor was his manly, mature voice—low, calm, experienced, very different from the thin ring or the hoarse shouts of boyish voices about the campus. The next thing he observed was the strong line of contrast below the young man's sandy hair—the very fair forehead which had been protected by his hat, and the red-dish brown of his face, which had evidently been exposed to a stronger sun than the spring sun of Hamilton. The boy was fine-looking, he saw—tall and presumably well built, though the shoulders of his stiff, heavy coat were so prepos-terously padded that the upper part of him seemed shut up in a case.

"I want to go to school here, Professor St. Peter, and I've come to ask your advice. I don't know anybody in the town."

"You want to enter the university, I take it? What high school are you from?"

"I've never been to high school, sir. That's the trouble."

"Why, yes. I hardly see how you can enter the university. Where are you from?"

"New Mexico. I haven't been to school, but I've studied. I read Latin with a priest down there."

St. Peter smiled incredulously. "How much Latin?"

"I read Cæsar and Virgil, the *Æneid*."

"How many books?"

"We went right through." He met the Professor's ques-tions squarely, his eyes were resolute, like his voice.

"Oh, you did." St. Peter stood his spade against the wall. He had been digging around his red-fruited thorn-trees. "Can you repeat any of it?"

The boy began: *"Infandum, regina, jubes renovare dolorem,"* and steadily continued for fifty lines or more, until St. Peter held up a checking hand.

"Excellent. Your priest was a thorough Latinist. You have a good pronunciation and good intonation. Was the Father by any chance a Frenchman?"

"Yes, sir. He was a missionary priest, from Belgium."

"Did you learn any French from him?"

"No, sir. He wanted to practise his Spanish."

"You speak Spanish?"

"Not very well, Mexican Spanish."

The Professor tried him out in Spanish and told him he

thought he knew enough to get credit for a modern language. "And what are your deficiencies?"

"I've never had any mathematics or science, and I write a very bad hand."

"That's not unusual," St. Peter told him. "But, by the way, how did you happen to come to me instead of to the registrar?"

"I just got in this morning, and your name was the only one here I knew. I read an article by you in a magazine, about Fray Marcos. Father Duchene said it was the only thing with any truth in it he'd read about our country down there."

The Professor had noticed before that whenever he wrote for popular periodicals it got him into trouble. "Well, what are your plans, young man? And, by the way, what is your name?"

"Tom Outland."

The Professor repeated it. It seemed to suit the boy exactly. "How old are you?"

"I'm twenty." He blushed, and St. Peter supposed he was dropping off a few years, but he found afterward that the boy didn't know exactly how old he was. "I thought I might get a tutor and make up my mathematics this summer."

"Yes, that could be managed. How are you fixed for money?"

Outland's face grew grave. "I'm rather awkwardly fixed. If you were to write to Tarpin, New Mexico, to inquire about me, you'd find I have money in the bank there, and you'd think I had been deceiving you. But it's money I can't touch while I'm able-bodied. It's in trust for someone else. But I've got three hundred dollars without any string on it, and I'm hoping to get work here. I've been bossing a section gang all winter, and I'm in good condition. I'll do anything but wait table. I won't do that." On this point he seemed to feel strongly.

The Professor learned some of his story that morning. His parents, he said, were "mover people," and both died when they were crossing southern Kansas in a prairie schooner. He was a baby and had been informally adopted by some kind people who took care of his mother in her last hours,—a locomotive engineer named O'Brien, and his wife. This engineer was transferred to New Mexico and took the foundling boy along with his own children. As soon as Tom was old enough to work, he got a job as call boy and did his share toward supporting the family.

"What's a call boy, a messenger boy?"

"No, sir. It's a more responsible position. Our town was an important freight division on the Santa Fé, and a lot of train men live there. The freight schedule is always changing, because it's a single track road and the dispatcher has to get the freights through when he can. Suppose you're a brakeman, and your train is due out at two A. M.; well, like as not, it will be changed to midnight, or to four in the morning. You go to bed as if you were going to sleep all night, with nothing on your mind. The call boy watches the schedule board, and half an hour before your train goes out, he comes and taps on your window and gets you up in time to make it. The call boy has to be on to things in the town. He must know when there's a poker game on, and how to slip in easy. You can't tell when there's a spotter about, and if a man's reported for gambling, he's fired. Sometimes you have to get a man when he isn't where he ought to be. I found there was usually a reason at home for that." The boy spoke with gravity, as if he had reflected deeply upon irregular behaviour.

Just then Mrs. St. Peter came out into the garden and asked her husband if he wouldn't bring his young friend in to lunch. Outland started and looked with panic toward the door by which he had come in; but the Professor wouldn't hear of his going, and picked up his telescope to prevent his escape. As he carried it into the house and put it down in the hall, he noticed that it was strangely light for its bulk. Mrs. St. Peter introduced the guest to her two little girls, and asked him if he didn't want to go upstairs to wash his hands. He disappeared; as he came back something disconcerting happened. The front hall and the front staircase were the only hard wood in the house, but as Tom came down the waxed steps, his heavy new shoes shot out from under him, and he sat down on the end of his spine with a thump. Little Kathleen burst into a giggle, and her elder sister

that she couldn't let him give his stones to the children. "They are worth a lot of money."

"I'd never sell them. They were given to me by a friend. I have a lot, and they're no use to me, but they'll make pretty playthings for little girls." His voice was so wistful and winning that there was nothing to do.

"Hold them still a moment," said the Professor, looking down, not at the turquoises, but at the hand that held them: the muscular, many-lined palm, the long, strong fingers with soft ends, the straight little finger, the flexible, beautifully shaped thumb that curved back from the rest of the hand as if it were its own master. What a hand! He could see it yet, with the blue stones lying in it.

In a moment the stranger was gone, and the St. Peter family sat down and looked at one another. He remembered just what his wife had said on that occasion.

"Well, this is something new in students, Godfrey. We ask a poor perspiring tramp boy to lunch, to save his pennies, and he departs leaving princely gifts."

Yes, the Professor reflected, after all these years, that was still true. Fellows like Outland don't carry much luggage, yet one of the things you know them by is their sumptuous generosity—and when they are gone, all you can say of them is that they departed leaving princely gifts.

With a good tutor, young Outland had no difficulty in making up three years' mathematics in four months. Latin, he owned, had been hard for him. But in mathematics, he didn't have to work, he had merely to give his attention. His tutor had never known anything like it. But St. Peter held the boy at arm's length. As a young teacher full of zeal, he had been fooled more than once. He knew that the wonderful seldom holds water, that brilliancy has no staying power, and the unusual becomes commonplace by a natural law.

In those first months Mrs. St. Peter saw more of their protégé than her husband did. She found him a good boarding-place, took care that he had proper summer clothes and that he no longer addressed her as "Ma'am." He came often to the house that summer, to play with the little girls. He would spend hours with them in the garden, making Hopi villages with sand and pebbles, drawing maps of the Painted Desert

and the Rio Grande country in the gravel, telling them stories, when there was no one by to listen, about the adventures
he had had with his friend Roddy.

"Mother," Kathleen broke out one evening at dinner,
"what do you think! Tom hasn't any birthday."

"How is that?"

"When his mother died in the mover wagon, and Tom was
a baby, she forgot to tell the O'Briens when his birthday was.
She even forgot to tell them how old he was. They thought
he must be a year and a half, because he was so big, but Mrs.
O'Brien always said he didn't have enough teeth for that."

St. Peter asked her whether Tom had ever said how it happened that his mother died in a wagon.

"Well, you see, she was very sick, and they were going West
for her health. And one day, when they were camped beside a
river, Tom's father went in to swim, and had a cramp or
something, and was drowned. Tom's mother saw it, and it
made her worse. She was there all alone, till some people
found her and drove her on to the next town to a doctor. But
when they got her there, she was too sick to leave the wagon.
They drove her into the O'Briens' yard, because that was
nearest the doctor's and Mrs. O'Brien was a kind woman.
And she died in a few hours."

"Does Tom know anything about his father?"

"Nothing except that he was a school-teacher in Missouri.
His mother told the O'Briens that much. But the O'Briens
were just lovely to him."

St. Peter had noticed that in the stories Tom told the children there were no shadows. Kathleen and Rosamond regarded his free-lance childhood as a gay adventure they would
gladly have shared. They loved to play at being Tom and
Roddy. Roddy was the remarkable friend, ten years older
than Tom, who knew everything about snakes and panthers
and deserts and Indians. "And he gave up a fine job firing on
the Santa Fé, and went off with Tom to ride after cattle for
hardly any wages, just to be with Tom and take care of him
after he'd had pneumonia," Kathleen told them.

"That wasn't the only reason," Rosamond added dreamily.
"Roddy was proud. He didn't like taking orders and living on
pay cheques. He liked to be free, and to sit in his saddle all

day and use it for a pillow at night. You know Tom said that, Kitty."

"Anyhow, he was noble. He was always noble, noble Roddy!" Kathleen finished it off.

After the first day, when he had walked into the garden and introduced himself, Tom never took up the story of his own life again, either with the Professor or Mrs. St. Peter, though he was often encouraged to do so. He would talk about the New Mexico country when questioned, about Father Duchene, the missionary priest who had been his teacher, about the Indians; but only with the two little girls did he ever speak freely and confidentially about himself. St. Peter used to wonder how the boy could afford to spend so much time with the children. All through that summer and fall he used to come in the afternoon and join them in the garden. In the winter he dropped in two or three evenings a week to play Five Hundred or to take a dancing-lesson.

There was evidently something enchanting about the atmosphere of the house to a boy who had always lived a rough life. He enjoyed the prettiness and freshness and gaiety of the little girls as if they were flowers. Probably, too, he liked being so attractive to them. A flush of pleasure would come over Tom's face—so much fairer now than when he first arrived in Hamilton—if Kathleen caught his hand and tried to squeeze it hard enough to hurt, crying: "Oh, Tom, *tell* us about the time you and Roddy found the water hole dry, and then afterward tell us about when the rattlesnake bit Henry!" He would whisper: "Pretty soon," and after a while, through the open windows, the Professor would hear them in the garden: the laughter and exclamations of the little girls, and that singularly individual voice of Tom's—mature, confident, seldom varying in pitch, but full of slight, very moving modulations.

He couldn't have wished for a better companion for his daughters, and they were teaching Tom things that he needed more than mathematics.

Sitting thus in his study, long afterward, St. Peter reflected that those first years, before Outland had done anything remarkable, were really the best of all. He liked to remember

the charming groups of three he was always coming upon,—
in the hammock swung between the linden-trees, in the
window-seat, or before the dining-room fire. Oh, there had
been fine times in this old house then: family festivals and
hospitalities, little girls dancing in and out, Augusta coming
and going, gay dresses hanging in his study at night, Christmas shopping and secrets and smothered laughter on the
stairs. When a man had lovely children in his house, fragrant
and happy, full of pretty fancies and generous impulses, why
couldn't he keep them? Was there no way but Medea's, he
wondered?

XI

ST. PETER had come in late from an afternoon lecture, and had just lighted his kerosene lamp to go to work, when he heard a light foot ascending the stairs. In a moment Kathleen's voice called: "May I interrupt for a moment, Papa?"

He opened the door and drew her in.

"Kitty, do you remember the time you sat out there with your bee-sting and your bottle? Nobody ever showed me more consideration than that, not even your mother."

Kathleen threw her hat and jacket into the sewing-chair and walked about, touching things to see how dusty they were. "I've been wondering if you didn't need me to come in and clean house for you, but it's not so bad as they report it. This is the first time I've called on you since you've been here alone. I've turned in from the walk more than once, but I've always run away again." She paused to warm her hands at the little stove. "I'm silly, you know; such queer things make me blue. And you still have Augusta's old forms. I don't think anything ever happened to her that amused her so much. And now, you know, she's quite sentimental about their being here. It's about Augusta that I came, Papa. Did you know that she had lost some of her savings in the Kinkoo Copper Company?"

"Augusta? Are you sure? What a shame!"

"Yes. She was sewing for me last week. I noticed that she seemed depressed and hadn't much appetite for lunch—which, you know, is unusual for Augusta. She was ashamed to tell any of us about it, because it seems she'd asked Louie's advice, and he told her not to invest in that company. But a lot of the people in her church were putting money into it, and of course that made it seem all right to her. She lost five hundred dollars, a fortune for her, and Scott says she'll never get a cent of it back."

"Five hundred dollars," murmured St. Peter. "Let me see, at three dollars a day that means one hundred and sixty-six days. Now what can we do about it?"

"Of course we must do something. I knew you'd feel that way, Father."

"Certainly. Among us, we must cover it. I'll speak to Rosamond to-night."

"You needn't, dear." Kathleen tossed her head. "I have been to her. She refuses."

"Refuses? She can't refuse, my dear. I'll have a word to say." The firmness of his tone, and the quick rush of claret colour under his skin, were a gratification to his daughter.

"She says that Louie took the trouble to speak to his banker and to several copper men before he advised Augusta; and that if she doesn't learn her lesson this time, she will do the same thing over again. Rosamond said they would do something for Augusta later, but she didn't say what."

"Leave Rosamond to me. I'll convince her."

"Even if you can do anything with her, she's determined to make Augusta admit her folly, and it can't be done that way. Augusta is terribly proud. When I told her her customers ought to make it up to her, she was very haughty and said she wasn't that kind of a sewing-woman; that she gave her ladies good measure for their money. Scott thought we could buy stock in some good company and tell her we had used our influence and got an exchange, but that she must keep quiet about it. We could manage some such little fib, she knows so little about business. I know I can get the Dudleys and the Browns to help. We needn't go to the Marselluses."

"Wait a few days. It's a disgrace to us as a family not to make it up ourselves. On her own account, we oughtn't to let Rosamond out. She's altogether too blind to responsibilities of that kind. In a world full of blunderers, why should Augusta have to pay scrupulously for her mistakes? It's very petty of Rosie, really!"

Kathleen started to speak, stopped and turned away. "Scott will give a hundred dollars," she said a moment later.

"That's very generous of him. I'll give another, and Rosie shall make up the rest. If she doesn't, I'll speak to Louie. He's an absolutely generous chap. I've never known him to refuse to give either time or money."

Kathleen's eyes suddenly brightened. "Why, Daddy, you have Tom's Mexican blanket! I never knew he gave it to you. I've often wondered what became of it." She picked up from

XII

St. Peter was breakfasting at six-thirty, alone, reading last night's letters while he waited for the coffee to percolate. It had been long since he had had an eight o'clock class, but this year the schedule committee had slyly put him down for one. "He can afford to take a taxi over now," the Dean remarked.

After breakfast he went upstairs and into his wife's room. "I have a rendezvous with a lady," he said, tossing an envelope upon her counterpane. She read a note from Mrs. Crane, the least attractive of the faculty ladies, requesting an interview with the Professor at his earliest convenience: as she wished to see him quite alone, might she come to his study in the old house, where she understood he still worked?

"Poor Godfrey!" murmured his wife.

"One ought not to joke about it——" St. Peter went into his own room to get a handkerchief and came back, taking up his suspended sentence. "I'm afraid it means poor Crane is coming up for another operation. Or, worse still, that the surgeons tell her another would be useless. It's like *The Pit and the Pendulum*. I feel as if the poor fellow were strapped down on a revolving disk that comes around under the knife just so often."

Mrs. St. Peter looked judicially at the letter, then at her husband's back. She didn't believe that surgery would be the subject of discussion when they met. Mrs. Crane had been behaving very strangely of late.

Doctor Crane had married a girl whom no other man ever thought of courting, a girl of whom people always said: "Oh, she's so *good*!" chiefly because she was so homely. They had three very plain daughters, and only Crane's salary to live upon. Doctors and surgeons kept them poor enough.

St. Peter kissed his wife and went forth quite unconscious of what was going on in her mind. During the morning he telephoned Mrs. Crane, and arranged a meeting with her at five o'clock. As the bell in the old house didn't work now, he waited downstairs on the front porch, to receive his visitor and conduct her up to his study. It was raining drearily, and rs. Crane arrived in a rubber coat, and a knitted sport *hat* belonging to one of her daughters. St. Peter took her wet umbrella and led her up the two flights of stairs.

"I'm not very well appointed to receive ladies, Mrs. Crane. This was the sewing-room, you know. There's Augusta's chair, which she insisted was comfortable."

"Thank you." Mrs. Crane sat down, took off her gloves, and tucked wisps of damp hair up under her crocheted hat. Her bleak, plain face wore an expression of grievance.

"I've come without my husband's knowledge, Doctor St. Peter, to ask you what you think can be done about our rights in the Outland patent. You know how my husband's health has crippled us financially, and we never know when his trouble may come on worse again. Myself, I've never doubted that you would see it is only right to share with us."

St. Peter looked at her in amazement. "But, my dear Mrs. Crane, how can I share with you what I haven't got? Tom willed his estate and royalties in a perfectly regular way. The fact that he named my daughter as his sole beneficiary doesn't affect me, any more than if he had named some relative of his own. I tell you frankly, I have never received one dollar from the Outland vacuum."

"It's all the same if it goes to your family, Doctor St. Peter. My husband must be considered in this matter. He spent days and nights working with Outland. Tom never could have worked his theory out without Robert's help. He said so, more than once, in my presence and in the presence of others."

"Oh, I believe that, Mrs. Crane. But the difficulty is that Tom didn't make any recognition of that assistance in his will."

Mrs. Crane had set her head and advanced her long chin with meek determination. "Well, this is how it was, Professor. Mr. Marsellus came here a stranger, to put in the Edison power plant, just at the time the city was stirred up about Outland's being killed at the front. Everybody was wanting to do something in recognition of the young man. You brought Mr. Marsellus to our house and introduced him. After that he came alone, again and again, and he got round my husband. Robert thought he was disinterested, and was only taking a

scientific interest, and he told him a great d
and Outland had been working on. Then Ros
came for the papers. Tom Outland had no lab   his
own. He was allowed the use of a room in the p   s building, at my husband's request. He wanted to be there, because
he constantly needed Robert's help. The first thing we knew,
your daughter's engagement to Marsellus was announced,
and then we heard that all Outland's papers had been given
over to him."

Here St. Peter anticipated her. "But, Mrs. Crane, your husband couldn't, and wouldn't, have kept Tom's papers. They
had to be given over to his executor, who was my daughter's
attorney."

"Well, I could have kept them, if he couldn't!"—Mrs.
Crane threw up her head as if to show that the worm had
turned at last—"kept them until justice was done us, and
some recognition had been made of my husband's part in all
that research work. If he had taken the papers to court then,
with all the evidence we have, we could easily have got an
equity. But Mr. Marsellus is very smooth. He flattered Robert
and got everything there was."

"But he didn't get anything from your husband. Outland's
papers and apparatus were delivered to his executor, as was
inevitable."

"That was a poor subterfuge," said Mrs. Crane, with deep
meaning. "You know how unworldly Robert is, and as an old
friend you might have warned us."

"Of what, Mrs. Crane?"

"Why, that Marsellus saw there was a fortune in the gas my
husband and his pupil had made, and we could have asked for
our equity before we gave your son-in-law a free hand with
everything."

St. Peter felt very unhappy. He began walking up and
down the little room. "Heaven knows I'd like to see Crane get
something out of it, but how? How? I've thought a great deal
about this matter, and I've blamed Tom for making that kind
of will. I don't think it occurred to the boy that the will
would ever be probated. He expected to come back from *the*
war and develop the thing himself. I doubt *whether* Robert,
with all his superior knowledge, *would* have known the twists

and turns by which the patent could be commercialized. It took a great deal of work and a special kind of ability to do that."

"A salesman's ability!" Mrs. Crane was becoming nasty.

"If you like; but certainly Robert would have been no man to convince manufacturers and machinists, any more than I would. A great deal of money was put into it, too, before any came back; every cent Marsellus had, and all he could borrow. He took heavy chances. Crane and I together could never have raised a hundredth part of the capital that was necessary to get the thing started. Without capital to make it go, Tom's idea was merely a formula written out on paper. It had lain for two years in your husband's laboratory, and would have lain there for years more before he or I would have done anything about it."

Mrs. Crane's dreary face took on more animation than he had supposed it capable of. "It had lain there because it belonged there, and was made there! My husband was done out of it by an adventurer, and his friendship for you tied his hands. I must say you've shown very little consideration for him. You might have warned us never to let those papers go. You see Robert getting weaker all the time and having those terrible operations, and our girls going shabby and teaching in the ward schools, and Rosamond riding about in a limousine and building country houses,—and you do nothing about it. You take your honours—you've deserved them, we never forget that—and move into your new house, and you don't remember what it is to be in straitened circumstances."

St. Peter drew his chair nearer to Mrs. Crane, and addressed her patiently. "Mrs. Crane, if you had any legal rights in the patent, I'd defend them against Rosamond as soon as against anyone else. I think she ought to recognize Dr. Crane's long friendship and helpfulness to Tom in some way. I don't see just how it can be done, but I feel it should be. And if you wish, I'll tell Rosamund how I feel. Why don't you put this matter before her?"

"I don't care to ask anything of Mrs. Marsellus. I wrote her some time ago, and she replied to me through her lawyer, saying that all claims against the Outland patent would be considered in due order. It's not worthy of a man in Robert's position to accept hush money from the Marselluses. We want justice, and my brother is confident the court will give it to us."

"Well, I suppose Bright knows more about what the courts will do than I. But if you've decided to go to law about it, why did you come to me?"

"There are some things the law don't cover," said Mrs. Crane mysteriously, as she rose and put on her gloves. "I wanted you to know how we feel about it."

St. Peter followed her downstairs and put up her umbrella for her, and then went back to his study to think it over. His friendship with Crane had been a strange one. Out in the world they would almost certainly have kept clear of each other; but in the university they had fought together in a common cause. Both, with all their might, had resisted the new commercialism, the aim to "show results" that was undermining and vulgarizing education. The State Legislature and the board of regents seemed determined to make a trade school of the university. Candidates for the degree of Bachelor of Arts were allowed credits for commercial studies; courses in book-keeping, experimental farming, domestic science, dress-making, and what not. Every year the regents tried to diminish the number of credits required in science and the humanities. The liberal appropriations, the promotions and increases in salary, all went to the professors who worked with the regents to abolish the purely cultural studies. Out of a faculty of sixty, there were perhaps twenty men who made any serious stand for scholarship, and Robert Crane was one of the staunchest. He had lost the Deanship of the College of Science because of his uncompromising opposition to the degrading influence of politicians in university affairs. The honour went, instead, to a much younger man, head of the department of chemistry, who was willing "to give the taxpayers what they wanted."

The struggle to preserve the dignity of the university, and their own, had brought St. Peter and Dr. Crane much together. They were, moreover, the only two men on the faculty who were doing research work of an uncommercial nature, and they occasionally dropped in on one another to exchange ideas. But that was as far as it went. St. Peter couldn't ask Crane to dinner; the presence of a bottle of claret on the table would have made him uncomfortable. Dr. Crane had all the prejudices of the Baptist community in which he grew up. He carried them with him when he went to study at a German university, and brought them back. But Crane knew that none of his colleagues followed his work so closely, and rejoiced at his little triumphs so heartily, as St. Peter.

St. Peter couldn't help admiring the man's courage; poor, ill, overworked, held by his conscience to a generous discharge of his duties as a teacher, he was all the while carrying on these tedious and delicate experiments that had to do with determining the extent of space. Fortunately, Crane seemed to have no social needs or impulses. He never went anywhere, except, once or twice a year, to a dinner at the President's house. Music disturbed him too much, dancing shocked him—he couldn't see why it was permitted among the students. Once, after Mrs. St. Peter had sat next him at the President's dinner-table, she said to her husband: "The man is too dreary! All evening his heavy underwear kept coming down below his cuffs, and he kept poking it back with his fore-finger. I believe he thinks it's wicked to live with even so plain a woman as Mrs. Crane."

After Tom Outland graduated from the university, he and Dr. Crane worked side by side in the Physics building for several years. The older man had been of great assistance to the younger, without doubt. Though that kind of help, the result of criticism and suggestion, is not easily reckoned in percentages, still St. Peter thought Crane ought to get something out of the patent. He resolved to see Louie about it. But first he had better talk with Crane himself, and try to dissuade him from going to law. His brother-in-law, Homer Bright, would be tempted by the publicity which an action involving the Outland patent would certainly bring him. But he would lose the case, and Crane would get nothing. Whereas Louie, if he were properly approached, would be generous.

St. Peter looked at his watch. He would go home now, and after dinner he would walk over to the Physics building, where his colleague worked every night. He never went to see Crane at his house if he could help it. He lived in the most depressing and unnecessary ugliness.

XIII

A T DINNER Lillian asked him no questions about his interview with Mrs. Crane, and he volunteered no information. She was not surprised, however, when he said he
would not stop for a cigar, as he was going over to the Physics laboratory.

He walked through the park, past the old house and across
the north end of the campus, to a building that stood off by
itself in a grove of pine-trees. It was constructed of red brick,
after an English model. The architect had had a good idea,
and he very nearly succeeded in making a good thing, something like the old Smithsonian building in Washington. But
after it was begun, the State Legislature had defeated him by
grinding down the contractor to cheap execution, and had
spoiled everything, outside and in. Ever since it was finished,
plumbers and masons and carpenters had been kept busy
patching and repairing it. Crane and St. Peter, both young
men then, had wasted weeks of time with the contractors, and
had finally gone before the Legislative committee in person to
plead for the integrity of that building. But nothing came of
all their pains. It was one of many lost causes.

St. Peter entered the building and went upstairs to a small
room at the end of a chain of laboratories. After knocking, he
heard the familiar shuffle of Crane's carpet slippers, and the
door opened.

Crane was wearing a grey cotton coat, shrunk to a rag by
washing, though he wasn't working with fluids or batteries
to-night, but at a roll-top desk littered with papers. The room
was like any study behind a lecture room; dusty books, dusty
files, but no apparatus—except a spirit-lamp and a little
saucepan in which the physicist heated water for his cocoa at
regular intervals. He was working by the glare of an unshaded
electric bulb of high power—the man seemed to have no feeling for comfort of any kind. He asked his visitor to sit down,
and to excuse him for a moment while he copied some entries
into a note-book.

St. Peter watched him scribbling with his fountain pen. The
hands that were so deft in delicate manipulations were white

XIV

$\mathbf{A}$T THE END of the semester, St. Peter went to Chicago with Rosamond to help her buy things for her country house. He had very much wanted to stay at home and rest — the university work seemed to take it out of him that winter more than ever before; but Rosamond had set her mind on his going, and Mrs. St. Peter told him he couldn't refuse. A Chicago merchant had brought over a lot of old Spanish furniture, and on this nobody's judgment would be better than St. Peter's. He was supposed to know a good deal about rugs, too. When his wife said a thing must be done, the Professor usually did it, from long-established habit. Her instincts about what one owed to other people were better than his.

Louie accompanied them to Chicago, where he was to join his brother, the one who was in the silk trade in China, and go on to New York with him for a family reunion. St. Peter was amused, and pleased, to see that Louie sincerely hated to leave them — with very little encouragement he would have sent his brother on alone and remained in Chicago with his wife and father-in-law. They all lunched together, after which the Professor and Rosamond took the Marsellus brothers to the LaSalle Street station. When Louie had again and again kissed his hand to them from the rear platform of the Twentieth Century observation car, and was rolled away in the very act of shouting something to his wife, St. Peter, who had so often complained that there was too much Louie in his life, now felt a sudden drop, a distinct sense of loss.

He took Rosamond's arm, and they turned away from the shining rails. "We must be diligent, Rosie. He expects wonders of us."

Scott McGregor got on the Blue Bird Express one afternoon, returning from a business trip for his paper. On entering the smoking-car, he came upon his father-in-law lying back in a leather chair, his clothes covered with dust, his eyes closed, a dead cigar hanging between the relaxed fingers of his dark, muscular hand. It gave Scott a start; he thought the Professor didn't look well.

"Hello, Doctor! What are you doing here? Oh, yes! the shopping expedition. Where's Rosamond?"

"In Chicago. At the Blackstone."

"Outlasted you, did she?"

"That's it." The Professor smiled apologetically, as if he were ashamed to admit it.

Scott sat down beside him and tried to interest him in one subject after another, without success. It occurred to him that he had never before seen the Professor when he seemed absolutely flattened out and listless. That was a bad sign; he was glad they were only half an hour from Hamilton. "The old chap needs rest," he reflected. "Rosamond's run him to death in Chicago. He oughtn't to be used as a courier, anyhow! I'm going to tell Kitty that we must look out for her father a little. The Marselluses have no mercy, and Lillian has always taken it for granted that he was as strong as three men."

That evening Mrs. St. Peter was standing by the French windows in the drawing-room, watching somewhat anxiously for her husband. The Chicago train was usually punctual, and surely he would have taken a cab from the station, for it was a raw February night with a freezing wind blowing off the lake. St. Peter arrived on foot, however. As he came through the gate, she could see by his walk and the set of his shoulders that he was very tired. She hurried to open the front door, and asked him why he hadn't come up in a taxi.

"Didn't think of it, really. I'm a creature of habit, and that's one of the things I never used to do."

"And in your lightest overcoat! I thought you only wore this one because you were going to buy a new fur coat in Chicago."

"Well, I didn't," he said rather shortly. "Let's omit the verb 'to buy' in all forms for a time. Keep dinner back a little, will you, Lillian? I want to take a warm bath and dress. I did get rather chilled coming up."

Mrs. St. Peter went to the kitchen, and, after a discreet interval, followed her husband upstairs and into his room.

"I know you're tired, but tell me one thing: did you find the painted Spanish bedroom set?"

"Oh, dear, yes! Several of them."

"And were they pretty?"

"Very. At least, I think I'd have found them so if I'd come upon them without so many other things. Too much is certainly worse than too little—of anything. It turned out to be rather an orgy of acquisition."

"Rosamond lost her head?"

"Oh, no! Perfectly cool. I should say she had a faultless purchasing manner. Wonder where a girl who grew up in that old house of ours ever got it. She was like Napoleon looting the Italian palaces."

"Don't be harsh. You had a nice little vacation, at any rate."

"A very expensive one, for a poor professor. And not much rest."

A look of sharp anxiety came into Mrs. St. Peter's face. "You mean," she breathed in a hushed voice, "that she let you——"

He cut in sharply. "I mean that I paid my way, as I hope always to be able to do. Any suggestion to the contrary might have been very graceful, but it would have been rejected. I am quite ready to permit myself a little extravagance to be of service to the women of my family. Any other arrangement is humiliating."

"Then that was why you didn't get your fur coat."

"That may have been one reason. I was not much in the humour for it."

Mrs. St. Peter went swiftly downstairs to make him a cocktail. She sensed an unusual weariness in him, and felt, as it were, the bitter taste on his tongue. A man, she knew, could get from his daughter a peculiar kind of hurt—one of the cruellest that flesh is heir to. Her heart ached for Godfrey.

When the Professor had been warmed and comforted by a good dinner, he lit a cigar and sat down before the hearth to read. After a while his wife saw that the book had slid to his knee, and he was looking into the fire. Studying his dark profile, she noticed that the corners of his funny eyebrows rose, as if he were amused by something.

"What are you thinking about, Godfrey?" she said presently. "Just then you were smiling—quite agreeably!"

"I was thinking," he answered absently, "about Euripides; how, when he was an old man, he went and lived in a cave by the sea, and it was thought queer, at the time. It seems that houses had become insupportable to him. I wonder whether it was because he had observed women so closely all his life."

the Professor's darkest secret. At the font he had been chris-tened Napoleon Godfrey St. Peter. There had always been a Napoleon in the family, since a remote grandfather got his discharge from the Grande Armée. Godfrey had abbreviated his name in Kansas, and even his daughters didn't know what it had been originally.

"I think, you know," he told his wife as he rose to go to bed, "that I'll get my second wind. But for the present I don't want anything very stimulating. Paris is too beautiful, and too full of memories."

XVI

O NE SATURDAY MORNING in the spring, when the Professor was at work in the old house, he heard energetic footsteps running up the uncarpeted stairway. Louie's voice called:

"*Cher Papa*, shall I disturb you too much?"

St. Peter rose and opened to him. Louie was wearing his golf stockings, and a purple jacket with a fur collar.

"No, I'm not going golfing. I changed my mind, but didn't have time to change my clothes. I want you to take a run out along the lake-shore with us. Rosie is going to lunch with some friends at the Country Club. We'll have a drive with her, and then drop her there. It's a glorious day." Louie's keen, interested eye ran about the shabby little room. He chuckled. "The old bear, he just likes his old den, doesn't he? I can readily understand. Your children were born here. Not your daughters—your sons, your splendid Spanish-adventurer sons! I'm proud to be related to them, even by marriage. And your blanket, surely that's a Spanish touch!" Louie pounced upon the purple blanket, threw it across his chest, and, moving aside the wire lady, studied himself in Augusta's glass. "And a very proper dressing-gown it would make for Louie, wouldn't it?"

"It was Outland's—a precious possession. His lost chum brought it up from Mexico."

"Was it Outland's, indeed?" Louie stroked it and regarded it in the glass with increased admiration. "I can never forgive destiny that I hadn't the chance to know that splendid fellow."

The Professor's eyebrows rose in puzzled interrogation. "It might have been awkward—about Rosie, you know."

"I never think of him as a rival," said Louie, throwing back the blanket with a wide gesture. "I think of him as a brother, an adored and gifted brother."

Half an hour later they were spinning along through the country, just coming green, Rosamond and her father on the back seat, Louie facing them. It struck the Professor that Louie had something on his mind; his restless bright eyes watched his wife narrowly, as if to seize an opportune moment.

"You know, Doctor," he said presently, "we've decided to give up our house before we go abroad, and cut off the rent. We'll move the books and pictures up to Outland (and our wedding presents, of course), and the silver we'll put in the bank. There won't be much of our present furniture that we'll need. I wonder if you could use any of it? And it has just occurred to me, Rosie," here he leaned forward and tapped her knee, "that we might ask Scott and Kathleen to come round and select anything they like. No use bothering to sell it, we'd get so little."

Rosamond looked at him in astonishment. It was very evident they had not discussed anything of this sort before. "Don't be foolish, Louie," she said quietly. "They wouldn't want your things."

"But why not?" he persisted playfully. "They are very nice things. Not right for Outland, but perfectly right for a little house. We chose them with care, and we don't want them going into some dirty second-hand shop."

"They won't have to. We can store them in the attic at Outland, Heaven knows it's big enough! You don't have to do anything with them just now."

"It seems a pity, when somebody might be getting the good of them. I know Scott could do very well with that chiffonier of mine. He admired it greatly, I remember, and said he'd never had one with proper drawers for his shirts."

Rosamond's lip curled.

"Don't look like that, Rosie! It's naughty. Stop it!" Louie reached forward and shook her gently by the elbows. "And how can you be sure the McGregors wouldn't like our things, when you've never asked them? What positive ideas she does get into her head!"

"They wouldn't want them because they are ours, yours and mine, if you will have it," she said coldly, drawing away from him.

Louie sank back into his seat and gave it up. "Why do you think such naughty things? I don't believe it, you know! You are so touchy. Scott and Kitty may be a little stand-offish, but it might very possibly make them feel better if you went at them nicely about this." He rallied and began to coax again. "She's got it into her head that the McGregors have a grudge, Doctor. There's nothing to it."

Rosamond had grown quite pale. Her upper lip, that was so like her mother's when she was affable, so much harder when she was not, came down like a steel curtain. "I happen to know, Louie, that Scott blackballed you for the Arts and Letters. You can call that a grudge or not, as you please."

Marsellus was visibly shaken. He looked sad. "Well, if he did, it wasn't very nice of him, certainly. But are you sure, Rosie? Rumours do go about, and people like to stir up family differences."

"It isn't people, and it's not rumour. I know it positively. Kathleen's best friend told me."

Louie lay back and shook with laughter. "Oh, the ladies, the ladies! What they do to each other, Professor!"

St. Peter was very uncomfortable. "I don't think I'd accept such evidence, Rosamond. I don't believe it of Scott, and I think Louie has the right idea. People are like children, and Scott's poor and proud. I think Louie's chiffonier would go to his heart, if Louie offered it to him. I'm afraid you wouldn't do it very graciously."

"Professor, I'll go to McGregor's office and put it up to him. If he scorns it, so much the worse for him. He'll lose a very handy piece of furniture."

Rosamond's paleness changed to red. Fortunately they were spinning over the gravel loops that led through shaven turf to the Country Club. "You can do as you like with your own things, Louie. But I don't want any of mine in the Mc-Gregors' bungalow. I know Scott's brand of humour too well, and the kind of jokes that would be made about them."

The car stopped. Louie sprang out and gave his arm to his wife. He walked up the steps to the door with her, and his back expressed such patient, protecting kindness that the Professor bit his lower lip with indignation. Louie came back looking quite grey and tired, and sank into the seat beside the Professor with a sadder-and-wiser smile.

"Louie," St. Peter spoke with deep feeling, "do you happen to have read a novel of Henry James, *The American*? There's a rather nice scene in it, in which a young Frenchman, hurt in a

alone in the house, writing on volumes three and four of his history. Tom was carrying on some experiments of his own, over in the Physics laboratory. He and St. Peter were often together in the evening, and on fine afternoons they went swimming. Every Saturday the Professor turned his house over to the cleaning-woman, and he and Tom went to the lake and spent the day in his sail-boat.

It was just the sort of summer St. Peter liked, if he had to be in Hamilton at all. He was his own cook, and had laid in a choice assortment of cheeses and light Italian wines from a discriminating importer in Chicago. Every morning before he sat down at his desk he took a walk to the market and had his pick of the fruits and salads. He dined at eight o'clock. When he cooked a fine leg of lamb, *saignant*, well rubbed with garlic before it went into the pan, then he asked Outland to dinner. Over a dish of steaming asparagus, swathed in a napkin to keep it hot, and a bottle of sparkling Asti, they talked and watched night fall in the garden. If the evening happened to be rainy or chilly, they sat inside and read Lucretius.

It was on one of those rainy nights, before the fire in the dining-room, that Tom at last told the story he had always kept back. It was nothing very incriminating, nothing very remarkable; a story of youthful defeat, the sort of thing a boy is sensitive about—until he grows older.

Tom Outland's Story

I

THE THING that side-tracked me and made me so late coming to college was a somewhat unusual accident, or string of accidents. It began with a poker game, when I was a call boy in Pardee, New Mexico.

One cold, clear night in the fall I started out to hunt up a freight crew that was to go out soon after midnight. It was just after pay day, and one of the fellows had tipped me off that there would be a poker game going on in the card-room behind the Ruby Light saloon. I knew most of my crew would be there, except Conductor Willis, who had a sick baby at home. The front windows were dark, of course. I went up the back alley, through a tumble-down ice house and a court, into a 'dobe room that didn't open into the saloon proper at all. It was crowded, and hot and stuffy enough. There were six or seven in the game, and a crowd of fellows were standing about the walls, rubbing the white-wash off on to their coat shoulders. There was a bird-cage hanging in one window, covered with an old flannel shirt, but the canary had wakened up and was singing away for dear life. He was a beautiful singer — an old Mexican had trained him — and he was one of the attractions of the place.

I happened along when a jack-pot was running. Two of the fellows I'd come for were in it, and they naturally wanted to finish the hand. I stood by the door with my watch, keeping time for them. Among the players I saw two sheep men who always liked a lively game, and one of the bystanders told me you had to buy a hundred dollars' worth of chips to get in that night. The crowd was fussing about one fellow, Rodney Blake, who had come in from his engine without cleaning up. That wasn't customary; the minute a man got in from his run, he took a bath, put on citizen's clothes, and went to a barber. This Blake was a new fireman on our division. He'd come up town in his greasy overalls and sweaty blue shirt, with his face streaked up with smoke. He'd been drinking; he smelled of it, and his eyes were out of focus. All the other men were clean and freshly shaved, and they were sore at Blake—said his hands were so greasy they marked the cards. Some of them wanted to put him out of the game, but he was a big, heavy-built fellow, and nobody wanted to be the man to do it. It didn't please them any better when he took the jack-pot.

I got my two men and hurried them out, and two others from the row along the wall took their places. One of the chaps who left with me asked me to go up to his house and get his grip with his work clothes. He'd lost every cent of his pay cheque and didn't want to face his wife. I asked him who was winning.

"Blake. The dirty boomer's been taking everything. But the fellows will clean him out before morning."

About two o'clock, when my work for that night was over and I was going home to sleep, I just dropped in at the card-room to see how things had come out. The game was breaking up. Since I left them at midnight, they had changed to stud poker, and Blake, the fireman, had cleaned everybody out. He was cashing in his chips when I came in. The bank was a little short, but Blake made no fuss about it. He had something over sixteen hundred dollars lying on the table before him in bank-notes and gold. Some of the crowd were insulting him, trying to get him into a fight and loot him. He paid no attention and began to put the money away, not looking at anybody. The bills he folded and put inside the band of his hat. He filled his overalls pockets with the gold, and swept the rest of it into his big red neckerchief.

I'd been interested in this fellow ever since he came on our division; he was close-mouthed and unfriendly. He was one of those fellows with a settled, mature body and a young face, such as you often see among working-men. There was something calm, and sarcastic, and mocking about his expression—that, too, you often see among working-men. When he had put all his money away, he got up and walked toward the door without a word, without saying good-night to anybody.

"Manners of a hog, and a dirty hog!" little Barney Shea yelled after him. Blake's back was just in the doorway; he hitched up one shoulder, but didn't turn or make a sound.

I slipped out after him and followed him down the street. His walk was unsteady, and the gold in his baggy overalls pockets clinked with every step he took. I ran a little way and caught up with him. "What are you going to do with all that money, Blake?" I asked him.

"Lose it, to-morrow night. I'm no hog for money. Damned barber-pole dudes!"

I thought I'd better follow him home. I knew he lodged with an old Mexican woman, in the yellow quarter, behind the round-house. His room opened on to the street, by a sky-blue door. He went in, didn't strike a light or make a stab at undressing, but threw himself just as he was on the bed and went to sleep. His hat stuck between the iron rods of the bed-head, the gold ran out of his pockets and rolled over the bare floor in the dark.

I struck a match and lit a candle. The bed took up half the room; on the dresser was a grip with his clean clothes in it, just as he'd brought it in from his run. I took out the clothes and began picking up the money; got the bills out of his hat, emptied his pockets, and collected the coins that lay in the hollow of the bed about his hips, and put it all into the grip. Then I blew out the light and sat down to listen. I trusted all the boys who were at the Ruby Light that night, except Barney Shea. He might try to pull something off on a stranger, down in Mexican town. We had a quiet night, however, and a cold one. I found Blake's winter overcoat hanging on the wall and wrapped up in it. I wasn't a bit sorry when the roosters began to crow and the dogs began barking all over Mexican town. At last the sun came up and turned the desert and the 'dobe town red in a minute. I began to shake the man on the bed. Waking men who didn't want to get up was part of my job, and I didn't let up on him until I had him on his feet.

"Hello, kid, come to call me?"

I told him I'd come to call him to a Harvey House breakfast. "You owe me a good one. I brought you home last night."

cows over here get the scent of them and make a break for the river. You'll have to watch 'em close when you bring 'em down."

I asked him whether nobody had ever gone over to get the lost cattle out.

Rapp glared at me. "Out of that mesa? Nobody has ever got into it yet. The cliffs are like the base of a monument, all the way round. The only way into it is through that deep canyon that opens on the water level, just where the river makes the bend. You can't get in by that, because the river's too deep to ford and too swift to swim. Oh, I suppose a horse could swim it, if cattle can, but I don't want to be the man to try."

I remarked that I had had my eye on the mesa all summer and meant to climb it.

"Not while you're working for the Sitwell Company, you don't! If you boys try any nonsense of that sort, I'll fire you quick. You'd break your bones and lose the herd for us. You have to watch them close to keep them from going over, I tell you. If it wasn't for that mesa, this would be the best winter range in all New Mexico."

After the foreman left us, we settled down to easy living and fine weather; blue and gold days, and clear, frosty nights. We kept the cattle off to the north and east and alternated in taking charge of them. One man was with the herd while the other got his sleep and did the cooking at the cabin. The mesa was our only neighbour, and the closer we got to it, the more tantalizing it was. It was no longer a blue, featureless lump, as it had been from a distance. Its sky-line was like the profile of a big beast lying down; the head to the north, higher than the flanks around which the river curved. The north end we could easily believe impassable—sheer cliffs that fell from the summit to the plain, more than a thousand feet. But the south flank, just across the river from us, looked accessible by way of the deep canyon that split the bulk in two, from the top rim to the river, then wound back into the solid cube so that it was invisible at a distance, like a mouse track winding into a big cheese. This canyon didn't break the solid outline of the mesa, and you had to be close to see that it was there at all. We faced the mesa on its shortest side; it was only about three miles long from north to south, but east and west it measured nearly twice that distance. Whether the top was wooded we couldn't see—it was too high above us; but the cliffs and canyon on the river side were fringed with beautiful growth, groves of quaking asps and piñons and a few dark cedars, perched up in the air like the hanging gardens of Babylon. At certain hours of the day, those cedars, growing so far up on the rocks, took on the bluish tint of the cliffs themselves.

It was light up there long before it was with us. When I got up at daybreak and went down to the river to get water, our camp would be cold and grey, but the mesa top would be red with sunrise, and all the slim cedars along the rocks would be gold—metallic, like tarnished gold-foil. Some mornings it would loom up above the dark river like a blazing volcanic mountain. It shortened our days, too, considerably. The sun got behind it early in the afternoon, and then our camp would lie in its shadow. After a while the sunset colour would begin to stream up from behind it. Then the mesa was like one great ink-black rock against a sky on fire.

No wonder the thing bothered us and tempted us; it was always before us, and was always changing. Black thunderstorms used to roll up from behind it and pounce on us like a panther without warning. The lightning would play round it and jab into it so that we were always expecting it would fire the brush. I've never heard thunder so loud as it was there. The cliffs threw it back at us, and we thought the mesa itself, though it seemed so solid, must be full of deep canyons and caverns, to account for the prolonged growl and rumble that followed every crash of thunder. After the burst in the sky was over, the mesa went on sounding like a drum, and seemed itself to be muttering and making noises.

One afternoon I was out hunting turkeys. Just as the sun was getting low, I came through a sea of rabbit-brush, still yellow, and the horizontal rays of light, playing into it, brought out the contour of the ground with great distinctness. I noticed a number of straight mounds, like plough furrows, running from the river inland. It was too late to examine them. I cut a scrub willow and stuck a stake into one of the ridges, to mark it. The next day I took a spade down to the plantation of rabbit-brush and dug around in the sandy soil. I came upon an old irrigation main, unmistakable, lined with hard smooth cobbles and 'dobe cement, with sluices where the water had been let out into trenches. Along these ditches I turned up some pieces of pottery, all of it broken, and arrowheads, and a very neat, well-finished stone pick-ax.

That night I didn't go back to the cabin, but took my specimens out to Blake, who was still north with the cattle. Of course, we both knew there had been Indians all over this country, but we felt sure that Indians hadn't used stone tools for a long while back. There must have been a colony of pueblo Indians here in ancient times: fixed residents, like the Taos Indians and the Hopis, not wanderers like the Navajos.

To people off alone, as we were, there is something stirring about finding evidences of human labour and care in the soil of an empty country. It comes to you as a sort of message, makes you feel differently about the ground you walk over every day. I liked the winter range better than any place I'd ever been in. I never came out of the cabin door in the morning to go after water that I didn't feel fresh delight in our snug quarters and the river and the old mesa up there, with its top burning like a bonfire. I wanted to see what it was like on the other side, and very soon I took a day off and forded the river where it was wide and shallow, north of our camp. I rode clear around the mesa, until I met the river again where it flowed under the south flank.

On that ride I got a better idea of its actual structure. All the way round were the same precipitous cliffs of hard blue rock, but in places it was mixed with a much softer stone. In these soft streaks there were deep dry watercourses which could certainly be climbed as far as they went, but nowhere did they reach to the top of the mesa. The top seemed to be one great slab of very hard rock, lying on the mixed mass of the base like the top of an old-fashioned marble table. The channels worn out by water ran for hundreds of feet up the cliffs, but always stopped under this great rimrock, which projected out over the erosions like a granite shelf. Evidently, it was because of this unbroken top layer that the butte was inaccessible. I rode back to camp that night, convinced that if we ever climbed it, we must take the route the cattle took, through the river and up the one canyon that broke down to water-level.

over everything we'd done, and examined everything minutely: the pottery, cloth, stone implements, and the remains of food. He measured the heads of the mummies and declared they had good skulls. He cut down one of the old cedars that grew exactly in the middle of the deep trail worn in the stone, and counted the rings under his pocket microscope. You couldn't count them with the unassisted eye, for growing out of a tiny crevice in the rock as that tree did, the increase of each year was so scant that the rings were invisible except with a glass. The tree he cut down registered three hundred and thirty-six years' growth, and it could have begun to grow in that well-worn path only after human feet had ceased to come and go there.

Why had they ceased? That question puzzled him, too. Smallpox, any epidemic, would have left unburied bodies. Father Duchene suggested what Dr. Ripley, in Washington, afterward surmised: that the tribe had been exterminated, not here in their stronghold, but in their summer camp, down among the farms across the river. Father Duchene had been among the Indians nearly twenty years then, he had seventeen Indian pueblos in his parish, and he spoke several Indian dialects. He was able to explain the use of many of the implements we found, especially those used in religious ceremonies. The night before he left us, he summed up the results of his week's study, something like this:

"The two square towers on the mesa top, to which you have given little attention, were unquestionably granaries. Under the stones and earth fallen from the walls, there is a quantity of dried corn on the ear. Not a great harvest, for life must have come to an end here in the summer, when the new crop was not yet garnered and the last year's grain was getting low. The semicircular ridge on the mesa top, which you can see distinctly among the piñons when the sun is low and brings it into high relief, is the buried wall of an amphitheatre, where probably religious exercises and games took place. I advise you not to dig into it. It is probably the most important thing here, and should be left for scholars to excavate.

"The tower you so much admire in the cliff village may have been a watch tower, as you think, but from the curious placing of those narrow slits, like windows, I believe it was used for astronomical observations. I am inclined to think that your tribe were a superior people. Perhaps they were not so when they first came upon this mesa, but in an orderly and secure life they developed considerably the arts of peace. There is evidence on every hand that they lived for something more than food and shelter. They had an appreciation of comfort, and went even further than that. Their life, compared to that of our roving Navajos, must have been quite complex. There is unquestionably a distinct feeling for design in what you call the Cliff City. Buildings are not grouped like that by pure accident, though convenience probably had much to do with it. Convenience often dictates very sound design.

"The workmanship on both the wood and stone of the dwellings is good. The shapes and decoration of the water jars and food bowls is better than in any of the existing pueblos I know, better even than the pottery made at Acoma. I have seen a collection of early pottery from the island of Crete. Many of the geometrical decorations on these jars are not only similar, but, if my memory is trustworthy, identical.

"I see your tribe as a provident, rather thoughtful people, who made their livelihood secure by raising crops and fowl— the great number of turkey bones and feathers are evidence that they had domesticated the wild turkey. With grain in their store-rooms, and mountain sheep and deer for their quarry, they rose gradually from the condition of savagery. With the proper variation of meat and vegetable diet, they developed physically and improved in the primitive arts. They had looms and mills, and experimented with dyes. At the same time, they possibly declined in the arts of war, in brute strength and ferocity.

"I see them here, isolated, cut off from other tribes, working out their destiny, making their mesa more and more worthy to be a home for man, purifying life by religious ceremonies and observances, caring respectfully for their dead, protecting the children, doubtless entertaining some feelings of affection and sentiment for this stronghold where they were at once so safe and so comfortable, where they had practically overcome the worst hardships that primitive man

the beginning. He advised me to go back to our Congress-man and get a letter to the Smithsonian Institution. I packed up my pottery and got out of the place, feeling pretty sore. The head clerk followed me down the corridor and asked me what I'd take for that little bowl he'd taken a fancy to. He said it had no market value, I'd find Washington full of such things; there were cases of them in the cellar at the Smith-sonian that they'd never taken the trouble to unpack, hadn't any place to put them.

I went back to my Congressman. This time he wasn't so friendly as before, but he gave me a letter to the Smithsonian. There I went through the same experience. The Director couldn't be seen except by appointment, and his secretary had to be convinced that your business was important before he would give you an appointment with his chief. After the first morning I found it difficult to see even the secretary. He was always engaged. I was told to take a seat and wait, but when he was disengaged he was hurrying off to luncheon. I would sit there all morning with a group of unfortunate people: girls who wanted to get typewriting to do, nice polite old men who wanted to be taken out on surveys and expeditions next summer. The secretary would at last come out with his over-coat on, and would hurry through the waiting-room reading a letter or a report, without looking up.

The office assistants cheered me along, and I kept this up for some days, sitting all morning in that room, studying the patterns of the rugs, and the shoes of the patient waiters who came as regularly as I. One day after the secretary had gone out, his stenographer, a nice little Virginia girl, came and sat down in an empty chair next to mine and began talking to me. She wasn't pretty, but her kind eyes and soft Southern voice took hold of me at once. She wanted to know what I had in my telescope, and why I was there, and where I came from, and all about it. Nearly everyone else had gone out to lunch—that seemed to be the one thing they did regularly in Washington—and we had the waiting-room to ourselves. I talked to her a good deal. Her name was Virginia Ward. She was a tiny little thing, but she had lovely eyes and such gentle ways. She seemed indignant that I had been put off so long after having come so far.

"Now you just let me fix it up for you," she said at last. "Mr. Wagner is bothered by a great many foolish people who waste his time, and he is suspicious. The best way will be for you to invite him to lunch with you. I'll arrange it. I keep a list of his appointments, and I know he is not engaged for luncheon to-morrow. I'll tell him that he is to lunch with a nice boy who has come all the way from New Mexico to inform the Department about an important discovery. I'll tell him to meet you at the Shoreham, at one. That's expensive, but it would do no good to invite him to a cheap place. And, remember, you must ask him to order the luncheon. It will maybe cost you ten dollars, but it will get you somewhere."

I felt grateful to the nice little thing,—she wasn't older than I. I begged her wouldn't she please come to lunch with me herself to-day, and talk to me.

"Oh, no!" she said, blushing red as a poppy. "Why, I'm afraid you think——"

I told her I didn't think anything but how nice she was to me, and how lonesome I was. She went with me, but she wouldn't go to any swell place. She told me a great many useful things.

"If you want to get attention from anybody in Washin'ton," she said, "ask them to lunch. People here will do almost anything for a good lunch."

"But the Director of the Smithsonian, for instance," I said, "surely you don't mean that the high-up ones like that——? Why would he want to bother with a cow-puncher from New Mexico, when he can lunch with scientists and ambassadors?"

She had a pretty little fluttery Southern laugh. "You just name a hotel like the Shoreham to the Director, and try it! There has to be somebody to pay for a lunch, and the scientists and ambassadors don't do that when they can avoid it. He'd accept your invitation, and the next time he went to dine with the Secretary of State he'd make a nice little story of it, and paint you up so pretty you'd hardly know yourself."

When I asked her whether I'd better take my pottery—it was there under the table between us—to the Shoreham to show Mr. Wagner, she tittered again. "I wouldn't bother. If you show him enough of the Shoreham pottery, that will be more effective."

The next morning, when the secretary arrived at his office, he stopped by my chair and said he understood he had an engagement with me for one o'clock. That was a good idea, he added: his mind was freer when he was away from office routine.

I had been in Washington twenty-two days when I took the secretary out to lunch. It was an excellent lunch. We had a bottle of Château d'Yquem. I'd never heard of such a wine before, but I remember it because it cost five dollars. I drank only one glass, and that pleased him too, for he drank the rest. Though he was friendly and talked a great deal, my heart sank lower, for he wouldn't let me explain my mission to him at all. He kept telling me that he knew all about the Southwest. He had been sent by the Smithsonian to conduct parties of European archæologists through all the show places, Frijoles and Canyon de Chelly, and Taos and the Hopi pueblos. When some Austrian Archduke had gone to hunt in the Pecos range, he had been sent by his chief and the German ambassador to manage the tour, and he had done it with such success that both he and the Director were given decorations from the Austrian Crown, in recognition of his services. Then I had to listen to a long story about how well he was treated by the Archduke when he went to Vienna with his chief the following summer. I had to hear about balls and receptions, and the names and titles of all the people he had met at the Duke's country estate. I was amazed and ashamed that a man of fifty, a man of the world, a scholar with ever so many degrees, should find it worth his while to show off before a boy, and a boy of such humble pretensions, who didn't know how to eat the *hors d'œvres* any more than if an assortment of cocoanuts had been set before him with no hammer.

Imagine my astonishment when, as he was drinking his liqueur, he said carelessly: "By the way, I was successful in arranging an interview with the Director for you. He will see you at four o'clock on Monday."

That was Thursday. I spent the time between then and Monday trying to find out something more about the kind of people I had come among. I persuaded Virginia Ward to go to the theatre with me, and she told me that it always took a long while to get anything through with the Director, that I mustn't lose heart, and she would always be glad to cheer me up. She lived with her mother, a widow lady, and they had me come to dinner and were very nice to me.

All this time I was living with a young married couple who interested me very much, for they were unlike any people I had ever known. The husband was "in office," as they say there, he had some position in the War Department. How it did use to depress me to see all the hundreds of clerks come pouring out of that big building at sunset! Their lives seemed to me so petty, so slavish. The couple I lived with gave me a prejudice against that kind of life. I couldn't help knowing a good deal about their affairs. They had only a small flat, and rented me one room of it, so I was very much in their confidence and couldn't help overhearing. They asked me not to mention the fact that I paid rent, as they had told their friends I was making them a visit. It was like that in everything; they spent their lives trying to keep up appearances, and to make his salary do more than it could. When they weren't discussing where she should go in the summer, they talked about the promotions in his department; how much the other clerks got and how they spent it, how many new dresses their wives had. And there was always a struggle going on for an invitation to a dinner or a reception, or even a tea-party. When once they got the invitation they had been scheming for, then came the terrible question of what Mrs. Bixby should wear.

The Secretary of War gave a reception; there was to be dancing and a great showing of foreign uniforms. The Bixbys were in painful suspense until they got a card. Then for a week they talked about nothing but what Mrs. Bixby was going to wear. They decided that for such an occasion she must have a new dress. Bixby borrowed twenty-five dollars from me, and took his lunch hour to go shopping with his wife and choose the satin. That seemed to me very strange. In New Mexico the Indian boys sometimes went to a trader's with their wives and bought shawls or calico, and we thought it rather contemptible. On the night of the reception the Bixbys set off gaily in a cab; the dress they considered a great success. But they had bad luck. Somebody spilt claret-cup on Mrs. Bixby's skirt before the evening was half over, and when they got home that night I heard her weeping and reproaching

opened his trunk and took out some underwear and socks and a couple of shirts. After he had put these into the bag, he slung it over one shoulder, and his canvas water-bag over the other. I let these preparations go on without a word. He went to the cupboard over the stove and put some sticks of chocolate into his pocket, then his pipe and a bag of tobacco. Presently I said he'd break his neck if he tried riding down the trail in the dark.

"I'm not riding the trail," he replied curtly. "I'm going down the quick way. My horse is grazing in Cow Canyon."

"I noticed the river's high. It's dangerous crossing," I remarked.

"I got over that way a few days ago. I'm surprised at you, using such common expressions!" he said sarcastically. "*Dangerous crossing*; it's painted on signboards all over the world!" He walked out of the cabin without looking back. I followed him to the V-shaped break in the rim rock, hardly larger than a man's body, where the spliced tree-trunks made a swinging ladder down the face of the cliff. I wanted to protest, but only succeeded in finding fault.

"You'll catch your knapsack on those forks and come to grief."

"That's my look-out."

By this time my eyes had grown accustomed to the darkness, and I could see Blake quite clearly—the stubborn, crouching set of his shoulders that I used to notice when he first came to Pardee and was drinking all the time. There was an ache in my arms to reach out and detain him, but there was something else that made me absolutely powerless to do so. He stepped down and settled his foot into the first fork. Then he stopped a moment and straightened his pack, buttoned his coat up to the chin, and pulled his hat on tighter. There was always a night draught in the canyon. He gripped the trunk with his hands. "Well," he said with grim cheerfulness, "here's luck! And I'm glad it's you that's doing this to me, Tom; not me that's doing it to you."

His head disappeared below the rim. I could hear the trees creak under his heavy body, and the chains rattle a little at the splicings. I lay down on the ledge and listened. I could hear him for a long way down, and the sounds were comforting to me, though I didn't realize it. Then the silence closed in. I went to sleep that night hoping I would never waken.

VII

THE NEXT MORNING the whinnying of my saddle-horse in the shed roused me. I took him down to the foot of the trail where I'd left my trunk, and packed my things up to the cabin on his back. I sat up late that night, waiting for Blake, though I knew he wouldn't come. A few days later I rode into Tarpin for news of him. Bill Hook showed me Roddy's horse. He had sold him to the barn for sixty dollars. The station-master told me Blake had bought a ticket to Winslow, Arizona. I wired the station-master and the dispatcher at Winslow, but they could give me no information. Father Duchene came along, on his rounds, and I told him the whole story.

He thought Blake would come back sometime, that I'd only miss him if I went out to look for him. He advised me to stay on the mesa that summer and get ahead with my studies, work up my Spanish grammar and my Latin. He had friends all along the Santa Fé, and he was sure we could catch Blake by advertising in the local papers along the road; Albuquerque, Winslow, Flagstaff, Williams, Los Angeles. After a few days with him, I went back to the mesa to wait.

I'll never forget the night I got back. I crossed the river an hour before sunset and hobbled my horse in the wide bottom of Cow Canyon. The moon was up, though the sun hadn't set, and it had that glittering silveriness the early stars have in high altitudes. The heavenly bodies look so much more remote from the bottom of a deep canyon than they do from the level. The climb of the walls helps out the eye, somehow. I lay down on a solitary rock that was like an island in the bottom of the valley, and looked up. The grey sage-brush and the blue-grey rock around me were already in shadow, but high above me the canyon walls were dyed flame-colour with the sunset, and the Cliff City lay in a gold haze against its dark cavern. In a few minutes it, too, was grey, and only the rim rock at the top held the red light. When that was gone, I could still see the copper glow in the piñons along the edge of the top ledges. The arc of sky over the canyon was silvery blue, with its pale yellow moon, and presently stars shivered into it, like crystals dropped into perfectly clear water.

I remember these things, because, in a sense, that was the first night I was ever really on the mesa at all—the first night that all of me was there. This was the first time I ever saw it as a whole. It all came together in my understanding, as a series of experiments do when you begin to see where they are leading. Something had happened in me that made it possible for me to co-ordinate and simplify, and that process, going on in my mind, brought with it great happiness. It was possession. The excitement of my first discovery was a very pale feeling compared to this one. For me the mesa was no longer an adventure, but a religious emotion. I had read of filial piety in the Latin poets, and I knew that was what I felt for this place. It had formerly been mixed up with other motives; but now that they were gone, I had my happiness unalloyed.

What that night began lasted all summer. I stayed on the mesa until November. It was the first time I'd ever studied methodically, or intelligently. I got the better of the Spanish grammar and read the twelve books of the *Æneid*. I studied in the morning, and in the afternoon I worked at clearing away the mess the German had made in packing—tidying up the ruins to wait another hundred years, maybe, for the right explorer. I can scarcely hope that life will give me another summer like that one. It was my high tide. Every morning, when the sun's rays first hit the mesa top, while the rest of the world was in shadow, I wakened with the feeling that I had found everything, instead of having lost everything. Nothing tired me. Up there alone, a close neighbour to the sun, I seemed to get the solar energy in some direct way. And at night, when I watched it drop down behind the edge of the plain below me, I used to feel that I couldn't have borne another hour of that consuming light, that I was full to the brim, and needed dark and sleep.

All that summer, I never went up to the Eagle's Nest to get my diary—indeed, it's probably there yet. I didn't feel the need of that record. It would have been going backward. I didn't want to go back and unravel things step by step. Perhaps I was afraid that I would lose the whole in the parts. At any rate, I didn't go for my record.

III

THE FAMILY DOCTOR knew all about St. Peter. It was summer, moreover, and he had plenty of time. He devoted several mornings to the Professor and made tests of the most searching kind. In the end he of course told St. Peter there was nothing the matter with him.

"What made you come to me, any discomfort or pain?"

"None. I simply feel tired all the time."

Dr. Dudley shrugged. "So do I! Sleep well?"

"Almost too much."

"Eat well?"

"In every sense of the word, well. I am my own *chef*."

"Always a *gourmet*, and never anything wrong with your digestive tract! I wish you'd ask me to dine with you some night. Any of that sherry left?"

"A little. I use it plentifully."

"I'll bet you do! But why did you think there was something wrong with you? Low in your mind?"

"No, merely low in energy. Enjoy doing nothing. I came to you from a sense of duty."

"How about travel?"

"I shrink from the thought of it. As I tell you, I enjoy doing nothing."

"Then do it! There's nothing the matter with you. Follow your inclination."

St. Peter went home well satisfied. He did not mention to Dr. Dudley the real reason for his asking for a medical examination. One doesn't mention such things. The feeling that he was near the conclusion of his life was an instinctive conviction, such as we have when we waken in the dark and know at once that it is near morning; or when we are walking across the country and suddenly know that we are near the sea.

Letters came every week from France. Lillian and Louie alternated, so that one or the other got off a letter to him on every fast boat. Louie told him that wherever they went, when they had an especially delightful day, they bought him a present. At Trouville, for instance, they had laid in dozens of

the brilliant rubber casquettes he liked to wear when he went
swimming. At Aix-les-Bains they found a gorgeous dressing-
gown for him in a Chinese shop. St. Peter was happy in his
mind about them all. He was glad they were there, and that
he was here. Their generous letters, written when there were
so many pleasant things to do, certainly deserved more than
one reading. He used to carry them out to the lake to read
them over again. After coming out of the water he would lie
on the sand, holding them in his hand, but somehow never
taking his eyes off the pine-trees, appliquéd against the blue
water, and their ripe yellow cones, dripping with gum and
clustering on the pointed tips like a mass of golden bees in
swarming-time. Usually he carried his letters home unread.

His family wrote constantly about their plans for next
summer, when they were going to take him over with them.
Next summer? The Professor wondered. . . . Sometimes he
thought he would like to drive up in front of Notre Dame, in
Paris, again, and see it standing there like the Rock of Ages,
with the frail generations breaking about its base. He hadn't
seen it since the war.

But if he went anywhere next summer, he thought it would
be down into Outland's country, to watch the sunrise break
on sculptured peaks and impassable mountain passes—to
look off at those long, rugged, untamed vistas dear to the
American heart. Dear to all hearts, probably—at least, calling
to all. Else why had his grandfather's grandfather, who had
tramped so many miles across Europe into Russia with the
Grande Armée, come out to the Canadian wilderness to forget the chagrin of his Emperor's defeat?

IV

THE FALL TERM of the university opened, and now the Professor went to his lectures instead of to the lake. He supposed he did his work; he heard no complaints from his assistants, and the students seemed interested. He found, however, that he wasn't willing to take the trouble to learn the names of several hundred new students. It wasn't worth while. He felt that his relations with them would be of short duration.

The McGregors got home from their vacation in Oregon, and Scott was much amused to find the Professor so doggedly anchored in the old house.

"It never struck me, Doctor, that you were a man who would be keeping up two establishments. They'll be coming home pretty soon, and then you'll have to decide where you are going to live."

"I can't leave my study, Scott. That's flat."

"Don't, then! Darn it, you've a right to two houses if you want 'em."

This encounter took place on the street in front of the house. The Professor went wearily upstairs and lay down on the couch, his refuge from this ever-increasing fatigue. He really didn't see what he was going to do about the matter of domicile. He couldn't make himself believe that he was ever going to live in the new house again. He didn't belong there. He remembered some lines of a translation from the Norse he used to read long ago in one of his mother's few books, a little two-volume Ticknor and Fields edition of Longfellow, in blue and gold, that used to lie on the parlour table:

> For thee a house was built
> Ere thou wast born;
> For thee a mould was made
> Ere thou of woman camest.

Lying on his old couch, he could almost believe himself in that house already. The sagging springs were like the sham upholstery that is put in coffins. Just the equivocal American way of dealing with serious facts, he reflected. Why pretend that it is possible to soften that last hard bed?

He could remember a time when the loneliness of death had terrified him, when the idea of it was insupportable. He used to feel that if his wife could but lie in the same coffin with him, his body would not be so insensible that the nearness of hers would not give it comfort. But now he thought of eternal solitude with gratefulness; as a release from every obligation, from every form of effort. It was the Truth.

One morning, just as St. Peter was leaving the house to go to his class-room, the postman handed him two letters, one addressed in Lillian's hand and one in Louie's. He put them into his pocket. The feel of them disturbed him. They were of a suspicious thinness—as if they didn't contain amusing gossip, but announced sudden decisions. He set off down the street, sniffing the lake-cooled morning air and trying to overcome a feeling of nervous dread.

All the morning those two letters lay in his breast pocket. Though they were so light, their effect was to make him drop his shoulders and look woefully tired. The weather, too, had changed, come on suddenly hot and sultry at noon, as if getting ready for a storm. When his classes were over and he was back in his study again, St. Peter felt no interest in lunch. He took out the two letters and ripped them open with his forefinger to have it over. Yes, all plans were changed, and by the happiest of expectations. The family were hurrying home to prepare for the advent of a young Marsellus. They would sail on the sixteenth, on the *Berengaria*.

Lillian added a postscript to the effect that by this same mail she was getting off a letter to Augusta, who would come to him for the keys of the new house. She would be the best person to open the house and arrange to have the cleaning done. She would take it entirely off his shoulders and see that everything was properly put in order.

They were sailing on the sixteenth, and this was the seventeenth; they were already on the water. The *Berengaria* was a five-day boat. St. Peter caught up his hat and light overcoat and started down the stairs. Half-way down, he stopped short, went back to his study, and softly shut the door behind him. He sat down, forgetting to take off his overcoat, though

DEATH COMES FOR THE ARCHBISHOP

"Auspice Maria!"
Father Vaillant's signet-ring

They were talking business; had met, indeed, to discuss an anticipated appeal from the Provincial Council at Baltimore for the founding of an Apostolic Vicarate in New Mexico—a part of North America recently annexed to the United States. This new territory was vague to all of them, even to the missionary Bishop. The Italian and French Cardinals spoke of it as *Le Mexique*, and the Spanish host referred to it as "New Spain." Their interest in the projected Vicarate was tepid, and had to be continually revived by the missionary, Father Ferrand; Irish by birth, French by ancestry—a man of wide wanderings and notable achievement in the New World, an Odysseus of the Church. The language spoken was French—the time had already gone by when Cardinals could conveniently discuss contemporary matters in Latin.

The French and Italian Cardinals were men in vigorous middle life—the Norman full-belted and ruddy, the Venetian spare and sallow and hook-nosed. Their host, Garcia Maria de Allande, was still a young man. He was dark in colouring, but the long Spanish face, that looked out from so many canvases in his ancestral portrait gallery, was in the young Cardinal much modified through his English mother. With his *caffè oscuro* eyes, he had a fresh, pleasant English mouth, and an open manner.

During the latter years of the reign of Gregory XVI, de Allande had been the most influential man at the Vatican; but since the death of Gregory, two years ago, he had retired to his country estate. He believed the reforms of the new Pontiff impractical and dangerous, and had withdrawn from politics, confining his activities to work for the Society for the Propagation of the Faith—that organization which had been so fostered by Gregory. In his leisure the Cardinal played tennis. As a boy, in England, he had been passionately fond of this sport. Lawn tennis had not yet come into fashion; it was a formidable game of indoor tennis the Cardinal played. Amateurs of that violent sport came from Spain and France to try their skill against him.

The missionary, Bishop Ferrand, looked much older than any of them, old and rough—except for his clear, intensely blue eyes. His diocese lay within the icy arms of the Great Lakes, and on his long, lonely horseback rides among his missions the sharp winds had bitten him well. The missionary was here for a purpose, and he pressed his point. He ate more rapidly than the others and had plenty of time to plead his cause,—finished each course with such dispatch that the Frenchman remarked he would have been an ideal dinner companion for Napoleon.

The Bishop laughed and threw out his brown hands in apology. "Likely enough I have forgot my manners. I am pre-occupied. Here you can scarcely understand what it means that the United States has annexed that enormous territory which was the cradle of the Faith in the New World. The Vicarate of New Mexico will be in a few years raised to an Episcopal See, with jurisdiction over a country larger than Central and Western Europe, barring Russia. The Bishop of that See will direct the beginning of momentous things."

"Beginnings," murmured the Venetian, "there have been so many. But nothing ever comes from over there but trouble and appeals for money."

The missionary turned to him patiently. "Your Eminence, I beg you to follow me. This country was evangelized in fifteen hundred, by the Franciscan Fathers. It has been allowed to drift for nearly three hundred years and is not yet dead. It still pitifully calls itself a Catholic country, and tries to keep the forms of religion without instruction. The old mission churches are in ruins. The few priests are without guidance or discipline. They are lax in religious observance, and some of them live in open concubinage. If this Augean stable is not cleansed, now that the territory has been taken over by a pro-gressive government, it will prejudice the interests of the Church in the whole of North America."

"But these missions are still under the jurisdiction of Mexico, are they not?" inquired the Frenchman.

"In the See of the Bishop of Durango?" added Maria de Allande.

The missionary sighed. "Your Eminence, the Bishop of Durango is an old man; and from his seat to Santa Fé is a distance of fifteen hundred English miles. There are no wagon roads, no canals, no navigable rivers. Trade is carried on by means of pack-mules, over treacherous trails. The desert down there has a peculiar horror; I do not mean thirst, nor Indian massacres, which are frequent. The very floor of the world is cracked open into countless canyons and arroyos, fissures in the earth which are sometimes ten feet deep, sometimes a thousand. Up and down these stony chasms the traveller and his mules clamber as best they can. It is impossible to go far in any direction without crossing them. If the Bishop of Durango should summon a disobedient priest by letter, who shall bring the Padre to him? Who can prove that he ever received the summons? The post is carried by hunters, fur trappers, gold seekers, whoever happens to be moving on the trails."

The Norman Cardinal emptied his glass and wiped his lips.

"And the inhabitants, Father Ferrand? If these are the travellers, who stays at home?"

"Some thirty Indian nations, Monsignor, each with its own customs and language, many of them fiercely hostile to each other. And the Mexicans, a naturally devout people. Untaught and unshepherded, they cling to the faith of their fathers."

"I have a letter from the Bishop of Durango, recommending his Vicar for this new post," remarked Maria de Allande.

"Your Eminence, it would be a great misfortune if a native priest were appointed; they have never done well in that field. Besides, this Vicar is old. The new Vicar must be a young man, of strong constitution, full of zeal, and above all, intelligent. He will have to deal with savagery and ignorance, with dissolute priests and political intrigue. He must be a man to whom order is necessary—as dear as life."

The Spaniard's coffee-coloured eyes showed a glint of yellow as he glanced sidewise at his guest. "I suspect, from your exordium, that you have a candidate—and that he is a French priest, perhaps?"

"You guess rightly, Monsignor. I am glad to see that we have the same opinion of French missionaries."

"Yes," said the Cardinal lightly, "they are the best missionaries. Our Spanish fathers made good martyrs, but the French Jesuits accomplish more. They are the great organizers."

"Better than the Germans?" asked the Venetian, who had Austrian sympathies.

"Oh, the Germans classify, but the French arrange! The French missionaries have a sense of proportion and rational adjustment. They are always trying to discover the logical relation of things. It is a passion with them." Here the host turned to the old Bishop again. "But your Grace, why do you neglect this Burgundy? I had this wine brought up from my cellar especially to warm away the chill of your twenty Canadian winters. Surely, you do not gather vintages like this on the shores of the Great Lake Huron?"

The missionary smiled as he took up his untouched glass. "It is superb, your Eminence, but I fear I have lost my palate for vintages. Out there, a little whisky, or Hudson Bay Company rum, does better for us. I must confess I enjoyed the champagne in Paris. We had been forty days at sea, and I am a poor sailor."

"Then we must have some for you." He made a sign to his major-domo. "You like it very cold? And your new Vicar Apostolic, what will he drink in the country of bison and *serpents à sonnettes*? And what will he eat?"

"He will eat dried buffalo meat and frijoles with chili, and he will be glad to drink water when he can get it. He will have no easy life, your Eminence. That country will drink up his youth and strength as it does the rain. He will be called upon for every sacrifice, quite possibly for martyrdom. Only last year the Indian pueblo of San Fernandez de Taos murdered and scalped the American Governor and some dozen other whites. The reason they did not scalp their Padre, was that their Padre was one of the leaders of the rebellion and himself planned the massacre. That is how things stand in New Mexico!"

"Where is your candidate at present, Father?"

"He is a parish priest, on the shores of Lake Ontario, in my diocese. I have watched his work for nine years. He is but thirty-five now. He came to us directly from the Seminary."

"And his name is?"

"Jean Marie Latour."

Maria de Allande, leaning back in his chair, put the tips of his long fingers together and regarded them thoughtfully.

"Of course, Father Ferrand, the Propaganda will almost certainly appoint to this Vicarate the man whom the Council at Baltimore recommends."

As this was Christmas Day, the two friends were speaking in their native tongue. For years they had made it a practice to speak English together, except upon very special occasions, and of late they conversed in Spanish, in which they both needed to gain fluency.

"And yet sometimes you used to chafe a little at your dear Sandusky and its comforts," the Bishop reminded him—"to say that you would end a home-staying parish priest, after all."

"Of course, one wants to eat one's cake and have it, as they say in Ohio. But no farther, Jean. This is far enough. Do not drag me any farther." Father Joseph began gently to coax the cork from a bottle of red wine with his fingers. "This I begged for your dinner at the hacienda where I went to baptize the baby on St. Thomas's Day. It is not easy to separate these rich Mexicans from their French wine. They know its worth." He poured a few drops and tried it. "A slight taste of the cork; they do not know how to keep it properly. However, it is quite good enough for missionaries."

"You ask me not to drag you any farther, Joseph. I wish," Bishop Latour leaned back in his chair and locked his hands together beneath his chin, "I wish I knew how far this is! Does anyone know the extent of this diocese, or of this territory? The Commandant at the Fort seems as much in the dark as I. He says I can get some information from the scout, Kit Carson, who lives at Taos."

"Don't begin worrying about the diocese, Jean. For the present, Santa Fé is the diocese. Establish order at home. To-morrow I will have a reckoning with the churchwardens, who allowed that band of drunken cowboys to come in to the midnight Mass and defile the font. There is enough to do here. *Festina lente*. I have made a resolve not to go more than three days' journey from Santa Fé for one year."

The Bishop smiled and shook his head. "And when you were at the Seminary, you made a resolve to lead a life of contemplation."

A light leaped into Father Joseph's homely face. "I have not yet renounced that hope. One day you will release me, and I will return to some religious house in France and end my days in devotion to the Holy Mother. For the time being, it is my destiny to serve Her in action. But this is far enough, Jean."

The Bishop again shook his head and murmured, "Who knows how far?"

The wiry little priest whose life was to be a succession of mountain ranges, pathless deserts, yawning canyons and swollen rivers, who was to carry the Cross into territories yet unknown and unnamed, who would wear down mules and horses and scouts and stage-drivers, to-night looked apprehensively at his superior and repeated, "No more, Jean. This is far enough." Then making haste to change the subject, he said briskly, "A bean salad was the best I could do for you; but with onion, and just a suspicion of salt pork, it is not so bad."

Over the compote of dried plums they fell to talking of the great yellow ones that grew in the old Latour garden at home. Their thoughts met in that tilted cobble street, winding down a hill, with the uneven garden walls and tall horse-chestnuts on either side; a lonely street after nightfall, with soft street lamps shaped like lanterns at the darkest turnings. At the end of it was the church where the Bishop made his first Communion, with a grove of flat-cut plane trees in front, under which the market was held on Tuesdays and Fridays.

While they lingered over these memories—an indulgence they seldom permitted themselves—the two missionaries were startled by a volley of rifle-shots and blood-curdling yells without, and the galloping of horses. The Bishop half rose, but Father Joseph reassured him with a shrug.

"Do not discompose yourself. The same thing happened here on the eve of All Souls' Day. A band of drunken cow-boys, like those who came into the church last night, go out to the pueblo and get the Tesuque Indian boys drunk, and then they ride in to serenade the soldiers at the Fort in this manner."

4

A BELL AND A MIRACLE

On the morning after the Bishop's return from Durango, after his first night in his Episcopal residence, he had a pleasant

Zumarraga and his Vicar instantly fell upon their knees among the flowers. On the inside of his poor mantle was a painting of the Blessed Virgin, in robes of blue and rose and gold, exactly as She had appeared to him upon the hill-side.

A shrine was built to contain this miraculous portrait, which since that day has been the goal of countless pilgrimages and has performed many miracles.

Of this picture Padre Escolastico had much to say: he affirmed that it was of marvellous beauty, rich with gold, and the colours as pure and delicate as the tints of early morning. Many painters had visited the shrine and marvelled that paint could be laid at all upon such poor and coarse material. In the ordinary way of nature, the flimsy mantle would have fallen to pieces long ago. The Padre modestly presented Bishop Latour and Father Joseph with little medals he had brought from the shrine; on one side a relief of the miraculous portrait, on the other an inscription: *Non fecit taliter omni nationi. (She hath not dealt so with any nation.)*

Father Vaillant was deeply stirred by the priest's recital, and after the old man had gone he declared to the Bishop that he meant himself to make a pilgrimage to this shrine at the earliest opportunity.

"What a priceless thing for the poor converts of a savage country!" he exclaimed, wiping his glasses, which were clouded by his strong feeling. "All these poor Catholics who have been so long without instruction have at least the reassurance of that visitation. It is a household word with them that their Blessed Mother revealed Herself in their own country, to a poor convert. Doctrine is well enough for the wise, Jean; but the miracle is something we can hold in our hands and love."

Father Vaillant began pacing restlessly up and down as he spoke, and the Bishop watched him, musing. It was just this in his friend that was dear to him. "Where there is great love there are always miracles," he said at length. "One might almost say that an apparition is human vision corrected by divine love. I do not see you as you really are, Joseph; I see you through my affection for you. The Miracles of the Church seem to me to rest not so much upon faces or voices or healing power coming suddenly near to us from afar off, but upon our perceptions being made finer, so that for a moment our eyes can see and our ears can hear what is there about us always."

Missionary Journeys

I

THE WHITE MULES

I̶N MID-MARCH, Father Vaillant was on the road, returning from a missionary journey to Albuquerque. He was to stop at the *rancho* of a rich Mexican, Manuel Lujon, to marry his men and maid servants who were living in concubinage, and to baptize the children. There he would spend the night. To-morrow or the day after he would go on to Santa Fé, halting by the way at the Indian pueblo of Santo Domingo to hold service. There was a fine old mission church at Santo Domingo, but the Indians were of a haughty and suspicious disposition. He had said Mass there on his way to Albuquerque, nearly a week ago. By dint of canvassing from house to house, and offering medals and religious colour prints to all who came to church, he had got together a considerable congregation. It was a large and prosperous pueblo, set among clean sand-hills, with its rich irrigated farm lands lying just below, in the valley of the Rio Grande. His congregation was quiet, dignified, attentive. They sat on the earth floor, wrapped in their best blankets, repose in every line of their strong, stubborn backs. He harangued them in such Spanish as he could command, and they listened with respect. But bring their children to be baptized, they would not. The Spaniards had treated them very badly long ago, and they had been meditating upon their grievance for many generations. Father Vaillant had not baptized one infant there, but he meant to stop to-morrow and try again. Then back to his Bishop, provided he could get his horse up La Bajada Hill.

He had bought his horse from a Yankee trader and had been woefully deceived. One week's journey of from twenty to thirty miles a day had shown the beast up for a wind-broken wreck. Father Vaillant's mind was full of material cares as he approached Manuel Lujon's place beyond Berna-lillo. The *rancho* was like a little town, with all its stables, corrals, and stake fences. The *casa grande* was long and low, with glass windows and bright blue doors, a *portale* running its full length, supported by blue posts. Under this *portale* the adobe wall was hung with bridles, saddles, great boots and spurs, guns and saddle blankets, strings of red peppers, fox skins, and the skins of two great rattlesnakes.

When Father Vaillant rode in through the gateway, children came running from every direction, some with no clothing but a little shirt, and women with no shawls over their black hair came running after the children. They all disappeared when Manuel Lujon walked out of the great house, hat in hand, smiling and hospitable. He was a man of thirty-five, settled in figure and somewhat full under the chin. He greeted the priest in the name of God and put out a hand to help him alight, but Father Vaillant sprang quickly to the ground.

"God be with you, Manuel, and with your house. But where are those who are to be married?"

"The men are all in the field, Padre. There is no hurry. A little wine, a little bread, coffee, repose—and then the ceremonies."

"A little wine, very willingly, and bread, too. But not until afterward. I meant to catch you all at dinner, but I am two hours late because my horse is bad. Have someone bring in my saddle-bags, and I will put on my vestments. Send out to the fields for your men, Señor Lujon. A man can stop work to be married."

The swarthy host was dazed by this dispatch. "But one moment, Padre. There are all the children to baptize; why not begin with them, if I cannot persuade you to wash the dust from your sainted brow and repose a little."

"Take me to a place where I can wash and change my clothes, and I will be ready before you can get them here. No, I tell you, Lujon, the marriages first, the baptisms afterward; that order is but Christian. I will baptize the children tomorrow morning, and their parents will at least have been married over night."

Father Joseph was conducted to his chamber, and the older boys were sent running off across the fields to fetch the men. Lujon and his two daughters began constructing an altar at

Bishop works as hard as I do, and his horse is little better than mine. You know he lost everything on his way out here, in a shipwreck at Galveston,—among the rest a fine wagon he had had built for travel on these plains. I could not go about on a mule like this when my Bishop rides a common hack. It would be inappropriate. I must ride away on my old mare."

"Yes, Padre?" Manuel looked troubled and somewhat aggrieved. Why should the Padre spoil everything? It had all been very pleasant yesterday, and he had felt like a prince of generosity. "I doubt if she will make La Bajada Hill," he said slowly, shaking his head. "Look my horses over and take the one that suits you. They are all better than yours."

"No, no," said Father Vaillant decidedly. "Having seen these mules, I want nothing else. They are the colour of pearls, really! I will raise the price of marriages until I can buy this pair from you. A missionary must depend upon his mount for companionship in his lonely life. I want a mule that can look at me like a Christian, as you said of these."

Señor Lujon sighed and looked about his barnyard as if he were trying to find some escape from this situation.

Father Joseph turned to him with vehemence. "If I were a rich *ranchero*, like you, Manuel, I would do a splendid thing; I would furnish the two mounts that are to carry the word of God about this heathen country, and then I would say to myself: *There go my Bishop and my Vicario, on my beautiful cream-coloured mules.*"

"So be it, Padre," said Lujon with a mournful smile. "But I ought to get a good many prayers. On my whole estate there is nothing I prize like those two. True, they might pine if they were parted for long. They have never been separated, and they have a great affection for each other. Mules, as you know, have strong affections. It is hard for me to give them up."

"You will be all the happier for that, Manuelito," Father Joseph cried heartily. "Every time you think of these mules, you will feel pride in your good deed."

Soon after breakfast Father Vaillant departed, riding Contento, with Angelica trotting submissively behind, and from his gate Señor Lujon watched them disconsolately until they disappeared. He felt he had been worried out of his mules, and yet he bore no resentment. He did not doubt Father Joseph's devotedness, nor his singleness of purpose. After all, a Bishop was a Bishop, and a Vicar was a Vicar, and it was not to their discredit that they worked like a pair of common parish priests. He believed he would be proud of the fact that they rode Contento and Angelica. Father Vaillant had forced his hand, but he was rather glad of it.

2

THE LONELY ROAD TO MORA

The Bishop and his Vicar were riding through the rain in the Truchas mountains. The heavy, lead-coloured drops were driven slantingly through the air by an icy wind from the peak. These raindrops, Father Latour kept thinking, were the shape of tadpoles, and they broke against his nose and cheeks, exploding with a splash, as if they were hollow and full of air. The priests were riding across high mountain meadows, which in a few weeks would be green, though just now they were slate-coloured. On every side lay ridges covered with blue-green fir trees; above them rose the horny backbones of mountains. The sky was very low; purplish lead-coloured clouds let down curtains of mist into the valleys between the pine ridges. There was not a glimmer of white light in the dark vapours working overhead—rather, they took on the cold green of the evergreens. Even the white mules, their coats wet and matted into tufts, had turned a slaty hue, and the faces of the two priests were purple and spotted in that singular light.

Father Latour rode first, sitting straight upon his mule, with his chin lowered just enough to keep the drive of rain out of his eyes. Father Vaillant followed, unable to see much,—in weather like this his glasses were of no use, and he had taken them off. He crouched down in the saddle, his shoulders well over Contento's neck. Father Joseph's sister, Philomène, who was Mother Superior of a convent in her native town in the Puy-de-Dôm, often tried to picture her

pueblo people for pesos. An Indian girl cooked his beans and cornmeal mush for him, he required little else. The girl was not very skilful, he said, but she was clean about her cooking. When the Bishop remarked that everything in this pueblo, even the streets, seemed clean, the Padre told him that near Isleta there was a hill of some white mineral, which the Indians ground up and used as whitewash. They had done this from time immemorial, and the village had always been noted for its whiteness. A little talk with Father Jesus revealed that he was simple almost to childishness, and very superstitious. But there was a quality of golden goodness about him. His right eye was overgrown by a cataract, and he kept his head tilted as if he were trying to see around it. All his movements were to the left, as if he were reaching or walking about some obstacle in his path.

After coming to the house by way of a garden full of parrots, Father Latour was amused to find that the sole ornament in the Padre's poor, bare little *sala* was a wooden parrot, perched in a hoop and hung from one of the roof-logs. While Father Jesus was instructing his Indian girl in the kitchen, the Bishop took this carving down from its perch to examine it. It was cut from a single stick of wood, exactly the size of a living bird, body and tail rigid and straight, the head a little turned. The wings and tail and neck feathers were just indicated by the tool, and thinly painted. He was surprised to feel how light it was; the surface had the whiteness and velvety smoothness of very old wood. Though scarcely carved at all, merely smoothed into shape, it was strangely lifelike; a wooden pattern of parrots, as it were.

The Padre smiled when he found the Bishop with the bird in his hand.

"I see you have found my treasure! That, your Grace, is probably the oldest thing in the pueblo—older than the pueblo itself."

The parrot, Father Jesus said, had always been the bird of wonder and desire to the pueblo Indians. In ancient times its feathers were more valued than wampum and turquoises. Even before the Spaniards came, the pueblos of northern New Mexico used to send explorers along the dangerous and difficult trade routes down into tropical Mexico to bring back upon their bodies a cargo of parrot feathers. To purchase these the trader carried pouches full of turquoises from the Cerrillos hills near Santa Fé. When, very rarely, a trader succeeded in bringing back a live bird to his people, it was paid divine honours, and its death threw the whole village into the deepest gloom. Even the bones were piously preserved. There was in Isleta a parrot skull of great antiquity. His wooden bird he had bought from an old man who was much indebted to him, and who was about to die without descendants. Father Jesus had had his eye upon the bird for years. The Indian told him that his ancestors, generations ago, had brought it with them from the mother pueblo. The priest fondly believed that it was a portrait, done from life, of one of those rare birds that in ancient times were carried up alive, all the long trail from the tropics.

Father Jesus gave a good report of the Indians at Laguna and Ácoma. He used to go to those pueblos to hold services when he was younger, and had always found them friendly.

"At Ácoma," he said, "you can see something very holy. They have there a portrait of St. Joseph, sent to them by one of the Kings of Spain, long ago, and it has worked many miracles. If the season is dry, the Ácoma people take the picture down to their farms at Acomita, and it never fails to produce rain. They have rain when none falls in all the country, and they have crops when the Laguna Indians have none."

2

JACINTO

Taking leave of Isleta and its priest early in the morning, Father Latour and his guide rode all day through the dry desert plain west of Albuquerque. It was like a country of dry ashes; no juniper, no rabbit brush, nothing but thickets of withered, dead-looking cactus, and patches of wild pumpkin—the only vegetation that had any vitality. It is a vine, remarkable for its tendency, not to spread and ramble, but to mass and mount. Its long, sharp, arrow-shaped leaves, frosted over with prickly silver, are thrust upward and crowded together; the whole rigid, up-thrust matted clump looks less like a plant than like a great colony of grey-green lizards, moving and suddenly arrested by fear.

As the morning wore on they had to make their way through a sand-storm which quite obscured the sun. Jacinto knew the country well, having crossed it often to go to the religious dances at Laguna, but he rode with his head low and a purple handkerchief tied over his mouth. Coming from a pueblo among woods and water, he had a poor opinion of this plain. At noon he alighted and collected enough greasewood to boil the Bishop's coffee. They knelt on either side of the fire, the sand curling about them so that the bread became gritty as they ate it.

The sun set red in an atmosphere murky with sand. The travellers made a dry camp and rolled themselves in their blankets. All night a cold wind blew over them. Father Latour was so stiff that he arose long before day-break. The dawn came at last, fair and clear, and they made an early start.

About the middle of that afternoon Jacinto pointed out Laguna in the distance, lying, apparently, in the midst of bright yellow waves of high sand dunes—yellow as ochre. As they approached, Father Latour found these were petrified sand dunes; long waves of soft, gritty yellow rock, shining and bare except for a few lines of dark juniper that grew out of the weather cracks,—little trees, and very, very old. At the foot of this sweep of rock waves was the blue lake, a stone basin full of water, from which the pueblo took its name.

The kindly Padre at Isleta had sent his cook's brother off on foot to warn the Laguna people that the new High Priest was coming, and that he was a good man and did not want money. They were prepared, accordingly; the church was clean and the doors were open; a small white church, painted above and about the altar with gods of wind and rain and thunder, sun and moon, linked together in a geometrical design of crimson and blue and dark green, so that the end of the church seemed to be hung with tapestry. It recalled to Father Latour the interior of a Persian chieftain's tent he had seen in a textile exhibit at Lyons. Whether this decoration had been done by Spanish missionaries or by Indian converts, he was unable to find out.

The Governor told him that his people would come to
Mass in the morning, and that there were a number of children to be baptized. He offered the Bishop the sacristy for the
night, but there was a damp, earthy smell about that chamber,
and Father Latour had already made up his mind that he
would like to sleep on the rock dunes, under the junipers.

Jacinto got firewood and good water from the Lagunas,
and they made their camp in a pleasant spot on the rocks
north of the village. As the sun dropped low, the light
brought the white church and the yellow adobe houses up
into relief from the flat ledges. Behind their camp, not far
away, lay a group of great mesas. The Bishop asked Jacinto if
he knew the name of the one nearest them.

"No, I not know any name," he shook his head. "I know
Indian name," he added, as if, for once, he were thinking
aloud.

"And what is the Indian name?"

"The Laguna Indians call Snow-Bird mountain." He spoke
somewhat unwillingly.

"That is very nice," said the Bishop musingly. "Yes, that is
a pretty name."

"Oh, Indians have nice names too!" Jacinto replied quickly,
with a curl of the lip. Then, as if he felt he had taken out on
the Bishop a reproach not deserved, he said in a moment:
"The Laguna people think it very funny for a big priest to be
a young man. The Governor say, how can I call him Padre
when he is younger than my sons?"

There was a note of pride in Jacinto's voice very flattering
to the Bishop. He had noticed how kind the Indian voice
could be when it was kind at all; a slight inflection made one
feel that one had received a great compliment.

"I am not very young in heart, Jacinto. How old are you,
my boy?"

"Twenty-six."

"Have you a son?"

"One. Baby. Not very long born."

Jacinto usually dropped the article in speaking Spanish,
just as he did in speaking English, though the Bishop had
noticed that when he did give a noun its article, he used the
right one. The customary omission, therefore, seemed to be

little Spanish, was apparently trying to get the point of the recital which made the Padres so merry. At any rate, he became distracted, and as he passed behind the senior priest of Zuñi, he tipped his full platter and spilled a stream of rich brown gravy over the good man's head and shoulders. Baltazar was quick-tempered, and he had been drinking freely of the fiery grape brandy. He caught up the empty pewter mug at his right and threw it at the clumsy lad with a malediction. It struck the boy on the side of the head. He dropped the platter, staggered a few steps, and fell down. He did not get up, nor did he move. The Padre from Zuñi was skilled in medicine. Wiping the sauce from his eyes, he bent over the boy and examined him.

"*Muerto*," he whispered. With that he plucked his junior priest by the sleeve, and the two bolted across the garden without another word and made for the head of the stairway. In a moment the Padres of Laguna and Isleta unceremoniously followed their example. With remarkable speed the four guests got them down from the rock, saddled their mules, and urged them across the plain.

Baltazar was left alone with the consequences of his haste. Unfortunately the cook, astonished at the prolonged silence, had looked in at the door just as the last pair of brown gowns were vanishing across the cloister. He saw his comrade lying upon the floor, and silently disappeared from the premises by an exit known only to himself.

When Friar Baltazar went into the kitchen he found it solitary, the turkey still dripping on the spit. Certainly he had no appetite for the roast. He felt, indeed, very remorseful and uncomfortable, also indignant with his departed guests. For a moment he entertained the idea of following them; but a temporary flight would only weaken his position, and a permanent evacuation was not to be thought of. His garden was at its prime, his peaches were just coming ripe, and his vines hung heavy with green clusters. Mechanically he took the turkey from the spit, not because he felt any inclination for food, but from an instinct of compassion, quite as if the bird could suffer from being burned to a crisp. This done, he repaired to his loggia and sat down to read his breviary, which he had neglected for several days, having been so occupied in the refectory. He had begrudged no pains to that sauce which had been his undoing.

The airy loggia, where he customarily took his afternoon repose, was like a birdcage hung in the breeze. Through its open archways he looked down on the huddled pueblo, and out over the great mesa-strewn plain far below. He was unable to fix his mind upon his office. The pueblo down there was much too quiet. At this hour there should be a few women washing pots or rags, a few children playing by the cisterns and chasing the turkeys. But to-day the rock top baked in the fire of the sun in utter silence, not one human being was visible—yes, one, though he had not been there a moment ago. At the head of the stone stairway, there was a patch of lustrous black, just above the rocks; an Indian's hair. They had set a guard at the trail head.

Now the Padre began to feel alarmed, to wish he had gone down that stairway with the others, while there was yet time. He wished he were anywhere in the world but on this rock. There was old Father Ramirez's donkey path; but if the Indians were watching one road, they would watch the other. The spot of black hair never stirred; and there were but those two ways down to the plain, only those . . . Whichever way one turned, three hundred and fifty feet of naked cliff, without one tree or shrub a man could cling to.

As the sun sank lower and lower, there began a deep, singing murmur of male voices from the pueblo below him, not a chant, but the rhythmical intonation of Indian oratory when a serious matter is under discussion. Frightful stories of the torture of the missionaries in the great rebellion of 1680 flashed into Friar Baltazar's mind; how one Franciscan had his eyes torn out, another had been burned, and the old Padre at Jamez had been stripped naked and driven on all fours about the plaza all night, with drunken Indians straddling his back, until he rolled over dead from exhaustion.

Moonrise from the loggia was an impressive sight, even to this Brother who was not over-impressionable. But to-night he wished he could keep the moon from coming up through the floor of the desert,—the moon was the clock which began things in the pueblo. He watched with horror for that golden rim against the deep blue velvet of the night.

The moon came, and at its coming the Ácoma people issued from their doors. A company of men walked silently across the rock to the cloister. They came up the ladder and appeared in the loggia. The Friar asked them gruffly what they wanted, but they made no reply. Not once speaking to him or to each other, they bound his feet together and tied his arms to his sides.

The Ácoma people told afterwards that he did not supplicate or struggle; had he done so, they might have dealt more cruelly with him. But he knew his Indians, and that when once they had collectively made up their pueblo mind . . . Moreover, he was a proud old Spaniard, and had a certain fortitude lodged in his well-nourished body. He was accustomed to command, not to entreat, and he retained the respect of his Indian vassals to the end.

They carried him down the ladder and through the cloister and across the rock to the most precipitous cliff—the one over which the Ácoma women flung broken pots and such refuse as the turkeys would not eat. There the people were assembled. They cut his bonds, and taking him by the hands and feet, swung him out over the rock-edge and back a few times. He was heavy, and perhaps they thought this dangerous sport. No sound but hissing breath came through his teeth. The four executioners took him up again from the brink where they had laid him, and, after a few feints, dropped him in mid-air.

So did they rid their rock of their tyrant, whom on the whole they had liked very well. But everything has its day. The execution was not followed by any sacrilege to the church or defiling of holy vessels, but merely by a division of the Padre's stores and household goods. The women, indeed, took pleasure in watching the garden pine and waste away from thirst, and ventured into the cloisters to laugh and chatter at the whitening foliage of the peach trees, and the green grapes shrivelling on the vines.

When the next priest came, years afterward, he found no ill will awaiting him. He was a native Mexican, of unpretentious tastes, who was well satisfied with beans and jerked meat, and let the pueblo turkey flock scratch in the hot dust that had once been Baltazar's garden. The old peach stumps kept sending up pale sprouts for many years.

BOOK FOUR

Snake Root

I

THE NIGHT AT PECOS

A MONTH after the Bishop's visit to Albuquerque and Ácoma, the genial Father Gallegos was formally suspended, and Father Vaillant himself took charge of the parish. At first there was bitter feeling; the rich *rancheros* and the merry ladies of Albuquerque were very hostile to the French priest. He began his reforms at once. Everything was changed. The holy-days, which had been occasions of revelry under Padre Gallegos, were now days of austere devotion. The fickle Mexican population soon found as much diversion in being devout as they had once found in being scandalous. Father Vaillant wrote to his sister Philomène, in France, that the temper of his parish was like that of a boys' school; under one master the lads try to excel one another in mischief and disobedience, under another they vie with each other in acts of loyalty. The Novena preceding Christmas, which had long been celebrated by dances and hilarious merry-making, was this year a great revival of religious zeal.

Though Father Vaillant had all the duties of a parish priest at Albuquerque, he was still Vicar General, and in February the Bishop dispatched him on urgent business to Las Vegas. He did not return on the day that he was expected, and when several days passed with no word from him, Father Latour began to feel some anxiety.

One morning at day-break a very sick Indian boy rode into the Bishop's courtyard on Father Joseph's white mule, Contento, bringing bad news. The Padre, he said, had stopped at his village in the Pecos mountains where black measles had broken out, to give the sacrament to the dying, and had fallen ill of the sickness. The boy himself had been well when he started for Santa Fé, but had become sick on the way.

The Bishop had the messenger put into the wood-house, an isolated building at the end of the garden, where the sisters of Loretto could tend him. He instructed the Mother Superior to pack a bag with such medicines and comforts for the sick as he could carry, and told Fructosa, his cook, to put up for him the provisions he usually took on horseback journeys. When his man brought a pack-mule and his own mule, Angelica, to the door, Father Latour, already in his rough riding-breeches and buckskin jacket, looked at the handsome beast and shook his head.

"No, leave her with Contento. The new army mule is heavier, and will do for this journey."

The Bishop rode out of Santa Fé two hours after the Indian messenger rode in. He was going direct to the pueblo of Pecos, where he would pick up Jacinto. It was late in the afternoon when he reached the pueblo, lying low on its red rock ledges, half-surrounded by a crown of fir-clad mountains, and facing a sea of junipers and cedars. The Bishop had meant to get fresh horses at Pecos and push on through the mountains, but Jacinto and the older Indians who gathered about the horseman, strongly advised him to spend the night there and start in the early morning. The sun was shining brilliantly in a blue sky, but in the west, behind the mountain, lay a great stationary black cloud, opaque and motionless as a ledge of rock. The old men looked at it and shook their heads.

"Very big wind," said the governor gravely.

Unwillingly the Bishop dismounted and gave his mules to Jacinto; it seemed to him that he was wasting time. There was still an hour before night-fall, and he spent that hour pacing up and down the crust of bare rock between the village and the ruin of the old mission church. The sun was sinking, a red ball which threw a copper glow over the pine-covered ridge of mountains, and edged that inky, ominous cloud with molten silver. The great red earth walls of the mission, red as brick-dust, yawned gloomily before him,—part of the roof had fallen in, and the rest would soon go.

At this moment Father Joseph was lying dangerously ill in the dirt and discomfort of an Indian village in winter. Why, the Bishop was asking himself, had he ever brought his friend to this life of hardship and danger? Father Vaillant had been frail from childhood, though he had the endurance resulting from exhaustless enthusiasm. The Brothers at Montferrand were not given to coddling boys, but every year they used to send this one away for a rest in the high Volvic mountains, because his vitality ran down under the confinement of college life. Twice, while he and Father Latour were missionaries in Ohio, Joseph had been at death's door; once so ill with cholera that the newspapers had printed his name in the death list. On that occasion their Ohio Bishop had christened him *Trompe-la-Mort*. Yes, Father Latour told himself, *Blanchet* had outwitted death so often, there was always the chance he would do it again.

Walking about the walls of the ruin, the Bishop discovered that the sacristy was dry and clean, and he decided to spend the night there, wrapped in his blankets, on one of the earthen benches that ran about the inner walls. While he was examining this room, the wind began to howl about the old church, and darkness fell quickly. From the low doorways of the pueblo ruddy fire-light was gleaming—singularly grateful to the eye. Waiting for him on the rocks, he recognized the slight figure of Jacinto, his blanket drawn close about his head, his shoulders bowed to the wind.

The young Indian said that supper was ready, and the Bishop followed him to his particular lair in those rows of little houses all alike and all built together. There was a ladder before Jacinto's door which led up to a second storey, but that was the dwelling of another family; the roof of Jacinto's house made a veranda for the family above him. The Bishop bent his head under the low doorway and stepped down; the floor of the room was a long step below the door-sill—the Indian way of preventing drafts. The room into which he descended was long and narrow, smoothly whitewashed, and clean, to the eye, at least, because of its very bareness. There was nothing on the walls but a few fox pelts and strings of gourds and red peppers. The richly coloured blankets of which Jacinto was very proud were folded in piles on the earth settle,—it was there he and his wife slept, near the fire-place. The earth of that settle became warm during the day and held its heat until morning, like the Russian peasants' stove-bed. Over the fire a pot of beans and dried meat was simmering. The burning piñon logs filled the room with sweet-smelling smoke.

Clara, Jacinto's wife, smiled at the priest as he entered. She ladled out the stew, and the Bishop and Jacinto sat down on the floor beside the fire, each with his bowl. Between them Clara put a basin full of hot corn-bread baked with squash seeds,—an Indian delicacy comparable to raisin bread among the whites. The Bishop said a blessing and broke the bread with his hands. While the two men ate, the young woman watched them and stirred a tiny cradle of deerskin which hung by thongs from the roof poles. Jacinto, when questioned, said sadly that the baby was ailing. Father Latour did not ask to see it; it would be swathed in layers of wrappings, he knew; even its face and head would be covered against drafts. Indian babies were never bathed in winter, and it was useless to suggest treatment for the sick ones. On that subject the Indian ear was closed to advice.

It was a pity, too, that he could do nothing for Jacinto's baby. Cradles were not many in the pueblo of Pecos. The tribe was dying out; infant mortality was heavy, and the young couples did not reproduce freely,—the life-force seemed low. Smallpox and measles had taken heavy toll here time and again.

Of course there were other explanations, credited by many good people in Santa Fé. Pecos had more than its share of dark legends,—perhaps that was because it had been too tempting to white men, and had had more than its share of history. It was said that this people had from time immemorial kept a ceremonial fire burning in some cave in the mountain, a fire that had never been allowed to go out, and had never been revealed to white men. The story was that the service of this fire sapped the strength of the young men appointed to serve it,—always the best of the tribe. Father Latour thought this hardly probable. Why should it be very arduous, in a mountain full of timber, to feed a fire so small that its whereabouts had been concealed for centuries?

There was also the snake story, reported by the early explorers, both Spanish and American, and believed ever since: that this tribe was peculiarly addicted to snake worship, that they kept rattlesnakes concealed in their houses, and somewhere in the mountain guarded an enormous serpent which they brought to the pueblo for certain feasts. It was said that they sacrificed young babies to the great snake, and thus diminished their numbers.

It seemed much more likely that the contagious diseases brought by white men were the real cause of the shrinkage of the tribe. Among the Indians, measles, scarlatina and whooping-cough were as deadly as typhus or cholera. Certainly, the tribe was decreasing every year. Jacinto's house was at one end of the living pueblo; behind it were long rock ridges of dead pueblo,—empty houses ruined by weather and now scarcely more than piles of earth and stone. The population of the living streets was less than one hundred adults.* This was all that was left of the rich and populous Cicuyè of Coronado's expedition. Then, by his report, there were six thousand souls in the Indian town. They had rich fields irrigated from the Pecos River. The streams were full of fish, the mountain was full of game. The pueblo, indeed, seemed to lie upon the knees of these verdant mountains, like a favoured child. Out yonder, on the juniper-spotted plateau in front of the village, the Spaniards had camped, exacting a heavy tribute of corn and furs and cotton garments from their hapless hosts. It was from here, the story went, that they set forth in the spring on their ill-fated search for the seven golden cities of Quivera, taking with them slaves and concubines ravished from the Pecos people.

As Father Latour sat by the fire and listened to the wind sweeping down from the mountains and howling over the plateau, he thought of these things; and he could not help wondering whether Jacinto, sitting silent by the same fire, was thinking of them, too. The wind, he knew, was blowing out of the inky cloud bank that lay behind the mountain at sunset; but it might well be blowing out of a remote, black past. The only human voice raised against it was the feeble wailing of the sick child in the cradle. Clara ate noiselessly in a corner, Jacinto looked into the fire.

The Bishop read his breviary by the fire-light for an hour. Then, warmed to the bone and assured that his roll of blankets was warmed through, he rose to go. Jacinto followed with the blankets and one of his own buffalo robes. They

*In actual fact, the dying pueblo of Pecos was abandoned some years before the American occupation of New Mexico.

went along a line of red doorways and across the bare rock to
the gaunt ruin, whose lateral walls, with their buttresses, still
braved the storm and let in the starlight.

2

STONE LIPS

It was not difficult for the Bishop to waken early. After midnight his body became more and more chilled and cramped.
He said his prayers before he rolled out of his blankets, remembering Father Vaillant's maxim that if you said your
prayers first, you would find plenty of time for other things
afterward.

Going through the silent pueblo to Jacinto's door, the
Bishop woke him and asked him to make a fire. While the
Indian went to get the mules ready, Father Latour got his
coffee-pot and tin cup out of his saddle-bags, and a round
loaf of Mexican bread. With bread and black coffee, he could
travel day after day. Jacinto was for starting without breakfast,
but Father Latour made him sit down and share his loaf.
Bread is never too plenty in Indian households. Clara was still
lying on the settle with her baby.

At four o'clock they were on the road, Jacinto riding the
mule that carried the blankets. He knew the trails through his
own mountains well enough to follow them in the dark. Toward noon the Bishop suggested a halt to rest the mules, but
his guide looked at the sky and shook his head. The sun was
nowhere to be seen, the air was thick and grey and smelled of
snow. Very soon the snow began to fall—lightly at first, but
all the while becoming heavier. The vista of pine trees ahead
of them grew shorter and shorter through the vast powdering
of descending flakes. A little after midday a burst of wind sent
the snow whirling in coils about the two travellers, and a
great storm broke. The wind was like a hurricane at sea, and
the air became blind with snow. The Bishop could scarcely
see his guide—saw only parts of him, now a head, now a
shoulder, now only the black rump of his mule. Pine trees by
the way stood out for a moment, then disappeared absolutely

in the whirlpool of snow. Trail and landmarks, the mountain itself, were obliterated.

Jacinto sprang from his mule and unstrapped the roll of blankets. Throwing the saddle-bags to the Bishop, he shouted, "Come, I know a place. Be quick, Padre."

The Bishop protested they could not leave the mules. Jacinto said the mules must take their chance.

For Father Latour the next hour was a test of endurance. He was blind and breathless, panting through his open mouth. He clambered over half-visible rocks, fell over prostrate trees, sank into deep holes and struggled out, always following the red blankets on the shoulders of the Indian boy, which stuck out when the boy himself was lost to sight.

Suddenly the snow seemed thinner. The guide stopped short. They were standing, the Bishop made out, under an overhanging wall of rock which made a barrier against the storm. Jacinto dropped the blankets from his shoulder and seemed to be preparing to climb the cliff. Looking up, the Bishop saw a peculiar formation in the rocks; two rounded ledges, one directly over the other, with a mouth-like opening between. They suggested two great stone lips, slightly parted and thrust outward. Up to this mouth Jacinto climbed quickly by footholds well known to him. Having mounted, he lay down on the lower lip, and helped the Bishop to clamber up. He told Father Latour to wait for him on this projection while he brought up the baggage.

A few moments later the Bishop slid after Jacinto and the blankets, through the orifice, into the throat of the cave. Within stood a wooden ladder, like that used in kivas, and down this he easily made his way to the floor.

He found himself in a lofty cavern, shaped somewhat like a Gothic chapel, of vague outline,—the only light within was that which came through the narrow aperture between the stone lips. Great as was his need of shelter, the Bishop, on his way down the ladder, was struck by a reluctance, an extreme distaste for the place. The air in the cave was glacial, penetrated to the very bones, and he detected at once a fetid odour, not very strong but highly disagreeable. Some twenty feet or so above his head the open mouth let in grey daylight like a high transom.

While he stood gazing about, trying to reckon the size of the cave, his guide was intensely preoccupied in making a careful examination of the floor and walls. At the foot of the ladder lay a heap of half-burned logs. There had been a fire there, and it had been extinguished with fresh earth,—a pile of dust covered what had been the heart of the fire. Against the cavern wall was a heap of piñon faggots, neatly piled. After he had made a minute examination of the floor, the guide began cautiously to move this pile of wood, taking the sticks up one by one, and putting them in another spot. The Bishop supposed he would make a fire at once, but he seemed in no haste to do so. Indeed, when he had moved the wood he sat down upon the floor and fell into reflection. Father Latour urged him to build a fire without further delay.

"Padre," said the Indian boy, "I do not know if it was right to bring you here. This place is used by my people for ceremonies and is known only to us. When you go out from here, you must forget."

"I will forget, certainly. But unless we can have a fire, we had better go back into the storm. I feel ill here already."

Jacinto unrolled the blankets and threw the dryest one about the shivering priest. Then he bent over the pile of ashes and charred wood, but what he did was to select a number of small stones that had been used to fence in the burning embers. These he gathered in his *serape* and carried to the rear wall of the cavern, where, a little above his head, there seemed to be a hole. It was about as large as a very big watermelon, of an irregular oval shape.

Holes of that shape are common in the black volcanic cliffs of the Pajarito Plateau, where they occur in great numbers. This one was solitary, dark, and seemed to lead into another cavern. Though it lay higher than Jacinto's head, it was not beyond easy reach of his arms, and to the Bishop's astonishment he began deftly and noiselessly to place the stones he had collected within the mouth of this orifice, fitting them together until he had entirely closed it. He then cut wedges from the piñon faggots and inserted them into the cracks between the stones. Finally, he took a handful of the earth that had been used to smother the dead fire, and mixed it with the wet snow that had blown in between the stone lips. With this thick mud he plastered over his masonry, and smoothed it with his palm. The whole operation did not take a quarter of an hour.

Without comment or explanation he then proceeded to build a fire. The odour so disagreeable to the Bishop soon vanished before the fragrance of the burning logs. The heat seemed to purify the rank air at the same time that it took away the deathly chill, but the dizzy noise in Father Latour's head persisted. At first he thought it was a vertigo, a roaring in his ears brought on by cold and changes in his circulation. But as he grew warm and relaxed, he perceived an extraordinary vibration in this cavern; it hummed like a hive of bees, like a heavy roll of distant drums. After a time he asked Jacinto whether he, too, noticed this. The slim Indian boy smiled for the first time since they had entered the cave. He took up a faggot for a torch, and beckoned the Padre to follow him along a tunnel which ran back into the mountain, where the roof grew much lower, almost within reach of the hand. There Jacinto knelt down over a fissure in the stone floor, like a crack in china, which was plastered up with clay. Digging some of this out with his hunting knife, he put his ear on the opening, listened a few seconds, and motioned the Bishop to do likewise.

Father Latour lay with his ear to this crack for a long while, despite the cold that arose from it. He told himself he was listening to one of the oldest voices of the earth. What he heard was the sound of a great underground river, flowing through a resounding cavern. The water was far, far below, perhaps as deep as the foot of the mountain, a flood moving in utter blackness under ribs of antediluvian rock. It was not a rushing noise, but the sound of a great flood moving with majesty and power.

"It is terrible," he said at last, as he rose.

"*Si, Padre.*" Jacinto began spitting on the clay he had gouged out of the seam, and plastered it up again.

When they returned to the fire, the patch of daylight up between the two lips had grown much paler. The Bishop saw it die with regret. He took from his saddle-bags his coffee-pot and a loaf of bread and a goat cheese. Jacinto climbed up to the lower ledge of the entrance, shook a pine tree, and filled the coffee-pot and one of the blankets with fresh snow. While his guide was thus engaged, the Bishop took a swallow of old Taos whisky from his pocket flask. He never liked to drink spirits in the presence of an Indian.

Jacinto declared that he thought himself lucky to get bread and black coffee. As he handed the Bishop back his tin cup after drinking its contents, he rubbed his hand over his wide sash with a smile of pleasure that showed all his white teeth.

"We had good luck to be near here," he said. "When we leave the mules, I think I can find my way here, but I am not sure. I have not been here very many times. You was scare, Padre?"

The Bishop reflected. "You hardly gave me time to be scared, boy. Were you?"

The Indian shrugged his shoulders. "I think not to return to pueblo," he admitted.

Father Latour read his breviary long by the light of the fire. Since early morning his mind had been on other than spiritual things. At last he felt that he could sleep. He made Jacinto repeat a *Pater Noster* with him, as he always did on their night camps, rolled himself in his blankets, and stretched out, feet to the fire. He had it in his mind, however, to waken in the night and study a little the curious hole his guide had so carefully closed. After he put on the mud, Jacinto had never looked in the direction of that hole again, and Father Latour, observing Indian good manners, had tried not to glance toward it.

He did waken, and the fire was still giving off a rich glow of light in that lofty Gothic chamber. But there against the wall was his guide, standing on some invisible foothold, his arms outstretched against the rock, his body flattened against it, his ear over that patch of fresh mud, listening; listening with supersensual ear, it seemed, and he looked to be supported against the rock by the intensity of his solicitude. The Bishop closed his eyes without making a sound and wondered why he had supposed he could catch his guide asleep.

The next morning they crawled out through the stone lips, and dropped into a gleaming white world. The snow-clad mountains were red in the rising sun. The Bishop stood looking down over ridge after ridge of wintry fir trees with the

nothing to us. They've got their own superstitions, and their minds will go round and round in the same old ruts till Judgment Day."

Father Latour remarked that their veneration for old customs was a quality he liked in the Indians, and that it played a great part in his own religion.

The trader told him he might make good Catholics among the Indians, but he would never separate them from their own beliefs. "Their priests have their own kind of mysteries. I don't know how much of it is real and how much is made up. I remember something that happened when I was a little fellow. One night a Pecos girl, with her baby in her arms, ran into the kitchen here and begged my mother to hide her until after the festival, for she'd seen signs between the *caciques*, and was sure they were going to feed her baby to the snake. Whether it was true or not, she certainly believed it, poor thing, and Mother let her stay. It made a great impression on me at the time."

BOOK FIVE

Padre Martinez

Bishop Latour, with Jacinto, was riding through the mountains on his first official visit to Taos—after Albuquerque, the largest and richest parish in his diocese. Both the priest and people there were hostile to Americans and jealous of interference. Any European, except a Spaniard, was regarded as a gringo. The Bishop had let the parish alone, giving their animosity plenty of time to cool. With Carson's help he had informed himself fully about conditions there, and about the powerful old priest, Antonio José Martinez, who was ruler in temporal as well as in spiritual affairs. Indeed, before Father Latour's entrance upon the scene, Martinez had been dictator to all the parishes in northern New Mexico, and the native priests at Santa Fé were all of them under his thumb.

It was common talk that Padre Martinez had instigated the revolt of the Taos Indians five years ago, when Bent, the American Governor, and a dozen other white men were murdered and scalped. Seven of the Taos Indians had been tried before a military court and hanged for the murder, but no attempt had been made to call the plotting priest to account. Indeed, Padre Martinez had managed to profit considerably by the affair.

The Indians who were sentenced to death had sent for their Padre and begged him to get them out of the trouble he had got them into. Martinez promised to save their lives if they would deed him their lands, near the pueblo. This they did, and after the conveyance was properly executed the Padre troubled himself no more about the matter, but went to pay a visit at his native town of Abiquiu. In his absence the seven Indians were hanged on the appointed day. Martinez now cultivated their fertile farms, which made him quite the richest man in the parish.

Father Latour had had polite correspondence with Martinez, but had met him only once, on that memorable occasion when the Padre had ridden up from Taos to strengthen the Santa Fé clergy in their refusal to recognize the new Bishop. But he could see him as if that were only yesterday,—the priest of Taos was not a man one would easily forget. One could not have passed him on the street without feeling his great physical force and his imperious will. Not much taller than the Bishop in reality, he gave the impression of being an enormous man. His broad high shoulders were like a bull buffalo's, his big head was set defiantly on a thick neck, and the full-cheeked, richly coloured, egg-shaped Spanish face—how vividly the Bishop remembered that face! It was so unusual that he would be glad to see it again; a high, narrow forehead, brilliant yellow eyes set deep in strong arches, and full, florid cheeks,—not blank areas of smooth flesh, as in Anglo-Saxon faces, but full of muscular activity, as quick to change with feeling as any of his features. His mouth was the very assertion of violent, uncurbed passions and tyrannical self-will; the full lips thrust out and taut, like the flesh of animals distended by fear or desire.

Father Latour judged that the day of lawless personal power was almost over, even on the frontier, and this figure was to him already like something picturesque and impressive, but really impotent, left over from the past.

The Bishop and Jacinto left the mountains behind them, the trail dropped to a plain covered by clumps of very old sage-brush, with trunks as thick as a man's leg. Jacinto pointed out a cloud of dust moving rapidly toward them,—a cavalcade of a hundred men or more, Indians and Mexicans, come out to welcome their Bishop with shouting and musketry.

As the horsemen approached, Padre Martinez himself was easily distinguishable—in buckskin breeches, high boots and silver spurs, a wide Mexican hat on his head, and a great black cape wound about his shoulders like a shepherd's plaid. He rode up to the Bishop and reining in his black gelding, uncovered his head in a broad salutation, while his escort surrounded the churchmen and fired their muskets into the air.

The two priests rode side by side into Los Ranchos de Taos, a little town of yellow walls and winding streets and green orchards. The inhabitants were all gathered in the square before the church. When the Bishop dismounted to enter the church, the women threw their shawls on the dusty pathway for him to walk upon, and as he passed through the kneeling congregation, men and women snatched for his hand to kiss the Episcopal ring. In his own country all this would have been highly distasteful to Jean Marie Latour. Here, these demonstrations seemed a part of the high colour that was in landscape and gardens, in the flaming cactus and the gaudily decorated altars,—in the agonized Christs and dolorous Virgins and the very human figures of the saints. He had already learned that with this people religion was necessarily theatrical.

From Los Ranchos the party rode quickly across the grey plain into Taos itself, to the priest's house, opposite the church, where a great throng had collected. As the people sank on their knees, one boy, a gawky lad of ten or twelve, remained standing, his mouth open and his hat on his head. Padre Martinez reached over the heads of several kneeling women, snatched off the boy's cap, and cuffed him soundly about the ears. When Father Latour murmured in protest, the native priest said boldly:

"He is my own son, Bishop, and it is time I taught him manners."

So this was to be the tune, the Bishop reflected. His well-schooled countenance did not change a shadow as he received this challenge, and he passed on into the Padre's house. They went at once into Martinez's study, where they found a young man lying on the floor, fast asleep. He was a very large young man, very stout, lying on his back with his head pillowed on a book, and as he breathed his bulk rose and fell amazingly. He wore a Franciscan's brown gown, and his hair was clipped short. At sight of the sleeper, Padre Martinez broke into a laugh and gave him a no very gentle kick in the ribs. The fellow got to his feet in great confusion, escaping through a door into the *patio*.

"You there," the Padre called after him, "only young men who work hard at night want to sleep in the day! You must have been studying by candle-light. I'll give you an examination in theology!" This was greeted by a titter of feminine laughter from the windows across the court, where the fugitive took refuge behind a washing hung out to dry. He bent his tall, full figure and disappeared between a pair of wet sheets.

"That was my student, Trinidad," said Martinez, "a nephew of my old friend Father Lucero, at Arroyo Hondo. He's a monk, but we want him to take orders. We sent him to the Seminary in Durango, but he was either too homesick or too stupid to learn anything, so I'm teaching him here. We shall make a priest of him one day."

Father Latour was told to consider the house his own, but he had no wish to. The disorder was almost more than his fastidious taste could bear. The Padre's study table was sprinkled with snuff, and piled so high with books that they almost hid the crucifix hanging behind it. Books were heaped on chairs and tables all over the house,—and the books and the floors were deep in the dust of spring sand-storms. Father Martinez's boots and hats lay about in corners, his coats and cassocks were hung on pegs and draped over pieces of furniture. Yet the place seemed overrun by serving-women, young and old,—and by large yellow cats with full soft fur, of a special breed, apparently. They slept in the window-sills, lay on the well-curb in the *patio*; the boldest came, directly, to the supper-table, where their master fed them carelessly from his plate.

When they sat down to supper, the host introduced to the Bishop the tall, stout young man with the protruding front, who had been asleep on the floor. He said again that Trinidad Lucero was studying with him, and was supposed to be his secretary,—adding that he spent most of his time hanging about the kitchen and hindering the girls at their work.

These remarks were made in the young man's presence, but did not embarrass him at all. His whole attention was fixed upon the mutton stew, which he began to devour with undue haste as soon as his plate was put before him. The Bishop observed later that Trinidad was treated very much like a poor relation or a servant. He was sent on errands, was told without ceremony to fetch the Padre's boots, to bring wood for the fire, to saddle his horse. Father Latour disliked his personality so much that he could scarcely look at him. His fat face was irritatingly stupid, and had the grey, oily look of soft cheeses. The corners of his mouth were deep folds in plumpness, like the creases in a baby's legs, and the steel rim of his spectacles, where it crossed his nose, was embedded in soft flesh. He said not one word during supper, but ate as if he were afraid of never seeing food again. When his attention left his plate for a moment, it was fixed in the same greedy way upon the girl who served the table — and who seemed to regard him with careless contempt. The student gave the impression of being always stupefied by one form of sensual disturbance or another.

Padre Martinez, with a napkin tied round his neck to protect his cassock, ate and drank generously. The Bishop found the food poor enough, despite the many cooks, though the wine, which came from El Paso del Norte, was very fair.

During supper, his host asked the Bishop flatly if he considered celibacy an essential condition of the priest's vocation.

Father Latour replied merely that this question had been thrashed out many centuries ago and decided once for all.

"Nothing is decided once for all," Martinez declared fiercely. "Celibacy may be all very well for the French clergy, but not for ours. St. Augustine himself says it is better not to go against nature. I find every evidence that in his old age he regretted having practised continence."

The Bishop said he would be interested to see the passages from which he drew such conclusions, observing that he knew the writings of St. Augustine fairly well.

"I have the telling passages all written down somewhere. I will find them before you go. You have probably read them with a sealed mind. Celibate priests lose their perceptions. No priest can experience repentance and forgiveness of sin unless he himself falls into sin. Since concupiscence is the most common form of temptation, it is better for him to know something about it. The soul cannot be humbled by fasts and prayer; it must be broken by mortal sin to experience forgiveness of sin and rise to a state of grace. Otherwise, religion is nothing but dead logic."

"This is a subject upon which we must confer later, and at some length," said the Bishop quietly. "I shall reform these practices throughout my diocese as rapidly as possible. I hope it will be but a short time until there is not a priest left who does not keep all the vows he took when he bound himself to the service of the altar."

The swarthy Padre laughed, and threw off the big cat which had mounted to his shoulder. "It will keep you busy, Bishop. Nature has got the start of you here. But for all that, our native priests are more devout than your French Jesuits. We have a living Church here, not a dead arm of the European Church. Our religion grew out of the soil, and has its own roots. We pay a filial respect to the person of the Holy Father, but Rome has no authority here. We do not require aid from the Propaganda, and we resent its interference. The Church the Franciscan Fathers planted here was cut off; this is the second growth, and is indigenous. Our people are the most devout left in the world. If you blast their faith by European formalities, they will become infidels and profligates."

To this eloquence the Bishop returned blandly that he had not come to deprive the people of their religion, but that he would be compelled to deprive some of the priests of their parishes if they did not change their way of life.

Father Martinez filled his glass and replied with perfect good humour. "You cannot deprive me of mine, Bishop. Try it! I will organize my own church. You can have your French priest of Taos, and I will have the people!"

With this the Padre left the table and stood warming his back at the fire, his cassock pulled up about his waist to expose his trousers to the blaze. "You are a young man, my Bishop," he went on, rolling his big head back and looking up at the well-smoked roof poles. "And you know nothing about Indians or Mexicans. If you try to introduce European civilization here and change our old ways, to interfere with the secret dances of the Indians, let us say, or abolish the bloody rites of the Penitentes, I foretell an early death for you. I advise you to study our native traditions before you begin your reforms. You are among barbarous people, my French-man, between two savage races. The dark things forbidden by your Church are a part of Indian religion. You cannot intro-duce French fashions here."

At this moment the student, Trinidad, got up quietly, and after an obsequious bow to the Bishop, went with soft, escap-ing tread toward the kitchen. When his brown skirt had dis-appeared through the door, Father Latour turned sharply to his host.

"Martinez, I consider it very unseemly to talk in this loose fashion before young men, especially a young man who is studying for the priesthood. Furthermore, I cannot see why a young man of this calibre should be encouraged to take orders. He will never hold a parish in my diocese."

Padre Martinez laughed and showed his long, yellow teeth. Laughing did not become him; his teeth were too large — distinctly vulgar. "Oh, Trinidad will go to Arroyo Hondo as curate to his uncle, who is growing old. He's a very devout fellow, Trinidad. You ought to see him in Passion Week. He goes up to Abiquiu and becomes another man; carries the heaviest crosses to the highest mountains, and takes more scourging than anyone. He comes back here with his back so full of cactus spines that the girls have to pick him like a chicken."

Father Latour was tired, and went to his room soon after supper. The bed, upon examination, seemed clean and com-fortable, but he felt uncertain of its surroundings. He did not like the air of this house. After he retired, the clatter of dish-washing and the giggling of women across the *patio* kept him awake a long while; and when that ceased, Father Martinez began snoring in some chamber near by. He must have left his door open into the *patio*, for the adobe parti-tions were thick enough to smother sound otherwise. The Padre snored like an enraged bull, until the Bishop decided to go forth and find his door and close it. He arose, lit his candle, and opened his own door in half-hearted resolution. As the night wind blew into the room, a little dark shadow fluttered from the wall across the floor; a mouse, perhaps. But no, it was a bunch of woman's hair that had been indolently tossed into a corner when some slovenly female toilet was made in this room. This discovery annoyed the Bishop exceedingly.

High Mass was at eleven the next morning, the parish priest officiating and the Bishop in the Episcopal chair. He was well pleased with the church of Taos. The building was clean and in good repair, the congregation large and devout. The delicate lace, snowy linen, and burnished brass on the altar told of a devoted Altar Guild. The boys who served at the altar wore rich smocks of hand-made lace over their scarlet surplices. The Bishop had never heard the Mass more impressively sung than by Father Martinez. The man had a beautiful baritone voice, and he drew from some deep well of emotional power. Nothing in the service was slighted, every phrase and gesture had its full value. At the moment of the Elevation the dark priest seemed to give his whole force, his swarthy body and all its blood, to that lifting-up. Rightly guided, the Bishop reflected, this Mexican might have been a great man. He had an altogether compelling personality, a disturbing, mysterious magnetic power.

After the confirmation service, Father Martinez had horses brought round and took the Bishop out to see his farms and live-stock. He took him all over his ranches down in the rich bottom lands between Taos and the Indian pueblo which, as Father Latour knew, had come into his possession from the seven Indians who were hanged. Martinez referred carelessly to the Bent massacre as they rode along. He boasted that there had never been trouble afoot in New Mexico that wasn't started in Taos.

They stopped just west of the pueblo a little before sunset,—a pueblo very different from all the others the Bishop had visited; two large communal houses, shaped like pyramids, gold-coloured in the afternoon light, with the purple mountain lying just behind them. Gold-coloured men in white burnouses came out on the stairlike flights of roofs, and stood still as statues, apparently watching the changing light on the mountain. There was a religious silence over the place; no sound at all but the bleating of goats coming home through clouds of golden dust.

These two houses, the Padre told him, had been continuously occupied by this tribe for more than a thousand years. Coronado's men found them there, and described them as a superior kind of Indian, handsome and dignified in bearing, dressed in deerskin coats and trousers like those of Europeans.

Though the mountain was timbered, its lines were so sharp that it had the sculptured look of naked mountains like the Sandias. The general growth on its sides was evergreen, but the canyons and ravines were wooded with aspens, so that the shape of every depression was painted on the mountain-side, light green against the dark, like symbols; serpentine, crescent, half-circles. This mountain and its ravines had been the seat of old religious ceremonies, honeycombed with noiseless Indian life, the repository of Indian secrets, for many centuries, the Padre remarked.

"And some place in there, you may be sure, they keep Popé's estufa, but no white man will ever see it. I mean the estufa where Popé sealed himself up for four years and never saw the light of day, when he was planning the revolt of 1680. I suppose you know all about that outbreak, Bishop Latour?"

"Something, of course, from the Martyrology. But I did not know that it originated in Taos."

"Haven't I just told you that all the trouble there ever was in New Mexico originated in Taos?" boasted the Padre. "Popé was born a San Juan Indian, but so was Napoleon a Corsican. He operated from Taos."

Padre Martinez knew his country, a country which had no written histories. He gave the Bishop much the best account he had heard of the great Indian revolt of 1680, which added such a long chapter to the Martyrology of the New World, when all the Spaniards were killed or driven out, and there was not one European left alive north of El Paso del Norte.

That night after supper, as his host sat taking snuff, Father Latour questioned him closely and learned something about the story of his life.

Martinez was born directly under that solitary blue mountain on the sky-line west of Taos, shaped like a pyramid with the apex sliced off, in Abiquiu. It was one of the oldest

Mexican settlements in the territory, surrounded by canyons so deep and ranges so rugged that it was practically cut off from intercourse with the outside world. Being so solitary, its people were sombre in temperament, fierce and fanatical in religion, celebrated the Passion Week by cross-bearings and bloody scourgings.

Antonio José Martinez grew up there, without learning to read or write, married at twenty, and lost his wife and child when he was twenty-three. After his marriage he had learned to read from the parish priest, and when he became a widower he decided to study for the priesthood. Taking his clothes and the little money he got from the sale of his household goods, he started on horseback for Durango, in Old Mexico. There he entered the Seminary and began a life of laborious study.

The Bishop could imagine what it meant for a young man who had not learned to read until long after adolescence, to undergo a severe academic training. He found Martinez deeply versed, not only in the Church Fathers, but in the Latin and Spanish classics. After six years at the Seminary, Martinez had returned to his native Abiquiu as priest of the parish church there. He was passionately attached to that old village under the pyramidal mountain. All the while he had been in Taos, half a lifetime now, he made periodic pilgrimages on horseback back to Abiquiu, as if the flavour of his own yellow earth were medicine to his soul. Naturally he hated the Americans. The American occupation meant the end of men like himself. He was a man of the old order, a son of Abiquiu, and his day was over.

On his departure from Taos, the Bishop went out of his way to make a call at Kit Carson's ranch house. Carson, he knew, was away buying sheep, but Father Latour wished to see the Señora Carson to thank her again for her kindness to poor Magdalena, and to tell her of the woman's happy and devoted life with the Sisters in their school at Santa Fé.

The Señora received him with that quiet but unabashed hospitality which is a common grace in Mexican households. She was a tall woman, slender, with drooping shoulders and lustrous black eyes and hair. Though she could not read, both her face and conversation were intelligent. To the Bishop's thinking, she was handsome; her countenance showed that discipline of life which he admired. She had a cheerful disposition, too, and a pleasant sense of humour. It was possible to talk confidentially to her. She said she hoped he had been comfortable in Padre Martinez's house, with an inflection which told that she much doubted it, and she laughed a little when he confessed that he had been annoyed by the presence of Trinidad Lucero.

"Some people say he is Father Lucero's son," she said with a shrug. "But I do not think so. More likely one of Padre Martinez's. Did you hear what happened to him at Abiquiu last year, in Passion Week? He tried to be like the Saviour, and had himself crucified. Oh, not with nails! He was tied upon a cross with ropes, to hang there all night; they do that sometimes at Abiquiu, it is a very old-fashioned place. But he is so heavy that after he had hung there a few hours, the cross fell over with him, and he was very much humiliated. Then he had himself tied to a post and said he would bear as many stripes as our Saviour—six thousand, as was revealed to St. Bridget. But before they had given him a hundred, he fainted. They scourged him with cactus whips, and his back was so poisoned that he was sick up there for a long while. This year they sent word that they did not want him at Abiquiu, so he had to keep Holy Week here, and everybody laughed at him."

Father Latour asked the Señora to tell him frankly whether she thought he could put a stop to the extravagances of the Penitential Brotherhood. She smiled and shook her head. "I often say to my husband, I hope you will not try to do that. It would only set the people against you. The old people have need of their old customs; and the young ones will go with the times."

As the Bishop was taking his leave, she put into his saddlebags a beautiful piece of lace-work for Magdalena. "She will not be likely to use it for herself, but she will be glad to have it to give to the Sisters. That brutal man left her nothing. After he was hung, there was nothing to sell but his gun and one burro. That was why he was going to take the risk of killing two Padres for their mules—and for spite against religion, maybe! Magdalena said he had often threatened to kill the priest at Mora."

At Santa Fé the Bishop found Father Vaillant awaiting him. They had not seen each other since Easter, and there were many things to be discussed. The vigour and zeal of Bishop Latour's administration had already been recognized at Rome, and he had lately received a letter from Cardinal Fransoni, Prefect of the Propaganda, announcing that the vicarate of Santa Fé had been formally raised to a diocese. By the same long-delayed post came an invitation from the Cardinal, urgently requesting Father Latour's presence at important conferences at the Vatican during the following year. Though all these matters must be taken up in their turn between the Bishop and his Vicar-General, Father Joseph had undoubtedly come up from Albuquerque at this particular time because of a lively curiosity to hear how the Bishop had been received in Taos.

Seated in the study in their old cassocks, with the candles lighted on the table between them, they spent a long evening.

"For the present," Father Latour remarked, "I shall do nothing to change the curious situation at Taos. It is not expedient to interfere. The church is strong, the people are devout. No matter what the conduct of the priest has been, he has built up a strong organization, and his people are devotedly loyal to him."

"But can he be disciplined, do you think?"

"Oh, there is no question of discipline! He has been a little potentate too long. His people would assuredly support him against a French Bishop. For the present I shall be blind to what I do not like there."

"But Jean," Father Joseph broke out in agitation, "the man's life is an open scandal, one hears of it everywhere. Only a few weeks ago I was told a pitiful story of a Mexican girl carried off in one of the Indian raids on the Costella valley. She was a child of eight when she was carried away, and was fifteen when she was found and ransomed. During all that time the pious girl had preserved her virginity by a succession of miracles. She had a medal from the shrine of Our Lady of Guadeloupe tied round her neck, and she said such prayers as she had been taught. Her chastity was threatened many times, but always some unexpected event averted the catastrophe. After she was found and sent back to some relatives living in Arroyo Hondo, she was so devout that she wished to become a religious. She was debauched by this Martinez, and he married her to one of his peons. She is now living on one of his farms."

"Yes, Christobal told me that story," said the Bishop with a shrug. "But Padre Martinez is getting too old to play the part of Don Juan much longer. I do not wish to lose the parish of Taos in order to punish its priest, my friend. I have no priest strong enough to put in his place. You are the only man who could meet the situation there, and you are at Albuquerque. A year from now I shall be in Rome, and there I hope to get a Spanish missionary who will take over the parish of Taos. Only a Spaniard would be welcomed there, I think."

"You are doubtless right," said Father Joseph. "I am often too hasty in my judgments. I may do very badly for you while you are in Europe. For I suppose I am to leave my dear Albuquerque, and come to Santa Fé while you are gone?"

"Assuredly. They will love you all the more for lacking you awhile. I hope to bring some more hardy Auvergnats back with me, young men from our own Seminary, and I am afraid I must put one of them in Albuquerque. You have been there long enough. You have done all that is necessary. I need you here, Father Joseph. As it is now, one of us must ride seventy miles whenever we wish to converse about anything."

Father Vaillant sighed. "Ah, I supposed it would come! You will snatch me from Albuquerque as you did from Sandusky. When I went there everybody was my enemy, now everybody is my friend; therefore it is time to go." Father Vaillant took off his glasses, folded them, and put them in their case, which act always announced his determination to retire. "So a year from now you will be in Rome. Well, I had rather be among my people in Albuquerque, that I can say honestly. But Clermont,—there I envy you. I should like to see my own mountains again. At least you will see all my family and bring me word of them, and you can bring me the vestments that my dear sister Philomène and her nuns have been making for me these three years. I shall be very glad to have them." He rose,

Martinez had for women, and they had never been rivals in the pursuit of their pleasures. After Trinidad was ordained and went to stay with his uncle, Father Lucero complained that he had formed gross habits living with Martinez, and was eating him out of house and home. Father Martinez told with delight how Trinidad sponged upon the parish at Arroyo Hondo, and went about poking his nose into one bean-pot after another.

When the Bishop could no longer remain deaf to the rebellion, he sent Father Vaillant over to Taos to publish the warning for three weeks and exhort the two priests to renounce their heresy. On the fourth Sunday Father Joseph, who complained that he was always sent *"à fouetter les chats,"* solemnly read the letter in which the Bishop stripped Father Martinez of the rights and privileges of the priesthood. On the afternoon of the same day, he rode over to Arroyo Hondo, eighteen miles away, and read a similar letter of excommunication against Father Lucero.

Father Martinez continued at the head of his schismatic church until, after a short illness, he died and was buried in schism, by Father Lucero. Soon after this, Father Lucero himself fell into a decline. But even after he was ailing he performed a feat which became one of the legends of the countryside,—killed a robber in a midnight scuffle.

A wandering teamster who had been discharged from a wagon train for theft, was picking up a living over in Taos and there heard the stories about Father Lucero's hidden riches. He came to Arroyo Hondo to rob the old man. Father Lucero was a light sleeper, and hearing stealthy sounds in the middle of the night, he reached for the carving-knife he kept hidden under his mattress and sprang upon the intruder. They began fighting in the dark, and though the thief was a young man and armed, the old priest stabbed him to death and then, covered with blood, ran out to arouse the town. The neighbours found the Padre's chamber like a slaughterhouse, his victim lying dead beside the hole he had dug. They were amazed at what the old man had been able to do.

But from the shock of that night Father Lucero never recovered. He wasted away so rapidly that his people had the horse doctor come from Taos to look at him. This veterinary was a Yankee who had been successful in treating men as well as horses, but he said he could do nothing for Father Lucero; he believed he had an internal tumour or a cancer.

Padre Lucero died repentant, and Father Vaillant, who had pronounced his excommunication, was the one to reconcile him to the Church. The Vicar was in Taos on business for the Bishop, staying with Kit Carson and the Señora. They were all sitting at supper one evening during a heavy rain-storm, when a horseman rode up to the *portale*. Carson went out to receive him. The visitor he brought in with him was Trinidad Lucero, who took off his rubber coat and stood in a full-skirted cassock of Arroyo Hondo make, a crucifix about his neck, seeming to fill the room with his size and importance. After bowing ceremoniously to the Señora, he addressed himself to Father Vaillant in his best English, speaking slowly in his thick felty voice.

"I am the only nephew of Padre Lucero. My uncle is verra seek and soon to die. She has vomit the blood." He dropped his eyes.

"Speak to me in your own language, man!" cried Father Joseph. "I can at least do more with Spanish than you can with English. Now tell me what you have to say of your uncle's condition."

Trinidad gave some account of his uncle's illness, repeating solemnly the phrase, "She has vomit the blood," which he seemed to find impressive. The sick man wished to see Father Vaillant, and begged that he would come to him and give him the Sacrament.

Carson urged the Vicar to wait until morning, as the road down into "the Hondo" would be badly washed by rain and dangerous to go over in the dark. But Father Vaillant said if the road were bad he could go down on foot. Excusing himself to the Señora Carson, he went to his room to put on his riding-clothes and get his saddle-bags. Trinidad, upon invitation, sat down at the empty place and made the most of his opportunity. The host saddled Father Vaillant's mule, and the Vicar rode away, with Trinidad for guide.

Not that he needed a guide to Arroyo Hondo, it was a place especially dear to him, and he was always glad to find a pretext for going there. How often he had ridden over there

Father Lucero related that Martinez, before his death, had entrusted to him a certain sum of money to be spent in masses for the repose of his soul, these to be offered at his native church in Abiquiu. Lucero had not used the money as he promised, but had buried it under the dirt floor of this room, just below the large crucifix that hung on the wall yonder.

At this point Father Vaillant again signalled to the women to withdraw, but as they took up their candles, Father Lucero sat up in his night-shirt and cried, "Stay as you are! Are you going to run away and leave me with a stranger? I trust him no more than I do you! Oh, why did God not make some way for a man to protect his own after death? Alive, I can do it with my knife, old as I am. But after?"

The Señora Gonzales soothed Father Lucero, persuaded him to lie back upon his pillows and tell them what he wanted them to do. He explained that this money which he had taken in trust from Martinez was to be sent to Abiquiu and used as the Padre had wished. Under the crucifix, and under the floor beneath the bed on which he was lying, they would find his own savings. One third of his hoard was for Trinidad. The rest was to be spent in masses for his soul, and they were to be celebrated in the old church of San Miguel in Santa Fé.

Father Vaillant assured him that all his wishes should be scrupulously carried out, and now it was time for him to dismiss the cares of this world and prepare his mind to receive the Sacrament.

"All in good time. But a man does not let go of this world so easily. Where is Conçeption Gonzales? Come here, my daughter. See to it that the money is taken up from under the floor while I am still in this chamber, before my body is cold, that it is counted in the presence of all these women, and the sum set down in writing." At this point, the old man started, as with a new hope. "And Christobal, he is the man! Christobal Carson must be here to count it and set it down. He is a just man. Trinidad, you fool, why did you not bring Christobal?"

Father Vaillant was scandalized. "Unless you compose yourself, Father Lucero, and fix your thoughts upon Heaven, I

shall refuse to administer the Sacrament. In your present state
of mind, it would be a sacrilege."

The old man folded his hands and closed his eyes in as-
sent. Father Vaillant went into the adjoining room to put on
his cassock and stole, and in his absence Conçeption Gonzales covered a small table by the bed with one of her own
white napkins and placed upon it two wax candles, and a
cup of water for the ministrant's hands. Father Vaillant came
back in his vestments, with his pyx and basin of holy water,
and began sprinkling the bed and the watchers, repeating
the antiphon, *Asperges me, Domine, hyssopo, et mundabor.*
The women stole away, leaving their lights upon the floor.
Father Lucero made his confession, renouncing his heresy
and expressing contrition, after which he received the Sacrament.

The ceremony calmed the tormented man, and he lay quiet
with his hands folded on his breast. The women returned and
sat murmuring prayers as before. The rain drove against the
window panes, the wind made a hollow sound as it sucked
down through the deep arroyo. Some of the watchers were
drooping from weariness, but not one showed any wish to go
home. Watching beside a death-bed was not a hardship for
them, but a privilege,— in the case of a dying priest it was a
distinction.

In those days, even in European countries, death had a
solemn social importance. It was not regarded as a moment
when certain bodily organs ceased to function, but as a dramatic climax, a moment when the soul made its entrance
into the next world, passing in full consciousness through a
lowly door to an unimaginable scene. Among the watchers
there was always the hope that the dying man might reveal
something of what he alone could see; that his countenance,
if not his lips, would speak, and on his features would fall
some light or shadow from beyond. The "Last Words" of
great men, Napoleon, Lord Byron, were still printed in gift-
books, and the dying murmurs of every common man and
woman were listened for and treasured by their neighbours
and kinsfolk. These sayings, no matter how unimportant,
were given oracular significance and pondered by those who
must one day go the same road.

The stillness of the death chamber was suddenly broken when Trinidad Lucero knelt down before the crucifix on the wall to pray. His uncle, though all thought him asleep, began to struggle and cry out, "A thief! Help, help!" Trinidad retired quickly, but after that the old man lay with one eye open, and no one dared go near the crucifix.

About an hour before day-break the Padre's breathing became so painful that two of the men got behind him and lifted his pillows. The women whispered that his face was changing, and they brought their candles nearer, kneeling close beside his bed. His eyes were alive and had perception in them. He rolled his head to one side and lay looking intently down into the candle-light, without blinking, while his features sharpened. Several times his lips twitched back over his teeth. The watchers held their breath, feeling sure that he would speak before he passed,—and he did. After a facial spasm that was like a sardonic smile, and a clicking of breath in his mouth, their Padre spoke like a horse for the last time:

"Comete tu cola, Martinez, comete tu cola!" (Eat your tail, Martinez, eat your tail!) Almost at once he died in a convulsion.

After day-break Trinidad went forth declaring (and the Mexican women confirmed him) that at the moment of death Father Lucero had looked into the other world and beheld Padre Martinez in torment. As long as the Christians who were about that death-bed lived, the story was whispered in Arroyo Hondo.

When the floor of the priest's house was taken up, according to his last instructions, people came from as far as Taos and Santa Cruz and Mora to see the buckskin bags of gold and silver coin that were buried beneath it. Spanish coins, French, American, English, some of them very old. When it was at length conveyed to a Government mint and examined, it was valued at nearly twenty thousand dollars in American money. A great sum for one old priest to have scraped together in a country parish down at the bottom of a ditch.

BOOK SIX

Doña Isabella

I

DON ANTONIO

BISHOP LATOUR had one very keen worldly ambition; to build in Santa Fé a cathedral which would be worthy of a setting naturally beautiful. As he cherished this wish and meditated upon it, he came to feel that such a building might be a continuation of himself and his purpose, a physical body full of his aspirations after he had passed from the scene. Early in his administration he began setting aside something from his meagre resources for a cathedral fund. In this he was assisted by certain of the rich Mexican *rancheros*, but by no one so much as by Don Antonio Olivares.

Antonio Olivares was the most intelligent and prosperous member of a large family of brothers and cousins, and he was for that time and place a man of wide experience, a man of the world. He had spent the greater part of his life in New Orleans and El Paso del Norte, but he returned to live in Santa Fé several years after Bishop Latour took up his duties there. He brought with him his American wife and a wagon train of furniture, and settled down to spend his declining years in the old ranch house just east of the town where he was born and had grown up. He was then a man of sixty. In early manhood he had lost his first wife; after he went to New Orleans he had married a second time, a Kentucky girl who had grown up among her relatives in Louisiana. She was pretty and accomplished, had been educated at a French convent, and had done much to Europeanize her husband. The refinement of his dress and manners, and his lavish style of living, provoked half-contemptuous envy among his brothers and their friends.

Olivares's wife, Doña Isabella, was a devout Catholic, and at their house the French priests were always welcome and were most cordially entertained. The Señora Olivares had made a pleasant place of the rambling adobe building, with its

gentlemen smoked. The banjo always remained a foreign instrument to Father Latour; he found it more than a little savage. When this strange yellow boy played it, there was softness and languor in the wire strings—but there was also a kind of madness; the recklessness, the call of wild countries which all these men had felt and followed in one way or another. Through clouds of cigar smoke, the scout and the soldiers, the Mexican *rancheros* and the priests, sat silently watching the bent head and crouching shoulders of the banjo player, and his seesawing yellow hand, which sometimes lost all form and became a mere whirl of matter in motion, like a patch of sand-storm.

Observing them thus in repose, in the act of reflection, Father Latour was thinking how each of these men not only had a story, but seemed to have become his story. Those anxious, far-seeing blue eyes of Carson's, to whom could they belong but to a scout and trail-breaker? Don Manuel Chavez, the handsomest man of the company, very elegant in velvet and broadcloth, with delicately cut, disdainful features,—one had only to see him cross the room, or to sit next him at dinner, to feel the electric quality under his cold reserve; the fierceness of some embitterment, the passion for danger.

Chavez boasted his descent from two Castilian knights who freed the city of Chavez from the Moors in 1160. He had estates in the Pecos and in the San Mateo mountains, and a house in Santa Fé, where he hid himself behind his beautiful trees and gardens. He loved the natural beauties of his country with a passion, and he hated the Americans who were blind to them. He was jealous of Carson's fame as an Indian-fighter, declaring that he had seen more Indian warfare before he was twenty than Carson would ever see. He was easily Carson's rival as a pistol shot. With the bow and arrow he had no rival; he had never been beaten. No Indian had ever been known to shoot an arrow as far as Chavez. Every year parties of Indians came up to the Villa to shoot with him for wagers. His house and stables were full of trophies. He took a cool pleasure in stripping the Indians of their horses or silver or blankets, or whatever they had put up on their man. He was proud of his skill with Indian weapons; he had acquired it in a hard school.

When he was a lad of sixteen Manuel Chavez had gone out with a party of Mexican youths to hunt Navajos. In those days, before the American occupation, "hunting Navajos" needed no pretext, it was a form of sport. A company of Mexicans would ride west to the Navajo country, raid a few sheep camps, and come home bringing flocks and ponies and a bunch of prisoners, for every one of whom they received a large bounty from the Mexican Government. It was with such a raiding party that the boy Chavez went out for spoil and adventure.

Finding no Indians abroad, the young Mexicans pushed on farther than they had intended. They did not know that it was the season when all the roving Navajo bands gather at the Canyon de Chelly for their religious ceremonies, and they rode on impetuously until they came out upon the rim of that mysterious and terrifying canyon itself, then swarming with Indians. They were immediately surrounded, and retreat was impossible. They fought on the naked sandstone ledges that overhang that gulf. Don José Chavez, Manuel's older brother, was captain of the party, and was one of the first to fall. The company of fifty were slaughtered to a man. Manuel was the fifty-first, and he survived. With seven arrow wounds, and one shaft clear through his body, he was left for dead in a pile of corpses.

That night, while the Navajos were celebrating their victory, the boy crawled along the rocks until he had high boulders between him and the enemy, and then started eastward on foot. It was summer, and the heat of that red sandstone country is intense. His wounds were on fire. But he had the superb vitality of early youth. He walked for two days and nights without finding a drop of water, covering a distance of sixty odd miles, across the plain, across the mountain, until he came to the famous spring on the other side, where Fort Defiance was afterward built. There he drank and bathed his wounds and slept. He had had no food since the morning before the fight; near the spring he found some large cactus plants, and slicing away the spines with his hunting-knife, he filled his stomach with the juicy pulp.

From here, still without meeting a human creature, he stumbled on until he reached the San Mateo mountain, north

rights of the Propaganda. Without more ado he threw on his old cloak over his cassock, and the three men set off through the red mud to the Olivares hacienda in the hills east of the town.

Father Joseph had not been to the Olivares' house since the night of the New Year's party, and he sighed as he approached the place, already transformed by neglect. The big gate was propped open by a pole because the iron hook was gone, the courtyard was littered with rags and meat bones which the dogs had carried there and no one had taken away. The big parrot cage, hanging in the *portale*, was filthy, and the birds were squalling. When O'Reilly rang the bell at the outer gate, Pablo, the banjo player, came running out with tousled hair and a dirty shirt to admit the visitors. He took them into the long living-room, which was empty and cold, the fireplace dark, the hearth unswept. Chairs and window-sills were deep in red dust, the glass panes dirty, and streaked as if by tear-drops. On the writing-table were empty bottles and sticky glasses and cigar ends. In one corner stood the harp in its green cover.

Pablo asked the Fathers to be seated. His mistress was staying in bed, he said, and the cook had burnt her hand, and the other maids were lazy. He brought wood and laid a fire.

After some time, Doña Isabella entered, dressed in heavy mourning, her face very white against the black, and her eyes red. The curls about her neck and ears were pale, too—quite ashen.

After Father Vaillant had greeted her and spoken consoling words, the young lawyer began once more gently to explain to her the difficulties that confronted them, and what they must do to defeat the action of the Olivares family. She sat submissively, touching her eyes and nose with her little lace handkerchief, and clearly not even trying to understand a word of what he said to her.

Father Joseph soon lost patience and himself approached the widow. "You understand, my child," he began briskly, "that your husband's brothers are determined to disregard his wishes, to defraud you and your daughter, and, eventually, the Church. This is no time for childish vanity. To prevent this outrage to your husband's memory, you must satisfy the court that you are old enough to be the mother of Mademoiselle Inez. You must resolutely declare your true age; fifty-three, is it not?"

Doña Isabella became pallid with fright. She shrank into one end of the deep sofa, but her blue eyes focused and gathered light, as she became intensely, rigidly animated in her corner,—her back against the wall, as it were.

"Fifty-three!" she cried in a voice of horrified amazement. "Why, I never heard of anything so outrageous! I was forty-two my last birthday. It was in December, the fourth of December. If Antonio were here, he would tell you! And he wouldn't let you scold me and talk about business to me, either, Father Joseph. He never let anybody talk about business to me!" She hid her face in her little handkerchief and began to cry.

Father Latour checked his impetuous Vicar, and sat down on the sofa beside Madame Olivares, feeling very sorry for her and speaking very gently. "Forty-two to your friends, dear Madame Olivares, and to the world. In heart and face you are younger than that. But to the Law and the Church there must be a literal reckoning. A formal statement in court will not make you any older to your friends; it will not add one line to your face. A woman, you know, is as old as she looks."

"That's very sweet of you to say, Bishop Latour," the lady quavered, looking up at him with tear-bright eyes. "But I never could hold up my head again. Let the Olivares have that old money. I don't want it."

Father Vaillant sprang up and glared down at her as if he could put common sense into her drooping head by the mere intensity of his gaze. "Four hundred thousand pesos, Señora Isabella!" he cried. "Ease and comfort for you and your daughter all the rest of your lives. Would you make your daughter a beggar? The Olivares will take everything."

"I can't help it about Inez," she pleaded. "Inez means to go into the convent anyway. And I don't care about the money. *Ah, mon père, je voudrais mieux être jeune et mendiante, que n'être que vieille et riche, certes, oui!*"

Father Joseph caught her icy cold hand. "And have you a

right to defraud the Church of what is left to it in your trust? Have you thought of the consequences to yourself of such a betrayal?"

Father Latour glanced sternly at his Vicar. *"Assez,"* he said quietly. He took the little hand Father Joseph had released and bent over it, kissing it respectfully. "We must not press this any further. We must leave this to Madame Olivares and her own conscience. I believe, my daughter, you will come to realize that this sacrifice of your vanity would be for your soul's peace. Looking merely at the temporal aspect of the case, you would find poverty hard to bear. You would have to live upon the Olivares's charity, would you not? I do not wish to see this come about. I have a selfish interest; I wish you to be always your charming self and to make a little *poésie* in life for us here. We have not much of that."

Madame Olivares stopped crying. She raised her head and sat drying her eyes. Suddenly she took hold of one of the buttons on the Bishop's cassock and began twisting it with nervous fingers.

"Father," she said timidly, "what is the youngest I could possibly be, to be Inez's mother?"

The Bishop could not pronounce the verdict; he hesitated, flushed, then passed it on to O'Reilly with an open gesture of his fine white hand.

"Fifty-two, Señora Olivares," said the young man respectfully. "If I can get you to admit that, and stick to it, I feel sure we will win our case."

"Very well, Mr. O'Reilly." She bowed her head. As her visitors rose, she sat looking down at the dust-covered rugs. "Before everybody!" she murmured, as if to herself.

When they were tramping home, Father Joseph said that as for him, he would rather combat the superstitions of a whole Indian pueblo than the vanity of one white woman.

"And I would rather do almost anything than go through such a scene again," said the Bishop with a frown. "I don't think I ever assisted at anything so cruel."

Boyd O'Reilly defeated the Olivares brothers and won his case. The Bishop would not go to the court hearing, but Father Vaillant was there, standing in the malodorous crowd (there were no chairs in the court room), and his knees shook under him when the young lawyer, with the fierceness born of fright, poked his finger at his client and said:

"Señora Olivares, you are fifty-two years of age, are you not?"

Madame Olivares was swathed in mourning, her face a streak of shadowed white between folds of black veil.

"Yes, sir." The crape barely let it through.

The night after the verdict was pronounced, Manuel Chavez, with several of Antonio's old friends, called upon the widow to congratulate her. Word of their intention had gone about the town and put others in the mood to call at a house that had been closed to visitors for so long. A considerable company gathered there that evening, including some of the military people, and several hereditary enemies of the Olivares brothers.

The cook, stimulated by the sight of the long *sala* full of people once more, hastily improvised a supper. Pablo put on a white shirt and a velvet jacket, and began to carry up from the cellar his late master's best whisky and sherry, and quarts of champagne. (The Mexicans are very fond of sparkling wines. Only a few years before this, an American trader who had got into serious political trouble with the Mexican military authorities in Santa Fé, regained their confidence and friendship by presenting them with a large wagon shipment of champagne—three thousand, three hundred and ninety-two bottles, indeed!)

This hospitable mood came upon the house suddenly, nothing had been prepared beforehand. The wineglasses were full of dust, but Pablo wiped them out with the shirt he had just taken off, and without instructions from anyone he began gliding about with a tray full of glasses, which he afterward refilled many times, taking his station at the side-board. Even Doña Isabella drank a little champagne; when she had sipped one glass with the young Georgia captain, she could not refuse to take another with their nearest neighbour, Ferdinand Sanchez, always a true friend to her husband. Everyone was gay, the servants and the guests, everything sparkled like a garden after a shower.

Father Latour and Father Vaillant, having heard nothing of

this spontaneous gathering of friends, set off at eight o'clock to make a call upon the brave widow. When they entered the courtyard, they were astonished to hear music within, and to see light streaming from the long row of windows behind the *portale*. Without stopping to knock, they opened the door into the *sala*. Many candles were burning. Señors were standing about in long frock-coats buttoned over full figures. O'Reilly and a group of officers from the Fort surrounded the sideboard, where Pablo, with a white napkin wrapped showily about his wrist, was pouring champagne. From the other end of the room sounded the high tinkle of the harp, and Doña Isabella's voice:

> *"Listen to the mocking-bird,*
> *Listen to the mocking-bird!"*

The priests waited in the doorway until the song was finished, then went forward to pay their respects to the hostess. She was wearing the unrelieved white that grief permitted, and the yellow curls were bobbing as of old—three behind her right ear, one over either temple, and a little row across the back of her neck. As she saw the two black figures approaching, she dropped her arms from the harp, took her satin toe from the pedal, and rose, holding out a hand to each. Her eyes were bright, and her face beamed with affection for her spiritual fathers. But her greeting was a playful reproach, uttered loud enough to be heard above the murmur of conversing groups:

"I never shall forgive you, Father Joseph, nor you either, Bishop Latour, for that awful lie you made me tell in court about my age!"

The two churchmen bowed amid laughter and applause.

BOOK SEVEN

The Great Diocese

THE BISHOP'S WORK was sometimes assisted, often impeded, by external events.

By the Gadsden Purchase, executed three years after Father Latour came to Santa Fé, the United States took over from Mexico a great territory which now forms southern New Mexico and Arizona. The authorities at Rome notified Father Latour that this new territory was to be annexed to his diocese, but that as the national boundary lines often cut parishes in two, the boundaries of Church jurisdiction must be settled by conference with the Mexican Bishops of Chihuahua and Sonora. Such conferences would necessitate a journey of nearly four thousand miles. As Father Vaillant remarked, at Rome they did not seem to realize that it was no easy matter for two missionaries on horseback to keep up with the march of history.

The question hung fire for some years, the subject of voluminous correspondence. At last, in 1858, Father Vaillant was sent to arrange the debated boundaries with the Mexican Bishops. He started in the autumn and spent the whole winter on the road, going from El Paso del Norte west to Tucson, on to Santa Magdalena and Guaymas, a seaport town on the Gulf of California, and did some seafaring on the Pacific before he turned homeward.

On his return trip he was stricken with malarial fever, resulting from exposure and bad water, and lay seriously ill in a cactus desert in Arizona. Word of his illness came to Santa Fé by an Indian runner, and Father Latour and Jacinto rode across New Mexico and half of Arizona, found Father Vaillant, and brought him back by easy stages.

He was ill in the Bishop's house for two months. This was the first spring that he and Father Latour had both been there

no one to instruct them, how can they get right? They are like seeds, full of germination but with no moisture. A mere contact is enough to make them a living part of the Church. The more I work with the Mexicans, the more I believe it was people like them our Saviour bore in mind when He said, *Unless ye become as little children.* He was thinking of people who are not clever in the things of this world, whose minds are not upon gain and worldly advancement. These poor Christians are not thrifty like our country people at home; they have no veneration for property, no sense of material values. I stop a few hours in a village, I administer the sacraments and hear confessions, I leave in every house some little token, a rosary or a religious picture, and I go away feeling that I have conferred immeasurable happiness, and have released faithful souls that were shut away from God by neglect.

"Down near Tucson a Pima Indian convert once asked me to go off into the desert with him, as he had something to show me. He took me into a place so wild that a man less accustomed to these things might have mistrusted and feared for his life. We descended into a terrifying canyon of black rock, and there in the depths of a cave, he showed me a golden chalice, vestments and cruets, all the paraphernalia for celebrating Mass. His ancestors had hidden these sacred objects there when the mission was sacked by Apaches, he did not know how many generations ago. The secret had been handed down in his family, and I was the first priest who had ever come to restore to God his own. To me, that is the situation in a parable. The Faith, in that wild frontier, is like a buried treasure; they guard it, but they do not know how to use it to their soul's salvation. A word, a prayer, a service, is all that is needed to set free those souls in bondage. I confess I am covetous of that mission. I desire to be the man who restores these lost children to God. It will be the greatest happiness of my life."

The Bishop did not reply at once to this appeal. At last he said gravely, "You must realize that I have need of you here, Father Joseph. My duties are too many for one man."

"But you do not need me so much as they do!" Father Joseph threw off his coverings and sat up in his cassock, putting his feet to the ground. "Any one of our good French priests from Montferrand can serve you here. It is work that can be done by intelligence. But down there it is work for the heart, for a particular sympathy, and none of our new priests understand those poor natures as I do. I have almost become a Mexican! I have learned to like *chili colorado* and mutton fat. Their foolish ways no longer offend me, their very faults are dear to me. I am *their man!*"

"Ah, no doubt, no doubt! But I must insist upon your lying down for the present."

Father Vaillant, flushed and excited, dropped back upon his pillows, and the Bishop took a short turn through the garden,—to the row of tamarisk trees and back. He walked slowly, with even, unhesitating pace, with that slender, un-rigid erectness, and the fine carriage of head, which always made him seem master of the situation. No one would have guessed that a sharp struggle was going on within him. Father Joseph's impassioned request had spoiled a cherished plan, and brought Father Latour a bitter personal disappointment. There was but one thing to do,—and before he reached the tamarisks he had done it. He broke off a spray of the dry lilac-coloured flowers to punctuate and seal, as it were, his renunciation. He returned with the same easy, deliberate tread, and stood smiling beside the army cot.

"Your feeling must be your guide in this matter, Joseph. I shall put no obstacles in your way. A certain care for your health I must insist upon, but when you are quite well, you must follow the duty that calls loudest."

They were both silent for a few moments. Father Joseph closed his eyes against the sunlight, and Father Latour stood lost in thought, drawing the plume of tamarisk blossom absently through his delicate, rather nervous fingers. His hands had a curious authority, but not the calmness so often seen in the hands of priests; they seemed always to be investigating and making firm decisions.

The two friends were roused from their reflections by a frantic beating of wings. A bright flock of pigeons swept over their heads to the far end of the garden, where a woman was just emerging from the gate that led into the school grounds; Magdalena, who came every day to feed the doves and to gather flowers. The Sisters had given her charge of the altar decoration of the school chapel for this month, and she came for the Bishop's apple blossoms and daffodils. She advanced in a whirlwind of gleaming wings, and Tranquilino dropped his spade and stood watching her. At one moment the whole flock of doves caught the light in such a way that they all became invisible at once, dissolved in light and disappeared as salt dissolves in water. The next moment they flashed around, black and silver against the sun. They settled upon Magdalena's arms and shoulders, ate from her hand. When she put a crust of bread between her lips, two doves hung in the air before her face, stirring their wings and pecking at the morsel. A handsome woman she had grown to be, with her comely figure and the deep claret colour under the golden brown of her cheeks.

"Who would think, to look at her now, that we took her from a place where every vileness of cruelty and lust was practised!" murmured Father Vaillant. "Not since the days of early Christianity has the Church been able to do what it can here."

"She is but twenty-seven or -eight years old. I wonder whether she ought not to marry again," said the Bishop thoughtfully. "Though she seems so contented, I have sometimes surprised a tragic shadow in her eyes. Do you remember the terrible look in her eyes when we first saw her?"

"Can I ever forget it! But her very body has changed. She was then a shapeless, cringing creature. I thought her half-witted. No, no! She has had enough of the storms of this world. Here she is safe and happy." Father Vaillant sat up and called to her. "Magdalena, Magdalena, my child, come here and talk to us for a little. Two men grow lonely when they see nobody but each other."

2

DECEMBER NIGHT

Father Vaillant had been absent in Arizona since midsummer, and it was now December. Bishop Latour had been going through one of those periods of coldness and doubt which, from his boyhood, had occasionally settled down upon his spirit and made him feel an alien, wherever he was. He attended to his correspondence, went on his rounds among the parish priests, held services at missions that were without pastors, superintended the building of the addition to the Sisters' school: but his heart was not in these things.

One night about three weeks before Christmas he was lying in his bed, unable to sleep, with the sense of failure clutching at his heart. His prayers were empty words and brought him no refreshment. His soul had become a barren field. He had nothing within himself to give his priests or his people. His work seemed superficial, a house built upon the sands. His great diocese was still a heathen country. The Indians travelled their old road of fear and darkness, battling with evil omens and ancient shadows. The Mexicans were children who played with their religion.

As the night wore on, the bed on which the Bishop lay became a bed of thorns; he could bear it no longer. Getting up in the dark, he looked out of the window and was surprised to find that it was snowing, that the ground was already lightly covered. The full moon, hidden by veils of cloud, threw a pale phosphorescent luminousness over the heavens, and the towers of the church stood up black against this silvery fleece. Father Latour felt a longing to go into the church to pray; but instead he lay down again under his blankets. Then, realizing that it was the cold of the church he shrank from, and despising himself, he rose again, dressed quickly, and went out into the court, throwing on over his cassock that faithful old cloak that was the twin of Father Vaillant's.

They had bought the cloth for those coats in Paris, long ago, when they were young men staying at the Seminary for Foreign Missions in the rue du Bac, preparing for their first voyage to the New World. The cloth had been made up into caped riding-cloaks by a German tailor in Ohio, and lined with fox fur. Years afterward, when Father Latour was about to start on his long journey in search of his Bishopric, that same tailor had made the cloaks over and relined them with squirrel skins, as more appropriate for a mild climate. These

medal, with a figure of the Virgin, he had in his pocket. He gave it to her, telling her that it had been blessed by the Holy Father himself. Now she would have a treasure to hide and guard, to adore while her watchers slept. Ah, he thought, for one who cannot read—or think—the Image, the physical form of Love!

He fitted the great key into its lock, the door swung slowly back on its wooden hinges. The peace without seemed all one with the peace in his own soul. The snow had stopped, the gauzy clouds that had ribbed the arch of heaven were now all sunk into one soft white fog bank over the Sangre de Cristo mountains. The full moon shone high in the blue vault, majestic, lonely, benign. The Bishop stood in the doorway of his church, lost in thought, looking at the line of black footprints his departing visitor had left in the wet scurf of snow.

3

SPRING IN THE NAVAJO COUNTRY

Father Vaillant was away in Arizona all winter. When the first hint of spring was in the air, the Bishop and Jacinto set out on a long ride across New Mexico, to the Painted Desert and the Hopi villages. After they left Oraibi, the Bishop rode several days to the south, to visit a Navajo friend who had lately lost his only son, and who had paid the Bishop the compliment of sending word of the boy's death to him at Santa Fé.

Father Latour had known Eusabio a long while, had met him soon after he first came to his new diocese. The Navajo was in Santa Fé at that time, assisting the military officers to quiet an outbreak of the never-ending quarrel between his people and the Hopis. Ever since then the Bishop and the Indian chief had entertained an increasing regard for each other. Eusabio brought his son all the way to Santa Fé to have the Bishop baptize him,—that one beloved son who had died during this last winter.

Though he was ten years younger than Father Latour, Eusabio was one of the most influential men among the Navajo people, and one of the richest in sheep and horses. In Santa

Fé and Albuquerque he was respected for his intelligence and authority, and admired for his fine presence. He was extremely tall, even for a Navajo, with a face like a Roman general's of Republican times. He always dressed very elegantly in velvet and buckskin rich with bead and quill embroidery, belted with silver, and wore a blanket of the finest wool and design. His arms, under the loose sleeves of his shirt, were covered with silver bracelets, and on his breast hung very old necklaces of wampum and turquoise and coral—Mediterranean coral, that had been left in the Navajo country by Coronado's captains when they passed through it on their way to discover the Hopi villages and the Grand Canyon.

Eusabio lived, with his relatives and dependents, in a group of hogans on the Colorado Chiquito; to the west and south and north his kinsmen herded his great flocks.

Father Latour and Jacinto arrived at the cluster of booth-like cabins during a high sandstorm, which circled about them and their mules like snow in a blizzard and all but obliterated the landscape. The Navajo came out of his house and took possession of Angelica by her bridle-bit. At first he did not open his lips, merely stood holding Father Latour's very fine white hand in his very fine dark one, and looked into his face with a message of sorrow and resignation in his deep-set, eagle eyes. A wave of feeling passed over his bronze features as he said slowly:

"My friend has come."

That was all, but it was everything; welcome, confidence, appreciation.

For his lodging the Bishop was given a solitary hogan, a little apart from the settlement. Eusabio quickly furnished it with his best skins and blankets, and told his guest that he must tarry a few days there and recover from his fatigue. His mules were tired, the Indian said, the Padre himself looked weary, and the way to Santa Fé was long.

The Bishop thanked him and said he would stay three days; that he had need for reflection. His mind had been taken up with practical matters ever since he left home. This seemed a spot where a man might get his thoughts together. The river, a considerable stream at this time of the year, wound among mounds and dunes of loose sand which whirled through the air all day in the boisterous spring winds. The sand banked up against the hogan the Bishop occupied, and filtered through chinks in the walls, which were made of saplings plastered with clay.

Beside the river was a grove of tall, naked cottonwoods— trees of great antiquity and enormous size—so large that they seemed to belong to a bygone age. They grew far apart, and their strange twisted shapes must have come about from the ceaseless winds that bent them to the east and scoured them with sand, and from the fact that they lived with very little water,—the river was nearly dry here for most of the year. The trees rose out of the ground at a slant, and forty or fifty feet above the earth all these white, dry trunks changed their direction, grew back over their base line. Some split into great forks which arched down almost to the ground; some did not fork at all, but the main trunk dipped downward in a strong curve, as if drawn by a bow-string; and some terminated in a thick coruscation of growth, like a crooked palm tree. They were all living trees, yet they seemed to be of old, dead, dry wood, and had very scant foliage. High up in the forks, or at the end of a preposterous length of twisted bough, would burst a faint bouquet of delicate green leaves—out of all keeping with the great lengths of seasoned white trunk and branches. The grove looked like a winter wood of giant trees, with clusters of mistletoe growing among the bare boughs.

Navajo hospitality is not intrusive. Eusabio made the Bishop understand that he was glad to have him there, and let him alone. Father Latour lived for three days in an almost perpetual sand-storm—cut off from even this remote little Indian camp by moving walls and tapestries of sand. He either sat in his house and listened to the wind, or walked abroad under those aged, wind-distorted trees, muffled in an Indian blanket, which he kept drawn up over his mouth and nose. Since his arrival he had undertaken to decide whether he would be justified in recalling Father Vaillant from Tucson. The Vicar's occasional letters, brought by travellers, showed that he was highly content where he was, restoring the old mission church of St. Xavier del Bac, which he declared to be the most beautiful church on the continent, though it had been neglected for more than two hundred years.

Since Father Vaillant went away the Bishop's burdens had grown heavier and heavier. The new priests from Auvergne were all good men, faithful and untiring in carrying out his wishes; but they were still strangers to the country, timid about making decisions, and referred every difficulty to their Bishop. Father Latour needed his Vicar, who had so much tact with the natives, so much sympathy with all their short-comings. When they were together, he was always curbing Father Vaillant's hopeful rashness—but left alone, he greatly missed that very quality. And he missed Father Vaillant's companionship—why not admit it?

Although Jean Marie Latour and Joseph Vaillant were born in neighbouring parishes in the Puy-de-Dôm, as children they had not known each other. The Latours were an old family of scholars and professional men, while the Vaillants were people of a much humbler station in the provincial world. Besides, little Joseph had been away from home much of the time, up on the farm in the Volvic mountains with his grandfather, where the air was especially pure, and the country quiet salu-tary for a child of nervous temperament. The two boys had not come together until they were Seminarians at Montfer-rand, in Clermont.

When Jean Marie was in his second year at the Seminary, he was standing on the recreation ground one day at the opening of the term, looking with curiosity at the new students. In the group, he noticed one of peculiarly unprom-ising appearance; a boy of nineteen who was undersized, very pale, homely in feature, with a wart on his chin and tow-coloured hair that made him look like a German. This boy seemed to feel his glance, and came up at once, as if he had been called. He was apparently quite unconscious of his homeliness, was not at all shy, but intensely interested in his new surroundings. He asked Jean Latour his name, where he came from, and his father's occupation. Then he said with great simplicity:

"My father is a baker, the best in Riom. In fact, he's a re-markable baker."

Young Latour was amused, but expressed polite appre-

bring with him a couple of good French stone-cutters. They will certainly be no more expensive than workmen from St. Louis. Now that I have found exactly the stone I want, my Cathedral seems to me already begun. This hill is only about fifteen miles from Santa Fé; there is an up-grade, but it is gradual. Hauling the stone will be easier than I could have hoped for."

"You plan far ahead," Father Vaillant looked at his friend wonderingly. "Well, that is what a Bishop should be able to do. As for me, I see only what is under my nose. But I had no idea you were going in for fine building, when everything about us is so poor—and we ourselves are so poor."

"But the Cathedral is not for us, Father Joseph. We build for the future—better not lay a stone unless we can do that. It would be a shame to any man coming from a Seminary that is one of the architectural treasures of France, to make another ugly church on this continent where there are so many already."

"You are probably right. I had never thought of it before. It never occurred to me that we could have anything but an Ohio church here. Your ancestors helped to build Clermont Cathedral, I remember; two building Bishops de la Tour back in the thirteenth century. Time brings things to pass, certainly. I had no idea you were taking all this so much to heart."

Father Latour laughed. "Is a cathedral a thing to be taken lightly, after all?"

"Oh, no, certainly not!" Father Vaillant moved his shoulders uneasily. He did not himself know why he hung back in this.

The base of the hill before which they stood was already in shadow, subdued to the tone of rich yellow clay, but the top was still melted gold—a colour that throbbed in the last rays of the sun. The Bishop turned away at last with a sigh of deep content. "Yes," he said slowly, "that rock will do very well. And now we must be starting home. Every time I come here, I like this stone better. I could hardly have hoped that God would gratify my personal taste, my vanity, if you will, in this way. I tell you, *Blanchet*, I would rather have found that hill of yellow rock than have come into a fortune to spend in charity. The Cathedral is near my heart, for many reasons. I hope you do not think me very worldly."

As they rode home through the sage-brush silvered by moonlight, Father Vaillant was still wondering why he had been called home from saving souls in Arizona, and wondering why a poor missionary Bishop should care so much about a building. He himself was eager to have the Cathedral begun; but whether it was Midi Romanesque or Ohio German in style, seemed to him of little consequence.

2

A LETTER FROM LEAVENWORTH

The day after the Bishop and his Vicar rode to the yellow rock the weekly post arrived at Santa Fé. It brought the Bishop many letters, and he was shut in his study all morning. At lunch he told Father Vaillant that he would require his company that evening to consider with him a letter of great importance from the Bishop of Leavenworth.

This letter of many pages was concerned with events that were happening in Colorado, in a part of the Rocky Mountains very little known. Though it was only a few hundred miles north of Santa Fé, communication with that region was so infrequent that news travelled to Santa Fé from Europe more quickly than from Pike's Peak. Under the shadow of that peak rich gold deposits had been discovered within the last year, but Father Vaillant had first heard of this through a letter from France. Word of it had reached the Atlantic coast, crossed to Europe, and come from there back to the Southwest, more quickly than it could filter down through the few hundred miles of unexplored mountains and gorges between Cripple Creek and Santa Fé. While Father Vaillant was at Tucson he had received a letter from his brother Marius, in Auvergne, and was vexed that so much of it was taken up with inquiries about the gold rush to Colorado, of which he had never heard, while Marius gave him but little news of the war in Italy, which seemed relatively near and much more important.

That congested heaping up of the Rocky Mountain chain

often think, Jean, how you were an unconscious agent in the
hands of Providence when you recalled me from Tucson. I
seemed to be doing the most important work of my life
there, and you recalled me for no reason at all, apparently.
You did not know why, and I did not know why. We were
both acting in the dark. But Heaven knew what was happening at Cripple Creek, and moved us like chessmen on the
board. When the call came, I was here to answer it—by a
miracle, indeed."

Father Latour put down his silver coffee-cup. "Miracles are
all very well, Joseph, but I see none here. I sent for you
because I felt the need of your companionship. I used my
authority as a Bishop to gratify my personal wish. That was
selfish, if you will, but surely natural enough. We are countrymen, and are bound by early memories. And that two friends,
having come together, should part and go their separate
ways—that is natural, too. No, I don't think we need any
miracle to explain all this."

Father Vaillant had been wholly absorbed in his preparations for saving souls in the gold camps—blind to everything
else. Now it came over him in a flash, how the Bishop had
held himself aloof from his activities; it was a very hard thing
for Father Latour to let him go; the loneliness of his position
had begun to weigh upon him.

Yes, he reflected, as he went quietly to his own room, there
was a great difference in their natures. Wherever he went, he
soon made friends that took the place of country and family.
But Jean, who was at ease in any society and always the flower
of courtesy, could not form new ties. It had always been so.
He was like that even as a boy; gracious to everyone, but
known to a very few. To man's wisdom it would have seemed
that a priest with Father Latour's exceptional qualities would
have been better placed in some part of the world where
scholarship, a handsome person, and delicate perceptions all
have their effect; and that a man of much rougher type would
have served God well enough as the first Bishop of New Mexico. Doubtless Bishop Latour's successors would be men of a
different fibre. But God had his reasons, Father Joseph devoutly believed. Perhaps it pleased Him to grace the beginning of a new era and a vast new diocese by a fine personality.

And perhaps, after all, something would remain through the years to come; some ideal, or memory, or legend.

The next afternoon, his wagon loaded and standing ready in the courtyard, Father Vaillant was seated at the Bishop's desk, writing letters to France; a short one to Marius, a long one to his beloved Philomène, telling her of his plunge into the unknown and begging her prayers for his success in the world of gold-crazed men. He wrote rapidly and jerkily, moving his lips as well as his fingers. When the Bishop entered the study, he rose and stood holding the written pages in his hand.

"I did not mean to interrupt you, Joseph, but do you intend to take Contento with you to Colorado?"

Father Joseph blinked. "Why, certainly. I had intended to ride him. However, if you have need for him here——"

"Oh, no. Not at all. But if you take Contento, I will ask you to take Angelica as well. They have a great affection for each other; why separate them indefinitely? One could not explain to them. They have worked long together."

Father Vaillant made no reply. He stood looking intently at the pages of his letter. The Bishop saw a drop of water splash down upon the violet script and spread. He turned quickly and went out through the arched doorway.

At sunrise next morning Father Vaillant set out, Sabino driving the wagon, his oldest boy riding Angelica, and Father Joseph himself riding Contento. They took the old road to the north-east, through the sharp red sand-hills spotted with juniper, and the Bishop accompanied them as far as the loop where the road wound out on the top of one of those conical hills, giving the departing traveller his last glimpse of Santa Fé. There Father Joseph drew rein and looked back at the town lying rosy in the morning light, the mountain behind it, and the hills close about it like two encircling arms.

"*Auspice, Maria!*" he murmured as he turned his back on these familiar things.

The Bishop rode home to his solitude. He was forty-seven years old, and he had been a missionary in the New World for twenty years—ten of them in New Mexico. If he were a parish priest at home, there would be nephews coming to him for help in their Latin or a bit of pocket-money; nieces to run into his garden and bring their sewing and keep an eye on his housekeeping. All the way home he indulged in such reflections as any bachelor nearing fifty might have.

But when he entered his study, he seemed to come back to reality, to the sense of a Presence awaiting him. The curtain of the arched doorway had scarcely fallen behind him when that feeling of personal loneliness was gone, and a sense of loss was replaced by a sense of restoration. He sat down before his desk, deep in reflection. It was just this solitariness of love in which a priest's life could be like his Master's. It was not a solitude of atrophy, of negation, but of perpetual flowering. A life need not be cold, or devoid of grace in the worldly sense, if it were filled by Her who was all the graces; Virgin-daughter, Virgin-mother, girl of the people and Queen of Heaven: *le rêve suprême de la chair*. The nursery tale could not vie with Her in simplicity, the wisest theologians could not match Her in profundity.

Here in his own church in Santa Fé there was one of these nursery Virgins, a little wooden figure, very old and very dear to the people. De Vargas, when he recaptured the city for Spain two hundred years ago, had vowed a yearly procession in her honour, and it was still one of the most solemn events of the Christian year in Santa Fé. She was a little wooden figure, about three feet high, very stately in bearing, with a beautiful though rather severe Spanish face. She had a rich wardrobe; a chest full of robes and laces, and gold and silver diadems. The women loved to sew for her and the silver-smiths to make her chains and brooches. Father Latour had delighted her wardrobe keepers when he told them he did not believe the Queen of England or the Empress of France had so many costumes. She was their doll and their queen, something to fondle and something to adore, as Mary's Son must have been to Her.

These poor Mexicans, he reflected, were not the first to pour out their love in this simple fashion. Raphael and Titian had made costumes for Her in their time, and the great masters had made music for Her, and the great architects had built cathedrals for Her. Long before Her years on earth, in the long twilight between the Fall and the Redemption, the pagan sculptors were always trying to achieve the image of a goddess who should yet be a woman.

Bishop Latour's premonition was right: Father Vaillant never returned to share his work in New Mexico. Come back he did, to visit his old friends, whenever his busy life permitted. But his destiny was fulfilled in the cold, steely Colorado Rockies, which he never loved as he did the blue mountains of the South. He came back to Santa Fé to recuperate from the illnesses and accidents which consistently punctuated his way; came with the Papal Emissary when Bishop Latour was made Archbishop; but his working life was spent among bleak mountains and comfortless mining camps, looking after lost sheep.

Creede, Durango, Silver City, Central City, over the Continental Divide into Utah,—his strange Episcopal carriage was known throughout that rugged granite world.

It was a covered carriage, on springs, and long enough for him to lie down in at night,—Father Joseph was a very short man. At the back was a luggage box, which could be made into an altar when he celebrated Mass in the open, under a pine tree. He used to say that the mountain torrents were the first road builders, and that wherever they found a way, he could find one. He wore out driver after driver, and his coach was repaired so often and so extensively that long before he abandoned it there was none of the original structure left.

Broken tongues and singletrees, smashed wheels and splintered axles he considered trifling matters. Twice the old carriage itself slipped off the mountain road and rolled down the gorge, with the priest inside. From the first accident of this kind, Father Vaillant escaped with nothing worse than a sprain, and he wrote Bishop Latour that he attributed his preservation to the Archangel Raphael, whose office he had said with unusual fervour that morning. The second time he rolled down a ravine, near Central City, his thigh-bone was broken just below the joint. It knitted in time, but he was lamed for life, and could never ride horseback again.

Before this accident befell him, however, he had one long visit among his friends in Santa Fé and Albuquerque, a renewal of old ties that was like an Indian summer in his life.

and without shame—and I am always a little cold—*un pé-dant*, as you used to say. If hereafter we have stars in our crowns, yours will be a constellation. Give me your blessing."

He knelt, and Father Vaillant, having blessed him, knelt and was blessed in turn. They embraced each other for the past—for the future.

BOOK NINE

Death Comes for the Archbishop

I

W HEN THAT DEVOUT NUN, Mother Superior Philomène, died at a great age in her native Riom, among her papers were found several letters from Archbishop Latour, one dated December 1888, only a few months before his death. *"Since your brother was called to his reward,"* he wrote, *"I feel nearer to him than before. For many years Duty separated us, but death has brought us together. The time is not far distant when I shall join him. Meanwhile, I am enjoying to the full that period of reflection which is the happiest conclusion to a life of action."*

This period of reflection the Archbishop spent on his little country estate, some four miles north of Santa Fé. Long before his retirement from the cares of the diocese, Father Latour bought those few acres in the red sand-hills near the Tesuque pueblo, and set out an orchard which would be bearing when the time came for him to rest. He chose this place in the red hills spotted with juniper against the advice of his friends, because he believed it to be admirably suited for the growing of fruit.

Once when he was riding out to visit the Tesuque mission, he had followed a stream and come upon this spot, where he found a little Mexican house and a garden shaded by an apricot tree of such great size as he had never seen before. It had two trunks, each of them thicker than a man's body, and though evidently very old, it was full of fruit. The apricots were large, beautifully coloured, and of superb flavour. Since this tree grew against the hillside, the Archbishop concluded that the exposure there must be excellent for fruit. He surmised that the heat of the sun, reflected from the rocky hill-slope up into the tree, gave the fruit an even temperature, warmth from two sides, such as brings the wall peaches to perfection in France.

The old Mexican who lived there said the tree must be two hundred years old; it had been just like this when his grandfather was a boy, and had always borne luscious apricots like these. The old man would be glad to sell the place and move into Santa Fé, the Bishop found, and he bought it a few weeks later. In the spring he set out his orchard and a few rows of acacia trees. Some years afterward he built a little adobe house, with a chapel, high up on the hill-side overlooking the orchard. Thither he used to go for rest and at seasons of special devotion. After his retirement, he went there to live, though he always kept his study unchanged in the house of the new Archbishop.

In his retirement Father Latour's principal work was the training of the new missionary priests who arrived from France. His successor, the second Archbishop, was also an Auvergnat, from Father Latour's own college, and the clergy of northern New Mexico remained predominantly French. When a company of new priests arrived (they never came singly) Archbishop S—— sent them out to stay with Father Latour for a few months, to receive instruction in Spanish, in the topography of the diocese, in the character and traditions of the different pueblos.

Father Latour's recreation was his garden. He grew such fruit as was hardly to be found even in the old orchards of California; cherries and apricots, apples and quinces, and the peerless pears of France—even the most delicate varieties. He urged the new priests to plant fruit trees wherever they went, and to encourage the Mexicans to add fruit to their starchy diet. Wherever there was a French priest, there should be a garden of fruit trees and vegetables and flowers. He often quoted to his students that passage from their fellow Auvergnat, Pascal: that Man was lost and saved in a garden.

He domesticated and developed the native wild flowers. He had one hill-side solidly clad with that low-growing purple verbena which mats over the hills of New Mexico. It was like a great violet velvet mantle thrown down in the sun; all the shades that the dyers and weavers of Italy and France strove for through centuries, the violet that is full of rose colour and is yet not lavender; the blue that becomes almost pink and then retreats again into sea-dark purple—the true Episcopal colour and countless variations of it.

In the year 1885 there came to New Mexico a young Seminarian, Bernard Ducrot, who became like a son to Father Latour. The story of the old Archbishop's life, often told in the cloisters and class-rooms at Montferrand, had taken hold of this boy's imagination, and he had long waited an opportunity to come. Bernard was handsome in person and of unusual mentality, had in himself the fineness to reverence all that was fine in his venerable Superior. He anticipated Father Latour's every wish, shared his reflections, cherished his reminiscences.

"Surely," the Bishop used to say to the priests, "God himself has sent me this young man to help me through the last years."

2

Throughout the autumn of the year '88 the Bishop was in good health. He had five French priests in his house, and he still rode abroad with them to visit the nearer missions. On Christmas eve, he performed the midnight Mass in the Cathedral at Santa Fé. In January he drove with Bernard to Santa Cruz to see the resident priest, who was ill. While they were on their way home the weather suddenly changed, and a violent rain-storm overtook them. They were in an open buggy and were drenched to the skin before they could reach any Mexican house for shelter.

After arriving home, Father Latour went at once to bed. During the night he slept badly and felt feverish. He called none of his household, but arose at the usual hour before dawn and went into the chapel for his devotions. While he was at prayer, he was seized with a chill. He made his way to the kitchen, and his old cook, Fructosa, alarmed at once, put him to bed and gave him brandy. This chill left him feverish, and he developed a distressing cough.

After keeping quietly to his bed for a few days, the Bishop called young Bernard to him one morning and said:

"Bernard, will you ride into Santa Fé to-day and see the Archbishop for me. Ask him whether it will be quite convenient if I return to occupy my study in his house for a short time. *Je voudrais mourir à Santa Fé.*"

The Bishop was recalling this saying of Molny's when a voice out of the present sounded in his ear. It was Bernard.

"A fine sunset, Father. See how red the mountains are growing; Sangre de Cristo."

Yes, Sangre de Cristo; but no matter how scarlet the sunset, those red hills never became vermilion, but a more and more intense rose-carnelian; not the colour of living blood, the Bishop had often reflected, but the colour of the dried blood of saints and martyrs preserved in old churches in Rome, which liquefies upon occasion.

3

The next morning Father Latour wakened with a grateful sense of nearness to his Cathedral—which would also be his tomb. He felt safe under its shadow; like a boat come back to harbour, lying under its own sea-wall. He was in his old study; the Sisters had sent a little iron bed from the school for him, and their finest linen and blankets. He felt a great content at being here, where he had come as a young man and where he had done his work. The room was little changed; the same rugs and skins on the earth floor, the same desk with his candlesticks, the same thick, wavy white walls that muted sound, that shut out the world and gave repose to the spirit.

As the darkness faded into the grey of a winter morning, he listened for the church bells,—and for another sound, that always amused him here; the whistle of a locomotive. Yes, he had come with the buffalo, and he had lived to see railway trains running into Santa Fé. He had accomplished an historic period.

All his relatives at home, and his friends in New Mexico, had expected that the old Archbishop would spend his closing years in France, probably in Clermont, where he could occupy a chair in his old college. That seemed the natural thing to do, and he had given it grave consideration. He had half expected to make some such arrangement the last time he was in Auvergne, just before his retirement from his duties as Archbishop. But in the Old World he found himself homesick for the New. It was a feeling he could not explain; a feeling that old age did not weigh so heavily upon a man in New Mexico as in the Puy-de-Dôm.

He loved the towering peaks of his native mountains, the comeliness of the villages, the cleanness of the country-side, the beautiful lines and the cloisters of his own college. Clermont was beautiful,—but he found himself sad there; his heart lay like a stone in his breast. There was too much past, perhaps . . . When the summer wind stirred the lilacs in the old gardens and shook down the blooms of the horse-chestnuts, he sometimes closed his eyes and thought of the high song the wind was singing in the straight, striped pine trees up in the Navajo forests.

During the day his nostalgia wore off, and by dinner-time it was quite gone. He enjoyed his dinner and his wine, and the company of cultivated men, and usually retired in good spirits. It was in the early morning that he felt the ache in his breast; it had something to do with waking in the early morning. It seemed to him that the grey dawn lasted so long here, the country was a long while in coming to life. The gardens and the fields were damp, heavy mists hung in the valley and obscured the mountains; hours went by before the sun could disperse those vapours and warm and purify the villages.

In New Mexico he always awoke a young man; not until he rose and began to shave did he realize that he was growing older. His first consciousness was a sense of the light dry wind blowing in through the windows, with the fragrance of hot sun and sage-brush and sweet clover; a wind that made one's body feel light and one's heart cry "To-day, to-day," like a child's.

Beautiful surroundings, the society of learned men, the charm of noble women, the graces of art, could not make up to him for the loss of those light-hearted mornings of the desert, for that wind that made one a boy again. He had noticed that this peculiar quality in the air of new countries vanished after they were tamed by man and made to bear harvests. Parts of Texas and Kansas that he had first known as open range had since been made into rich farming districts, and the air had quite lost that lightness, that dry aromatic odour. The moisture of plowed land, the heaviness of labour and growth and grain-bearing, utterly destroyed it; one could breathe that only on the bright edges of the world, on the great grass plains or the sage-brush desert.

That air would disappear from the whole earth in time, perhaps; but long after his day. He did not know just when it had become so necessary to him, but he had come back to die in exile for the sake of it. Something soft and wild and free, something that whispered to the ear on the pillow, lightened the heart, softly, softly picked the lock, slid the bolts, and released the prisoned spirit of man into the wind, into the blue and gold, into the morning, into the morning!

4

Father Latour arranged an order for his last days; if routine was necessary to him in health, it was even more so in sickness. Early in the morning Bernard came with hot water, shaved him, and helped him to bathe. They had brought nothing in from the country with them but clothing and linen, and the silver toilet articles the Olivares had given the Bishop so long ago; these thirty years he had washed his hands in that hammered basin. Morning prayers over, Magdalena came with his breakfast, and he sat in his easy-chair while she made his bed and arranged his room. Then he was ready to see visitors. The Archbishop came in for a few moments, when he was at home; the Mother Superior, the American doctor. Bernard read aloud to him the rest of the morning; St. Augustine, or the letters of Madame de Sevigné, or his favourite Pascal.

Sometimes, in the morning hours, he dictated to his young disciple certain facts about the old missions in the diocese; facts which he had come upon by chance and feared would be forgotten. He wished he could do this systematically, but he had not the strength. Those truths and fancies relating to a bygone time would probably be lost; the old legends and customs and superstitions were already dying out. He wished now that long ago he had had the leisure to write them down, that he could have arrested their flight by throwing about them the light and elastic mesh of the French tongue.

He had, indeed, for years, directed the thoughts of the

young priests whom he instructed to the fortitude and devotion of those first missionaries, the Spanish friars; declaring that his own life, when he first came to New Mexico, was one of ease and comfort compared with theirs. If he had used to be abroad for weeks together on short rations, sleeping in the open, unable to keep his body clean, at least he had the sense of being in a friendly world, where by every man's fireside a welcome awaited him.

But the Spanish Fathers who came up to Zuñi, then went north to the Navajos, west to the Hopis, east to all the pueblos scattered between Albuquerque and Taos, they came into a hostile country, carrying little provisionment but their breviary and crucifix. When their mules were stolen by Indians, as often happened, they proceeded on foot, without a change of raiment, without food or water. A European could scarcely imagine such hardships. The old countries were worn to the shape of human life, made into an investiture, a sort of second body, for man. There the wild herbs and the wild fruits and the forest fungi were edible. The streams were sweet water, the trees afforded shade and shelter. But in the alkali deserts the water holes were poisonous, and the vegetation offered nothing to a starving man. Everything was dry, prickly, sharp; Spanish bayonet, juniper, greasewood, cactus; the lizard, the rattlesnake,—and man made cruel by a cruel life. Those early missionaries threw themselves naked upon the hard heart of a country that was calculated to try the endurance of giants. They thirsted in its deserts, starved among its rocks, climbed up and down its terrible canyons on stone-bruised feet, broke long fasts by unclean and repugnant food. Surely these endured *Hunger, Thirst, Cold, Nakedness*, of a kind beyond any conception St. Paul and his brethren could have had. Whatever the early Christians suffered, it all happened in that safe little Mediterranean world, amid the old manners, the old landmarks. If they endured martyrdom, they died among their brethren, their relics were piously preserved, their names lived in the mouths of holy men.

Riding with his Auvergnats to the old missions that had been scenes of martyrdom, the Bishop used to remind them that no man could know what triumphs of faith had happened there, where one white man met torture and death

the terraced peach orchards so dear to them. When they saw
all that was sacred to them laid waste, the Navajos lost heart.
They did not surrender; they simply ceased to fight, and were
taken. Carson was a soldier under orders, and he did a soldier's brutal work. But the bravest of the Navajo chiefs he did
not capture. Even after the crushing defeat of his people in
the Canyon de Chelly, Manuelito was still at large. It was
then that Eusabio came to Santa Fé to ask Bishop Latour to
meet Manuelito at Zuñi. As a priest, the Bishop knew that it
was indiscreet to consent to a meeting with this outlawed
chief; but he was a man, too, and a lover of justice. The request came to him in such a way that he could not refuse it.
He went with Eusabio.

Though the Government was offering a heavy reward for
his person, living or dead, Manuelito rode off his own reser-
vation down into Zuñi in broad daylight, attended by some
dozen followers, all on wretched, half-starved horses. He had
been in hiding out in Eusabio's country on the Colorado
Chiquito.

It was Manuelito's hope that the Bishop would go to Washington and plead his people's cause before they were utterly
destroyed. They asked nothing of the Government, he told
Father Latour, but their religion, and their own land where
they had lived from immemorial times. Their country, he explained, was a part of their religion; the two were inseparable.
The Canyon de Chelly the Padre knew; in that canyon his
people had lived when they were a small weak tribe; it had
nourished and protected them; it was their mother. Moreover, their gods dwelt there—in those inaccessible white
houses set in caverns up in the face of the cliffs, which were
older than the white man's world, and which no living man
had ever entered. Their gods were there, just as the Padre's
God was in his church.

And north of the Canyon de Chelly was the Shiprock, a
slender crag rising to a dizzy height, all alone out on a flat
desert. Seen at a distance of fifty miles or so, that crag presents the figure of a one-masted fishing-boat under full sail,
and the white man named it accordingly. But the Indian has
another name; he believes that rock was once a ship of the air.
Ages ago, Manuelito told the Bishop, that crag had moved

through the air, bearing upon its summit the parents of the Navajo race from the place in the far north where all peoples were made,—and wherever it sank to earth was to be their land. It sank in a desert country, where it was hard for men to live. But they had found the Canyon de Chelly, where there was shelter and unfailing water. That canyon and the Shiprock were like kind parents to his people, places more sacred to them than churches, more sacred than any place is to the white man. How, then, could they go three hundred miles away and live in a strange land?

Moreover, the Bosque Redondo was down on the Pecos, far east of the Rio Grande. Manuelito drew a map in the sand, and explained to the Bishop how, from the very beginning, it had been enjoined that his people must never cross the Rio Grande on the east, or the Rio San Juan on the north, or the Rio Colorado on the west; if they did, the tribe would perish. If a great priest, like Father Latour, were to go to Washington and explain these things, perhaps the Government would listen.

Father Latour tried to tell the Indian that in a Protestant country the one thing a Roman priest could not do was to interfere in matters of Government. Manuelito listened respectfully, but the Bishop saw that he did not believe him. When he had finished, the Navajo rose and said:

"You are the friend of Cristobal, who hunts my people and drives them over the mountains to the Bosque Redondo. Tell your friend that he will never take me alive. He can come and kill me when he pleases. Two years ago I could not count my flocks; now I have thirty sheep and a few starving horses. My children are eating roots, and I do not care for my life. But my mother and my gods are in the West, and I will never cross the Rio Grande."

He never did cross it. He lived in hiding until the return of his exiled people. For an unforeseen thing happened:

The Bosque Redondo proved an utterly unsuitable country for the Navajos. It could have been farmed by irrigation, but they were nomad shepherds, not farmers. There was no pasture for their flocks. There was no firewood; they dug mesquite roots and dried them for fuel. It was an alkaline country, and hundreds of Indians died from bad water. At

last the Government at Washington admitted its mistake—
which governments seldom do. After five years of exile, the
remnant of the Navajo people were permitted to go back to
their sacred places.

In 1875 the Bishop took his French architect on a pack trip
into Arizona to show him something of the country before he
returned to France, and he had the pleasure of seeing the Navajo horsemen riding free over their great plains again. The
two Frenchmen went as far as the Canyon de Chelly to be-
hold the strange cliff ruins; once more crops were growing
down at the bottom of the world between the towering sandstone walls; sheep were grazing under the magnificent cottonwoods and drinking at the streams of sweet water; it was like
an Indian Garden of Eden.

Now, when he was an old man and ill, scenes from those
bygone times, dark and bright, flashed back to the Bishop:
the terrible faces of the Navajos waiting at the place on the
Rio Grande where they were being ferried across into exile;
the long streams of survivors going back to their own country, driving their scanty flocks, carrying their old men and
their children. Memories, too, of that time he had spent with
Eusabio on the Little Colorado, in the early spring, when the
lambing season was not yet over,—dark horsemen riding
across the sands with orphan lambs in their arms—a young
Navajo woman, giving a lamb her breast until a ewe was
found for it.

"Bernard," the old Bishop would murmur, "God has been
very good to let me live to see a happy issue to those old
wrongs. I do not believe, as I once did, that the Indian will
perish. I believe that God will preserve him."

8

The American doctor was consulting with Archbishop S——
and the Mother Superior. "It is his heart that is the trouble
now. I have been giving him small doses to stimulate it, but
they no longer have any effect. I scarcely dare increase them;
it might be fatal at once. But that is why you see such a
change in him."

The change was that the old man did not want food, and that he slept, or seemed to sleep, nearly all the time. On the last day of his life his condition was pretty generally known. The Cathedral was full of people all day long, praying for him; nuns and old women, young men and girls, coming and going. The sick man had received the Viaticum early in the morning. Some of the Tesuque Indians, who had been his country neighbours, came into Santa Fé and sat all day in the Archbishop's courtyard listening for news of him; with them was Eusabio the Navajo. Fructosa and Tranquilino, his old servants, were with the supplicants in the Cathedral.

The Mother Superior and Magdalena and Bernard attended the sick man. There was little to do but to watch and pray, so peaceful and painless was his repose. Sometimes it was sleep, they knew from his relaxed features; then his face would assume personality, consciousness, even though his eyes did not open.

Toward the close of day, in the short twilight after the candles were lighted, the old Bishop seemed to become restless, moved a little, and began to murmur; it was in the French tongue, but Bernard, though he caught some words, could make nothing of them. He knelt beside the bed: "What is it, Father? I am here."

He continued to murmur, to move his hands a little, and Magdalena thought he was trying to ask for something, or to tell them something. But in reality the Bishop was not there at all; he was standing in a tip-tilted green field among his native mountains, and he was trying to give consolation to a young man who was being torn in two before his eyes by the desire to go and the necessity to stay. He was trying to forge a new Will in that devout and exhausted priest; and the time was short, for the *diligence* for Paris was already rumbling down the mountain gorge.

When the Cathedral bell tolled just after dark, the Mexican population of Santa Fé fell upon their knees, and all American Catholics as well. Many others who did not kneel prayed in their hearts. Eusabio and the Tesuque boys went quietly away to tell their people; and the next morning the old Archbishop lay before the high altar in the church he had built.

SHADOWS ON THE ROCK

Contents

Vous me demandez des graines de fleurs de ce pays. Nous en faisons venir de France pour notre jardin, n'y en ayant pas ici de fort rares ni de fort belles. Tout y est sauvage, les fleurs aussi bien que les hommes.

Marie de l'Incarnation

(LETTRE À UNE DE SES SŒURS)

Québec, le 12 août, 1653

BOOK ONE

The Apothecary

O NE AFTERNOON late in October of the year 1697, Euclide
 Auclair, the philosopher apothecary of Quebec, stood
on the top of Cap Diamant gazing down the broad, empty
river far beneath him. Empty, because an hour ago the flash
of retreating sails had disappeared behind the green island
that splits the St. Lawrence below Quebec, and the last of the
summer ships from France had started on her long voyage
home.

As long as *La Bonne Espérance* was still in sight, many of
Auclair's friends and neighbours had kept him company on
the hill-top; but when the last tip of white slid behind the
curving shore, they went back to their shops and their kitch-
ens to face the stern realities of life. Now for eight months the
French colony on this rock in the North would be entirely cut
off from Europe, from the world. This was October; not a
sail would come up that wide waterway before next July. No
supplies; not a cask of wine or a sack of flour, no gunpowder,
or leather, or cloth, or iron tools. Not a letter, even—no
news of what went on at home. There might be new wars,
floods, conflagrations, epidemics, but the colonists would
never know of them until next summer. People sometimes
said that if King Louis died, the Minister would send word
by the English ships that came to New York all winter, and
the Dutch traders at Fort Orange would dispatch couriers to
Montreal.

The apothecary lingered on the hill-top long after his fellow
townsmen had gone back to their affairs; for him this sever-
ance from the world grew every year harder to bear. It was a
strange thing, indeed, that a man of his mild and thoughtful
disposition, city-bred and most conventional in his habits,
should be found on a grey rock in the Canadian wilderness.
Cap Diamant, where he stood, was merely the highest ledge
of that fortified cliff which was "Kebec,"—a triangular headland wedged in by the joining of two rivers, and girdled
about by the greater river as by an encircling arm. Directly

little tired. While his daughter was bringing in the roast, Auclair poured a glass of red wine for her and one of white for himself.

"Papa," she said as he began to carve, "what is the earliest possible time that Aunt Clothilde and Aunt Blanche can get our letters?"

Auclair deliberated. Every fall the colonists asked the same question of one another and reckoned it all anew. "Well, if *La Bonne Espérance* has good luck, she can make La Rochelle in six weeks. Of course, it has been done in five. But let us say six; then, if the roads are bad, and they are likely to be in December, we must count on a week to Paris."

"And if she does not have good luck?"

"Ah, then who can say? But unless she meets with very heavy storms, she can do it in two months. With this west wind, which we can always count on, she will get out of the river and through the Gulf very speedily, and that is sometimes the most tedious part of the voyage. When we came over with the Count, we were a month coming from Percé to Quebec. That was because we were sailing against this same autumn wind which will be carrying *La Bonne Espérance* out to sea."

"But surely the aunts will have our letters by New Year's, and then they will know how glad I was of my béret and my jerseys, and how we can hardly wait to open the box upstairs. I can remember my Aunt Blanche a little, because she was young and pretty, and used to play with me. I suppose she is not young now, any more; it is eight years."

"Not young, exactly, but she will always have high spirits. And she is well married, and has three children who are a great joy to her."

"Three little cousins whom I have never seen, and one of them is named for me! Cécile, André, Rachel." She spoke their names softly. These little cousins were almost like playfellows. Their mother wrote such long letters about them that Cécile felt she knew them and all their ways, their individual faults and merits. Cousin Cécile was seven, very studious, *bien sérieuse*, already prepared for confirmation; but she would eat only sweets and highly spiced food. André was five, truthful and courageous, but he bit his nails.

Rachel was a baby, in the midst of teething when they last heard of her.

Cécile would have preferred to live with Aunt Blanche and her children when she should go back to France; but by her mother's wish she was destined for Aunt Clothilde, who had long been a widow of handsome means and was much interested in the education of young girls. The face of this aunt Cécile could never remember, though she could see her figure clearly,—standing against the light, she always seemed to be, a massive woman, short and heavy though not exactly fat,—square, rather, like a great piece of oak furniture; always in black, widow's black that smelled of dye, with gold rings on her fingers and a very white handkerchief in her hand. Cécile could see her head, too, carried well back on a short neck, like a general or a statesman sitting for his portrait; but the face was a blank, just as if the aunt were standing in a doorway with blinding sunlight behind her. Cécile was once more trying to recall that face when her father interrupted her.

"What are we having for dessert tonight, my dear?"

"We have the cream cheese you brought from market yesterday, and whichever conserve you prefer; the plums, the wild strawberries, or the gooseberries."

"Oh, the gooseberries, by all means, after chicken."

"But, Papa, you prefer the gooseberries after almost everything! It is lucky for us we can get all the sugar we want from the Count. Our neighbours cannot afford to make conserves, with sugar so dear. And gooseberries take more than anything else."

"There is something very palatable about the flavour of these gooseberries, a bitter tang that is good for one. At home the gooseberries are much larger and finer, but I have come to like this bitter taste."

"En France nous avons tous les légumes, jusqu'aux dattes," murmured Cécile. She had never seen a date, but she had learned that phrase from a book, when she went to day-school at the Ursulines.

Immediately after dinner the apothecary went into the front shop to post his ledger, while his daughter washed the dishes with the hot water left in an iron kettle on the stove, where the birch-wood fire was now smouldering coals. She had

"would you allow me to speak to the Count? He is kind to children, and I believe he would get Jacques some shoes."

II

That afternoon Cécile ran up the hill with a light heart. She was always glad of a reason for going to the Château,—often slipped into the courtyard merely to see who was on guard duty. Her little friend Giorgio, the drummer boy, was at his post on the steps before the great door, and the moment he saw Cécile he snatched his drumsticks from his trousers pocket and executed a rapid flourish in the air above his drum, making no noise. Cécile laughed, and the boy grinned. This was an old joke, but they still found it amusing. Giorgio was stationed there to announce the arrival of the commanding officer, and of all distinguished persons, by a flourish on his drum. The drum-call echoed amazingly in the empty court, could be heard even in the apothecary shop down the hill, so that one always knew when the Count had visitors.

Cécile told the soldier on duty that she would like to see Picard, the Count's valet, and while she waited for him, she went up the steps to talk with Giorgio and to ask him if his cold were better, and when he had last heard from his mother.

The boy's real name was Georges Million; his family lived over on the Île d'Orléans, and his father was a farmer, Canadian-born. But the old grandfather, who was of course the head of the house, had come from Haute-Savoie as a drummer in the Carignan-Salières regiment. He played the Alpine horn as well, and still performed on the flute at country weddings. This grandson, Georges, took after him,—was musical and wanted nothing in the world but a soldier's life. When he was fifteen, he came into Quebec and begged the Governor to let him enter the native militia. He was very small for his age, but he was a good-looking boy, and the Count took him on as a drummer until he should grow tall enough to enlist. He put him into a blue coat, high boots, and a three-cornered hat, and stationed him at the door to welcome visitors. For some reason the Count always called him Giorgio, and that had become his name in Quebec.

Giorgio's life was monotonous; his duties were to keep clean and trim, and to stand perfectly idle in a draughty court-yard for hours at a time. There were very few distinguished persons in Quebec, and not all of those were on calling terms with Count Frontenac. The Intendant, de Champigny, came to the Château when it was necessary, but his relations with the Count were formal rather than cordial. Sometimes, in-deed, he brought Madame de Champigny with him, and when they rolled up in their *carrosse*, Giorgio had a great op-portunity. Old Bishop Laval, who would properly have been announced by the drum, had not crossed the threshold of the Château for years. The new Bishop had called but twice since his return from France. Dollier de Casson, Superior of the Sulpician Seminary at Montreal, was a person to be greeted by the drum, and so was Jacques Le Ber, the rich merchant. Sometimes Daniel du Lhut, the explorer in command of Fort Frontenac, came to Quebec, and, very rarely, Henri de Tonti,—that one-armed hero who had an iron hook in place of a hand. For all Indian chiefs and messengers, too, Giorgio could beat his drum long and loud. This form of welcome was very gratifying to the savages. But often the days passed one after another when the drummer had no one to salute but the officers of the fort, and life was very dull for him.

When a friendly soldier was on guard, Cécile would often run in to give the drummer boy some cardamon seeds or raisins from her father's shop, and to gossip with him for a while. This afternoon their talk was cut short by the arrival of the Count's valet, through whom one approached his master. Picard had been with the Count since the Turkish wars, and Cécile had known him ever since she could remember. He took her by the hand and led her into the Château and upstairs to the Count's private apartment in the south wing.

The apartment was of but two rooms, a dressing-cabinet and a long room with windows on two sides, which was both chamber and study. The Governor was seated at a writing-table in the south end, a considerable distance from his fire-place and his large curtained bed. He was nearly eighty years old, but he had changed very little since Cécile could remem-ber him, except that his teeth had grown yellow. He still walked, rode, struck, as vigorously as ever, and only two years ago he had gone hundreds of miles into the wilderness on one of the hardest Indian campaigns of his life. When Picard spoke to him, he laid down his pen, beckoned Cécile with a long forefinger, put his arm about her familiarly, and drew her close to his side, inquiring about her health and her father's. As he talked to her, his eyes took on a look of uneasy, mocking playfulness, with a slightly sarcastic curl of the lips. Cécile was not afraid of him. He had always been one of the important figures in her life; when she was little she used to like to sit on his knee, because he wore such white linen, and satin waistcoats with jewelled buttons. He took great care of his person when he was at home. Nothing annoyed him so much as his agent's neglecting to send him his supply of lavender-water by the first boat in the spring. It vexed him more than a sharp letter from the Minister, or even from the King.

After replying to his courtesies Cécile began at once:

"Monsieur le Comte, you know little Jacques Gaux, the son of La Grenouille?"

The old soldier nodded and sniffed, drooping the lid slightly over one eye, — an expression of his regard for a large class of women. She understood.

"But he is a good little boy, Monsieur le Comte, and he cannot help it about his mother. You know she neglects him, and just now he is very badly off for shoes. I am knitting him some stockings, but the shoes we cannot manage."

"And if I were to give you an order on the cobbler? That is soon done. It is very nice of you to knit stockings for him. Do you knit your own?"

"Of course, monsieur! And my father's."

The old Count looked at her from out his deep eye-sockets, and felt for the hard spots on her palm. "You are content down there, keeping house for your father? Not much time for play, I take it?"

"Oh, everything we do, my father and I, is a kind of play."

He gave a dry chuckle. "Well said! Everything we do is. It gets rather tiresome, — but not at your age, perhaps. I am very well pleased with you, Cécile, because you do so well for your father. We have too many idle girls in Kebec, and I cannot say that Kebec is exceptional. I have been about the world a great deal, and I have found only one country where the women like to work,—in Holland. They have made an ugly country very pretty." He slipped a piece of money into her hand. "That is for your charities. Get the frog's son what he needs, and Picard will give Noël Pommier an order for his shoes. And is there nothing you would like for yourself? I have never forgot what a brave sailor you were on the voyage over. You cried only once, and that was when we were coming into the Gulf, and a bird of prey swooped down and carried off a little bird that perched on one of our yardarms. I wish I had some sweetmeats; you do not often pay me a visit."

"Perhaps you would let me look at your glass fruit," Cécile suggested.

The Count got up and led her to the mantelpiece. Between the tall silver candlesticks stood a crystal bowl full of glowing fruits of coloured glass: purple figs, yellow-green grapes with gold vine-leaves, apricots, nectarines, and a dark citron stuck up endwise among the grapes. The fruits were hollow, and the light played in them, throwing coloured reflections into the mirror and upon the wall above.

"That was a present from a Turkish prisoner whose life I spared when I was holding the island of Crete," the Count told her. "It was made by the Saracens. They blow it into those shapes while the glass is melted. Every piece is hollow; that is why they look alive. Here in Canada it reminds one of the South. You admire it?"

"More than anything I have ever seen," said Cécile fervently.

He laughed. "I like it myself, or I should not have taken so much trouble to bring it over. I think I must leave it to you in my will."

"Oh, thank you, monsieur, but it is quite enough to look at it; one would never forget it. It is much lovelier than real fruit." She curtsied and thanked him again and went out softly to where Picard was waiting for her in the hall. She wished that she could some time go there when the Count was away, and look as long as she pleased at the glass fruit and at the tapestries on the walls of the long room. They were

"It will not keep you awake, as it did the first time I told you? We must not grieve about these things that happened long ago,—and this happened when the Count was in Canada the first time, while your grandfather and grandmother were both living.

"Poor old Bichet had lodged in our cellar since I was a boy. He was a knife-grinder and used to go out every day with his wheel on his back, and he picked up a few sous at his trade. But he could never have kept himself in shoes, having to walk so much, if your grandfather had not given him his old ones. He paid us nothing for his lodging, of course. He had his bed on the floor in a dry corner of our cellar, where the sirops and elixirs were kept. In very cold weather your grandmother would put a couple of bricks among the coals when she was getting supper, and old Bichet would take these hot bricks down and put them in his bed. And she often saved a cup of hot soup and a piece of bread for the old man and let him eat them in the warm kitchen, for he was very neat and cleanly. When I had any spending-money, or when I was given a fee for carrying medicines to some house in the neighbourhood, I always saved a little for the old knife-grinder. He was reserved and uncomplaining and never inflicted his troubles upon us, though he must have had many. On Saturdays, when your grandmother cooked a joint and had a big fire, she used to heat a kettle of water for him, and he carried it down to his corner and washed himself. He was a Christian and went to mass. He was a kind man, gentle to creatures below him,—for there were those even worse off.

"Now, on the rue du Figuier stood a house that had long been closed, for the family had gone to live at Fontainebleau, and the empty coach-house was used as a store-room for old pieces of furniture. The care-taker was a careless fellow who went out to drink with his cronies and left the place unguarded. In the coach-house were two brass kettles which had lain there for many years, doing nobody any good. Bichet must have seen them often, as he went in and out to sharpen the care-taker's carving-knife.

"One night, when this fellow was carousing, Bichet carried off those two pots. He took them to an iron-monger and sold them. Nobody would ever have missed them; but Bichet had an enemy. Near us there lived a degenerate, half-witted boy of a cruel disposition. He tortured street cats, and even sparrows when he could catch them. Old Bichet had more than once caught him at his tricks and reproved him and set his victims at liberty. That boy was cunning, and he used to spy on Bichet. He saw him carrying off those brass kettles and reported him to the police. Bichet was seized in the street, when he was out with his grindstone, and taken to the Châtelet. He confessed at once and told where he had sold the pots. But that was not enough for the officers; they put him to torture and made him confess to a lifetime of crime; to having stolen from us and from the Frontenac house—which he had never done.

"Your grandfather and I hurried to the prison to speak for him. Your grandfather told them that a man so old and infirm would admit anything under fright and anguish, not knowing what he said; that a confession obtained under torture was not true evidence. This infuriated the Judge. If we would take oath that the prisoner had never stolen anything from us, they would put him into the strappado again and make him correct his confession. We saw that the only thing we could do for our old lodger was to let him pass quickly. Luckily for Bichet, the prison was overcrowded, and he was hanged the next morning.

"Your grandmother never got over it. She had for a long while struggled with asthma every winter, and that year when the asthma came on, she ceased to struggle. She said she had no wish to live longer in a world where such cruelties could happen."

"And I am like my grandmother," cried Cécile, catching her father's hand. "I do not want to live there. I had rather stay in Quebec always! Nobody is tortured here, except by the Indians, in the woods, and they know no better. But why does the King allow such things, when they tell us he is a kind King?"

"It is not the King, my dear, it is the Law. The Law is to protect property, and it thinks too much of property. A couple of brass pots, an old saddle, are reckoned worth more than a poor man's life. Christ would have forgiven Bichet, as He did the thief on the cross. We must think of him in

beautiful part of the afternoon. They thought they would like
to go down once more. With a quick push-off their sled shot
down through constantly changing colour; deeper and deeper
into violet, blue, purple, until at the bottom it was almost
black. As they climbed up again, they watched the last flames
of orange light burn off the high points of the rock. The slender spire of the Récollet chapel, up by the Château, held the
gleam longest of all.

Cécile saw that Jacques was cold. They were not far from
Noël Pommier's door, so she said they would go in and get
warm.

The cobbler had pulled his bench close to the window and
was making the most of the last daylight. Cécile begged him
not to get up.

"We have only come in to get warm, Monsieur Pommier."

"Very good. You know the way. Come here, my boy, let me
see whether your shoes keep the snow out." He reached for
Jacques's foot, felt the leather, and nodded. Cécile passed into
the room behind the shop, called to Madame Pommier in her
kitchen, and asked if they might sit by her fire.

"Certainly, my dear, find a chair. And little Jacques may
have my footstool; it is just big enough for him. Noël," she
called, "come put some wood on the fire, these children are
frozen." She came in bringing two squares of maple sugar—
and a towel for Jacques to wipe his fingers on. He took the
sugar and thanked her, but she saw that his eyes were fixed
upon a dark corner of the room where a little copper lamp
was burning before some coloured pictures. "That is my
chapel, Jacques. You see, being lame, I do not get to mass very
often, so I have a little chapel of my own, and the lamp burns
night and day, like the sanctuary lamp. There is the Holy
Mother and Child, and Saint Joseph, and on the other side are
Sainte Anne and Saint Joachim. I am especially devoted to the
Holy Family."

Drawn out by something in her voice, Jacques ventured a
question.

"Is that why this is called Holy Family Hill, madame?"

Madame Pommier laughed and stooped to pat his head.
"Quite the other way about, my boy! I insisted upon living

here because the hill bore that name. My husband was for settling in the Basse Ville, thinking it would be better for his trade. But we have not starved here; those for whom the street was named have looked out for us, maybe. When we first came to this country, I was especially struck by the veneration in which the Holy Family was held in Kebec, and I found it was so all out through the distant parishes. I never knew its like at home. Monseigneur Laval himself has told me that there is no other place in the world where the people are so devoted to the Holy Family as here in our own Canada. It is something very special to us."

Cécile liked to think they had things of their own in Canada. The martyrdoms of the early Church which she read about in her *Lives of the Saints* never seemed to her half so wonderful or so terrible as the martyrdoms of Father Brébeuf, Father Lalemant, Father Jogues, and their intrepid companions. To be thrown into the Rhone or the Moselle, to be decapitated at Lyon,—what was that to the tortures the Jesuit missionaries endured at the hands of the Iroquois, in those savage, interminable forests? And could the devotion of Sainte Geneviève or Sainte Philomène be compared to that of Mother Catherine de Saint-Augustin or Mother Marie de l'Incarnation?

"My child, I believe you are sleepy," said Madame Pommier presently, when both her visitors had been silent a long while. She liked her friends to be entertaining.

Cécile started out of her reverie. "No, madame, but I was thinking of a surprise I have at home, and perhaps I had better tell you about it now. You remember my Aunt Clothilde? I am sure my mother often talked to you of her. Last summer she sent me a box on *La Licorne*: a large wooden box, with a letter telling me not to open it. We must not open it until the day before Christmas, because it is a crèche; so, you see, we shall have a Holy Family, too. And we have been hoping that on Christmas Eve, before the midnight mass, Monsieur Noël will bring you to see it. You have not been in our house, you know, since my mother died."

"Noël, my son, what do you say to that?"

The cobbler had come in from the shop to light his candle at the fire.

"The invitation is for you too, Monsieur Noël, from my father."

The cobbler smiled and stood with the stump of candle in his hand before bending down to the blaze.

"That can be managed, and my thanks to monsieur your father. If there is snow, I will push my mother down in her sledge, and if the ground is naked, I will carry her on my back. She is no great weight."

"I shall like to see the inside of your house again, Cécile. I miss it. I have not been there since that time when your mother was ill, and Madame de Champigny sent her carriage to convey me."

Cécile remembered the time very well. It was after old Madame Pommier was crippled; Madame Auclair had long been too ill to leave the house. There was then only one closed carriage in Quebec, and that belonged to Madame de Champigny, wife of the Intendant. In some way she heard that the apothecary's sick wife longed to see her old friend, and she sent her *carrosse* to take Madame Pommier to the Auclairs'. It was a mark of the respect in which the cobbler and his mother were held in the community.

When Jacques and Cécile ran out into the cold again, from the houses along the tilted street the evening candlelight was already shining softly. Up at the top of the hill, behind the Cathedral, that second afterglow, which often happens in Quebec, had come on more glorious than the first. All the western sky, which had been hard and clear when the sun sank, was now throbbing with fiery vapours, like rapids of clouds; and between, the sky shone with a blue to ravish the heart,—that limpid, celestial, holy blue that is only seen when the light is golden.

"Are you tired, Jacques?"

"A little, my legs are," he admitted.

"Get on the sled and I will pull you up. See, there's the evening star—how near it looks! Jacques, don't you love winter?" She put the sled-rope under her arms, gave her weight to it, and began to climb. A feeling came over her that there would never be anything better in the world for her than this; to be pulling Jacques on her sled, with the tender, burning sky before her, and on each side, in the dusk, the kindly lights from neighbours' houses. If the Count should go back with the ships next summer, and her father with him, how could she bear it, she wondered. On a foreign shore, in a foreign city (yes, for her a foreign shore), would not her heart break for just this? For this rock and this winter, this feeling of being in one's own place, for the soft content of pulling Jacques up Holy Family Hill into paler and paler levels of blue air, like a diver coming up from the deep sea.

VIII

On the morning of the twenty-fourth of December Cécile lay snug in her trundle-bed, while her father lit the fires and pre- pared the chocolate. Although the heavy red curtains had not yet been drawn back, she knew that it was snowing; she had heard the crunch of fresh snow under the Pigeon boy's feet when he brought the morning loaf to the kitchen door. Even before that, when the bell rang for five o'clock mass, she knew by its heavy, muffled tone that the air was thick with snow and that it was not very cold. Whenever she heard the early bell, it was as if she could see the old Bishop with his lantern at the end of the bell-rope, and the cold of the church up there made her own bed seem the warmer and softer. In winter the old man usually carried a little basin as well as his lantern. It was his custom to take the bowl of holy water from the font in the evening, carry it into his kitchen, and put it on the back of the stove, where enough warmth would linger through the night to keep it from freezing. Then, in the morning, those who came to early mass would not have a mere lump of ice to peck at. Monseigneur de Laval was very particular about the consecrated oils and the holy water; it was not enough for him that people should merely go through the forms.

Cécile did not always waken at the first bell, which rang in the coldest hour of the night, but when she did, she felt a peculiar sense of security, as if there must be powerful protec- tion for Kebec in such steadfastness, and the new day, which was yet darkness, was beginning as it should. The punctual bell and the stern old Bishop who rang it began an orderly procession of activities and held life together on the rock, though the winds lashed it and the billows of snow drove over it.

With the sound of the crackling fire a cool, mysterious fragrance of the forest, very exciting because it was under a roof, came in from the kitchen,—the breath of all the fir boughs and green moss that Cécile and Blinker had brought in yesterday from the Jesuits' wood. Today they would unpack the crèche from France,—the box that had come on *La Licorne* in midsummer and had lain upstairs unopened for all these months.

Auclair brought the chocolate and placed it on a little table beside his daughter's bed. They always breakfasted like this in winter, while the house was getting warm. This morning they had finally to decide where they would set out the crèche. Weeks ago they had agreed to arrange it in the deep window behind the sofa,—but then the sofa would have to be put on the other side of the room! This morning they found the thought of moving the sofa, where Madame Auclair used so often to recline, unendurable. It would quite destroy the harmony of their salon. The room, the house indeed, seemed to cling about that sofa as a centre.

There was another window in the room,—seldom uncurtained, because it opened directly upon the side wall of the baker's house, and the outlook was uninteresting. It was narrow, but Auclair said he could remedy that. As soon as his shop was put in order, he would construct a shelf in front of the window-sill, but a little lower; then the scene could be arranged in two terraces, as was customary at home.

Cécile spent the morning covering the window and the new shelf with moss and fir branches until it looked like a corner in the forest, and at noon she waylaid Blinker, just getting up from his bed behind the baker's ovens, and sent him to go and hunt for Jacques.

When Blinker returned with the boy, he himself looked in through the door so wistfully that Cécile asked him to come and open the box for her in the kitchen. There were a great number of little figures in the crate, each wrapped in a sheath of straw. As Blinker took them one at a time out of the straw and handed them to Cécile, he kept exclaiming: "Regardez,

ma'm'selle, un beau petit âne!" . . . "Voilà, le beau mouton!"
Cécile had never seen him come so far out of his shell; she
had supposed that his shrinking sullenness was a part of
him, like his crooked eyes or his red hair. When all the figures
were unwrapped and placed on the dining-table in the salon,
Blinker gathered up the straw and carried it with the crate
into the cellar. She had thought that would be the last of him,
but when he came back and stood again in the doorway, she
hadn't the heart to send him away. She asked him to come in
and sit down by the fire. Her mother had never done that,
but today there seemed no way out of it. The fête which she
meant so especially for Jacques, turned out to be even more
for Blinker.

Jacques, indeed, was so bewildered as to seem apathetic,
and was afraid to touch anything. Only when Cécile directed
him would he take up one of the figures from the table and
carry it carefully to the window where she was making the
scene. The Holy Family must be placed first, under a little
booth of fir branches. The Infant was not in His Mother's
arms, of course, but lay rosy and naked in a little straw-lined
manger, in which he had crossed the ocean. The Blessed Virgin wore no halo, but a white scarf over her head. She looked
like a country girl, very naïve, seated on a stool, with her
knees well apart under her full skirt, and very large feet. Saint
Joseph, a grave old man in brown, with a bald head and wrinkled brow, was placed opposite her, and the ox and the ass
before the manger.

"Those are all that go inside the stable," Cécile explained,
"except the two angels. We must put them behind the manger; they are still watching over Him."

"Is that the stable, Cécile? I think it's too pretty for a stable," Jacques observed.

"It's a little *cabine* of branches, like those the first missionaries built down by Notre Dame des Anges, when they
landed here long ago. They used to say the mass in a little
shelter like that, made of green fir boughs."

Jacques touched one of the unassorted figures on the table
with the tip of his finger. "Cécile, what are those animals?"

"Why, those are the camels, Jacques. Did you never see

hear you! There are so many sacred relics, and they are always working cures."

"The sacred relics are all very well, my dear, and I do not deny that they work miracles,—but not through the digestive tract. Mother de Saint-Augustin meant well, but she made a mistake. If she had given her heretic a little more ground bone, she might have killed him."

"Are you sure?"

"I think it probable. It is true that in England, in every apothecary shop, there is a jar full of pulverized human skulls, and that terrible powder is sometimes dispensed in small doses for certain diseases. Even in France it is still to be found in many pharmacies; but it was never sold in our shop, not even in my grandfather's time. He had seen a proof made of that remedy. A long while ago, when Henry of Navarre was besieging Paris, the people held out against him until they starved by hundreds. I have heard my grandfather tell of things too horrible to repeat to you. The famine grew until there was no food at all; people killed each other for a morsel. The bakers shut their shops; there was not a handful of flour left, they had used all the forage meant for beasts; they had made bread of hay and straw, and now that was all gone. Then some of the starving went to the cemetery of the Inno- cents, where there was a great wall of dry bones, and they ground those bones to powder and made a paste of it and baked it in ovens; and as many as ate of that bread died in agony, as if they had swallowed poison. Indeed, they had swallowed poison."

"But those were ordinary bones, maybe bones of wicked people. That would be different."

"No bones are good to be taken into the stomach, Cécile. God did not intend it. The relics of the saints may work cures at the touch, they may be a protection worn about the neck; those things are outside of my knowledge. But I am the guardian of the stomach, and I would not permit a patient to swallow a morsel of any human remains, not those of Saint Peter himself. There are enough beautiful stories about Mother de Saint-Augustin, but this one is not to my liking."

Cécile could only hope it would never happen that her father and Mother Juschereau would enter into any discussion of miraculous cures. Her father must be right; but she felt in her heart that what Mother Juschereau told her had certainly occurred, and the English sailor had been converted by Father Brébeuf's bone.

III

"Ma'm'selle, have you heard the news from Montreal?"

Blinker had just come in for his soup, and Cécile saw that he was greatly excited.

No, she had heard nothing; what did he mean?

"Ma'm'selle, there has been a miracle at Montreal. The recluse has had a visit from the angels,—the night after Epiphany, when there was the big snow-storm. That day she broke her spinning-wheel, and in the night two angels came to her cell and mended it for her. She saw them."

"How did you hear this, Blinker?"

"Some men got in from Montreal this morning, in dog-sledges, and they brought the word. They brought letters, too, for the Reverend Mother at the Ursulines'. If you go there, you will likely hear all about it."

"You are sure she saw the angels?"

He nodded. "Yes, when she got up to pray, at midnight. They say her wheel was mended better than a carpenter could do it."

"The men didn't say which angels, Blinker?"

He shook his head. He was just beginning his soup. Cécile dropped into one of the chairs by the table. "Why, one of them might have been Saint Joseph himself; he was a carpenter. But how was it she saw them? You know she keeps her spinning-wheel up in her work-room, over the cell where she sleeps."

"Just so, ma'm'selle, it is just so the men said. She goes into the church to pray every night at midnight, and when she got up on Epiphany night, she saw a light shining from the room overhead, and she went up her little stair to see what was the matter, and there she found the angels."

"Did they speak to her?"

"The men did not say. Maybe the Reverend Mother will know."

"I will go there tomorrow, and I will tell you everything I hear. It's a wonderful thing to happen, so near us—and in that great snow-storm! Don't you like to know that the angels are just as near to us here as they are in France?"

Blinker turned his head, glancing all about the kitchen as if someone might be hiding there, leaned across the table, and said to her in such a mournful way:

"Ma'm'selle, I think they are nearer."

When he had drunk his little glass and gone away for the last time, Cécile went in and told her father the good news from Montreal. He listened with polite interest, but she had of late begun to feel that his appreciation of miracles was not at all what it should be. They were reading Plutarch this winter, and tonight they were in the middle of the life of Alexander the Great, but her thoughts strayed from the text. She made so many mistakes that her father said she must be tired, and, gently taking the book from her, continued the reading himself.

Later, while she was undressing, her father filled the kitchen stove with birch logs to hold the heat well through the night. He blew out the candles, and himself got ready for bed. After he had put on his night-cap and disappeared behind his curtains, Cécile, who had feigned to be asleep, turned over softly to watch the dying fire, and with a sigh abandoned herself to her thoughts. In her mind she went over the whole story of the recluse of Montreal.

Jeanne Le Ber, the recluse, was the only daughter of Jacques Le Ber, the richest merchant of Montreal. When she was twelve years old, her parents had brought her to Quebec and placed her in the Ursuline convent to receive her education. She remained here three years, and that was how she belonged to Quebec as well as to Ville-Marie de Montréal. Sister Anne de Sainte-Rose saw at once that this pupil had a very unusual nature, though her outward demeanour was merely that of a charming young girl. The Sister had told Cécile that in those days Jeanne was never melancholy, but warm and ardent, like her complexion; gracious in her manner, and not at all shy. She was at her ease with strangers,—all distinguished visitors to Montreal were entertained at her father's house. But underneath this exterior of pleasing girlhood,

Sister Anne felt something reserved and guarded. While she was at the convent, Jeanne often received gifts and attentions from her father's friends in Quebec; and from home, boxes of sweets and dainties. But everything that was sent her she gave away to her schoolmates, so tactfully that they did not realize she kept nothing for herself.

Jeanne completed her studies at the convent, returned home to Montreal, and was in a manner formally introduced to the world there. Her father was fond of society and lavish in hospitality; proud of his five sons, but especially devoted to his only daughter. He loved to see her in rich apparel, and selected the finest stuffs brought over from France for her. Jeanne wore these clothes to please him, but whenever she put on one of her gay dresses, she wore underneath it a little haircloth shirt next her tender skin.

Soon after Jeanne's return from school her father and uncle gave to the newly-completed parish church of Montreal a rich lamp of silver, made in France, to burn perpetually before the Blessed Sacrament. The Le Bers' house on Saint Paul street was very near the church, and from the window of her upstairs bedroom Jeanne could see at night the red spark of the sanctuary lamp showing in the dark church. When everyone was asleep and the house was still, it was her custom to kneel beside her casement and pray, the while watching that spot of light. *"I will be that lamp,"* she used to whisper. *"I will be that lamp; that shall be my life."*

Jacques Le Ber announced that his daughter's dowry would be fifty thousand gold écus, and there were many pretendants for her hand. Cécile had often heard it said that the most ardent and most favoured of these was Auclair's friend Pierre Charron, who still lived next door to the Le Bers in Montreal. He had been Jeanne's playfellow in childhood.

Jeanne's shining in the *beau monde* of Ville-Marie de Montréal was brief. For her the only real world lay within convent walls. She begged to be allowed to take the vows, but her father's despair overcame her wish. Even her spiritual directors, and that noble soldier-priest Dollier de Casson, Superior of the Sulpician Seminary, advised her against taking a step so irrevocable. She at last obtained her parents' consent to imitate the domestic retreat of Sainte Catherine of Siena, and at seventeen took the vow of chastity for five years and immured herself within her own chamber in her father's house. In her vigils she could always look out at the dark church, with the one constant lamp which generous Jacques Le Ber had placed there, little guessing how it might affect his life and wound his heart.

Upon her retirement Jeanne had explained to her family that during the five years of her vow she must on no account speak to or hold communication with them. Her desire was for the absolute solitariness of the hermit's life, the solitude which Sainte Marie l'Égyptienne had gone into the desert of the Thebais to find. Her parents did not believe that a young girl, affectionate and gentle from her infancy, could keep so harsh a rule. But as time went on, their hearts grew heavier. From the day she took her vow, they never had speech with her or saw her face, — never saw her bodily form, except veiled and stealing down the stairway like a shadow on her way to mass. Jacques Le Ber no longer gave suppers on feast-days. He stayed more and more in his counting-room, drove about in his sledge in winter, and cruised in his sloop in summer; avoided the house that had become the tomb of his hopes.

Before her withdrawal Jeanne had chosen an old serving-woman, exceptional for piety, to give her henceforth such service as was necessary. Every morning at a quarter to five this old dame went to Jeanne's door and attended her to church to hear early mass. Many a time Madame Le Ber concealed herself in the dark hallway to see her daughter's muffled figure go by. After the return from mass, the same servant brought Jeanne her food for the day. If any dish of a rich or delicate nature was brought her, she did not eat it, but fasted.

She went always to vespers, and to the high mass on Sundays and feast-days. On such occasions people used to come in from the neighbouring parishes for a glimpse of that slender figure, the richest heiress in Canada, clad in grey serge, kneeling on the floor near the altar, while her family, in furs and velvet, sat in chairs in another part of the church.

At the end of five years Jeanne renewed her vow of seclusion for another five years. During this time her mother died.

On her death-bed she sent one of the household to her daughter's door, begging her to come and give her the kiss of farewell.

"Tell her I am praying for her, night and day," was the answer.

When she had been immured within her father's house for almost ten years, Jeanne was able to accomplish a cherished hope; she devoted that *dot*, which no mortal man would ever claim, to build a chapel for the Sisters of the Congregation of the Blessed Virgin. Behind the high altar of this chapel she had a cell constructed for herself. At a solemn ceremony she took the final vows and entered that cell from which she would never come forth alive. Since that time she had been known as la recluse de Ville-Marie.

Jeanne's entombment and her cell were the talk of the province, and in the country parishes where not much happened, still, after two years, furnished matter for conversation and wonder. The cell, indeed, was not one room, but three, one above another, and within them the solitaire carried on an unvarying routine of life. In the basement cubicle was the grille through which she spoke to her confessor, and by means of which she was actually present at mass and vespers, though unseen. There, through a little window, her meagre food was handed to her. The room above was her sleeping-chamber, constructed by the most careful measurements for one purpose; her narrow bed against the wall was directly behind the high altar, and her pillow, when she slept, was only a few inches from the Blessed Sacrament on the other side of the partition.

The upper cell was her atelier, and there she made and embroidered those beautiful altar-cloths and vestments which went out from her stone chamber to churches all over the province: to the Cathedral at Quebec, and to the poor country parishes where the altar and its ministrant were alike needy. She had begun this work years before, in her father's house, and had grown very skilful at it. Old Bishop Laval, so sumptuous in adorning his Cathedral, had more than once expressed admiration for her beautiful handiwork. When her eyes were tired, or when the day was too dark for embroidering, she spun yarn and knitted stockings for the poor.

In her work-room there was a small iron stove with a heap of faggots, and in the most severe cold of winter the recluse lit a little fire, not for bodily comfort, but because her fingers became stiff with the cold and lost their cunning,—indeed, there were sometimes days on which they would actually have frozen at their task. Every night at midnight, winter and summer, Jeanne rose from her cot, dressed herself, descended into her basement room, opened the grille, and went into the church to pray for an hour before the high altar. On bitter nights many a kind soul in Montreal (and on the lonely farms, too) lay awake for a little, listening to the roar of the storm, and wondered how it was with the recluse, under her single coverlid.

She bore the summer's heat as patiently as the winter's cold. Only last July, when the heat lay so heavy in her chamber with its one small window, her confessor urged her to quit her cell for an hour each day after sunset and take the air in the cloister garden, which her window looked out upon.

She replied: *Ah, mon père, ma chambre est mon paradis terrestre; c'est mon centre; c'est mon élément. Il n'y a pas de lieu plus délicieux, ni plus salutaire pour moi; point de Louvre, point de palais, qui me soit plus agréable. Je préfère ma cellule à tout le reste de l'univers.*

For long after the night when Cécile first heard of the angels' visit to Mademoiselle Le Ber, the story was a joy to her. She told it over and over to little Jacques on his rare visits. Throughout February the weather was so bad that Jacques could come only when Blinker (who was always a match for 'Toinette) went down and brought him up Mountain Hill on his back. The snows fell one upon another until the houses were muffled, the streets like tunnels. Between the storms the weather was grey, with armies of dark clouds moving across the wide sky, and the bitter wind always blowing. Quebec seemed shrunk to a mere group of shivering spires; the whole rock looked like one great white church, above the frozen river.

By many a fireside the story of Jeanne Le Ber's spinning-wheel was told and re-told with loving exaggeration during that severe winter. The word of her visit from the angels went abroad over snow-burdened Canada to the remote parishes. Wherever it went, it brought pleasure, as if the recluse herself had sent to all those families whom she did not know some living beauty,—a blooming rose-tree, or a shapely fruit-tree in fruit. Indeed, she sent them an incomparable gift. In the long evenings, when the family had told over their tales of Indian massacres and lost hunters and the almost human intelligence of the beaver, someone would speak the name of Jeanne Le Ber, and it again gave out fragrance.

The people have loved miracles for so many hundred years, not as proof or evidence, but because they are the actual flowering of desire. In them the vague worship and devotion of the simple-hearted assumes a form. From being a shapeless longing, it becomes a beautiful image; a dumb rapture becomes a melody that can be remembered and repeated; and the experience of a moment, which might have been a lost ecstasy, is made an actual possession and can be bequeathed to another.

IV

One night in March there was a knock at the apothecary's door, just as he was finishing his dinner. Only sick people, or strangers who were ignorant of his habits, disturbed him at that hour. Peeping out between the cabinets, Cécile saw that the visitor was a thick-set man in moccasins, with a bearskin coat and cap. His long hair and his face covered with beard told that he had come in from the woods.

"Don't you remember me, Monsieur Auclair?" he asked in a low, sad voice. "I am Antoine Frichette; you used to know me."

"It is your beard that changes you, Antoine. Sit down."

"Ah, it is more than that," the man sighed.

"Besides, I thought you were in the Montreal country,— out from the Sault Saint-Louis, wasn't it?"

"Yes, monsieur, I went out there, but I had no luck. My brother-in-law died in the woods, and I got a strain that made me no good, so I came back to live with my sister until I am cured."

"Your brother-in-law? Not Michel Proulx, surely? I am grieved to hear that, Antoine. He cannot well be spared here. We have few such good workmen."

"But you see, monsieur, no building goes on in Kebec in the winter, and there was the chance to make something in the woods. But he is dead, and I am not much better. I got down from Montreal only today,—we had a hard fight coming in this snow. I came to you because I am a sick man. I tore something loose inside me. Look, monsieur, can you do anything for that?" He stood up and unbuttoned his bearskin jacket. A rupture, Auclair saw at once,—and for a woodsman that was almost like a death-sentence.

Yes, he told Frichette, he could certainly do something for him. But first they would be seated more comfortably, and have a talk. He took the poor fellow back into the sitting-room and gave him his own arm-chair by the fire.

"This is my daughter, Cécile, Antoine; you remember her. Now I will give you something to make you feel better at once. This is a very powerful cordial, there are many healing herbs in it, and it will reach the sorest spot in a sick man. Drink it slowly, and then you must tell me about your bad winter."

The woodsman took the little glass between his thick fingers and held it up to the fire-light. *"C'est jolie, la couleur,"* he observed childishly. Presently he slid off his fur jacket and sat in his buckskin shirt and breeches. When he had finished the cordial, his host filled his glass again, and Antoine sighed and looked about him. *"C'est tranquille, chez vous, comme toujours,"* he said with a faint smile. "I bring you a message, monsieur, from Father Hector Saint-Cyr."

"From Father Hector? You have seen him? Come, Cécile, Antoine is going to tell us news of our friend." Auclair rose and poured a little cordial for himself.

"He said he will be here very soon, God willing, while the river is still hard. He had a letter from the new Bishop telling him to come down to Kebec. He asked me to say that he invited himself to dinner with you. He is a man in a thousand, that priest. We have been through something together. But that is a long story."

"Begin at the beginning, Frichette, my daughter and I have

all evening to listen. So you and Proulx went into the woods, out from the Sault?"

"Yes, we went early in the fall, when the hunting was good, and we took Joseph Choret from Three Rivers. We put by plenty of fish, as soon as it was cold enough to freeze them. We meant to go up into the Nipissing country in the spring, and trade for skins. The Nipissings don't come to the settlements much, and I know a little of their language. We made a good log house in the fall, good enough, but you know what a man my brother-in-law was for hewing; he wasn't satisfied. When the weather kept open, before Christmas, he wanted to put in a board floor. I cannot say how it happened. You know yourself, monsieur, what a man he was with the ax,—he hewed the beams for Notre Dame de la Victoire when he was but a lad, and how many houses in Kebec didn't he hew the beams and flooring for? He could cut better boards with his ax than most men can with a saw. He was not a drinking man, either; never took a glass too much. Very well; one day out there he was hewing boards to floor our shack, and something happens,—the ax slips and lays his leg open from the ankle to the knee. There is a big vein spouting blood, and I catch it and tie it with a deer-gut string I had in my pocket. Maybe that gut was poisoned some way, for the wound went bad very soon. We had no linen, so I dressed it with punk wood, as the Indians do. I boiled pine chips and made turpentine, but it did no good. He got black to the thigh and began to suffer agony. The only thing that eased him was fresh snow heaped on his leg. I don't know if it was right, but he begged for it. After Christmas I saw it was time to get a priest.

"It was three days' journey in to the Sault mission, and the going was bad. There wasn't snow enough for snowshoes,— just enough to cover the roots and trip you. I took my snowshoes and grub-sack on my back, and made good time. The second day I came to a place where the trees were thin because there was no soil, only flint rock, in ledges. And there one big tree, a white pine, had blown over. It hadn't room to fall flat, the top had caught in the branches of another tree, so it lay slanting and made a nice shelter underneath, like a shanty, high enough to stand in. The top was still fresh and green and made thick walls to keep out the wind. I cleared away some of the inside branches and had a good sleep in there. Next morning when I left that place, I notched a few trees as I went, so I could find it when I brought the priest back with me. Ordinarily I don't notch trees to find my way back. When there is no sun, I can tell directions like the Indians."

Here Auclair interrupted him. "And how is that, Antoine?"

Frichette smiled and shrugged. "It is hard to explain,—by many things. The limbs of the trees are generally bigger on the south side, for example. The moss on the trunks is clean and dry on the north side,—on the south side it is softer and maybe a little rotten. There are many little signs; put them all together and they point you right.

"I got to the mission late the third night and slept in a bed. Early the next morning Father Hector was ready to start back with me. He had two young priests there, but he would go himself. He carried his snowshoes and a blanket and the Blessed Sacrament on his back, and I carried the provisions— smoked eels and cold grease—enough for three days. We slept the first night in that shelter under the fallen pine, and made a good start the next day. That was Epiphany, the day of the big snow all over Canada. When we had been out maybe two hours, the snow began to fall so thick we could hardly see each other, and I told Father Hector we better make for that shelter again. It took us nearly all day to get back over the ground we had covered in two hours before the storm began. By God, I was glad to see that thin place in the woods again! I was afraid I'd lost it. There was our tree, heaped over with snow, with the opening to the south still clear. We crept in and got our breath and unrolled our blankets. A little snow had sifted in, but not much. It had packed between the needles of that pine top until it was like a solid wall and roof. It was warm in there; no wind got through. Father Hector said some prayers, and we rolled up in our blankets and slept most of the day and let the storm come.

"Next day it was still snowing hard, and I was afraid to start out. We ate some lard, and an eel apiece, but I could see the end of our provisions pretty soon. We were thirsty and ate the snow, which doesn't satisfy you much. Father Hector said prayers and read his breviary. When I went to sleep, I heard him praying to himself, very low,—and when I wakened he was still praying, just the same. I lay still and listened for a long while, but I didn't once hear an Ave Maria, and not the name of a saint could I make out. At last I turned over and told Father Hector that was certainly a long prayer he was saying. He laughed. 'That's not a prayer, Antoine,' he says; 'that's a Latin poem, a very long one, that I learned at school. If I am uncomfortable, it diverts my mind, and I remember my old school and my comrades.'

" 'So much the better for you, Father,' I told him. 'But a long prayer would do no harm. I don't like the look of things.'

"The next day the snow had stopped, but a terrible bitter wind was blowing. We couldn't have gone against it, but since it was behind us, I thought we'd better get ahead. We hadn't food enough to see us through, as it was. That was a cruel day's march on an empty belly. Father Hector is a good man on snowshoes, and brave, too. My pack had grown lighter, and I wanted to carry his, but he would not have it. When it began to get dark, we made camp and ate some cold grease and the last of our eels. I built a fire, and we took turns, one of us feeding the fire while the other slept. I was so tired I could have slept on into eternity. Father Hector had to throw snow in my face to waken me.

"Before daylight the wind died, but the cold was so bitter we had to move or freeze. It was good snowshoeing that day, but with empty bellies and thirst and eating snow, we both had colic. That night we ate the last of our lard. I wasn't sure we were going right,—the snow had changed the look of everything. When Father Hector took off the little box he carried that held the Blessed Sacrament, I said: 'Maybe that will do for us two, Father. I don't see much ahead of us.'

" 'Never fear, Antoine,' says he, 'while we carry that, Some-one is watching over us. Tomorrow will bring better luck.'

"It did, too, just as he said. We were both so weak we made poor headway. But by the mercy of God we met an Indian. He had a gun, and he had shot two hares. When he saw what a bad way we were in, he made a fire very quick and cooked the hares,—and he ate very little of that meat himself. He

said Indians could bear hunger better than the French. He
was a kind Indian and was glad to give us what he had.
Father Hector could speak his language, and questioned him.
Though I had never seen him before, he knew where our
shack was, and said we were pointed right. But I told him I
was tired out and wanted a guide, and I would pay him well
in shot and powder if he took us in.

"We got back to our shack six days after we left the mission, and they were the six worst days of the winter. My
brother-in-law was very bad. He died while Father Hector
was there, and had a Christian burial. The Indian took Father
Hector back to the mission. Soon after that I got this strain in
my side, and I lost heart. I left our stores for Joseph Choret to
trade with, and I went down to the Sault and then to Montreal. I found a sledge party about to come down the river,
and they brought me to Kebec. Now I am here, what can you
do for me, Monsieur Auclair?"

The apothecary's kindly tone did not reassure Frichette. He
looked searchingly into his face and asked:

"Will it grow back, my inside, like it was?"

Auclair felt very sorry for him. "No, it will not grow back,
Antoine. But tomorrow I will make you a support, and you
will be more comfortable."

"But not to carry canoes over portages, I guess? No? Nor
to go into the woods at all, maybe?" He sank back in the
chair. "Then I don't know how I'll make a living, monsieur. I
am not clever with tools, like my brother-in-law."

"We'll find a way out of that, Antoine."

Frichette did not heed him. "It's a funny thing," he went
on. "A man sits here by the warm fire, where he can hear the
bell ring for mass every morning and smell bread baked fresh
every day, and all that happened out there in the woods seems
like a dream. Yet here I am, no good any more."

"*Courage, mon bourgeois,* I am going to give you a good
medicine."

Frichette shook his head and spread his thick fingers apart
on his knees. "There is no future for me if I cannot paddle a
canoe up the big rivers any more."

"Perhaps you can paddle, Antoine, but not carry."

Antoine rose. "In this world, who paddles must carry, monsieur. Good night, Mademoiselle Cécile. Father Hector will be surprised to see how you have grown. He thinks a great deal about that good dinner you are going to give him, I expect. You ask him if it tastes as good as those hares the Indian cooked for him when he was out with Frichette."

V

Father Hector Saint-Cyr was not long in following his messenger. On the day of his arrival in Kebec he stopped at the apothecary shop, but, Auclair being out, he saw only Cécile, and they arranged that he should come to dinner the following evening.

He came after hearing vespers at the Cathedral, attended to the door of the pharmacy by a group of Seminarians, who always followed him about when he was in town. This was his first meeting with Auclair, and there was a cordial moisture in the priest's eyes as he embraced his old friend and kissed him on both cheeks.

"How many times on my way from Ville-Marie I have enjoyed this moment in anticipation, Euclide," he declared. "Only solitary men know the full joys of friendship. Others have their family; but to a solitary and an exile his friends are everything."

Father Hector was the son of a noted family of Aix-en-Provence; his good breeding and fine presence were by no means lost upon his Indian parishioners at the Sault. The savages, always scornful of meekness and timidity, believed that a man was exactly what he looked. They used Father Hector better than any of his predecessors because he was strong and fearless and handsome. If he was humble before Heaven, he was never so with his converts. He took a high hand with them. If one were drunk or impertinent, he knocked him down. More than once he had given a drunken Indian a good beating, and the Indian had come and thanked him afterwards, telling him he did quite right.

Cécile thought it a great honour to entertain a man like Father Hector at their table, and she was much gratified by his frank enjoyment of everything; of the fish soup with which she had taken such pains, and the wood doves, cooked in a casserole with mushrooms and served with wild rice. Her father had brought up from the cellar a bottle of fine old Burgundy which the Count had sent them for New Year's. She scarcely ate at all herself, for watching their guest.

When Auclair said that this dinner was to make up to Father Hector for the one he missed on Epiphany, he laughed and protested that on Epiphany he had dined very well.

"Smoked eels and cold lard—what more does a man want in the woods? It was on the day following that we began to feel the pinch,—and the next day, and the next. Frichette made a great fuss about it, but certainly it was not the first time either he or I had gone hungry. If one had not been through little experiences of that kind, one would not know how to enjoy a dinner like this." He reached out and put his hand lightly on Cécile's head. "How I wish you could keep her from growing up, Euclide!"

She blushed with joy at the touch of that large, handsome hand which the Indians feared.

"Yes," he went on, looking about him, "these are great occasions in a missionary's life. The next time I am overtaken by a storm in the woods, the recollection of this evening will be food and warmth to me. I shall see it in memory as plainly as I see it now; this room, so like at home, this table with everything as it should be; and, most of all, the feeling of being with one's own kind. How many times, out there, I shall live over this evening again, with you and Cécile." Father Hector tasted his wine, inhaling it with a deep breath. "Very clearly, Euclide, it was arranged in Heaven that I should be a missionary in a foreign land. I am peculiarly susceptible to the comforts of the fireside and to the charm of children. If I were a teacher in the college at home, where I have many young nieces and nephews, I should be always planning for them. I should sink into nepotism, the most disastrous of the failings of the popes."

Auclair had to remind Cécile when it was time to bring in the dessert. She had quite forgot where they were in the dinner, so intent was she upon Father Hector's talk, upon watching his brown face and white forehead, with a sweep of black hair standing out above it.

"And now, Cécile," said her father, "shall we tell Father

Hector our secret? Next autumn the Count expects to return to France, and we go with him. We think you have been a missionary long enough; that it is time for you to become a professor of rhetoric again. We expect you to go back with us,—or very soon afterwards."

Father Hector smiled, but shook his head. "Ah, no. Thank you, but no. I have taken a vow that will spoil your plans for me. I shall not return to France."

Auclair had put his glass to his lips, but set it down untasted. "Not return?" he echoed.

"Not at all, Euclide; never."

"But when my wife was here, you both used to plan—"

"Ah, yes. That was my temptation. Now it is vanquished." He sat for a moment smiling. Then he began resolutely:

"Listen, my friend. No man can give himself heart and soul to one thing while in the back of his mind he cherishes a desire, a secret hope, for something very different. You, as a student, must know that even in worldly affairs nothing worth while is accomplished except by that last sacrifice, the giving of oneself altogether and finally. Since I made that final sacrifice, I have been twice the man I was before."

Auclair felt disturbed, a little frightened. "You have made a vow, you say? Is it irrevocable?"

"Irrevocable. And what do you suppose gave me the strength to make that decision? Why, merely a good example!" At this point Father Hector glanced at Cécile and saw that she had almost ceased to breathe in her excitement; that her eyes, in the candlelight, were no longer blue, but black. Again he put out his hand and touched her head. "See, she understands me! From the beginning women understand devotion, it is a natural grace with them; they have only to learn where to direct it. Men have to learn everything.

"There was among the early missionaries, among the martyrs, one whom I have selected for my especial reverence. I mean Noël Chabanel, Euclide. He was not so great a figure as Brébeuf or Jogues or Lalemant, but I feel a peculiar sympathy for him. He perished, you remember, in the great Iroquois raid of '49. But his martyrdom was his life, not his death.

"He was a little different from all the others,—equal to

them in desire, but not in fitness. He was only thirty years of age when he came, and was from Toulouse, that gracious city.

"Chabanel had been a professor of rhetoric like me, and like me he was fond of the decencies, the elegancies of life. From the beginning his life in Canada was one long humiliation and disappointment. Strange to say, he was utterly unable to learn the Huron language, though he was a master of Greek and Hebrew and spoke both Italian and Spanish. After five years of devoted study he was still unable to converse or to preach in any Indian tongue. He was sent out to the mission of Saint Jean in the Tobacco nation, as helper to Father Charles Garnier. Father Garnier, though not at all Chabanel's equal in scholarship, had learned the Huron language so thoroughly that the Indians said there was nothing more to teach him, — he spoke like one of themselves.

"His humiliating inability to learn the language was only one of poor Chabanel's mortifications. He had no love for his converts. Everything about the savages and their mode of life was utterly repulsive and horrible to him; their filth, their indecency, their cruelty. The very smell of their bodies revolted him to nausea. He could never feel toward them that long-suffering love which has been the consolation of our missionaries. He never became hardened to any of the privations of his life, not even to the vermin and mosquitos that preyed upon his body, nor to the smoke and smells in the savage wigwams. In his struggle to learn the language he went and lived with the Indians, sleeping in their bark shelters, crowded with dogs and dirty savages. Often Father Chabanel would lie out in the snow until he was in danger of a death self-inflicted, and only then creep inside the wigwam. The food was so hateful to him that one might say he lived upon fasting. The flesh of dogs he could never eat without becoming ill, and even corn-meal boiled in dirty water and dirty kettles brought on vomiting; so that he used to beg the women to give him a little uncooked meal in his hand, and upon that he subsisted.

"The Huron converts were more brutal to him than to Father Garnier. They were contemptuous of his backwardness in their language, and they must have divined his excessive sensibility, for they took every occasion to outrage it. In the wigwam they tirelessly perpetrated indecencies to wound him. Once when a hunting party returned after a long famine, they invited him to a feast of flesh. After he had swallowed the portion in his bowl, they pulled a human hand out of the kettle to show him that he had eaten of an Iroquois prisoner. He became ill at once, and they followed him into the forest to make merry over his retchings.

"But through all these physical sufferings, which remained as sharp as on the first day, the greatest of his sufferings was an almost continual sense of the withdrawal of God. All missionaries have that anguish at times, but with Chabanel it was continual. For long months, for a whole winter, he would exist in the forest, every human sense outraged, and with no assurance of the nearness of God. In those seasons of despair he was constantly beset by temptation in the form of homesickness. He longed to leave the mission to priests who were better suited to its hardships, to return to France and teach the young, and to find again that peace of soul, that cleanliness and order, which made him the master of his mind and its powers. Everything that he had lost was awaiting him in France, and the Director of Missions in Quebec had suggested his return.

"On Corpus Christi Day, in the fifth year of his labours in Canada and the thirty-fifth of his age, he cut short this struggle and overcame his temptation. At the mission of Saint Matthias, in the presence of the Blessed Sacrament exposed, he made a vow of perpetual stability (*perpetuam stabilitatem*) in the Huron missions. This vow he recorded in writing, and he sent copies of it to his brethren in Kebec.

"Having made up his mind to die in the wilderness, he had not long to wait. Two years later he perished when the mission of Saint Jean was destroyed by the Iroquois,—though whether he died of cold in his flight through the forest, or was murdered by a faithless convert for the sake of the poor belongings he carried on his back, was not surely known. No man ever gave up more for Christ than Noël Chabanel; many gave all, but few had so much to give.

"It was perhaps in memory of his sufferings that I, in my turn, made a vow of perpetual stability. For those of us who are unsteadfast by nature, who have other lawful loves than our devotion to our converts, it is perhaps the safest way. My sacrifice is poor compared with his. I was able to learn the Indian languages; I have a house where I can, at least, pray in solitude; I can keep clean, and am seldom hungry, except by accident in the journeys I have to make. But Noël Chabanel—ah, when your faith is cold, think of him! How can there be men in France this day who doubt the existence of God, when for the love of Him weak human beings have been able to endure so much?"

Cécile looked up at him in bewilderment. "Are there such men, Father?" she whispered.

"There are, my child,—but it is the better for you if you have never heard of them."

Presently it was time that Father Hector should get back to Monseigneur de Saint-Vallier's Palace, where he was lodged during his stay in Quebec.

"And your books, Father Hector? Will you not take them back to the Sault with you? If I leave Canada before you visit Quebec again, what shall I do with them?" Auclair opened a cabinet and pointed to a row of volumes bound in vellum. Father Hector's eyes brightened as he looked at them, but he shook his head.

"No, I shall not take them this time. If you go away, give them to Monseigneur l'Ancien to keep for me. If they could be eaten, or worn on the back, he would give them to the poor, certainly. But Greek and Latin texts will be safe with him. I will not say good-bye, for I shall come tomorrow to lay in a supply of medicines for my mission."

After Auclair had disappeared behind his bed-curtains that night, he lay awake a long while, regretting that a man with Father Hector's gifts should decide to live and die in the wilderness, and wondering whether there had not been a good deal of misplaced heroism in the Canadian missions,—a waste of rare qualities which did nobody any good.

"Ah, well," he sighed at last, "perhaps that is the box of precious ointment which was acceptable to the Saviour, and I am like the disciples who thought it might have been used better in another way."

This solution allowed him to go to sleep.

VI

About the middle of March, soon after Father Hector's visit, the weather went sick, as it were. The air suddenly grew warm and springlike, and for three days there was a continuous downpour of rain. The deep snow drank it up like a thirsty sponge, but never melted. Not a patch of ground showed through, even on the hill-sides. But the snow darkened; everything grew grey like faintly smoked glass. The ice in the river broke up before Quebec, and olive-green water carried grey islands of ice and snow slowly northward. The great pine forests, across the river and on the western sky-line, were no longer bronze, but black. The only colours in the world were black and white and grey, — bewildering variations of clouded white and grey. The Laurentian mountains, to the north, sometimes showed a little blue in their valleys, when the fogs thinned enough to let them be seen. After the interval of rain everything froze hard again and stayed frozen, — but no fresh snow fell. The white winter was gone. Only the smirched ruins of winter remained, mournful and bleak and impoverished, frozen into enduring solidity.

Behind the Auclairs' little back yard and the baker's, the cliff ran up to the Château in a perpendicular wall, and the face of it was overgrown with wild cherry bushes and knotty little Canadian willows. It was up there that one looked, from the back door, for the first sign of spring. But all through April those stumps and twigs were so forbidding, so black and ugly, that Cécile often wondered whether anything short of a miracle of the old-fashioned kind could ever make the sap rise in them again.

A great many people in the town were sick at this time, and Cécile herself caught a cold and was feverish. Her father wrapped her in blankets and made her sit with her feet in a hot mustard bath while she drank a great quantity of sassafras tea. Then he put her to bed and entertained her with an

account of the cures his father and grandfather had effected
with sassafras. It was one of the medicinal plants of the New
World in which he had great faith. It had been first brought
to Europe by Sir Walter Raleigh, he said, and had been for a
time a very popular remedy in France. Even when it went out
of fashion, the pharmacy on the Quai des Célestins had remained loyal to it, and continued to use sassafras after it became expensive because of infrequent supply. His father got it
from London, where it still came in occasional shipments
from the Virginia colony.

Cécile was kept in bed for three days,—in her father's big
bed, with the curtains drawn back, while her father himself
attended to all the household duties. He was an accomplished
cook, and continual practice in making medicines kept his
hand expert in handling glass and earthenware and in regulat-
ing heat. He debated the advisability of sending for Jeanette,
the laundress, or of asking Madame Pigeon to come in and
help him. *"Mais non, nous sommes plus tranquilles comme ça,"* he
decided. That was the important thing—tranquillity. In the
evenings he read aloud to his daughter; and even when he
was in the shop, she could hear everything his clients had to
say, so she was not dull. If her father was disengaged for a
moment, he came in to chat with her. They talked about
Father Hector, and of how soon they could hope for green
salads in the market, and of whether it could be true that
Pierre Charron was home from the Great Lakes already, since
there was a rumour that he had been seen in Montreal.

It was a pleasant and a novel experience to lie warm in
bed while her father was getting dinner in the kitchen, and
to feel no responsibility at all; to listen to the drip of the
rain, to watch the grey daylight fade away in the salon, and
the firelight grow redder and redder on the old chairs and
the sofa, on the gilt picture-frames and the brass candlesticks. But her mind roamed about the town and was dreamily conscious of its activities and of the lives of her friends;
of the dripping grey roofs and spires, the lighted windows
along the crooked streets, the great grey river choked with
ice and frozen snow, the never-ending, merciless forest beyond. All these things seemed to her like layers and layers of
shelter, with this one flickering, shadowy room at the core.

They dined on the little table beside the bed (as they so often breakfasted even when she was well), and after dinner her father closed the door so that she would not be disturbed by the noise he made in washing the dishes, or even by Blinker's visit. It was while he was thus alone in the kitchen that he had, one evening, a strange interview with Blinker.

When Blinker had finished his tasks, he asked timidly if monsieur would please give him a little of that medicine again, to make him sleep.

Auclair looked at him doubtfully.

"How long is it you have not been sleeping?"

"Oh, a long time! Please, monsieur, give me something."

"Sit down, Jules. What is the matter? You are strong and healthy. You do not overeat. I cannot understand why you have this trouble. Perhaps you have something on your mind."

"Perhaps."

"That will often keep one awake. I am not a man to meddle, but if you told me what worries you, I should know better what to do for you."

Blinker's head drooped. He looked very miserable.

"Monsieur, I am an unfortunate man. If I told you, you might put me out."

"You have told your confessor?"

"It was not a sin. Not what they call a sin. It was a misfortune."

"Well, we will never put you out, Jules, be sure of that."

Blinker, with his hands knotted on his knees, seemed to be trying to bring something up out of himself. "Monsieur," he said at last, "I am unfortunate. I was brought up to a horrible trade. I was a torturer in the King's prison at Rouen."

Auclair started, but he caught himself quickly.

"Well, Jules," he said quietly, "that, too, is the King's service."

"*Sale service, monsieur,*" the poor wretch exclaimed bitterly, "*sale métier!* It was my father who did those things,—he was under the chief, he had to do it. I was afraid of him, for he was a hard man. I had no chance to learn another trade. Nobody wanted the prison folks about. In the street people would curse us. My father gave me brandy when he made me help him, all I could hold. He said it was right to punish the wicked, but I could never get used to it. Then something dreadful happened." Blinker was shivering all over.

Auclair poured him a glass of spirits and put some more wood into the stove. "You had better get it out, my boy. That will help you," he told him.

Hard as it was for Blinker to talk, he managed to tell his story. In Rouen there was a rough sort of woman who lived down near the river and did washing. She was honest, but quarrelsome; her neighbours didn't like her. She had a little son who was a bad boy, and she often thrashed him. When he grew older, he struck back, and they used to fight, to the great annoyance of the neighbours. One summer this boy disappeared. A search was made for him. His mother was examined, and contradicted herself. The neighbours remembered hearing angry shouts and a smashing of bottles one night; they began to say she had done away with him. Someone made an accusation. The laundress was taken before the examiners again, but was sullen and refused to talk. She was put to the torture. After half an hour she broke down and confessed that she had killed her son, had put his body into a sack with stones and dragged it to the river. A few weeks later she was hanged.

Not long afterwards Blinker began to have trouble with his lower jaw, some decomposition of the bone; pieces of bone came out through his cheek. For weeks he never lay down, but walked the floor all night. Sometimes when he was full of brandy, he could doze in a chair for half an hour.

But he had another misery, harder to bear than his jaw. This was the first time he had ever suffered great pain, and ghosts began to haunt him. The faces of people he had put to torture rose before him, faces he had long forgotten. When everybody else was asleep, he could think of nothing but those faces. He told himself it was the law of the land and must be right; someone had to do it. But they never gave him any peace.

The suppuration in his jaw stopped at last. The scars on his face had begun to heal, when that murdered boy came back,—walked insolently in the streets of Rouen. The truth came out. After his quarrel with his mother he had hidden himself away on a boat tied up to the wharf, had got to Le Havre undiscovered, and there shipped as *mousse* on a bark bound for the West Indies. He made the voyage and came home.

Blinker began to walk the floor at night again, just as when his jaw was at its worst. How many of the others had been innocent? He could never get the big washer-woman's screams out of his ears. He would have made away with himself then, but he was afraid of being punished after death. If he dropped asleep from exhaustion, he would dream of her. He had only one hope; that miserable boy's adventure had put a thought into his head. If he could get away to a new country, where nobody knew him for the executioner's son, perhaps he would leave all that behind and forget it. That was why he had come to Kebec. But sometimes, he never knew when or why, these things would rise up out of the past . . . faces . . . voices . . . even words, things they had said.

"They are inside me, monsieur, I carry them with me." Blinker closed his eyes and slowly dropped his head forward on his hands.

"Your sickness was a good chance for you, my poor fellow. Suffering teaches us compassion. There are some in Kebec, in high places, who have not learned that yet. If Monseigneur de Saint-Vallier had ever known chagrin and disappointment, he would not cross the old Bishop as he does. I will give you something to make you sleep tomorrow, but afterwards you will not need anything. When God sent you that affliction in your face, he showed his mercy to you. And, by the way, who is your confessor?"

"Father Sébastien, at the Récollets'. But I have wanted to tell you, monsieur, ever since All Souls' Eve. I came back late with my buckets, and the door there was a little open,—you were telling Ma'm'selle about the old man who stole the brass pots. I wanted to make away with myself—but you said something. You said the law was wrong, not us poor creatures. Monsieur, I never hurt an animal to amuse myself, as some do. I was brought up to that trade." Blinker stopped and wiped the sweat out of his eyes with his sleeve.

The poor fellow had begun to give off a foul odour, as creatures do under fear or anguish. Auclair watched with

amazement the twisted face he saw every day above an armful
of wood,—grown as familiar to him as an ugly piece of furniture,—now become altogether strange; it brought to his
mind terrible weather-worn stone faces on the churches at
home,—figures of the tormented in scenes of the Last Judgment. He hastened to measure out a dose of laudanum. After
Blinker had gone out of the kitchen door, he made the sign of
the cross over his own heart before he blew out the candle
and went in to his daughter.

Cécile was flushed and excited; she had been crying, he
saw.

"Oh father, why were you so long with Blinker, and what
was he telling you? He sounded so miserable!"

Her father put her head back on the pillow and smoothed
her hair. "He was telling me all his old troubles, my dear, and
when you are well again, I will tell them to you. We must be
very kind to him. Your mother was right when she said there
was no harm in him. Tomorrow I will go to Father Sébastien,
and between us we will cure his distress."

"Then it was not a crime? You know some people say he
was in the galleys in France."

"No, he was never in the galleys. He was one of the unfortunate of this world. You remember, when Queen Dido offers
Æneas hospitality, she says: *Having known misery, I have
learned to pity the miserable.* Our poor wood-carrier is like
Queen Dido."

The next morning Cécile's recovery began. As soon as she
had drunk her chocolate, her father brought a pair of woollen
stockings and told her to put them on. When she looked up
at him wonderingly, he said:

"I have something to show you."

He wrapped her in a blanket, took her up in his arms, and
carried her into the kitchen, where the back door stood open.

"Look out yonder," he said, "and presently you will see
something."

She looked out at the dreary cliff-side with its black, frozen
bushes and dirty snow, and long, grey icicles hanging from
the jagged rocks. She wondered if there could be yellow buds

on the willows, perhaps; but they were still naked, like stiff black briars.

Suddenly there was a movement up there, a flicker of something swift and slender in the grey light, against the grey, granulated snow,—then a twitter, a scolding anxious protest. Now she knew why her father had smiled so confidently when he lifted her out of bed.

"Oh, Papa, it is our swallow! Then the spring is coming! Nothing can keep it back now." She put her head down on his shoulder and cried a little. He pretended not to notice it, but stood holding her fast, patting her back, so muffled in folds of blanket.

"She is hunting her old nest, up among the crags. I cannot see whether it is still there. But if it has been blown away, she can easily build herself another. She can get mud, because there is a thaw every day now about noon, and the dead leaves are sticking up wherever the snow melts."

"Is she the only one? Is she all alone?"

"She is the only one here this morning, but her friends will be close behind. Listen, how she scolds!"

"Father," said Cécile suddenly, "where has she been, our swallow? Where, do you think?"

"Oh, far away in the South! Somewhere down there where Robert de La Salle was murdered. By the Gulf of Mexico, perhaps."

"And in France where do the swallows go in winter?"

"Very far. Across the Mediterranean to Algérie, where the oranges grow."

"Has our swallow been where there are oranges? Do they grow by the Gulf of Mexico? Oh, Papa, I wish I could see an orange, on its little tree!"

"You will see them when we go home. There are fine old orange-trees growing under glass in our own parish, and they are brought out into the courtyards in summer."

"But couldn't we possibly grow one here in Quebec? The Jesuits have such great warm cellars; I am sure they could, if they tried."

Her father laughed as he carried her back to bed. "I am afraid not even the Jesuits could do that! Now I am going to leave you for a little while. I will put a card on the door announcing that we are closed until noon. You are so much better, that I can make my visit to the Hôtel Dieu this morning."

"And on your way, Papa, will you stop and tell Monseigneur l'Ancien that our swallow has come? For his book, you know."

Ever since he first came out to Canada, old Bishop Laval had kept a brief weather record, noting down the date of the first snowfall, when the river froze over, the nights of excessive cold, the storms and the great thaws. And for nearly forty years now he had faithfully recorded the return of the swallow.

BOOK FOUR

Pierre Charron

I

IT WAS THE FIRST DAY of June. Before dawn a wild calling and twittering of birds in the bushes on the cliff-side above the apothecary's back door announced clear weather. When the sun came up over the Île d'Orléans, the rock of Kebec stood gleaming above the river like an altar with many candles, or like a holy city in an old legend, shriven, sinless, washed in gold. The quickening of all life and hope which had come to France in May had reached the far North at last. That morning the Auclairs drank their chocolate with all the doors and windows open.

Euclide was at his desk, making up little packets of saffron flowers to flavour fish soups, when a slender man in buck-skins, with a quick swinging step, crossed the threshold and embraced him before he had time to rise. He was not a big fellow, this Pierre Charron, hero of the fur trade and the coureurs de bois, not above medium height, but quick as an otter and always sure of himself. When Auclair, after returning his embrace with delight, drew back to look at him and asked him how he was, he threw up his chin and answered:

"Je me porte bien, comme toujours."

"And have you had a good winter, Pierre?"

"But yes. I always have a good winter, monsieur. I see to it."

"And how do you happen to be down so early?"

Charron's face changed. He frowned. "That is not so good. My mother was ailing. They brought me word, out to Michilimackinac, so I returned to Montreal in March. She was better; the Sisters of the Congregation had been taking care of her. But I did not leave her again. No one can nurse her so well as I. I stayed at home and let the other fellows have my spring trade this year. I can afford it."

"But I must hear about your mother's ailment, my son; and first let me call Cécile. She will not want to lose even a minute of your visit."

"I see your grand neighbour has come home," Pierre observed.

"Oh yes, last September. But you must have heard? People say he brought such beautiful things for his house; furniture and paintings and tapestry and silver dishes. Wouldn't you love to see the inside of his Palace?"

"Not a bit! He is too French for me." Charron threw up his chin.

Cécile laughed. "But my father is French, and so is Father Hector; you like them."

"Oh, that is different. But the man over there goes against me. He smells of Versailles. The old man is my Bishop. But I could do without any of them."

"Hush, Pierre Charron! You are foolish to quarrel with the priests. I love Father Hector. You can't say he isn't a brave man."

Pierre shrugged. "Oh, he is brave enough. All the same, he's a little too Frenchified for me. You and I are Canadians, monkey. We were born here."

"Why, I wasn't at all! You know that."

"Well, if you weren't you couldn't help it. You got here early. You were very little when I first saw you with your mother. Cécile, every autumn, before I start for the woods, I have a mass said at the *paroisse* in Ville-Marie for madame your mother."

Cécile pressed his hand softly and drew closer to him. Whenever Charron spoke of her mother, or of his own, his voice lost its tone of banter; he became respectful, serious, simple. It was clear enough that for him the family was the first and final thing in the human lot; and it was so engrafted with religion that he could only say: "Very well; religion for the fireside, freedom for the woods."

As they passed the end of the long Seminary building, the door of the garden stood open, and within they saw Bishop Laval, walking up and down the sanded paths, his breviary open in his hand. It was a very small garden; a grass plot in the centre, a row of Lombardy poplars along the wall, some lilac bushes, now in bloom, a wooden seat with no back under a crooked quince-tree. The old man caught sight of

Pierre, though he walked so noiselessly,—beckoned to him and called out his name. The Bishop knew everyone along the river so well that it was said he could recognize a lost child by the family look in its face.

Pierre snatched off his cap and they went inside the garden door. Monseigneur inquired after the health of Madame Charron, and of the aged nun Marguerite Bourgeoys. And had Pierre heard whether Mademoiselle Le Ber was in health?

Not directly. He supposed she was as usual; he had heard nothing to the contrary.

The Bishop breathed heavily, like a tired horse. "All the sinners of Ville-Marie may yet be saved by the prayers of that devoted girl," he said with a certain meaning in his tone. "And you, my son, have you been to your confessor since your return from the woods?"

Pierre said respectfully that he had. The Bishop then turned to Cécile and placed his hand upon her head, with the rare smile which always seemed a little sad on his grim features.

"And here we have a child who borrows money,—and of a poor priest, too! Why did you never come to pay me back my twenty sous?"

"But Monseigneur l'Ancien, I gave them to Houssart, the very day after!"

"I know you did, my child, but I should have liked it better if you had come to me when you paid your debt. You are not afraid of me?"

"Oh, no, Monseigneur! But you are always occupied, and I did not know whether you liked to have children come."

"I do. I like it very much. Make me a visit here in my garden some morning at this hour, and I will share my lilacs with you; they are coming on now. Bring the little boy, if you like. I hear from the Pommiers that you and your father are making a good boy of him, and that is very commendable in you."

During the rest of the short walk to the cobbler's, Pierre asked what the Bishop meant by the twenty sous, but he seemed to pay little attention to the story; he was rather overcast, indeed. It was not until he greeted Madame Pommier that he recovered his high spirits.

and lit his pipe, which had gone out. "You know, monsieur, three times in the woods my comrades have thought it was all over with me; a powder explosion, my canoe going down under me in the rapids, and then the gunshot wound I had in the Count's last campaign. I have remembered that promise; for I have certainly been delivered from sudden death. I remember, too, her voice when she said those words,—it was still her own voice, which made people love to go to her father's house, and one felt gay if she but spoke one's name. And now it is harsh and hollow like an old crow's—terrible to hear!"

Auclair began to wonder whether Pierre might have had anything to drink before he came to dinner. "Now you are talking wildly, my boy. We cannot know what her voice is like now."

"I know," said Charron sullenly. He crossed the room to the door of the enclosed staircase, and examined it to see that it was shut. "The little one cannot hear, up there? No?" He sat down and leaned forward, his elbows on the table. "I know. I have heard her. I have seen her."

"Pierre, you have not done anything irreverent, that the nuns will never forgive?" Auclair was alarmed by the very thought that the sad solitaire, who asked for nothing on this earth but solitude, had perhaps been startled.

Charron was too much excited and too sorry for himself at that moment to notice his friend's apprehensions.

"It was like this," he went on presently. "You know, because of my mother, this year I got back to Montreal early, months before my time. There is not much to do there, God knows, except to be a pig, and I never behave like dirt in my mother's town. We live so near the chapel of the Congregation that I can never get the recluse out of my mind. You remember there were two weeks of terrible cold in March, and it made me wretched to think of her walled up there. No, don't misunderstand me!" Charron's eyes came back from their far-away point of vision and fixed intently, distrustfully, on his friend's face. "All that is over; one does not love a woman who has been dead for nearly twenty years. But there is such a thing as kindness; one wouldn't like to think of a dog that had been one's playfellow, much less a little girl, suffering from cold those bitter nights. You see, there are all those early memories; one cannot get another set; one has but those." Pierre's voice choked, because something had come out by chance, thus, that he had never said to himself before. The candles blurred before Auclair a little, too. God was a witness, he murmured, that he knew the truth of Pierre's remark only too well.

After he had relit his pipe and smoked a little, Charron continued. "You know she goes into the church to pray before the altar at midnight. Well, I hid myself in the church and saw her. It is not difficult for a man who has lived among the Indians; you slide into the chapel when an old sacristan is locking up after vespers, and stay there behind a pillar as long as you choose. It was a long wait. I had my fur jacket on and a flask of brandy in my pocket, and I needed both. God's Name, is there any place so cold as churches? I had to move about to keep from aching all over,—but, of course, I made no noise. There was only the sanctuary lamp burning, until the moon came round and threw some light in at the windows. I knew when it must be near midnight, you get to have a sense of time in the woods. I hid myself behind a pillar at the back of the church. I felt a little nervous, sorry I had come, perhaps.—At last I heard a latch lift,—you could have heard a rabbit breathe in that place. The iron grille beside the altar began to move outward. She came in, carrying a candle. She wore a grey gown, and a black scarf on her head, but no veil. The candle shone up into her face. It was like a stone face; it had been through every sorrow."

Charron stopped and crossed himself. He shut his eyes and dropped his head in his hands. "My friend, I could remember a face!—I could remember Jeanne in her little white furs, when I used to pull her on my sled. Jacques Le Ber would have burned Montreal down to keep her warm. He meant to give her every joy in the world, and she has thrown the world away. . . . She put down her candle and went toward the high altar. She walked very slowly, with great dignity. At first she prayed aloud, but I scarcely understood her. My mind was confused; her voice was so changed,—hoarse, hollow, with the sound of despair in it. Why is she unhappy, I ask you? She is, I know it! When she prayed in silence, such sighs broke from her. And once a groan, such as I have never heard; such despair—such resignation and despair! It froze everything in me. I felt that I would never be the same man again. I only wanted to die and forget that I had ever hoped for anything in this world.

"After she had bowed herself for the last time, she took up her candle and walked toward that door, standing open. I lost my head and betrayed myself. I was well hidden, but she heard me sob.

"She was not startled. She stood still, with her hand on the latch of the grille, and turned her head, half-facing me. After a moment she spoke.

"*Poor sinner*, she said, *poor sinner, whoever you are, may God have mercy upon you! I will pray for you. And do you pray for me also.*

"She walked on and shut the grille behind her. I turned the key in the church door and let myself out. No man was ever more miserable than I was that night."

III

Ever since Cécile could remember, she had longed to go over to the Île d'Orléans. It was only about four miles down the river, and from the slopes of Cap Diamant she could watch its fields and pastures come alive in the spring, and the bare trees change from purple-grey to green. Down the middle of the island ran a wooded ridge, like a backbone, and here and there along its flanks were cleared spaces, cultivated ground where the islanders raised wheat and rye. Seen from the high points of Quebec, the island landscape looked as if it had been arranged to please the eye,—full of folds and wrinkles like a crumpled table-cloth, with little fields twinkling above the dark tree-tops. The climate was said to be more salubrious than that of Quebec, and the soil richer. All the best vegetables and garden fruits in the market came from the Île, and the wild strawberries of which Cécile's father was so fond. Giorgio, the drummer boy, had often told her how well the farmers lived over there; and about the great eel-fishings in the autumn, when the islanders went out at night with torches and seined eels by the thousand.

Pierre Charron had a friend on the island, Jean Baptiste Harnois, the smith of Saint-Laurent, and he meant to go over and pay him a visit this summer, before he went back to Montreal. He had promised to take Cécile along,—every time he came to the shop, he reminded her that they were to make this excursion. One fine morning in the last week of June he dropped in to say that the wind was right, and he would start for the island in about an hour, to be gone for three days.

Very well, Auclair told him, Cécile would be ready.

"But three days, father!" she exclaimed; "can you manage for yourself so long? You bought so many things at the market for me to cook."

"I can manage. You must go by all means. You may not have such a chance again."

"Good," said Pierre. "I will be back in an hour. And she must bring a warm coat; it will be cold out on the water."

Cécile had never gone on a voyage before,—had never slept a night away from home, except during the Phips bombardment, when she and her mother had taken refuge at the Ursuline convent, along with the other women and children from the Lower Town.

"What shall I take with me, Father? I am so distracted I cannot think!"

"The little valise that was your mother's will hold your things. You will need a night-gown, and a pair of stockings, and a clean cotton blouse, and some handkerchiefs; I should think that would be all. And I will give you a package of raisins as a present for Madame Harnois."

She ran upstairs and began to pack her mother's bag, finding it hard to assemble her few things in her excitement.

"Are you ready, Cécile?" her father presently called from the foot of the stairs.

"I am not sure, Father—I think so. I wish I had known yesterday."

"Then you would not have slept all night. Come along, and I will put the raisins in your valise."

Pierre was waiting, seated on the long table that served as a counter. Her father looked into her bag to see that she had the proper things, then handed it to him. Cécile put on her cap and coat. Auclair kissed her and wished them *bon voyage*. "Take good care of her, Pierre."

Pierre touched his hand to his black forelock. "As you would yourself, monsieur." He pushed Cécile out of the door before him.

"Papa," she called back, "you will not forget to keep the fire under the soup? It has been on only an hour."

Pierre's boat was a light shallop with one sail. He rowed out far enough to catch the breeze and then sat in the stern, letting the wind and current carry them. He had made a change in his clothes during the hour he was absent from the shop, Cécile noticed (later in the day she wondered why!), had put on a white linen shirt and knotted a new red silk neckerchief about his throat. He soon took off his knitted cap, lit his pipe, and lounged at his ease. On one shore stretched the dark forest, on the other the smiling, sunny fields that ran toward Beaupré. Behind them the Lower Town grew smaller and smaller; the rock of Kebec lost its detail until they could see only Cap Diamant, and the Château, and the spires of the churches. The sunlight on the river made a silver glare all about the boat, and from the water itself came a deep rhythmic sound, like something breathing.

"Think of it, Pierre, in all these years I have never been on the river before!" Such a stretch of lost opportunity as life seemed just then!

Pierre smiled. "Not so many years, at that! Your father is over-cautious, maybe, but squalls come up suddenly on this river, and most of these young fellows had as lief drown as not. I'd rather you never went with anyone but me. If you like it, you can go with me any time."

"But I'd like to go the other way,—to Montreal, and up those rivers that are full of rapids. I want to go as far as Michilimackinac."

"Some time, perhaps. We'll see how you like roughing it."

Cécile asked what he had in the stone jug she saw in the bow, along with his blanket and buckskin coat.

"That is brandy, for the smith. But it will come back full of good country wine. He makes it from wild grapes. The wild grapes on the island are the best in Canada; Jacques Cartier named it the Île de Bacchus because he found such fine grapes growing in the woods. That ought to please you, with all your Latin!"

"Are you like Mother Juschereau, do you think it wrong for a girl to know Latin?"

"Not if she can cook a hare or a partridge as well as Mademoiselle Auclair! She may read all the Latin she pleases. But I expect you won't like the food at the Harnois', *à la campagnarde*, you know,—they cook everything in grease. As for me, it doesn't matter. When you can go to an Indian feast and eat dogs boiled with blueberries, you can eat anything."

Cécile shuddered. "I don't see how you can do it, Pierre. I should think it would be easier to starve."

"Oh, do you, my dear? Try starving once; it's a long business. I've known the time when dog meat cooked in a dirty pot seemed delicious! But the worst food I ever swallowed was what they call *tripe de roche*. I went out to Lac la Mort with some Frenchmen early in the spring once. They were a green lot, and they let most of our provisions get stolen on the way. As soon as we reached the lake, we were caught in a second winter; a heavy snow, and everything frozen. No game, no fish. We had to fall back on *tripe de roche*. It's a kind of moss that grows on the rocks along the lake, something like a sponge; the cold doesn't kill it, when everything else is frozen hard as iron. You gather it and boil it, and it's not so bad as it goes down,—tastes like any boiled weed. But afterwards—oh, what a stomach-ache! The men sat round tied up in a knot. We had about a week of that stuff. We scraped the hair off our bear skins and roasted them, that time. But it's a truth, monkey, I wouldn't like a country where things were too soft. I like a cold winter, and a hot summer. My father used to boast that in Languedoc you were never out of sight of a field or a vineyard. That would mean people everywhere around you, always watching you! No hunting,—they put you in jail if you shoot a partridge. Even the fish in the streams belong to somebody. I'd be in prison in a week there."

The settlement at Saint-Laurent was Pierre's destination. After he had passed the point at Saint-Pétronille and turned into the south channel, a sweet, warm odour blew out from the shore, very like the smell of ripe strawberries. Each time

her,—they hadn't any, but wiped their sweaty faces on their sleeves or their skirts. Several of her handkerchiefs had come from her aunts, and she was very fond of them, but she parted with them gladly and only wished she had more things to give the children.

She could scarcely believe in her good fortune when Pierre's boat actually left the shore and he began pulling out into the river, while the Harnois children stood waving to them from the cove.

"We needn't hurry, eh?" Pierre asked.

"Oh, no! I love being on the river," she replied unsteadily. He asked no further questions, but handled his oars, singing softly to himself. Of course, she thought sadly, he would never want to take her anywhere again. She used to dream that one day he might take her to Montreal in his boat, perhaps even to see the great falls at Niagara.

As soon as they were out of the south channel and had cleared the point of the island, they could see the rock of Kebec and the glare of the sun on the slate roofs. Cécile began to struggle with her tears again. It was as if she were home already. For a long while it did not grow much plainer; then it rose higher and higher against the sky.

"Now I can see the Château, and the Récollet spire," she cried. "And, oh, Pierre, there is the Seminary!"

"Yes? It's a fine building, but I never had any particular affection for it." He saw that she was much too happy to notice his banter.

Soon they could see the spire of Notre Dame de la Victoire—and then they were in the shadow of the rock itself. When she stepped upon the shore, Cécile remembered how Sister Catherine de Saint-Augustin, when she landed with her companions, had knelt down and kissed the earth. Had she been alone, she would have loved to do just that. They went hand in hand up La Place street, across the market square, down Notre Dame street beside the church, and into Mountain Hill. It was wonderful that everything should be just the same, when she had been away so long! Pierre did not bother her with questions, but she knew he was watching her closely. She was ashamed, but it couldn't be helped; some things are stronger than shame.

When they burst in upon her father, he was seated at his desk, rolling pills on a sheet of glass.

"What, back already?" He did not seem so overjoyed as Cécile had thought he would be.

"Yes, monsieur," Pierre replied carelessly, "we were a little bored in the country, both of us."

How grateful she was for that *"tous les deux!"* She might have known Pierre would not betray her.

"Father," she said as she kissed him again, "please ask Pierre Charron to come to dinner tonight. I want to make something very nice for him. I've given him a lot of trouble."

After Pierre was gone, and she had peeped into the salon and the kitchen to see that everything was as she had left it, Cécile came back into the shop.

"Father, Pierre took it on himself, but it was my fault we came home. I didn't like country life very well. I was not happy."

"But aren't they kind people, the Harnois? Haven't they kind ways?"

"Yes, they have." She sighed and put her hand to her forehead, trying to think. They had kind ways, those poor Harnois, but that was not enough; one had to have kind things about one, too. . . .

But if she was to make a good dinner for Pierre, she had no time to think about the Harnois. She put on her apron and made a survey of the supplies in the cellar and kitchen. As she began handling her own things again, it all seemed a little different,—as if she had grown at least two years older in the two nights she had been away. She did not feel like a little girl, doing what she had been taught to do. She was accustomed to think that she did all these things so carefully to please her father, and to carry out her mother's wishes. Now she realized that she did them for herself, quite as much. Dogs cooked with blueberries—poor Madame Harnois' dishes were not much better! These coppers, big and little, these brooms and clouts and brushes, were tools; and with them one made, not shoes or cabinet-work, but life itself. One made a climate within a climate; one made the days,—the complexion, the special flavour, the special happiness of each day as it passed; one made life.

Suddenly her father came into the kitchen. "Cécile, why did you not call me to make the fire? And do you need a fire so early?"

"I must have hot water, Papa. It is no trouble to make a fire." She wiped her hands and threw her arms about him. "Oh, Father, I think our house is so beautiful!"

BOOK FIVE

The Ships from France

I

A T FOUR O'CLOCK in the morning Cécile was sitting by her
upstairs window, dressed and wide awake. Across the
river there was already a red and purple glow above the black
pines; but overhead spread the dark night sky, like a tent with
its flap up, letting in a new day,—the most important day of
the year.

Word had come down by land that five ships from France
had passed Tadousac and were beating up the river against
head winds. During the night the wind had changed; Cécile
had only to hold her handkerchief outside her window and
watch it flutter, to reassure herself that a strong breeze was
blowing in from the east, and the ships would be in today.
She wondered how her father could go on sleeping. Nicho-
las Pigeon and Blinker had been up all night, making a
great deal of noise as they turned out one baking after another to feed the hungry sailors. The smell of fresh bread
was everywhere, very tempting to one who had been awake
so long.

At last she heard a door below open softly, and she ran
down the stairs to the salon and out into the kitchen, where
her father was just beginning to make his fire.

"Oh, Father, the wind is right! I knew it would come! Yesterday all the nuns at the Ursulines' were praying for the wind
to change. How soon do you suppose they will get in? You
remember last year it rained all day when the first ships came.
But today will be beautiful. I expect Kebec will look very fine
to them."

"No better than they will to us, certainly. But there is no
hurry. They will not be along for hours yet."

Cécile told him she had been awake nearly all night and
was very hungry, so would he please hurry the chocolate. She
herself ran out through the board fence that divided their
back yard from the Pigeons', to get a loaf from Blinker, as it

"Oh, no! One is best in one's own country. I run back to Saint-Malo after my last trip, and tie up there for the winter."

"But that must add to your difficulties, Monsieur Pondaven."

"It is nothing to me. I know the Channel like my own town. All my equipage are glad to get home. They are all Malouins. I should not know how to manage with men from another part."

"You Malouins stick together like Jesuits," Pierre declared. "Yet by your own account you were not so well treated there that you need love the place."

Captain Pondaven smiled an artless smile. "Perhaps that is the very reason! He means, Monsieur Auclair, that the town brought me up like a stepmother. My father was drowned, fishing off Newfoundland, and my mother died soon afterwards. With us, when an orphan boy is twelve years old, he is given a suit of clothes and a chest and is sent to sea as a *mousse*. They sent me out with a hard master my first voyage. But when I came back from Madagascar and showed how my ears were torn and my back was scarred, the townspeople took up my case and got my papers changed. My townspeople did not do so badly by me. When I was ready for a command, they saw that I had my chance. They put their money behind me, and I have been half-owner in my boat for five years now."

Though she liked the Captain very much and gave polite attention to his talk, Cécile's mind was on the parrot. He sat forgotten on the back of the chair, attached to his master's belt by a long cord. He seemed of a sullen disposition—there was nothing gay and bird-like about him. Neither was he so brilliant as she had expected. He was all grey, except for rose-coloured tail-feathers, and his plumage was ruffled and untidy, for he was moulting. He gave no sign of his peculiar talent, but sat as silent as the stuffed alligator at home, never moving except to cock his head on one side. When the leek soup put a temporary stop to conversation, she ventured a question.

"And what is your parrot's name, if you please, Monsieur Pondaven?"

The Captain looked up from his plate and smiled at her.

"His name is Coco, mademoiselle, and he will make noise enough presently. He is a little shy with strangers, not seeing many on board."

Then the shell-fish came on, and Auclair asked the Captain what people at home thought of the King's peace with the English.

He said he did not know what the inland people thought. "But with us on the coast it will make little difference. The King cannot make peace on the sea. Our people will take an English ship whenever they have a chance. They are looking for good plunder this summer. We must have our revenge for the ships they took from us last year."

"They are fine seamen, the English," Pierre Charron declared. Cécile had noticed that he was in one of his perverse moods, when he liked to tease and antagonize everyone a little.

The Captain answered him mildly. "Yes, they are good sailors, but we usually get the better of them. They are a blasphemous lot and have no respect for good manners or religion. That never pays."

Auclair reminded him that last summer the English had captured one of the boats bound for Canada.

"I remember well, *Le Saint-Antoine*, and the Captain is a friend of mine. They took the boat into Plymouth and sold her at auction. Many of our merchants lost heavily. Your Bishop, Monseigneur de Saint-Vallier, had sent some things for the missions over here by *Le Saint-Antoine*. Some bones of the saints and other holy relics were packed in an oak chest, and the Captain, out of respect, put it in his own cabin. The English, when they plundered the ship, came upon this chest and supposed it was treasure. When they opened it, they were furious. After committing every possible sacrilege they took the relics to the cook's galley and threw them into the stove where their dinner was cooking."

Cécile asked whether no punishment had come upon those sailors.

"Not at the time, mademoiselle, but I shouldn't like to put to sea with such actions on my soul,—and I am no coward, either."

"*Sales cochons anglais, sales cochons!*" said another voice, and

He was thinking of this as he stood by the fire, awaiting his master's pleasure. At last the Governor pushed back his papers and turned to him.

"Euclide," he began, "I am afraid I cannot promise you much for the future. When the last ships came in, I had no doubt that I should go home on one of them,—and you and your daughter with me. By *La Vengeance* the Minister sends me a letter concerning the peace of Rijswijk, but ignores my petition for recall. He assures me of His Majesty's esteem, and of his desire to reward my services more substantially in the future. The future, for a man of my age, is an inconsiderable matter. His Majesty prefers that I shall die in Quebec."

The Count rose and walked to the window behind his desk, where he stood looking down at the ships anchored in the river, already loading for departure. As he stood there lost in reflection, Auclair thought he seemed more like a man revolving plans for a new struggle with fortune than one looking back upon a life of brilliant failures. The Count had the bearing of a fencer when he takes up the foil; from his shoulders to his heels there was intention and direction. His carriage was his unconscious idea of himself,—it was an armour he put on when he took off his night-cap in the morning, and he wore it all day, at early mass, at his desk, on the march, at the Council, at his dinner-table. Even his enemies relied upon his strength.

"I have never been a favourite," he said, turning round suddenly. "I have not the courtier's address. Without that, a military man cannot go far nowadays. Perhaps I offended His Majesty by trying to teach him geography. Nothing is more unpopular at Court than the geography of New France. They like to think of Quebec as isolated, French, and Catholic. The rest of the continent is a wilderness, and they prefer to disregard it. Any advance to the westward costs money— and Quebec has already cost them enough."

The Count returned to his desk, sat down, and went on talking in the impersonal, remote tone which he often adopted with his apothecary. Indeed, Auclair's chief service to his patron was not to administer drugs, but to listen occasionally, when the Governor felt lonely, to talk of places and persons,—talk which would have been incomprehensible to anyone else in Kebec.

"After my reappointment to Canada I had two audiences with His Majesty. The first was at Versailles, when he was full of a project to seize New York and the Atlantic seaports from the English. I was not averse to such an enterprize, but I explained some of the difficulties. With a small fleet and a few thousand regulars, I would gladly have undertaken it.

"My second audience was at Fontainebleau, shortly before we embarked from La Rochelle. The King received me very graciously in his cabinet, but he was no longer in a conqueror's mood; he had consulted the treasury. When I referred to the project he had advanced at our previous meeting, he glanced at the clock over his fireplace and remarked that it was the hour for feeding the carp. He asked me to accompany him. An invitation to attend His Majesty at the feeding of the carp is, of course, a compliment. We went out to the carp basins. I like a fine pond of carp myself, and those at Fontainebleau are probably the largest and fiercest in France. The pages brought baskets of bread, and His Majesty threw in the first loaves. The carp there are monsters, really. They came grunting and snorting like a thousand pigs. They piled up on each other in hills as high as the rim of the basin, with all their muzzles out; they caught a loaf and devoured it before it could touch the water. Not long before that, a care-taker's little girl fell into the pond, and the carp tore her to pieces while her father was running to the spot. Some of them are very old and have an individual renown. One old creature, red and rusty down to his belly, they call the Cardinal.

"Well, after the ravenous creatures had been fed by the royal hand, the King accompanied me a little way down the chestnut avenue. He wished me God-speed and said adieu. I took my departure by the great gate, where my carriage waited, and the King went back to the carp pond. That was my last interview with my royal master. That was the end of his bold project to snatch the seaports from the English and make this continent a French possession, as it should be. I sailed without troops, without money, to do what I could. Unfortunately for you, I brought you with me." The Count unlocked a drawer of his desk. He took out a leather bag and dropped it on his pile of correspondence. From its weight and the sound it made, Auclair judged it contained gold pieces.

"When I persuaded you to come out here," the Governor continued, "I promised you a return. I have already seen the captain of *Le Soleil d'Afrique* and bespoken his best cabin in case I have need of it. As you know, I am always poor, but in that sack there is enough for you to begin a modest business at home. If I were in your place, I should get my belongings together and embark the day after tomorrow."

"And you, Monsieur le Comte?"

"It is just possible that I may follow you next year. If not, Kebec is as near heaven as any place."

"Then I prefer to wait until next year also." Auclair spoke quietly, but without hesitation. "I came to share your fortunes."

The Governor frowned. "But you have your daughter's future to consider. At the present moment, I can in some degree assure you another start in the world. But if I terminate my days here, you will be adrift, and I doubt if you will ever get home at all. You are not very adept in practical matters, Euclide."

Auclair flushed faintly. "I have made my choice, patron. I remain in Kebec until you leave it. And I have no need for that," indicating the leather bag. "You pay me well for my services."

When the apothecary left the chamber, the Count looked after him with a shrug, and a smile in which there was both contempt and kindness. He remembered an incident very long ago: He had just come home from the foreign wars, and had nearly ruined himself providing a new coach and horses and liveries to make a suitable re-entrance in the world. The first time he went abroad in his new carriage, to pay calls in the fashionable part of Paris, the occupants of every coach he passed either were looking the other way, or saluted him carelessly, as if they had seen him only the day before. Not even a driver or a footman glanced twice at his fine horses. The gatekeepers and equerries at the houses where he stopped were insolently indifferent. Late in the afternoon, when he was crossing the Pont-Neuf at the crowded hour, in a stream of coaches, he saw among the foot-passengers the first admirers of his splendour: an old man and a young boy, gazing up and following his carriage with eager eyes—the grandfather and grandson who lived in the pharmacy next his stables and were his tenants.

II

The Count de Frontenac awoke suddenly out of a curious dream—a dream so vivid that he could not at once shake it off, but lay in the darkness behind his bed-curtains slowly realizing where he was. The sound of a church-bell rang out hoarse on the still air: yes, that would be the stubborn old man, Bishop Laval, ringing for early mass. He knew that bell like a voice. He was, then, in Canada, in the Château on the rock of Kebec; the St. Lawrence must be flowing seaward beneath his windows.

In his dream, too, he had been asleep and had suddenly awakened; awakened a little boy, in an old farm-house near Pontoise, where his nurse used to take him in the summer. He had been awakened by fright, a sense that some danger threatened him. He got up and in his bare feet stole to the door leading into the garden, which was ajar. Outside, in the darkness, stood a very tall man in a plumed hat and huge boots—a giant, in fact; the little boy's head did not come up to his boot-tops. He had no idea who the enormous man might be, but he knew that he must not come in, that everything depended upon his being kept out. Quickly and cleverly the little boy closed the door and slid the wooden bar,—he had no trouble in finding it, for he knew the house so well. But there was the front door,—he was sleeping in the wing of the cottage, and that front door was three rooms away. Still barefoot, he went softly and swiftly through the kitchen and the living-room to the hallway behind that main door, which could be fastened by an iron bolt. It was pitch-dark, but he did not fumble, he found the bolt at once. It was rusty, and stuck. He felt how small and weak his hands were—of that he was very conscious. But he turned the bolt gently back and forth in its hasp to loosen the rust-flakes, and coaxed it into the iron loop on the door-jamb which made it fast. Then he felt suddenly faint. He wiped the sweat from his face with the sleeve of his night-gown, and waited. That terrible man on the other side of the door; one could hear him moving about in the currant bushes, pulling at the rose-vines on the wall. There were other doors—and windows! Every nook and corner of the house flashed through his mind; but for the moment he was safe. The broad oak boards and the iron bolt were between him and the great boots that must not cross the threshold. While he stood gathering his strength, he awoke in another bed than the one he had quitted a few moments ago, but he was still covered with sweat and still frightened. He did not come fully to himself until he heard the call of the old Bishop's bell-clapper. Then he knew where he was.

Of all the houses he had slept in all over the world, in Flanders, Holland, Italy, Crete, why had he awakened in that one near Pontoise, and why had he remembered it so well? His bare feet had avoided every unevenness in the floor; in the dark he had stepped without hesitation from the earth floor of the kitchen, over the high sill, to the wooden floor of the living-room. He had known the exact position of all the furniture and had not stumbled against anything in his swift flight through the house. Yet he had not been in that house since he was eight years old. For four summers his nurse, Noémi, had taken him there. It was her property, but on her son's marriage the daughter-in-law had become mistress, according to custom. Noémi had taken care of him from the time he was weaned until he went to school. His own mother was a cold woman and had little affection for her children. Indeed, the Count reflected, as he lay behind his bed-curtains recovering from his dream, no woman, probably, had ever felt so much affection for him as old Noémi. Not all women had found him so personally distasteful as his wife had done; but not one of his mistresses had felt more than a passing inclination for him. Tenderness, uncalculating, disinterested devotion, he had never known. It was in his stars that he was not to know it. Noémi had loved his fine strong little body, grieved when he was hurt, watched over him when he was sick, carried him in her arms when he was tired. Now, when he was sick indeed, his mind, in sleep, had gone back to that woman and her farm-house on the Oise.

It struck him that a dream of such peculiar vividness signified a change in himself. A change had been coming on all summer—during the last few months it had progressed very fast. When from his windows he saw the last sail going out between the south shore and the Île d'Orléans, he knew he would never live to see those boats come back. Now, after this dream, he decided to make his will before another night fell.

Of late the physical sureness and sufficiency he had known all his life had changed to a sense of limitation and uncertainty. He had no wish to prolong this state. There was no one in this world whom he would be sorry to leave. His wife, Madame de la Grange Frontenac, he had no desire to see again, though he would will to her the little property he had, as was customary. Once a year she wrote him a long letter, telling him all the gossip of Paris and informing him of the changes which occurred there. From her accounts it appeared that the sons of most of his old friends had turned out badly enough. He could not feel any very deep regret that his own son had died in youth,—killed in an engagement in the Low Countries many years ago.

The Count himself was ready to die, and he would be glad to die here alone, without pretence and mockery, with no troop of expectant relatives about his bed. The world was not what he had thought it at twenty—or even at forty.

He would die here, in this room, and his spirit would go before God to be judged. He believed this, because he had been taught it in childhood, and because he knew there was something in himself and in other men that this world did not explain. Even the Indians had to make a story to account for something in their lives that did not come out of their appetites: conceptions of courage, duty, honour. The Indians had these, in their own fashion. These ideas came from some unknown source, and they were not the least part of life.

In spiritual matters the Count had always accepted the authority of the Church; in governmental and military matters he stoutly refused to recognize it. He had known absolute unbelievers, of course; one, a witty and blasphemous scapegrace, the young Baron de La Hontan, he had sheltered here in the Château, under the noses of two Bishops. But it was for his clever conversation, not for his opinions, that the Count offered La Hontan hospitality.

When the grey daylight began to sift through the hangings of his bed, Count Frontenac rang for Picard to bring his coffee.

"I shall not get up today, Picard," he remarked. "You may shave me in bed. Afterwards, go to the notary and fetch him here to transact some business with me. Stop at the apothecary shop on your way, and tell Monsieur Auclair I shall not need him until four o'clock."

When Auclair arrived in the afternoon, he found his patron still in bed, in his dressing-gown. To his inquiries the Count replied carelessly:

"Oh, I do very well indeed! I find myself so comfortable that I have almost decided to stay in bed for the rest of my life. I have been making my will today, and that reminded me of a promise I once gave your daughter. That bowl of glass fruit on the mantel: do not forget to take it to her when you go home tonight, with my greetings. She has always admired it. And there is another matter. In the leather chest in my dressing-room you will find a large package wrapped in brown Holland. It is table linen that I brought out from Île Savary. Tonight, when you will not be observed, I wish you to take it home with you for safe keeping. Upon Cécile's marriage, you will present it to her from me. Why do you look sober, Euclide? You know very well that I must soon change my climate, as the Indians say, and this Château will be in other hands. I merely arrange to dispose of my personal belongings as I wish."

"Monsieur le Comte, if you would permit me to try the remedy I suggested yesterday——"

"Tut-tut! We will have no more remedies. A little repose and comfort. The machine is worn out, certainly; but if we let it alone, it may go a little longer, from habit. When you come up tonight, you may bring me something to make me sleep, however. These long hours of wakefulness do a man no good. Draw up a chair and sit down by the fire, where I can speak to you without shouting. If you are to be in constant attendance here, you cannot be forever standing."

Picard was called to put more wood on the fire, and after he withdrew the Governor lay quiet for a time. The grey light of the rainy afternoon grew so pale that Auclair could no longer see his patient's face, and supposed he had fallen asleep. But suddenly he spoke.

"Euclide, do you know the church of Saint-Nicholas-des-Champs, out some distance?"

"Certainly, Monsieur le Comte. I remember it very well."

"Many of my family are buried there; a sister of whom I was fond. I shall be buried here, in the chapel of the Récollets, but I should like my heart to be sent back to France, in a box of lead or silver, and buried near my sister in Saint-Nicholas-des-Champs. I have left instructions to that effect in my will, but I prefer to tell you, as I suppose you will have to attend to it. That is all we need say on the subject.

"Monseigneur de Saint-Vallier called here today, but as I was engaged with the notary, he left word that he would make his visit of ceremony tomorrow. I should be pleased if some indisposition were to keep him at home. If he looks for any apologies or recantations from me, he will be disappointed. The old one will not bother me with civilities." Auclair heard the Count chuckle. "The old one knows where he stands, at least, and never bends his neck. All the same, a better man for this part of the world than the new one. Saint-Vallier belongs at the Court—where he came from."

The Count fell into reflection, and his apothecary sat silent, waiting for his dismissal. Both were thinking of a scene outside the windows, under the low November sky—but the river was not the St. Lawrence. They were looking out on the Pont-Marie, and the hay-barges tied up at the Port-au-Foin. On an afternoon like this the boatmen would be covering the hay-bales with tarpaulins, Auclair was thinking, and about this time the bells always rang from the Célestins' and the church of Saint-Paul.

When the fire fell apart and Auclair got up to mend it, the Count spoke again, as if he knew perfectly well what was in the apothecary's mind. "The Countess de Frontenac writes me that the Île Saint-Louis has become a very fashionable quarter. I can remember when it was hardly considered a respectable place to live in,—when they first began building there, indeed!"

"And my grandfather could remember when it was a wood-pile, patron; before the two islands were joined into one. He was never reconciled to the change, poor man. He always thought it the most convenient place for the wood-supply of our part of Paris."

III

One dark afternoon in November Cécile was sitting in the front shop, knitting a stocking. She sat in her own little chair, placed beside her father's tall stool, on which she had put a candle, as the daylight was so thick. Though the street outside was wet and the fog brown and the house so quiet, and though the Count was ill up in the Château, she was not feeling dull, but happy and contented. As she knitted and watched the shop, she kept singing over Captain Pondaven's old song, about the three ships that came

A Saint-Malo, beau port de mer,
Chargés d'avoin', chargés de bléd,

No more boats from France would come to Quebec as late as this, even her father admitted that, and his herbarium had been put back on the high shelves of the cabinet, where it belonged. As soon as those dried plants were out of sight, the house itself changed; everything seemed to draw closer together, to join hands, as it were. Cécile had polished the candlesticks and pewter cups, rubbed the table and the bed-posts and the chair-claws with oil, darned the rent in her father's counterpane. A little more colour had come back into the carpet and the curtains, she thought. Perhaps that was only because the fire was lit in the salon every evening now, and things always looked better in the fire-light. But no, she really believed that everything in the house, the furni-ture, the china shepherd boy, the casseroles in the kitchen, knew that the herbarium had been restored to the high shelves and that the world was not going to be destroyed this winter.

A life without security, without plans, without preparation

for the future, had been terrible. Nothing had gone right this fall; her father had not put away any wood-doves in fat, or laid in winter vegetables, or bought his supply of wild rice from the Indians. "But we will manage," she sometimes whispered to her trusty poêle when she stuffed him with birch and pine.

Cécile tended the shop alone every afternoon now. A notice on the door requested messieurs les clients to be so good as to call in the morning, as the pharmacien was occupied elsewhere in the afternoon. Nevertheless clients came in the afternoon, especially country people, and her father placed all the most popular remedies on one shelf and marked them clearly, so that Cécile could dispense them when they were called for.

This afternoon, just as she was about to go for another candle, she thought she heard her father coming home; but it proved to be Noël Pommier, the cobbler, who wanted a mixture of rhubarb and senna that M. Auclair sometimes made up for his mother.

Cécile sprang up and told him it was ready at hand, plainly marked. *"Et préféréez-vous les pilules, ou le liquide, Monsieur Noël?"*

"Les pilules, s'il vous plaît, mademoiselle. Et votre père?"

"He is always at the Château after three o'clock. The Governor had been indisposed for two weeks now."

"Everyone knows that, mademoiselle," said the cobbler with a sigh. "Everyone is offering prayers for his recovery. It will be bad for all of us if anything goes wrong with the Count."

"Never fear, monsieur! My father is giving him every care, and he grows a little stronger each day."

"God grant it, mademoiselle. Picard is very much discouraged about his master. He says he cannot shave himself any more and does not look like himself. Picard thinks he ought to be bled."

"Oh, Monsieur Pommier, I wish you could hear what my father has to say to that! And what does Picard know about medicine? But he is not the only one. Other people have tried to persuade my father to bleed the Governor, but he is as firm as a rock."

"I have no doubt Monsieur Auclair knows best, Mademoiselle Cécile; but people will talk at such times, when a public man is ill."

Pommier had scarcely gone when her father came in, with a dragging step and a mournful countenance.

"Papa," said Cécile as she brought him his indoor coat, "I know you are tired, but the dinner will soon be ready. Sit down by the fire and rest a little. And, Father, won't you try to look a little more confident these days? The people watch you, and when you have a discouraged air, they all become discouraged."

"You think so?" He spoke anxiously.

"I am sure of it, Papa. I can tell by the things they say when they call here in your absence. You must look as if the Governor were much, much better."

"He is not. He is failing all the time." Her father sighed. "But you are right. We must put on a better face for the public."

Cécile kissed him and went into the kitchen. Just as she was moving the soup forward to heat, she heard a sharp knock at the shop door. Her father answered it, and Bishop de Saint-Vallier entered. Auclair hurriedly brought more candles into the shop and set a chair for his visitor. After preliminary civilities the Bishop came to the point.

"I have called, Monsieur Auclair, to inquire concerning the Governor's condition. Do you consider his illness mortal?"

"Not necessarily. If he were ten years younger, I should not consider it serious. However, he has great vitality and may very easily rally from this attack."

The Bishop frowned and stroked his narrow chin. He was clearly in some perplexity. "When I called upon the Comte de Frontenac some days ago, he stated that his recovery would be a matter of a week, at most. In short, he refused to consider his indisposition seriously, though to my eyes the mark of death was clearly upon him. Does he really believe he will recover?"

"Very probably. And that is a good state of mind for a sick man."

"Monsieur Auclair," Saint-Vallier spoke up sharply, "I feel that you evade me. Do you yourself believe that the Count will recover?"

"I must ask your indulgence, Monseigneur, but in a case like the Count's a medical adviser should not permit himself to believe in anything but recovery. His doubts would affect the patient. If the Count still has the vital force I have always found in him, he will recover. His organs are sound."

Saint-Vallier seemed to pay little heed to this reply. His eyes had been restlessly sweeping the room from floor to ceiling and now became fixed intently upon one point—on the stuffed alligator, as it happened. He began to speak rapidly, with gracious rise and fall of the voice, but in his most authoritative manner.

"If the Governor's illness is mortal, and he does not realize the fact, he should be brought to realize it. He has a great deal to put right with Heaven. He has used his authority and his influence here for worldly ends, rather than to strengthen the kingdom of God in Septentrional France!" For the first time he flashed a direct glance at the apothecary.

Auclair bowed respectfully. "Such matters are beyond me, Monseigneur. The Governor does not discuss his official business with me."

"But there is always open discussion of these things! Of the Governor's stand on the brandy traffic, for example, which is destroying our missions. I have denounced his policy openly from the pulpit, and on occasions when I noted that you were present in the church. You cannot be ignorant of it."

"Oh, upon that subject the Governor has also spoken publicly. Everyone knows that he considers it an unavoidable evil."

Saint-Vallier drew himself up in his chair and adopted an argumentative tone. "And why unavoidable? You doubtless refer to his proposition that the Indians will sell their furs only to such traders as will supply them with brandy?"

"Yes, Monseigneur; and since the English and Dutch traders give them all the brandy they want, and better prices for their skins as well, we must lose the fur trade altogether if we deny them brandy. And our colony exists by the fur trade alone."

"That is our unique opportunity, Monsieur l'apothicaire, to sacrifice our temporal interests for the glory of God, and impress by our noble example the Dutch and English."

"If Monseigneur thinks the Dutch traders can be touched by a noble example—" Auclair smiled and shook his head. "But these things are all beyond me. I know only what everyone knows,—though I have my own opinions."

"If the Count's illness is as serious as it seems to me, Monsieur Auclair, he should be given an opportunity to acknowledge his mistakes before the world as well as to Heaven. Such an admission might have a salutary influence upon the administration which will follow his. Since he relies upon you, it is your duty to apprise him of the gravity of his condition."

Auclair met Saint-Vallier's glittering, superficial glance and plausible tone rather bluntly.

"I shall do nothing to discourage my patient, Monseigneur, any more than I shall bleed him, as many good people urge me to do. The mind, too, has a kind of blood; in common speech we call it hope."

The Bishop flushed—his sanguine cheeks were apt to become more ruddy when he was crossed or annoyed. He rose and gathered the folds of his cloak about him. "It is time your patient dropped the stubborn mask he has worn so long, and began to realize that none of his enterprises will benefit him now but such as have furthered the interests of Christ's Church in this Province. I have seen him, and I believe he is facing eternity."

Auclair expressed himself as much honoured by the Bishop's visit and accompanied him to the door, holding it open that the light might guide him across the street to the steps of his episcopal Palace. When he returned to the salon, Cécile was bringing in the soup.

"I began to think Monseigneur de Saint-Vallier would never go, Papa. How people do bother us about everything since the Count is ill! I am glad we can keep them away from him, at least."

Her father sat down and took a few spoonfuls of soup. "Why, I find I am quite hungry!" he declared. "And when I came home, I did not think I could eat at all. For some reason, our neighbour's visit seems to have made me more cheerful."

"That is because you were so resolute with him, Father!"

He smiled at her between the candles.

"What restless eyes he has, Cécile; they run all over everything, like quicksilver when I spill it. He kept looking in again and again at your glass fruit, there on the mantel. Do you know, I believe he drew some conclusion from that; he has seen it at the Château, of course. These men who are trained at Court all become a little crafty; they learn to put two and two together. I have always believed that is why our patron never got advancement at Versailles: he is too downright."

IV

It was late afternoon, and Cécile was alone—as she was nearly always now. The Count had died last night. Today her father had gone to the Château to seal his heart up in a casket, so that it could be carried back to France according to his wish. It was already arranged that Father Joseph, Superior of the Récollets, should take the casket to Montreal, then to Fort Orange, and down the river to New York, where the English boats came and went all winter. On one of those boats he would go to England, cross over to France, and journey to Paris with the Count's heart, to bury it in the Montmort chapel at Saint-Nicholas-des-Champs.

Auclair had been gone all the afternoon, and Cécile knew that he would come home exhausted from sorrow, from his night of watching, and from the grim duty which had taken him today to the Count's death-chamber. Cécile regarded this rite with awe, but not with horror; autopsies, she knew, must be performed upon kings and queens and all great people after death. That was the custom. Her father would have the barber-surgeon to help him,—though they were not very good friends, because they disagreed about bleeding people.

The barber complained that the meddlesome apothecary took the bread out of his mouth.

Many times that afternoon Cécile went out to the doorstep and looked up at the Château. A light snow was falling, and the sky was grey. It was very strange to look up at those windows in the south end, and to know that there was no friend, no protection there. She felt as if a strong roof over their heads had been swept away. She was not sure that they would even have a livelihood without the Count's patronage. Their sugar and salt and wine, and her father's Spanish snuff, had always come from the Count's storehouses. The colonists paid very little for their remedies; if they brought a basket of eggs, or a chicken, or a rabbit, they thought they were treating their medical man very handsomely. But what she most dreaded was her father's loneliness. He had lived under the Count's shadow. The Count was the reason for nearly everything he did, — for his being here at all.

About four o'clock, as the darkness began to close in, Cécile put more wood on the fire in the salon and set some milk to warm before it. There was very little to eat in the house. Her father had not been to market for a week. Running to the door every few minutes, she at last saw him coming down the hill, with his black bag full of deadly poisons. He looked grey and sick as she let him in. Before he threw his black bag into the cupboard, he took out of it a lead box, rudely soldered over. She looked at it solemnly.

"Yes," he said, "it is all we have left of him. Father Joseph will set out for France in two days. I am in charge of this box until it starts upon its journey."

He placed it in the cabinet where he kept his medical books, then went into the salon and sank down in his chair by the fire. Cécile knelt on the floor beside him, resting her arms upon his knee. He bent and leaned his cheek for a moment on her shingled brown hair.

"So it is over, my dear," he sighed softly. "It has lasted a lifetime, and now it is over. Since I was six years old, the Count has been my protector, and he was my father's before me. To my mother, and to your mother, he was always courteous and considerate. He belonged to the old order; he cherished those beneath him and rendered his duty to those above

him, but flattered nobody, not the King himself. That time
has gone by. I do not wish to outlive my time."

"But you wish to live on my account, don't you, Father? I
do not belong to the old time. I have got to live on into a
new time; and you are all I have in the world."

Her father went on sadly: "The Count and the old Bishop
were both men of my own period, the kind we looked up to
in my youth. Saint-Vallier and Monsieur de Champigny are of
a different sort. Had I been able to choose my lot in the
world, I would have chosen to be like my patron, for all his
disappointments and sorrows; to be a soldier who fought for
no gain but renown, merciful to the conquered, charitable to
the poor, haughty to the rich and overbearing. Since I could
not be such a man and was born in an apothecary shop, it was
my good fortune to serve such a man and to be honoured by
his confidence."

Cécile slipped quietly away to pour the warm milk into a
cup, and with it she brought a glass of brandy. Her father
drank them. He said he would want no dinner tonight, but
that she must prepare something for herself. Without noticing
whether she did so or not, he sat in a stupor of weariness,
dreaming by the fire. The scene at the Château last night
passed again before his eyes.

The Count had received the Sacrament in perfect consciousness at seven o'clock. Then he sank into a sleep which
became a coma, and lay for three hours breathing painfully,
with his eyes rolled back and only a streak of white showing
between the half-open lids. A little after ten o'clock he suddenly came to himself and looked inquiringly at the group
around his bed; there were two nursing Sisters from the
Hôtel Dieu, the Intendant and Madame de Champigny, Hector
de Callières, Auclair, and Father Joseph, the Récollets' Superior, who had heard the Count's confession and administered
the last rites of the Church. The Count raised his eyebrows
haughtily, as if to demand why his privacy was thus invaded.
He looked from one face to another; in those faces he read
something. He saw the nuns upon their knees, praying. He
seemed to realize his new position in the world and what was
now required of him. The challenge left his face,—a dignified
calm succeeded it. Father Joseph held the crucifix to his lips.

He kissed it. Then, very courteously, he made a gesture with his left hand, indicating that he wished every one to draw back from his bed.

"This I will do alone," his steady glance seemed to say.

All drew back.

"Merci," he said distinctly. That was the last word he spoke. While the group of watchers stood four or five feet away from the bed, wondering, they saw that his face had become altogether natural and lost all look of suffering. He breathed softly for a few moments, then breathed no more. One of the nuns held a feather to his lips. Madame de Champigny got a mirror and put it close to his mouth, but there was no cloud on it. Auclair laid his head down on his patron's chest; there all was still.

As Auclair was returning home after midnight, under the glitter of the hard bright northern stars, he felt for the first time wholly and entirely cut off from France; a helpless exile in a strange land. Not without reason, he told himself bitterly as he looked up at those stars, had the Latin poets insisted that thrice and four times blessed were those to whom it befell to die in the land of their fathers.

While Auclair sat by the fire thinking of these things, numb and broken, Cécile was lying on the sofa, wrapped up in the old shawl Madame Auclair had used so much after she became ill. She, too, was thinking of what they had lost. They would indeed have another winter in Quebec; but everything was changed almost as much as if they had gone away. That sense of a strong protector had counted in her life more than she had ever realized. To be sure, they had not called upon the Count's authority very often; but to know that they could appeal to him at any moment meant security, and gave them a definite place in their little world.

The hours went by. Her father did not speak or move, not even to fix the fire, which was very low. For once, Cécile herself had no wish to set things right. Let the fire burn out; what of it?

At last there came a knock at the door, not very loud, but insistent,—urgent, as it were. Auclair got up from his chair.

"Whoever it is, send him away. I can see no one tonight." He went into the kitchen and shut the door behind him.

Cécile was a little startled, — death made everything strange. She took a candle into the shop, set it down on the counter, and opened the door. Outside there, against the snow, was the outline of a man with a gun strapped on his back. She had thrown her arms around him before she could really see him, — the set of his shoulders told her who it was.

"Oh, Pierre, Pierre Charron!" She began to cry abandonedly, but from joy. Never in all her life had she felt anything so strong and so true, so real and so sure, as that quick embrace that smelled of tobacco and the pine-woods and the fresh snow.

"*Petite tête de garçon!*" he muttered running his hand over her head, which lay on his shoulder. "There, don't try to tell me. I know all about it. I started for Kebec as soon as I heard the Count was sinking. Today, on the river, I passed the messengers going to Montreal; they called the word to me. And your father?"

"I don't know what to do, Pierre. It is worse with him than when my mother died. There seems to be no hope for us."

"I understand," he stroked her soothingly. "I knew this would be a blow to him. I said to myself in Ville-Marie: 'I must be there when it happens.' I came as quickly as I could. Never did I paddle so fast. The breeze was against me, there was no chance of a sail. I had only a half-man to help me —Antoine Frichette, you remember? That poor fellow for whom your father made the belly-band. He did his best, but since his hurt he has no wind. I'm here at last, to be of any use I can. Command me." He had loosed the big kerchief from his neck, and now he gently wiped her cheeks dry with it. Turning her face about to the candlelight, he regarded it intently.

"I wish you would go to him, Pierre. He is in the kitchen."

He kissed her softly on the forehead, unslung his gun, and went out into the kitchen. He, too, closed the door behind him. In the few moments while she was left alone in the shop, Cécile opened the outer door again and looked up toward the Château. The falling snow and the darkness hid it from sight; but she had once more that feeling of security, as if the strong roof were over them again; over her and the shop and the salon and all her mother's things. For the first time she realized that her father loved Pierre for the same reason he had loved the Count; both had the qualities he did not have himself, but which he most admired in other men.

When they came in from the kitchen, Charron had his arm over Auclair's shoulder.

"Cécile," he called, "je n'ai pas de chance. Evidently I am too late for supper, and I have not had a morsel since I broke camp before daybreak."

"Supper? But we have had no supper here tonight. We had no appetite. I will make some for you, at once. There is not much in the house, I am afraid; my father has not been to market. Smoked eels, perhaps?"

Charron made a grimace. "Detestable! Even I can do better than that. I shot a deer for our supper in the forest last night, and I brought a haunch along with me,—outside, in my bag. What else have you?"

"Not much." Cécile felt deeply mortified to confess this, though it was not her fault. "We have some wild rice left from last year, and there are some carrots. We always have preserves, and of course there is soup."

"Excellent; all that sounds very attractive to me at the moment. You attend to everything else, but by your leave I will cook the venison in my own way. It's enough for us all, and there will be good pickings left for Blinker."

When Charron went out to get his game-bag, Auclair whispered to his daughter: "Are we really so destitute, my child? Do the best you can for him. I will open a box of the conserves from France."

He now seemed very anxious about his dinner, and she could not forbear a reproachful glance at the head of the house, who had been so neglectful of his duties.

"And you, Monsieur Euclide," said Pierre, when he came back with the haunch in his hand, "you ought to produce something rather special from your cellar for us."

"It shall be the best I have," declared his host.

The supper lasted until late. After the dessert the apothecary opened a bottle of heavy gold-coloured wine from the South.

"This," he said, "is a wine the Count liked after supper. His family was from the South, and his father always kept on hand wines that were brought up from Bordeaux and the Rhone vineyards. The Count inherited that taste." He sighed heavily.

"Euclide," said Charron, "tomorrow it may be you or I; that is the way to look at death. Not all the wine in the Château, not all the wines in the great cellars of France, could warm the Count's blood now. Let us cheer our hearts a little while we can. Good wine was put into the grapes by our Lord, for friends to enjoy together."

When it was almost midnight, the visitor said he was too tired to go hunt a lodging, and would gladly avail himself of the invitation, often extended, but never before accepted, of spending the night here and sleeping on the sofa in the salon.

Cécile, in her upstairs bedroom, turned to slumber with the weight of doubt and loneliness melted away. Her last thoughts before she sank into forgetfulness were of a friend, devoted and fearless, here in the house with them, as if he were one of themselves. He had not a throne behind him, like the Count (it had been very far behind, indeed!), not the authority of a parchment and seal. But he had authority, and a power which came from knowledge of the country and its people; from knowledge, and from a kind of passion. His daring and his pride seemed to her even more splendid than Count Frontenac's.

Epilogue

ON THE SEVENTEENTH DAY of August 1713, fifteen years after the death of Count Frontenac, the streets of Quebec and the headland overlooking the St. Lawrence were thronged with people. By the waterside the Governor-General and Monsieur Vaudreuil, the Intendant, with all the clergy, regular and secular, the magistrates, and the officers from the garrison, stood waiting to receive a long-expected guest. Down the river lay a ship from France, *La Manon*, unable to come in against the wind. A small boat had been sent out to bring in one of her passengers. As the little boat drew near the shore, all the cannon on the fortifications, and the guns on the vessels anchored in the roadstead, thundered a salute of welcome to Monseigneur de Saint-Vallier, at last returning to his people after an absence of thirteen years.

When the prelate put foot upon the shore of Quebec, the church-bells began to ring, and continued to ring while the Governor-General, the Intendant, and the Archidiacre made addresses of welcome. The Indendant's carriage stood ready to convey the Bishop, but he preferred, characteristically, to ascend on foot to the Cathedral in the Upper Town, surrounded by the clergy and preceded by drums and hautbois.

Euclide Auclair, the old apothecary, standing before his door on Mountain Hill to watch the procession, was shocked at the change in Monseigneur de Saint-Vallier. When he sailed for France thirteen years ago, he was a very young man of forty-seven; now he came back a very old man of sixty. Every physical trait by which Auclair remembered the handsome and arrogant churchman had disappeared. He would never have recognized, in this heavy, stooped, lame old man going up the hill, the slender and rather dramatic figure he had so often seen mounting the steps of the episcopal Palace across the way. The narrow, restless shoulders were fat and bent; the Bishop carried his head like a man broken to the yoke.

Auclair watched the procession until the turn of the way shut Monseigneur de Saint-Vallier from sight, then went back to his shop and sat down, overcome. The thirteen years which for him had passed quietly, happily, had been bitter ones for the wandering Bishop. Nine years ago Saint-Vallier was on his way back to Canada after one of his long absences, when his ship, *La Seine*, was captured by the English, taken into London, and sold at auction. The Bishop himself was declared a prisoner of state, and was sequestered in a small English town near Farnham until the French King should ransom him.

Politics intervened: King Louis had lately seized and imprisoned the Baron of Méan, Dean of the Cathedral of Liège. The German Emperor was much offended at this, and besought Queen Anne not to release the Bishop of Quebec under any other terms than as an exchange for the Baron of Méan. For five years Saint-Vallier remained a prisoner of state in England, until King Louis at last set the Baron of Méan at liberty and recalled the Bishop of Quebec to France. But this did not mean that he was free to return to Canada. During his captivity his enemies in Quebec and Montreal had been busy, had repeatedly written the Minister, Pontchartrain, that the affairs of the colony went better with the Bishop away; that the King would be assisting his Canadian subjects by keeping Saint-Vallier in France. This the King did. He kept him, indeed, almost as long as the Queen of England had done.

That period of detention in France had sobered and saddened the wilful Bishop. His captivity in England he could ascribe to the hostilities of nations; to himself and to others he was able to put a very good face on it. But he could not pretend that he was kept in France for any other reason than that he was not wanted in Quebec. He had to admit to the Minister that he had made mistakes; that he had not taken the wise course with the Canadian colonists. Only by unceasing importunities, and by working upon the sympathies of Madame de Maintenon, who had always befriended him, had he ever wrung from the King permission to sail back to his diocese.

On this day of his return, even his enemies were softened at seeing how the man was changed. In place of his former assurance he seemed to wear a leaden mantle of humility; he climbed heavily up the hill to the Cathedral as if he were treading down the mistakes of the past.

Auclair, the apothecary, on the other hand, had scarcely changed at all. His delicate complexion had grown a trifle sallow from staying indoors so much, but the years which had made the Bishop an old man had passed lightly over the apothecary. Even his shop was still the same; perhaps a trifle dustier than it used to be, and opposite his counter there was a new cabinet screwed fast to the wall, full of brilliant sea-shells, starfish and horseshoe crabs, dried seaweed and branches of coral. Everyone looked at this case on entering the shop,—there was something surprising and unexpected about such a collection. It suggested the South and blue seas far away.

On the third day after the Cathedral had welcomed its long absent shepherd, that prelate himself came to call upon the apothecary, arriving at the door on foot and unattended. He greeted Auclair with friendliness and took the proffered chair, admitting that he felt the summer heat in Quebec more than he used to do.

"But you yourself, Monsieur Auclair, are little altered. I rejoice to see that God has preserved you in excellent health."

Auclair hastened to bring out a glass of fortifying cordial, and the Bishop accepted it gratefully. While he drank it, Auclair regarded him. It was unfortunate that Saint-Vallier, of all men, should have grown heavy—it took away his fine carriage. His once luxuriant brown hair was thin and grey, his triangular cheeks had become full and soft, like an old woman's, and they were waxy white. Between them, the sharp chin had almost disappeared.

"I have been thinking how fortunate I shall be to have you for my neighbour once more, Monseigneur," said Auclair. "Every spring I have given some little advice to the workmen who were attending to your garden, and I have often wished you could see your shrubs coming into bloom."

The Bishop smiled faintly and shook his head.

"Ah, monsieur, I shall not live in the episcopal Palace again. Perhaps that was a mistake; I should have waited to understand the designs of Providence more perfectly."

"Not live in your own residence, Monseigneur? That will be a great disappointment to all of us. The building is in excellent condition."

The Bishop again shook his head. "I find myself too poor now to maintain such an establishment. I suppose you do not know anyone who would care to rent the Palace? The rental would be very helpful to me in my present undertakings. No, I shall reside at the Hôpital Général.* My good daughters there have arranged un petit appartement of two rooms which will meet my needs very well. I shall reside with them for the remainder of my life, God willing. Their chaplain is old and must soon retire, and I shall take his place. The office of chaplain will be quite compatible with my other duties."

Auclair was amazed. "In a hospital the duties of a chaplain are considerable, are they not?"

"But very congenial to me—" (the old man folded his hands over the kerchief he had taken out to wipe his brow) —"to celebrate the morning mass for the sisters and to hear their confessions; to administer the consolations of the Church to the sick and the dying. As chaplain I shall be in daily attendance upon the unfortunate, as is my wish."

Auclair sat silent for some moments, stroking his short beard in perplexity. Evidently nothing in his former relations with Monseigneur de Saint-Vallier was a guide for future intercourse. He changed the subject and began to speak of happenings in Quebec during the Bishop's absence, of common acquaintances who had died in that time, among them old Monseigneur de Laval.

Saint-Vallier sighed. "Would it had been permitted me to return in time to thank him for the labours he underwent for my flock during the years of my captivity, and to close his eyes at the last. I can never hope to be to this people all that my venerable predecessor became, through his devotion and his long residence among them. But I shall be with them now for as long as God spares me, and I hope to be deserving of their affection."

At this moment a countrywoman appeared at the door. She was about to withdraw when she saw what visitor the apothecary was entertaining, but the Bishop called her back and

---

*Some years before he sailed for France in 1770, Bishop de Saint-Vallier had founded the Hôpital Général, for the aged and incurable. The hospital still stands today, much enlarged; the wards which Saint-Vallier built and the two small rooms in which he lived until his death are unchanged.

insisted that his host attend to her needs. He waited patiently in his chair while she bought fox-glove water for her dropsical father-in-law, and liquorice for her baby's cough. While he was serving her, Auclair wondered how he could give a turn to the Bishop's talk and learn from him what was going on at home. When the farmer woman had gone, he took the liberty of questioning his visitor directly.

"You have been at Versailles lately, Monseigneur? And how are things there, pray tell me?"

"Very sad since the death of the young Duc and Duchesse de Bourgogne last year. The King will never recover from that double loss. In the Duc, his grandson, he foresaw a wise and happy reign for France; and the young Duchesse had been the idol of his heart ever since she first came to them from Savoie. She was the life of the Court,—as dear to Madame de Maintenon as to the King. The official mourning is over, but the Court mourns, nevertheless."

Auclair nodded. "And the King, I suppose, is an old man now."

"Yes, the King is old. He still comes down to supper to the music of twenty-four violins, still works indefatigably with his ministers; there is dancing and play and conversation in the Salle d'Apollon every evening. His Court remains the most brilliant in Europe,—but his heart is not in it. There is no one left who can charm away his years and his cares as the little Duchesse de Bourgogne did, and nothing can make him forget for one hour the death of the Duc de Bourgogne. All Christendom, monsieur, has suffered an incalculable loss in the death of that pious prince."

"They died within a few days of each other, we heard."

Saint-Vallier bowed his head. "They were buried in the same tomb, and their little son with them."

"There is still talk of poison?"

"Popular opinion accuses the Duc d'Orléans. Their second son, an infant in arms, showed the same symptoms of poisoning, but he survived."

"Ah," said Auclair, "a bad situation! The King is seventy-seven, and the Dauphin a child in arms. That will mean a long regency. I suppose the young Duc de Berry will fill that office?"

"God grant it, monsieur, God spare him!" exclaimed the Bishop fervently. "If any mischance were to befall the Duc de Berry, then that arch-atheist and suspected poisoner the Duc d'Orléans would be regent of France!" Saint-Vallier's voice cracked at a high pitch.

Auclair crossed himself devoutly. "I should have liked to see my King once more. He has been a great King. Is he much altered in person?"

"He is old. I had a private interview with His Majesty last November, late in the afternoon, when he was taking his exercise in the Parc of Versailles. We had scarcely begun our conference when a wind arose, stripping the trees that were already half-bare. The King invited me to go indoors to his cabinet, remarking that it distressed him now to hear the autumn winds and to see the leaves fall. That seemed to me to indicate a change."

"Yes," said Auclair, "that tells a story."

"Monsieur," began the Bishop sadly, "we are in the beginning of a new century, but periods do not always correspond with centuries. At home the old age is dying, but the new is still hidden. I felt the same condition in England, during my long captivity there. There is now no figure in the world such as our King was thirty years ago. The changes in the nations are all those of the old growing older. You have done well to remain here where nothing changes. Here with you I find everything the same." He glanced about the shop and peered into the salon. "And the little daughter, whom I used to see running in and out?"

"She is married, to our old friend Pierre Charron of Ville-Marie. He has built a commodious house in the Upper Town, beyond the Ursuline convent. They are well established in the world."

"You live alone, then?"

"For part of the year. Perhaps you remember a little boy whom my daughter befriended, Jacques Gaux? His mother was a loose woman—she died in your Hôpital Général, some years ago. The boy is now a sailor, and when he is in Quebec, between voyages, he lives with me. He occupies my daughter's little chamber upstairs." Auclair pointed to the cabinet of shells and corals. "He brings me these things back from his voyages; he is in the West India trade. I should like to keep him here all the time; but his father was a sailor—it is natural."

"No," said the Bishop, "I do not recall him. But your daughter I remember with affection. Heaven has blessed her with children?"

The apothecary's eyes twinkled. "Four sons already, Monseigneur. She is bringing up four little boys, the Canadians of the future."

"Ah yes, the Canadians of the future,—the true Canadians."

There was something in Saint-Vallier's voice as he said this which touched Auclair's heart; a note humble and wistful, something sad and defeated. Sometimes a neighbour whom we have disliked a lifetime for his arrogance and conceit lets fall a single commonplace remark that shows us another side, another man, really; a man uncertain, and puzzled, and in the dark like ourselves. Had his visitor not been a Bishop, Auclair would have reached out and grasped his hand and murmured: "Courage, mon bourgeois," as he did to down-hearted patients. The two men sat together in a warm and friendly silence until Saint-Vallier rose and said he must be going. "I shall have the pleasure of confirming your grandsons, I hope? They will live to see better times than ours."

Auclair accompanied him to the door and watched him tread his way up the hill and round the turn of the street. Then he went back to his desk with the feeling that old feuds were forgotten. He would have a great deal to tell Cécile when he went to supper there tonight. She would be quicker than anyone to sense the transformation in their old neighbour, who had built himself an episcopal residence approached by twenty-four stone steps, and who now proposed to spend the rest of his life in two small rooms in the hospital out on the river Charles. To be sure, the Bishop was a little theatrical in his humility, as he had been in his grandeur; but that was his way, Auclair reflected, and, after all, nobody can help his way. If a man admits his mistakes, that is a great deal, when he is a proud man and a Dauphinois—always a stiff-necked race.

While he was closing his shop and changing his coat to go up to his daughter's house, he thought over much that his visitor had told him, and he believed that he was indeed fortunate to spend his old age here where nothing changed; to watch his grandsons grow up in a country where the death of the King, the probable evils of a long regency, would never touch them.

LUCY GAYHEART

Book I

IN HAVERFORD on the Platte the townspeople still talk of Lucy Gayheart. They do not talk of her a great deal, to be sure; life goes on and we live in the present. But when they do mention her name it is with a gentle glow in the face or the voice, a confidential glance which says: "Yes, you, too, remember?" They still see her as a slight figure always in motion; dancing or skating, or walking swiftly with intense direction, like a bird flying home.

When there is a heavy snowfall, the older people look out of their windows and remember how Lucy used to come darting through just such storms, her muff against her cheek, not shrinking, but giving her body to the wind as if she were catching step with it. And in the heat of summer she came just as swiftly down the long shaded sidewalks and across the open squares blistering in the sun. In the breathless glare of August noons, when the horses hung their heads and the workmen "took it slow," she never took it slow. Cold, she used to say, made her feel more alive; heat must have had the same effect.

The Gayhearts lived at the west edge of Haverford, half a mile from Main Street. People said "out to the Gayhearts' " and thought it rather a long walk in summer. But Lucy covered the distance a dozen times a day, covered it quickly with that walk so peculiarly her own, like an expression of irrepressible light-heartedness. When the old women at work in their gardens caught sight of her in the distance, a mere white figure under the flickering shade of the early summer trees, they always knew her by the way she moved. On she came, past hedges and lilac bushes and woolly-green grape arbours and rows of jonquils, and one knew she was delighted with everything; with her summer clothes and the air and the sun and the blossoming world. There was something in her nature that was like her movements, something direct and unhesitating and joyous, and in her golden-brown eyes.

They were not gentle brown eyes, but flashed with gold sparks like that Colorado stone we call the tiger-eye. Her skin was rather dark, and the colour in her lips and cheeks was like the red of dark peonies—deep, velvety. Her mouth was so warm and impulsive that every shadow of feeling made a change in it.

Photographs of Lucy mean nothing to her old friends. It was her gaiety and grace they loved. Life seemed to lie very near the surface in her. She had that singular brightness of young beauty: flower gardens have it for the first few hours after sunrise.

We missed Lucy in Haverford when she went away to Chicago to study music. She was eighteen years old then; talented, but too careless and light-hearted to take herself very seriously. She never dreamed of a "career." She thought of music as a natural form of pleasure, and as a means of earning money to help her father when she came home. Her father, Jacob Gayheart, led the town band and gave lessons on the clarinet, flute, and violin, at the back of his watch-repairing shop. Lucy had given piano lessons to beginners ever since she was in the tenth grade. Children liked her, because she never treated them like children; they tried to please her, especially the little boys.

Though Jacob Gayheart was a good watchmaker, he wasn't a good manager. Born of Bavarian parents in the German colony at Belleville, Illinois, he had learned his trade under his father. He came to Haverford young and married an American wife, who brought him a half-section of good farm land. After her death he borrowed money on this farm to buy another, and now they were both mortgaged. That troubled his older daughter, Pauline, but it did not trouble Mr. Gayheart. He took more pains to make the band boys practise than he did to keep up his interest payments. He was a town character, of course, and people joked about him, though they were proud of their band. Mr. Gayheart looked like an old daguerreotype of a minor German poet; he wore a moustache and goatee and had a fine sweep of dark hair above his forehead, just a little grey at the sides. His intelligent, lazy hazel eyes seemed to say: "But it's a very pleasant world, why bother?"

He managed to enjoy every day from start to finish. He got up early in the morning and worked for an hour in his flower garden. Then he took his bath and dressed for the day, selecting his shirt and necktie as carefully as if he were going to pay a visit. After breakfast he lit a good cigar and walked into town, never missing the flavour of his tobacco for a moment. Usually he put a flower in his coat before he left home. No one ever got more satisfaction out of good health and simple pleasures and a blue-and-gold band uniform than Jacob Gayheart. He was probably the happiest man in Haverford.

2

It was the end of the Christmas holidays, the Christmas of 1901, Lucy's third winter in Chicago. She was spending her vacation at home. There had been good skating all through Christmas week, and she had made the most of it. Even on her last afternoon, when she should have been packing, she was out with a party of Haverford boys and girls, skating on the long stretch of ice north of Duck Island. This island, nearly half a mile in length, split the river in two,—or, rather, it split a shallow arm off the river. The Platte River proper was on the south side of this island and it seldom froze over; but the shallow stream between the island and the north shore froze deep and made smooth ice. This was before the days of irrigation from the Platte; it was then a formidable river in flood time. During the spring freshets it sometimes cut out a new channel in the soft farm land along its banks and changed its bed altogether.

At about four o'clock on this December afternoon a light sleigh with bells and buffalo robes and a good horse came rapidly along the road from town and turned at Benson's corner into the skating-place. A tall young man sprang out, tied his horse to the hitch-bar, where a row of sleighs already stood, and hurried to the shore with his skating-shoes in his hand. As he put them on, he scanned the company moving over the ice. It was not hard to pick out the figure he was looking for. Six of the strongest skaters had left the others behind and were going against the wind, toward the end of the island. Two were in advance of the rest, Jim Hardwick and Lucy Gayheart. He knew her by her brown squirrel jacket and fur cap, and by her easy stroke. The two ends of a long crimson scarf were floating on the wind behind her, like two slender crimson wings.

Harry Gordon struck out across the ice to overtake her. He, too, was a fine skater; a big fellow, the heavy-weight boxer type, and as light on his feet as a boxer. Nevertheless he was a trifle winded when he passed the group of four and shot alongside Jim Hardwick.

"Jim," he called, "will you give me a turn with Lucy before the sun goes down?"

"Sure, Harry. I was only keeping her out of mischief for you." The lad fell back. Haverford boys gave way to Harry Gordon good-naturedly. He was the rich young man of the town, and he was not arrogant or overbearing. He was known as a good fellow; rather hard in business, but liberal with the ball team and the band; public-spirited, people said.

"Why, Harry, you said you weren't coming!" Lucy exclaimed as she took his arm.

"Didn't think I could. I did, though. Drove Flicker into a lather getting out here after the directors' meeting. This is the best part of the afternoon, anyway. Come along." They crossed hands and went straight ahead in two-step time.

The sun was dropping low in the south, and all the flat snow-covered country, as far as the eye could see, was beginning to glow with a rose-coloured light, which presently would deepen to orange and flame. The black tangle of willows on the island made a thicket like a thorn hedge, and the knotty, twisted, slow-growing scrub-oaks with flat tops took on a bronze glimmer in that intense oblique light which seemed to be setting them on fire.

As the sun declined, the wind grew sharper. They had left the skating party far behind. "Shan't we turn?" Lucy gasped presently.

"Not yet. I want to get into that sheltered fork of the island. I have some Scotch whisky in my pocket; that will warm you up."

"How nice! I'm getting a little tired. I've been out a long while."

The end of the island forked like a fish's tail. When they had rounded one of these points, Harry swung her in to the shore. They sat down on a bleached cottonwood log, where the black willow thicket behind them made a screen. The interlacing twigs threw off red light like incandescent wires, and the snow underneath was rose-colour. Harry poured Lucy some whisky in the metal cup that screwed over the stopper; he himself drank from the flask. The round red sun was falling like a heavy weight; it touched the horizon line and sent quivering fans of red and gold over the wide country. For a moment Lucy and Harry Gordon were sitting in a stream of blinding light; it burned on their skates and on the flask and the metal cup. Their faces became so brilliant that they looked at each other and laughed. In an instant the light was gone; the frozen stream and the snow-masked prairie land became violet, under the blue-green sky. Wherever one looked there was nothing but flat country and low hills, all violet and grey. Lucy gave a long sigh.

Gordon lifted her from the log and they started back, with the wind behind them. They found the river empty, a lonely stretch of blue-grey ice; all the skaters had gone. Harry knew by her stroke that Lucy was tired. She had been out a long while before he came, and she had made a special effort to skate with him. He was sorry and pleased. He guided her in to the shore at some distance from his sleigh, knelt down and took off her skating shoes, changed his own, and with a sudden movement swung her up in his arms and carried her over the trampled snow to his cutter. As he tucked her under the buffalo robes she thanked him.

"The wind seems to have made me very sleepy, Harry. I'm afraid I won't do much packing tonight. No matter; there's tomorrow. And it was a good skate."

On the drive home Gordon let his sleigh-bells (very musical bells, he had got them to please Lucy) do most of the talking. He knew when to be quiet.

Lucy felt drowsy and dreamy, glad to be warm. The sleigh was such a tiny moving spot on that still white country settling into shadow and silence. Suddenly Lucy started and struggled under the tight blankets. In the darkening sky she had seen the first star come out; it brought her heart into her throat. That point of silver light spoke to her like a signal, released another kind of life and feeling which did not belong here. It overpowered her. With a mere thought she had reached that star and it had answered, recognition had flashed between. Something knew, then, in the unknowing waste: something had always known, forever! That joy of saluting what is far above one was an eternal thing, not merely something that had happened to her ignorance and her foolish heart.

The flash of understanding lasted but a moment. Then everything was confused again. Lucy shut her eyes and leaned on Harry's shoulder to escape from what she had gone so far to snatch. It was too bright and too sharp. It hurt, and made one feel small and lost.

3

The following night, Sunday evening, all the boys and girls who had been at home for the vacation were going back to school. Most of them would stop at Lincoln; Lucy was the only one going through to Chicago. The train from the west was due to leave Haverford at seven-thirty, and by seven o'clock sleighs and wagons from all directions were driving toward the railway station at the south end of town.

The station platform was soon full of restless young people, glancing up the track, looking at their watches, as if they could not endure their own town a moment longer. Presently a carriage drawn by two horses dashed up to the siding, and the swaying crowd ran to meet it, shouting.

"Here she is, here's Fairy!"

"Fairy Blair!"

"Hello, Fairy!"

Out jumped a yellow-haired girl, supple and quick as a kitten, with a little green Tyrolese hat pulled tight over her curls. She ripped off her grey fur coat, threw it into the air for the boys to catch, and ran down the platform in her travelling suit—a black velvet jacket and scarlet waistcoat, with a skirt very short indeed for the fashion of that time. Just then a man came out from the station and called that the train would be twenty minutes late. Groans and howls broke from the crowd.

"Oh, hell!"

"What in thunder can we do?"

The green hat shrugged and laughed. "Shut up. Quit swearing. We'll wake the town."

She caught two boys by the elbow, and between these stiffly overcoated figures raced out into the silent street, swaying from left to right, pushing the boys as if she were shaking two saplings, and doing an occasional shuffle with her feet. She had a pretty, common little face, and her eyes were so lit-up and reckless that one might have thought she had been drinking. Her fresh little mouth, without being ugly, was really very naughty. She couldn't push the boys fast enough; suddenly she sprang from between the two rigid figures as if she had been snapped out of a slingshot and ran up the street with the whole troop at her heels. They were all a little crazy, but as she was the craziest, they followed her. They swerved aside to let the town bus pass.

The bus backed up to the siding. Mr. Gayheart alighted and gave a hand to each of his daughters. Pauline, the elder, got out first. She was short and stout and blonde, like the Prestons, her mother's people. She was twelve years Lucy's senior. (Two boys, born between the daughters, died in childhood.) It was Pauline who had brought her sister up; their mother died when Lucy was only six.

Pauline was talking as she got out of the bus, urging her father to hurry and get the trunk checked. "There are always a lot of people in the baggage room, and it takes Bert forever to check a trunk. And be sure you tell him to get it onto this train. When Mrs. Young went to Minneapolis her trunk lay here for twenty-four hours after she started, and she didn't get it until . . ." But Mr. Gayheart walked calmly away and lost the story of Mrs. Young's trunk. Lucy remained standing beside her sister, but she did not hear it either. She was thinking of something else.

Pauline took Lucy's arm determinedly, as if it were the right thing to do, and for a moment she was silent. "Look, there's Harry Gordon's sleigh coming up, with the Jenks boy driving. Do you suppose he is going east tonight?"

"He said he might go to Omaha," Lucy replied carelessly.

"That's nice. You will have company," said Pauline, with the rough-and-ready heartiness she often used to conceal annoyance.

Lucy made no comment, but looked in through a window at the station clock. She had never wanted so much to be moving; to be alone and to feel the train gliding along the smooth rails; to watch the little stations flash by.

Fairy Blair, in her Tyrolese hat, came back from her run quite out of breath and supported by the two boys. As she passed the Gayheart sisters she called:

"Off for the East, Lucy? Wish I were going with you. You musical people get all the fun." As she and her overcoated props came to a standstill she watched Lucy out of the tail of her eye. They were the two most popular girls in Haverford, and Fairy found Lucy frightfully stuffy and girly-girly. Whenever she met Harry Gordon she tossed her head and flashed at him a look which plainly said: "What in hell do you want with *that?*"

Mr. Gayheart returned, gave his daughter her trunk check, and stood looking up at the sky. Among other impractical pursuits he had studied astronomy from time to time. When at last the scream of the whistle shivered through the still winter air, Lucy drew a quick breath and started forward. Her father took her arm and pressed it softly; it was not wise to show too much affection for his younger daughter. A long line of swaying lights came out of the flat country to the west, and a moment later the white beam from the headlight streamed along the steel rails at their feet. The great locomotive, coated with hoar-frost, passed them and stopped, panting heavily.

Pauline snatched her sister and gave her a clumsy kiss. Mr. Gayheart picked up Lucy's bag and led the way to the right car. He found her seat, arranged her things neatly, then stood looking at her with a discerning, appreciative smile. He liked pretty girls, even in his own family. He put his arm around her, and as he kissed her he murmured in her ear: "She's a nice girl, my Lucy!" Then he went slowly down the car and got off just as the porter was taking up the step. Pauline was already in a fret, convinced that he would be carried on to the next station.

In Lucy's car were several boys going back to the University at Lincoln. They at once came to her seat and began talking to her. When Harry Gordon entered and walked down the aisle, they drew back, but he shook his head.

"I'm going out to the diner now. I'll be back later."

Lucy shrugged as he passed on. Wasn't that just like him? Of course he knew that she, and all the other students, would have eaten an early supper at the family board before they started; but he might have asked her and the boys to go out to the dining-car with him and have a dessert or a Welsh rabbit. Another instance of the instinctive unwastefulness which had made the Gordons rich! Harry could be splendidly extravagant upon occasion, but he made an occasion of it; it was the outcome of careful forethought.

Lucy gave her whole attention to the lads who were so pleased to have it. They were all about her own age, while Harry was eight years older. Fairy Blair was holding a little court at the other end of the car, but distance did not muffle her occasional spasmodic laugh—a curious laugh, like a bleat, which had the effect of an indecent gesture. When this mirth broke out, the boys who were beside Lucy looked annoyed, and drew closer to her, as if protesting their loyalty. She was sorry when Harry Gordon came back and they went away. She received him rather coolly, but he didn't notice that at all. He began talking at once about the new street-lamps they were to have in Haverford; he and his father had borne half the cost of them.

Harry sat comfortably back in the Pullman seat, but he did not lounge. He sat like a gentleman. He had a good physical presence, whether in action or repose. He was immensely conceited, but not nervously or aggressively so. Instead of being a weakness in him, it amounted to a kind of strength.

Such easy self-possession was very reassuring to a mercurial, vacillating person like Lucy.

Tonight, as it happened, Lucy wanted to be alone; but ordinarily she was glad to meet Harry anywhere; to pass him in the post-office or to see him coming down the street. If she stopped for only a word with him, his vitality and unfailing satisfaction with life set her up. No matter what they talked about, it was amusing. She felt absolutely free with him, and she found everything about him genial; his voice, his keen blue eyes, his fresh skin and sandy hair. People said he was hard in business and took advantage of borrowers in a tight place; but neither his person nor his manner gave a hint of such qualities.

While he was chatting confidentially with her about the new street-lamps, Harry noticed that Lucy's hands were restless and that she moved about in her seat.

"What's the matter, Lucy? You're fidgety."

She pulled herself up and smiled. "Isn't it silly! Travelling always makes me nervous. But I'm not very used to it, you know."

"You're in a hurry to get back. I can tell," he nodded knowingly. "How about the opera this spring? Will you let me come on for a week and go with me every night?"

"Oh, that will be splendid! But I don't know about every night. I'm teaching now, you see. I'm much busier than I was last year."

"We can fix that all right. I'll make a call on Auerbach. I got on with him first-rate. I told him I had known you ever since you were a youngster." Harry chuckled and leaned forward a little. "Do you know the first time I ever saw you, Lucy? It was in the old skating-rink. I suppose Haverford was about the last town on earth to have a skating-rink."

"But that was ages ago. The old rink was pulled down before your bank was built."

"That's right. Father and I were staying at the hotel. We had come on to look the town over. One afternoon I was passing the rink and I heard a piano going, so I went in. An old man was playing a waltz, *Hearts and Flowers* I think they called it. There were a bunch of people on the floor, but I picked you out first shot. You must have been about thirteen, with your hair down your back. You had on a short skirt and a skin-tight red jersey, and you were going like a streak. I thought you had the prettiest eyes in the world—Still think so," he added, puckering his brows, as if he were making a grave admission.

Lucy laughed. Harry was cautious, even in compliments.

"Oh, thank you, Harry! I had such good times in that old rink. I missed it terribly after it was pulled down. Pauline wouldn't let me go to dances then. But I don't remember you very well until you began to pitch for Haverford. Everyone was crazy about your in-curves. Why did you give up base-ball?"

"Too lazy, I guess." He shrugged his smooth shoulders. "I liked playing ball, though. But now about the opera. You'll keep the first two weeks of April open for me? I can't tell now just when I'll be able to run on."

Young Gordon was watching Lucy as they talked, and thinking that he had about made up his mind. He wasn't rash, he hadn't been in a hurry. He didn't like the idea of marrying the watchmaker's daughter, when so many brilliant opportunities were open to him. But as he had often told himself before, he would just have to swallow the watch-maker. During the two winters Lucy had been away in Chi-cago, he had played about with lots of girls in the cities where his father's business took him. But there was simply nobody like her,—for him, at least.

Tomorrow he would have to deal with a rather delicate sit-uation. Harriet Arkwright, of the St. Joseph Arkwrights, was visiting a friend in Omaha, and she had telephoned him to come on and take her to a dance. He had carried things along pretty far with Miss Arkwright. Her favour was flattering to a small-town man. She was a person of position in St. Joe. Her father was president of the oldest banking house, and she had a considerable fortune of her own, from her mother. If she was twenty-six years old and still unmarried, it was not from lack of suitors. She had been in no hurry to tie herself up. She managed her own property very successfully, travelled a good deal, liked her independence. A woman of the world, Harry considered her; good style, always at her ease, had a kind of authority that money and social position give. But she was

plain, confound it! She looked like the men of her family.
And she had a hard, matter-of-fact voice, which never kindled
with anything; slightly nasal. Whatever she spoke of, she di-
vested of charm. If she thanked him for his gorgeous roses,
her tone deflowered the flowers.

Harry liked to play with the idea of how such a marriage
would affect his future, but he had never tried to make himself believe that he was in love with Harriet. Strangely
enough, the only girl who gave him any deep thrill was this
same Lucy, who lived in his own town, was poor as a church
mouse, never flattered him, and often laughed at him. When
he was with her, life was different; that was all.

And she was growing up, he realized. All through the
Christmas vacation he had felt a change in her. She was perhaps a trifle more reserved. At the dance, on New Year's Eve,
he thought she held herself away from him just a little—and
from everyone else. She wasn't cold, she had never looked
lovelier, never been more playfully affectionate toward her old
friends. But she was not there in the old way. All evening her
eyes shone with something she did not tell him. The moment
she was not talking to someone, that look came back. And in
every waltz she seemed to be looking over his shoulder at
something—positively enchanting! . . . whereas there was
only the same old crowd, dancing in the Masonic Hall, with a
"crash" over the Masonic carpet. He would not soon forget
that New Year's Eve. It had brought him up short. Lucy
wasn't an artless, happy little country girl any longer; she was
headed toward something. He had better be making up his
mind. Even tonight, here on the train, when she seemed to
give him her whole attention, she didn't, really.

The porter came for Gordon's bags, and said they were
pulling into Omaha. Lucy went out to the vestibule with
Harry, and they talked in low tones during the stop. He
stood holding her hand and looking down at her with that
blue-eyed friendliness which seemed so transparent and uncalculating, until the porter called "All aboard!" Harry kissed
her on the cheek and stepped down to the station platform.
Lucy waved to him through the window while the train was
pulling out.

Gordon got into a horse cab and started for his hotel. His

chin was lowered in his muffler, and he smiled at the street-
lights as the cab rattled along. Yes, he told himself, he must
use diplomacy with Miss Arkwright for a while longer. Her
stock was going down. He meant to commit the supreme
extravagance and marry for beauty. He meant to have a wife
other men would envy him.

Lucy undressed quickly, got into her berth, and turned off
the lights. At last she was alone, lying still in the dark, and
could give herself up to the vibration of the train,—a rhythm
that had to do with escape, change, chance, with life hurrying
forward. That sense of release and surrender went all over her
body; she seemed to lie in it as in a warm bath. Tomorrow
night at this time she would be coming home from Clement
Sebastian's recital. In a few hours one could cover that incalculable distance; from the winter country and homely neighbours, to the city where the air trembled like a tuning-fork
with unimaginable possibilities.

Lucy carried in her mind a very individual map of Chicago:
a blur of smoke and wind and noise, with flashes of blue
water, and certain clear outlines rising from the confusion; a
high building on Michigan Avenue where Sebastian had his
studio—the stretch of park where he sometimes walked in
the afternoon—the Cathedral door out of which she had seen
him come one morning—the concert hall where she first
heard him sing. This city of feeling rose out of the city of fact
like a definite composition,—beautiful because the rest was
blotted out. She thought of the steps leading down from the
Art Museum as perpetually flooded with orange-red sunlight;
they had been like that one stormy November afternoon
when Sebastian came out of the building at five o'clock and
stopped beside one of the bronze lions to turn up the collar of
his overcoat, light a cigarette, and look vaguely up and down
the avenue before he hailed a cab and drove away.

In the round of her day's engagements, hurrying about
Chicago from one place to another, Lucy often came upon
spots which gave her a sudden lift of the heart, made her
feel glad before she knew why. Tonight, lying in her berth,
she thought she would be happy to be going back, even if

Clement Sebastian were no longer there. She would still be going back to "the city," to the place where so many memories and sensations were piled up, where a window or a doorway or a street-corner with a magical meaning might at any moment flash out of the fog.

4

The next morning Lucy was in Chicago, in her own room, unpacking and putting her things to rights. She lived in a somewhat unusual manner; had a room two flights up over a bakery, in one of the grimy streets off the river.

When she first came to Chicago she had stayed at a students' boarding-house, but she didn't like the pervasive informality of the place, nor the Southern gentlewoman of fallen fortunes who conducted it. She told her teacher, Professor Auerbach, that she would never get on unless she could live alone with her piano, where there would be no gay voices in the hall or friendly taps at her door. Auerbach took her out to his house, and they consulted with his wife. Mrs. Auerbach knew exactly what to do. She and Lucy went to see Mrs. Schneff and her bakery.

The Schneff bakery was an old German landmark in that part of the city. On the ground floor was the bake shop, and a homely restaurant specializing in German dishes, conducted by Mrs. Schneff. On the top floor was a glove factory. The three floors between, the Schneffs rented to people who did not want to take long leases; travelling salesmen, clerks, railroad men who must be near the station. The food in the bakery downstairs was good enough, and there were no table companions or table jokes. Everyone had his own little table, attended to his own business, and read his paper. Lucy had taken a room here at once, and for the first time in her life she could come and go like a boy; no one fussing about, no one hovering over her. There were inconveniences, to be sure. The lodgers came and went by an open stairway which led up from the street beside the front door of the restaurant; the winter winds blew up through the halls—burglars might come, too, but so far they never had. There was no parlour in which Lucy could receive callers. When she went anywhere with one of Auerbach's students, the young man waited for her on the stairway, or met her in the restaurant below.

This morning Lucy was glad as never before to be back with her own things and her own will. After she had unpacked, she arranged and rearranged; nothing was too much trouble. The moment she had shut the door upon the baggage man, she seemed to find herself again. Out there in Haverford she had scarcely been herself at all; she had been trying to feel and behave like someone she no longer was; as children go on playing the old games to please their elders, after they have ceased to be children at heart. Coming up from the station, through a pecking fall of sleet, she wondered whether something she had left in this room might have vanished in her absence; might not be there to welcome her. It was here she had come the night after she first heard Clement Sebastian, and here she had brought back all her chance glimpses of him. These four walls held all her thoughts and feelings about him. Her memories did not stand out separately; they were blended and pervasive. They made the room seem larger than it was, quieter and more guarded; gave it a slight austerity.

Since she was going to Sebastian's recital tonight, Lucy had her dinner early, in the restaurant below. When she came upstairs again, it was not yet time to dress. She put on her dressing-gown, turned out the gas light, and lay down to reflect.

Only three months ago, early in October, Professor Auerbach had told her that his old friend, Clement Sebastian, was in Chicago, and that she must hear him—probably he would not be there long. He was a man one couldn't afford to miss. But Lucy had little money and many wants; a baritone voice didn't seem to be one of the most vehement. She missed his first recital without regret, though afterwards the newspaper notices, and the talk she heard among the students, aroused her curiosity. The following week he gave a benefit recital for the survivors of a mine disaster. Auerbach got a single ticket for her, and she went alone. She had dressed here, in this room, without much enthusiasm, rather reluctant to go out again after a tiring day. She had turned on the steam heat and put out the gas and gone downstairs, anticipating nothing.

Sebastian's personality had aroused her, even before he began to sing, the moment he came upon the stage. He was not young, was middle-aged, indeed, with a stern face and large, rather tired eyes. He was a very big man; tall, heavy, broadshouldered. He took up a great deal of space and filled it solidly. His torso, sheathed in black broadcloth and a white waistcoat, was unquestionably oval, but it seemed the right shape for him. She said to herself immediately: "Yes, a great artist should look like that."

The first number was a Schubert song she had never heard or even seen. His diction was one of the remarkable things about Sebastian's singing, and she did not miss a word of the German. A Greek sailor, returned from a voyage, stands in the temple of Castor and Pollux, the mariners' stars, and acknowledges their protection. He has steered his little boat by their mild, protecting light, *eure Milde, eure Wachen*. In recognition of their aid he hangs his oar as a votive offering in the porch of their temple.

The song was sung as a religious observance in the classical spirit, a rite more than a prayer; a noble salutation to beings so exalted that in the mariner's invocation there was no humbleness and no entreaty. *In your light I stand without fear, O august stars! I salute your eternity.* That was the feeling. Lucy had never heard anything sung with such elevation of style. In its calmness and serenity there was a kind of large enlightenment, like daybreak.

After this invocation came five more Schubert songs, all melancholy. They made Lucy feel that there was something profoundly tragic about this man. The dark beauty of the songs seemed to her a quality in the voice itself, as kindness can be in the touch of a hand. It was as simple as that—like light changing on the water. When he began *Der Doppelgänger*, the last song of the group (*Still ist die Nacht, es ruhen die Gassen*), it was like moonlight pouring down on the narrow street of an old German town. With every phrase that picture deepened—moonlight, intense and calm, sleeping on old human houses; and somewhere a lonely black cloud in the night sky. *So manche Nacht in alter Zeit?* The moon was gone, and the silent street. — And Sebastian was gone, though Lucy had not been aware of his exit. The black cloud that had passed over the moon and the song had obliterated him, too. There was nobody left before the grey velvet curtain but the red-haired accompanist, a lame boy, who dragged one foot as he went across the stage.

Through the rest of the recital her attention was intermittent. Sometimes she listened intently, and the next moment her mind was far away. She was struggling with something she had never felt before. A new conception of art? It came closer than that. A new kind of personality? But it was much more. It was a discovery about life, a revelation of love as a tragic force, not a melting mood, of passion that drowns like black water. As she sat listening to this man the outside world seemed to her dark and terrifying, full of fears and dangers that had never come close to her until now.

A note on the program said there would be no encores. After the last number, when the singer had repeatedly come back to acknowledge applause, the lights above the stage were turned out. But the audience remained seated. A French basso from the New York opera, who happened to be in town, occupied a stage box with a party of friends. He kept calling:

"Clément! Clément!"

At last the baritone came back, his coat on his arm and his hat in his hand. He bowed to his colleague, the bass, then turned aside and spoke through the stage door. The lame boy appeared; they had a word together under the applause. Sebastian walked to the front of the stage in the half-darkness and began to sing an old setting of Byron's *When We Two Parted*; a sad, simple old air which required little from the singer, yet probably no one who heard it that night will ever forget it.

Lucy had come home and up the stairs, into this room, tired and frightened, with a feeling that some protecting barrier was gone — a window had been broken that let in the cold and darkness of the night. Sitting here in her cloak, shivering, she had whispered over and over the words of that last song:

> When we two parted,
>   In silence and tears,
> Half broken-hearted,
>   To sever for years,
>
> Pale grew thy cheek and cold,
>   Colder thy kiss;
> Surely that hour foretold
>   Sorrow to this.

It was as if that song were to have some effect upon her own life. She tried to forget it, but it was unescapable. It was with her, like an evil omen; she could not get it out of her mind. For weeks afterwards it kept singing itself over in her brain. Her forebodings on that first night had not been mistaken; Sebastian had already destroyed a great deal for her. Some people's lives are affected by what happens to their person or their property; but for others fate is what happens to their feelings and their thoughts—that and nothing more.

The following day Lucy had questioned Paul Auerbach about Sebastian, at first timidly, then fiercely. What was his history? What had he been like as a boy? What made him different from other singers?

"Oh, but," said Professor Auerbach calmly, "Clement is very exceptional; he is a fine artist." This exasperated her. It was like saying, This is a black horse, or, This is a tall tree. Auerbach promised her that she should meet him some time, but it never seemed to come off.

Then one afternoon, a few days before the Christmas vacation, Auerbach came into the back room where Lucy was just finishing with a pupil and told her he had a surprise for her. Sebastian would be here at the studio at ten o'clock tomorrow morning. His accompanist, James Mockford, was to have an operation on his hip when he got home to England, and for the present his doctor wanted him to spend his mornings in bed. He might be able to keep his concert dates, if he got rid of the routine work. Sebastian was looking for someone to accompany him in his practice hours. He was coming tomorrow to try out several of Auerbach's pupils, and Lucy would have a chance to play for him.

"He wants someone young and teachable, not somebody who will try to teach him. I think you might please him, Lucy. I spoke for you."

That night, of course, she slept very little. She had never been nervous when Auerbach asked her to play for his friends; he had told her this was because she was not ambitious,—that it was her greatest fault. But this time it was different. If she didn't please Sebastian, she would probably never meet him again. If she did please him—But that possibility frightened her more than the other. For an ordinary singer she thought she could do very well; but she could never play for him. She hadn't it in her. By five o'clock in the morning she had decided not to appear at the studio at all; she would decline the risk.

With her breakfast, courage revived. To this day she could not remember how she ever got to Auerbach's studio, but she arrived there. As she approached the door, she heard Sebastian singing the *"Largo al Factotum"* from the *Barber of Seville*. It must be John Patterson at the piano. She slipped in quietly. It was an easier entrance than she had hoped for. When the aria was over, Auerbach introduced her. Sebastian was easy and kindly. He took her hand and looked straight into her eyes.

"Shall we set to work at once, Miss Gayheart, or had you rather wait a bit, while Mr. Schneller and I try our luck?"

"I'd rather try now, if you please," she said decidedly.

He laughed. "And get it over with? Don't be nervous. It's no great matter. We might try this same aria. I seemed not to do it very well."

Poor young Patterson flushed under his sandy hair; he knew what that meant.

"Have you ever played the piano accompaniment?" Sebastian asked as she sat down.

"I haven't happened to. But I've heard the opera."

When they finished he began turning over his music. "Now suppose we take something quite different." He put an aria from Massenet's *Hérodiade*, *"Vision fugitive,"* on the rack before her.

Afterwards he called Mr. Schneller, and Lucy sat in a deep corner of the sofa, remembering the mistakes she had made.

Presently she heard Sebastian thanking the two young men and telling Auerbach they were a credit to him.

"Now, my boys, I won't keep you any longer. We will have another practice morning one of these days. I'm going to detain Miss Gayheart; she was a little nervous and I want her to try again." He shook hands with Schneller and Patterson, and they left. Then he took Auerbach's arm and walked with him toward the sofa where Lucy was sitting. "On the whole, Paul, I think Miss Gayheart would be the best risk. She is a little uncertain, but she has much the best touch."

Auerbach spoke up for her.

"She's not usually uncertain. I was surprised when she went wrong in the Massenet. She reads well at sight."

"I was frightened, Mr. Auerbach," Lucy said feebly.

The large man in the double-breasted morning coat stood before her and smiled encouragingly. "I know when people are frightened, my dear. I've seen it before. The point is, you do not make ugly sounds; that puts me out more than anything. After the holidays you must come to my studio and we'll try an hour's practice together. That's the only way to arrive at anything. Just when do you get back from your vacation?"

On the 3rd of January, she told him.

"Very well, shall we say January 4th, at ten o'clock, in my studio on Michigan Avenue?" He took a notebook from his pocket and wrote it down. "You might take the score of *Elijah* with you and glance over it." Again he looked at her intently, with real kindness in his eyes. "Good-bye, Miss Gayheart, and a pleasant holiday."

That was the last time she had seen him.

Tonight she would hear his Schubert program, and tomorrow morning at ten she was to be at his studio.

Lucy sprang up from her bed; it was almost time to start for the concert. She slipped into her only evening dress and put on the velvet cloak she had bought just before she went home for Christmas. It was very pretty, she thought, and becoming (she had quite impoverished herself to have it), but it was not very warm. Tonight there was a bitter wind blowing off the Lake, but she was going to have a cab—anyway, she was not afraid of the cold. She rather liked the excitement of winding a soft, light cloak about her bare arms and shoulders and running out into a glacial cold through which one could hear the hammer-strokes of the workmen who were thawing out switches down on the freight tracks with gasoline torches. The thing to do was to make an overcoat of the cold; to feel one's self warm and awake at the heart of it, one's blood coursing unchilled in an air where roses froze instantly.

5

The recital this evening was given in a small hall, before an audience made up of Germans and Jews. Lucy arrived very early and was able to change her seat (which was near Auerbach's) for one at the back of the house, in the shadow of a pillar, where she could feel very much alone. She had never heard *Die Winterreise* sung straight through as an integral work. For her it was being sung the first time, something newly created, and she attributed to the artist much that belonged to the composer. She kept feeling that this was not an interpretation, this was the thing itself, with one man and one nature behind every song. The singing was not dramatic, in any way she knew. Sebastian did not identify himself with this melancholy youth; he presented him as if he were a memory, not to be brought too near into the present. One felt a long distance between the singer and the scenes he was recalling, a long perspective.

This evening Lucy tried to give some attention to the accompanist—there was good reason, surely, if she were to attempt to take his place tomorrow! Even at the other concert she had felt that she had never heard anyone play for the voice so well. *Die Krähe, Der Wegwiser* . . . there was something uncanny in that young man's short, insinuating fingers. She admired him, but she didn't like him. Was she jealous, already? No, something in his physical personality set her on edge a little. He was picturesque—too picturesque. He had the very white skin that sometimes goes with red hair, and tonight, as he sat against an olive-green velvet curtain, his features seemed to disappear altogether. His face looked like a handful of flour thrown against the velvet. His head was rather flat behind the ears, and his red hair seemed to clasp it in a wreath of curls that were stiff but not tight. She thought she remembered plaster casts in the Art Museum with just such curls. For some reason she didn't like the way he moved across the stage. His lameness gave him a weak, undulating walk, "like a rag walking," she thought. It was contemptible to hold a man's infirmity against him; besides, if this young man weren't lame, she would not be going to Sebastian's studio tomorrow,—she would never have met him at all. How strange it was that James Mockford's bad hip should bring about the most important thing that had ever happened to her!

After the concert Paul Auerbach, in his old-fashioned dress coat and white lawn tie, came up to her. "I am going back to the artists' room, Lucy. Would you like to go with me?"

She hesitated. "No, thank you, Mr. Auerbach. I'd rather not. Will he really expect me tomorrow, do you think?"

6

The next morning Lucy was walking across the city toward Michigan Avenue. She was happy, she was frightened,— couldn't keep her attention on anything. Her mind had got away from her and was darting about in the sunlight, over the tops of the tall buildings. Exactly at ten o'clock she went into the Arts Building and told the hall porter she had an engagement with Mr. Sebastian. He rang for the elevator, and she was taken up to the sixth storey. When she lifted the brass knocker, Sebastian himself opened the door.

"I was expecting you," he said with a nod. "I knew you were in town, for I saw you in my audience last night, hiding behind a pillar. Did you like the concert?" He took her coat from her and hung it up. "Better take off your hat, too; you'll be more comfortable."

The music room opened directly off the entry hall, with only a doorway between. As she walked into it, Lucy noticed it was a big room, full of sunlight, and that the general colour was dark red; the rugs and curtains and chairs. The piano stood at the front, between two windows.

Sebastian saw that she was not looking at anything; probably she was frightened again.

"Shall we begin? We can talk afterwards. We'll work a little on the *Elijah*. I have to go to St. Paul to sing it with an oratorio society very soon, and I've not looked at it for a long while."

When she sat down at the piano, he put the music on the rack, turning over the pages. "Before we begin with my part, we might run through the tenor's aria, here. It's much too high for me, of course, but I like to sing it." He pointed to the page and began: *"If with all your heart you truly seek Him."*

"That's a nice introduction to the whole thing, isn't it? Now we'll take it up just here," he leaned over her and indicated with his finger.

He walked up and down in his elkskin shoes as he sang, his hands in the pockets of his smoking-jacket. Lucy had no thought for anything but the score in front of her. An hour and a half went by very quickly. Just when she thought things were going better, he put his hand on her shoulder.

"Enough for today, Miss Gayheart. Very good for a first trial. Shall we begin at the same hour tomorrow? And don't become agitated when you make mistakes. What I most want is elasticity. You must learn to catch a hint quickly in the tempi. When I'm eccentric, catch step with me. I have a reason, or think I have. Now suppose we sit down over here by the fire and have a glass of port and a biscuit. We've been working very hard."

She rose and went to the chair he pointed out. She suddenly felt tired. Sebastian lowered the heavy window-shades a little, until the sunshine fell only on the rugs and the brass fire-irons. He brought a tray with a decanter and glasses and sat down opposite her, lounging back in his chair with his feet to the fire.

"Have you ever heard the *Elijah* well given, Miss Gayheart?"

Lucy told him she had never heard it given at all.

He smiled indulgently. "Mendelssohn is out of fashion just now. Who is the fashion? Debussy, I suppose? You've noticed that people are interested in music chiefly to have something to talk about at dinner parties?"

Lucy murmured she couldn't say as to that; she didn't go to dinner parties, and she didn't know anyone in Chicago except Professor Auerbach and a few of his students.

"And in your own part of the country isn't it so?"

"I think my father is the only person in our town who is much interested in music. He leads the town band and gives lessons on the clarinet."

"Your father is a music-teacher?"

"Not exactly. He's a watchmaker by trade, but he plays the clarinet and flute very well, and the violin a little."

"German, of course? That's good. A German watchmaker who plays the flute seems to me a comfortable sort of father to have."

He asked her how she happened to come to Chicago, and to study with Auerbach. She felt that his questions were not perfunctory, that he really wanted to know something about her life, and she got over her shyness.

While they were talking, the outer door opened softly, and a little man in a stiffly starched white jacket and noiseless tennis shoes, carrying several coats on hangers, darted through the room and disappeared into the sleeping-chamber beyond.

"That is Giuseppe, my valet," Sebastian explained. "Come in and see how well he does for me." He opened the door and took Lucy into his sleeping-room. "Giuseppe, this is the Signorina who is coming to play for me until Mr. Mockford is better. I want her to see how we live."

"*Si, si, signore.*" Giuseppe smiled eagerly and stepped back from the clothes-closet, pointing to the rows of coats and trousers very much as if he were a guide in a picture gallery. When he thought she had observed them sufficiently, he flourished his hand toward the dressing-table and toward a bed of faultless contour.

"Yes, he keeps everything very neat. If you went through my bureau drawers, you'd find them just like your own. He makes my breakfast too, and brings it up to me."

Giuseppe stood holding his hands clasped in front of his stomach, smiling like a little boy being praised. His face seemed almost like a boy's. But his hair, Lucy noticed, was thin and faded, and his high red forehead (shaped like a bowl) was seamed by deep lines from left to right. A moment later, when he had gone to the far end of the music room to put fresh coal on the fire, Lucy asked Sebastian whether Giuseppe had been with him long.

"I picked him up in London, on the way over. He used to be valet de chambre in an hotel in Florence. I've never had better service. Think of it, he has got all those lines on his forehead worrying about other people's coats and boots and breakfasts. I haven't a friend in the world who would do for me what that little man would."

Something in the way he said this made Lucy feel a trifle downcast. She almost wished she were Giuseppe. After all, it was people like that who counted with artists—more than their admirers.

When she left the studio a few moments later she found the Italian in the little entrance hall, before a table drawer which was divided into compartments. Into these he was putting away gloves; into one white gloves, into another tan, into another grey. A man must be rich and successful indeed to live in such beautiful order, she thought.

When she reached her own room after lunch, she looked about it with affection and compassion. She pulled down the shades, opened the window a little, and threw herself upon the bed, too tired to sit up and too much excited to sleep. Things she had scarcely noticed at the time came rushing through her mind: the dressing-gown thrown on a chair, the silver on the dressing-table, the spongy softness of the rose-coloured blankets the valet was smoothing on the bed, and those gloves in the table drawer. Evidently nothing ever came near Sebastian to tarnish his personal elegance. She had never known a man who lived like that.

Harry Gordon was rich, to be sure; he owned carriages and blooded horses, sleighs and guns, and he had his clothes made in Chicago. But his things stood out, and weren't a part of himself. His overcoats were harsh to touch, his hats were stiff. He was crude, like everyone else she knew. An upstanding young man, they called him at home, easy and masterful in his own town, but in a big city he took on a certain self-importance, as if he were afraid of being ignored in the crowd. She remembered just how Sebastian looked when he stood against the light in his heelless shoes and old velvet jacket. He would be equal to any situation in the world. He had a simplicity that must come from having lived a great deal and mastered a great deal. If you brushed against his life ever so lightly it was like tapping on a deep bell; you felt all that you could not hear.

7

It was settled that, for the present, Lucy should go to the studio every day when Sebastian was in town. In the morning she awoke with such lightness of heart that it seemed to her she had been drifting on a golden cloud all night. After she had lain still for a few moments to feel the physical pleasure of coming up out of sleep, she would run down a cold hallway and take her bath before the other occupants on her floor were stirring. When she entered the bakery downstairs, the savour of coffee was delightful to her. Mrs. Schneff served the early comers herself, in a blue gingham dress and a white apron. She asked Lucy "how come" she ate more breakfast now than she used to. Lucy laughed and told her she was making more money now. "Dat is goot," said the plump bakeress approvingly.

After breakfast Lucy went upstairs and put her room in order. She could never make her bed look so high and smooth as Giuseppe's, but that was because she had no boxsprings, or blankets soft as fur.

The weather was miraculous, for January. She always started very early for Michigan Avenue, and had an hour or so to walk along the Lake front before she went into the Arts Building. There was very little ice in the water that January, and the blue floor of the Lake, wrinkled with gold, seemed to be the day itself, stretching before her unspent and beautiful. As she walked along, holding her muff against her cheek on the wind side, it was hard to believe there was anything in the world she could not have if she wanted it. The sharp air that blew off the water brought up all the fire of life in her; it was like drinking fire. She had to turn her back to it to catch her breath.

At ten o'clock she went into the studio and brought the freshness of the morning weather to a man who rose late and did not go abroad until noon. She warmed her hands at the coal grate while he finished his cigarette. If Sebastian had been slow in dressing, Giuseppe answered her knock, his dust-cloth on his arm, and hung up her coat, telling her that the *maestro* would be out *subito, subito.* He called her Signorina Lucia. After she and Sebastian set to work, Giuseppe went in to do the bedroom, leaving the door open a little so that he could listen.

One morning when Sebastian finished singing *"It is enough . . . I am not better than my fathers,"* Lucy turned impulsively on her stool to look at him. She never allowed herself to make any comment (she knew he wouldn't like it), but often she had to make some bodily movement to break the tension. There in the doorway of the sleeping-chamber stood Giuseppe, his red hands crossed over his stomach, his head inclined, his sharp face and quick little eyes melted into repose and gravity. He caught up the laundry bag from behind the door, and pausing just a moment on the ball of his foot, looked Sebastian straight in the eye. *"Ecco una cosa molto bella!"* he brought out in a husky voice, before he vanished through the entry hall.

Lucy found she clung to Giuseppe as if he were a protector among things that were new and strange. Several times she met him in the street, going on errands in a grey overcoat much too long for him and a hard felt hat. On seeing her he would snatch off his hat, and his face, his whole body, indeed, would express astonishment and delight, as if it were wonderful, almost supernatural, that they should encounter one another thus.

Her acquaintance with Giuseppe progressed rapidly, but with Sebastian she seemed to get little further than on the first day. He kept well behind his courteous, half-playful, and rather professional manner,—a manner so perfected that it could go on representing him when he himself was either lethargic or altogether absent. His amiability puzzled Lucy, and rather discouraged her.

When she used to see Sebastian by chance occasionally, on the street or in the Park, his face seemed to her forbidding. Sometimes she thought it stern and indifferent, but more than once it had struck her as melancholy. In the studio there was none of that. He met her with a smile, and throughout the morning was friendly and affable. Yet she went away feeling that the other man, whom she used to see secretly, was his real self.

Trivial, accidental things gradually broke down his reserve. Once, as she was coming down the Lake side of Michigan Avenue, just before she crossed to the Arts Building, she happened to glance up, and saw Sebastian standing at an open window, looking down at her. He leaned out a little and waved his hand. After that he was at the window almost every morning. This made a difference in the way he greeted her at the door; it was as if they had already met in the street and were coming into the studio together. There was a keener interest in his eyes when he took her hand, and he looked down into her face as if she were bringing him something that pleased him. He once told her so, indeed. She had just put her hat on the hall table. He took it up, stroked the brown fur, and ran his finger-tips along the slender, drooping red feather.

"You know, I like to see this little red feather coming down the street. I watch for it, and should be terribly disappointed if it didn't come. You seem to find walking in the cold the most delightful thing imaginable. Montaigne says somewhere that in early youth the joy of life lies in the feet. You recall that passage to me, Lucy. I had forgotten it."

He often told her amusing stories. It was not a habit of his, but he liked to hear her laugh. He never remarked upon this (compliments, he believed, had a disastrous effect upon any charming natural expression), but he provoked it for his own pleasure. A beautiful laugh was rare, certainly; after she left him he used to screw up his eyes and try to imitate it in his mind. Nothing about her drew him to her so much as this purely unconscious physical response.

Lucy knew more or less about Sebastian's outside life from his telephone conversations. When she left the piano, he always made her rest before she went out into the cold. He sat down and talked to her, but they were very often interrupted by the telephone,—the house operator put no calls through until after eleven-thirty. Lucy could not help hearing his replies and learning something about his engagements, his business affairs, who his friends were. With women his talk was usually gentle and soothing, as if the lady at the other end were in a flurry, or very insistent. He told the most transparent lies in refusing invitations, didn't seem to try to make them plausible. But he always said something agreeable; asked to be remembered to the lady's charming daughter, or thanked her for recommending a book which he had liked very much. Every day his concert agent, Morris Weisbourn, called him up as soon as his wire was open. Their talk was usually very brief. But one morning when he answered Weisbourn's call Lucy heard a sudden change in Sebastian's voice.

"What's that, Morris? When did this letter come? . . . No, she wrote me nothing about it. We don't discuss business matters in our correspondence, that is what you are for. . . . Send a draft for the amount she mentions, and get it off to-day, not later. . . . Of course I can. Simply let the bills go over. . . . Very well, then meet me at the Auditorium for lunch, and I'll write a cheque for it."

When he came back from the telephone he lit another cigarette and took up the story he had been telling her about his first meeting with Debussy. But there was something bleak and unnatural in his smile, and Lucy hurried away.

She knew, as well as if a name had been mentioned, that the woman who had written for money was Mrs. Sebastian, and she thought it a shame. He always spoke of his wife in a very chivalrous way, and admiringly. She had heard him explain over the telephone, to a friend just arrived from the Orient, that Mrs. Sebastian was not with him because she dreaded the Chicago winter climate. When he happened to tell Lucy about something he and his wife had done or seen, he seemed to recall it with pleasure, became animated and gay. But she felt sure that things were not like that with them now. Perhaps this was why he was unhappy.

His manner, when she was with him, was that of a man who has an easy, if somewhat tolerant, enjoyment of life. Some of the people who telephoned him he seemed really fond of, and she knew that he was attached to James Mockford, "one of the few friends who have lasted through time and change," as he once remarked. But he seemed very careful

never to come too close to people. She believed he was disappointed in something—or in everything.

She had been playing for him nearly three weeks, when
quite by accident she saw again that side of him which
his genial manner usually covered. One evening Giuseppe
knocked at her door, bringing a note from Sebastian. He
would not be at the studio tomorrow morning, as he had to
attend the funeral services of a friend.

Lucy looked through the evening paper and found that
Madame Renée de Vignon, a French singer, returning from
California, had died in her hotel last night after an illness of
only twenty-four hours. There would be a funeral service for
her at eleven o'clock in the small Catholic church near her
hotel. Afterwards her body would be sent back to France.

The next morning, a little before the hour announced, Lucy
stole into the church. There were not a great many people
there, and in the dusky light she easily found Sebastian. He
was kneeling, with his hand over his face. When the organ
began to play softly, and the doors were opened and held
back to admit the pallbearers, he lifted his head and turned in
his seat to face the coffin, carried into the church on the
shoulders of six men. A company of priests and censer-bearers
went with it up the aisle toward the altar. As it moved forward, Sebastian's eyes never left it; turning his head slowly,
he followed it with a look that struck a chill to Lucy's heart.
It was a terrible look; anguish and despair, and something
like entreaty. All faces were turned reverently toward the
procession, but his stood out from the rest with a feeling
personal and passionate. He had forgotten himself, forgotten
where he was and that there were people who might stare at
him. It seemed to Lucy that a wave of black despair had
swept into the church, carrying him and that black coffin up
the aisle together, while the clergy and worshippers were unconscious of it. Had this woman been a very dear friend? Or
was it death itself that seemed horrible to him—death in a
foreign land, in a hotel, far from everything one loved?

During the service he remained kneeling. From time to
time he drew out a handkerchief and wiped his forehead, but
he did not lift his face or his broad black shoulders until the
coffin was carried back toward the door. As it passed him, he

gave it one long, dull look, out of half-closed eyes. He was among the first to leave the church. When Lucy reached the steps outside, she could see him far down the street, walking rapidly, his back straight and stiff.

Once before, in November (how long ago it seemed!), she had seen him coming out of a church, the Cathedral, when she happened to be passing. He merely came out of the door, down the steps, and turned straight north, without looking about for a cab as he usually did. She felt sure, by the look on his face, that he was coming from some religious observance. She went into the Cathedral; there was no service going on, there were not a dozen people in the building; but she knew that he had been there with a purpose that had to do with the needs of his soul.

8

Usually Sebastian and Mockford went out of town at the end of the week to give a recital somewhere. Sebastian often telephoned the young man, making appointments for the evening or afternoon, but Mockford never dropped in upon them in the morning, and Lucy was glad of it. She had never met him, or seen him except on the concert stage. One morning when Sebastian handed her some songs from *Die Winterreise* and asked her to look them over, she sighed and shook her head.

"It won't be much use, I'm afraid. After hearing Mr. Mockford play them, I think the best I can do is just to read them off."

Sebastian laughed. "Jimmy is a little genius with those, isn't he? I doubt if Schubert ever heard them played so well. In his mind, perhaps. Jimmy's not especially good with Mozart or the Italian composers; but in the true German Lieder, whatever he does seems to be right. I've got a great many hints from him."

On the day Sebastian was to leave for his concert engagements in Minnesota and Wisconsin, Lucy went to the studio to tell him good-bye. It was Mockford who opened the door for her and asked her to come in. She drew back and would have run away if she could.

"No, come in, Miss Gayheart. It is Miss Gayheart, isn't it? Clément has gone down to Allston's studio for a moment. Please allow me." He took her coat, waited for her to go into the music room, and limped in after her.

While he was pulling up a chair for her and poking the coal fire, she saw him by daylight for the first time. She had thought of him as a very young man, a youth, indeed. This morning he did not seem young, but wiry and rather hard. Even his white skin looked harder, somewhat rubbery, and there was a yellow glint in it where the razor had not bit close. His copper-red hair fitted his head so snugly that it might have been a well-made wig.

"I'm glad to meet you, Miss Gayheart. Glad to have an opportunity to thank you for filling in." He sat down and looked at Lucy, looked her over deliberately, and she looked at him. When they had met at the door, the light was behind him and she could not see his eyes. They might be called hazel, perhaps, but this morning they were frankly green; a cool, sparkling green, with something restless in them. He was the first to break down in the searching look they gave each other. He rose quickly and softly and lowered the window-shades a little. On the way back to his chair, he began talking:

"I'm very upset to be fussing with doctors and dropping out like this. Neither of us had looked forward to this American season with much pleasure. However, he seems to be getting on very well with you."

"I don't know as to that. I've no experience. I do the best I can." Lucy could not tell whether he meant to be patronizing, or whether he was merely ill at ease. She felt that he had disliked her instantly, as she had him.

"Oh, he rather fancies breaking in a new person. The difficulty is that Clément can never work with anyone who isn't personally sympathetic to him. The odds are always against our being able to pick up one of that sort on short notice."

Lucy flushed, but said nothing. She was looking at his white, freckled hands, lying on the red velvet arms of the chair. The fingers were square and unusually short for a pianist, but the breadth of palm was remarkable.

"He gives a good account of you"—Mockford shot her a green glance—"and since you do get on, it may be a good thing for him—a change. He doesn't find much to divert him here. The truth is, he's bored to death. I wasn't for his coming over at all. But he needs the money. And he'd be bored anywhere just now. It's only fair to say that you're not hearing the artist we know at home and on the Continent."

"You have been with him a long while, Mr. Mockford?"

"Yes, off and on, a long while," he said carelessly. "There have been interregnums. Mrs. Sebastian takes a fancy to a new pianist now and then, and Clément tries him out. So far they've not been altogether satisfactory."

"She is musical then, Mrs. Sebastian?"

"Oh, naturally! She is one of Sir Robert Lester's daughters." He glanced at Lucy to see whether this enlightened her. It did not, so he murmured: "He was one of our best conductors. The pianist has to make it go with her as well as with Clément, if you mean that."

Lucy coloured again. "No, I did not mean that. I only wanted to know if she is much interested in—in that side of him."

"In all sides, I should say. She was accustomed to direct things in her father's household. It becomes her very well." He wrinkled up his short nose and squinted as if a strong light had been flashed in his face.

There was a kind of fascination about Mockford, Lucy thought. He looked as if he were made up for the stage, yet there he sat in perfectly conventional clothes, except for a green silk shirt and green necktie. He couldn't help looking theatrical; he was made so, and she couldn't tell whether or not he liked being unusual. His manner was a baffling mixture of timidity and cheek. One thing was clear; he was uncomfortable in her company, and certainly she was in his. She was about to rise when she heard a fumbling at the door. It was not Sebastian, however, but the hall porter, with the railway tickets. He gave them to Mockford, told him at what hour their train left, and just when he would have a cab downstairs for them.

As soon as he was gone, Lucy rose and said she couldn't

her a cheque, without any word, in a note written to Auerbach. It was much too large, and made her feel as if she were being paid off. She hadn't cashed it; it lay in her top bureau drawer.

She had been very busy; had managed to get in four lessons with Auerbach, besides giving the usual time to her pupils, and she had practised resolutely. But her heart was not in it. Probably he had found a pianist who suited him better, or perhaps James Mockford felt well enough to take up his work again. That day at the studio, when Mockford was standing behind her holding her coat, she had happened to glance at the mirror over the table and caught a strange smile flickering over his face; as if he had a safe card up his sleeve.

On the tenth morning of Sebastian's absence Lucy awoke late because the room was dark. It was storming outside, and there was a snowdrift on her floor beneath the open window. She put on her dressing-gown, swept up the snow with a whisk-broom and a newspaper, turned on the heat, and got back into bed to wait until the room was warm. As she lay there thinking of nothing in particular, she was startled by a knock on her door, and a boy's voice called: "Western Union!"

When the rubber-caped boy was gone, Lucy stood looking at the yellow envelope before she tore it open. She felt sure that it was from Sebastian, and it happened to be the first telegram she had ever received in her life.

> *Hope you can be at the studio Thursday morning usual hour. Greetings.*
>
> *Sebastian*

Thursday; that was tomorrow. Lucy stuck the telegram in her mirror and hurriedly began to dress. She was thinking that years from now, when she would probably be teaching piano to the neighbours' children in Haverford, nothing would recall this part of her life so vividly, or make it seem so real, as that slip of paper.

When she went down to the bakery Mrs. Schneff greeted her with a broad smile. "You eat a good breakfast today, I expect? The telegraph boy come in here to inquire, but I see you ain't got no bad news anyway."

No, Lucy told her, it was something pleasant.

"Dat's good. Now you eat a good breakfast. I don't like to see you git worried like." She wiped off a table with her apron, and spread a clean napkin over it.

A little later Lucy put on her high overshoes and hurried to the bank to cash her cheque. Then she went to a department store and bought a new dress for the studio, a pretty one, with a silk blouse and embroidered jacket. As she walked home, carrying her parcels with her, she stopped at a flower shop and got a bunch of violets.

She spent the afternoon putting her clothes and bureau drawers in order. At four o'clock she went over to Auerbach's studio to give a lesson. When she came back, her room was almost dark; the air was fresh from the window she had left a little open, and full of the smell of violets. Like spring, it was, to one coming in out of the wintry streets. She sat down in the dusk before the grey square of window-glass to rest.

Yesterday she had been like someone waiting in a doctor's office; it was not living, it was time passing. There was a strange heaviness under whatever she did, as if she had swallowed lead. Today everything was soft, tranquil. There was a kindness in the air one breathed. Everyone in the shops had seemed kind. Life ought always to be like this.

Presently, when even the square of window was dark, she lit the gas and sat down at the piano, beginning to play over some songs from *Die schöne Müllerin*, which Sebastian had been practising before he left. She was thinking that he must be already on his way home, settled in his stateroom and rushing through the great snowy country up there . . . full of forests and lakes, she had heard tell.

10

The city was very sloppy on the morning after the snow-storm, and Lucy did not take her usual walk along the Lake; she was afraid of splashing her new dress. She went straight to the Arts Building. How glad she was to greet the hall porter, and to step into the elevator once more!

"I haven't bothered you for some time, have I, George? Mr. Sebastian is home again?"

"Yes, miss. He got in early yesterday morning."

Lucy was astonished. He got back yesterday? Why, the telegram had come yesterday, saying he would arrive today—but no, the message didn't really say that, she remembered. He must have sent it just before he got on the train at St. Paul. She hadn't noticed the date. How strange, when he could have sent her word from this building yesterday! However, that was probably his way of doing things,—and she was already at the studio door.

Sebastian opened it, in his elkskins and short jacket as usual, but he looked younger and fresher than when he went away. He laughed as she came in, and dropped both hands lightly on her shoulders.

"And here she is! Let me have a look at you, and tell me whether you have been a good girl all this while. A new dress, too; such a pretty one!"

While he detained her in the entry hall, she vaguely noticed a heavy fragrance of fresh flowers in the air. Going into the music room, she saw that the tea table had been moved from its usual place beside the coal grate, and on it stood a large primrose-tinted vase, full of cream-coloured roses and heavy, drooping sprays of acacia. She exclaimed and stopped to look at them on her way to the piano. They were rich and opulent beyond anything she had ever seen.

"Yes, a kind lady, an old friend, stopped over in Chicago yesterday and called on me. This morning, on her way to the train, she brought me those, just as they are."

Lucy had never seen mimosa except in florists' windows, and she lingered over it; it seemed like a whole garden from the South. "I think that lady must have been a sweetheart," she murmured.

Sebastian smiled. "Perhaps. And perhaps she remembers things as sweeter than they were. That often happens. And it's a mercy, too!" He was arranging the music for her. "We will begin *Die schöne Müllerin* and go straight along until we are tired. I feel like work this morning."

She thought she had never heard him sing so beautifully, but she was much too timid to say so. He went through the cycle before he stopped. Then he brought out his bottle of port and they sat down before the fire. He began to tell her

about his concerts in the North, and said he liked engagements with singing societies.

"Many singers don't, you know. But I always feel such
a friendliness in the people of the chorus; and I like them, especially when they sing well. In Minneapolis the sopranos
were very good. The basses, too; most of them Germans
and Swedes. The people in choral societies really get something out of music, something to help them through their
lives, not something to talk about. Plumbers and brewers
and bank clerks and dressmakers, they wouldn't be there unless it meant something; it cuts one night out of their week all
winter."

Just then he was called to the telephone to speak with his
agent. When he came back, Lucy was again bending over the
flowers. He picked up the vase and stood holding it between
himself and the light.

"Yes, they're nice, aren't they? Very suggestive: youth, love,
hope—all the things that pass." He turned around to the fire
and took up the cigarette he had left on the mantel.

In that moment while he seemed absent-minded Lucy
slipped into the hall and put on her coat and hat. She came
back to say good-bye. He was still standing by the grate,
smoking, more approachable than usual; but when he took
her hand he was clearly thinking about something else.

"Mr. Sebastian," she asked him, her face breaking into a
smile, "didn't you ever get any pleasure out of being in
love?"

He shook his head slowly, frowned with his brows and
smiled with his lips. "N-n-no, not much." Then turning to
find an ash-tray, he said mischievously: "Why?—Do you?"

Lucy found herself at the door with her hand on the knob.
She wanted nothing so much as to be outside, but for some
reason she stopped and turned to face him, without seeing
him at all.

"Yes, I do. And nobody can spoil it."

She could hear her own voice, small and cracked because
there was no breath behind it. Once outside the door she did
not ring for the elevator, but ran down the five flights of stairs
as fast as she could.

When she was a little girl she used to run away after she

had been scolded, along the country road that led toward
the Platte, faster and faster, as if she could leave hurt feelings behind. Now in the same way she went hurrying across
the city, splashing the new dress she had meant to take
care of. She was crying, and she did not care who saw
her. She would never go back to the studio. If she couldn't
keep her feelings to herself, she must stay away. All the
same, it was heartless of him to make fun of her; it was just
the kind of thing she would never have expected of him. He
had been seeing a woman who was rich and beautiful and
cultivated, who had everything that she had not. His spirits
were high, and his vanity had been flattered; he found Lucy
Gayheart amusing. The moment she saw those flowers she
had felt a sudden uneasiness, and a vague envy of the unknown person who had a right to send him roses worth their
weight in gold. Until today she could not have imagined that
he would ever be unkind to her; indifferent, perhaps, but not
unkind. Moreover, he was mistaken. She didn't care for him
in that way. She didn't want anything from him; she didn't
even want him to be too much aware of her. Why had he said
that?

When Lucy was almost home she suddenly stopped and
stood still, looked down into the mud with intense amazement on her face. It was quite possible that he had not meant
at all what she thought! What did he know about her life,
after all? He might easily take it for granted that she had a
sweetheart among the students. She was pretty, at an age
when it is quite natural to be in love. Older men often teased
young girls in that way as a compliment. Her shoulders relaxed, and she walked on slowly.

Then perhaps everything was all right, or would be but for
that stupid speech she had made at the door. Oh, why had
she exposed her wound and her anger! How often Pauline
had told her that one day she would come to grief from blurting out everything she felt.

She had not been in her own room half an hour when a
messenger boy came with a telegram. He said the answer was
prepaid, and he must wait for it. She tore open the envelope
with a feeling of dread. It was from Sebastian, asking whether

she could meet him for tea at the Auditorium at five o'clock. He added the word "important."

She couldn't, just then, bear the thought of seeing him. Fortunately, she had a sound reason for refusing. She wrote a truthful answer.

"I am sorry, but I have to give a lesson for Professor Auerbach at five."

She did not want to sign her name, but the messenger boy insisted that it was necessary. After he was gone, she looked from the yellow sheet in her hand to the other telegram on her dresser, which had come only yesterday. What had happened in the meantime? She gave it up; she was too tired to think. Let chance take its way. She lay down and slept for nearly two hours. When she got up at four o'clock to go to Auerbach's studio she was quite herself again.

Lucy kept her pupil longer than usual that afternoon. Mr. Auerbach came to the door and asked her to stop at his study before she left the building. When she went there, she found Clement Sebastian seated by Auerbach's desk, talking to him. He rose as she entered and held out his hand. He said he wanted to see her about tomorrow's work, and as she had no telephone he had thought he might reach her through Auerbach. "I have a cab waiting outside, so I may as well take you home, we can talk on the way. And now I shall find where this young lady lives, Paul. To me her number indicates the middle of the Chicago River."

When they were seated in the cab he came to the point at once.

"Now, my dear, whatever did you mean by flying off like that this morning? One is always saying things of that sort to young people. It's not in very good taste, perhaps, but it's customary, and we've grown used to it—surely *you* must be used to it! Why were you so annoyed?"

Lucy looked out of the carriage window. She found it rather difficult to explain.

"I don't know, Mr. Sebastian. I felt ashamed afterwards. I think it must have been something in the way you said it. I was startled. Please never think of it again. I know you didn't mean anything unkind."

"Unkind? Lucy, my dear! Come, we must trust each other more than that. We mustn't have little clouds creeping over our mornings. We can't afford it. Sailing dates come soon enough, and then we'll be sorry."

As they turned a corner the green lights of the bakery windows came into view. In a moment the cab stopped.

"So this is where you live! If you won't come over to me for tea, I shall come here and have coffee with you. A very substantial place it looks." He accompanied her to the foot of the linoleum-covered wooden stairs and stood for a moment, holding his hat in his hand and smiling down into her face. His eyes still had that livelier look she had noticed in the morning. "Till tomorrow, then? And I'll be as solemn as an owl. No joking with Lucy!"

The next morning it was Giuseppe who opened the door for her, beaming and rapidly exploding into speech. By this time she could understand him pretty well. Sebastian had given her an Italian grammar one day, and told her she might as well pick up what she could. Giuseppe explained that Sebastian had been called upstairs to see Signor Cunningham, who was ill, but would return in a moment. Meanwhile she must sit down and get warm. He dropped on his knees and began blowing the fire. Then he went on with his dusting, telling her all the while what good fortune it was for her, so young, to work with a great artist like Sebastian. Education was everything in this world; if his father had been able to send him to school, he would not now *fare il cameriere*. For the first time it occurred to Lucy that even this smiling little man might have his regrets. And had he, in his uncanny way, sensed that something went wrong yesterday?

II

One Sunday afternoon near the end of February Lucy was sitting in her room looking out at the back of the next building, which came close to her window, — a blank wall of bricks painted grey. Sunday was the only day in which she had much time for reflection. She gave lessons all day on Saturday, but on Sunday she was free.

This morning she was wondering how a month, nearly two months, indeed, could have slipped by so quickly. A strange kind of life she had been leading. For two hours, five days of the week, she was alone with Sebastian, shut away from the rest of the world. It was as if they were on the lonely spur of a mountain, enveloped by mist. They saw no one but Giuseppe, heard no one; the city below was blotted out. Then, after eleven-thirty, the city began poking in its fingers. The telephone began to buzz, and she heard him build up the rest of his day and his evening. At about twelve she got into the elevator and dropped down into Chicago again.

The weather, which everyone grumbled about, had been exactly the right weather for her. The dark, stormy mornings made the warmth and quiet toward which she hurried seem all the richer. The dirty streets, as she crossed the town through sleet and snow, were like narrow rivers, shut in by grey cliffs where the light was always changing, and she herself was a twig or a leaf swept along on the current. As soon as she reached the studio, that excitement and sense of struggle vanished; her mind was like a pair of dancing balances brought to rest. Something quieted her like a great natural force. Things took on their right relation, the trivial and disturbing shut out. Life was resolved into something simple and noble—yes, and joyous; a joyousness which seemed safe from time or change, like that in Schubert's *Die Forelle*, which Sebastian often sang.

Lucy stopped looking at the streaks of rain against the grey wall, went to her shabby piano, and played that song again and again. There were other songs which she associated more closely with Sebastian himself, but this one was like the studio, like the hours they spent there together. No matter where in the world she should ever hear it, it would always drop her down again into that room with the piano between two big windows, the coal fire glowing behind her, the Lake reaching out before her, and the man walking carelessly up and down as he sang.

On this same Sunday Sebastian himself was going through a bad time. He happened to have no out-of-town engagement, so he was in Chicago, in his studio. This day, with a brutal rain beating on brutal buildings, had been one of slowly rising misery.

In the morning paper he had read a dispatch from Geneva, announcing the death of an old friend and fellow student, at a sanatorium in Savoy. He hadn't even known that Larry MacGowan was ill; there had been a coldness between them for the last few years. But the moment his eyes fell on that black headline the feeling of estrangement vanished as if it had never been. The reality was their ardent, generous young friendship, their student days together—which were only yesterday, after all. He put down the newspaper softly, as if he were afraid of wakening someone. It was like reading his own death notice. Like it? It was just that. The obituary would serve for both—for their good days.

Nothing had ever made Sebastian admit to himself that his youth was forever and irrevocably gone. He had clung to a secret belief that he would pick it up again, somewhere. This was a time of temporary lassitude and disillusion, but his old feeling about life would come back; he would turn a corner and confront it. He would waken some morning and step out of bed the man he used to be. Now, all in a moment, it came over him that when people spoke of their dead youth they were not using a figure of speech. The thing he was looking for had gone out into the wide air, like a volatile essence, and he was staring into the empty jar. Emptiness, that was the feeling: the very objects in his studio seemed to draw farther apart, and to regard each other more coldly. MacGowan had slipped out of all this; grey skies, falling rain, chilled affections. Everything in this room, in this city and this country, had suddenly become unfamiliar and unfriendly.

The lid once off, he began remembering everything, and everything seemed to have gone wrong. Life had so turned out that now, when he was nearing fifty, he was without a country, without a home, without a family, and very nearly without friends. Surely a man couldn't congratulate himself upon a career which had led to such results. He had missed the deepest of all companionships, a relation with the earth itself, with a countryside and a people. That relationship, he knew, cannot be gone after and found; it must be long and deliberate, unconscious. It must, indeed, be a way of living. Well, he had missed it, whatever it was, and he had begun to believe it the most satisfying tie men can have. Friendships? Larry was the man he had cared for most. Among women? There was little for sweet reflection in that chapter. He had married the woman he loved, and for years they had been happy; now they were both better off when they had the Atlantic between them. The thing which had estranged them was not at all the conventional situation supposed to arise between an artist and his wife. It was jealousy, perhaps, but not of the usual sort.

As they had no children, Sebastian had taken into their house a talented boy, almost a child when he came, who had no home and no parents; the orphan of a couple who had both sung at the Opéra Comique. He was a charming boy, and devoted to Madame Sebastian. But she had taken a strong dislike to him and treated him harshly. The lad was sensitive, and so adoring of her that her severity amounted to cruelty. After a year and a half Sebastian could endure the situation no longer, and sent Marius away to a good school. But this did not mend matters; he had seen a side of his wife's nature which he had never before suspected; it had changed his feeling for her. She sensed this, and was bitter. He missed the boy and used to go into Paris to see him; even this she resented. He came to America, to Chicago, where he was born, though he had left it at eighteen and had lived abroad most of the time since.

Sebastian had been sitting by the fire for hours. He had smoked until his throat was dry, and his thoughts had wandered over a great part of the surface of the earth. He had dragged the bottom, and brought up nothing worth remembering. His mind could not find a comfortable position to lie in. He remembered Macbeth's *Oh, full of scorpions is my mind, dear wife!* Wasn't there one lovely, unspoiled memory? — In the present wasn't there somewhere a flower or a green bough that he could hold close and breathe its freshness? His glance wandered toward the piano; perhaps there was one!

Sebastian got up and opened the windows wide, wound a scarf about his throat, and walked up and down the room while the wind blew out the tobacco smoke. He was thinking about Lucy; that perhaps he wouldn't have got so far down this morning if she had been there for an hour. It was dangerous to go for sympathy to a young girl who was in love with one, but Lucy was different. As he paced back and forth he told himself that hers was quite another kind of feeling than the one he had encountered under so many disguises. It seemed complete in itself, not putting out tentacles all the while. He had sometimes thought of her as rather boyish, because she was so square. It was more like a chivalrous loyalty than a young passion. He didn't believe she would ever be guilty of those uncatalogued, faint treacheries which vanity makes young people commit. He didn't believe she would ever use his name for her own advantage—not even in a harmless way, to make herself interesting to a crowd of students, for instance. That was a good deal to say for a young thing with her living to make, struggling to get a foothold in a slippery world. He hadn't met with just that kind of delicacy before, in man or woman. When she gave him a quick shy look and the gold sparks flashed in her eyes, he read devotion there, and the fire of imagination; but no invitation, no appeal. In her companionship there was never the shadow of a claim. On the contrary, there was a spirit which disdained advantage.

He suddenly noticed that the place had grown very cold. His watch said five o'clock; he must have been on his feet for nearly an hour. The air of the room had freshened, and something within him had freshened. The contraction in his chest, the bitter taste in his mouth were gone. He shut the windows and went into his bedroom to change his clothes. In a quarter of an hour he came out in a dinner jacket and put on his overcoat. Downstairs he hailed the first cab he saw and gave the driver Lucy's number.

When he got out before the bakery he told the cabman to wait. First he glanced into the restaurant, thinking she might already have come down for her supper. Then he went up the two flights of stairs. He would not have known at which door to knock, but behind one of them he heard a piano with a bad tone; *Die Forelle*. He smiled, and when she had finished he knocked gently.

"Who is it?"

"It's Sebastian, Miss Gayheart. May I see you for a moment?"

Lucy glanced despairingly about the room; but it was dark, he couldn't see anything. She pulled her dressing-gown tight and opened the door a little way.

"I shouldn't bother you on Sunday, should I? But won't you come out to dinner with me tonight, if you've no other engagement? I've had a melancholy day, and I dread dining alone."

"Why, certainly, Mr. Sebastian. I'll have to dress, but it won't take long."

"Don't hurry, take all the time you want. It's still very early. I'll wait for you downstairs in the cab. And I'll go into the bakery and buy a bun, so the good woman can see that you are driving off with a staid, respectable person."

Lucy shut the door and lit the gas. She had only the same old evening dress, the black net she had worn to all his concerts. However, she told herself, if it was well-dressed women he wished to dine with, there were plenty he could ask. He must know she hadn't any clothes, and if he didn't mind, she didn't.—But she would have given a great deal to have a new dress to put on for him.

When they went into the hotel dining-room she was glad to find that it was nearly empty; he wouldn't have to conduct a shabby girl through a roomful of smart people. While they were waiting for the soup he smiled for the first time.

"I'm afraid I startled you, turning up uninvited like that. I've been sticking in the studio all day. Did you happen to notice in the morning paper that Larry MacGowan died yesterday in a sanatorium in Savoy? We were the closest of friends, long ago. We were students together."

The day of Madame de Vignon's funeral flashed up in Lucy's mind. She could only murmur that she was sorry he had had bad news.

"And I am sorry in the wrong way. I am sorry for myself. Years ago if I had seen that thing in brutal type, I would have lain down and cried like a boy. Things happen to our friendships; that's the worst about living. Young people can't know what it means."

The waiter came with the soup and wine. When he was gone, Sebastian began to talk again.

"We had drifted apart, and for no good reason. Five years ago he came to visit me in France. My wife and I had been having our little place at Chantilly done over, and we were very pleased with it. I had looked forward to Larry's visit, but it didn't turn out well. He didn't like our house or our servants or our friends, or anything else. He showed it plainly, and I was disappointed and piqued. Our parting was cold. I think he must have been breaking up even then. He was difficult about everything, and he made criticisms that hurt one's feelings."

"Did you never see him afterwards?"

"Never. Other troubles came along, soon enough. We exchanged a few letters, the kind which mean nothing. The dispatch said he died in a sanatorium in the mountains above Sallanches. He and I took a walking trip through that very country one summer when we were in our early twenties. He must have recalled those days, when he was ill up there. We used to lie down on the hillsides and look up at those mountains, with our knapsacks under our heads, for hours together. We always got up very early and went out on our balconies before sunrise, while the light was changing on the peaks, and called good-morning to each other. I can't help wondering why he didn't wish to see me again. Why didn't he send for me last summer, I wonder?"

Sebastian drank a good deal of wine, and he told Lucy more about his own life than he had ever done before: how he had met Larry MacGowan on the steamer when he first left Chicago and was on his way abroad to study. He soon found that MacGowan also was going over to study, and under the same master. When they landed at Cherbourg they were already friends. They took a studio together in Paris and lived at the same pension.

Sebastian lingered a long while over his dinner. The dining-room was almost empty when they at last left it and took a cab for Lucy's part of the town. He slipped his arm through hers and pressed her hand gratefully. "You were kind to give me this evening, Lucy. I wanted to talk to someone; and I wanted it to be you. No one else."

She turned to him quickly and caught his sleeve. "Oh, Mr. Sebastian, I wish you didn't ever have to be sad! I am happy whenever I think about you, and so are lots of people. You have everything other people are struggling for. You don't value it enough, truly you don't!" She stopped because she knew she was talking foolishly.

Sebastian was listening not to what she said, but to the rush of feeling in her warm young voice. There is no way to define that ring of truth in a voice, he was thinking, and no mistaking it. He took the hand on his sleeve and held it between both his own. "Do I seem sad to you, Lucy? Everyone has disappointments. I'm sometimes lonely over here. Not in the mornings, when we are working together; then I feel quite like myself. That reminds me: tomorrow morning I must spend with my agent. Perhaps you can come in at five o'clock and have tea with me? I should like that."

The cab turned the corner, and the greenish-white lights in the bakery windows came into view. Sebastian took her to the foot of the stairway. "Remember," he said, "tomorrow is a holiday for you, and you are to sleep late and dream of something very nice. Perhaps you will dream that we are both twenty, and are taking a walking trip in the French Alps. And I shall call to you at daybreak from my balcony!"

12

The next afternoon Lucy was walking slowly over toward Michigan Avenue. She had never loved the city so much; the city which gave one the freedom to spend one's youth as one pleased, to have one's secret, to choose one's master and serve him in one's own way. Yesterday's rain had left a bitter, springlike smell in the air; the vehemence that beat against her in the street and hummed above her had something a little wistful in it tonight, like a plaintive hand-organ tune. All the lovely things in the shop windows, the furs and jewels, roses and orchids, seemed to belong to her as she passed them. Not to have wrapped up and sent home, certainly; where would she put them? But they were hers to live among.

At last it was five o'clock, the grey twilight was gone, and she turned toward the Arts Building. She was frightened as she went up in the elevator, and tried not to think at all. She lifted the brass knocker, and Sebastian opened the door. Before she had time to speak, just as she was, in her hat and coat, he took her in his arms.

They stood for a long while without moving, in the dusky little hall among overcoats and walking-sticks. Lucy felt him take everything that was in her heart; there was nothing to hold back any more. His soft, deep breathing seemed to drink her up entirely, to take away all that was timid, uncertain, bewildered. Something beautiful and serene came from his heart into hers; wisdom and sadness. If he took her secret, he gave her his in return; that he had renounced life. Nobody would ever share his life again. But he had unclouded faith in the old and lovely dreams of man; that he would teach her and share with her. When they went into the music room, neither of them had spoken.

The tea things were set out before the fire. The kettle had almost boiled dry, and Sebastian went to fill it, leaving Lucy alone in a room which she seemed unable to enter. The piano and the book-shelves were far away, out of reach; and she was far away from herself. She felt as if everything were on the point of vanishing. Now that he knew, he might think it his duty to let her go. He could sweep her existence blank with one word.

He came back, came and stood before her, but she could not look up until she heard her name.

"Don't be frightened, Lucy. I am not going to make love to you. Though it's true enough I love you." He sat down on the arm of her chair. "Why do you crouch away from me like that? And your little hands are so cold. What are you afraid of?"

"I don't know—of things being different. Maybe you won't let me come and play for you any more. Please don't send me away. I won't be a bother."

"Send you away? I'm afraid I'm not so unselfish. Perhaps I ought. But it isn't as if you were really in love. I am quite old enough to be your father, you know. You are merely growing up,—and finding things. It was just that freshness which charmed me, I thought. But now I believe I love everything about you, Lucy. The mornings used to be dull and heavy here. You brought something sweet into them. I began to watch for you from the window, and when I caught sight of you tripping along in the wind, my heart grew lighter. I love young ardour, young fire. I had a nice boy in my house once; but he had to go away to school. What a difference you have made in my life here! When you knocked, it was like spring-time coming in at the door. I went to work with more spirit because things were new and wonderful to you."

Lucy pressed her face against his shoulder to hide the tears of happiness. When she heard him tell her that she had given him something! — and only a little while ago that had seemed the most extravagant of all hopes, so foolish that she was ashamed of it, even in the dark. Lying there she felt herself drifting again into his breathing, into his heart-beats. She knew this could not last; in a moment she must gather herself up and be herself again. Yet she knew, too, that it would last a lifetime.

There was a light, familiar knock at the door. She drew away and went over to the fireplace. Giuseppe always knocked like that before he entered with his latch-key. He stuck his head in and asked whether the Signore was ready to dress.

Sebastian told him to come in and lay his clothes out quickly. "I have a dinner engagement, Lucy, and I shall take you home on the way. Wait here for me a few moments. I shan't be long."

He disappeared with Giuseppe, and Lucy sat down in the chair she had quitted. She sat without stirring, her hands lying open in her lap, listening to the faint noises that came up from the street.

In twenty minutes Sebastian came out in his dinner coat. "Can you change as quickly as that, Lucy?" He was standing before the fire, putting on his white gloves, when a latch-key scratched at the door. It opened, and in walked James Mock-ford, also in a dinner coat; a silk hat on the back of his head and a cane in his hand. Seeing Lucy, he removed his hat and bowed.

"Come in, Jimmy! Where did you drop from?" Sebastian called jovially. Mockford was already in, and Lucy thought he needed no encouragement. There was something impertinent about the way he entered the room.

"From my lodgings. I'm dining with friends, and I thought you might give me a lift in your cab."

Sebastian laughed, as if he liked his coolness. "Sorry, but I'm afraid you'll have to purchase a cab for yourself tonight. I'm taking Miss Gayheart home. However, if you choose to wait here, I suppose I might come back for you."

"Thanks. I'll wait." Mockford put his overcoat and hat on the piano and limped over to the table, where he began eating the sandwiches that had been meant for tea. He looked into each of the two unused cups and wrinkled his nose. Lucy watched him in amazement. She wondered whether he did use white paint, or a liquid powder, on his face at night. He glanced at Sebastian over his plate of sandwiches.

"Wearing a ribbon, I see?"

"The dinner is given for the Belgian Minister."

This time Lucy thought Sebastian spoke rather frigidly. She noticed a tiny purple knot in his lapel. Giuseppe brought his overcoat.

Mockford finished the sandwiches and wiped his fingers.

"How long shall you be gone?"

"Oh, I can stop for you in twenty minutes or so."

"Will you send the hall porter up for me when you come? I don't care to stand about down there on my bad leg. Good night, Miss Gayheart." He half rose when she got up to go, but dropped back immediately. As she went out, she saw him stretched in the deepest chair, his lame foot on the couch, a cigarette hanging loosely between his lips.

"Mustn't let Mockford get on your nerves," Sebastian told her, as he got into the cab after her and shut the door. He patted Lucy's arm soothingly when she tried to protest. "Oh, my dear, I can read your face like a book! You haven't much skill in dissimulation. Jimmy is rather brassy at times,—fault of his early training. He came out of the slums, really. Mrs. Sebastian found him for me. A friend of her father discovered this queer, talented, tricky boy. He's all right at bottom, but he's not well. That makes him peevish. Just now he's fighting with me; for his rights, he says. Some of his cronies have put it into his head that he ought to be printed on my programs as 'assisting artist' instead of accompanist. I won't have it, and he's sulky."

Lucy wanted to say a great deal, but she only brought out: "In general, then, you think he's—loyal?"

Sebastian laughed. "Loyal? As loyal as anyone who plays second fiddle ever is. We mustn't expect too much!"

13

Lucy used to be sorry that her birthday came in March. In Chicago it was the most disagreeable season of the year; and at home, in Haverford, it was always cheerless enough. The ice on the Platte had either disappeared or gone rotten, so there was no skating. The wind never stopped blowing, and the air was full of dust from the ploughed fields and sand from the river banks. But this year March was the happiest month she had ever known.

Sebastian was getting up his programs for his April concert tour in the East, and every morning was important. It was much more as if he were really living at the studio now. He kept the place full of flowers and growing plants because he found Lucy liked them. When he opened the door for her, he met her with a kiss. That embrace, often playful but never hurried, seemed to bring them at once into complete understanding: every sound, every silence, had the beauty of intimacy and confidence. The air one breathed in that room was different from any other in the world. Lucy thought there was even a special kind of light there, which kept a soft tint of gold, though the fog was brown and the smoke hung low outside. The weather was consistently bad. The ice cakes ground upon each other in the Lake, rain and wet snow beat down upon the city, high winds strewed the streets with broken umbrellas. But when she reached the Arts Building the elevator took her up into an untroubled climate.

It was at night, when she was quiet and alone, that she got the greatest happiness out of each day—after it had passed! Why this was, she never knew. In the darkness she went over every moment of the morning again. Nothing was lost; not a phrase of a song, not a look on his face or a motion of his hand. In these quiet hours she had time to reflect, and to realize that the few weeks since the 4th of January were longer than the twenty-one years that had gone before. Life, it seemed, could not be measured by years.

It was not that she had been discontented before. She had been happy ever since she first came to Chicago; thought herself fortunate to have escaped from a little town to a city, and to work with a kind and conscientious man like Paul Auerbach. But that time was far away. She began a new life on the night when she first heard Clement Sebastian. Until that night she had played with trifles and make-believes.

Since then she had changed so much in her thoughts, in her ways, even in her looks, that she might wonder she knew herself—except that the changes were all in the direction of becoming more and more herself. She was no longer afraid to like or to dislike anything too much. It was as if she had found some authority for taking what was hers and rejecting what seemed unimportant.

One morning Sebastian brought out an old English song, *She Never Told Her Love*. He sang it over several times, walking up and down and smiling to himself: *But let concealment, like a worm i' the bud, feed on her damask cheek.*

He stopped beside the piano and bent down, bringing his face close to Lucy's.

"It doesn't feed on yours, my dear!"

She started and put her hand quickly to her cheek. "But— why should it? I have nothing to conceal!"

"Nothing? Nothing troubles you?"

"How can you ask me?" She looked up at him in astonishment. "When I live my life out under your eyes every day?"

"Don't you sometimes feel it's a waste, living your life out?"

"Not for me, it isn't. Have we finished?"

"Once again, please."

As Lucy got up from the piano, she drew a long breath. "I've never heard that song before. The words are lovely, too."

Sebastian laughed. "Oh, yes? And there are plenty more where those came from." He went to the bookcase, ran his finger along a row of small red leather volumes, and pulled one out of its place. "Take it along. You'll find the lines of this song, and others. Lots of lovely words." He sometimes used that teasing tone, as if she were a child.

Lucy blushed. She had read it, certainly, and had thought it a rather foolish comedy, where everybody was pretending and nobody was in earnest. Until she began to play for Sebastian she had never known that words had any value aside from their direct meaning.

14

Soon after Sebastian left for his Eastern tour, Lucy got a letter from Harry Gordon: he was coming on for a week of the opera, and she must remember her promise. In those days the New York opera company came to Chicago for several weeks every spring. Last year she had been glad to go to the opera with Harry. But now everything was different: she didn't want to see him, didn't want to be reminded of Haverford or of anything that lay behind her. She was going to the Public Library every day now, to hunt through the newspapers for notices of Sebastian's concerts; that took time. Her life was exactly as she wanted it, and Harry would spoil it. He would manage to prove to her that she had been living in a dream, that she was Lucy Gayheart and had been fooling herself all this while.

In his letter Harry asked where he could meet her. She knew he hated calling for her at the bakery. Sebastian didn't mind waiting in the restaurant downstairs when he came to take her out to dinner, but it annoyed Harry. She sent a note to the hotel where he would be stopping, telling him to meet her at Auerbach's studio on Monday, after her lessons. Auerbach's show studio was used as a reception room, when he was not giving a lesson there. His private office opened behind it. Across the hall was a much bleaker room, with a north light, where Lucy heard the younger pupils, and practised if she had a vacant hour.

On Monday afternoon when Lucy came out from this back studio she found Auerbach himself in the reception room, entertaining Harry Gordon, and they seemed to be getting on very well together. As she crossed the room toward him, she suddenly felt pleased with Harry. He came to meet her with such a jolly smile, fresh and ruddy and well turned-out in his new grey clothes. In a flash she was conscious of the thing she had always liked best in him, the fine physical balance which made him a good dancer and a tireless skater. Paul Auerbach seemed as pleased at their meeting as Lucy was herself. He was plainly reluctant to have Harry's call cut short, urged him to come in again, suggested that Lucy bring him out to his house to see Mrs. Auerbach.

As he walked to the door with them, he asked Harry when he had arrived. Harry replied that he had come in "by the morning train," without betraying the fact that he had already been in Chicago three days. He had written his tailor to have two suits ready for the last fitting, and he made no calls until these were sent to his hotel. He wanted to wear exactly what well-dressed men in Chicago were wearing.

After they left the studio, Harry said they must go somewhere for dinner. "Shall we go early, or do you want to dress and have me call for you later?"

"Oh, no! We can dine in state tomorrow evening, before the opera. I'd rather you took me to some quiet place where we can talk."

"Anything you like. We mean to have one good time this week, don't we, Lucy?"

Lucy remembered that when Harry was out for a good time he swept one along with him, just as he did in a polka or a schottish. She liked to do those rather violent, jumpy dances with him; he had a good sense of rhythm and put so much lift and spring behind his partner.

When she got home that evening, Lucy told herself that it was nice to see Harry again. She hated the idea of throwing over old friends. She was thinking, as she undressed, that Harry would be very intelligent if he were not so conceited; it was a kind of mental near-sightedness, and kept him from seeing what didn't immediately concern him. But tonight she hadn't minded that he was pleased with himself, because he was pleased with everything. He hadn't made the countryman's mistake of finding fault with the service and the food. He had tipped the waiters generously, without fumbling or ostentation. He had insisted upon a drive along Michigan Avenue before they came home—a hopeful sign!

With the Gordons, who had good horses and carriages of their own, a hired carriage was regarded as a painful extravagance and meant the shortest route. She thought she must have forgotten how much she liked to hear Harry talk—for his voice, chiefly. No matter what he was saying, you could guess his real feeling from his voice, once you knew its several disguises. There was the genial, confidential tone, just tinged by regret, with which he refused a loan to a man who needed it. And there was the other friendliness, not so very different (a little less concerned, indeed), but that was real.

The next evening, for *Aida*, Harry appeared in his new dress clothes, very handsome and correct. Lucy had been teaching all afternoon and was rather tired when they drove to his hotel for dinner, but his good spirits revived her. At the opera they had excellent seats; Harry had written for them weeks ago. He was in his most engaging mood, and didn't once try to ridicule things which she "held sentimentally sacred," as he said. He enjoyed the music, and the audience, and being with Lucy. His enthusiasm for the tenor was sincere; the duet in the third act was, he whispered, his idea of music. He beat time softly to the triumphal march, and didn't mind that the trumpets played off pitch.

When he said good-night to Lucy at the foot of her staircase, she could honestly tell him that she loved going to the opera with him.

15

On the morning after they heard *Otello*, Lucy cut out her practising because Harry had asked her to take him through the Art Museum. It was a rather gentle, sunny morning, and as they walked over toward Michigan Avenue they stopped to do a little shopping. Lucy caught at every pretext for delay. Last year when they went through the Museum together they had disagreed violently about almost everything, and had come away in a bad humour. Marshall Field's was a much better place for Harry, and it was fun choosing handkerchiefs and neckties for him. But he kept looking at his watch, and got her to the galleries soon after they were open. He was careful not to make any comments that would irritate her; she could actually feel caution in his step and voice. What a fury she must have been last spring! Not once did she catch that smart squint in his eyes. He did, occasionally, square his shoulders before a picture and twist his mouth awry, as if he would like to call the painter's bluff; but he did not try to be funny. When they reached a loan exhibit of French Impressionists he broke down, and began pointing out figures that were not correctly drawn.

"Now, you'll admit, Lucy—" he would begin persuasively.

"Certainly I admit, but I don't think it matters. I don't know anything about pictures, but I think some are meant to represent objects, and others are meant to express a kind of feeling merely, and then accuracy doesn't matter."

"But anatomy is a fact," he insisted, "and facts are at the bottom of everything."

She did not answer him impatiently, as she would have done once, but bent her head a little and spoke in a quiet voice which disconcerted him. "Are they, Harry? I'm not so sure."

He didn't reply to this. Something in her tone had made him feel very tenderly toward her. She must be tired, he thought. He saw a door open, leading to one of the stone porticos at the back of the building, that looked on the Lake. He touched Lucy's elbow.

"Let's go out on that balcony and get some fresh air."

The morning had grown warmer, but a mist had come up which hid the sky-line. The water was faintly blue, and above it everything was soft; a silvery mist with changing blue and green at the heart of it, far out. Even the grey gulls flew by on languid wings. The air felt full of spring showers. On a morning like this . . . Lucy felt an ache come up in her throat. When she looked off at that soft promise of spring, spring already happening in the colours of the sky before it had come on earth, such a longing awoke in her that it seemed as if it would break her heart. That happiness she had so lately found, where was it? Everything threatened it, the way of the world was against it. It had escaped her. She had lost it as one can lose a ravishing melody, remembering the mood of it, the kind of joy it gave, but unable to recall precisely the air itself. And she couldn't breathe in this other kind of life. It stifled her, woke in her a frantic fear—the fear of falling back into it forever. If only one could lose one's life and one's body and be nothing but one's desire; if the rest could melt away, and that could float with the gulls, out yonder where the blue and green were changing!

A far-away voice was saying something about lunch. She came back with a start.

"No, Harry, please. I have a headache, and I want to get home as quickly as I can. If I am to go with you tonight, I must lie down and try to get over this."

All that afternoon Lucy stayed quietly in her room. She told herself that she would see Harry Gordon's vacation through and do her best for him. There shouldn't be one flash of temper to regret afterwards. It wasn't his fault that she had changed so much. She was sorry now that she had ever let him come at all, but she must make the best of it. She had enjoyed going to four operas, one right after another. She hadn't heard a great many in her life; she was too busy and too poor. They had listened like two young people who had good seats and who were there to be pleased with everything. Tonight they would hear *Traviata*, and for tomorrow, Saturday, they had chosen the matinée instead of the evening performance, because Lucy had never heard *Lohengrin*, and she especially wanted to.

16

Saturday was a windy, bright April day. There were boys on the streets selling violets and daffodils, and all the barrel-organs were out playing *O Sole Mio!* Lucy was in high spirits and felt sure of a happy ending—Harry was leaving to-morrow.

It chanced that Lucy had never heard even the prelude to *Lohengrin* played by an orchestra; the first measures caught her unaware. Before the first act was half over she was longing to be alone; this wasn't the kind of opera to be hearing with Harry. She found herself leaning away from him as far as possible. The music kept bringing back things she used to feel

before the evening performance. Harry found a table to his taste and ordered champagne to be brought with the soup, remarking that it was never too early for a good thing. "When I have a place of my own, I shall keep plenty of it on hand—for special occasions."

He talked a good deal through dinner, said he hated going home tomorrow, but he had to relieve his father in the bank. His father wanted to get down to Hot Springs for his rheumatism. He thanked Lucy for having given him so much of her time. "Music doesn't mean much to me without you, except to remind me of you."

She threw him a smile. She had less colour than usual. She was dreadfully tired. Thank God tonight was the end of it! She had gone her limit, and now she wanted to be left alone with her own life.

The dinner seemed to be dragging on, even the dessert didn't end it. Harry ordered liqueurs and lit a cigar. He leaned across the table and took up Lucy's gloves, which were lying by her plate.

"And now, Lucy—" Something affectionate and masterful in his voice made her dread what was coming. "And now isn't it about time we got down to business? We know each other pretty well. You've had your little fling. You want to see the world, but you'll see it a lot better with me. Why waste any more time? This is April; I should think we might be married in May. Oh, June if you like! But we mustn't let another summer slip by."

Lucy frowned and avoided his eyes. "Nonsense, Harry. I'm not ready to marry anyone. I won't be, for a long while."

He put his open palm down heavily on the table. "But I am! Just ready. And we've always known we would do it some day, both of us."

She gave a dry laugh. "Have we? Why, you haven't been sure of yourself half the time!"

Harry chuckled guiltily. "Most of the time I've been sure." Then he looked at her with a singular straightforwardness, looked quite through the professional geniality which usually gleamed over his eyes like a pair of spectacles. "All the time I've been sure at bottom. I have never been able to believe in any sort of happy life except with you. That's the truth."

Lucy felt it was the truth. She could find nothing to say.

"Everything will be just as you wish it. You shall have the kind of house you like, and the kind of friends. I want the life you'd naturally make for yourself,—and it's the only life I do want."

She was trapped. He was looking straight and talking straight. When he was like this she was afraid of him. It seemed unfair to sit there and let him take off all his jocular masks and show her a naked man who had perhaps never been exposed to any eye before. She must stop him before he went any further. She thrust out her hands across the table.

"Don't, Harry, please! It's no use. Everything has changed this winter. My life is tied up with somebody else. It's done. I have no choice. I love another man."

Gordon seemed not to understand her at first.

"But—what's all this? Another man? And he lets you play about with me all week? You're trying to fool me, Lucy!" He looked at her with a threat in his eyes.

She had fallen into this; she must get out of it, get it over. "No, I'm not. He's away. It's the man I work for, play accompaniments for. I'm not the same person I used to be. I didn't mean to tell anyone, but I can't let you go on making plans."

While she was speaking, the harshness on Gordon's face slowly melted. A twinkle came in his eyes, as if he had found the catch in the puzzle. He so far forgot himself that he put his hand down over Lucy's and held it firmly when she tried to draw it away.

"Now, Lucy! Every girl falls in love with her singing teacher, but I thought you, for one, had escaped!"

She felt her cheeks burn with anger. "He's not my singing teacher! He's a great artist," she muttered, angrier still because this sounded so childish.

"Very well, I've no objection; the greater the better! But you'll soon recover, my dear." He refused to be annoyed. He was glowing with tolerance. She gave him a defiant look and managed to get her hand away. He considered a moment, then leaned forward and spoke softly, in a confident, teasing tone. "Now see here, Lucy, how far has this nonsense gone?"

The dining-room swam and tilted before Lucy's eyes. "How far?" she broke out in a flash of scorn. "How far? All the way; all the way! There's no going back. Can't you understand *anything*?" She did not see his face, her eyes were blind as if she were looking into a furnace. But she knew that he got up and left the table.

When she had recovered herself a little, she saw him at the other end of the room, talking to the head waiter. He put something in the waiter's hand and walked out of the dining-room.

Lucy drank some ice-water slowly. She was ashamed that she had lied. She had tried to tell him the truth about a feeling; but a feeling meant nothing to him, he had to be clubbed by a situation. She supposed it was just his coarse good-nature, his readiness to accept as a negligible truancy anything not actually compromising, that had driven her beyond herself. It was as if he had brought all his physical force, his big well-kept body, to ridicule something that had no body, that was a faith, an ardour.—Why had she ever tried to be nice to him, when she knew all the while he was like that? Well, it was over now, and she hoped she had cut through his stupidity and conceit. It seemed that she had, since he did not come back.

After about a quarter of an hour the head waiter came to her table and, bending down, spoke to her in a way which made an awkward situation seem quite usual and in order.

"Mr. Gordon said, miss, that if he were not back from the telephone in ten minutes, you should not wait for him. He said you would understand."

"Yes, thank you." Lucy caught up her gloves, and her bag, in which there was no money at all. "The check?" she stammered.

"The check is paid, miss. Shall I call a cab for you?"

"Yes, please."

He gave an order to one of the service boys, and held her cloak for her. "You will find it very warm outside, miss, like a summer evening. We have had good weather for the opera season; and last year it was so bad!" He spoke without an accent, but his voice and intonation were unmistakably Italian. He took Lucy through the long dining-room with an air of authority, as if he were conducting some important person-age, and at the door motioned one of his subordinates to put her into her carriage. She had not even a quarter to give the boy who brought the cab. Harry Gordon had walked off like that, leaving her to get home as best she could. What a coward, what a boor! She had some money at home, in her bureau drawer; but suppose she didn't have? She might walk home for all he cared.

When the cab stopped before the bakery, she asked the cab-man whether he could come upstairs for his fare. "I'm too tired to bring it down, driver."

"Sure, miss. I got a weight. Just sit still while I fasten my hitch-strap." He helped her up the two flights and thanked her for his tip.

17

The next morning Lucy awoke sick and sore. She wanted not to be alone for a moment, and hurried over to Auerbach's studio—perhaps he would have time to give her a lesson.

He met her with a newspaper in his hand. "Look at this, Lucy; Clement is advertised to give a second recital in New York on the 3rd of May. He will scarcely get here before he goes back again. Remarkable success he has had."

That was the important thing. She felt better at once; noth-ing else mattered, when all was going well with Sebastian. Auerbach himself seemed more wide awake than usual; and for the next few days he gave Lucy the kind of attention and criticism he was usually too easy-going to give anyone. Under his heavy domesticity and middle-aged content there was a discriminating musical intelligence—not often brought to the front. As for Lucy, she was working to forget something. But at odd moments that sickening last scene with Harry Gordon would come back upon her and make her angry and ashamed. She hadn't lied often in her life, she was too proud. And that was such a cheap, crawling, shabby lie! It was like boasting she had a claim on Sebastian, when she had none. She had used his name in a way that she could never tell him, and her ears burned whenever she thought of it. How could she have said such a thing? She considered writing to Harry, but that was difficult. She composed letters to him when she should have been asleep, and the next day put off writing them.

One evening when she went downstairs to get her dinner, she found Giuseppe walking up and down outside, in front of the open stairway. He was wearing a black coat and looked small and grave and important. Off went his hat, and as he stood bareheaded, he broke into such a rush of speech that she could not understand him at all; she caught only that Signor Weisbourn had come to the studio about something urgent. She held up her hand and begged him to speak slowly.

"*Scusi, signorina.*" He put on his hat and began again. Sebastian had written Mr. Weisbourn that all his plans were changed. He had accepted some engagements in England and would sail on the 4th of May, the day after his second New York recital.

Here Lucy interrupted. "But this is the last week of April, Giuseppe. Isn't he coming back here at all?"

"*Si, signorina,* for three days." Sebastian would arrive to-morrow, Friday, and would leave Chicago on Monday night. Giuseppe was to sail with him and would be with him until the engagements in England were over. Then he was going to Italy to see his father. He had been packing all day, to close the studio for the summer. Mr. Weisbourn had not asked him to communicate with Lucy; he had come on his own responsibility, thinking she might have arrangements to make or plans to change.

"No, there is nothing to arrange, Giuseppe. I have no plans. I wish I were going with you."

"And I, signorina, just as we were! It will be like that again when we come back in October. A summer is soon gone."

Lucy could not let Giuseppe go away; not until she had grown a little used to the news he brought, until she had time to take it in. She walked him round and round the block, asking him trivial questions about his preparations, his packing—was the piano gone? No, he had received no orders about the piano.

It was the crowded hour in the crowded part of the city, everyone going home from work. She and Giuseppe could scarcely hear each other speak for the clatter of truck wheels on the dirty pavements. Troops of screaming children on roller skates came streaking down the sidewalk, but Lucy hardly noticed them. She tried to keep close to Giuseppe, and everything around them was blank. An enormous emptiness had opened on all sides of her. This well-disposed little man seemed to be the only person who had thought of her at all. Even he, in his mind, was already outward bound. He began to tell her about the boat, *Wilhelm der Grosse*, on which they were to sail; its length, its tonnage, how many passengers it carried. He would be with the maestro in England and then they would go to France: before he started for Florence he would see the maestro's house at Chantilly, and his dogs, and the Signora Sebastian, who was the daughter of a mi-lord, did Lucy know?

As they came round the corner of the block after many circlings, Lucy felt too tired to hear any more, and was glad to say good-night. She forgot to thank him for coming. She did not go in for dinner, but went languidly upstairs to her room.

So there would be no return; only another departure. Just now she wished she had never met Sebastian at all. It would have been better only to have heard him, to have seen him at a distance, and to carry away a memory unclouded by personal disappointments. There was nothing sure or safe in this life she was leading. She had been sailing along in the air, like a little boy's kite; the wind drops, and the kite comes down in the dirty street, among the drays and roller skates.

There had been that one month, to be sure, when she lived under a golden canopy among spring flowers, while the March winds and rain threatened outside the windows. Then she was never afraid of cruel surprises. Perhaps that was all she was to have in this world; some people got very little. It was strange, to feel everything slipping away from one and to have no power to struggle, no right to complain. One had to sit with folded hands and see it all go. You couldn't, after all, live above your level: with good luck you might, for a few breaths, hold yourself up in that more vital air, but you dropped back; down, down into flatness, and it was worse than if you had never been out of it. She had known that he was to sail in June—but that had seemed years away. She had never thought about it for more than a moment. She hadn't taken it in that after he went the days and hours would no longer carry her anywhere.

On Saturday morning Lucy was sitting in Sebastian's studio. Both Sebastian and Auerbach were there; they had been in consultation for some time before Lucy was sent for. They were talking to her, about her, around her. Sometimes she listened and sometimes she did not. Finding Auerbach there had made her indifferent to everything.

She had known one of these men so long and the other so intimately—and now she seemed a stranger to both. She felt as if she were applying for a position of some sort, and not very likely to get it. Moreover, she didn't want it, whatever it was. She had not the faintest stirring of any wish or desire; and she did not believe in anything they were saying.

The first shock came when she was told that Sebastian would not be in Chicago next winter, but in New York. Lucy, they said, was to go on in November, and work with him there as she had done here. He and Auerbach had decided that she must stay in Chicago this summer, to study in preparation for next season. Auerbach himself was not going away; he was economizing in order to take his family abroad next year. This studio was leased until October, the rent paid. Sebastian suggested that she move into it as soon as he left it; it would be much cooler than the place where she was living.

Lucy had been listening to them without comment, but now she spoke.

"No, I couldn't leave my own room, Mr. Sebastian. I'm used to it, and I feel at home there."

"But you would get the Lake breezes here. Chicago is very hot, you know. And you would soon feel at home—if you don't already!"

She shook her head. "No, I couldn't do that. I wouldn't feel like myself, moving in here."

Auerbach began to reason with her, but Sebastian cut him short. "No, Paul, we mustn't press it. You'll surely be willing to use this place as a studio, Lucy? You won't leave a good piano standing here idle?"

Yes, she would be glad to work at his piano. "But I must have a little time to think about these things."

"We haven't a great deal of time, Lucy. I don't like to go away leaving you up in the air. This isn't the summer for you to go into the country and vegetate. We want you to prepare seriously for next season. Paul understands what I think you need most, and he has promised to give you a great deal of attention."

At this point Auerbach rose to go. He stood holding his hat for a moment, smiling down at the girl's discouraged face.

"I think you'll let Clement persuade you, Lucy. A winter in New York would be a fine thing for you. Then maybe in the spring you can go over to Vienna with my family. My wife has often said how she wished you could go with us." The two men went out to the elevator. They were still talking about her, Lucy knew. She wished they would both go away and leave her here to cry. Everything they wanted her to do seemed out of her reach.

Sebastian came back and stood over her where she sat limp in a corner of the sofa.

"Oh, what a morning! First, Paul is so slow to see things; and then Lucy so unwilling to see things. Why aren't you just a little pleased? Don't you want to play for me any more? Or are you so fond of Chicago you can't leave it?"

"Next winter is a long time away." Lucy looked up and smiled. She was feeling more pleased already. "And May was very near. I guess I'm disappointed to lose it."

"Oh, May would have been dragging out preparations that can be made in two days! Your summer was really the first thing to arrange. Next season is going to be an important one for me. For you, too, I hope. A winter in New York, at your age—you don't know what is waiting for you! And you'll like working with my new accompanist."

"Then Mr. Mockford—?"

"Is not coming back." Sebastian went over to his writing-desk and began hunting for something, speaking to her over his shoulder. "He doesn't know it yet. We shall arrange all that in England. I intend to see that he's well placed, but he has been with me too long. He and Weisbourn have been putting up some pretty little tricks on me. So I am going to have a new agent and a new accompanist. The best thing about this concert tour has been a revival of interest, in here, I mean," he tapped his chest. "I've met so many old friends who are still interested. Those things are contagious." He put a letter in his pocket and came back to the sofa. "Ah, now you are looking like Lucy again! You are beginning to believe in all these nice things I've thought out for you?"

"No, I wasn't thinking about them. I was thinking about you. It seems to me that something good has happened to you."

"Dear child!" For the first time after this long absence he gathered her up in his arms. "Now something good has happened to me! And something good has come back to me."

18

On the last evening Lucy got to the Arts Building just as James Mockford was arriving in a cab, followed by an express cart. Besides his travelling luggage, he brought with him a rusty little tin trunk and a large lounge chair, which he asked Sebastian to store, as he was giving up his lodgings. Mockford's entrance caused some confusion. Giuseppe dragged the trunk back into the bedroom, beckoning Lucy to follow him. He whispered to her that later he would get the ugly chair out of the way, so that she would not have to look at it. He meant to leave the music room very nice for her, not like a second-hand shop. She had noticed before that Giuseppe disliked Mockford. He once said to her, when Sebastian's favourite cigarette-case was not to be found, that, since he was responsible for the place, no one but he should have a latchkey, *no one!*—with a murderous flash in his quick eyes.

After Morris Weisbourn had arrived, and they were all gathered in the music room, Mockford was the only person altogether cheerful. He was so pleased to be leaving Chicago that he made himself agreeable even to Lucy. Sebastian was at the bookcase behind the piano, going over a pile of music. Giuseppe, who had been so delighted to be starting for home, and to be sailing on a big boat, had lost his enthusiasm. He stood in the background among the trunks, his hands crossed before him, solemn and hushed, as if he were waiting for a coffin to be carried out. They were all, of course, impatiently expecting the transfer men who were to come and get the luggage. The air in the room was heavy and hot—no breeze, though all the windows were open. Out over the Lake the sky was black, and from time to time there was a low growl of thunder.

Sebastian called Lucy to his corner and began giving her some directions, to which she tried to listen. But she was distracted by Weisbourn and Mockford, who were talking very loud, as if they wished everything they said to be heard. They had seated themselves by an open window and were finishing the last bottle of port. Weisbourn must have been drinking before he came; his dark blue cheeks looked very thick, and his eyes were small. The moment they sat down together they had been overtaken by the brotherly affection which beams from two schemers who have done each other a good turn.

"And when you are to be operate, you will send me a cable? So?"

Sebastian shot a glance of amusement at the two from behind the piano. Lucy saw their wine-glasses touch, one in the round fat hand, the other in the white freckled one.

Just then came heavy sounds and knocking at the door. Giuseppe flew to admit the baggage men. "Thank God!" Sebastian murmured. As soon as the trunks had gone down, he put on his topcoat and turned to Mockford and Weisbourn.

"Gentlemen, I have some calls to make, and I am going to take Miss Gayheart home. I shan't be back here. I will meet you at the station. Giuseppe will take the hand luggage down at eleven. Leave the keys with the doorman."

The cab Sebastian customarily used had been waiting outside half an hour. He told the driver to open the windows and take them out to the Park.

"You are worn out with all the fuss, and so am I," he said as they drove up the avenue. He drew her head over on his shoulder. "There. Shut your eyes and rest. We have three hours, all our own." He felt her soft young body take the line of his as she lay against him. She breathed lightly, like a child sleeping. He, too, closed his eyes. The warm night air blew in over their faces. After a while it began to smell of trees and new-cut grass, and the confused city noises died away.

Sebastian felt a wet splash on his face. He put his hand out of the window; it was raining a little. Then it came down harder, a fierce spring shower.

"Asleep, Lucy?"

"No."

"We were glad to get away, weren't we? But I've grown fond of that studio. I like to think it's not going to be shut up dumb and dusty all summer, that you'll be coming and going. I shall be thinking of you. When I am at sea, I shall look at my watch every morning and figure the difference in time and tell myself whether you have opened the piano yet."

Lucy buried her face closer, her hand on his shoulder tightened. She felt the tears rising and could not hold them back.

"I ought to do better than this. I'm so sorry!" she quavered.

"Never mind, dear. Cry if you feel like it. Perhaps I shall cry with you."

"It's only because I'm so afraid."

"Afraid again? Of what?"

"Oh, that you'll never come back! Something tells me you won't."

"That's because you are just beginning, and are not used to good-byes. They hurt, sometimes, even after one has gone through a great many." Sebastian felt a heaviness of heart; he scarcely knew whether on her account or his own. He was wondering whether there was not some way of escape from his life: from concerts and hotels, from Mockford, and his wife, and his place in France, from his friends in England, from everything he was and had. In what stretched out before him there was nothing he wanted very much. And this youth and devotion would not be the same when he came back, he knew; what he held against his heart was for tonight only. It was a parting between two who would never meet again.

Lucy knew what he was thinking. She felt a kind of hopeless despair in the embrace that tightened about her. As they passed a lamp-post she looked up, and in the flash of light she saw his face. Oh, then it came back to her! The night he sang *When We Two Parted* and she knew he had done something to her life. Presentiments like that one were not meaningless;

they came out of the future. *Surely that hour foretold sorrow to this.* They were going to lose something. They were both clinging to it and to each other, but they must lose it.

Presently Sebastian stopped the carriage and told the driver he could wait for them. He took Lucy's arm and they walked for a long while up and down the winding gravel paths, the bitter fragrance of young lilac leaves coming sharp into their faces at every turn. The rain had stopped, but the dripping bushes showered them with waterdrops. Their hands and faces were wet; it was good to feel. There was not a star to be seen, but the blackness above them was soft and velvety between the scattered park lights. Sebastian was telling Lucy that perhaps next summer they would be walking under night skies far away from here. If she went abroad with the Auerbachs, he would join them in Vienna. There were a great many things he would like to show her for the first time; gardens—forests—mountains.

They had turned back toward the carriage, the wet gravel crushing softly under their feet. As he came under one of the lamp-posts, he slipped out his watch. He said nothing to Lucy, but he gave the cabman her street-number. They drove back into the heart of the city in silence, as they had come away from it.

At the bakery entrance Sebastian got out and followed Lucy up the two flights of stairs to her own door. In the dim hall light he took her face in his hands and looked into it for a long moment. Lucy felt the old terror coming back; *to sever for years.* . . . She couldn't bear it any longer.

"Go," she whispered, "go now!" She scarcely felt his arms, his lips; she could only think that in a moment he would not be there at all. He held her closer and closer, and then he let her go. She stood just inside her door, leaning against it, listening to his quick heavy tread down the first stairway—the second—then she heard the cab door slam.

Sebastian knew she was listening. He shut the door violently to end her suspense. A last signal. He sank back in the seat and closed his eyes as the cab lumbered off. Against the rumble of the wheels he spoke aloud to himself. What he said was:

"Ein schöner Stern ging auf in meiner Nacht."

19

One hot morning in the middle of May, Lucy was putting fresh lavender bags in her bureau drawers. Lifting a pile of muslin underclothes, she came upon an unopened letter—a letter from Haverford, from Pauline! She laughed, but she was ashamed, really! It had come a week ago, when she was just beginning to practise in Sebastian's studio, trying to feel at her ease there, and she was afraid of anything that might dishearten her. Pauline's letters often had that effect, so she tucked this one out of sight for the moment,—and then forgot all about it. She thought, as she took it up and looked at it, that perhaps she hadn't made a mistake in forgetting! The letter was thick and bulky (a bad sign), and the handwriting on the envelope looked, even more than usual, like eggs rolling downhill. Pauline had inherited so many German characteristics—what a pity she couldn't have inherited a German script!

As Lucy opened the letter some newspaper clippings fell out. Pauline announced the theme at once. Harry Gordon was married! Married to Miss Arkwright of St. Joe, and they had started for Alaska on their wedding trip. Everyone in Haverford was "talking." People thought he had treated Lucy very badly. It was a great shock to her old friends. They had always believed his "intentions" were serious. They were asking Pauline what had happened, and she didn't know what to say. What did Lucy wish her to say, "under the circumstances"?

Lucy tore the letter to bits and threw it into the wastebasket. So Harry thought he would show her, did he? Such haste must have inconvenienced Miss Arkwright a trifle; but that wouldn't bother Harry, if he had his revenge. He must have given her about a week's notice! The announcement in the *St. Joseph Gazette* said they were to live in Haverford! That would certainly be dull for the bride. She crumpled the clipping and threw it after the letter.

"It would be a joke," she said to herself, "if Harry has gone and married Miss Arkwright more on my account than her own."

She laughed, but all the same that announcement left a bitter taste in her mouth. As she got ready to walk over to the studio, she was thinking that she had lost an old friend; and she had told him the kind of falsehood that made her think poorly of herself.

When she reached the Arts Building the hall porter's smile, hand to cap, changed the colour of her thoughts. George, the elevator man, held his car back to tell her there was a storm on its way from Duluth. The attendants about the place were devoted to Sebastian, and they admired Lucy. That was pleasant. They liked to see her come and go; so many of the studios were empty now.

Lucy hung her hat and jacket exactly where she used to put her winter things. Giuseppe had left one of Sebastian's raincoats hanging in the entry hall, and a collection of walking-sticks in the rack. She went into the music room, opened the windows, and stood breathing in the fresh air and looking out at the glittering blue water.

She had not begun to come here at once after Sebastian went away,—not, indeed, until she had a note from him, written on the boat and sent back by the tug. He began:

"It is eleven o'clock here. That means that you have just got to the studio and are opening the piano. I shall listen to hear that you do not begin lazily. I still feel more there than here."

An hour after that letter came, she used her latch-key for the first time. Not for a moment had the place seemed forlorn or deserted. To her it was full of the man himself. All her companionship with him was shut up there, and the future was beginning to live there,—the future in which she couldn't help believing. She came here by his wish; the quiet and comfort of the place were his kindness. She was thus lifted up above the sweating city streets because of his concern for her. Those ardent early-summer days, with heat that still had an edge of freshness, were glorious days for work. She had never had such a piano at her command, or so definite a purpose to direct her.

The weeks flew by, but Lucy flew faster than they. The heavy July heat made no drain on her vitality. This was the first summer she had spent in the city, and she found it stimulating; no hotter than Haverford, and God knew how much less dull! She seemed to be carried along on a rushing river, and was constantly saluting beautiful things on the shore. She couldn't stop to see them very clearly, but they were there, flashing on the right or the left. And when the morning was over, and she was tired, she was glad to creep home through the heat and do her darning or put ribbons in her nightgowns.

Auerbach had very few pupils in the summer months, and he gave her a great deal of time. He liked to have her with him, and urged her to spend her week-ends with his family. He had a house of his own out on the South Shore, and a garden. From the first green of spring, he rose very early and worked for two hours in his garden before he went into the city to his classes. His wife got up and made his breakfast, long before the children or the housemaid were awake. She told Lucy that as you got older there wasn't so much you could do for your husband any more, and it was nice to give him a good breakfast while you had the house to yourself.

Auerbach inquired after Harry Gordon occasionally. He liked the young man, and he had hopes for Lucy in that direction. She never told him of Harry's marriage. She was hurt, though she pretended to be scornful. He hadn't really a right to marry; he had belonged for years to Lucy Gayheart!

One Sunday morning they were sitting in the shade under Auerbach's grape arbour. Auerbach, in his shirt-sleeves, began to question her.

"I think you have changed your mind, Lucy. You would rather go on with the kind of work you do with Clement than teach?"

As Lucy made no reply, he continued.

"You must remember that Clement is very exceptional. Most singers are not interesting to work with, and they don't want to pay much. For the platform they always have a man."

Still Lucy said nothing. She bit her lip and looked out of the end of the arbour at the yellow squash blossoms. Auerbach smiled.

"Perhaps you have another plan, eh? The big Westerner? That would please me very well."

"You are mistaken, Mr. Auerbach. That is only a friend-ship."

"Maybe so. But I wouldn't be sorry to see it come to something else. In the musical profession there are many disappointments. A nice house and garden in a little town, with money enough not to worry, a family—that's the best life."

"You think so because you live in a city. Family life in a little town is pretty deadly. It's being planted in the earth, like one of your carrots there. I'd rather be pulled up and thrown away."

Auerbach shook his head. "No, you wouldn't. I've heard young people talk like that before. You will learn that to live is the first thing."

Lucy asked him if there were not more than one way of living.

"Not for a girl like you, Lucy; you are too kind. Even for women with great talent and great ambition—I don't know. Some have good success, but I don't envy them."

The next morning, when Lucy opened the windows in the studio and looked across at the Lake, she told herself that she wasn't going out to the Auerbachs' any more. It dampened her spirits. He was a heavy, thorough, German music-teacher, and there he stopped.

20

Lucy often spent the long hot evenings in Sebastian's music room, lying on the sofa, with the big windows open and the lights turned out. And how strange it was that she should be there, after all! Only last Christmas, when she went home, she had never been inside this room, and had thought herself fortunate to catch a glimpse of Sebastian coming out of the doorway downstairs.

This summer there would be no slowing-down to the village pace. No walking about the town for hours and hours in the moonlight: down to the post-office and home again; out to the little Lutheran church at the north end. At this hour she used often to be sitting on the church steps, looking up at that far-away moon; everything so still about

her, everything so wide awake within her. When she couldn't
sit still any longer, there was nothing to do but to hurry
along the sidewalks again; diving into black tents of shadow
under the motionless, thick-foliaged maple trees, then out
into the white moonshine. And always one had to elude
people. Harry and the town boys had their place, but on
nights like this she liked to be alone. She wondered she
hadn't worn a trail in the sidewalks about the Lutheran
church and the old high school. She wondered that her heart
hadn't burst in those long vacations, when there was no human image she could hold up against the summer night;
when she was alone out there, looking up at the moon from
the bottom of a well. She loved her own little town, but it
was a heart-breaking love, like loving the dead who cannot
answer back.

Now the world seemed wide and free, like the Lake out
yonder. She was not always struggling against something, she
was going with something much stronger than herself. It was
not that this new life was without pain. But there was nothing empty or meaningless in it, nothing that was not sweet to
remember; not even that last night when they had walked
under the dripping trees and breathed in the bitter darkness
together.

From the very beginning there had been the shadow of
some sorrow over her love for this man, even before she knew
him at all. When she used to get only a glimpse of him now
and then, on the street, on the steps of the Art Museum, coming out of the Cathedral, it was the look of loneliness and
disappointment in his face that had drawn her heart after him.
Now, when he was far away, she sometimes went into the
church where the service for Madame de Vignon was held
and where she had seen Sebastian pray so long and fervently.
It was a place sacred to sorrows she herself had never known;
but she knelt in the spot where he had knelt, and prayed for
him.

She heard from Sebastian occasionally, short notes, not
love-letters; a few words about his engagements or about her
own studies. There was always something meant for her
alone; an anecdote, a memory, a sentence about a place which
had stirred him—a human word. He kept her informed as to

his itinerary, so that she always knew where he was. He had finished his summer's work in Munich, and was going to the Italian lakes for his holiday.

21

One morning Mrs. Paul Auerbach came out into the garden and told her husband that his breakfast was ready. It was September, and he was cutting his grapes.

While she was bringing in his coffee he sat down and opened the morning paper. She heard him call to her, and knew by his voice that something terrible had happened. She ran into the dining-room. Paul did not speak, but pointed to the newspaper spread out on the table. Mrs. Auerbach saw the headlines and sank into a chair beside him. Together they read the cablegram from Milan.

Yesterday Clement Sebastian and James Mockford were drowned when their boat capsized in a sudden storm on Lake Como. There were three in the boat, Sebastian, his accompanist, and Gustave Wiertz, the Belgian violinist. The accident was seen from the shore, and two row-boats immediately put out from Cadenabbia, but only Wiertz was rescued. His account of the accident followed:

The breeze had stopped altogether, but they had not taken down their sail. When the hurricane from the mountains broke upon them, the boat was turned over immediately. Wiertz himself was struck by the boom and thrown out a considerable distance. He sank, and when he came up saw his two companions struggling in the water. He felt no alarm for Sebastian, who was a strong swimmer. Mockford could not swim and was apparently terrified; he had locked his arms about Sebastian's neck. Wiertz thought Sebastian would be able to control a man so much lighter, so he swam toward the boats coming out from shore. The water was so cold that he was already growing numb, and he did not look over his shoulder again. When he was pulled into the first row-boat, the two heads had disappeared. The second rescue party went on, believing that the two men might be clinging to the overturned sail-boat. But they found no one. Mockford must have fastened himself to his companion with a strangle-

Ramsay's house, but it was all she could do to sit through a short call. Her throat closed up, and her mind seemed frozen stiff. Her old friend could not help her—only one person in Haverford could help her. She was going to the post-office now on the chance of seeing him, as she had gone on many another morning. All the business men went for their mail at about half past nine. Suddenly she remembered that the school-bell had rung a long while ago. She might be too late; she hurried faster.

The double doors of the post-office were hooked back because of the warm weather. Men were going in and coming out. Lucy went to her father's box and slowly turned the combination lock about, purposely getting it wrong. She was waiting for someone. In a few moments Harry Gordon came in. The bank lock-box was a little way beyond Jacob Gayheart's. He passed behind Lucy without seeing her, opened his box, and threw the letters into a leather bag he carried. As he turned to leave, Lucy stood directly in his way.

"Good morning, Harry."

He looked up, pulled off his hat, and exclaimed: "Why, *good* morning, Lucy!" As if he were very much surprised to see her here; as if she had never been away and never come back; as if there had never been any special friendship between them. His voice had just that impersonal cordiality he had with unimportant customers or their womenfolk. She might have been a girl from one of the farms on which he held a claim he would gladly be rid of. And his eyes seemed to look at her through thick glasses, though he never wore any. Keen, sparkling, pale blue eyes, as cold as icicles. He was not stiff with her,—perfectly casual; and he went out of the post-office and down the street with that easy, confident stride with which he used to go out on the diamond in old baseball days, when he was the best pitcher in the Platte valley and Lucy was a little girl watching from the grandstand.

Again and again since she came back to Haverford they had met like this; and it was always just the same: the same affectation of surprise, the same look, the same tone of voice—to one who knew all the shades of his voice so well. If he had been embarrassed or curt, she might have got round it. But there was no breaking through this particular manner of his. Poor farmers couldn't break through it when Harry proposed a settlement little to their advantage and much to his own. He had a natural vigorous heartiness which was as convincing as his fresh complexion. It was so open and unlike the manner of a skinflint, that a slow-witted man couldn't realize he had agreed to a hard bargain until it was over and he was driving home in his wagon.

If she could only get a message to him, Lucy was thinking as she walked away. She wanted little more than a friendly look when he passed her on the street, the sort of look he used to give her, careless and jolly. It would be enough if he would stop on the street-corner occasionally and tell her a funny story in his real voice, which very few people ever heard, and look at her with the real kindness that used to be like a code sign between them whenever they met.

Lucy did not go directly home, though she knew Pauline was waiting for the morning paper. She went up to the north end of town, to the little Lutheran church, and sat down on the steps. It lay higher than the rest of Haverford, at the edge of the open country, and one could look out over the low hills, chequered with brown, furrowed wheat-fields, to the windings of the Platte River. She sat down there because she was tired, and then she forgot to think about the time. The sunlight fell warm on the wooden steps. An osage orange hedge shut out the only house that was near by, and the place was quiet and friendly. Presently she heard a bell,— the school-bell! Then it must be eleven o'clock. She hurried home as fast as she could.

Pauline was in the dining-room, setting the table. Lucy went straight to her.

"I'm sorry I forgot to bring the paper home, Pauline. I went for a walk and was gone longer than I meant to be."

"Oh, that's all right!" said Pauline in the cheery tone which meant that it wasn't right at all.

Lucy put the paper down and went quickly upstairs to her own room. Good heavens, why had she become so sensitive to people's voices! Everyone she met spoke to her in an unnatural, guarded tone. Her father's seemed to be the only honest voice in town.

Pauline called to her that lunch was ready. She came downstairs and took her place at the table, opposite her sister. Mr. Gayheart always lunched in town, at the Bohemian beer saloon. Pauline brought in a platter of mutton chops; the coffee-pot and vegetables were already on the table. "Any important letters?" she asked as she sat down.

"Important? No." Lucy supposed she must mean a letter calling her back to Chicago.

Pauline chattered away. As a little girl Lucy had trained herself to close her mind when her sister went rambling on. (Even then it had seemed to her that most women talked too much.) Now, as then, she tried to keep her mind on something outside the house. Pauline had a very informal way of eating when they were alone; neglected her food to talk, and then gobbled. Lucy couldn't dismiss things of that kind lightly as she used to. They chafed her and made her shrink into herself.

Suddenly Pauline came out with something which she really wanted to say, and then Lucy heard her.

"There, I nearly forgot after all! Mrs. Ramsay telephoned and said she very particularly wanted you to come in this evening. She wants just you, because I was there last week, the day after Madge came. You know we *all* liked Madge. Can you realize she has a boy in college this year?"

"Yes, I remember him. We called him Toddy. His real name was Theodore, wasn't it? I suppose I'll have to go."

"Of course you will. You were always a special favourite." Pauline gave a generous emphasis to this sentence. And it was generous of her, Lucy admitted; for Mrs. Ramsay had always treated Pauline like Pauline and Lucy like Lucy. But was generosity ever a grace when it came with a pull? Wasn't it like the quality of mercy and the gentle dew? Her sister broke in upon her reverie.

"Lucy, you're not eating anything again! That's why you've lost your colour. You know, it's not becoming to you to be pale. There's a new preparation of cod-liver oil—"

Lucy interrupted her firmly. "Pauline, I took that medicine when I first came home to please you, not because I thought it would do me any good. It doesn't help people to eat when they are not hungry. I worked too hard last summer, and had a kind of nervous smash-up at the end of it. The only thing that will help me is to be alone a great deal. That's why I came home, and why I don't go to see people. That's why I begged you to leave the orchard, too. I didn't lose my job, as some of our friends seem to think. My coming away put Professor Auerbach to a great deal of trouble. But he wouldn't let me try to work when I was sick."

"Well, Lucy," said Pauline as she began gathering up the dishes, "that's the most reasonable explanation of things you've given me yet. Of course I want to help you to get well. But if you expect people to help you, you must tell them a little about what is the matter. And you certainly have kept us in the dark."

"I know." Lucy spoke contritely, but she drew closer back within herself and looked at the floor. "I'm not a very reasonable person. You've had a good deal to put up with. I think I'm beginning to get a little steadier."

Pauline had spoken kindly, and she still meant to be kind when she went on:

"You must be plain and outspoken with your own folks, Lucy, and not theatrical. We aren't that kind, and we don't know how to behave."

"Yes, I understand, Pauline." Lucy spoke very low. She was not angry, but she went upstairs to her own room without once meeting her sister's eyes.

A few moments later Pauline saw her go out of the house carrying an old carriage robe, and disappear into the apple orchard behind the garden.

2

All afternoon Lucy lay in the sun under a low-branching apple tree, on the dry, fawn-coloured grass. The orchard covered about three acres and sloped uphill. From the far end, where she was lying, Lucy looked down through the rows of knotty, twisted trees. Little red apples still clung to the boughs, and a few withered grey-green leaves. The orchard had been neglected for years, and now the fruit was not worth picking. Through this long, soft, late-lingering autumn Lucy had spent most of her time out here.

Lucy had been at home only a few weeks when she was awakened one morning by the sound of an ax. She listened languidly for a moment, then suddenly realized that it wasn't somebody chopping wood. The sound was not like that at all; there was no vibration. The ax was cutting into something alive. She sprang out of bed, caught up a dressing-gown, and ran to her father's big room at the back of the house, which looked out over the yard and the orchard. Her father was in the bathroom, shaving. From his window she could see a man in the orchard, cutting down an apple tree. She ran down the back stairs to the kitchen, where Pauline was getting breakfast, and told her to go out to the orchard, quick! Someone was cutting a tree.

Pauline looked sidewise out of her rather small eyes. Her voice was not quite natural as she tried to answer carelessly.

"I told Poole to come today, but I didn't tell him to come so early. I'm sorry if I wakened you."

"But what's the matter with the tree? Why is he cutting it?"

Pauline broke an egg into the hot saucepan. "Hadn't I told you we are going to clear away the old orchard?"

"Clear away— Oh, where is Father?"

Startled by the frantic note in her sister's voice, Pauline pushed the eggs to the back of the stove and turned round.

"Father has agreed to it. You surely must know, Lucy, that he turns in very little money toward the running of this house. My onion crops have done a good deal for us. I am having the orchard cut down this fall and the ground prepared, so that I can put it into onions and potatoes in the spring. I can't be going out to the farms all the time to look things over, and I'm sure the tenants cheat me. But here I can have a crop under my eyes and make a good thing of it. I have to turn some trick, to keep the place going."

"But, Pauline, don't do it this fall. Don't do it now, when I'm so miserable!"

"Try to be reasonable, Lucy. I've made all the arrangements, and if I put it off I lose a year's crop."

Lucy was still scarcely awake. She caught Pauline's chubby hand and broke out wildly: "I can't stand it, I can't! It's all I have in the world just now. Leave it this year, and I'll pay you back what you lose, truly I will. I'll soon be making money again, and I'll pay you every cent. Pauline, go out and send that man away! Listen, it's down! He'll begin on another. I can't stand it!" Lucy dropped into a chair, and her head sank upon her bare arms on the kitchen table. Her hair was hanging in two braids over her shoulders which were shaking with bitter sobs. Pauline frowned darkly, but her own eyes filled with tears. She couldn't doubt the desperateness of Lucy's distress, and she looked so helpless. Not since she was a child had she ever begged for anything like that. Pauline bent over the table and gave her sister an awkward, spasmodic hug.

"There, there, Sister. I didn't know you would take it so hard. I'll let it stand till next fall. But won't you feel just the same about it then?"

Lucy lifted her face. "I won't be here then. I'll be off making my living, somewhere. I know you have to make up for Father's easy ways." She said this very low, and swallowed a lump in her throat. "But if you'll just—just humour me this year, you'll never be sorry. Some time you'll understand."

"All right, my dear. I'll go and send Poole away. And you go upstairs now and put your clothes on. Take this cup of coffee along, and drink it while you dress."

Lucy took it with gratitude, and went up the back stairs slowly, meekly, like a child who has been whipped until, as they say, its will is broken.

At the top of the stairs, before the door of his bedroom, stood a man who was also afraid of Pauline. He was freshly shaven, in a clean shirt, with bay rum on his greying hair and goatee. He took the coffee-cup from Lucy, put it on his dresser, and then took her in his arms. He kissed her with love, as he always did when he kissed her at all, on her lips and eyes and hair. He said not a word, but, keeping his arm around her, went with her to her own door, carrying the coffee.

3

As Lucy was coming in from the orchard just before sunset, she found Pauline waiting for her on the back porch, with a cape over her shoulders.

"Lucy, you'll take cold, you shouldn't be out there after four o'clock without a coat on. I never could make you wear clothes enough when you were little. It's just the same now. Mrs. Ramsay called up again and wants to speak to you. You will have to go there tonight."

Lucy said she supposed she must. There was only one thing she really liked to do in the evening. She and her father had been playing some sonatas of Mozart after he came home from the shop. He had a harsh tone on the violin, but he seemed to enjoy playing with her so much that she enjoyed it, too.

After supper she walked toward the town and turned into the street that people jokingly called Quality Street, because Mrs. Ramsay lived at one end of it and the Gordons at the other. Mrs. Ramsay was sitting in her high-backed chair beside the big front window, the shades up and the silk curtains drawn back. This had always been her way, though her house was so near the sidewalk that every passer-by could gaze in; her neighbours sometimes said it looked as if she were giving a reception to the street. As a little girl Lucy had loved to come to this house; such comfortable rooms, old-fashioned furniture, and soft, flowered carpets. She used to like the feeling that here there was a long distance between the parlour and the kitchen, that they were not always being mixed up together as they were at home. Mrs. Ramsay was then the only woman in town who kept two maids; now Mrs. Harry Gordon kept a man and his wife, Pauline had told her.

Lucy kissed Mrs. Ramsay's cheek and sat down at her side, on the bamboo stool with the red cushion where she used to sit when she was learning to crochet. Nothing ever changed in this house, and there was something in the air of it that one was glad to come back to. The house had some reality, had colour and warmth, because the woman who made it and ruled it had those things in her nature.

"Lucy, dear, you aren't treating me as well as you always used to. Have I grown too old for you, at last?"

Lucy murmured that she didn't like to visit her friends when she was dull and out of sorts. She had stayed in the city and worked all summer, and that didn't turn out very well.

"When fall came, I was not good for anything. My teacher's wife packed my things for me—and I let her do it, think of that!"

Mrs. Ramsay patted her hand. So it wasn't that Lucy had displeased her teacher and been sent away, as some people said.

"Well, my dear, if you don't feel like talking, you might come in and play for me sometimes. I had the piano tuned as soon as I heard you were home. And there it stands. Madge never touches it."

Lucy brightened. "Would you like that? I think I would! We have only the old upright at home, you know. The one in father's shop is a little better, but it bothers me to have people coming in and out. I didn't use to mind it when I was a girl."

"A girl? Good gracious, what are you now, I'd like to know? No, you mustn't practise much while you are at home. You look tired, my dear, and you walk tired. You need a long rest in country air, and there's no air like the Platte valley. Denver's too high, and Chicago's too low. There are no autumns like ours, anywhere. The fall we spent in Scotland, I count lost out of my life. Mr. Ramsay would have it, and he got enough of it!"

Yes, Lucy said, she was glad to be at home. A whole year of the city had been too much.

"But it was a good year, wasn't it? You must have been enjoying your work, or you wouldn't have stayed. And I hope you had plenty of fun along with it. I don't like to see young people with talent take it too seriously. Life is short; gather roses while you may. I'm sure you gathered a few."

Lucy smiled indulgently. "A few."

"Make it as many as you can, Lucy. Nothing really matters but living. Get all you can out of it. I'm an old woman, and I know. Accomplishments are the ornaments of life, they come second. Sometimes people disappoint us, and sometimes we disappoint ourselves; but the thing is, to go right on living. You've hardly begun yet. Don't let a backward spring discourage you. There's a long summer before you, and everything rights itself in time."

Lucy sat wondering why it was she could not talk to her

playing chess by telephone with a celebrated player who was
visiting a cousin in North Platte. To be sure, he didn't often
have a chance to match his skill with such an opponent.

Mr. Gayheart had let the shop get so dusty that it wasn't a
pleasant place to practise in. The space round the piano was
full of broken music-stands and brass instruments that were
never cleaned, and the walls were hung with dusty band uniforms. It embarrassed Lucy when people came in for watches
and clocks that should have been repaired weeks ago.

If she stayed at home to practise, there were so many things
to put her out. She was restless now, and trifles got on her
nerves. No matter how orderly she managed to keep her own
room, she couldn't help being aware that just on the other
side of that thin partition her sister's room was in confusion.
There was no doubting it, for Pauline left her door open. It
was Pauline's custom not to make her bed until noon; she
managed to get out of it in the morning without throwing off
the blankets, leaving it like a mole-hill, with the very shape of
her body.

"Lucy," she said one morning, "what's got into you, to be
turning your mattress and sweeping your room every day?
You never used to be so fussy."

"A little Italian showed me how a sleeping-room ought to
be kept. I learned something besides music last winter," Lucy
replied as she went downstairs.

Pauline squinted. That remark nettled her, really hurt her
feelings. She kept recalling it for days afterwards.

Lucy did what she could on the shop piano in the morning,
and every afternoon she walked; through the town, and out
the road to the north, where the land lay high and she could
look down over the Platte valley. She began to notice things
about the country that she had never taken much heed of
before. She believed she was bidding the country good-bye
this winter, and that made her eye more searching. One thing
she watched for, every afternoon. Long before sunset an un-
accountable pink glow appeared in the eastern sky, about
half-way between the zenith and the horizon. It was not a
cloud, it had not the depth of a reflection: it was thin and
bright like the colour on a postcard. On sunny afternoons it
was sure to be there, a pink rouge on the hard blue cheek of

the sky. From her window she could watch this colour come above the tall, wide-spreading cottonwood trees of the town park, where her father led the band concerts in summer. Did that pink flush use to come there, in the days when she was running up and down these sidewalks, or was it a new habit the light had taken on?

If there was anyone in Haverford who could tell her, it would be Harry Gordon. He was the only man here who noticed such things, and he was deeply, though unwillingly, moved by them. When she used to go duck-shooting with him she had found that he knew every tree and shrub and plant they ever came upon. Harry kept that side of himself well hidden. He could feel things without betraying himself, because he was so strong. If only she could have that strength behind her instead of against her! It was more than physical strength; it was something that could keep up to the bitter end, that could take hold and never let go. She was so without any such power that even to think of it heartened her a little. Perhaps some day they would be friends again. He was conceited and hard to teach, but she believed he would go on learning about life; because he had more depth than the people around him, and never pretended to like anything he didn't like. Quite the other way; he played at being a common fellow, and he wasn't. He was full of that energy which moves quietly, but always moves. It might get a man almost anywhere, she thought. And the people who hadn't it, even those with nice tastes, like her father, never got anywhere.

10

The weeks can be very long in the Platte valley, Lucy found. She began to feel trapped, shut up in a little town in winter. That long, soft, brooding autumn had been like a kind companion. Now the hard facts of country life were upon her. The weather grew windy and bitter cold; the town and all the country round were the colour of cement. The tides that raced through the open world never came here. There was never anything to make one leap beyond oneself or to carry one away. One's mind got stuffy, like the houses.

doors, out in the road, hurrying away from the house and walking toward the country. And she was carrying some-thing, in a black bag. Could it be her skating-shoes?

Pauline caught up a shawl and ran out into the yard.

"Lucy!" she called; then louder: "Lucy, wait!"

But Lucy never turned. She seemed, indeed, to quicken her pace. Pauline went back into the house. "Just the way she used to run off when she was little!" She dropped her shawl. "I wonder if she knows the old skating-place was ruined last spring when the river changed its bed? She'll have her walk for nothing."

Surely she wouldn't be crazy enough to try the ice out there? The bank had been torn up by the flood, and anyone could see that the river itself now flowed where the shallow arm used to be. Pauline considered telephoning the livery man to drive out after Lucy and tell her she wouldn't find any skating. But Lucy might be very much annoyed at any such interference. Probably it was the walk she wanted. Pauline re-membered how she used to shut her eyes to Lucy's truancies; the child usually got over her tempers out on the highroad, but if she were shut up for a punishment it only made her worse.

11

Lucy found the walking bad enough. The roads had been rutted during the thaw, and afterwards the deep cuts made by the wagon-wheels had frozen hard. Yesterday's snowfall had packed into them. Her foot kept catching in the walls of the ruts. On either side of the wheel-tracks the mud had frozen in jagged ridges, rough and sharp like mushroom coral. Since yesterday few countrymen had been abroad, and the horses' hoofs had not yet broken down these frozen incrustations. Lucy couldn't remember that her feet had ever got so cold when she was walking; but this was not walking, really, it was plodding, and breaking through.

She was going west, directly against the wind, and she had often to turn and stand still to catch her breath. After she was a mile out of town, not a single sleigh or wagon passed her. It was still too early for the farmers who had gone to town in the morning to be driving homeward. The country looked very dreary, certainly. If only the sun would break through! But it made a mere glassy white spot in the low grey sky. In that cold light even the fresh snow looked grey, and the frozen weeds sticking up through it. In the draws, between the low hills, thickets of wild plum bushes were black against the drifts; they should have been thatched with yesterday's snow, but today's sharp wind had stripped them bare.

After the first mile Lucy began to feel very tired. The wind seemed to blow harder out here in the open country; it brought the tears to her eyes, and she had to keep wiping them away to see the road clearly. At last she determined to beg a ride from anyone who came by, even if he were going toward town. It was almost too cold to skate; and there would be the long walk home.

She had got over another mile when she heard the sound of sleigh-bells behind her. She turned her back to the wind, and listened. Only one man in the country had such bells. It must be Harry Gordon. There was no place to hide; she wouldn't hide. Perhaps this was the chance she had been hoping for. She stepped behind a telephone post and waited. She felt even colder than before, and her heart beat fast. She was afraid, after all. There he came in his cutter, over the brow of a hill, down into a draw where he was lost to sight, then out on the very hill upon which she was standing. She stepped into the middle of the road, in front of him, and held up her hand. He pulled in his horses and stopped.

"Harry, could you give me a lift as far as Thompson's pasture? I find it's pretty rough walking." She was standing with her back to the wind, her skirts blown forward, holding her muff against her cheek. She looked very slight and appealing out there all alone.

Harry's eyes were watery from the cold; he seemed more than ever to look at her through glasses. He began in that voice of cheery friendliness which meant nothing at all, with the usual shade of surprise in it:

"Well, now, I'm just awfully sorry, but I'm not going out that way at all! I turn north right here at the corner. I have an important appointment with a man up in Harlem. I'm nearly an hour late as it is, and I've got to make up time on the road.

Wish I weren't in such a hurry." He touched his fur cap with his glove and drove on.

Lucy sent just one cry after him, angry and imperious, "Harry!" as if she had the right to call him back. His big shoulders never moved. His sharp-shod horses trotted on, the sleigh-bells singing, and turned north at the section corner a hundred yards away. The cutter with the upright seated figure moved along against the grey snow-drifted pasture land until at last it disappeared behind a group of distant straw stacks.

When Lucy next stopped to take breath, she found herself a long way nearer the river bend. For a moment she had leaned against the telephone post back yonder, but only for a moment. Such a storm of pain and anger boiled up in her that she felt strong enough to walk into the next county. Her blood was racing, and she was no longer conscious of the cold. She forgot to look where she put her feet; they took care of themselves.

She couldn't have imagined such rudeness, such an insult! She was young, she was strong, she would show them they couldn't crush her. She would get away from these people who were cruel and stupid—stupid as the frozen mud in the road. If she let herself think, she would cry. She must not give in to it, she must hurry on.

When she reached the river bank she sat down just long enough to take off her walking-shoes, and put on the other pair with skates attached. Her hands trembled so that she could scarcely pull the leather laces taut and tie them. She was angry with herself, too. That she should have given him the chance to leave her in the road, as he had left her in the dining-room that night in Chicago! But how could anyone be armed against such boorishness and spite? Catching up a stick, she got to her feet and took a few long strokes close to the shore. She was not looking about her, she saw nothing—she would get away from this frozen country and these frozen people, go back to light and freedom such as they could never know.

Without looking or thinking she struck toward the centre for smoother ice. A soft, splitting sound brought her to herself in a flash, and she saw dark lines running in the ice about her. She turned sharply, but the cracks ran ahead of her. A sheet of ice broke loose and tipped, and she plunged to her waist into cold water.

Lucy was more stimulated than frightened; she had got herself into a predicament, and she must keep her wits about her. The water couldn't be very deep. She still had both elbows on the ice; as soon as she touched bottom she could manage. (It never occurred to her that this was the river itself.) She was groping cautiously with her feet when she felt herself gripped from underneath. Her skate had caught in the fork of a submerged tree, half-buried in sand by the spring flood. The ice cake slipped from under her arms and let her down.

At half-past three, when the wind had grown so bitter, Pauline telephoned her father to drive out and pick Lucy up on the west road. Mr. Gayheart went to the livery barn a few doors from his shop and told Gullford, the driver, to put in two horses. Then he asked his friend the tailor to go with him for a sleigh-ride. Mr. Gayheart was not a man to look for trouble. But as they drove on and on and still did not meet his daughter, he grew uneasy.

When they reached the place on the shore from which the young people used to go skating, they found the ice out in the stream cracked and broken. So she couldn't have tarried here. She must have taken some other road, or gone to pay a call at one of the farms. The driver noticed something, out where the ice was bad; he said it looked like a red scarf.

Mr. Gayheart jumped out of the sleigh. He contradicted Gullford, but begged him to look again, to go out on the ice.

"I'm a little afraid to go out there, Mr. Gayheart; it's rotten. But don't get excited. Stay where you are, and I'll have a look around."

Gullford went slowly along the shore, considering what was to be done. He knew that was a scarf out there. Presently he stopped and bent over. Under a willow bush at the river's edge he found a pair of shoes and overshoes. He called Schneider, the tailor, and asked him to stay here with Mr.

how many memories of their youth went back to the music-teacher who had lived so long, and lived happily, in spite of misfortunes!

It was sad, too, to see the last member of a family go out; to see a chapter closed, and a once familiar name on the way to be forgotten. There they were, the Gayhearts, in that little square of ground, the new grave standing open. Mr. Gayheart would lie between his long-dead wife and his daughter Lucy; the young people could not remember her at all. Pauline they remembered; she lay on Lucy's left. There were two little mounds in the lot; sons who died in childhood, it was said. And now the story was finished: no grandchildren, complete oblivion.

While the prayers were being read, someone whispered that it was almost as if Lucy's grave had been opened; the service brought back vividly that winter day long ago when she had been laid to rest here, so young, so lovely, and, everyone vaguely knew, so unhappy. It was like a bird being shot down when it rises in its morning flight toward the sun. The townspeople remembered that as the saddest funeral that had ever drawn old and young together in this cemetery.

By the time the grave was filled in and the flowers were heaped over it, the sun had set, and a low streak of red fire burned along the edge of the prairie. The crusted snow in the open fields turned rose-colour. The automobiles began slowly to back out, and the people who had come on foot turned their steps homeward. In the company walking toward the town, one man withdrew from the slow-moving crowd. Forsaking the road, he struck off alone across a fenced pasture; a tall man of solid frame, walking deliberately, his hands in the pockets of his overcoat, his head erect, his shoulders straight. To a stranger he would have given an impression of loneliness and strength—tried and seasoned strength. He has need of it, for he has much to bear.

2

Harry Gordon went directly from the cemetery to his bank and called up his house by telephone. The maid answered.

Would she tell Mrs. Gordon that he must finish up some business he had laid aside to go to the funeral. He would have supper sent in from the hotel and would not be home until late.

This done, he went through a hallway to his private office. The first Gordon bank in Haverford was a wooden building. When the brick bank was built, Harry's father had the old building pushed back to the rear, and for years used it as a storehouse. Harry, after his marriage, had fitted it up for a study and private office. At first it had looked like any country lawyer's office; oak tables, shelves that held old ledgers and financial reports. Gradually, almost stealthily, he had made it more comfortable, and as the years went on he spent more and more time there. The room was heated by the bank furnace, but he had put in a fireplace where he burned coke when the steam got low after banking hours.

This evening when he came in, Gordon lit a fire before he took off his overcoat. He unlocked a cupboard, got out his whisky and a siphon of soda, and sat down by the fire. Pouring himself a drink, he swallowed it slowly. Then he lit a cigar and with a long sigh settled deep into his chair. His well-set, vigorous frame relaxed. As he lay against the leather cushions he looked tired, — tired and beaten.

He had just buried the last close personal friend he had in the world. He was not, he thought with a grim smile, likely to make new ones at fifty-five. How differently life had turned out from the life young Harry Gordon planned in the days when he used to step out on the diamond to pitch his famous in-curve, with all the boys and girls calling to him from the bleachers!

For the last eight years he had played chess with old Mr. Gayheart two or three evenings every week. He had become a good chess-player, quite Gayheart's equal. After Pauline's death left the old man alone, Gordon managed to drop in at his shop every day, if only for a moment. Chess had become one of his fixed habits. They played in Gayheart's shop, never at the house. They talked no more than good chess-players usually do. Gordon had watched games between players of international renown when he was abroad during the war, and Mr. Gayheart liked to hear him tell of them over and over.

Like many other men whose lives were dull or empty, Harry Gordon "threw himself," as the phrase went, enthusiastically into war work; Red Cross, Food Conservation. Finally he went over himself with an ambulance unit which he had helped to finance. He was gone for eight months, and his wife took his place as president of the bank and manager of all his business interests. That was probably the happiest period of her life; she was a born woman of affairs.

For Gordon himself that absence did a great deal; ever since he came back the townspeople had felt a change in him. His friendship with old Mr. Gayheart grew closer and warmer—like a son's regard, indeed. At home he played his part better. He and his wife seemed more companionable; went out together, had guests to dinner. The air in their big, slippery-floored many-bathroomed house was not so chill as it used to be. And in business Gordon was more consistent. For some years before he went away he had brought on himself a reputation for eccentricity; this had gone so far as to affect his credit. At one time he would be sharp and tricky, barely keeping inside the law. At another he would let everything go, as if he felt a contempt for his business and were shuffling it off in the easiest way. Conservative men had begun to doubt his judgment.

Since his return from France he had devoted himself seriously to the bank, as his father had done, and he became more like his father. You knew where to find him now, Milton Chase said. There had been a stretch of time back there when Gordon's erratic decisions wore his cashier thin and bald.

Milton Chase probably knew more about his chief than anyone else did, but he didn't pretend to understand him. He had found it very agreeable to work under Mrs. Gordon. She was a reasonable woman. When he gave her the facts about any proposition that came up, he could pretty well tell in advance what she would think about it. But Harry had sprung too many surprises on him. On the surface there was perfect accord between Gordon and his cashier, but deep down Milton was chafed by a secret distrust. What was he to think when one of the most self-centred of men began to give not only his time but his money to the Red Cross? And worse was to follow. On the morning when Harry called Milton into the room behind the bank and told him that he was going to France with the hospital unit, the cashier went to pieces and said he didn't know whether he could face his responsibility; he'd have to take a few days off and think it over.

In the course of the years queer things had happened which Milton could never explain; things which were out of order, which ought not to occur in business. For instance, a shocking scene had come about when they were foreclosing on Nick Wakefield. Nick had been one of the gay young fellows who used to play about with Lucy Gayheart. He inherited a big farm from his father, but he was a town boy, didn't like heavy work, and he failed as a farmer. When the bank was shutting down on him, Nick nerved himself with plenty of alcohol and came in to have it out with Harry Gordon. The game was up, and he might as well have his say. It was a very unseemly thing to occur in a bank. Nick was full of bitter talk. He made several ugly accusations, more or less true, and ended with a taunt which brought the cold sweat out on Milton's brow, as he sat trying to look small in his cage.

"You're ready to hit a man when he's down," Nick shouted, clenching his fists and standing up to Harry, "but you're a damned coward, for all your big chest. Afraid to go to poor Lucy Gayheart's funeral, weren't you, big man? Beat it for Denver! I guess there was a reason, all right!"

Milton had expected the ceiling to fall—he prayed that it might. But what happened was stranger. Gordon made figures on his desk pad for a moment. Then he turned in his chair and looked at Nick. He spoke to him in a voice that was really kind, without any contemptuous jollying in it:

"There are some names I wouldn't mention in your state of health, Nick. You're loaded, and you'll be sorry for this tomorrow. Come in then and finish what you have to say to me."

The bank sold Nick Wakefield out, but on terms more lenient than Milton Chase thought proper.

His own body grew marvellously free and light, and there was a snapping sparkle in his blood that made him set his teeth.

In the absolute stillness of the night (it was getting toward twelve), Gordon heard the bank telephone ringing again and again. That would be his wife, calling up to know what had become of him. He did not answer the telephone, but he covered the last glowing lumps of the coke fire, put on his overcoat, and started for home.

He is not a man haunted by remorse; all that he went through with long ago. He enjoys his prosperity and his good health. Lucy Gayheart is no longer a despairing little creature standing in the icy wind and lifting beseeching eyes to him. She is no longer near, beside his sleigh. She has receded to the far horizon line, along with all the fine things of youth, which do not change.

4

The day after Mr. Gayheart's funeral was Sunday. Harry and his cashier, Milton Chase, met at the bank by appointment, to go for a walk. People looked out of their windows to see them go by. Everyone is used to the fact that Milton seems older than Harry. When his youthful good looks withered, they left his cheeks thin and his nose too long. He walks jerkily, with short uneven steps, as if he had left some unfinished business behind him. Harry still has the firm, deliberate tread with which he has come and gone about these streets for nearly a lifetime.

The two men are going "out to the Gayhearts'," as people still say. The town has not grown in these twenty-five years, it has shrunk. The old Gayheart place is still half-farm, lying at the extreme west edge of Haverford, where the sidewalk ends. Beyond, there is only country road. It is a walk Gordon often takes on a Sunday afternoon.

When he was a young lad, newly come to Haverford with his father, one summer evening he was riding out that road on his bicycle. The cement gang had been at work there all day, laying this very sidewalk which was never to go any farther. They had finished smoothing the wet slabs, stretched mason's cord on low stakes all about them as a warning to passers-by to keep off, and gone home for supper. When Harry came along on his wheel, he noticed a slip of a girl in boy's overalls, barefoot, running about the flower garden, watering it with a length of rubber hose. Instantly he recognized her as the same girl he had seen in the skating-rink, gliding about to the music in her red jersey. He got off his bicycle and walked, pushing it beside him. She had not seen him. Suddenly she dropped the hose, glanced back at the house to make sure no one was observing her, and darted forward. She cleared the mason's cord and ran over those wet slabs—one, two, three steps, then out into the weeds beside the road, almost in front of Harry. She looked up at him and laughed.

"Don't tell on me, please!" With that she scampered up the dusty road and into the Gayheart yard by the driveway.

After all these years the three footprints were still there in the sidewalk; the straight, slender foot of a girl of thirteen, delicately and clearly stamped in the grey-white composition. The travel of the years had not made them fainter. To be sure, there was never a great deal of walking out this way; people came out here only when they were going to see the Gayhearts. Gordon had never heard anyone speak of these footprints; perhaps no one knew who made them. They were light, in very low relief; unless one were looking for them, one might not notice them at all. The Gayheart lots had not been well kept for a long while. In summer the wild sunflowers grew up on either side of the walk and hung over it; tufts of alfalfa, escaped from the near-by pasture, encroached upon it, and a wild vetch with sprays of lavender-pink blossoms, like fingers, came up there every year and climbed the sunflower stalks, making a kind of wattle all along the two slabs marked by those swift impressions. For to Harry Gordon they did seem swift: the print of the toes was deeper than the heel; the heel was very faint, as if that part of the living foot had just grazed the surface of the pavement. Was there really some baffling suggestion of quick motion in those impressions, Gordon often wondered, or was it merely because he had seen them made, that to him they always had a look of

II

At the hour when Sapphira Dodderidge Colbert was leaving the breakfast table in her wheel-chair, a short, stalwart woman in a sunbonnet, wearing a heavy shawl over her freshly ironed calico dress, was crossing the meadows by a little path which led from the highroad to the Mill House. She was a woman of thirty-six or -seven, though she looked older—looked so much like Henry Colbert that it was not hard to guess she was his daughter. The same set of the head, enduring yet determined, the broad, highly coloured face, the fleshy nose, anchored deeply at the nostrils. She had the miller's grave dark eyes, too, set back under a broad forehead.

After crossing the stile at the Mill House, Mrs. Blake took the path leading back to the negro cabins. She must stop to see Aunt Jezebel, the oldest of the Colbert negroes, who had been failing for some time. Mrs. Blake was always called where there was illness. She had skill and experience in nursing; was certainly a better help to the sick than the country doctor, who had never been away to any medical school, but treated his patients from Buchan's Family Medicine book.

On being told that Aunt Jezebel was asleep, Mrs. Blake passed the kitchen (separated from the dwelling by thirty feet or so), and entered the house by the back door which the servants used when they carried hot food from the kitchen to the dining-room in covered metal dishes. As she went down the long carpeted passage toward Mrs. Colbert's bedchamber, she heard her mother's voice in anger—anger with no heat, a cold, sneering contempt.

"Take it down this minute! You know how to do it right. Take it *down*, I told you! Hairpins do no good. Now you've hurt me, stubborn!"

Then came a smacking sound, three times: the wooden back of a hairbrush striking someone's cheek or arm. Mrs. Blake's firm mouth shut closer as she knocked. The same voice asked forbiddingly:

"Who is there?"

"It's only Rachel."

As Mrs. Blake opened the door, her mother spoke coolly to

a young girl crouching beside her chair: "You may go now. And see that you come back in a better humour."

The girl flitted by Mrs. Blake without a sound, her face averted and her shoulders drawn together.

Mrs. Colbert in her wheel-chair was sitting at a dressing-table before a gilt mirror, a white combing-cloth about her shoulders. This she threw off as her daughter entered.

"Take a chair, Rachel. You're early." She spoke politely, but she evidently meant "too early."

"Yes, I'm earlier than I calculated. I stopped to see old Jezebel, but she was asleep, so I came right on in."

Mrs. Colbert smiled. She was always amused when people behaved in character. Sooner than disturb a sick negro woman, Rachel had come in to disturb her at her dressing hour, when it was understood she did not welcome visits from anyone. How like Rachel!

For all Mrs. Blake could see, her mother's grey-and-chestnut hair was in perfect order; combed up high from the neck and braided in a flat oval on the crown, with wavy wings coming down on either side of her forehead.

"You might get me a fresh cap out of the upper drawer, Rachel. I hate a frowsy head in the morning. Thank you. I can arrange it." She pinned the small frill of ribbon and starched muslin over the flat oval. "Now," she said affably, "you might turn me a little, so that I can see you."

Her chair was carved walnut, with a cane back and down-curved arms: one of the dining-room chairs, made over for her use by Mr. Whitford, the country carpenter and coffin-maker. He had cushioned it, and set it on a walnut platform with iron castors underneath. Mrs. Blake turned it so that her mother sat in the sunlight and faced the east windows instead of the looking-glass.

"Well, I suppose it is a good thing Jezebel can sleep so much?"

Mrs. Blake shook her head. "I can't get her to eat anything. She's weaker every day. She'll not last long."

Mrs. Colbert smiled archly at her daughter's solemn face. "She has managed to last a good while: something into ninety years. I shouldn't care to last that long, should you?"

"No," Mrs. Blake admitted.

brooms, spades and hoes, and the rag dolls and home-made toy wagons of the negro children. Except in a downpour of rain, the children were always playing there, in company with kittens, puppies, chickens, ducks that waddled up from the millpond, turkey gobblers which terrorized the little darkies and sometimes bit their naked black legs.

When Sapphira Dodderidge Colbert first moved out to Back Creek Valley with her score of slaves, she was not warmly received. In that out-of-the-way, thinly settled district between Winchester and Romney, not a single family had ever owned more than four or five negroes. This was due partly to poverty—the people were very poor. Much of the land was still wild forest, and lumber was so plentiful that it brought no price at all. The settlers who had come over from Pennsylvania did not believe in slavery, and they owned no negroes. Mrs. Colbert had gradually reduced her force of slaves, selling them back into Loudoun County, whither they were glad to return. Her husband had needed ready money to improve the old mill. Here there were no large, rich farms for the blacks to work, as there were in Loudoun County. Many field-hands were not needed.

Sapphira Dodderidge usually acted upon motives which she disclosed to no one. That was her nature. Her friends in her own county could never discover why she had married Henry Colbert. They spoke of her marriage as "a long step down." The Colberts were termed "immigrants,"—as were all settlers who did not come from the British Isles. Old Gabriel Colbert, the grandfather, came from somewhere in Flanders. Henry's own father was a plain man, a miller, and he trained his eldest son to that occupation. The three younger sons were birds of a very different feather. They rode with a fast fox-hunting set. Being shrewd judges of horses, they were welcome in every man's stable. They were even (with a shade of contempt and only occasionally) received in good houses; —not the best houses, to be sure. Henry was a plain, hard-working, little-speaking young man who stayed at home and helped his father. With his father he regularly attended a dis-senting church supported by small farmers and artisans. He was certainly no match for Captain Dodderidge's daughter.

True, when Sapphira's two younger sisters were already married, she, at the age of twenty-four, was still single. She saved her face, people said, by making it clear that she was bound down by the care of her invalid father. Captain Dodderidge had been seriously hurt while out hunting; in taking a stone wall, his horse had fallen on him. He survived his injury for three years. After his death, when the property was divided, Sapphira announced her engagement to Henry Colbert, who had never gone to her father's house except on matters of business. After the Captain was crippled and ailing, he often sent for young Henry to advise him about selling his grain, to write his business letters, and to keep an eye on the nominal steward. He had great confidence in Henry's judgment.

Sapphira was usually present at their business conferences, and took some part in their discussions about the management of the farm lands and stock. It was she who rode over the estate to see that the master's orders were carried out. She went to the public sales on market days and bought in cattle and horses, of which she was a knowing judge. When the increase of the flocks or the stables was to be sold, she attended to it with Henry's aid. When the increase of the slave cabins was larger than needed for field and house service, she sold off some of the younger negroes. Captain Dodderidge never sold the servants who had been with his family for a long while. After they were past work, they lived on in their old cabins, well provided for.

When Sapphira announced her engagement, the family friends were more astonished than if she had declared her intention of marrying the gardener. They quizzed the negro servants, who declared that Mr. Henry had never been so much as asked into the parlour. They had never "caught" him talking to Miss Sapphy outside her father's room, much less courting her. After all these years the strangeness of this marriage still came up in conversation when old friends got together. Fat Lizzie, the cook, had whispered to the neighbours on Back Creek: "Folks back home says it seem like Missy an' Mr. Henry wasn't scarcely acquainted befo' de weddin', nor very close acquainted evah since. Him bein' kep' so close at de mill," she would add suavely.

Since she did marry Henry, it was not hard to explain why Sapphira had moved away from her native county, where his plain manners, his calling, vague ancestry, even his Lutheran connections, would have made her social position rather awkward. Once removed several days' journey from her old friends, she could go back to visit them without embarrassment. The miller's unbending, somewhat uncouth figure need never appear upon the scene at all.

The bride chose Back Creek for her place of exile because she owned a very considerable property there, willed to her by an uncle who died when she was still a young girl. On this Back Creek estate there was a mill. It had stood there for some generations, since Revolutionary times.

This farm (and a great tract of forest land afterward sold off) had been deeded by Thomas, Lord Fairfax, to a Nathaniel Dodderidge who came out to Virginia with Fairfax in 1747. Fairfax's actual possessions in the colony were immense; something like five million acres of forest and mountain which had never been surveyed, watered by rivers, great and small, which had never been explored except by the Indians and were nameless except for their unpronounceable Indian names. There was discontent in the Virginia Assembly that so large a territory should be held in one grant. When Fairfax established his final residence in the Shenandoah Valley, he quieted this dissatisfaction by deeding off portions of his estate to desirable settlers, laying out towns, and in every way encouraging immigration.

To Nathaniel Dodderidge he deeded a tract of land on Back Creek. Neither Nathaniel nor any of his descendants had ever lived on this land. It was only after the capture of Quebec by young General Wolfe in 1759 that the mountainous country between Winchester and Romney was altogether safe for settlers. Bands of Indians under French captains had burned and slaughtered as near Back Creek as the Capon River.

When the danger of Indian raids was over, someone (his name was lost) built a water mill where Henry Colbert's mill now stood. All through the Revolutionary War and ever since, a mill on that site had served the needs of the scattered settlers. The Dodderidges had let the Mill Farm to tenants for successive generations. Sapphira's father had never seen the place. But before his death Sapphira herself, attended by a groom, rode up a four days' journey on horseback to look over her inheritance. One morning she arrived at the Back Creek post office, where a spare room was kept for travellers. Sapphira unpacked her saddle-bags and settled herself for a stay of several days. She rode all over the Mill Farm and the timber land; had a friendly interview with the resident miller and told him she could not renew his lease, which had barely a year to run.

Before Sapphira's marriage to Henry Colbert, carpenters were sent out from Winchester to pull down the old mill house (it was scarcely more than a cabin), and to build the comfortable dwelling which now stood there. When the new house was completed, Sapphira's household goods were carted up from Chestnut Hill and settled in it. She and Henry Colbert were married at Christ Church, in Winchester, and drove directly to the new Mill House on Back Creek, omitting the elaborate festivities which customarily followed a wedding.

Though it was often said that Miss Dodderidge had broken away from her rightful station, she by no means dropped out of the lives of her family or lost touch with her friends. Until her illness came upon her, she made every year a long visit to the sister who lived at Chestnut Hill, the old estate in Loudoun County. Even now she was always driven to Winchester in March, to stay with her sister Sarah until after Easter. There she attended all the services at Christ Church, where Lord Fairfax, the first patron of the Virginia Dodderidges, was buried beneath the chancel. With the help of her brother-in-law and a cane she limped to the family pew, though she was obliged to remain seated throughout the service.

She was a comely figure in the congregation, clad in black silk and white fichu. From lack of exercise she had grown somewhat stout, but she wore stays of the severest make and carried her shoulders high. Her serene face and lively, shallow blue eyes smiled at old friends from under a black velvet bonnet, renewed or "freshened" yearly by the town milliner. She had not at all the air of a countrywoman come to town. No

She told him to the post office, so he turned west. When he had gone a mile, he slowed his horses to a walk. There was Mrs. Blake's house, standing under four great maple trees, in a neat yard with a white paling fence. Two little girls ran out, calling: "Good morning, Gran'ma!"

Jefferson stopped the carriage, and Mrs. Colbert asked after their mother.

"Ma ain't at home," said the older child. "She's gone over to Peughtown. Mrs. Thatcher's dreadful sick. They came for Ma in the night, and brought a horse for her."

"So you are all by yourselves? Suppose you get in and take a ride to the post office?"

The children shot quick glances at each other. The younger one, who was only eight, said timidly: "We've got just our old dresses on, Gran'ma."

Her grandmother laughed. "Oh, never mind, this time! Jump in, the horses don't like to stand. Molly's curls are nice, anyhow."

The children climbed into the carriage, delighted at their good luck. Sometimes, when their grandmother was driving of a Sunday morning, she stopped and took them and their mother as far as the Baptist church; but very seldom had they driven out with her by themselves. This was Saturday, and Molly wished that all her schoolmates could be loitering along the road to see them go by. Her real name was Mary, but since she promised to be a pretty girl, her grandmother had taken a fancy to her and called her Molly. It was understood that this name was Mrs. Colbert's special privilege; her mother and her schoolmates called her Mary. Her little sister was the only one who dared to use Grandmother's name for her.

Uncle Jeff drew his horses up before the long, low, white-painted house where the postmistress lived and performed her official duties. The postmistress herself threw an apron over her head and came out to the carriage. She and Mrs. Colbert greeted each other with marked civility. They held very different opinions on one important subject.

Mrs. Colbert drew from her reticule the letter she had written a few hours ago. "I brought this letter up to you myself, Mrs. Bywaters, because it is important, and I hope you will put it into the mailbag yourself."

"Certainly, Mrs. Colbert. Nobody but me ever handles the mail here. The bag goes from my hands into the stage-driver's. I see you've got your little granddaughters along today."

"Yes, Mrs. Bywaters, this is a pleasant day for a drive. I'd heard you had your house new painted. How nice it looks!"

"Thank you. I had trouble enough getting it done, but it's over at last. I had to tear down all my honeysuckle vines and lay them on the ground. I'm hoping they're not much hurt."

"I hope not, indeed. They were a great ornament to your house, especially the coral honeysuckle. Now, Jefferson, we will stop at the store for a minute. Good day to you, Mrs. Bywaters."

The country store stood across the road from the post office. The storekeeper saw the carriage stop, and came out. Mrs. Colbert asked him to bring her a pound of stick candy, half wintergreen and half peppermint. Both little girls tried to look unconscious, but while their grandmother was talking to the storekeeper, Betty pinched Mary softly to express her feelings. The candy was brought out in a brown paper parcel, but it was not given to them until their grandmother let them out at their own gate. They thanked her very prettily for the candy and the drive.

"Jefferson, you may take me down the turnpike, and out to Mrs. Cowper's on the Peughtown road. I want to ask after my carpets."

As she drove along, Mrs. Colbert was thinking it was fortunate that for once her daughter had been called to nurse in a prosperous family like the Thatchers, who would see that she was well repaid; if not in money, in hams or bacon or a bolt of good cloth. Usually she was called out to some bare mountain cabin where she got nothing but thanks, and likely as not had to take along milk and eggs and her own sheets for the poor creature who was sick. Rachel was poor, and it was not much use to give her things. Whatever she had she took where it was needed most; and Mrs. Colbert certainly didn't intend to keep the whole mountain.

After a few miles of jolting over a rough by-road, she stopped for a call on Mrs. Cowper, the carpet-weaver. At the Mill House all worn-out garments, discarded table linen, and old sheets were cut into narrow strips, sewn together, and wound into fat balls. This was the darkies' regular evening work in winter. When a great many balls of these "carpet-rags" had accumulated, they were sent, with hanks of cotton chain, to Mrs. Cowper, who dyed them with logwood, copperas, or cochineal, then wove them into stout carpets, striped or plain.

V

As soon as the Mistress had left the house, Till and her daughter Nancy fell to and began to give her bedroom a thorough cleaning; pushed the bed out from the wall, and washed the closet floors. All the windows were opened, and the rugs before the wash-basin stand and the dressing-table were carried into the back yard and beaten.

After Nancy had pinned a clean antimacassar on the back of the wheel-chair and put the Mistress's slippers ready at the foot of it, her mother said they might as well "give the parlour a lick" before the carriage got back.

The two women, their heads tied up in red cotton handkerchiefs, went into the parlour and rolled up the green paper shades, painted with garden scenes and fountains. The sunlight streamed into the room. The parlour was long in shape, not square, with a low ceiling, the brick fireplace in the middle, under a wide mantel shelf. Horsehair chairs and sofas sat about with tidies on their backs and arms. Captain Dodderidge's old mahogany desk filled one corner. Every inch of the floor was covered by a heavy Wilton carpet, figured with pink roses and green leaves. It was somewhat worn, as it had been "brought over" by Sapphira's mother when she first came out to Virginia. Upon this carpet the two brooms went swiftly to work.

The room had an air of settled comfort and stability; visitors sensed that at once. The deep-set windows made one feel the thickness of the walls. A child could climb up into one of those windows and make a playhouse. Every afternoon Mrs. Colbert was brought into the parlour and sat here for several hours before supper. Here she could watch the light of the sinking sun burn on the great cedars that grew along the farther side of the creek, across from the mill. In winter weather, when the snow was falling over the flower garden and the hedges, that long room, with its six windows and its warm hearth, was a pleasant place to be.

With Nancy at one end and Till at the other, the parlour was soon swept. Till never dawdled over her work. The housekeeper at Chestnut Hill had taught her that the shuffling foot was the mark of an inferior race. After the sweeping came the dusting.

"Now, Nancy, run and fetch me a kitchen chair and a clean soft rag. I want to git at the po'traits, which I didn't have time to do last week." Any other servant on the place would have stepped coolly on one of the fat horsehair chair-bottoms,—if, indeed, she had thought it worth while to dust the pictures at all, now that the Mistress could no longer reach up and run her fingers along the frames.

When the wooden chair was brought, Till mounted and wiped, first the canvases, then their heavy gilt frames. Her daughter stood gazing up at them: Master and Mistress twenty years ago. Mistress in a garnet velvet gown and real lace, wearing her long earrings and a garnet necklace: a vigorous young woman with chestnut hair and a high colour in her cheeks. The Master in a stock and broadcloth coat, his bushy black hair standing up as it often did now, his face broad and ruddy; he had changed very little. Nancy thought these pictures wonderful. She hoped the painter was really her father, as some folks said. Old Jezebel, her great-grandmother, had whispered to her that was why she had straight black hair with no kink in it.

Anyway, Nancy knew Uncle Jeff wasn't her father, though she always called him "Pappy" and treated him with respect. Her mother had no children by Uncle Jeff, and fat Lizzie, the cook, had left Nancy in no doubt as to the reason. When Nancy was a little girl, Lizzie had coaxed her off into the bushes one Sunday to help her pick gooseberries. There she told her how Miss Sapphy had married Till off to Jeff because he was a "capon man." The child was puzzled, and thought this meant that Jeff had come from somewhere up on the Capon River. But Lizzie made the facts quite clear. Miss Sapphy didn't want a lady's maid to be "havin' chillun all over de place,—always a-carryin' or a-nussin' 'em." So she married Till off to Jeff and "made it wuth her while, the niggers reckoned." Till got the light end of the work and the best of everything. And Lizzie didn't believe that talk about the painter man; she told Nancy that one of Mr. Henry's brothers was her real father. From that day Nancy had felt a horror of Lizzie. She tried not to show it, but Lizzie knew, and she got back at the stuck-up piece whenever she had a chance. She set her own daughter, Bluebell, to spy on Till's girl.

Nancy had never asked Till who her father was. She admired her mother and took pride in what she called her mother's "nice ways." The girl had a natural delicacy of feeling. Ugly sights and ugly words sickened her. She had Till's good manners—with something warmer and more alive. But she was not courageous. When the servants were gossiping at their midday dinner in the big kitchen, if she sensed a dirty joke coming, she slipped away from the table and ran off into the garden. If she felt a reprimand coming, she sometimes lied: lied before she had time to think, or to tell herself that she would be found out in the end. She caught at any pretext to keep off blame or punishment for an hour, a minute. She didn't tell falsehoods deliberately, to get something she wanted; it was always to escape from something.

Nancy was startled out of her reflections about her mysterious father by her mother's voice.

"Now, honey, if I was you, I'd make a nice egg-nog when you hear the carriage comin', an' I'd carry it in to the Mistress when she's got out of the coach an' into her room. I'd take it to her on the small silvah salvah, with a white napkin and some cold biscuit."

Nancy caught her breath, and looked downcast. "Lizzie, she don't like to have me meddlin' round the kitchen to do anything."

"I'll be out around the kitchen, an' Lizzie dassent say anything to *me*. An' if I was you, I wouldn't carry a tray to Missus with no haing-dawg look. I'd smile, an' look happy to serve her, an' she'll smile back."

Nancy shook her head. Her slender hands dropped limp at her side. "No she won't, Mudder," very low.

"Yes she will, if you smile right, an' don't go shiverin' like a drownded kitten. In all Loudoun County Miss Sapphy was knowed for her good mannahs, an' that she knowed how to treat all folks in their degree."

The daughter hesitated, but did not answer. For nearly a year now she had seemed to have no degree, and her mistress had treated her like an untrustworthy stranger. Before that, ever since she could remember, Miss Sapphy had been very kind to her, had liked her and had shown it. As they were leaving the parlour, Nancy murmured, more to herself than to her mother:

"I knows that fat Lizzie's at the bottom of it, somehow. She's always got a pick on me."

VI

THE MILL stood on the west bank of Back Creek: the big water-wheel hung almost over the stream itself. The creek ran noisily along over a rough stone bottom which here and there churned the dark water into foam. For the most part it was wide and shallow, though there were deep holes between the ledges. The dam, lying in the green meadows above the mill, was fed by springs, and a race conveyed the water to the big wooden wheel.

In the second storey of the mill flour and unground grain were stored; there it was safe in times of high water. The "miller's room," on the first floor, was a recognized feature of every mill in those days; the man in charge slept there and kept an eye on the property, even when no grinding was going on at night. Henry Colbert had no foreman. He himself occupied the room, using it both as sleeping-chamber and office. Years ago he spent the night at the mill only in times of night grinding or high water. But latterly the mill room had become more and more the place where he actually lived.

The mill room was all that was left of the original building which stood there in Revolutionary times. The old chimney was still sound, and the miller used the slate-paved fireplace in cold weather. The floor was bare; old boards, very wide, ax-hewn from great trees before the day of sawmills. There was no ceiling but the floor of the storeroom above, with its heavy, ax-dressed crossbeams. This wooden ceiling, its beams, and the wooden walls of the room were freshly whitewashed every spring. The miller's furniture was whitewashed, so to speak, day by day, by the flour-dust which sifted down from overhead, and through every crack and crevice in the doors and walls. Each morning Till's Nancy swept and dusted the flour away.

Here the miller had arranged everything to his own liking. The square windows were furnished with paper blinds, to keep out the four-o'clock summer dawn if he had been up late the night before. His narrow bed had been made of chestnut wood by Mr. Whitford, the neighbourhood carpenter and cabinet-maker, and it was a good piece of work. Bed-cords, hitched about neat knobs, took the place of springs. On the tightly drawn cords lay the mattress; a feather "tick" in winter, a corn-shuck one in summer. His "secretary" was also of chestnut. (Whitford liked to work in that wood.) It was both writing-desk and bookcase. Above the desk four shelves held ledgers and account books,—and a curious assortment of other books as well. The high chest of drawers at which the miller shaved stood between the two west windows, looking toward the house, and his small wood-framed looking-glass hung from a nail driven in the plank wall behind. At seven o'clock every morning little Zach ran down from the house with the master's shaving water in a steaming iron teakettle.

When Henry Colbert first took over the mill, his silent unconvivial nature was against him. A miller was expected to be jovial; to produce whisky, or at least applejack, when a man made a small payment on a long account. In time his neighbours found that though the new miller was stingy of speech, he was not tight with his purse-strings.

One rainy March day at about four o'clock in the afternoon (in Virginia one said four o'clock in the "evening") the miller was sitting at his secretary, going through his ledger. His purpose was to check off the names of debtors to whom he would not, under any circumstance, extend further credit. He found so many of these names already checked once, and even twice, that after frowning over his accounts for a long while, he leaned back in his chair and rubbed his chin. When people were so poor, what was a Christian man to do? They were poor because they were lazy and shiftless,—or, at best, bad managers. Well, he couldn't make folks over, he guessed. And they had to eat. While he sat thinking, Sampson, his head mill-hand, appeared at the door, which was often left ajar in the daytime.

"Mr. Henry, little Zach jist run down from de house sayin' de Mistress would like you to come up, if you ain't too busy."

The miller closed his ledger, glad to escape. "Anything amiss, Sampson?"

"No, sah, I don't reckon so. Zach, he said she was waitin' in de parlour."

Colbert changed his old leather jacket for a black coat, brushed the flour-dust off his broad hat, and walked up through the cold spring drizzle which was making the grass green.

He found his wife dressed for the afternoon, with a lace cap on her head and her rings on her fingers, having her tea by the fire. (When she heard him open the front door she poured his cup, smuggling in a good tot of Jamaica rum, since he didn't take cream.) Before he sat down, he took up a plate of toasted biscuit from the hearth and offered it to his wife. He drank his tea in a few swallows, though it was very hot.

"Thank you, Sapphy. That takes the chill out of a body's bones. It does get damp down there at the mill. Could you spare me another cup?"

Munching his biscuit, he watched her pour the tea. When she reached down for a small red cruet, well concealed on the lower deck of the table, he laughed and rubbed his hands together. "That's why it tastes so good! I must try to get up here oftener when you're having your tea. But it's just about this time of day the farmers come in. The good ones are at work all morning, and the poor sticks never get around to anything at all till the day's 'most gone."

"I'm sure the Master would always be very welcome company in the evenings," replied Mrs. Colbert, lifting her eyebrows, whether archly or ironically it would be hard to say.

"Don't you put on with me, Sapphy." He reached down to the hearth for another biscuit. "You're the master here, and I'm the miller. And that's how I like it to be."

His wife looked at him with an indulgent smile, and shook her head. She stirred her tea gently for a few moments in silence. A log fell apart in the fire and shot up tall flames; the miller put the ends together with the tongs. "Henry," she said suddenly, "do you realize it's getting on towards Easter?"

"And you haven't set out yet," he added. "Have you given up going for this year?"

"No, I wouldn't disappoint Sister Sarah. But Jezebel's been so low. I shouldn't like to be away from home when it happened. I thought she would have gone before this."

Colbert glanced up in surprise. "Well, you needn't put

808 SAPPHIRA AND THE SLAVE GIRL

yourself out on Jezebel's account. She may hang on till harvest. It seems like life won't let go of her."

"If you feel that way, what's to hinder my going this Friday? Then I would have all Holy Week with Sarah, and if I get no bad news from home I might stay a week longer. Sarah always entertains after Easter, you know, and I would meet my old friends."

"I can see no objection. The roads ought to be good, if this drizzle don't set into a hard rain. While you're in town you might have the carriage painted. It needs it."

"That's a good idea. And this year I think I shall take Nancy along instead of Till. It would smarten her up, to see how people do things in town."

He considered a moment. "Very well, if you leave Till to look after my place down there. Don't try any more Bluebell on me!"

His wife replied with her most ladylike laugh, a flash of fun in it. "Poor Bluebell! Is she never to have a chance to learn? Why are you so set against her?"

"I can't abide her, or anything about her. If there is one nigger on the place I could thrash with my own hands, it's that Bluebell!"

The Mistress threw up her hands; this time she laughed so heartily that the rings on her fingers glittered. It was a treat to hear her husband break out like this.

"Well, Henry," as she wiped her eyes with a tiny handkerchief, "I will own to you that if it wasn't for Lizzie's feelings, I'd send that lazy girl off the place tomorrow. I'd give her away! But we've got the only good cook west of Winchester, and so we have to have Bluebell. Lizzie would always be in the sulks, and when a cook is out of temper she can spoil every dish, just by a turn of the hand. We would never sit down to a good dinner again. Besides, your Baptists would miss Lizzie and Bluebell in the hymns. And they are always being sent for to sing at funerals. I like to hear them myself, of a summer night."

The miller rose, put another log on the fire, and, by way of an attention, righted the clumsy wheel-chair a little. He took his wife's plump hand and patted it. "Thank you for having me up, Sapphy. It's done me good. The mill room gets very

damp between seasons, and I forget to have Tap make a fire.
You might send for me a little oftener." He turned up his
coat-collar and reached for his hat, but his wife interfered.

"Go and get your shawl out of the hall press. Don't go back
to the mill and sit in a damp coat. It's folly to expose yourself.
You ought to have a fire every day this weather."

He went into the hall and returned with a great shawl of
fine Scotch wool. It had once been dark green, but time and
weather had put a dull gold cast into it. He folded it three-
cornered, so that it covered his coat, and went out into the
drizzle. Military men and prosperous townsmen wore overcoats, but farmers and countrymen wore heavy shawls, fastened with a large shawl-pin.

Sapphira sat looking out at the dripping trees and the thick
amethyst clouds which hung low over the mill and blurred
the tall cedars across the creek. She smiled faintly; it occurred
to her that when they were talking about Bluebell, both she
and Henry had been thinking all the while about Nancy.
How much, she wondered, did each wish to conceal from the
other?

Such speculations were mildly amusing for a woman who
did not read a great deal, and who had to sit in a chair all day.

She had given little time to reflection in the years when she
was having her children and bringing them up. Even after
they were married and gone, the management of the place
had kept her busy. Every year there was the gardening and
planting, butchering time and meat-curing. Summer meant
preserving and jelly-making, the drying of cherries and cur-
rants and sweet corn and sliced apples for winter. In those
days she often rode her mare to Winchester of a Saturday to
be there for the Sunday service. It was because she had been
so energetic, and such a good manager, that even from an
invalid's chair she was still able to keep her servants well in
hand.

BOOK II

Nancy and Till

I

ON THURSDAY MORNING two leather coach trunks were brought down from the garret, and Nancy was allowed, for the first time, to pack them, under Till's direction. Besides the trunks, there was a handy Whitford-made wooden box for shoes, as the poor Mistress had to carry so many pairs. The bandboxes were to go inside the carriage.

By eleven o'clock on Friday morning Mrs. Colbert was dressed and bonneted. All the household gathered round the carriage to see her off. Fat Lizzie brought the lunch-box, for light refreshment on the road to Winchester. The miller came up from the mill to lift his wife into the carriage. Nancy, in her Sunday bonnet and shawl, stood by, expecting to sit on the box with Uncle Jeff, but Mrs. Colbert told her she was to ride inside. The servants called good wishes as Jeff drove off, and Henry walked beside the coach as far as the mill. Nancy had cast an appealing glance at her mother when she learned she was to sit beside the Mistress. But Till knew the Dodderidge manners; if the girl was taken as a companion, she would be treated as such.

After Till had closed the Mistress's room, she went down to the mill to "straighten up" for Mr. Henry. She had her own sense of the appropriate, and she thought the miller's room right for him, in the same way that Captain Dodderidge's saddle room had always been right. She approved of the polished chestnut bedstead, and the counterpane in large blue and white squares, woven by the same Mrs. Cowper who made carpets. The four brass candlesticks, by which the miller read after dark, were clean and shining; only a little tallow from last night had dripped down the stems. The deep chair beside the reading-table was made of bent hickory withes, very strong and well fitted to the back. Till had wanted to make cushions for this chair, but the Master told her cushions

were for women. She was glad to see that Nancy had kept
Mr. Henry's copper pieces bright: she knew he set great store
by these.

Between the whitewashed uprights that held the board
walls together, the miller had fitted wooden shelves. On these
he kept sharp and delicate tools, which the mill-hands were
on no account allowed to touch, and a row of copper bowls
and tankards which had been his grandfather's.

Nancy had been keeping the mill room in order ever since
she was twelve years old. There was nothing down there that
could be damaged or broken, the Mistress had remarked to
Till; yet the work would be training of a sort.

This morning Till examined everything critically; the bed-
cords, the sheets and blankets, the hand wash-basin, the
drawer with soap and towels for the miller's private use. She
couldn't have kept the room better herself, she thought. On
her way back to the house Till fell to wondering for the
hundredth time why Nancy had fallen out of favour with the
Mistress. To be sure, until lately Miss Sapphy had pampered
the girl too much; but it wasn't a Dodderidge trait to turn
on anybody they had once taken a fancy to. Nancy herself,
Till knew, suspected fat Lizzie as the trouble-maker, but she
had never said why.

Old Washington could have given Till some hint as to how
this change in the Mistress had come about; but Washington
was close-mouthed. Long service had taught him that tattling
was sure to get a house-man into trouble.

Nearly a year ago, in the month of May, an unfortunate
incident had occurred. The Mistress, sitting at the table after
her husband had finished his breakfast and gone to the mill,
heard loud voices from the kitchen. The windows and doors
were open to let the fresh spring air blow through the house.
She recognized fat Lizzie's rolling tones and suspected she
was bullying one of the other servants. Washington was
standing behind the Mistress's chair. She beckoned him to
help her rise, took his arm, and limped painfully to the back
door.

This was what she heard (not Lizzie's voice, now, but
Nancy's): "You dasn't talk to me that way, Lizzie. I won't
bear it! I'll go to the Master."

wraps. Whenever the manservant heard the crunch of wheels on the driveway and threw open the front door. . . .

Just then Till heard a very different sound, close at hand. Old Jeff came shuffling along in the dusk. He stopped and stood uneasily before the seated figure.

"It's a-gittin' right late, deery," he said in his squeaky voice.

III

As his wife was always in Winchester for Holy Week, the miller customarily took his Easter dinner with his daughter and granddaughters. This year Easter Sunday fell early (the twenty-third of March), but it was a bright, sun-shiny morning, and warm for the season. He walked across the meadow to accompany Mrs. Blake and her little girls to church. The children told him joyfully that Mr. Fairhead, the preacher (who was also their schoolmaster), was coming to dinner. It would be like a party; for Mr. Fairhead was not old and dismal like most preachers, and did not say a long grace while the chicken was getting cold.

The church was a forlorn weather-boarded building with neither spire nor bell, standing on a naked hillside where the rains had washed winding gutters in the gravelly slope. It had once been painted red, but the boards were now curling from lack of paint. It looked like an abandoned factory left to the mercy of the weather. In the basement underneath, the coun-try day school was kept.

The miller and his daughter went up four warped plank steps and entered the church. Once within, they separated. All the men and boys sat on one side of the aisle, the girls and women on the other. The pews were long benches, with backs but no cushions. There was no floor covering of any kind, there were no blinds at the dusty windows. The peaked shingle roof was supported by whitewashed rafters. Up under this roof, over the front door, was the gallery where the coloured people sat. It was a rule among the farmers who owned slaves to send them to church on Sunday.

While Mrs. Blake knelt for a few moments in silent prayer, Mary and Betty sat restlessly trying to peep over the hats and sunbonnets in front of them to catch sight of their dear Mr. Fairhead, who was in the splint-bottom chair behind the pulpit, waiting for his congregation to assemble.

When the scuffling tramp of heavy shoes on the bare floor had ceased, Mr. Fairhead rose and said: "Let us pray." He closed his eyes and began his invocation. In the untempered light which poured through the bare windows he looked a very young man indeed, with rosy cheeks and yellow hair. He had been sent out into the backwoods to teach the country school and to "fill the pulpit," though he had not yet been ordained. During the long summer vacations he lived in Winchester and read divinity with old Doctor Sollers, coming out to Back Creek on horseback every Saturday to conduct the Sunday service.

After the prayer he gave out the hymn, read it aloud slowly and distinctly, since many of his congregation could not read. When he closed his hymnbook, the congregation rose. Old Andrew Shand, a Scotchman with wiry red hair and chin whiskers, officially led the singing. He struck his tuning-fork on the back of a bench and began: "There is a Land of Pure Delight," at a weary, drawling pace. But the Colbert negroes, and the miller himself, immediately broke away from Shand and carried the tune along. Mr. Fairhead joined in, looking up at the gallery. For him the singing was the living worship of the Sunday services; the negroes in the loft sang those bright promises and dark warnings with such fervent conviction. Fat Lizzie and her daughter, Bluebell, could be heard above them all. Bluebell had a pretty soprano voice, but Lizzie sang high and low with equal ease. The congregation downstairs knew what a "limb" she was, but no one, except Andy Shand, ever complained because she took a high hand with the hymns. The old people who couldn't read could "hear the words" when Lizzie sang. Neither could Lizzie read, but she knew the hymns by heart. Mr. Fairhead often wondered how it was that she sounded the letter "r" clearly when she sang, though she didn't when she talked.

> Could wé but stánd where Móses stóod
>   And víew the lándscape ó'er
> Not Jórdan's stréam nor deáth's cold flóod
>   Would fríght us fróm that shóre.

When Lizzie rolled out the last verse and sat down, the young preacher looked up at the gallery, not with a smile, exactly, but with appreciation. He often felt like thanking her.

As for Andy Shand, he hated Lizzie and all the Colbert negroes. His animosity extended to the Colberts themselves; even about Mrs. Blake he was "none so sure."

After the congregation was dismissed, Mr. Fairhead and the miller walked down the road together, deep in conversation. Mrs. Blake and her girls followed behind. She knew her father enjoyed the company of an educated man like Fairhead; that was why she had asked the preacher to dinner. Their talk, as she listened to it, was plain farmer talk, to be sure; about the early season, and the prospects for wheat and hay. Presently the miller began to ask about the country school and Mr. Fairhead's pupils. There were bright boys among them, the young man insisted, some who rode over to school from as far as Peughtown. There were even boys from the mountain who would do fairly well if they had half a chance. There was Casper Flight—Here Colbert held up his hand.

"Never say Flight to me, Mr. Fairhead. I've ground that man's miserable bit of corn and buckwheat ten years for nothing, and on top of that he hangs around the mill and steals honest men's grist. My Sampson has caught him time and again crawling down from the storeroom at night with a bag in his hand."

"I know all about him, Mr. Colbert. But if you could see how that corn and buckwheat was raised, you wouldn't grudge grinding it for nothing. They've got no horse, and this boy Casper breaks up the ground in their corn patch and buckwheat field himself. He pulls the plough, and his mother follows at the plough handles and holds the share in the earth. Last spring I got Mr. Giffen up on the ridge to lend Casper a horse, to put in his buckwheat. His father came home unexpectedly, knocked the boy down, took the horse out of the plough, and rode up to Capon River to go fishing."

"I'm glad you told me, sir. If there's any good can come out of the Flights, God knows I'd like to help it along. I could give this boy work around the place in busy times, but you know none of those mountain boys will work along with coloured hands."

"Yes, I know." Mr. Fairhead sighed. "It's the one thing

they've got to feel important about—that they're white. It's pitiful."

Whenever Colbert had a talk with David Fairhead, he wished he could see more of him. He had several times asked the young man to supper at the Mill House, but he observed that Fairhead was not at ease in Sapphira's company. He was shy and on his guard, and Sapphira had seemed possessed to puzzle him with light ironies. Since he was from Pennsylvania, she considered him an inferior. Yet her manner with inferiors (with the cobbler, the butcher, the weaver, the storekeeper) was irreproachable. When the old broom-pedlar or the wandering tinsmith happened along, they were always given a place at the dinner table, and she knew just how to talk to them. But with Fairhead she took on a mocking condescension, as if she were all the while ridiculing his simplicity. Therefore, Henry figured it out, she did not really regard him as an inferior, but as an equal—of the wrong kind. Fairhead boarded with Mrs. Bywaters, at the post office, and Sapphira knew that he was "Northern" at heart. She laughed and told Henry she could "smell it on him."

Oh, yes, she admitted, he was not an ignoramus, like the country schoolteachers who had been there before him. She was glad Mary and Betty had a teacher who did not chew tobacco in the schoolroom or speak like the mountain people. He had doubtless been raised a gentleman—of the Pennsylvania kind. But he was a mealy-mouth, say what you would; and if she made him uncomfortable, it was because he hadn't the wit to come back at her. "How can I talk to a man who blushes every time I poke fun at him, or at anybody else? You'd better give it up, Henry." So the schoolmaster was not invited to the Mill House again.

BOOK III

Old Jezebel

I

O N THE FIRST DAY after her return from town Mrs. Colbert summoned Till and told her she meant to go out to see Aunt Jezebel this morning. "I will have a look around the yard first. Send Nancy in to dress me, and tell Tap to have the boys here in about an hour."

The "boys" were young negroes whom Tap called in from the barn or the fields to help him carry the Mistress. On each side of her chair were two iron rings; into these the boys thrust dressed hickory saplings and bore Mrs. Colbert about the place. Tap was one of the mill-hands, but he loved to wait on ladies. He was a handsome boy, and he knew the Mistress thought so. He used to make his assistants clean up on these occasions. "Take off dat sweaty ole rag an' put on a clean shirt fo' de Missus."

This morning the sunshine was so bright that the Mistress carried a tiny parasol with a jointed handle. Her bearers took her along the brick walks bordered by clipped boxwood hedges,—which were dark as yew except for the yellow-green tips of new growth. Mrs. Colbert visited all the flower-beds. The lilac arbour was now in bud, the yellow roses would soon be opening. The Mistress sent Tap for her shears and cut off sprays from the mock-orange bushes, which were filling the air with fragrance. With these in her lap she moved on, until she was carried into old Jezebel's cabin and her chair put down beside the bed.

"You know who it is, don't you, Aunt Jezebel?"

"Co'se I does, Miss Sapphy! Ain't I knowed you since de day you was bawn?" The old woman turned on her side to see her mistress better.

She had wasted since Sapphira saw her last. As she lay curled up in bed, she looked very like a lean old grey monkey. (She had been a tall, strapping woman.) Her grizzled wool was twisted up in bits of rag. She was toothless, and her black skin had taken on a greyish cast. Jezebel thought she was about ninety-five. She knew she was eighteen when she was captured and sold to a British slaver, but she was not sure how many years passed before she learned English and began to keep account of time.

Mrs. Colbert put the sprays of syringa down on the pillow, close to the old woman's face. "The mock-oranges are out, I thought you'd like to smell them. There's not a man on the place can tend the shrubs like you did."

"Thank 'ee, mam. I hepped you set out most all de shrubs on dis place, didn' I? Wasn't nothin' when we first come here but dat ole white lilack tree."

"Those were good times, Auntie. I've been house-bound for a long while now, like you."

"Oh, Missy, cain't dem doctors in Winchester do nothin' fur you? What's dey good fur, anyways?" She broke off with a wheeze.

"There now, you mustn't talk, it catches your breath. We must take what comes to us and be resigned."

"Yes'm, I'se resigned," the old woman whispered.

Mrs. Colbert went on soothingly: "When I sit out on the porch on a day like this, and look around, I often think how we used to get up early and rake over the new flower-beds and transplant before it got hot. And you used to run down to the creek and break off alder branches, and we'd stick them all around the plants we'd set out, to keep the sun off. I expect you remember those things, too."

The old negress looked up at her and nodded.

"Now I'm going to read you a Psalm that will hearten us both." Mrs. Colbert took from her reticule her glasses-case and a Prayer Book, but she opened neither as she repeated: "The Lord is my shepherd."

Jezebel watched her intently, her eyes shining bright under eyelids thin as paper.

When the Mistress finished the Psalm, she called for Nancy, who was waiting in the cabin kitchen in case she might be needed.

"Are the boys outside?"

Then she turned again to the bed. "Have you quilts enough, Jezebel? Do they keep you warm?"

"Yes, Missy, the niggahs is mighty good to me. Dey keeps a flatiron to my feet, an' a bag a hot salt undah my knees. Lizzie, she sends Bluebell down to set wid me a lot. Dat he'ps to pass de time. Her an' Bluebell comes and sings to me, too."

"But Till tells me you don't eat anything. You must eat to keep up your strength."

"Don't want nothin', Missy."

"Can't you think of anything that would taste good to you? Now think a minute, and tell me. Isn't there something?"

The old woman gave a sly chuckle; one paper eyelid winked, and her eyes gave out a flash of grim humour. "No'm, I cain't think of nothin' I could relish, lessen maybe it was a li'l pickaninny's hand."

Nancy, crouching in a corner, broke out with a startled cry and ran to the foot of the bed. "Oh, she's a-wanderin' agin! She wanders turrible now. Don't stay, Missy! She's out of her haid!"

Mrs. Colbert raised her eyes and gave the girl a cold, steady look. "No need for you to be speaking up. I know your granny through and through. She is no more out of her head than I am." She turned back again to the bed, took up Jezebel's cold grey claw, and patted it. "Good-bye till another time, Auntie. Now you must turn over and have a nap."

She beckoned to the four hands standing outside, and they came with their hickory poles and carried her away.

II

JEZEBEL was the only one of the Colbert negroes who had come from Africa. All the others were, as they proudly said, Virginians; born and raised on the Dodderidge place or on the estates of their Loudoun County neighbours. But Jezebel was brought over from Guinea, that gold coast of the slave-traders, in the seventeen-eighties—about twenty years before the importation of slaves became illegal. She was sold to her first master on the deck of a British slaver in the port of Baltimore.

Her native village in Africa lay well inland, some four days' journey from the sea. It was raided and destroyed by a coast tribe which early in the history of the traffic had become slave-hunters for the slavers. That night of fire and slaughter, when she saw her father brained and her four brothers cut down as they fought, old Jezebel now remembered but dimly. It was all over in a few hours; of the village nothing was left but smoking ashes and mutilated bodies. By morning she and her fellow captives were in leg chains and on their march to the sea.

When they reached the coast they were kept in the stockade only long enough to be stripped, shaved all over the body, and drenched with sea water. An English vessel, the *Albert Horn*, lay at anchor out in the gulf, with nearly a full cargo of negroes stowed on board. The wind was good, and the skipper was waiting impatiently for the booty of this last raid.

Jezebel and the other captives were rowed out in small boats and put on board in leg chains; they came from a fierce cannibal people, and had not been broken in by weeks of discipline in the stockade.

When the *Albert Horn* was under sail, and the blue lines of the inland mountains began to grow dim, the fetters were taken off the female captives. They were not likely to make trouble.

The *Albert Horn*, built for the slave trade, had two decks. The negroes were stowed between the upper and lower decks, on a platform as long and as wide as the vessel; but there was only three feet ten inches between the shelf on which they lay and the upper deck which roofed them over. The slaves made the long voyage of from two to three months in a sitting or recumbent position, on a plank floor, with very little space, if any, between their bare bodies. The males were stowed forward of the main hatch, the women aft. All were kept naked throughout the voyage, and their heads and bodies were shaved every fortnight. As there was no drainage of any sort, the slaves' quarters, and the creatures in them, got very foul overnight. Every morning the " 'tween decks" and its inmates were cleaned off with streams of sea water from the hose. The Captain of the *Albert Horn* was not a brutal man, and his vessel was a model slaver. Except in rough weather, the males, ironed two and two, were allowed out on the lower deck for a few hours while their platform was being scrubbed and fumigated. At the same time, the women were turned out on the lower after deck without chains.

On the first night after the *Albert Horn* got under way, the sailors gave Jezebel the name she had borne ever since. When the two hands detailed to watch the after 'tween decks had seen that all the females were lying in the spaces assigned to them, they put out their lanterns and went on deck to take the air. A little later the second mate, hearing shrieks and screams from the women's quarters, ran down from his cabin to find the guards flogging a girl they had dragged out from a heap of rolling, howling blacks.

"It's this here Jezebel made all the row, sir," one of the men panted.

The mate made a dash and drove at her throat to throttle her, but she was too quick for him. She snapped like a mastiff and bit through the ball of his thumb.

Next morning the mate felt an ominous throbbing in his hand. He reported the fracas to the Captain, saying he didn't see anything for it but to throw the female gorilla overboard. She could never be tamed.

The skipper feared his mate might be in for a bad infection; but he had a third interest in the cargo, and he wasn't anxious to throw any of it overboard. He thought he would like to see a girl who could stand up against two men and the cat.

"Clean her off and put a bridle on her, and bring her up,"

he told the mate. Himself, he never went near the slave deck; he couldn't stand the smell.

Jezebel was brought up in heavy irons for his inspection. Her naked back was seamed with welts and bloody cuts, but she carried herself with proud indifference, and there was no plea for mercy in her eyes. The skipper told the seamen in charge to loosen the noose round her neck. As he walked up and down, smoking his pipe, he looked her well over. He judged this girl was worth any three of the women,—as much as the best of the men. Anatomically she was remarkable, for an African negress: tall, straight, muscular, long in the legs. The skipper had a kind of respect for a well-shaped creature; horse, cow, or woman. And he respected anybody who could take a flogging like that without buckling.

He gave orders that Jezebel was not to go back between decks. She was to be kept on the upper deck in all weathers, fastened with a light chain to the deck rail. She was to be given a sailor's jacket to cover her wounds, and at night she was to be provided with a tarpaulin.

After she was thus isolated, the girl gave no more trouble,—though she always laughed aloud when the second mate passed with his arm in a sling. The voyage was long and rough. Jezebel was knocked about and drenched by heavy seas, and was sometimes seasick, but she made no complaint. When the seamen hosed out the scupper, she took off her jacket and invited the stream of salt water over her body. Except for a few long scars on her back and thighs, there was nothing now to show what had happened the first night she came on board.

When the *Albert Horn* at last reached Baltimore, her skipper kept her out at anchor until buyers from Maryland and Virginia could be notified and arrive. Jezebel, he noticed, regarded the water line of the city with lively curiosity, quite different from the hopeless indifference on the faces of her fellow captives.

"She'll make the best sale of the lot," he told the mate.

In the first boat-load of purchasers who came out to inspect the skipper's cargo, there was a Dutch dairy farmer. He brought with him the country doctor of his neighbourhood. The dairyman and his friend, the doctor, were in no hurry.

They looked over a great number of negroes. To Jezebel they gave a searching physical examination, talking together in the low Dutch vernacular, and asking no questions of the skipper. The dairyman called attention to the whip scars on her body, and beckoned the second mate.

"Disposition?" he asked.

"The niggers who captured her did that. She put up a fight. Strong as an ox."

The Dutchman himself looked very like an ox, but the doctor looked kind and shrewd. He fumbled in his pocket and brought out a deerskin pouch, from which he took two squares of maple sugar. One he put in his own mouth, and smacked his lips. The other he offered to Jezebel with a questioning smile. She opened her jaws. At this the second mate, standing by, looked the other way. The doctor put the sugar on Jezebel's tongue. She crunched it, grinned, and stuck out her tongue for more. The doctor gave his friend the deciding nod. The Dutchman paid the skipper's price, took Jezebel into Baltimore, and stowed her in the heavy wagon in which he had come to town.

When he reached home, he set about breaking in his new wench. On the journey from Baltimore he had discovered that her personal manners were too strong for even a Dutch farmer's household, so he lodged her in the haymow over the cow barn. She learned to milk the cows and to do all the stable work, but she was kept in the barn and was never allowed to touch the butter. The dairy farmer died in an outbreak of smallpox; his widow promptly sold Jezebel. She had been owned by several masters and had learned some English before the Dodderidge farm steward bought her. She went to the Dodderidges the year that Sapphira was born, and had been in the family ever since.

Until Jezebel was eighty years old, Sapphira had entrusted her to oversee the gardens at the Mill Farm. As late as last spring she still got out to sit in the sun and watch the boys who did the shrubbery and shaped the hedges. In wintertime she stayed in her cabin, sewed carpet-rags, and patched the farm-hands' shirts and breeches. She meted out justice by giving a slack boy a rough seat in his breeches, and a likely boy a smooth seat. When Manuel, since dead, had come to her

will tell you how many loaves of light bread[1] to bake, and there must be plenty of corn bread, and sugar-cakes and ginger-cakes. Master is going to invite all Mr. Lockheart's niggers to come over and sit up, and likely some of Jezebel's grandchildren will come out from Winchester."

"Yes *mam!*" Lizzie rolled her eyes that shone like black-and-white china marbles. "Yes mam! I sho'ly will put my bes' foot for'ard fo' ole Aunt Jezebel an' all de yeahs she carry. But dat triflin' li'l Manuel wa'nt no 'count nohow, an' his pappy not much bettah—"

Mrs. Colbert held up her plump hand. "That will do, Lizzie. Remember this; if you don't do me credit at Jezebel's wake, I will send Bluebell back to Loudoun County for good, as sure as I sit here."

Lizzie put her two hands over her great bosom as if she were taking an oath. Sending Bluebell over to Loudoun County meant selling her there, and Lizzie knew it.

A few moments later Mrs. Blake, passing the kitchen on her way to Jezebel's cabin, heard Lizzie's malicious giggle. She stopped and looked in at the door. Lizzie was whispering to Bluebell, who sat drooping over the kitchen table, her elbows spread wide apart, as she sat day in and day out, supposedly helping her mother.

The Colberts, like all well-to-do families, had their own private burying-ground. It lay in a green field, and was enclosed by a wall,—flat slabs of brown stone laid one upon another, with a gate of wrought iron. A wide gravelled path divided the square plot in two halves. On one side were the family graves, with marble headstones. On the other side was the slaves' graveyard, with slate headstones bearing single names: "Dolly," "Thomas," "Manuel," and so on.

The mounds of masters and servants alike were covered with thick mats of myrtle. At this season innumerable sprays of new green shoots and starlike pale-blue blossoms shot out from the dark creeping vines which clung so close to the earth.

On Saturday afternoon the procession formed to carry Jezebel to the end of all her journeyings. Everyone was in black;

[1]"Light" bread meant bread of wheat flour, in distinction from corn bread.

the family, the neighbours from up and down the Creek, the Colbert negroes, and the slaves from down in the Hayfield country. Mrs. Blake's little girls had few dresses of any kind, so they were draped in black shawls lent by their grandmother. Mrs. Colbert herself wore the black crêpe she reserved for funerals. She was carried in her chair, and the miller, in his Sunday coat, walked beside her. They followed immediately behind the coffin, which was borne by four of Jezebel's great-grandsons, come out from Winchester.

While they stood about the grave, Mr. Fairhead made a short address. He recalled Jezebel's long wanderings; how she had come from a heathen land where people worshipped idols and lived in bloody warfare, to become a devout Christian and an heir to all the Promises. Perhaps her long old age had been granted her that she might fill out in years the full measure of a Christian life. After his last prayer, Lizzie and Bluebell sang "In the Sweet By and By," and the company dispersed. Jefferson and Washington, as the oldest servants, stayed behind with the great-grandsons to fill up the grave.

That night there was a big supper in the kitchen for the Colbert negroes and all the visitors; a first and second sitting at table. The darkies were always gay after a funeral, and this funeral had pleased everyone. "Miss Sapphy sho'ly give Jezebel a beautiful laying away," they all agreed.

Washington, serving his master and mistress in the big house, noticed that they, too, were more animated than usual, expressing their satisfaction that things had gone so well and that Jezebel's young kinsmen had been able to come and carry her. The Master sat long at table; had two helpings of pudding and drank four cups of tea. When at last he rose, his wife said persuasively:

"Surely you don't mean to go back to the mill tonight, Henry, with your good clothes on."

"Yes, I think I must. I have been away all day. I want to speak to those boys from town and give them a little money. They will be starting back late tonight. Good night, Sapphira. I expect you are tired, and I hope you sleep well."

"The same to you," she said with a placid smile, which

"Yes mam, yes mam! Whassa matter, Missy?"

Nancy's sleepy, startled voice. Mrs. Colbert dropped back in her chair and drew a long, slow breath. It was over. Her shattered, treacherous house stood safe about her again. She was in her own room, wakened out of a dream of disaster. — But she must see it through, what she had begun.

"Nancy, I'm taken bad. Run out to the kitchen and blow up the coals and put the kettle on. Then go for your mother. I must get my feet into hot water."

Nancy scurried down the long hall and out to the kitchen. She was wide awake now, and alarmed. She wasn't a girl to hold a grudge.

Till came, sooner than her mistress would have thought possible. Nancy brought the foot-tub and the big iron tea-kettle. Till sat on the floor rhythmically stroking her mistress's swollen ankles and knees, murmuring: "It's all right, Missy. They is no worse than common. It's just a chill you caught, waitin' out there by the graveside."

When the Mistress was again put to bed, Till begged to stay with her. But Mrs. Colbert, comforted by the prompt-ness and sympathy of her servants, thanked them both, said the pain was gone now, and she would sleep better alone. As they helped her from her chair she had looked once more from her window: the miller's lights were still burning in the west room of the mill. Was the man worrying over some law-suit he had never told her about, she wondered? Or was he, perhaps, reading his religious books? She knew he pondered at times upon how we are saved or lost. That was the disad-vantage of having been raised a Lutheran. In her Church all those things had been decided long ago by heads much wiser than Henry's. She had married the only Colbert who had a conscience, and she sometimes wished he hadn't quite so much.

Behind the square of candlelight down there, the miller, in his mill clothes, was sitting with his Bible open on the table before him, but he was no longer reading. Jezebel's life, as Mr. Fairhead had summed it up, seemed a strange instance of predestination. For her, certainly, her capture had been a de-liverance. Yet he hated the whole system of slavery. His father had never owned a slave. The Quakers who came down from Pennsylvania believed that slavery would one day be abolished. In the North there were many people who called themselves abolishers.

Henry Colbert knew he had a legal right to manumit any of his wife's negroes; but that would be an outrage to her feelings, and an injustice to the slaves themselves. Where would they go? How would they live? They had never learned to take care of themselves or to provide for tomorrow. They were a part of the Dodderidge property and the Dodderidge household. Of all the negro men on the place, Sampson, his head mill-hand, was the only one who might be able to get work and make a living out in the world. He was a tall, straight mulatto with a good countenance, thoughtful, intelligent. His head was full behind the ears, shaped more like a melon lying down than a peanut standing on end. Colbert trusted Sampson's judgment, and believed he could get a place for him among the Quaker mills in Philadelphia. He had considered buying Sampson from Sapphira and sending him to Pennsylvania a free man.

Three years ago he had called Sampson into his room one night, and proposed this plan to him. Sampson did not interrupt; he stood in his manly, responsible way, listening intently to his master. But when it was his turn to speak, he broke down. This was his home. Here he knew everybody. He didn't want to go out among strangers. Besides, Belle, his wife, was a slack worker, and his children were little. He could never keep them in a city as well off as they were here. What ever had put such a notion in Mister Henry's head? Wasn't he real smart about his work? Belle, he knew, wasn't much account to help down at the house, but she was good to the chillun, an' she didn't do no harm. Anyhow, he'd a'most sooner leave the chillun than leave the mill, when they'd got everything fixed up so nice and could bolt finer white flour than you could buy in town.

"I guess I'd miss you more than you'd miss the mill, Sampson. We'll say no more about it, if that's how you feel," said the miller, rising and putting his hand on Sampson's shoulder. There it ended. Sampson never afterward referred to this proposal, nor did his master.

On this night after Jezebel's burial, Henry Colbert had been reading over certain marked passages in the Book he accepted as a complete guide to human life. He had turned to all the verses marked with a large S. Joseph, Daniel, and the prophets had been slaves in foreign lands, and had brought good out of their captivity. Nowhere in his Bible had he ever been able to find a clear condemnation of slavery. There were injunctions of kindness to slaves, mercy and tolerance. *Remember them in bonds as bound with them.* Yes, but nowhere did his Bible say that there should be no one in bonds, no one at all. — And Henry had often asked himself, were we not all in bonds? If Lizzie, the cook, was in bonds to Sapphira, was she not almost equally in bonds to Lizzie?

The miller knew the hour must be getting late. His big silver watch he had left up at the house, on his wife's dressing-table. But he and the negroes could tell time by the stars. At this season of the year, if the Big Dipper had set under the dark spruce-clad hills behind Rachel's house, it would be past midnight. He opened his north window and looked out. Yes, the Dipper had gone down. The air of the soft, still, spring night came in at the window. There was no sound but the creek, pouring steadily over its rocky bottom. As he stood there, he repeated to himself some verses of a favourite hymn:

> God moves in a mysterious way
>   His wonders to perform.
>
> * * * * * * * *
>
> Deep in unfathomable mines
>   Of never failing skill,
> He treasures up His bright designs
>   And works His sovereign will.

We must rest, he told himself, on our confidence in His design. Design was clear enough in the stars, the seasons, in the woods and fields. But in human affairs—? Perhaps our bewilderment came from a fault in our perceptions; we could never see what was behind the next turn of the road. Whenever he went to Winchester, he called upon a wise old Quaker. This man, though now seventy, firmly believed that in his own lifetime he would see one of those great designs accomplished; that the Lord had already chosen His heralds and His captains, and a morning would break when all the black slaves would be free.

BOOK IV

Sapphira's Daughter

I

ONE BREEZY AFTERNOON Mrs. Blake was footing it round the last loop of the "Double S," on her way to Timber Ridge. At the end of the steep grade she sat down on a mossy stump, took off her sunbonnet, and gave herself up to enjoyment of the spring day.

In the deep ravine below the road a mountain stream rushed coffee brown, throwing up crystal rainbows where it gurgled over rock ledges. On the steep hillside across the creek the tall forest trees were still bare,—the oak leaves no bigger than a squirrel's ear. From out the naked grey wood the dogwood thrust its crooked forks starred with white blossoms—the flowers set in their own wild way along the rampant zigzag branches. Their unexpectedness, their singular whiteness, never loses its wonder, even to the dullest dweller in those hills. In all the rich flowering and blushing and blooming of a Virginia spring, the scentless dogwood is the wildest thing and yet the most austere, the most unearthly.

Mrs. Blake was thinking this out to herself as she sat on the stump. She gave scarcely a glance at the wild honeysuckle all about her, growing low out of the gravelly soil, pink and rose colour, with long, trembling stamens which made each blossom look like a brilliant insect caught in flight. When at last she took her basket and travelled upward, she left the turnpike and followed a by-road along the crest of the Ridge. Up here the soil was better; planted fields and little green meadows lay along her path. May apples grew in the damp spots; their blossoms, like tiny pond lilies, gave out a heavy, almost sickening sweetness. Here and there stood a well-built farmhouse, with carefully tended yard and garden. Along the rail fences the locust trees were in bloom. The breeze caught their perfume and wafted it down the road. Every Virginian remembers those locusts which grow along the highways: their cloud-shaped masses of blue-green foliage and heavy drooping clusters of cream-white flowers like pea blossoms. Excepting the very old trees, the giants, the locusts look yielding and languid, like the mountain boy lounging against the counter when he goes to the country store. Yet, from the time they are big enough to cut, they make the toughest fence posts a farmer can find, and in the timber trade the yellow locust is valued for its resistance to moisture.

From the Ridge road Mrs. Blake could look down over hills and valleys, as if she were at the top of the world. She liked to go up there at any time of the year, and she liked to go on foot and alone. Even in her best days, before her husband died, when she lived in Washington and never came home to Back Creek for a visit, she used sometimes to be homesick for these mountains and the high places. This afternoon she was on the Ridge in answer to a sick call, but it was not a serious one, and she meant to enjoy herself.

Last evening a pale little girl, barefoot, in a carefully mended dress, had slipped silently into Mrs. Blake's kitchen without knocking. For all that her hair was braided and her face was washed, she was a distressful little creature, with dark circles about her eyes. There was something at once furtive and innocent in her face. She told Mrs. Blake how Granny let the flatiron fall on her foot t'other day, an' now her toe was festerin'. Would Miz Blake maybe come up an' see if they ought to send for Doctor Brush? And now Mrs. Blake was on her way to see. She had bandages and turpentine ointment and arnica in her basket; but she had also a fruit jar full of fresh-ground coffee, half a baking of sugar cakes, and a loaf of "light" bread. The poor folks on the Ridge esteemed coffee and wheat bread great delicacies. This visit was not to be entirely wasted on a sore foot. Indeed, Mrs. Blake suspected that the foot was maybe not very bad, and that old Mrs. Ringer had sent for her because she had not seen her for a long time and wanted a visit with her.

Mrs. Blake herself looked forward to this visit. Mrs. Ringer was better company than many people who were more fortunate; who came of better blood, and had farms and raised sheep and pigs for market. There were some families on the

Ridge who were comfortably off, owned a few negroes to do the work, and held themselves very high. If you called at the Pembertons', for instance, you were kept waiting half an hour in the parlour while the ladies dressed and powdered their faces. When at last they appeared, with their mourning-bordered handkerchiefs and jet earrings, they minded their manners so carefully that the talk was very dull.

Now, Mandy Ringer had lived a hard life, goodness knew, but misfortune and drudgery had never broken her spirit. She was as thin as a grasshopper, and as lively as one. She had probably never spent a dull day. When she woke in the morning, she got into her calico dress in a flash and ran out to see what her garden had done overnight. Then she took a bucket and went to milk Sukey in the shed. Her son, though he was a cripple, would have done it for her, but in that country it was the custom for the women to do the milking. Mrs. Ringer wouldn't have trusted either of her two daughters to take care of Sukey. That little white-faced cow kept the log house going when everything else failed, and her calves brought in the only actual money the old woman ever saw.

Mrs. Ringer was born interested. She got a great deal of entertainment out of the weather and the behaviour of the moon. Any chance bit of gossip that came her way was a godsend. The rare sight of a strange face was a treat: a pedlar with a pack on his back, or a medicine-vendor come from across the Alleghenies with his little cart. Mrs. Ringer couldn't read or write, as she was frank to tell you, but the truth was she could read everything most important: the signs of the seasons, the meaning of the way the wood creatures behaved, and human faces. She once said to Mrs. Blake when they were talking things over: "If the Lord'll jist let me stay alive, mam, an' not put me down into a dirty hole, I kin bear anything."

She had borne a good deal, certainly. Her son was a poor cripple, and both her daughters had been "fooled." That seldom occurred twice, even in the most shiftless households. Disgrace to the womenfolk brought any family very low in that country. But Mandy Ringer couldn't stay crushed for long. She came up like a cork,—probably with no better excuse than that the sun came up. Her spirits bubbled into the light like a spring and spread among the cresses.

Rachel Blake had always been drawn toward expansive, warm-hearted people. And she had known many such folks in her time, when she lived in Washington City before her husband died.

As she turned in at a low log house with a big outside rock chimney, Mrs. Ringer, her foot done up in rags, hopped lightly to the door to greet her.

"Now ain't you most a angel to come all the way up the hills to see us! I declare I had a'most give you up, but Lawndis he tole me not to despair. An' he would go so fur as to shave fur you."

At this a brown-skinned man with a crooked back and a clubfoot came forward. "Yes, Miz Blake, when the wind turned an' blowed the clouds away, I reckoned you'd be along to see Mother." His voice was mellow and grave, and there was true courtesy in the way he looked at the visitor, placed a chair for her, and relieved her of her basket.

Mrs. Blake examined the sore foot and declared there was nothing worse than a bad bruise. She applied her ointment and a clean bandage, and took from her basket a pair of old carpet slippers. "You'll be easy in these, Mrs. Ringer. Put them on and keep them on. Don't on any account go about barefoot. Now I'm a little weary after my walk, and if Lawndis will kindle a fire I'm going to make some coffee for us."

After the son had a fire going, he took up his hat. "If you'll excuse me, Miz Blake, I'll go out in the garden an' do some weedin'. You and Mother'll feel freer to talk by yourselves. She ain't seen much comp'ny lately." He limped out of the house, careful not to put on his hat until he was well outside the door.

Mrs. Ringer spread a white cloth on the kitchen table and got out her blue chiney cups and plates. Before the water was boiling Lawndis came back with a stone crock in his hands. "Here, Mother. I seem to remember Miz Blake don't like her coffee without cream. If you'll skim some off, I'll take the crock back to the springhouse. We got a real cold springhouse, mam, better'n most folks up here. It's quite a piece away, but that's where the spring is."

"Your son surely has nice manners, Mrs. Ringer," remarked Mrs. Blake, as she watched him limping across the garden with the milk.

"Yes'm, Lawndis is a good boy, if I do say it. An' he gits a power a' work done, fur a lame man. Ain't it a pity I didn't have no luck with my gals?"

This was a delicate subject. Mrs. Blake did not wish to discuss it. "Where are the girls today?" she asked politely, as if there were nothing queer about them.

"Ginnie, she's got work up at Capon Springs, helpin' clean the hotel fur summer visitors. Up there they ain't heered about her trouble, maybe. I don't know where Marge is this minute, but she's likely off in the woods some'ers, 'shamed to have you see her. It would all a-been different, Miz Blake, if my Lawndis was a strong man. Then he could a-tracked down the fellers an' fit with 'em, an' made 'em marry his sisters. But them raskels knowed my pore gals hadn't nobody to stand up fur 'em. Fellers is skeered to make free with a gal that's got able men folks to see she gits her rights."

Mrs. Blake still sought to avoid discussing these misfortunes, since there was nothing she could do to remedy them. She said blandly: "Well, whatever happened, I know Lawndis would never be hard on his sisters. Now do tell me, Mrs. Ringer, who did you name your boy after? I've often wondered, and never thought to ask you."

"Lawndis? Why, after the preacher. Can't you remember, when you was a little girl there come a preacher a-holdin' revivals through these parts? He held meetin's every night fur a week an' more at Bethel Church, an' I never missed a sermon. I ain't never heered sich sermons before nor since. When the next baby come, I called him after that preacher."

Yes, Mrs. Blake remembered the preacher; he wore a long-tailed coat, even on horseback, and his name was Leonidas Bright. The hill people could do queer things with unfamiliar names.

At this moment the pale little girl who had come to Mrs. Blake's yesterday stole down the ladder from the loft over the kitchen and shyly approached the table. In her hand was a little wooden box full of quartz crystals she had picked up on the stony hillsides.

"Is these di'monds, Miz Blake, mam? Kin I sell 'em fur money?"

"No, child, I'm afraid they're not diamonds. They're just as pretty, though."

"Now, Becky, what need you come troublin' Miz Blake fur? I tole you they ain't di'monds. You run back upstairs an' mind the baby, an' here's a cake fur you Miz Blake fetched me. Is he asleep?"

"Yes'm."

Mrs. Blake slipped the child a second cake, and she went noiselessly up the ladder.

The grandmother gave a cackling little laugh. "That's the fashion up here now. Since the Bethel robbery everybody thinks they kin make a fortin sellin' somethin'. It's come down even to pore Becky."

"What robbery are you talkin' about, Mrs. Ringer?"

Mrs. Ringer put down the cup halfway to her lips. "You ain't meanin' you never heered of the Bethel communion service bein' stole?"

"I surely never heard a word about it."

Mrs. Ringer's face glowed. "Well, I'm su'prised, mam! It's a disgrace to us all up here, an' we can't hardly talk of nothin' else. Last Sunday night, after preachin', the whole communion service, the silver plate an' the silver goblet an' the little pitchers, was taken. An' now his triflin' relations is tryin' to put it off on Casper Flight, as good a boy as ever lived, because he has the door key so he kin sweep out the church an' keep it clean. Now we all know a winder was broke out the night the deed was done, so what has Casper's key got to do with it, I'd like to know? Would he break a winder, when he had a key?"

Mrs. Blake was thoroughly interested. "You mean the Flight boy that comes to Mr. Fairhead's school? Why, his teacher can't say enough good of him."

"That's him I mean. He's bein' persecuted by them louts of cousins of his'n, them ugly Keyser boys that runs a still. Who's they to act up for the church, when they was never inside one? Unless"—here Mrs. Ringer paused and shook her finger at Mrs. Blake as she added impressively—"unless they was inside Bethel Church last Sunday night, after meetin'."

"But why are the Keysers trying to put it on Casper? You say they're cousins."

"Now, Miz Blake, who kin hate worse'n cousins? We all know that. They hates him jist on account of his bein' a good boy, and tryin' to make somethin' of hisself, walkin' all the way down to Back Creek to learn to read an' write. Nobody in their fam'ly could ever read 'n' write, an' damned if anybody ever will. It's pure spite, an' I tell Lawndis I know Buck Keyser broke that winder an' clomb in an' robbed the Lord, as well as if I'd seen him do it. He's got them things hid away some'ers, an' one day he'll tromp over the Alleghenies where he ain't knowed, an' sell 'em."

Mrs. Blake sniffed audibly. "Well, he won't get much for 'em. That Bethel communion set ain't silver at all. It's plated stuff, and poor plate at that, I can tell you."

Mrs. Ringer started in her chair. "Is that so, Miz Blake! Now, nobody but you would a-knowed. Lordy me, I wisht I could a-had your chance, mam. It's city life that learns you, an' I'd a-loved it! So with all their deviltry they ain't got no fortin hid away, an' fur all the talk they've raised, it don't amount to much more'n pore Becky's di'monds! There is a kind-a justice in this world after all, now ain't there?"

Their talk turned naturally to the classic example of belated justice: the murder of the pedlar at the red brick house on the Ridge Road, and its exposure after twenty years. While Mrs. Ringer was telling all she remembered of the two wretched women who had killed the pedlar for his pack, Lawndis appeared at the door, sweaty and panting.

"Maw, I'm afeered them Keysers is got Casper. I heered trouble over in the woods, an' Buck's big haw-haw. He's got the meanest laff ever was, when he's out fur devilment. I'm a-goin' over."

Mrs. Ringer sprang up. "Then I'm a-goin' with ye."

"No you ain't, Maw. You're lamed with your foot."

"I reckon I'm no lamer'n you air. Come along, Miz Blake, we'll all go. They ain't no business in our woods."

Mrs. Blake picked up her basket. "Take one of Lawndis' canes, Mandy, and spare your foot all you can." She set out with the two cripples, down the garden, past the springhouse, and over toward the wood where they heard ugly, taunting voices.

They had not gone far when they came upon the three Keysers and their captive. A young boy, perhaps fifteen or sixteen, was stripped naked to the waist and bound tight to a chestnut sapling. Three men were lounging about the tree making fun of him. The brother called Buck had his sleeves rolled up and his shirt open, showing a thick fleece of red hair on his chest and forearms. He was laughing and cracking a lash of plaited cowhide thongs. The boy tied to the tree said not a word in answer to Buck's taunting questions. He made no sound at all, did not even look up when Mrs. Blake came swishing through the bushes. For all he had set his teeth tight together, she could see his lower jaw trembling.

Mrs. Ringer spoke first. "Now what air you Keysers up to?"

Big Buck had a very smooth way with him when he took the trouble. He had certainly not expected to see Mrs. Blake from Back Creek, and her appearance put a different light on things. He pulled off his hat and spoke easy.

"Nothin' but a fam'ly matter, folks. This young feller's been charged with takin' the communion set. His maw's a Keyser, an' it's fur us to settle with him. You know yourselves his paw's no account, an' that Baptist preacher he goes to school to don't seem to a-learned him to keep his hands off things. Time fur the fam'ly to learn him a little. He's got to tell where them things is hid."

Mrs. Blake had kept a steady eye on Buck, and now she spoke.

"Then you'd better go and get 'em, Buck Keyser, and put 'em back where they belong, for they're poor plated stuff, and you'll get nothing for them but trouble."

Buck's face didn't change, but his two brothers looked at each other.

"That's what I'm after doin', Miz Blake, onct I git 'em out-a him." With that he swung his lash and gave Casper a cut on the bare shoulder. The boy made no sound, but poor Lawndis was so worked upon that he burst out crying and threw his arms round the prisoner to shield him with his own back. "Don't you dast hit him agin! I can't fight ye, I'm jist a pore mock of a man, but you'll have to finish me afore you tech him."

Mrs. Blake knew Lawndis would be sick for a week after such an outbreak. "Shame on you, Buck Keyser!" she said, going up to him and putting her hand on his hairy arm. "It's Lawndis will get the most punishment out of this, and you know it. What did you come on their place for, to act your foolishness? What have you got against Lawndis?"

"We ain't got nothing agin Lawndis. This whimperin' boy come hidin' in the Ringer woods, 'cause he's a coward an' can't take a lickin'. We was after him, an' come on him here, that's how. Don't act the fool, Lawndis. I'll take care of my kin some'ers out-a your woods. He'll git his ticklin' when there's no ladies around. Come on, boys. Good day to you, Miz Blake."

Mrs. Blake told Lawndis to go back to the house and drink the coffee that was left. While the two women untied the Flight boy and hunted for his shirt, Mrs. Ringer whispered: "Like as not they brought him into our woods a purpose. They was feelin' devilish, an' what's the good a-actin' devilish if nobody sees you? They knows Lawndis is soft that-a-way, an' can't see a sparrer fall. It's a mercy you was here, Miz Blake. I reckon they don't want to git in too bad with your Paw."

On her way down the "Double S" and the "holler" road, Mrs. Blake told herself she must have a talk with David Fairhead about Casper. Perhaps it wasn't wise to encourage him. "I don't know whether that boy's strong enough to master what's around him," she said to herself. "A man's got to be stronger'n a bull to get out of the place he was born in. I just hope I won't dream tonight the way Casper stood against that tree, with his lower jaw tremblin'."

II

To see Mrs. Blake working about her house and garden, a stranger would scarcely guess that she had lived the happiest years of her life in Washington, and had known a wider experience of the world than her more worldly mother.

Rachel was sixteen years old when Michael Blake rode through Frederick County soliciting votes. He was already a member of the Virginia State Legislature, and was a nominee for the United States Congress. He spent some days at the Mill Farm, where he was warmly welcomed. Henry Colbert approved of Blake's record and his principles, and the Mistress was charmed by his good manners, his handsome face and blue eyes. When he said good-bye and rode up into the Capon River country, she missed him.

In two weeks he came back to the Mill Farm. He had made up his mind. He had made it up, indeed, on his first visit, but he had disclosed his intentions to no one, not even to Rachel. When, on this second visit, he asked the miller and Sapphira for their daughter's hand, they were speechless from astonishment. After the interview in which they gave their consent, Mrs. Colbert retired to her room and bolted the door for an hour to regain her composure.

She had never hoped for anything so good for Rachel. She had often doubted whether she would succeed in getting her married at all. Two older daughters she had married very well. But she could see nothing in this girl likely to be attractive to young men. Rachel was well-enough looking, in her father's masterful way, but no one could call her pretty. She was reserved to a degree which her mother called sullenness, and she had decided opinions on matters which did not concern women at all. She was her father's favourite; that was natural, since she was just like him. But this happy, fair-complexioned young Blake, with his warm laugh and mellow voice— Well, Mrs. Colbert reflected, there is no accounting for tastes. Blake was Irish, and the Irish often leap before they look.

When she had recovered herself, Mrs. Colbert sat down to write the amazing news to her sisters.

While she was at her desk, the young man was with Rachel. He had found her in the flower garden, separating tufts of clove pinks. He wiped her hands on his handkerchief and led her into the lilac arbour. Seated beside her on the rustic bench, he told her his story in the manner of the period.

On the first night of his first visit, he said, when he sat opposite her at the supper table, it all happened. He had watched her face in the candlelight and found it hard to reply to her mother's friendly questions, or to keep his mind on the conversation. He had stayed on at the house until he was afraid he might wear out his welcome. After he rode away, he could think of nothing but Rachel whenever he was alone. He was thirty years old, and had never before met a girl whom he wished to marry. Indeed, he admitted, he "liked his liberty." Now everything was different. Her father and mother had given their consent. But he must have her own, spoken from the heart.

"Do you think you could come to love me, really love me, Rachel?" His voice was wistful, almost sad.

She looked up and met his blue eyes fearlessly, something intense flashed into her own. "I do already, Michael."

"My sweetheart! May I have one kiss?"

She put her hands on his shoulders, holding him back, and with that almost fierce devotion still shining in her eyes said pleadingly: "Please, Michael, please! Not until the words have been said."

No reply could have made him happier. He caught her two hands and buried his face in them.

This was in the eighteen-thirties, when loose manners were very loose, and the proprieties correspondingly strict. Young bachelors who were free in their morals were very exacting that the girl they chose for a wife should be virginal in mind as well as in body. The worst that could be said of an unmarried girl was that "she knew too much."

Immediately after Michael's election as Representative for the —th District, the young couple were married and went to Washington to live in a small rented house. The devotion Michael read in Rachel's eyes when she refused him the betrothal kiss soon became her whole life: there was nothing of her left outside it. In every sense he was her first love. More than that, he had taken her from a home where she had never been happy. She felt for him all that was due to a rescuer and a saviour. Until he came, her heart was cold and frozen.

When Rachel was twelve years old, she had chanced to overhear a conversation which coloured her thoughts and feelings ever afterward. In those days she used often to walk to the post office to get the mail, although she knew this annoyed her mother. Rachel was deeply attached to the postmistress, then a young woman who had lately been left a widow with three little boys. One morning she was sitting on Mrs. Bywaters's shady front porch, behind the blooming honeysuckle vines, when she saw a handsome old gentleman ride up to the hitch-post, dismount, and tie his horse. That was Mr. Cartmell, Mrs. Bywaters's father. As he walked up the gravel path to the porch steps, his daughter saw him and came out to greet him. They went into the house together, leaving the door open behind them. Rachel liked to listen to Mr. Cartmell; his talk had a flavour of old-fashioned courtesy.

"I came with something on my mind today, daughter," he began. "Your mother and I think you have it too hard up here, since Jonah went. What with looking after the mail, and attending to your children and the housework, there is too much for one woman to do. Our old neighbour, Mr. Longfield, tells me he is willing to part with one of Abigail's daughters. But he would never sell her off to strangers. In busy seasons your mother often hires her from the Longfields, and finds her capable and willing. I would like to buy Mandy for you, and bring her up here myself. You would have a smart girl to help you, and she would have a good home."

There was a pause. Then Mrs. Bywaters said:

"Could we hire Mandy from the Longfields for a couple years, maybe?"

"I made such a proposal to Mr. Longfield, but he needs a considerable sum of money at once. He is forced to sell Mose, his body servant, into Winchester. You will remember our neighbour was somewhat inclined to extravagance. He has got behind."

Another pause. "You have never owned any slaves yourself, Father," she said thoughtfully, as if considering.

"You know my feeling on that matter, Caroline. But down with us, in the Round Hill neighbourhood, it is always easy to hire help from farmers who have too many negroes. Up here there are few slave-owners, and a raw white girl from the mountains would be of little help to you."

This time there was no pause. Mrs. Bywaters spoke quietly but firmly. "It's kindly thought of you, Father, and kindly spoken. But neither you nor I have ever owned flesh and blood, and I will not begin it. I am young and strong, and I'll make shift to manage. Peace of mind is what I value most."

Little Rachel Colbert, sitting breathless on the porch, heard Mr. Cartmell rise from his squeaky splint-bottom chair and say: "You are my own daughter, Caroline. We will manage." The deep emotion in his voice, and the hush which followed, made Rachel realize that she had been eavesdropping, listening to talk that was private and personal. She fled swiftly through the yard and out to the road. Her feet must have found the way home, for she gave no heed to where she was going. A feeling long smothered had blazed up in her—had become a conviction. She had never heard the thing said before, never put into words. It was the *owning* that was wrong, the relation itself, no matter how convenient or agreeable it might be for master or servant. She had always known it was wrong. It was the thing that made her unhappy at home, and came between her and her mother. How she hated her mother's voice in sarcastic reprimand to the servants! And she hated it in contemptuous indulgence. Till and Aunt Jezebel were the only blacks to whom her mother never spoke with that scornful leniency.

After that morning on Mrs. Bywaters's porch, Rachel was more than ever reserved and shut within herself. Her two aunts disapproved of her; she dreaded the yearly visit to them. At home, she knew that all the servants were fond of her mother, in good or ill humour, and that they were not fond of her. She was not at all what the darkies thought a young lady should be. Till's good manners were barely sufficient to conceal her disappointment in Miss Sapphy's youngest daughter.

*   *   *

Michael Blake had dropped from the clouds, as it were, to deliver Rachel from her loneliness, from life in a home where she had not a single confidant. She often wondered how she had borne that life at all. Once settled in the narrow rented house on R Street, she no longer brooded upon real or imagined injustices. Her mind and energy, and she was endowed with both, were wholly given to making for Michael the kind of home he wanted, and doing it on very little money.

Representative Blake was, he admitted, "fond of the pleasures of the table." Rachel became expert in cookery. Everything he liked, done as he liked, appeared in season on his dinner table. He lunched at an oyster bar near the Capitol, and dined at eight in the evening. His wife had the whole day to prepare his favourite dishes. She put herself under the instruction of a free mulatto woman from New Orleans, whose master had manumitted her when he was dying in Washington. Sarah now made her living by cooking for dinner parties.

Every morning, on his way to the Capitol, Michael stopped at the big market and sent home the choicest food of the season. In those days the Washington markets were second to none in the world for fish and game: wild ducks, partridges, pheasants, wild turkeys . . . the woods were full of wildfowl. The uncontaminated bays and rivers swarmed with fish: Potomac shad, Baltimore oysters, shrimps, scallops, lobsters, and terrapin. In the spring the Dutch truck gardeners brought in the first salads and asparagus and strawberries.

A group of Louisiana planters who came to Washington every winter kept Michael's cellar supplied with good wines. These Southerners often dined at the Blakes', grateful for an escape from the bleakness of Washington hotels. They usually brought with them a young French officer who had some humble post at the French Legation. Too poor to marry, Chénier lived wretchedly in a boarding-house. His devotion to Mrs. Blake and her good dinners became a positive embarrassment, the subject of many a jest at Michael's breakfast table.

The planters came up to Washington unaccompanied by their families. At the round dinner table in the Blakes' narrow dining-room would be seated five or six men, never more

"It's been a right busy time on the place, Aunt Sapphy."
He was still standing beside her chair. She reached out and
felt his palm. "I don't find any calluses."

He laughed gaily. "Oh, we have plenty of field-hands—too
many!"

Washington came in with the tea-tray and put it on the
table beside the Mistress. The visitor drew up a chair and sat
down opposite his aunt, crossing his legs and falling into an
attitude of easy indolence which diverted her. She liked a dash
of impudence in young men whom she considered attractive;
and Martin, she was thinking, was the best favoured of the
younger Colberts. Just then she happened to notice that his
boots were very dusty.

"Why, Martin, didn't you ride your mare out?"

"No, ma'am. I came on the stage and walked over from the
tollgate."

"The stage? You must have been very uncomfortable. Why
didn't you ride Merrylegs, and send your box by the stage?
It's a pleasant ride."

"I sold Merrylegs this spring. Had a good offer and needed
the money."

While he helped himself to sandwiches she studied his face.

"Are you sure you sold her, Mart?" she asked shrewdly.

He had not expected this question. He gave her a quick
glance, and ducked his head with a grin which seemed to say:
"You've caught me now!"

"Well, anyhow, I parted with her, Aunt Sapphy."

"Cards, I'll be bound!"

"No, honour bright. It was a racing bet. I'm not much of a
card man. But I lose my head at the races." He looked at her
frankly, holding out his teacup with an "If you please." Easy,
confidential, a trifle free in manner, as if she were not an old
woman and an invalid. That was how she liked it. She told
herself that Martin's visit would be very refreshing. She almost believed she had urged him to come solely because she
liked to have young people about.

"No matter. We can let you have a mount. Henry keeps a
good riding horse to go in to Winchester on business. He
doesn't like to be bothered with the carriage. I always pre-

ferred to go on horseback when I went to town for Sunday service."

"You pretty nearly lived on horseback, didn't you? Oh, down with us they still tell about how you used to take the fences."

"Yes, I liked riding, but I never gave myself over body and soul to horses, as the Bushwells appear to do."

"That's right. They just live for the stables. The house and grounds would shock you now. People say they used to keep the place up as long as you went to visit there. But Chestnut Hill has never been the same since old Matchem died."

Till appeared at the door and said that Martin's box had come.

Mrs. Colbert beckoned her. "Call Nancy to take Mr. Martin up to his room and unpack his things for him. She keeps your uncle's room at the mill, Martin, and she will do yours, and look after your laundry. Young men are none too orderly, I seem to remember. Now I will rest for an hour before supper."

Martin went up the wide staircase leading from the long hall. Upstairs he saw an open door, and a young mulatto girl standing at attention outside.

"And are you Nancy? Good evening, Nancy. I hear you are going to take care of me." He stood still and looked hard at her.

A wave of pink went over her gold-coloured cheeks, and her eyes fell. "If I can please you, sir," she said quietly, waiting for him to enter the chamber.

"Oh, you do please me!" he laughed.

Going into the room, Martin glanced about: large, airy, not too much furniture, canopy bed with fresh muslin curtains. He opened one of the front windows and looked out over the yard, the mill, the woods across the creek. Beyond the woods the blue, wavy slopes of the North Mountain lay against the sky. The upper porch ran along outside the room; he put one leg out through the open window. "Am I allowed to go on the veranda, girl? Very strict rules in this house, I've heard tell."

"Certainly, sir. There's a door in the hall goes out to the upper porch," she said quickly, correcting an implied reproach on the house.

Martin drew in his foot. "That will be more convenient. And now you can unpack my trunk."

"It's locked, sir."

"Lordy, I forgot!" His sole-leather trunk had been placed on a chair. He unlocked it and threw back the lid. "There. Now you put my clothes where you think they ought to go, and I'll watch you, so I'll know where to find them." He pulled off his coat and waistcoat, threw them on the bed, and sat down in the usual guest-chamber rocking-chair. Nancy took the discarded upper garments and hung them in the clothes-press. She opened the bureau drawers and stood timidly hesitating before the trunk.

"Would you like your collars an' neckcloths kept in the upper drawer, sir?"

He was just lighting a cigar. "Follow your own notion. We have a slut of a housekeeper at home. I never know where to find anything."

She went noiselessly to work, moving back and forth between the bureau and the press. Young Colbert sat with his feet on the low window sill, enjoying his cigar.

"Does my aunt object to smoking?" he asked presently.

"Oh, no, sir! She likes to have the gen'lemen smoke."

After putting away the shirts and nightshirts, Nancy lifted the top tray and stood perplexed by the confusion she found below.

"If you don't mind, sir, I'll take the coats an' pants downstairs direc'ly, an' press 'em."

"That's a good idea."

The shoes and boots she found stuffed full of dirty socks and soiled underwear. She made a bundle of the rumpled linen and put it outside the door. She was embarrassed because the guest watched her so closely.

"Anybody ever tell you you're a damned pretty girl, Nancy?" she heard as she stooped over the trunk.

"No, sir."

Martin would have done better to change his tone. But he did not see her face, and went on teasingly:

"You tryin' to make me believe none of these country jakes around here been makin' up to you? You can't fool me!"

"There's good, kind folks on Back Creek, Mr. Martin."

"You don't say, honey!" Martin laughed, stretching his loose shoulders.

Nancy didn't like his laugh, not at all! She took up an armful of coats and trousers, snatched the pile of soiled linen outside the door, and vanished so quickly that when the young man turned from throwing his cigar end out of the window, he was amazed to find her gone.

shining all about her and bend down the branches over her head. The morning air was still so fresh that the sunlight on her bare feet and legs was grateful. She was light-hearted this morning. She loved to pick cherries, and she loved being up in a tree. Someway no troubles followed a body up there; nothing but the foolish, dreamy, nigger side of her nature climbed the tree with her. She knew she had left half her work undone, but here nobody would find her out to scold her. The leaves over her head laughed softly in the wind; maybe they knew she had run away.

She was in no hurry to pick the cherries. She ate the ripest ones and dropped the hard ones into her basket. Presently she heard someone singing. She sat very still and gently released the branch she was holding down. He was coming from the stables, she thought.

> *Down by de cane-brake, close by de mill,*
> *Dar lived a yaller gal, her name was Nancy Till.*

Should she scramble down? Likely as not he would go along the path through the garden, and then he could not see her from the smokehouse. He wouldn't come prowling around back here among the weeds. But he did. He came through the wet grass straight toward the cherry trees, his straw hat in his hand, singing that old darky song.

Martin had gone to the kitchen to complain that Nancy had not done his room, and Bluebell told him Nancy was out picking cherries. There never was a finer morning for picking cherries or anything else, he was thinking, as he went out to the kitchen garden and round the stables. He didn't really intend to frighten the girl, though he owed her one for the trick she played him yesterday.

"Good morning, Nancy," he called up to her as he stood at the foot of the tree. "Cherries are ripe, eh? Do you know that song? Can you sing, like Bluebell?"

"No, sir. I can't sing. I got no singin' voice."

"Neither have I, but I sing anyhow. Can't help it on a morning like this. Come now, you're going to give me something, Nancy."

His tone was coaxing, but careless. She somehow didn't feel scared of him as he stood down there, with his head thrown back. His eyes were clear this morning, and jolly. He didn't look wicked. Maybe he only meant to tease her anyhow, and she just didn't know how young men behaved over in the racing counties.

"Aren't you going to give me something on such a pretty day? Let's be friends." He held up his hand as if to help her down.

She didn't move, but she laughed a soft darky laugh and dropped a bunch of cherries down to him.

"I don't want cherries. They're sour, and I want something sweet."

"No, Mr. Martin. The sour cherries is all gone. These is blackhearts."

"Stop talking about cherries. You look awful pretty, sitting up there."

Nancy giggled nervously. Martin was smiling all the time. Maybe he was just young and foolish like, not bad.

"Who's your beau, anyhow, Nancy Till?"

"Ain't got none."

"You goin' to be a sour old maid?"

"I reckon I is."

"Now who in the world is that scarecrow, comin' on us?"

Nancy followed his eyes and looked back over her shoulder. The instant her head was turned Martin stepped lightly on the chair, caught her bare ankles, and drew her two legs about his cheeks like a frame. Nancy dropped her basket and almost fell out of the tree herself. She caught at the branch above her and clung to it.

"Oh, please get down, Mr. Martin! Do, please! Somebody'll come along, an' you'll git me into trouble."

Martin laughed. "Get you into trouble? Just this? This is nothin' but to cure toothache."

The girl had gone pale. She was frightened now, but she couldn't move, couldn't pull herself up with him holding her so hard. Everything had changed in a flash. He had changed, and she couldn't collect her wits.

"Please, Mr. Martin, please let me git down."

Martin framed his face closer and shut his eyes. "Pretty soon.—This is just nice.—Something smells sweet—like May apples." He seemed murmuring to himself, not to her,

seen Mr. Martin standin' at the foot of the tree. Before we come, he'd been standin' on the cheer Nancy took to climb up with. I seen the mud off his boots on the cheer-bottom. The gal was scared fo' sho', Mr. Henry. She was tremblin' like a leaf an' taken sick like. I took her down, an' Jeff hepped her to the cabin. I may be wrong, but I didn't like it."

The miller's face had taken on a dark flush. "I'll keep an eye on my nephew, Sampson. Sometimes a girl will make a fuss over nothing, you know."

"Yes, sir. I never seen Nancy do nothin' free nor unbecomin' when she comes an' goes."

"Nor have I. She's a good girl, and I'll look after her."

"Thank you, sir. Good night, Mr. Henry." Sampson withdrew, but his face told that he was not reassured.

The miller closed his book and began to move slowly about the room. In a flash he realized that from the first he had distrusted his nephew, though he had never thought of him in connection with Nancy. To him Nancy was scarcely more than a child. It was his habit to refer to her in that way. In reality, of course, she was a young woman. His three daughters had married when they were younger than Nancy was now. Wrath flamed up in him as he paced the floor; against his nephew and the father who begot him, against all his brothers and the Colbert blood. His own father he could hold in reverence; he was an honest man, and the woman who shared his laborious and thrifty life was a good woman. But there must have been bad blood in the Colberts back on the other side of the water, and it had come to light in his three brothers and their sons. He knew the family inheritance well enough. He had his share of it. But since his marriage he had never let it get the better of him. He had kept his marriage vows as he would keep any other contract.

The miller got very little sleep that night. When the first blush of the early summer dawn showed above the mountain, he rose, put on his long white cotton milling coat, and went to bathe in the shallow pool that always lay under the big mill-wheel. This was his custom, after the hot, close nights which often made sleep unrefreshing in summer. The chill of the water, and the rays of gold which soon touched the distant hills before the sun appeared, restored his feeling of physical vigour. He came back to his room, leaving wet foot-prints on the floury floor behind him. Having dressed and shaved, he put on his hat and walked down along the mill-race toward the dam. He did not know why, but he felt strongly disinclined to see Nancy this morning. He did not wish to be there when she came to the mill; it would not be the same as yesterday. Something disturbing had come between them since then.

For years, ever since she was a child, Nancy had seemed to him more like an influence than a person. She came in and out of the mill like a soft spring breeze; a shy, devoted creature who touched everything so lightly. Never before had anyone divined all his little whims and preferences, and been eager to gratify them. And it was for love, from dutiful affection. She had nothing to gain beyond the pleasure of seeing him pleased.

Now that he must see her as a woman, enticing to men, he shrank from seeing her at all. Something was lost out of that sweet companionship; for companionship it had been, though it was but a smile and a glance, a greeting in the fresh morning hours.

II

I T WAS A LITTLE past midnight, and Sapphira had been asleep for an hour or more, when she was rudely awakened. Nancy had burst in at her door and was calling out, like someone startled.

"Yes, Miss Sapphy, here I is. Whassa matter, mam?"

"Nothing at all is the matter. Have you gone crazy, Nancy, waking me up out of my sleep like this?"

"Oh, you called out, Missy. You sho'ly did. An' I was havin' bad dreams about you."

"Be more careful what you eat, and don't come to me with your bad dreams. You know if I'm once wakened it's hard for me to get to sleep again."

"I'm dreadful sorry, Missy. I was sure I heard you callin', an' I feared you was taken bad, maybe. No, mam, I won't come in thoughtless agin. Maybe I better run down to Ma's cabin tonight, if I'm a-goin' to be res'less an' disturb you?"

"You go right back to your own bed, and control yourself properly. I won't have such crazy behaviour."

"Yes, mam." Nancy went out and closed the door softly behind her. She sat down on her pallet and wrapped a quilt about her shoulders. She did not lie down; she would wait until it was time to roll up her bed and put it in the back closet. Her rushing in upon her mistress had been a ruse. She had heard no call, but she had heard something—a cautious, barefoot step on the wide stairway which led from the upper chambers down into the open hall where she lay on her pallet before the Mistress's door. The stair treads always creaked a little; the dampness of the air kept the wood from drying thoroughly.

When the Mistress sent her back to bed, Nancy told herself that if she heard that stealthy step again, she would run down the hall and out the back door, over to her mammy's cabin. She believed someone upstairs was listening as intently as she. It was a horrible feeling. If she had the start of him, she knew she could outrun him. But then there was the curved oak banister of the stairway, smooth as glass; anybody could slide down it without making a sound. Once he was in the hall, she wouldn't have the start of him. He would be there.

At last the first grey daylight came through the wide windows at the foot of the stairs. It gave her a feeling of safety so sweet that she cuddled her head in her pillow and dozed a little. For hours the object of her terror had been fast asleep in his upstairs chamber. When he heard the sound of voices in his aunt's room, he had shrugged his shoulders and gone back to bed.

As the grey light grew stronger, Nancy rose very softly and dressed,—a simple process, since in summer she went barefoot and slept in her sleeveless "shimmy" (chemise). She had only to tie her petticoat round her waist and slip her calico dress over her head. She tiptoed down the long hall and ran out into the flower garden. The sun was just coming up over the mountain. Fleecy pink clouds were scattered about the sky, and the distant hills had turned gold. A curling mist hung over the low meadows down by the mill dam. The dew from the shrubbery was dripping in splashes upon the brick walks, and on the boxwood hedges the silvery spiderwebs trembled with glistening waterdrops. The tea roses and bleeding-hearts hung heavy, as if they would never rise again. Nobody was stirring in the negro cabins; their overgrowth of trumpet vines and gourd vines was so wet that by running into them you could take a shower bath. It made your skin pretty, washing your face and arms in the dew.

Oh, this was a beautiful place! Nancy didn't believe there was a lovelier spot in the world than this right here. She felt so joyful that her heart beat as hard as it did last night when she was scared. She loved everybody in those vine-covered cabins, everybody. This morning she would be glad to see even fat Lizzie and Bluebell. After all, they were home folks. And down yonder was the mill, *"and the Master so kind and so true."* That was in a song Miss Sapphy used to sing before she got sick, and to Nancy those words had always meant Mister Henry. Was it possible that she might have lost all this happiness last night, the night just gone? But it was still hers: the home folks and the home place and the precious feeling of belonging here. Maybe that fright back there in the dark hall had been just a bad dream. Out here it didn't seem true.

Look-a-there! the smoke was coming out of Sampson's chimley a'ready. He was up, getting breakfast for his children, and his wife, who managed to be sick most of the time. All the niggers knew that Sampson not only got the breakfast: in the small hours of the night he baked all the bread for his family. What patience the man had! And he never raised his low, kind voice against anybody.

One morning, soon after the above incident, the miller found his wife sitting alone at breakfast, and learned that his nephew had ridden off to Winchester for the day.

"I hope he won't use my horse too hard," he remarked. "When is he coming back?"

"Tomorrow, I think."

The miller was silent for a moment, then said with a shade of impatience, "How long is Mart going to hang around here, anyway?"

"We can't very well ask our kin how long they intend to stay with us, can we?"

"Maybe not, but he's been here about six weeks, and that's a long visit."

Sapphira smiled. "I remember my father used to tell how Benjamin Franklin said: *'Hospitality, like fish, stinks after three days.'* That may be true in the North, but we don't feel that way in Virginia, I hope."

"Sapphira, I've had about enough of Martin's company. I never liked his father's ways, and I don't like his. What does he want here, anyway?"

"Maybe the boy wants a refuge,—from creditors."

"Or from the men of families where he's brought disgrace," her husband muttered.

She shook her finger at him. "Now, don't be too hard on him, Henry. Your brothers were all like that, you know. And Martin has a gentlemanly side which they had not. I am certainly not very lively company for a young blade to spend his evenings with, but if he is dull here he never shows it. Certainly I shall miss him when he is gone."

"Well, if you take pleasure in his company, I shan't say anything. But he will demoralize the servants. His way with the young darkies is too free. He goes into the woods across the creek to hunt mushrooms with that trifling Bluebell."

"If the servants go wrong from any visitor in the house, it's their own fault. I think they know their place better. Bluebell is a lazy, lying nigger as ever was, but I've found her smart enough to look out for herself. I doubt whether Martin would so demean himself, but it's no affair of mine." Sapphira laughed softly. It was almost as good as a play, she was thinking; the way whenever she and her husband were thinking of Nancy, they invariably talked about Bluebell.

only a little spell now. They kept in line, but they certainly advanced more slowly. A cheering "Halloo" rang out across the field. The men stopped and straightened up with a grateful sigh, looking toward the Mill House stile. Yonder came young Martin, carrying in each hand a gallon jug, and behind him came Nancy and Bluebell and Nelly and Trudy and little Zach, all with baskets.

It was the custom for the mowers to have their dinner in the field. The scythes were left beside the swath last cut, and the hands gathered in the shade under a wide-spreading maple tree. In every hayfield one big tree was left for that purpose. It was always called "the mowers' tree."

After they had spread a red tablecloth on the grass and laid out the provisions, the women went away. The jugs Martin had brought were full of cold tea. The Master poured himself a full gourd, but the men drank from the jug,—it went round from mouth to mouth.

As they fell to their dinner, a pitiful figure of a negro came toward the group, not approaching directly, but circling to right and left and looking down in the grass as if he were hunting for some lost object. The darkies grinned and nudged one another. "Dar's Tansy Dave. 'Bout time he was drappin' 'long."

The Master spoke to Sampson. "Call him up, poor fellow."

In a voice that was quiet and yet carried far, the yellow man called: "Master says hurry up, Dave, or there won't be nothin' left."

The scarecrow man, bare-legged, his pants torn away to the knee, his shirt a dirty rag, approached slowly, his head hanging down. He muttered something about "been havin' a sort-a spell lately, an' didn't know as he ought-a eat nothin'."

The Master spoke up: "This is a good dinner, Dave. Set down an' eat all you want. We've got plenty."

Dave's mournful face brightened as he looked hungrily at what was spread on the red cloth. He took the chunks of corn bread and fried middling meat Sampson handed him, and drew apart from the others; just on the edge of the shade line he sat down and ate his food.

After dinner the hands lay under the tree and slept for an

hour; lay on their backs, with their old hats over their faces. The miller sat leaning against the trunk and watched the ragged visitor steal across the mown field and hide himself in the sassafras bushes along the rail fence. He was thinking it was a dreary business to be responsible for other folks' lives. Time was when poor Dave, that half-witted ghost of a man, was one of the happiest boys on the place. He and Tap were the ringleaders in all the farm festivals. Dave was very clever with his mouth-organ, and he used to play for the darkies to dance on the hard-packed earth in the back yard. It was six years now since he began to go to pieces.

Six years ago a lady from Baltimore, Mrs. Morrison, had come to board with a relative three miles down the creek. She brought with her her coloured maid, Susanna, who used to come over to dance with the Colbert darkies. She was a taking wench, with big soft eyes and an irresistible giggle— light on her feet, and a pretty dancer. Colbert and Sapphira sometimes went out to watch her dance, while Dave played his mouth-organ, and the other darkies "patted" with their hands. Dave always escorted her home. Lizzie told the Mistress that every night after supper Dave changed his shirt and went down the creek to court Susanna, and before he started he rolled over and over in the tansy bed, "to make hisself smell sweet." The nickname "Tansy Dave" had stuck to him long after he ceased to go a-courting, and after he no longer tried to make hisself smell sweet.

When Mrs. Morrison was packing to go back to the city, Dave came to Sapphira and begged her to buy Susanna, so that he could marry her. They were "promised," he said, and Susanna wanted to stay. At first his mistress laughed at him. But he cried like a little boy; threw himself on the floor and declared he "would run away and foller her if she was took off on the cars." Mrs. Colbert was melted by the boy's desperation; she told him to get up and behave himself, and she would think it over. She did think it over, and talked about it to Henry that night. Both agreed it would be foolish to buy another girl, when they had too many already. But early next morning Sapphira wakened her husband to tell him she had decided to buy Susanna if the woman would take a reasonable price for her. The girl was a good seamstress, and she could do all the fine sewing about the house.

Sapphira ordered the carriage and drove away soon after breakfast. The miller doubted her success, but he said nothing. Susanna's mistress had once come to the Baptist church, and he did not like her arrogant manner, or the look of her. She had a small, hard face, white as flour.

When Sapphira returned, she sent down to the mill for her husband. She was greatly put out. The woman had told her at once that she thoroughly disapproved of slave-owning. When her late husband's shipping interests took him from Bath, Maine, to Baltimore, she had found it necessary to purchase two negroes for house service. In Baltimore there was no other way to get good servants. She would not sell Susanna at any price. The girl was trained for work in a town house. And after she got back to Baltimore she would never think of this crazy nigger again.

Susanna and her mistress left the neighbourhood, and Dave ran away as he had threatened. He walked to Winchester and got on the "cars." When he reached Harpers Ferry and was told he must wait there for the big train that went on to Washington, he lost heart. After a few days he came wandering home, but he was never the same boy again. He went from bad to worse; spent days, often weeks, in the mountains, wherever there was a still and moonshine whisky. Nowadays he lived in the mountains the summer through. In the fall he came down to the mill to borrow Sampson's gun and go hunting. Dave could perfectly imitate the call of the wild turkey, and he brought those wary birds home for the table; the Mistress was very fond of them. Colbert often wondered at Sapphira's forbearance with Dave. When he traded his clothes for whisky and slunk home without a shirt on his back, she would make him go wash himself in the creek, burn his rags, and put on a whole pair of pants and a new "hickory" shirt. Soon he would disappear again and not come back till winter. Taylor was pretty sure to find him in the barn some morning after the first hard freeze, buried deep in the hay. Sapphira saw that he was clothed and fed through the winter. Even Lizzie had pity on him, but she would not let him come into the kitchen to eat with the other hands. She filled a little bucket with victuals and handed it out to him.

The men finished cutting the long meadow before sundown. That night the miller excused himself early from the supper table, admitting that he was tired. He would "limber up" in a few days, he told his wife, but tonight his arms and back ached from unaccustomed exercise.

Once in his room at the mill, he threw himself upon his bed and lay still, watching the lingering twilight die. He looked forward to the next two weeks, which would take the soreness out of his back and mind. It was good for him to be out in the fields; to feel his strength drunk up by the earth and sun, and to set the pace for younger men at cutting grass and wheat.

This was a troubled time for Henry Colbert when he was alone with his thoughts. He was too often preoccupied with what Sampson had told him. Now and then the actual realization of Martin's designs would flash into his mind. The poison in the young scamp's blood seemed to stir something in his own. The Colbert in him threatened to raise its head after long hibernation. Not that he was afraid of himself. For nothing on earth, even by a glance, would he trouble that sweet confidence and affection which had been a comfort to him for so long. But it was not now the comforting thing it had been. Now he tried to avoid Nancy. Her light step on the old ax-dressed boards of the mill floor, her morning smile, did not bring the lift of spirit they used to bring.

He told himself that in trying to keep a close watch on Martin, he had begun to see through Martin's eyes. Sometimes in his sleep that preoccupation with Martin, the sense of almost being Martin, came over him like a black spell.

How was he to get rid of the fellow? In those days, and in that country, a man could not put his nephew out of the house unless he had flagrantly outraged hospitality. The miller had thought seriously of trying to buy Martin off. That seemed the likeliest possibility, though the approach would be awkward: offering a near kinsman money to clear out of the neighbourhood. Nevertheless he had gone to Winchester the week before the hay was ripe, and had drawn from the bank a larger sum of money than he customarily kept on hand. It was now locked in his secretary drawer. He liked to feel that it was there, ready.

Before he undressed for the night Colbert took from the shelf a book he often read, John Bunyan's *Holy War*,—a copy printed in Glasgow in 1763. He opened the book at a passage relating to the state of the town of Mansoul after Diabolus had entered her gates and taken up his rule there:

> "Also things began to grow scarce in Mansoul: now the things that her soul lusted after were departing from her. Upon all her pleasant things there was a blast, and a burning instead of a beauty. Wrinkles now, and some shews of the shadow of death, were upon the inhabitants of Mansoul. And now, O how glad would Mansoul have been to enjoyed quietness and satisfaction of mind, though joined with the meanest condition in the world."

Next he turned to the pages describing the state of Mansoul after she had been retaken and reclaimed by Prince Emmanuel, the Son of God:

> "When the town of Mansoul had thus far rid themselves of their enemies, and of the troublers of their peace, a strict commandment was given out, that yet my Lord Willbewill, should search for, and do his best, to apprehend what Diabolonians were yet alive in Mansoul. . . . He also apprehended Carnalsense, and put him in hold; but how it came about I cannot tell, but he brake prison and made his escape; yea, and the bold villain will not yet quit the town, but lurks in the Diabolonian Dens at days, and haunts like a Ghost, honest men's houses at nights."

In this book he found consolation. An honest man, who had suffered much, was speaking to him of things about which he could not unbosom himself to anyone.

BOOK VII

Nancy's Flight

I

THE WHEAT HARVEST was nearly over. Nancy and her companions had been carrying dinner to the mowers, in the big wheat field on the other side of Back Creek. On her way home Nancy slipped from the company and ran through Mrs. Blake's yard to her kitchen door. Mary and Betty had finished washing the dishes, and their mother was preparing to roast coffee beans in the oven. After one look at Nancy's face, she told the children they could go down the road and watch Grandfather cutting his wheat. When they were gone, she turned to the yellow girl.

"What's the matter now, child? Has that scamp been pestering you again? Set down and tell me."

Nancy dropped into a chair. "Oh, I'm most drove out-a my mind, I cain't bear it no longer, 'deed I cain't! I gets no rest night nor day. I'm goin' to throw myself into the millpawnd, I am!" She bowed her head on her arms and broke into sobs.

"Hush, hush! Don't talk so, Nancy, it's wicked. Stop your crying, and tell me about it." She stood over the girl, stroking her quivering shoulders until the sobs grew more throaty and, as it were, dried up. Nancy lifted her face.

"Miz' Blake, you's the only one I got to talk to. He's just after me night an' day, till I wisht I'd never been bawn."

"I guess a good many of us wish that, sometimes. But we come right again, and bear our lot. Have you said anything to my father?"

"How could I, Miz' Blake? I'd die a' shame to speak it before that good ole man. I got nobody I kin come to but you."

"Then you must try to make it plain to me, Nancy. Can't you keep out of his way?"

"It's worst at night, Miz' Blake. You know I sleeps outside Miss Sapphy's door, an' he's right over me, at the top of the stairs. One night I heard him comin' down the stairs in his

only in their relation to herself. She was born that way, and had been brought up that way.

Yet one must admit inconsistencies. There was her singular indulgence with Tansy Dave, her real affection for Till and old Jezebel, her patience with Sampson's lazy wife. Even now, from her chair, she took some part in all the celebrations that darkies love. She liked to see them happy. On Christmas morning she sat in the long hall and had all the men on the place come in to get their presents and their Christmas drink. She served each man a strong toddy in one of the big glass tumblers that had been her father's. When Tap, the mill boy, smacked his lips and said: "Miss Sapphy, if my mammy's titty had a-tasted like that, I never would a-got weaned," she laughed as if she had never heard the old joke before.

When the darkies were sick, she doctored them, sent linen for the new babies and had them brought for her to see as soon as the mother was up and about. Recalling these things and trying to be fair to her mother, Mrs. Blake suddenly rose from her chair and said aloud:

"No, it ain't put on; she believes in it, and they believe in it. But it ain't right."

II

BY THE NEXT morning's stage Mrs. Bywaters sent an important letter to David Fairhead, asking him to come out to Back Creek as soon as possible. He rode up to her gate next evening on his old grey horse. That night Mrs. Blake and Mr. Whitford, the carpenter, met at the post office to confer with him. When they were seated in the postmistress's private parlour, where they would not be disturbed, Mrs. Blake revealed her bold purpose. Mrs. Bywaters sat by to encourage her.

To the two women the plan seemed a desperate undertaking. No negro slave had ever run away from Back Creek, or from Hayfield, or Round Hill, or even from Winchester. But Mr. Fairhead was reassuring. He told them the underground railroad was now busier than ever before. The severe Fugitive Slave Law, passed six years ago, had by no means prevented slaves from running away. Its very injustice had created new sympathizers for fugitives, and opened new avenues of escape. From as far away as Louisiana, negroes were now reaching Canada; the railroads and the lake steamboats helped them. If a negro once got into Pennsylvania or Ohio, he seldom failed to go through.

Fairhead explained to Mrs. Blake how simple it would be to get Nancy from Winchester to Martinsburg, and from there into Pennsylvania. While she sat by, he wrote a letter to his cousin in Martinsburg, who would be very glad to assist her. This letter would go off by the stage tomorrow morning.

Mr. Whitford said he could manage for Mrs. Blake as far as Winchester. He had a light canvas-covered spring-wagon in which he carried coffins to distant burying-grounds. Chairs for two women could be put inside under the canvas, and they could make the drive to town unseen by anyone. Travelling late at night, they would reach Winchester in good time to take the morning stage for Martinsburg.

Mrs. Blake went home greatly reassured. But the hardest thing to arrange, the interview she most dreaded, was still before her.

III

MR. WHITFORD was to be at Mrs. Blake's house at one o'clock in the morning. Starting at that hour, he would be unlikely to meet travellers on the road, and he would get into Winchester well before daylight. He and his passengers were to have an early breakfast with the old Quaker who was a friend of the miller and of Mr. Fairhead. From the Quaker's house they would take the stage for Martinsburg. If Mrs. Blake chanced to meet an acquaintance on the street or in the stage, it was quite natural that she should be going to Martinsburg on a visit, attended by her mother's maid.

Nancy was to come over to Mrs. Blake's about midnight. When all was still at the Mill House, she got up from her pallet, dressed in the dark, and slipped out of the back door, carrying her shoes and stockings in one hand, and in the other an old pillowcase stuffed with her spare clothes and her few belongings.

When she got to the stile, she sat down behind it and put on her shoes. It was the dark of the moon, and anyone crossing the meadow could not easily be recognized. But if she met anyone, the fact that she was wearing her winter shawl and a hat would arouse curiosity. To travel as Mrs. Blake's lady's maid, she must be dressed for town. Her hat was an old black turban of Mrs. Colbert's. Till had put a red feather on it when Nancy accompanied her mistress to Winchester at Easter.

Mrs. Blake was sitting on her doorstep, waiting, and her house was dark. She drew a sigh of relief when she saw a figure come out of the meadow and cross the road. She met Nancy at the gate, took her into the parlour, pulled down the blinds, and lighted a candle.

"Now, Nancy, here's my old carpet sack. I'm going to give it to you for your own, and you can pack away in it whatever you've got in your bundle there. From now on we must look spruce, like we was going visiting. I'm glad you've got a feather in your hat. It's real becoming to you, and it was a good hat in the first place, when Mother got it. I see you've brought along one of the old reticules. That will be handy to carry the letters I've written out for you to show to the Quaker folks, and maybe to the railroad men, telling how you're a deserving girl and I stand behind you. But when I give you your money, in Martinsburg, you must put it in your stockings. Never let it off your body."

"Oh, Miz' Blake, the reticule ain't mine! Miss Sapphy give it to me yisterday, with three pairs a-her good silk stockings for me to darn. I did mean to darn 'em today, but some way I jist couldn't git down to it. I been kind-a flighty in the haid like. I'll mend 'em as soon as I git there, an' send 'em back by stage, or somehow." Nancy was nervously packing the carpet-bag as she spoke.

Mrs. Blake glanced up, and then stepped quickly into the kitchen to get command of herself. She thought how vague, even to her, was this "there" that Nancy spoke of—*there* was Canada, wasn't it? Mrs. Blake herself had never been farther north than Baltimore. She had always thought of Boston as very, very far north. And Montreal was away, away longer off than Boston. And Nancy spoke of sending things back by stage! For a moment she felt her courage sink.

When she returned to the parlour, she set about straightening the tidies on the chairs, speaking over her shoulder in a matter-of-fact tone. "You better leave your darning right here. I'll mend 'em up neatly and send 'em over. Things often get lost on the stage. Listen! There's Mr. Whitford for sure. He's stopped his horses at our gate. I'll get my things on."

A few minutes later Mrs. Blake walked out of her door in her Sunday best, even to black gloves, and Nancy walked behind her, carrying the carpet sack. Mr. Whitford helped them into the back of his wagon and then untied his horses. Very soon the team splashed through Back Creek. Mrs. Blake had a moment of apprehension and glanced at Nancy. But the girl seemed worn out and dulled by the day's excitement; her head drooped forward on her knees as if she were dozing. It was not until they were passing the old Elliot place, and a jolt over a limestone ledge threw her chair to one side, that she wakened up.

The houses along the road were all dark. The first lighted windows were in the disreputable tavern near Hoag Creek, a

were tied tight, and her money safe in her stockings. In a flash she knew she had said the wrong thing. The girl wilted altogether.

"Oh, Miz' Blake, please mam, take me home! I can't go off amongst strangers. It's too hard. Let me go back an' try to do better. I don't mind Miss Sapphy scoldin'. Why, she brought me up, an' now she's sick an' sufferin'. Look at her pore feet. I ought-a borne it better. Miz' Blake, please mam, I want to go home to the mill an' my own folks."

"Now don't talk foolish. What about Martin?"

"I kin keep out-a his way, Miz' Blake. He won't be there always. I can't bear it to belong nowheres!"

"You've been a brave girl right along, an' you mustn't fail me now. I took a big risk to get you this far. If we went back, Mother would never forgive you—nor me. It would be worse than before. These Quaker folks will be kind to you, an' you'll be bright an' happy, like you used to be. If you ain't happy when you get to your journey's end, I'll fetch you back somehow. Don't give way, after all Mr. Fairhead and Mr. Whitford have done for you. Remember, you were ready to throw yourself in the mill dam."

"Yes'm," the girl breathed. But Mrs. Blake didn't believe she had heard her at all. She couldn't take anything in; her mind was frozen with homesickness and dread. After that they sat in silence.

The nerve-racking suspense did not go on much longer. Through the rushing of the river Mrs. Blake thought she heard the rattle of wheels and hoofs over a stony road.

"Listen, I believe they're coming now. Listen!" She hurried out of the cabin, dragging Nancy after her.

An old chaise emerged from the dark wood, and the driver got out. He was a coloured man, she knew at once from his voice; a negro preacher, as it proved, and a freed man. In greeting Mrs. Blake he took off an old beaver hat, which he wore as the sign of his calling.

"Is this Miz' Blake? I'm 'fraid I kep' you waitin', mam. I had some trouble on de way. De road, from Williamsport on, is very bad, an' they's been heavy rains. De folks sent me along to drive, 'cause Reverend Fairhead wrote how de gal was young an' easy skeered. I am a minister of de gospel, well known hereabouts, an' dey figgered she wouldn't feel so strange wid me."

"I'm glad you came, Uncle. The girl's lost heart a little. She's never been away from home before, an' she's afraid with strangers."

The tall black man turned to Nancy and put a hand on her shoulder. "Dey ain't strangers, where you're goin', honey. Dey calls theyselves Friends, an' dey is friends to all God's people. You'll be treated like dey had raised you up from a chile, an' you'll be passed along on yo' way from one kind fambly to de next. Dey got a letter all 'bout you from de Reverend Fairhead, an' dey all feels 'quainted. We must be goin' now, chile. We want to git over the line into Pennsylvany as early tomorrer as we kin." There was something solemn yet comforting in his voice, like the voice of prophecy. When he gave Nancy his hand, she climbed into the chaise. He put her bag in after her, then turned to Mrs. Blake, still holding his hat over his chest.

"An' you, lady, the Lawd will sho'ly bless you, fo' He said Hisself: Blessed is the merciful."

He untied his team and waited a moment, but Nancy never said a word; not to him, not to Mrs. Blake. She had stood dumb all the while the old man spoke to her, as if she were drugged; indeed she was, by the bitterest of all drugs. The preacher clucked to his horses, seeing that the girl had no word of farewell to say. But as they started off, Mrs. Blake called out to her:

"Good-bye, Nancy! We shall meet again."

BOOK VIII

The Dark Autumn

I

Mrs. Bywaters's youngest son walked into Mrs. Blake's yard one morning with a letter. She was sitting in her parlour by an open window, sewing. He took off his cap and went to speak to her through the window:

"Good day, Mrs. Blake. I brought a letter for you. Mother said it must have been slipped into the letter-box late last night, for she didn't find it till she was stamping the mail for the stage this morning. She thought it might be important, so she sent me down with it."

"Thank you, Jonathan. That was real thoughtful of your mother."

After Jonathan went away, Mrs. Blake sat contemplating the envelope he had brought. It was addressed in her mother's neat handwriting. She had heard nothing from the Mill Farm since her return from Winchester by stage three days ago—except from Bluebell. That spineless darky girl (doubtless sent by Lizzie) had come across the meadow after dark and guilelessly asked Mrs. Blake if she had seen nothin' of Nancy lately. Nobody at home had seen her, an' they was a-gittin' right worried. Taylor he thought they ought to drag the mill dam, but Trudy said maybe she was a-stayin' over to Miz Blake's, or was some'ers Miz Blake knowed about.

No, Mrs. Blake knew nothing of Nancy's whereabouts, and Bluebell had better run along home, as Mrs. Blake was going to a prayer meeting at the church.

"Yes'm. I's a-goin'. We cain't find out nothin' at home, 'cause Miss Sapphy ain't once spoke Nancy's name since we foun' her bed empty one mawnin'. An' Till ain't spoke her name, nuther. When Maw axed her where was Nancy, she jist tole her to mind her business. But we 'speck Till had some talk wid de Missus, 'cause right from the fust day Till's been doin' Master's room an' Mr. Martin's. Seem like Till don't miss her gal much. Las' night when Taylor axed her mus' he drag de mill dam, she tole him he could do what he pleased, an' not to come pesterin' her."

Mrs. Blake resolutely put on her bonnet and pointed to the kitchen door. When Bluebell went out, she shut it behind her and drew the bolt. This was the only word she had had from the mill people.

The letter Jonathan had brought was doubtless something final, since it bore a stamp and came through the post office. People on Back Creek did not send letters to their neighbours through the post. A note to be sent up or down the road was not even put into an envelope. It was folded, turned down at one corner, and carried to the addressee by one of the boys or girls about the place. Government stamps were considered an extravagance. At last Mrs. Blake opened the letter and read:

> *Mistress Blake is kindly requested to make no further visits at the Mill House.*
>
> *Sapphira Dodderidge Colbert*

Well, that was best, Mrs. Blake agreed, as she folded up the paper. Her mother would meet this situation with dignity, as she had met other misfortunes. She would not set the slave-catchers on to track Nancy. She would not question anyone. She knew, of course, that the girl could never have got away without help, and this letter told that she understood who had contrived her escape. The Colbert darkies must know that Mrs. Blake's house had been closed for two days, and that Mary and Betty stayed with Mrs. Bywaters while their mother was away. She was sorriest for the hurt this would be to her mother's pride. Nancy's disappearance would be the talk of the neighbourhood. Every time Mrs. Colbert drove out she would meet inquiring faces. The whisperings and surmises among her own servants would be a trial to her. Mrs. Blake knew how her mother hated to be overreached or outwitted, and she was sorry to have brought another humiliation to one who had already lost so much: her activity on horse and foot, her fine figure and rosy complexion.

The property loss Mrs. Colbert would bear lightly. Tansy Dave was certainly a property loss, and she had never complained or tried to punish him. But if he had actually run away and stayed in Baltimore, his mistress would likely enough have had him seized and brought back.

A girl like Nancy, refined and very pretty, skilful with her needle and in chamber work, would easily fetch a thousand dollars, maybe more. But Mrs. Blake did her mother the justice to believe that this money out was not the thing that cut to the quick. She unfolded the letter again, and as she looked at it, tears rose slowly to her eyes.

"It's hard for a body to know what to do, sometimes," she murmured to herself. "I hate to mortify her. Maybe I ought to a-thought about how much she suffers, and her poor feet, like Nancy said to me that night in the dark cabin by that roaring river. Maybe I ought to have thought and waited."

All through the month of August Mrs. Blake was busy sewing for her girls, to get them ready for school. She saw no one from the Mill House except her father, who walked home with her from church every Sunday. Nancy's name was never mentioned between them.

One Sunday morning fat Lizzie caught Mrs. Blake outside the church door and came at her. "Howdy, Miz Blake. Now maybe you knows when Nancy is comin' home? I axed Miss Sapphy only yiste'day, an' she says to me she s'posed Nancy'd come back from Ches'nut Hill when she was sent fur. Now Tap come up wid a nigger from Ches'nut Hill in Winchester, an' he tells Tap dey ain't never seen sight a' Nancy down dar. It begins to look like Taylor's right, an' she drownded herse'f in de dam. He says dat's all a pack a' lies 'bout dem risin' to de top in fo' days. She might easy a-ketched on a big root an' be down dar still."

By this time a dozen eager listeners had gathered round, and Mrs. Blake gave Lizzie a dark look. "Here comes your master. You had better ask him."

Lizzie turned and saw the miller coming up the path. With a "God a'mighty!" she hurried into the church and up the narrow stairs to the gallery as fast as a woman of her figure could go.

After the first October frosts, when everyone went into the woods to gather chestnuts and hickory nuts, Mrs. Blake and her two little girls happened to come upon a nutting party from the Mill House. Till was among them. She met Mrs. Blake with such warmth as she seldom betrayed and called her by her given name.

"It's surely nice to lay eyes on you agin, Miss Rachel. It does me good to see you lookin' fine and hearty."

Mrs. Blake asked after her mother's health.

"I'm right worried about her, Miss Rachel. Doctor Clavenger comes out from Winchester every week to see her. Sometimes he draws the water off, an' then she's easier. She don't git up for breakfast no more. She stays in bed all day till I dresses her an' takes her into the parlour for tea."

Their talk was suddenly interrupted by shouts and scrambling. Tap, the nimblest of the mill boys, had climbed a tall chestnut tree and was thrashing the branches with a pole. The little darkies shouted as the nuts showered down, and all the women fell on their knees and began scratching among the dried leaves and stuffing the nuts into their bags and baskets. Till and Mrs. Blake picked side by side, and once when they were bending over close together, Till asked in a low, cautious murmur: "You ain't heard nothin', Miss Rachel?"

"Not yet. When I do hear, I'll let you know. I saw her into good hands, Till. I don't doubt she's in Canada by this time, amongst English people."

"Thank you, mam, Miss Rachel. I can't say no more. I don't want them niggers to see me cryin'. If she's up there with the English folks, she'll have some chance."

II

No one on Back Creek could remember a finer autumn; frosts before sunrise, summer heat at noon, chill nights. All morning the mountain lay in a soft blue haze, and in the afternoon broad fans of heavy golden sunlight warmed its back and flanks. The colour on the hillsides, in the low meadows, and along the streams had never been more brilliant. Little rain fell in October, and the trees held their leaves. The great maples in Mrs. Blake's yard were like blazing torches; scarlet leaves fluttered softly down to the green turf, leaving the boughs above still densely covered.

With November the weather changed. Heavy rains set in. There was scarcely a clear day. The earth was soon soaked, the meadows became boggy, and all the streams rose. Back Creek overflowed its low banks and rushed yellow and foaming into the mill road. The schoolroom under the Baptist Church, set deep in the hillside, became very damp. Suddenly David Fairhead's school was closed; nearly half his pupils were in bed with ulcerated throats or diphtheria.

It was a rare winter when there was not an outbreak of diphtheria in Hayfield or Back Creek or Timber Ridge. This year it came before winter began. Doctor Brush rode with his saddle-bags all day long from house to house, never bothering to wash his hands when he came or went. His treatment was to scour throats with a mixture of sulphur and molasses, and to forbid his patients both food and water. If he found "white spots," he declared the case diphtheria, and the patient was starved until the spots were gone. Few children survived his treatment.

Late one evening in the week after the school had been closed, Mr. Whitford was driving his covered spring-wagon along the big road, carrying two coffins up to Timber Ridge. As he passed Mrs. Blake's house he saw that her front door stood wide open, and a flickering light came from the parlour windows. This was a signal to passers-by that help of some sort was needed within. As he slowed his team, Mrs. Blake herself ran out into the road to hail him.

"We're in trouble here, Mr. Whitford. Both my girls are

sick, and I want you to carry word to the post office. Yes sir, they've been ailing with colds since yesterday, but tonight, just after supper, they were taken very bad. Maybe Mrs. Bywaters can come down to help me. And maybe she can send one of her boys along with you to hunt for the doctor. He's likely somewhere on the ridge. I daren't leave the house, and not a soul has come along the road till you."

"I'll get somebody here in no time, Mrs. Blake. Don't you worry, mam." Mr. Whitford whipped up his horses.

At the post office there was a brief consultation between Mrs. Bywaters and David Fairhead. Most people, though not all, believed that diphtheria was "catching." Clearly the postmistress, who had to be on duty and see people every day, should not go where there was a contagious disease. Fairhead said he would go: Whitford could carry him back to Mrs. Blake's, then drive up to Timber Ridge, deliver his coffins, and trail Doctor Brush until he found him.

When Fairhead reached Mrs. Blake's house, he found her in an upstairs bedroom, holding the wash-basin for Betty, who was nauseated. After she laid the child back on her pillow, she rose and said: "Oh, I'm glad it's you, David." She fronted him with a strange, dark look which frightened him. He was very fond of these children. He stood still and tried to think. Mrs. Blake had got the girls into their nightgowns, braided their hair, and put them into two cots in the room they shared together. Fairhead told her he felt sure they ought not to be in the same room.

"There's the spare room, across the hall, David. The bed's made up. You can carry Mary over and put her in it."

Toward morning Mr. Whitford brought word that Doctor Brush would stop at Mrs. Blake's about sun-up, if she would have a good breakfast and plenty of coffee ready for him. The doctor came, looked down the girls' throats, found his "white spots," and seated himself in the dining-room to enjoy his breakfast. Immediately David Fairhead started for the mill.

The miller was standing before his little looking-glass, in the act of shaving, when Fairhead called to him through the open window.

"Mr. Colbert, I've come from Mrs. Blake's house. Both her little girls are sick with bad throats. Doctor Brush is over

and taken for granted: her long illness, with all its discomforts, and the intrepid courage with which she had faced the inevitable. He reached out for her two hands and buried his face in her palms. She felt his tears wet on her skin. For a long while he crouched thus, leaning against her chair, his head on her knee.

He had never understood his wife very well, but he had always been proud of her. When she was young, she was fearless and independent, she held her head high and made this Mill House a place where town folks liked to come. After she was old and ill, she never lowered her flag; not even now, when she knew the end was not far off. He had seen strong men quail and whimper at the approach of death. He, himself, dreaded it. But as he leaned against her chair with his face hidden, he knew how it would be with her; she would make her death easy for everyone, because she would meet it with that composure which he had sometimes called heartlessness, but which now seemed to him strength. As long as she was conscious, she would be mistress of the situation and of herself.

After this long silence, in which he seemed to know that she followed his thoughts, he lifted his head, still holding fast to her hands, and spoke falteringly. "Yes, dear wife, do let us have Rachel here. You are a kind woman to think of it. You are good to a great many folks, Sapphy."

"Not so good as Rachel, with her basket!" She turned it off lightly, tweaking his ear.

"There are different ways of being good to folks," the miller held out stubbornly, as if this idea had just come to him and he was not to be teased into letting go of it. "Sometimes keeping people in their place is being good to them."

"Perhaps. We would all do better if we had our lives to live over again." She was silent for a moment, then added thoughtfully: "Take it all in all, though, we have had many happy years here, and we both love the place. Neither of us would be easy anywhere else."

BOOK IX

Nancy's Return

(*Epilogue — Twenty-five years later*)

I

TWENTY-FIVE YEARS had passed since Mrs. Blake took her mother's slave girl across the Potomac. The Civil War, which came on so soon after Nancy ran away, was long gone by when Back Creek folks saw the yellow girl again.

In all that time the country between Romney and Winchester had changed very little. The same families were living on their old places. There were new people at the Colbert mill, of course, and several new brick houses with ambitious porticos now stood on the turnpike between Winchester and Timber Ridge. But the wooden foot-bridge over Back Creek hung just as it did in the Colberts' time, a curious "suspension" bridge, without piles, swung from the far-reaching white limb of a great sycamore that grew on the bank and leaned over the stream. Mrs. Bywaters, though now an old woman, was still the postmistress. She had not been removed in the "carpetbag" period, when so many questionable Government appointments were made. During the war years, when Federal troops were marching up and down the valley, her well-known Northern sympathies stood the Confederate soldiers in good stead. When they were home on leave, they could always hide from search parties in her rambling garrets. Her house was exempt from search.

The war made few enmities in the country neighbourhoods. When Willie Gordon, a Rebel boy from Hayfield, was wounded in the Battle of Bull Run, it was Mr. Cartmell, Mrs. Bywaters's father, who went after him in his hay-wagon, got through the Federal lines, and brought him home. While the boy lay dying from gangrene in a shattered leg (Doctor Brush never attempted an amputation, and Doctor Clavenger was far away on Lee's staff), the Hayfield people, regardless of political differences, came in relays, night and day, and did the only thing that relieved his pain a little: they carried cold water from the springhouse and with a tin cup poured it steadily over his leg for hours at a time.

Mr. Whitford's son enlisted in the Northern army, as his father's son might be expected to do. His nearest neighbour, Mr. Jeffers, had a son in Ashby's cavalry. The fathers remained friends, worked their bordering fields, and talked to each other across the rail fence as they had always done. Both men admired young Turner Ashby of Fauquier County, who held the Confederate line from Berkeley Springs to Harpers Ferry,—so near home that word of his brilliant cavalry exploits came out to Back Creek with the stage-driver. The war news from distant places came slowly, sometimes long after the event, but Stonewall Jackson and Ashby, both operating in Frederick County, gave people plenty to talk about.

Ashby fell in the second year of the war, shot through the heart after his horse had been killed under him, leading a victorious charge near Harrisonburg, on the sixth day of June. Even today, if you should be motoring through Winchester on the sixth of June, and should stop to see the Confederate cemetery, you would probably find fresh flowers on Ashby's grave. He was all that the old-time Virginians admired: *Like Paris handsome and like Hector brave.* And he died young. "Shortlived and glorious," the old Virginians used to say.

After Lee's surrender, the country boys from Back Creek and Timber Ridge came home to their farms and set to work to reclaim their neglected fields. The land was still there, but few horses were left to work it with. In the movement of troops to and fro between Romney and Winchester, all the livestock had been carried away. Even the cocks and hens had been snapped up by the foragers.

The Rebel soldiers who came back were tired, discouraged, but not humiliated or embittered by failure. The country people accepted the defeat of the Confederacy with dignity, as they accepted death when it came to their families. Defeat was not new to those men. Almost every season brought defeat of some kind to the farming people. Their cornfields, planted by hand and cultivated with the hoe, were beaten down by hail, or the wheat was burned up by drouth, or cholera broke out among the pigs. The soil was none too fertile, and the methods of farming were not very good.

The Back Creek boys were glad to be at home again; to see the sun come up over one familiar hill and go down over another. Now they could mend the barn roof where it leaked, help the old woman with her garden, and keep the wood-pile high. They had gone out to fight for their home State, had done their best, and now it was over. They still wore their army overcoats in winter, because they had no others, and they worked the fields in whatever rags were left of their uniforms. The day of Confederate reunions and veterans' dinners was then far distant.

When Nancy came back after so many years, though the outward scene was little changed, she came back to a different world. The young men of 1856 were beginning to grow grey, and the children who went to David Fairhead's basement school were now married and had children of their own.

This new generation was gayer and more carefree than their forbears, perhaps because they had fewer traditions to live up to. The war had done away with many of the old distinctions. The young couples were poor and extravagant and jolly. They were much given to picnics and camp-meetings in summer, sleighing parties and dancing parties in the winter. Every ambitious young farmer kept a smart buggy and a double carriage, but these were used for Sunday church-going and trips to Winchester and Capon Springs. The saddle-horse was still the usual means of getting about the neighbourhood. The women made social calls, went to the post office and the dressmaker, on horseback. A handsome woman (or a pretty girl) on a fine horse was a charming figure to meet on the road; the close-fitting riding-habit with long skirt, the little hat with the long plume. Cavalry veterans rose in the stirrup to salute her as she flashed by.

The actual scene of the meeting had been arranged for my benefit. When I cried because I was not allowed to go downstairs and see Nancy enter the house, Aunt Till had said: "Never mind, honey. You stay right here, and I'll stay right here. Nancy 'll come up, and you'll see her as soon as I do." Mrs. Blake stayed with us. My mother went down to give Nancy the hand of welcome.

I heard them talking on the stairs and in the hall; my parents' voices excited and cordial, and another voice, low and pleasant, but not exactly "hearty," it seemed to me, — not enough so for the occasion.

Till had already risen; when the stranger followed my mother into the room, she took a few uncertain steps forward. She fell meekly into the arms of a tall, gold-skinned woman, who drew the little old darky to her breast and held her there, bending her face down over the head scantily covered with grey wool. Neither spoke a word. There was something Scriptural in that meeting, like the pictures in our old Bible.

After those few moments of tender silence, the visitor released Aunt Till with a gentle stroke over her bent shoulders, and turned to Mrs. Blake. Tears were shining in the deep creases on either side of Mrs. Blake's nose. "Well, Nancy, child, you've made us right proud of you," she said. Then, for the first time, I saw Nancy's lovely smile. "I never forget who it was took me across the river that night, Mrs. Blake."

When Nancy laid aside her long black coat, I saw with astonishment that it was lined with grey fur, from top to toe! We had no coats like that on Back Creek. She took off her turban and brushed back a strand of her shiny, blue-black hair. She wore a black silk dress. A gold watch-chain was looped about her neck and came down to her belt, where the watch was tucked away in a little pocket.

"Now we must sit down and talk," said my mother. That was what one always said to visitors. While they talked, I looked and listened. Nancy had always been described to me as young, gold-coloured, and "lissome"—that was my father's word.

"Down by de cane-brake, close by de mill, Dar lived a yaller

gal—" That was the picture I had carried in my mind. The
stranger who came to realize that image was forty-four years
old. But though she was no longer lissome, she was other
things. She had, I vaguely felt, presence. And there was a
charm about her voice, though her speech was different from
ours on Back Creek. Her words seemed to be too precise,
rather cutting in their unfailing distinctness. Whereas Mrs.
Blake used to ask me if she should read to me from my
"hist'ry book" (*Peter Parley's Universal*), Nancy spoke of the
his-to-ry of Canada. I didn't like that pronunciation. Even my
father said "hist'ry." Wasn't that the right and easy way to say
it? Nancy put into many words syllables I had never heard
sounded in them before. That repelled me. It didn't seem a
friendly way to talk.

Her speech I counted against her. But I liked the way she
sat in her chair, the shade of deference in her voice when
she addressed my mother, and I liked to see her move about,
—there was something so smooth and measured in her
movements. I noticed it when she went to get her hand-
bag, and opened it on the foot of my bed, to show us the
pictures of her husband and three children. She spoke of her
mistress as Madam, and her master as Colonel Kenwood.
The family were in England for the spring, and that was
why Nancy was able to come home and visit her mother.
She could stay exactly six weeks; then she must go back to
Montreal to get the house ready for the return of the family.
Her husband was the Kenwoods' gardener. He was half
Scotch and half Indian.

Nancy was to be at our house for the midday dinner. Then
she would walk home with her mother, to stay with her in the
old cabin of her childhood. The "new miller," as he was still
called, though he had now been running the mill for some
seventeen years, was a kind man from over the Blue Ridge.
He let Till stay on in her cabin behind the Mill House, work
her own garden patch, and even keep a pig or two.

When my mother and father and Mrs. Blake went down to
dinner, Nancy and Till sat where they were, hand in hand,
and went on talking as if I were not there at all. Nancy was
telling her mother about her husband and children, how they

had a cottage to themselves at the end of the park, and how the work was divided between the men and the maids.

Suddenly Till interrupted her, looking up into her face with idolatrous pride.

"Nancy, darlin', you talks just like Mrs. Matchem, down at Chestnut Hill! I loves to hear you."

Presently they were called downstairs to the second table, to eat the same dinner as the family, served by the same maid (black Moses' Sally). My mother gave me an egg-nog to quiet me and pulled down the blinds. I was tired out with excitement and went to sleep.

During her stay on Back Creek Nancy came often with her mother to our house. She used to bring a small carpetbag, with her sewing and a fresh apron, and insisted upon helping Mrs. Blake and Moses' Sally in whatever housework was under way. She begged to be allowed to roast the coffee. "The smell of it is sweeter than roses to me, Mrs. Blake," she said laughing. "Up there the coffee is always poor, so I've learned to drink tea. As soon as it's browned, I'll grind a little and make us all a cup, by your leave."

Our kitchen was almost as large as a modern music-room, and to me it was the pleasantest room in the house,—the most interesting. The parlour was a bit stiff when it was not full of company, but here everything was easy. Besides the eight-hole range, there was a great fireplace with a crane. In winter a roaring fire was kept up in it at night, after the range fire went out. All the indoor and outdoor servants sat round the kitchen fireplace and cracked nuts and told stories until they went to bed.

We had three kitchen tables: one for kneading bread, another for making cakes and pastry, and a third with a zinc top, for dismembering fowls and rabbits and stuffing turkeys. The tall cupboards stored sugar and spices and groceries; our farm wagons brought supplies out from Winchester in large quantities. Behind the doors of a very special corner cupboard stood all the jars of brandied fruit, and glass jars of ginger and orange peel soaking in whisky. Canned vegetables, and the preserved fruits not put down in alcohol, were kept in a very cold cellar: a stream ran through it, actually!

Till and Nancy usually came for dinner, and after the dishes were washed they sat down with Mrs. Blake in the wooden rocking-chairs by the west window where the sunlight poured in. They took out their sewing or knitting from the carpet-bag, and while the pound cake or the marble cake was baking in a slow oven, they talked about old times. I was allowed to sit with them and sew patchwork. Sometimes their talk was puzzling, but I soon learned that it was best never to inter-rupt with questions,—it seemed to break the spell. Nancy wanted to know what had happened during the war, and what had become of everybody,—and so did I.

While she sat drawing her crochet hook in and out, she would say: "And what ever did become of Lizzie and Bluebell after Miss Sapphy died?"

Then Till would speak up: "Why, ain't I told you how Mr. Henry freed 'em right after Missy died, when he freed all the niggers? But it was hard to git rid of free niggers befo' the war. He surely had a sight a' trouble gittin' shet of them two! Even after he'd got Lizzie a good place at the Taylor House hotel in Winchester, they kep' makin' excuse to stay on, hangin' 'round the kitchen. In the end he had to drive 'em into town himself an' put 'em down at the hotel, an' tole 'em fur the las' time they wasn't needed at the mill place no more. You know he never did like them two niggers. He took a wonderful lot a' trouble gittin' good places fur his people. You remembers Sampson, honey?"

"Why, of course I do, Mother. He was Master's steadiest man." At this moment Till would likely be on her feet in a twinkle with: "Before I begin on Sampson, I'll just turn the bread fur you, Mrs. Blake. I seem to smell it's about ready."

When all the pans had been changed about, Till would sit down and continue:

"Well, Mr. Henry got Sampson a wonderful good place up in Pennsylvany, in some new kind of mill they calls roller mills. He's done well, has Sampson, an' his children has turned out well, they say. Soon as the war was over, Sampson come back here, just to see the old place. The new miller treated him real clever, and let him sleep in old Master's mill room—he don't use it only like a kind of office, to see folks. Sampson come to my cabin every day he was here, to eat my

Chronology

1873   Born December 7 in Back Creek Valley, near Winchester, Virginia, in the home of maternal grandmother, Rachel Seibert Boak, first child of Charles Fectigue Cather (b. 1848) and Mary Virginia ("Jennie") Boak Cather (b. 1850). Named Wilella for aunt who died of diptheria; called "Willie" by parents. (Cather family had emigrated from Northern Ireland and settled in the Winchester area after the Revolutionary War. Maternal grandfather, William Boak, served in the Virginia House of Delegates, and two of Cather's Boak uncles fought in the Confederate Army.) Father, who had studied law but never practiced, raises sheep for sale in Baltimore and Washington.

1874   Family moves to grandfather William Cather's nearby farm, Willow Shade, accompanied by Rachel Boak. Father manages his father's sheep farm until 1883 (later Cather often will accompany him on his rounds).

1877   Grandparents William and Caroline Cather emigrate with three daughters to Webster County, Nebraska, where their son George and his wife, Frances, are successful farmers. Brother Roscoe born.

1879–82   Strongly affected by reunion of household servant and her daughter, who had escaped from slavery to Canada before the Civil War. Taught to read by Grandmother Boak from the Bible, *Pilgrim's Progress*, and *Peter Parley's Universal History*. Listens to stories told by local women who come to Willow Shade to make quilts, especially Mary Ann Anderson, whose mildly retarded daughter, Marjorie (Margie), works for the Cathers as a housemaid. Brother Douglass born 1880 and sister Jessica in 1881. Begins to call herself "Willa Love Cather," claiming to be named after uncle William Seibert Boak, killed in the Civil War, and the Dr. Love who had attended her birth.

1883   When sheep barn burns down and grandfather refuses to rebuild, Willow Shade is sold. Family, along with Rachel Boak, Marjorie Anderson and her brother, and cousins Bess Seymour and Will Andrews, moves to the Nebraska

Divide (the high plains between the Republican and Little Blue rivers) and lives for a year and a half on grandparents' farm. Mother becomes ill and suffers a miscarriage. Distressed at first by change from sheltered to exposed landscape "as bare as a piece of sheet iron," Cather soon adapts to the prairie. Briefly attends school during winter. Visits homesteads of immigrant settlers from Scandinavia, Russia, Germany, France, and Bohemia and develops friendships with pioneer farm women; listens to stories of their homelands. Ill for part of year (possibly with mild case of polio), but makes full recovery.

1884   In September father sells livestock and farm equipment and family moves into small frame house in Red Cloud, prairie town sixteen miles southeast. Household includes Rachel Boak, Marjorie Anderson, and Bess Seymour. Father opens a real estate and loan office and Cather attends school. Meets Englishman William Ducker, a storekeeper who teaches her Greek and Latin (they read Virgil, Ovid, Homer, and Anacreon together), and the Wieners, French- and German-speaking neighbors who introduce her to European literature. Discovers romantic adventure fiction and enjoys becoming "Caesar or Napoleon at will."

1885   Sees plays for the first time at newly opened Red Cloud Opera House. Becomes close friends with the Miner sisters (Mary, Margie, Irene, and Carrie), daughters of a local storekeeper, and participates in amateur theatricals with them (will retain lifelong ties with Irene and Carrie).

1888   Brother James is born and mother is ill. Cather crops her long hair and adopts male dress (maintains this appearance for four years); calls herself "William Cather, M.D." ("I was determined then to be a surgeon") and "William Cather, Jr." Interest in science leads to experiments with dissection and vivisection, attracting criticism from neighbors. Enters in friend's album her ideal of happiness as "amputating limbs" and favorite pastime as "slicing toads." Plays Beauty's father in *The Beauty and the Beast*, performed with friends at the Opera House. Begins personal library with Pope's translation of *The Iliad* (soon includes Jacob Abbott's *Histories of Cyrus the Great and Alexander the Great*, George Eliot's *The Spanish Gypsy*,

Thomas Carlyle's *Sartor Resartus*, and Shakespeare's *Antony and Cleopatra*).

1890   June, graduates from Red Cloud High School in class of three and delivers speech "Superstition versus Investigation" in defense of scientific inquiry and experimentation. September, moves to Lincoln and enrolls as a second-year student in the Latin School, two-year preparatory school of the University of Nebraska. Sister Elsie born.

1891   First published essay, "Concerning Thos. Carlyle," appears March 1 in the *Nebraska State Journal* (signed "W.C."), submitted by her English instructor; appears unsigned in the university paper *Hesperian*. Becomes more interested in literature than in science. September, matriculates as freshman at the University of Nebraska, where she studies Greek (for three years, including Pindar, Homer, Herodotus, drama and lyric poetry), Latin (for two years), Anglo-Saxon, Shakespeare and other Elizabethan dramatists, Browning and other 19th-century writers (including Tennyson, Emerson, Hawthorne, and Ruskin), French (reads Daudet, Gautier, Balzac, Racine, and Taine), German (for one year), as well as courses in history, philosophy, rhetoric, journalism, chemistry, and mathematics; is particularly drawn to French literature and to the classics. Friends and fellow students include Louise Pound, Mariel Gere, and Dorothy Canfield. Becomes active in student publications and literary, debating, and theatrical societies, and attends the theater. Changes middle name from "Love" to "Lova." In November essay "Shakespeare and Hamlet" published in the *Nebraska State Journal*.

1892   May, first short story, "Peter," published in Boston literary weekly *The Mahogany Tree* after submission by another teacher. First poem, "Shakespeare: A Freshman Theme," published in the June *Hesperian*. (Will publish short fiction in the *Hesperian* throughout her university career.) Before returning to Red Cloud for the summer, writes Louise Pound expressing her love and declaring it unfair that intense female friendship should be "unnatural"; signs the letter "William." Becomes literary editor of the *Hesperian* in fall and appears in two plays. Brother John Esten (Jack)

Garden Lodge," "The Marriage of Phædra," "Paul's Case") and three most recent magazine works, published by McClure, Phillips & Co. Spends the summer in the West with Isabelle McClung: visits Douglass in Cheyenne, camps with Roscoe in the Black Hills, and stays with parents in Red Cloud for a month. Goes to New York for a week at end of summer, sees S. S. McClure and stays with Edith Lewis. Returns to Pittsburgh at start of school year. Attends birthday dinner for Mark Twain on December 5 at Delmonico's in New York.

1906   Accepts offer from S. S. McClure of job at *McClure's Magazine* when several staff members, including Ida Tarbell and Lincoln Steffens, resign to form a rival publication. Moves to New York in late spring and lives in the same Greenwich Village apartment building as Edith Lewis at 60 Washington Square South. Colleagues at *McClure's* include Viola Roseboro, Witter Bynner, Ellery Sedgwick, Cameron Mackenzie, and eventually Edith Lewis (who later described life at the magazine as "working in a high wind" in which S. S. McClure was the "storm center").

1907   Moves to Boston on assignment for *McClure's*, verifying, researching, and extensively rewriting Georgine Milmine's *The Life of Mary Baker G. Eddy and the History of Christian Science*. Lives in the Parker House hotel, then moves to an apartment on Chestnut Street. Enjoys an active social life, meeting editor Ferris Greenslet, poet Louise Imogen Guiney, novelist Margaret Deland, and attorney Louis Brandeis and his wife, Alice. Publishes four stories in 1907 (three in *McClure's* and one in *Century*) and a poem, "The Star Dial," in which she assumes the persona of Sappho.

1908   In March meets Annie Fields, widow of Boston publisher James T. Fields, and Sarah Orne Jewett at Fields' Beacon Hill home at 148 Charles Street—the "house of memories." Develops close friendships with both women, visiting often in Boston, Thunderbolt Hill (Fields' summer home in Manchester, Massachusetts), and Jewett's home in South Berwick, Maine. Travels to Europe in late spring with Isabelle McClung, spending several weeks in Italy. Returns to New York in fall and moves into an apartment at 82 Washington Place with Edith Lewis. Becomes managing editor of *McClure's*. November, Jewett writes of her "delight" in "On the Gull's Road," which appears in the December *McClure's*. ("It makes me the more sure that you are far on your road toward a fine and long story of very high class.") Cather writes Jewett of her nervous exhaustion and despair that her literary talents are not developing. Jewett reassures Cather of her artistic promise, praising "The Sculptor's Funeral," and urging her to find the "time and quiet to perfect your work."

1909 January, rejects several poems submitted by future playwright Zoë Akins; the two women begin a lifelong correspondence and friendship. Publishes "The Enchanted Bluff," story drawing on her Nebraska past, in the April *Harper's*. May, travels to London to solicit manuscripts and contact authors for *McClure's*. Meets drama critic William Archer, H. G. Wells, and Ford Madox Ford, and attends the theater with Lady Gregory. Sarah Orne Jewett dies, June 24. Cather writes Fields that life is "dark and purposeless" without her. Visits Red Cloud in September and October. Returns to New York and assumes sole responsibility for editing *McClure's* when S. S. McClure leaves for Europe. Gives 1875 as year of birth in her first submission to *Who's Who*.

1910 Meets Elizabeth Sergeant, a young Bryn Mawr graduate who had submitted an article on sweatshop workers to *McClure's*. Sergeant becomes close friend and literary confidante for several years.

1911 February, suffers attack of mastoiditis and spends several weeks in the hospital. Travels to England for *McClure's* after recovery. Visits South Berwick in the spring, where she stays with Sarah Orne Jewett's sister, Mary. Meets Elizabeth Sergeant in Gloucester, Massachusetts, and the two visit Annie Fields in Boston. Returns to Boston in May for a week with Fields and in June again visits South Berwick. Annie Fields' edition of *Letters of Sarah Orne Jewett*, including correspondence with Cather, appears. Over the summer begins *Alexander's Bridge*, novel portraying a Western-born engineer's discomfort with his upperclass Eastern world. Takes leave of absence from *McClure's* in October and spends three months with Isabelle McClung in Cherry Valley, New York; there she rests, revises *Alexander's Bridge*, and writes "The Bohemian Girl" and finishes "Alexandra," two stories with Western settings. Sends *Alexander's Bridge* to *McClure's* under pseudonym "Fanny Cadwallader," revealing her identity when it is accepted. Returns to New York at the end of the year but decides not to go back to the magazine.

1912   *Alexander's Bridge* published as *Alexander's Masquerade* in *McClure's* in three installments beginning in February. Ferris Greenslet accepts the novel for Houghton Mifflin, and it appears in May (under original title) to mixed reviews, most critics noting its indebtedness to Henry James. Brings "The Bohemian Girl" to Cameron Mackenzie, new managing editor at *McClure's*, who offers $750 for the story; Cather accepts only $500, the standard payment during her editorship. After several weeks of illness leaves in March to visit brother Douglass in Winslow, Arizona, and spends the next few months exploring the Southwest—the beginning of a strong attachment to this region. Visits Indian ruins, explores canyons and cliff dwellings, and attends a Hopi snake dance. Becomes infatuated with young Mexican man living in Winslow and writes to Elizabeth Sergeant describing his beauty and elegance. Spends June in Nebraska where she sees the wheat harvest for the first time in several years. Stays with the McClungs in Pittsburgh through the fall, writing short story "The White Mulberry Tree," then combining it with "Alexandra" to form basis of *O Pioneers!*

1913   January, returns to New York and moves with Edith Lewis into seven-room apartment at 5 Bank Street. They hire Josephine Bourda, a Frenchwoman, to cook and keep house for them. Begins ghost-writing S. S. McClure's autobiography, working from his spoken reminiscences. June, *O Pioneers!*, dedicated to Sarah Orne Jewett, published by Houghton Mifflin Company to enthusiastic critical reception. Travels to childhood home in Virginia with Isabelle McClung in September and spends the fall in Pittsburgh working on *The Song of the Lark*. *My Autobiography*, credited solely to McClure, runs in *McClure's* from October to May 1914 (published as a book by Frederick A. Stokes Co. in September 1914). Returns to New York in November. Interviews (for *McClure's*) and becomes friends with Wagnerian soprano Olive Fremstad.

1914   Hospitalized in February for blood poisoning resulting
        from hat-pin scratch. Spends most of the year in Pitts-
        burgh writing *The Song of the Lark*, with summer visits to
        Olive Fremstad in Maine and to Nebraska and the South-
        west.

1915   Saddened by Annie Fields' death in February. Continues
        working on *The Song of the Lark* and sends most of the
        manuscript to Ferris Greenslet at Houghton Mifflin in
        March. Spends summer in the Southwest with Edith
        Lewis, traveling to Mesa Verde, Taos, and Santa Fe, and
        returns to Pittsburgh in the fall. Judge McClung dies in
        October and Cather stays with Isabelle through the win-
        ter. *The Song of the Lark* published by Houghton Mifflin
        in October to good reviews, including H. L. Mencken's
        announcement that "Miss Cather, indeed, here steps defi-
        nitely into the small class of American novelists who are
        seriously to be reckoned with."

1916   Isabelle McClung marries violinist Jan Hambourg in
        April. Cather is surprised and devastated. "The Book-
        keeper's Wife" published in the May *Century* and "The
        Diamond Mine" in the October *McClure's*. Signs with lit-
        erary agent Paul Reynolds and resolves to let him handle
        placement of short fiction and serialization. Accompanied
        by Edith Lewis, returns to Santa Fe and Taos in the sum-
        mer and goes alone to visit brother Roscoe in Wyoming,
        stopping off in Red Cloud on the way east. Returns to
        Bank Street in fall and works on *My Ántonia*. Commis-
        sions artist W. T. Benda to do the illustrations and con-
        sults with him frequently. Fights to keep illustrations
        when Houghton Mifflin balks at their cost.

1917   "A Gold Slipper" appears in the January *Century*. Visits
        Lincoln in June to accept first honorary degree, a Doctor
        of Letters from the University of Nebraska (others hon-
        ored include fellow graduates Roscoe Pound and General
        Pershing). Visits Isabelle and Jan Hambourg at the Shat-
        tuck Inn in Jaffrey, New Hampshire, and stays through
        the summer and fall, working on *My Ántonia* in a tent
        pitched in a meadow.

1918   Ill for several weeks in January and February; progress on
        My Ántonia slows. "Ardessa" appears in the May *Century*.

painted by Léon Bakst; finds it unflattering. *A Lost Lady*
published by Alfred A. Knopf in September, and by December is in sixth printing (50,000 copies). *One of Ours*
has four additional printings (20,400 copies). Earns
$19,000 in royalties from Knopf for year.

1924   Knopf sells film rights to *A Lost Lady* to Warner Brothers
for $12,000. Cather agrees to edit a two-volume collection
of Sarah Orne Jewett's fiction for Houghton Mifflin.
Meets D. H. Lawrence, who comes to Bank Street for tea.
June, receives honorary degree from the University of
Michigan. Summers on Grand Manan and goes to Jaffrey
in the fall. Works on the Jewett edition and *The Professor's
House*. Introduction to Daniel Defoe's *The Fortunate Mistress* appears in new Knopf edition.

1925   Film version of *A Lost Lady* opens. Dismayed, Cather re-
solves never to permit another screen adaptation of her
work. "Uncle Valentine" serialized, beginning in the February *Woman's Home Companion*. March, attends birthday
dinner for Robert Frost in New York and presents him
with copy of the recently published *The Best Short Stories
of Sarah Orne Jewett*. April, receives letter from F. Scott
Fitzgerald informing her that similar passages concerning
the heroine's attractiveness in *A Lost Lady* and *The Great
Gatsby* suggest a "case of apparent plagiarism," but that he
had written his before reading her novel. Cather replies
that she finds no cause for suspicion. "Katherine Mans-
field" appears in *The Borzoi, 1925*, collection of essays published by Knopf. Works on *My Mortal Enemy*. Writes
introductions to Gertrude Hall's *The Wagnerian Romances*
and the Knopf edition of Stephen Crane's *Wounds in the
Rain*. *The Professor's House* serialized in *Collier's* beginning
in June and published by Knopf in September. Buys a
mink coat with *Collier's* money and tells a friend that "her
professor" has made the purchase. Travels with Edith
Lewis to the Southwest for the summer. Stays in Mabel
Dodge Luhan's guest house in Taos for two weeks and
visits D. H. and Frieda Lawrence on their ranch. Reads
Father W. J. Howlett's *Life of the Right Reverend Joseph P.
Machebeuf*, biography of 19th-century French missionary
in the Southwest. Spends fall in Jaffrey working on *Death
Comes for the Archbishop*, drawn in part from Howlett's
book. Has cottage built for her on Grand Manan.

1926   Revises introduction to *My Ántonia* for new edition pub-
        lished by Houghton Mifflin. Returns with Edith Lewis to
        New Mexico for the summer. Visits Acoma and the Mesa
        Encantada and stays in Mary Austin's house in Santa Fe.
        Stops in Red Cloud to visit her sick mother on the way
        home. Works on *Death Comes for the Archbishop* in July
        while in residence at the MacDowell Colony in Peterboro,
        New Hampshire. Spends fall in Jaffrey. *My Mortal Enemy*
        published by Knopf in October. Finishes *Death Comes for
        the Archbishop* and obtains from Knopf one-time increase
        in royalties from 15 to 16 percent.

1927   *Death Comes for the Archbishop* serialized in *The Forum* Jan-
        uary–June, published by Knopf in September. Summer
        trip through Big Horn Mountains in Wyoming is cut
        short when father suffers severe attack of angina; returns
        to New York after visit to Red Cloud. Moves with Edith
        Lewis to the Grosvenor Hotel, 35 Fifth Avenue, when
        Bank Street apartment house is torn down. (Intends stay
        to be temporary, but lives there for five years.) Spends the
        fall in Jaffrey and returns to Red Cloud for Christmas.

1928   Returns to New York in late February. Father dies of
        heart attack, March 3. Travels to Red Cloud for the fu-
        neral and stays several weeks, experiencing, along with
        grief, renewed sense of connection to her family and past.
        Returns to New York in late April after stopping off at
        the Mayo Clinic for treatment. Writes story "Neighbour
        Rosicky." Becomes ill with influenza. June, receives hon-
        orary degree from Columbia University. Spends summer
        on Grand Manan. Rereads Francis Parkman's histories
        during visit to Quebec City with Edith Lewis and meets
        Abbé Henri Arthur Scott, Canadian ecclesiastical histo-
        rian. Fall, begins *Shadows on the Rock* in New York. Re-
        turns to Quebec at Thanksgiving for two weeks of further
        research on Frontenac era. Marjorie Anderson dies and is
        buried in the Cather family plot. December, mother has
        paralytic stroke while staying with family in California.

1929   Spends spring in Long Beach, California, with her
        mother, who is partially paralyzed and unable to speak.
        Tries to work on *Shadows on the Rock* but finds concentra-
        tion difficult due to intense distress over mother's condi-
        tion. Elected to National Institute of Arts and Letters.

June, receives honorary degree from Yale University. Visits
Quebec and spends summer on Grand Manan. Goes to
Jaffrey in fall, then returns to New York before spending
Christmas in Quebec.

1930   Visits mother, now in Pasadena sanatorium, in the spring.
"Neighbor Rosicky" serialized in the *Woman's Home Companion* (April–May). Sails for France in May with Edith
Lewis. Stays with the Hambourgs in Paris and tours Brittany with them. Introduced by Jan Hambourg to Moshe
and Marutha Menuhin and their children Yehudi, Heph-
zibah, and Yaltah. Meets and talks with Madame Franklin
Grout, Flaubert's niece, in hotel dining room in Aix-les-
Bains (reminiscence of encounter, "A Chance Meeting,"
appears in February 1933 *Atlantic Monthly*). Sails to Quebec in September and spends most of fall there and in
Jaffrey. November, awarded Howells Medal for Fiction by
the American Academy of Arts and Letters for *Death
Comes for the Archbishop*. December, finishes *Shadows on the
Rock*.

1931   Spends spring in Pasadena with mother; writes "Two
Friends." Receives honorary degrees from the University
of California at Berkeley and from Princeton University.
Spends summer on Grand Manan. Writes "Old Mrs. Harris," featuring characters based on grandmother, mother,
and herself. Mother dies August 30. Cather is unable to
leave Grand Manan in time to attend funeral; writes Dorothy Canfield: "I feel a good deal like a ghost." *Shadows
on the Rock* published in August by Knopf. Reviews are
unenthusiastic, but sales reach 160,000 by Christmas.
Travels to Red Cloud for family reunion at Christmas (her
last visit to Nebraska); continues to send money and food
to several local farm families severely affected by the
Depression. (Will also contribute regularly to fund for
support of now-destitute S. S. McClure, organized by Ida
Tarbell.)

1932   "Two Friends" appears in the July *Woman's Home Companion*. Refuses Houghton Mifflin permission to sell film
rights to *The Song of the Lark*. "Old Mrs. Harris" (under
title "Three Women") serialized in the *Ladies' Home Journal*, September–November. Vacations on Grand Manan in
summer, stays at Jaffrey in fall. *Obscure Destinies*, collection

comprised of "Neighbour Rosicky," "Old Mrs. Harris,"
and "Two Friends," published by Knopf in August.
Friendship deepens with Menuhin children, who regard
her as "Aunt Willa"; reads Shakespeare, walks in Central
Park with them. December, moves to new apartment at
570 Park Avenue despite continuing unhappiness with
New York (remains in city partially because of Edith
Lewis's job as copywriter at J. Walter Thompson advertising agency); encouraged by Josephine Bourda's return as
housekeeper and cook (works for Cather until her return
to France in 1935).

1933   Wins first Prix Femina Américain, prestigious French literary award, for *Shadows on the Rock*, after being nomi-
nated by panel of American women writers and literary
figures. Begins work on *Lucy Gayheart*. June, receives honorary degree from Smith College. Spends summer on
Grand Manan and fall in Jaffrey. Enjoys visit during island
stay from niece Mary Virginia Auld, daughter of sister Jessica. Sprains tendons in right wrist, which becomes chron-
ically inflamed (inflammation later spreads to left hand).
Condition, which persists for remainder of her life, often
necessitates an immobilizing brace and drastically inter-
feres with writing of fiction, since she finds it impossible
to dictate anything except correspondence.

1934   Finishes *Lucy Gayheart* in spring. Spends summer on
Grand Manan, and at Jaffrey, in fall, begins short story
"The Golden Wedding." Angered by new Warner Brothers film version of *A Lost Lady*, begins to take legal measures to prevent further screen adaptations of her work
(eventually writes prohibitory provision into will). Sells
serial rights to *Lucy Gayheart* to raise money for friends in
Nebraska.

1935   *Lucy Gayheart* serialized in *Woman's Home Companion*
March–July, published by Knopf in August. Reviewers
accuse Cather of "supine romanticism" and criticize her
for ignoring contemporary social problems. March, Isabelle Hambourg arrives in the United States, seriously ill
with kidney disease. Cather visits her daily in hospital in
New York for three weeks. Goes to Chicago with the
Hambourgs in late spring; after six weeks in Italy with
Edith Lewis during summer, rejoins Hambourgs after

their return to France. Stays with them in Paris for two months. November, returns to New York.

1936 Spends summer on Grand Manan entertaining nieces Mary Virginia Auld and Margaret and Elizabeth (Roscoe Cather's twin daughters). *Not Under Forty*, collection of essays on literature, published by Knopf in November. In introduction expressing alienation from modern American life since the war, writes "the world broke in two in 1922 or thereabouts" and that she belongs to the former half. Writes "The Old Beauty" in autumn.

1937 Spends year helping Houghton Mifflin prepare the Library Edition of her collected works. Eliminates all stories before *Youth and the Bright Medusa*, and *O Pioneers!* becomes Volume I. Extensively cuts *The Song of the Lark*, which appears as Volume II, and places *Alexander's Bridge* and *April Twilights* together as Volume III. (Twelve volumes published by 1938.) Vacations on Grand Manan with nieces. When "The Old Beauty" is accepted by *Woman's Home Companion* without enthusiasm, Cather withdraws manuscript and makes no further attempt to arrange magazine publication. Begins work on *Sapphira and the Slave Girl* in fall, drawing heavily upon childhood memories and family stories from Virginia. Douglass Cather visits on her birthday.

1938–39 Hand injury recurs. Develops friendship with young British aristocrat and writer Stephen Tennant. In the spring visits Virginia childhood home with Edith Lewis. Elected to American Academy of Arts and Letters. Greatly distraught at deaths of brother Douglass in June and Isabelle Hambourg in October. Writes to Zoë Akins: "I think people often write books for just one person, and for me Isabelle was that person." Spends fall in Jaffrey but has trouble writing and is distressed at damage done to woods by recent hurricane. Works on *Sapphira* in New York into July of 1939, unwilling to interrupt work for a vacation.

1940 Deeply dismayed by surrender of French Army in June. September, finishes *Sapphira and the Slave Girl* while on Grand Manan. Writes Canfield: "I cannot tell you how much pleasure I had in listening to those voices which had been nonexistent for me for so many years, when other sounds silenced them." Develops friendship with Norwegian novelist Sigrid Undset (that "undaunted exile") after introduction by Alfred and Blanche Knopf. *Sapphira and the Slave Girl* published by Knopf on birthday. Spends Christmas holidays in the French Hospital in New York for treatment of right hand.

1941   Travels to San Francisco in spring to see brother Roscoe, who is recovering from a heart attack. Visits Victoria, British Columbia, and returns home by the Canadian Pacific Railroad. Begins novel set in Avignon, France. (Works on it intermittently over several years but is unable to make progress due to recurring hand pain and other health problems.) Enters the French Hospital in New York for week of rest in autumn.

1942   July, has gall bladder and appendix removed at Presbyterian Hospital. Recovers from operation but never regains full health. Fall, spends several weeks at the Williams Inn in Williamstown, Massachusetts, registered as "Miss Carter" to protect privacy. Follows war news closely and is deeply distressed by sense that civilization is crumbling.

1943   Unable to travel to Grand Manan due to war conditions. Spends summer (and the three succeeding) at the Asticou Inn on Mount Desert, an island off Maine. Receives hundreds of letters from servicemen reading her books in special armed forces editions and tries to answer some of them.

1944   Writes "Before Breakfast." Receives Gold Medal of the National Institute of Arts and Letters. Embraces S. S. McClure, now 87, during ceremony.

1945   Writes story "The Best Years" during summer in Maine (appears with "The Old Beauty" and "Before Breakfast" in *The Old Beauty and Others*, published by Knopf in 1948). Brother Roscoe dies.

1946   Writes Zoë Akins of her physical and spiritual weakness since Roscoe's death. Has influenza in spring and spends month in Atlantic City convalescing. Informs Houghton

Reynolds, her agent, sold the serial rights to *Collier's* for $10,000. The novel, heavily edited and truncated, appeared in nine installments in the June 6, 13, 20, 27, July 4, 11, 18, 25, and August 1 numbers of the magazine. Cather finished reading the proofs for the book version by the end of June, and it was published on September 4, 1925. The first printing of 20,000 copies (plus 225 copies signed by Cather) was shipped on August 7; a second printing of 10,000 copies soon followed. By late October, 55,000 copies had been sold. Cather made a few revisions in the Autograph Edition of the novel, brought out by Houghton Mifflin in 1938, but most of the differences between the two editions were caused by the imposition of the Houghton Mifflin house style. None of the revisions for the Autograph Edition was included in the ninth printing of the first edition in 1942, although in that printing Cather changed Tom Outland's "bulkheaded vacuum" to "Outland engine," and "vacuum" to either "engine" or "patent." Though these later revisions, reflecting the difference in aircraft terminology in 1942 from what it was in 1925, were probably made by Cather, she no doubt was acting on someone else's suggestion. Another change in the first edition was made in 1949 in the 10th printing, when the dedication to Jan Hambourg was deleted. This volume prints the text of the first edition, first printing.

Cather's work on *Death Comes for the Archbishop* began soon after her return to New York from New Mexico in the fall of 1925. By the end of April 1926, before going once more to New Mexico, she had finished half the novel, and on her return to New York in July she met with her agent Paul Reynolds and Henry Leach, editor of *The Forum*, to discuss terms for serialization. In September a final agreement was reached: *The Forum* would begin serialization of the novel in January 1927, using about three-fourths of the text divided into six installments, for each of which Cather would receive $500. The last installment was sent by Cather to *The Forum* before Christmas 1926; the novel was serialized from January through June 1927. The sections omitted in the magazine version were all of Book Five, "Padre Martinez," part one of Book Seven, "The Month of Mary," and part one of Book Eight, "Cathedral." Other lines were dropped, and there are numerous differences in wording, punctuation, and spelling from the book version. Cather read proofs for Knopf while the novel was running in *The Forum*. Three printings were shipped before the publication date of September 2, 1927: the first of 25,000 copies in July, of which 20,000 were immediately bound and the remaining 5,000 bound by August 5; a second printing was completed on August 11; and a third printing was completed on August 19 (an error was corrected in this printing). All together, 34 printings were made from the first-edition plates, including four in the Modern Library series, the last of which was made in 1934. An illustrated second edition was published by Knopf on November 9, 1929, but no revisions were made in this edition until the fifth printing in May 1940, when Cather inserted many of the changes she had earlier made in the Autograph Edition of the novel, published by Houghton Mifflin in 1938. Most of the differences between the first edition and the Autograph Edition reflect the house style preferences at Houghton Mifflin, but other changes were made because of technical errors pointed out to Cather by others, such as the description of water in an open trough traveling up an arroyo, or errors of fact, such as the correct site of the gold rush that took place in the period covered by the novel. A fourth edition, the paperback Armed Services edition, was published in 1943 and was based on the fifth printing of the second Knopf edition, which had incorporated the revisions made in the Autograph Edition, but Cather took no part in it. A fifth edition was published by Knopf in January 1945, incorporating some of the corrections from the Autograph Edition (the water in the open trough going uphill and the site of the gold rush), with a few additional revisions, but basically following the first edition text. This is the edition from which all subsequent printings and editions are drawn. Because the first printing of the first edition, published by Knopf in September 1927, is closest to Cather's own style, that text is printed here, and some of the revisions are included in the notes to this volume.

Soon after visiting Quebec City in the summer of 1928, Cather began working on *Shadows on the Rock*, and she completed it late in 1930. The novel was not serialized. She began reading proofs for the book early in 1931 in New York City and finished reading them in California in March. The book was published by Alfred A. Knopf on August 1, 1931. Two printings, a first of 25,700 copies and a second of 40,000, were printed in June for Knopf, and 51,800 were printed for the Book-of-the-Month Club. By the end of the year more than 167,600 copies had been shipped. Cather did not make corrections in later printings of this edition, and she made very few when she prepared the novel for the Autograph Edition, published by Houghton Mifflin in 1938. Almost all of the differences between the two editions are again caused by the imposing of the Houghton Mifflin house style. The first book edition is printed here.

Cather started work on *Lucy Gayheart* in the spring of 1933 and completed it in July 1934. Because she wanted the extra money she could earn by having the novel serialized, Cather postponed book publication until after it had appeared in *The Woman's Home Companion* from March through June 1935. There are numerous differences between the serial version and the book version, many of these caused by the editorial practices of the magazine. As usual, Cather gave more attention to the preparation of the book version. *Lucy Gayheart* was published by Alfred A. Knopf on August 1, 1935. The first printing of 25,000 copies and the second printing of 27,500 copies were printed and bound at the same time; the second printing has a notice on the copyright page that the first and second printings took place before publication. No corrections were made in later printings of the first edition, and no substantive changes were made in the Autograph Edition, published by Houghton Mifflin in 1938. The text of the first book edition is printed here.

Cather began writing *Sapphira and the Slave Girl* in the spring of 1937 but had to put it aside to work on the Autograph Edition for Houghton Mifflin. After visiting in May 1938 the sites in Virginia where the novel is set, her work on it was again interrupted by the deaths of her brother Douglass and her friend Isabelle McClung Hambourg. She resumed work on the novel in the summer of 1939 and was able to finish it in August 1940. The novel was not serialized, and in September she read proofs. The book was published on her birthday, December 7, 1940, by Alfred A. Knopf in a first

printing of 50,000 copies. The Book-of-the-Month Club dis-
tributed nearly 220,000 copies in January, and by March 15,
1941, Alfred Knopf reported that more than 65,000 copies had
been sold to the trade. A new edition of *Sapphira and the
Slave Girl* was published by Houghton Mifflin in 1941 for inclusion in the Autograph Edition of Cather's works, but
Cather herself does not seem to have made any revisions for
this edition; the differences between the first and second editions are confined to Houghton Mifflin's usual changes in
punctuation, spelling, and capitalization. The text of the first
edition is printed here.

This volume presents the texts of the original printings
chosen for inclusion here but does not attempt to reproduce
features of their typographic design, such as the display
capitalization of chapter openings. The texts are printed without change, except for the correction of typographical errors.
Spelling, punctuation, and capitalization are often expressive
features, and they are not altered, even when inconsistent or
irregular. The following is a list of typographical errors corrected, cited by page and line number: 70.22, Dalzell's; 87.24,
altogether.; 97.7, every-; 127.30, Applehoff; 128.1, Applehoff;
163.7, pompuosity; 166.36, moved; 174.21, Agusta; 196.9,
worldiness; 205.7, come; 252.1, VI; 288.37, happned; 311.14,
suppper; 436.6, From; 471.24, your; 515.13, Auclaire's; 621.33,
hay-bale; 662.15, peoples'; 671.25, Or; 822.31, Moses; 866.2,
Zack.

Notes

In the notes that follow, the reference numbers denote page and line of this volume (the line count includes chapter headings). No note is made for material found in a standard desk-reference book. Quotations from Shakespeare have been keyed to *The Riverside Shakespeare*, ed. G. Blakemore Evans (Boston: Houghton Mifflin, 1974). Notes at the foot of the page in the text are Cather's own. For more detailed notes, references to other studies, and further biographical background than is included in the Chronology, see: E. K. Brown and Leon Edel, *Willa Cather* (New York: Alfred A. Knopf, Inc., 1953; Avon Books, 1980); Joan Crane, *Willa Cather: A Bibliography* (Lincoln: University of Nebraska Press, 1982); Sharon O'Brien, *Willa Cather: The Emerging Voice* (New York: Oxford University Press, 1987); James Woodress, *Willa Cather: A Literary Life* (Lincoln: University of Nebraska Press, 1987).

A LOST LADY

1.2–4   " . . . *Come,* . . . *night.*"]   *Hamlet* IV.v.71–73.

2.2   *Jan Hambourg*]   The husband of Cather's friend Isabelle McClung Hambourg.

11.23–24   Some . . . *Companion*]   The popular children's magazine (1827–1929) founded by Nathaniel Willis began in 1867 to offer a large choice of "premium gifts," such as magic lanterns, chemistry sets, printing presses, and boxes of tools, to readers for selling new subscriptions.

14.34   "St. Elmo."]   Best-selling romantic novel (1867) by Augusta Jane Evans (1835–1909).

16.12–13   democrat wagon]   A light, high cart with several seats, one behind the other, often drawn by two horses.

41.26   glittering . . . Mariner's]   Cf. "The Rime of the Ancient Mariner" (1798), lines 3, 13, 228, by Samuel Taylor Coleridge (1772–1834).

44.11   Bohn classics]   The Classical Library, a series published by British bookseller Henry George Bohn (1796–1884).

44.18–22   Byron . . . Meister"]   The poem "Don Juan" (1819–24), considered scandalous during the Victorian period because of its overt sexuality and frequently expurgated or left out of collected editions of Byron's work; *The History of Tom Jones* (1749), a novel by Henry Fielding (1707–54), and *Wilhelm Meister* (1795–1829) by Goethe (1749–1832).

44.35   *Heroides*]   Also known as the *Epistulae Heroidum* (*Letters of*

then in the museum there, tells the story of William (1028–87) of Normandy's conquest of England. According to legend, it was made by his wife, Queen Matilda (d. 1083), and her handmaids.

160.35   *L'Espoir*]   Hope.

161.15   *Matrimonio Segreto*]   *The Secret Marriage*, a comic opera in two acts by Domenico Cimarosa (1749–1801), first performed in Vienna in 1792.

162.33   *haricots verts*]   Green beans.

165.22–29   *Æneid . . . dolorem,"*]   Aeneas's response (Book 2, line 3) to Dido's request to hear the story of his travels: "Queen, you ask me to renew unspeakable grief."

166.10   Fray Marcos]   Marcos de Niza (c. 1495–1558), a Franciscan missionary and explorer, served in Mexico and led expeditions to New Mexico and Arizona (1539–40).

166.36   "mover people"]   People migrating westward.

172.17   Five Hundred]   A card game usually played by three people.

173.10   no . . . Medea's,]   In the Greek legend and in Euripedes' tragedy, Medea, betrayed by Jason, kills their two children.

176.17–18   wooden . . . other.]   *Amis et Amile*, a 12th-century French chanson de geste, is concerned with the devotion of two friends.

178.20–21   *The Pit . . . Pendulum.*]   A short story (1843) by Edgar Allan Poe (1809–49).

179.22   vacuum]   Changed to "patent" in the ninth printing. Later reference also changed, page 187.24 in this volume.

189.33   *My . . . men.*]   *Antony and Cleopatra* IV .v.16–17.

192.29–30   hurt . . . heir to.]   Cf. *Hamlet* III.i.61–62.

195.37   *Beaux-fils*]   Sons-in-law.

206.14   *saignant,*]   Bloody, rare.

212.14   hanging . . . Chicago]   During what came to be known as the Haymarket Riot (May 4, 1886), a crowd assembled in Chicago's Haymarket Square to protest the police shooting of several striking laborers the previous day. A bomb was thrown, rioting ensued, and seven policemen and four workers were killed. Although the bomb-thrower was not found, Judge Joseph Gary sentenced eight men to death for inciting violence. Four were hanged, one committed suicide, and the remaining three were pardoned in 1893 by the new governor, John P. Altgeld, who called the trial unjust.

212.26–27   *Robinson . . . Travels*]   *The Life and strange and surprising Ad-*

ventures of Robinson Crusoe (1719) by Daniel Defoe (1660–1731) and *Gulliver's Travels* (1726) by Jonathan Swift (1667–1745).

254.19   grotto . . . spring] The nymph's grotto on the African shore where Aeneas and his Trojan sailors find shelter in Book I., lines 166–68.

255.23   "an extravagant . . . stranger."] *Othello* I.i.136.

255.25–26   *"He . . . them!"*] Cf. Psalm 39:6.

256.20   Fray Garces' manuscript] *Diario y Derrotero* (1777) (*Diary of a Way of Life*) of Father Garces (1738–81), a Franciscan missionary and martyr killed by the Yuma Indians on the banks of the Colorado River.

264.31–34   For . . . camest.] Cf. Henry Wadsworth Longfellow's translation from the Anglo-Saxon, "The Grave": "For thee was a house built / Ere thou wast born, / For thee a mould meant / Ere thou of mother camest."

265.28   *Berengaria*] An ocean liner, originally named the *Impereator*, built in 1912 for the Hamburg-American line and then ceded by Germany to Britain in 1920. Rechristened the *Berengaria* by the Cunard and White Star Lines, the ship sailed the Southampton–Cherbourg–New York route until 1938. Willa Cather was one of its passengers.

DEATH COMES FOR THE ARCHBISHOP

On November 23, 1927, Cather wrote the following letter to *Commonweal*, a Catholic magazine:

To the editor of *The Commonweal:*— You have asked me to give you a short account of how I happened to write *Death Comes for the Archbishop*.

When I first went into the Southwest some fifteen years ago, I stayed there for a considerable period of time. It was then much harder to get about than it is today. There were no automobile roads and no hotels off the main lines of railroad. One had to travel by wagon and carry a camp outfit. One travelled slowly, and had plenty of time for reflection. It was then very difficult to find anyone who would tell me anything about the country, or even about the roads. One of the most intelligent and inspiriting persons I found in my travels was a Belgian priest, Father Haltermann, who lived with his sister in the parsonage behind the beautiful old church at Santa Cruz, New Mexico, where he raised fancy poultry and sheep and had a wonderful vegetable and flower garden. He was a florid, full-bearded farmer priest, who drove about among his eighteen Indian missions with a spring wagon and a pair of mules. He knew a great deal about the country and the Indians and their traditions. He went home during the war to serve as a chaplain in the French Army, and when I last heard of him he was an invalid.

The longer I stayed in the Southwest, the more I felt that the story of the Catholic Church in that country was the most interesting of all its stories. The old mission churches, even those which were abandoned and in ruins,

duction of tithing and resigned his office in 1856 but continued to act unofficially as pastor. Excommunicated by Lamy in 1858, he headed a schismatic church until his death.

295.11   *CHEZ LUI*]   At his home.

298.10–11   *Ave Maris Stella*]   "Hail, Star of the Sea," a hymn to the Virgin Mary traditionally associated with the feast of the Annunciation (March 25).

298.15–16   *Monseigneur . . . bougies.*]   Monseigneur is served! So, Jean, will you bring the candles.

299.29–30   *soupiàre . . . pommes sautées*]   Soup-tureen; sautéed potatoes.

300.32   *Festina lente.*]   "Make haste slowly." From Suetonius (fl. A.D. 120), *Divus Augustus*, 25.

302.7–8   St. John Lateran]   Now officially called the Basilica of the Savior, but still known as the Lateran; one of the principal basilicas of Rome and the residence of the popes before the papacy moved from Rome to Avignon in 1307.

303.39   Guadaloupe]   The spelling is changed to "Guadalupe" throughout the text in both the Autograph Edition and the fifth edition.

305.21   shrine . . . Spain]   In Guadalupe, Extremadura, west-central Spain. The cult was transferred to Mexico after the apparitions to Juan Diego, and Our Lady of Guadalupe Hidalgo was declared patron of New Spain by Pope Benedict XIV in 1754.

310.1   *sala*]   Living, or drawing, room.

315.37   Puy-de-Dôm]   The spelling is changed throughout the text to "Puy-de-Dôme" in all the later versions.

324.5–6   Sisters of Loretto]   An order founded in Ireland in 1822.

325.8   Plenary . . . Baltimore]   The first of three in Baltimore, convened in 1852. Plenary Councils, composed of bishops and other territorial church leaders (ordinaries) called by the Holy See, are legislative bodies whose acts must be agreed to by the Vatican and are valid for the territories that the ordinaries oversee.

325.28   Padre Gallegos]   José Manuel Gallegos (1815–75), religious and political leader, served in the Nuevo Mexico Assembly 1843–46. Excommunicated by Bishop Lamy for concubinage, he devoted himself to political causes and was elected as the territorial representative to the U.S. House of Representatives in 1853. His re-election in 1855 was challenged and the seat awarded in 1856 to Miguel Otero, a political associate of Lamy.

335.31–33   rock . . . armour.]   Half the population of the Ácoma pueblo was killed and part of their village burned when an outbreak against the Spanish was subdued in 1599.

335.38–39   Christ . . . Church.] Matthew 16:18–19.

336.1–2   Hebrews . . . God.] Cf., for example, 2 Samuel 22:2, 32; Psalms 18:2, 31, 46; 42:9.

336.36–38   Creation . . . confusion.] Cf. Genesis 1:1–13.

342.31–32   St. John's Day.] The Feast of Saint John the Baptist, June 24.

345.30   great . . . 1680] The revolt of Pueblo Indians, led by Popé, a medicine man of the San Juan tribe, against the Spanish conquerors and missionaries who were forcibly suppressing native religious practices. Killing more than 400 colonists and 21 Franciscan missionaries, the Pueblos forced the Spanish to retreat from Santa Fe to El Paso and remained independent until the Spanish returned in the 1690s.

350.9   *Trompe-la-Morte*] Death's cheat.

361.19–22   Padre . . . murder] Martinez, cooperating with the U.S. government, helped suppress the anti-American uprising of 1847. The court-martial of the leaders was held in his home.

366.38   bloody . . . Penitentes] The Brotherhood of Penitents, a lay religious society active in New Mexico and southern Colorado, is distinguished by its painful penitential rites. Holy Week ceremonies include flagellation with cactus whips and the bearing of crosses. It was condemned by the archbishop of Santa Fe in 1889.

368.11   surplices] Changed to "cassocks" in later versions.

369.18   estufa] An underground chamber in which a fire is kept constantly burning, where the Pueblo Indian men assemble for social, communal, or religious purposes.

376.13   *à fouetter les chats*] To stir up the cats.

378.15–24   Its original . . . that.] The Autograph Edition corrects to: "Its original source was so high, indeed, that by merely laying a closed wooden trough up the face of the cliff, the Mexicans conveyed the water some hundreds of feet to an open ditch at the top of the precipice. Father Vaillant had often stopped to watch the imprisoned water leaping out into the light like a thing alive, just where the steep trail down into the Hondo began." The passage differs from this in minor ways in other corrected editions.

381.11   *Asperges . . . mundabor.*] "Sprinkle me, Lord, with hyssop, and I shall be cleansed," a reminder of baptism.

393.37–38   *Ah . . . oui!*] Ah, my father, I would much rather be young and poor than old and rich, yes, indeed!

394.4   *Assez*] Enough.

396.13–14   *"Listen . . . mocking-bird!"*]   Song written by Septimus Winner (1827–1902) under the pen name Alice Hawthorne.

397.7   Gadsden Purchase]   Wedge of territory, 45,535 square miles in area, now the southernmost regions of New Mexico and Arizona, purchased from Mexico in 1853 for $10 million.

399.32   *Alma Mater redemptoris!*]   "Kind Mother of the Redeemer."

402.6   *Unless . . . children*]   Matthew 18.3.

408.35–36   Sacrament]   Changed to "Sacrifice" in later versions.

409.27–28   *And . . . Heaven.*]   Cf. Matthew 18:4, 19:30, 20:16; Luke 9:48.

423.5   old . . . Avignon]   Gothic palace built as papal residence during the location of the papacy in Avignon, 1309–77.

425.23   Pike's Peak]   In 1850, gold was discovered at Ralston Creek near what is now Denver, and in 1858 prospecting began in the region. Some gold was found in Cherry Creek, and in the winter of 1858–59, exaggerated accounts of the discovery appeared in the press, and the rush to find gold began. Although the area was 75 miles from Pike's Peak, it was the best known landmark and the region was called "Pike's Peak Gold Country." In May 1859, the first rich gold vein was found in the mountains at what is now Central City.

425.30   Cripple Creek]   Changed to "Cherry Creek" in later versions. The gold strike at Cripple Creek occurred in 1891.

425.35   war in Italy]   In January 1859 France and Piedmont formed an alliance directed against Austrian rule in northern Italy. Austria responded by declaring war in April 1859, but was defeated twice during the summer and ceded most of Lombardy to Piedmont in November 1859. Austria's defeat undermined its influence throughout Italy, and in 1860–61 Piedmont annexed, through war, diplomacy, and plebiscites, extensive territory, including almost all of the Papal States, leading to the establishment of the Kingdom of Italy in 1861. French intervention preserved papal rule in Rome and the surrounding coastal plain until 1870, when France's defeat in the Franco-Prussian War permitted Italy to occupy Rome. Pius XI, however, refused to recognize the Italian government and considered himself "imprisoned" in the Vatican until his death in 1878.

426.4–6   Frémont . . . horses.]   The Western explorer John Charles Frémont (1813–90) led an expedition into the San Juan Mountains of Colorado during the harsh winter of 1848–49 in an attempt to find passes for a possible southern railway route to California. Eleven men died and the rest found their way back to Taos in small groups, where Kit Carson helped them recover.

426.8   near Cripple Creek]   Changed to "along Cherry Creek" in the Autograph Edition and the second edition, fifth printing, and the Knopf fifth edition.

426.13   Cripple Creek]   Changed to "Colorado" in editions and printing noted above.

426.16   Cherry Creek]   Changed to "Denver City" in editions and printing noted above.

427.29–30   consecration . . . hands]   During the ordination service, the priest's hands are anointed.

429.6   breviary . . . Mass]   Changed to "breviary and his missal" in the Autograph Edition and the fifth printing of the second edition. Omitted in the fifth edition.

430.7   at Cripple Creek]   Corrected to "on Cherry Creek" in all later versions.

432.16   *le rêve . . . chair*]   The highest dream of the flesh.

433.32   preservation . . . Raphael]   The archangel Raphael, whose name means "God has healed," is the guide of Tobias in the Book of Tobit in the Apocrypha.

439.38   *Je . . . Fé.*]   I would like to die in Santa Fe.

440.19   *mon fils*]   My son.

442.4   Sangre de Cristo]   Blood of Christ.

445.30–31   *Hunger*, . . . Paul]   Cf. 1 Corinthians 4.11, 11.27

450.26   *Allons! . . . L'invitation du voyage!*]   Let's go! . . . The invitation to the journey!

SHADOWS ON THE ROCK

464.1–7   *Vous . . . 1653.*]   "You ask me for some flower seeds from this country. We have them sent from France for our garden, as those here are neither very rare nor very beautiful. Everything is wild here, the flowers as well as the men. Marie of the Incarnation (letter to one of her sisters), Quebec, 12 August, 1653." The mystic Marie de l'Incarnation (1599–1672), originally named Marie Guyard, one of the first woman missionaries to the New World, arrived in Quebec in 1639 and became the first mother superior of an

engrave this name forever in your heart and imprint it on your brow and I will preserve you from sudden death, as I do for all those who do the same.'"

520.23–24   Je . . . savez!]   I'm the mother, you know!

524.27–29   *"Priez . . . tré-pas-sés!"*]   Pray for the dead, you who rest, pray for the dead.

526.36   *Inferretque deos Latio*]   "And he brought his gods to Latium." *Aeneid*, Book I, line 6.

528.34   Saint Joachim]   Husband of Anne and father of the Virgin Mary.

529.15–16   Father Brébeuf, . . . Jogues]   Gabriel Lalemant (1610–49) was sent to Quebec in 1646 and served as assistant to Jean de Brébeuf (1593–1649) among the Hurons. The Jesuit missionaries were tortured to death by the Iroquois who attacked their village during their war on the Huron Nation (1648–49). Another Jesuit, Isaac Jogues (1607–46), who had also worked with Brébeuf, was captured by the Iroquois in 1642, tortured, and kept as a slave until his rescue in 1643. In 1646, while returning on a second visit after an earlier successful political mission to the Mohawks, he was killed by the Mohawk Clan of the Bear who believed a box he had left behind contained magic intended to harm them.

532.40–533.1   Regardez . . . mouton!]   Look, Ma'm'selle, a beautiful little donkey! . . . There's the beautiful sheep!

534.28   paroisse]   Parish church.

534.28–29   reveillon]   Christmas revels.

536.14   Non . . . toujours,]   No, it's for always.

536.20   C'est ça,]   That's so.

544.15–16   Henry . . . Paris]   Henry IV, King of France (1589–1610), besieged Paris May–August 1590, during the Wars of Religion. He was forced to retreat when the Spanish came to the aid of the Catholic League.

546.27–28   Jeanne . . . Montreal]   The recluse Jeanne Le Ber (1662–1714) entered a cell in the church of Notre Dame in 1695. She became known for her embroidery of church tapestries, altar cloths, and vestments.

547.40   Sainte Catherine of Siena]   The youngest child of a dyer in Siena, Tuscany, Catherine (1347?–80), against her parents' wishes, refused to marry and devoted herself to a life of prayer and penance at home. When she became a Dominican tertiary, she spent years in solitude before beginning her work in the world as a nurse, spiritual leader, and mediator of Church disputes. In 1970 she was declared a Doctor of the Church.

548.11–12   Sainte . . . Thebais]   Saint Mary of Egypt, a fifth-century penitent, probably legendary, who, after a divine vision, spent her life as a hermit in the desert.

550.20–24   *Ah, . . . l'univers.*]   Ah, my father, my chamber is my earthly paradise; it is my center; it is my element. There is no place sweeter or more salutary for me; neither the Louvre nor a palace would be more agreeable. I prefer my cell to all the rest of the universe.

552.24   *C'est . . . couleur,*]   It's pretty, the color.

552.28   *C'est . . . toujours,*]   It's peaceful at your home, as always.

556.34   *Courage, mon bourgeois*]   Courage, my good man.

560.12   the Tobacco nation]   The Tionnontates, belonging to a linguistic group that also included the Iroquois, the Hurons, and the Neutral Nation or Attionidarons, were called the Petun (Tobacco) nation by the French because they cultivated tobacco.

560.12–13   Father Charles Garnier]   Garnier (1605?–49), a Jesuit missionary, came to Quebec in 1636 and served in the Huron missions until he was killed by the Iroquois.

564.18   *Mais . . . ça,*]   But no, we are more tranquil like this.

565.35–36   *Sale . . . métier!*]   Dirty service . . . dirty trade.

567.2   *mousse*]   Ship's boy, cabin-boy.

568.23–25   Queen . . . *miserable*]   *Aeneid*, Book I, line 630: "Non ignara mali miseris succurrere disco."

571.23   *Je . . . toujours.*]   I am doing well, as always.

572.2   *tablier*]   Apron.

583.7–8   *à la campagnarde*]   Country-style.

586.27   sagamite]   A kind of porridge made from coarse hominy.

589.7   *tous les deux!*]   Both (all two).

593.9   *pays*]   Region.

594.38   Monsieur le Dauphin]   Louis, the Grand Dauphin (1661–1711), eldest son of Louis XIV and heir to the French throne.

594.39–40   Duc . . . Savoie]   Louis (1682–1712), son of the Grand Dauphin and grandson of Louis XIV, married Marie-Adélaide de Savoie (1685–1712) on December 7, 1697.

595.1   *mais baien sage*]   But very wise (i.e., good, grown-up).

595.1   The war . . . standstill;]   The War of the Grand Alliance (1688–97)—also known as the War of the League of Augsburg, and in the New World colonies as King William's War—between France and the League of

671.19–20   *Ecco . . . bella!*]   What a very beautiful thing!

681.26   *Die schöne Müllerin*]   *The Fair Maid of the Mill*, a song-cycle for male voice and piano composed by Schubert in 1823. The songs are settings of the cycle of poems by Wilhelm Müller.

686.27   *fare il cameriere*]   Be a waiter.

687.25   *Die Forelle*]   *The Trout.*

689.15   Opéra Comique]   The second opera house of Paris, home to the operatic genre *opéra comique*, a form that includes spoken dialogue and a wide variety of musical forms.

689.33–34   Macbeth's . . . *wife!*]   *Macbeth*, III.ii.36.

698.18–20   *She . . . cheek.*]   *Twelfth Night*, II.iv.110–113.

701.11   *Aida*]   Opera (1871) by Giuseppe Verdi (1813–1901).

701.27   *Otello*]   An opera (1816) by Rossini.

703.21–23   *Traviata . . . Lohengrin*]   *La Traviata* (1853) (*The Lady Gone Astray* or *The Fallen Woman*) by Verdi, and *Lohengrin* (1850) by Richard Wagner (1813–83).

703.28   *O Sole Mio!*]   "O My Sun!", a popular concert song (1899) by Giovanni Capurro and Eduardo Di Capua.

717.40   *Ein schöner . . . Nacht.*]   A beautiful star appears in my night.

733.5–12   "*Oh . . . realm.*"]   Airs from *Elijah*.

737.29–30   gather . . . may]   Cf. "To the Virgins to Make Much of Time" by Robert Herrick (1591–1674), line 1: "Gather ye rosebuds while ye may."

745.19   *The Bohemian Girl*]   Opera by Irish composer Michael Balfe (1808–70), first performed in London in 1843 and popular in the 19th century. It is also the title of a short story (1911) by Cather.

745.27   *Die Fledermaus*]   An operetta (1874) (*The Bat*) by Austrian composer Johann Strauss (1825–99).

745.27   *La Belle Hélène*]   An operetta (1864) by Jacques Offenbach (1819–80).

746.33   "I . . . halls,"]   Song from *The Bohemian Girl*, Act II, libretto by Alfred Bunn (1796?–1860).

SAPPHIRA AND THE SLAVE GIRL

779.25   Back Creek]   Small farming community near Winchester, Virginia, where Cather was born, now renamed Gore after her great-aunt Sidney Gore.

782.7–8   You . . . sale,]   In Virginia, upon marriage a woman's property (including slaves) legally became her husband's.

784.20   Buchan's . . . book]   *Domestic Medicine; or The Family Physician* (1769), a popular text by Scottish physician William Buchan (1729–1805).

790.37   dissenting church]   A "dissenting" church was a non-Anglican Protestant church.

792.30–32   capture . . . settlers]   James Wolfe (1727–1759) defeated the French general Montcalm on the Plains of Abraham above Quebec in 1759, gaining the crucial victory that ended the French and Indian Wars and secured the North American continent for the English. Both generals were mortally wounded in the conflict.

815.37   Mercy, . . . companion]   In *The Pilgrim's Progress*, Part II (1684), Christiana, accompanied by her neighbor Mercy, begins the pilgrimage to the Celestial City undertaken by her husband Christian in Part I.

822.13–14   "There . . . Delight,"]   By Isaac Watts (1674–1748), in *Horae Lyricae* (1706).

822.23   "limb"]   An epithet applied to a mischievous child or ill-tempered adult, abbreviated from "limb of the devil."

826.33   "The Lord . . . shepherd."]   Psalm 23:1.

828.8   twenty . . . illegal]   Acts prohibiting the slave trade were passed in the United States and Great Britain in 1807.

833.36   middling meat]   Pork between the hams and shoulder; sometimes salt pork.

835.17   "In . . . By,"]   Hymn by Samuel F. Bennett and J. P. Webster.

840.8–9   *Remember . . . them*]   Hebrews 13:3.

840.25–31   God . . . will.]   By William Cowper (1731–1800), Number 35 in the *Olney Hymns* (1779) by Cowper and John Newton.

850.23   an' can't . . . fall]   Cf. Matthew 10:29–30, Luke 12:6–7.

859.14   New York *Tribune*]   A daily newspaper founded in 1841 and edited by the social reformer and anti-slavery advocate Horace Greeley (1811–72).

859.14–15   Government . . . indiscreet]   Post office appointments were patronage positions, controlled by the administration in power and its local supporters, in this case the anti-abolitionist Democrats.

867.17–18   Tidewater Virginia] The low-lying coastal plain of eastern Virginia, where the first English settlements were located and where the slave-holding plantation aristocracy flourished in the 18th and 19th centuries.

878.16–17   *Down . . . Till.*] Lines from the 19th-century American folk song "Nancy Till."

881.17–18   'Home . . . Warming.'] "Home, Sweet Home," an air composed by Henry Rowley Bishop for the opera *Clari* (1823), lyrics by John Howard Payne, was an immediate success in England and soon after in the United States. "The Gipsy's Warning" is a 19th-century folk song.

888.22–23   Benjamin . . . *days.*'] "Fish & Visitors stink in 3 days." *Poor Richard's Almanack*, January 1736.

901.15–16   Fugitive Slave Law] The Fugitive Slave Act of 1850, a more stringent version of the Fugitive Slave Act of 1793, imposed heavy penalties on persons who helped runaway slaves, but was resisted by abolitionists and countered in many Northern states by the passage of "personal liberty laws." The foremost injustice of the 1850 law was that it denied alleged fugitives any jury trial. Their cases were instead heard by federal commissioners who received $5 if they decided for the defendant and $10 if they decided for the claimant.

904.31–32   *Not . . . knowledge*] Cf. Matthew 10:29–30 and Luke 12:6–7.

911.20   Blessed . . . merciful] From the Sermon on the Mount. Cf. Matthew 5:7.

927.29   Battle . . . Run] The battles of Bull Run, called First and Second Manassas in the South, were fought on July 21, 1861, and August 29–30, 1862, near Manassas Junction, a railroad center about 30 miles southwest of Washington, D.C. Both were Confederate victories.

933.9   *Peter Parley's Universal*] One in a series of more than 100 books for children written by publisher Samuel Griswold Goodrich (1793–1860) and his staff under the name Peter Parley.

CATALOGING INFORMATION

Cather, Willa, 1873–1947.
  Later Novels.
  Edited by Sharon O'Brien

  (The Library of America ; 49)
  Contents: A lost lady—The professor's house—
  Death comes for the Archbishop—Shadows on the
  rock—Lucy Gayheart—Sapphira and the slave girl.
  I. Title: A lost lady. II. Title: The professor's house.
  III. Title: Death comes for the Archbishop.
  IV. Title: Shadows on the rock. V. Title: Lucy Gayheart.
  VI. Title: Sapphira and the slave girl. VII. Series.
PS3505.A87A6   1990   89–64130
813'.52—dc20
ISBN 0–940450–52–6 (alk. paper)

For a list of titles in The Library of America, write to:
The Library of America
14 East 60th Street
New York, New York 10022

This book is set in 10 point Linotron Galliard,
a face designed for photocomposition by Matthew Carter
and based on the sixteenth-century face Granjon. The paper
is acid-free Ecusta Nyalite and meets the requirements for perma-
nence of the American National Standards Institute. The binding
material is Brillianta, a 100% woven rayon cloth made by
Van Heek-Scholco Textielfabrieken, Holland. The com-
position is by Haddon Craftsmen, Inc., and The
Clarinda Company. Printing and binding
by R. R. Donnelley & Sons Company.
Designed by Bruce Campbell.